AGAINST
A
DARK
BACKGROUND

Iain M. Banks

BANTAM BOOKS
NEW YORK · TORONTO
LONDON · SYDNEY · AUCKLAND

AGAINST A DARK BACKGROUND

A Bantam Spectra Book

PUBLISHING HISTORY

First Published in Great Britain by Macdonald & Co.
Bantam edition / August 1993
Bantam reissue edition / July 1995

SPECTRA *and the portrayal of a boxed "s" are trademarks of Bantam Books, a*
division of Bantam Doubleday Dell Publishing Group, Inc.

All rights reserved.
Copyright © 1993 by Iain M. Banks.
Cover art copyright © 1993 by Paul Youll.
No part of this book may be reproduced or transmitted in any
form or by any means, electronic or mechanical, including
photocopying, recording, or by any information storage and
retrieval system, without permission in writing from the publisher.
For information address: Bantam Books.

ISBN 0-553-29225-0

Published simultaneously in the United States and Canada

Bantam Books are published by Bantam Books, a division of Bantam Doubleday Dell
Publishing Group, Inc. Its trademark, consisting of the words "Bantam Books" and
the portrayal of a rooster, is Registered in U.S. Patent and Trademark Office and in
other countries. Marca Registrada. Bantam Books, 1540 Broadway, New York, New
York 10036.

PRINTED IN THE UNITED STATES OF AMERICA

RAD   0 9 8 7 6 5 4 3 2

For Dave McCartney

Contents

3. A TROPHY OF A PAST DISPUTE

Prologue

S he put her chin on the wood below the window. The wood was cold and shiny and smelled. She knelt on the seat; it smelled too, but different. The seat was wide and red like the sunset and had little buttons that made deep lines in it and made it look like somebody's tummy. It was dull outside and the lights were on in the cable car. There were people skiing on the steep slopes beneath. She could see her own face looking back at her in the glass; she started to make faces at herself.

After a while the glass in front of her face went misty. She reached up and wiped it. Somebody in another car, going down the hill, waved at her. She ignored them. The hills and the white trees tipped slowly back and forward.

The cable car swung gently as it rose through the mountain air toward the cloud base. The trees and runs on the slopes beneath were equally white; a fresh snowfall and freezing fog blowing up the valley overnight had coated the branches and needles of the trees with a crisp white wrap of crystals. Skiers cut and scythed through the new plumpness of the fall, engraving a carved text of blue-white lines onto the bulging fresh page of snow.

She watched the child for a moment. She was kneeling on the button-hide seat, looking out. Her ski suit was garish pink, fur trimmed. Her gloves, hanging from her sleeves on lengths of cord, were a clashing mauve. Her little boots were orange. It was a foul-looking combination (especially so here in Frelle, northern Caltasp's supposedly most exclusive and certainly its most snobbish resort), but—she suspected—probably less psyche damaging than the tantrum and sulk that would inevitably have resulted had her daughter not been allowed to choose her own skiing outfit. The girl wiped at the window, frowning.

She wondered what the child was frowning at and turned to see another cable car passing them on the way down, twenty meters or so away. She put her hand out and moved it through the girl's black hair, pulling some of the curls away from her face. She didn't seem to notice; she just kept gazing out of the window. Such a serious face for a little girl.

She smiled, remembering when she had been that age. She could recall being five; she had memories from about as far back as three, but they were vague and inchoate; flashes of memory illuminating a dark landscape of forgotten past.

But she could remember being conscious of being five; even remember her fifth birthday party and the fireworks over the lake.

How she had wanted to be older then; to be grown-up and stay up late and go to dances. She had hated being young, hated always being told what to do, hated the way adults didn't tell you everything. And hated, too, some of the stupid things they *did* tell you, like, These are the best days of your life. You could never believe at the time that adults had any idea—beyond mischief—what they were talking about. You had to be an adult, with all an adult's cares and responsibilities, before you could appreciate the struggling ignorance that adults termed "innocence," and—usually forgetting the way they, too, had felt at the time—the captivity of childhood they called "freedom."

It was a very ordinary tragedy, she supposed, but no less a cause for regret because it was so common. Like a hint, a foretaste of grief, it was an original, even unique, experience for everyone it affected, no matter how often it had happened in the past to others.

And how *did* you avoid it? She had tried so hard not to make the same mistakes with her own daughter that she felt her parents had made with her, but sometimes she heard herself scolding the girl and thought, *That's what my mother said to me.*

Her husband didn't feel the same way, but then he had been brought up differently, and anyway, didn't really have that much to do with the child's upbringing. These old families. Hers had been rich and influential and probably quite unbearable in its own power-deranged way, but it had never displayed quite the degree of almost willful eccentricity Kryf's had down the generations.

She looked at her wrist screen and turned down the heating in her boots, which were quite cozy now. Midday. Kryf would probably just be getting up, ringing for breakfast and having his butler read him the news while a footman proffered a selection of clothes from which to choose that afternoon's attire. She smiled, thinking of him, then realized that she was looking across the car at Xellpher. The bodyguard—the only other occupant of the car—was solid and dark as some old-fashioned stove, and smiling a little too.

She gave a small laugh and put her hand to her mouth.

"M'lady?" Xellpher said.

She shook her head. Outside, behind Xellpher, an outcrop of rocks ridged above the trees, caked in whiteness but streaked with naked black rock, a dark foreign body among the sheets and pillows of the snow. The cable car rose to meet the clouds and was enveloped by them.

A mast went past, gray and quick outside, and the cable car whirred and bumped on its wheels for a second or so, then continued its silent, burringly smooth ascent, seemingly nodding to itself as it was hauled on upward past ranks of trees like the ghosts of some great descending army.

It went all gray. A gray post went by and the car rocked. The view stayed gray. There were some trees and she could see the other cable, but that was all. She looked around, annoyed. Xellpher smiled at her. She didn't smile back. There was a cliff behind him, black bits in the white snow.

She turned back to the window and rubbed, hoping to see better. She watched a cable car appear out of the mists above, coming down on the other cable to meet them.

The cable car began to slow down.

The car slowed and stopped.

"Oh dear," she said, looking up at the varnished ceiling of the car.

Xellpher stood up, frowning. He looked at the cable car on the descending cable, which had stopped almost level with them. She looked at it too. The car hung, swaying, just as theirs was. It appeared to be empty. Xellpher turned and looked at the cliff on the other side, visible through the mist thirty or forty meters away. She saw his eyes narrow and experienced the first faint twinge of fear as she followed his gaze to the cliff.

There was an impression—perhaps imagined—of movement among some trees at the top of the cliff. Xellpher glanced back at the cable car hanging across from them and took a pair of multisights from his skiing jacket. She was still watching the cliff, like him. Something did move among the trees, roughly level with them. Xellpher adjusted a control on the side of the sights.

She stuck her nose against the window. It was very cold. Mummy had told her once that a bad little girl had stuck her nose against a very cold window one day and it had stuck there—frozen! Stupid girl. The car on the other cable stopped rocking. She saw somebody in it. They peeked up, holding something long and dark, then they crouched down again so she couldn't see them anymore.

Xellpher crouched down, putting the sights away and reaching out to take both her hands and pull her toward him. He glanced at the child as he said, "I'm sure there's nothing to worry about, my lady, but it might be best to sit down here on the floor, just for a moment."

She squatted down on the scuffed boards of the car, her head below the level of the car windows. She reached up and gently pulled the child off the seat. She struggled for a second, said, "*Mummy . . .*" in her demanding voice.

"Ssh," she told her, cuddling her against her chest.

Still squatting, Xellpher waddled over toward the car's doors, taking his communicator out of his pocket as he did so.

All the windows burst at once, spraying them with glass. The car shuddered.

She heard herself scream, clutching the child to her and falling down to the floor of the car. She bit the scream off. The car shook as more shots slammed into it. In the sudden silence, Xellpher murmured something; then there were a series of sharp concussions. She looked up to see Xellpher firing his handgun out the shattered window toward the cliff. More shots cracked into the car, blasting splinters of wood into the air and puffing dust and little bits of foam from the hide seat coverings.

Xellpher ducked, then jumped up, firing back for a moment, then diving to the floor and changing the clip in his gun. Shots tore into the car, smacking the metal and making it hum. She could taste the odor produced by Xellpher's gun, acrid and burnt at the back of her throat. She glanced down at the child, wide-eyed but unharmed beneath her.

"Code zero, repeat, code zero," Xellpher said into the communicator during a brief lull in the firing. He slipped the machine back into his pocket. "I'll open the door on the lee side," he told her loudly but calmly over the noise of puncturing metal and whining ricochets. "The drop is only ten meters onto snow. It might be safer to jump than stay here." The firing thrummed against the car, juddering it. Xellpher grimaced and lowered his head as a cloud of wood fragments sprayed off the wall by one smashed window. "When I open the door," he told her, "throw the child out first, then drop yourself. Do you understand?"

She nodded, afraid to try speaking. The taste at the back of her throat was not the smoke from his gun; it was fear.

He pushed himself back across the wooden slats to the door; the firing went on, sporadic gusts of furious noise and vibration. Xellpher smashed something, reached and pulled; the door swung in and along the wall. She could see their skis in their bins on the outside of the car, chopped off at window level by the gunfire. Xellpher looked out.

His head burst open; it was as though his body had been hit by some invisible cannonball, throwing it back from the opened door and thumping against the other wall of the cable car.

She couldn't see properly. She started screaming only as she realized the warm sticky stuff in her eyes was his blood.

Another shot from that side tore some of the seats out and sent them bouncing to the floor; the whole car shook and swayed. She cuddled the child, hearing her scream and hearing her own screams, then she looked up as another blast set the car rocking from side to side again. She crawled toward the door.

The blow was astonishing, beyond comprehension. It was as though she had been hit by a train, by a power hammer, by a comet. It hit somewhere below her chest; she had no idea where. She couldn't move. In an instant she knew she was dead; she could have believed she had been torn in half.

The child was screaming beneath her. Almost at the door. She knew the girl was screaming because she could see her mouth, her face, but she couldn't hear anything. Everything seemed to be getting very dark. The door was so close, but she couldn't move. The child dragged herself from under her, and she had to struggle to keep her head up, using one of her arms to support herself.

Child stood there, shouting something, face puffed and tear streaked. So close to the door, but she couldn't move. Ending now. No way to bring up a child. Silly, stupid, cruel people; like children, like poor children. Forgive them. No idea what's next, if anything. Nor they. But forgive. Poor children. All of us, poor frightened children. Fate, nothing in your grubby creed's worth this. . . .

The grenade flew threw the door, hit Xellpher's body, and landed clicking on the slatted floor behind the child. The child hadn't seen it. She wanted to tell her to pick it up and throw it away, but she couldn't get her mouth to work. The child kept screaming at her, bending down and screaming at her.

She reached up and with the last of her strength pushed the screaming child out the door, a second before the grenade exploded.

Sharrow fell howling to the snow.

1.

FROM
A
GLASS
SHORE

1

Overture

La, la, la, la-la;
Can you see-ee any clearer from a glass shore?
Hmm, hmm, hmm, hmm-hmm . . .

One line was all that came back to her. She stood on a
fused beach with her arms folded, her boot heels
scuffing the grainy, scratch-dulled surface, her gaze sweeping the flat horizons, and she half whispered, half sang that
one remembered line.

It was the slack water of the atmosphere, when the day
winds blowing onto the land had died, and the night breeze,
delayed by a warmth-lidding overcast, had yet to be born
from the inertia of archipelagic air.

Seaward, at the edge of a dark canopy of overhanging
cloud, the sun was setting. Red-tinged waves fell toward the
glass beach, and surf frothed on the scoured slope, to be
blown away along the curved blade of shore toward a distant
line of dully glinting dunes. A smell of brine saturated the
air; she breathed deeply, then started to walk along the
beach.

She was a little above average height. Her trousered
legs looked slim beneath her thin jacket; black hair spilled
thick and heavy down her back. When she turned her head
a little, the red light of the sunset made one side of her face

look flushed. Her heavy, knee-length boots made rasping noises as she walked. And as she walked, she limped; a soft bias in her tread like weakness.

". . . see-ee any clearer . . ." She sang softly to herself, pacing along the glass shore of Issier, wondering why she'd been summoned here, and why she had agreed to come.

She took out an antique watch and looked at the time, then made a tutting noise and stuffed the watch back into her pocket. She hated waiting.

She kept walking, heading along the tipped shelf of fused sand toward the hydrofoil. She'd left the aging, secondhand craft moored—maybe a little dubiously, now that she thought about it—to some indecipherable piece of junk a hundred paces or so along that unlikely shore. The hydrofoil, its arrowhead shape just a smudge in the dimness, glittered suddenly as it rocked in the small waves hitting the beach, chrome lines reflecting the ruddy glare of the day's dying light.

She stopped and looked down at the motley red-brown glass surface, wondering just how thick the layer of fused silicate was. She kicked at it with the toe of one boot. The blow hurt her toes, and the glass looked undamaged. She shrugged, then turned around and walked the other way.

Her face, seen from a distance, looked calm; only somebody who knew her well would have detected a certain ominousness about that placidity. Her skin was pale under the sunset's red reflection. Her brows were black curves under a wide forehead and a crescent of swept-back hair, her eyes large and dark, and her nose long and straight—a column to support the dark arches of those brows. Her mouth—set in a tight, compressed line—was narrow. Wide cheekbones helped balance a proud jaw.

She sighed once more and sang the line from the song again under her breath. The tight line of her mouth relaxed then, becoming small, full lips.

Ahead of her, a couple of hundred paces up the beach, she could see the tall, boxy shape of an old automatic beachcomber. She walked toward it, eyeing the ancient machine suspiciously. It sat, silent and dark on its rubber tracks, apparently deactivated for lack of flotsam, waiting for the next tide to provide it with fresh stimulus. Its battered, decrepit casing was streaked with seabird droppings glowing pink in the sunset light, and while she watched, a foam-white bird landed briefly on the flat top of the machine, sat for a moment, then flew away inland.

She took out the old watch again, inspected it, and made a little growling noise at the back of her throat. The waves beat at the margin of the land, hissing like static.

She would walk, she decided, almost as far as the beachcomber, then she would turn around, head back to the hydrofoil, and go. Whoever had set up the rendezvous probably wasn't coming after all. It might even be a trap, she thought, glancing round at the line of dunes, old fears returning. Or a hoax; somebody's idea of a joke.

She got within twenty paces of the old beachcombing machine, then turned, walking away with her just-a-little-crippled walk and singing her little, monotonous tune, relic of some-or-other postatomic.

The rider appeared suddenly on the crest of a large dune, fifty meters to her right. She stopped and stared.

The sand-colored animal was man-high at its broad, muscled shoulders; its narrow waist held a glittering saddle, and its massive rump was covered in a silvery cloth. It put its great wide tawny head back, reins jingling; it snorted and stamped its front paws. Its rider, dark on dark against the dull weight of cloud, nudged the big animal forward. It put its head down and snorted again, testing the shard-fringe where the sand at the top of the dune became glass. The beast shook its head, then trod carefully down the edge of sand to the hollow between two dunes at the urging of its rider; his cloak billowed out behind him as though hardly lighter than the air he moved through.

The man muttered something, stuck his heels into the beast's flank; the animal flinched as the spur terminals connected and sent little involuntary shivers of muscle movement up its great flanks. It put one broad paw tentatively onto the glass, then two; its rider made encouraging noises. Still snorting nervously, the animal took a couple of steps on the inclined deck of the shore, then—with a noise like an enormous whimper—it skidded, tottered, and sat heavily on its rump, almost unseating its rider. The animal put its head back and roared.

The man jumped quickly from the animal; his long cloak snagged briefly on the high saddle, and he landed awkwardly on the glass surface, almost falling. His mount was making sudden lurching attempts to get back up, paws skittering over the slick surface. The man collected his cloak about him and strode purposefully to the woman who was standing with one hand under the opposite armpit, the other hand up at her forehead, as though shading her eyes while she looked down at the beach. She was shaking her head.

The man was tall, thin beneath his riding britches and tight jacket, and had a pale, narrow face, topped with black curls and edged with a neatly trimmed black beard. He walked up to her. He looked, perhaps, a few years older than she was.

"Sharrow," he said, smiling. "Cousin; thank you for coming." It was a cultured, refined voice, and quiet but nevertheless assured. He put his hands out to hers, squeezing them briefly, then letting go.

"Geis," she said, looking over his shoulder at the bellowing mount as it finally got shakily to its feet. "What are you doing with that animal?"

Geis glanced back at the beast. "Breaking it in," he said with a grin that slowly faded. "But really, it's just a way of getting here to tell you . . ." He shrugged and gave a small, regretful laugh. "Hell, Sharrow, it's a melodramatic message: you're in danger."

"Perhaps a phone call would have been quicker, then."

"I had to see you, Sharrow; it's more important than some phone call."

She looked at the saddled animal, sniffing experimentally at the anchor-grass lining the nearest dune. "A taxi, then," she suggested. Her voice was soft and possessed a heavy smoothness.

Geis smiled. "Taxis are so . . . vulgar, don't you find?" he said with a trace of irony.

"Hmm, but why the . . ." She gestured at the animal.

"It's a bandamyion. Fine animal."

"Yes, well—why the bandamyion?"

Geis shrugged. "I just bought it. Like I say, I'm breaking it in." He made a dismissive gesture with a gauntleted hand. "Look, never mind the animal. This is more than mildly urgent."

She sighed. "Okay—what?"

He took a deep breath, then breathed, "The Huhsz."

She was silent for a moment; then she shrugged and

looked away. "Oh, them." She scratched at the glass beach with the toe of her boot.

"Yes," Geis said quietly. "My people at the World Court say there's a deal being arranged that means they'll get their . . . their hunting Passports, probably very soon. In a matter of days, perhaps."

Sharrow nodded, not looking at her cousin. She crossed her arms and started to walk slowly along the beach. Geis took off his gauntlets and—after a glance at the ruminating bandamyion—followed her.

"Sorry I have to be the one to tell you, Sharrow."

"That's all right," she said.

"I don't think there's any more we can do. I've got the family lawyers working on an appeal, and my corporate people are giving all the help they can—there's a chance we can injunct on grounds of due notice—but it looks like the Stehrins have dropped their objections and the Nul Church Council is withdrawing its demurrance action. The rumor is the Huhsz have done a land deal in Stehrin, carving up some enclave, and the Church has been bought off, either with straight credit or the offer of a relic."

Sharrow said nothing; she kept walking along the beach, staring down. Geis made a resigned gesture with his hands. "It's all blown up so suddenly; I thought we had those assholes tied up for years, but the Court's fast-tracked the whole matter, sidelined cases that have waited generations." He sighed. "And of course it's Llocaran's turn to provide the Court President this session. Their nominee is actually from Lip City."

"Yes, Lip City," Sharrow said. "I imagine they are still upset about that damn Lazy Gun." She gazed ahead to the dimly glinting shape of her distant hydrofoil.

(And in her mind saw again the line of desert hills beyond the stone balustrade of the hotel-room balcony, and the faint crease of dawn-light above suddenly swamped by the stuttering pulses of silent fire from beyond the horizon. She had watched—dazed and dazzled and wondering—as that distant eruption of annihilation had lit up the face of her lover.)

Geis's voice sounded tired as he said, "Actually, I think the Huhsz must have got to one of the justiciaries. There's been talk of one of the old guys being found in a snuff parlor a few days ago. I wouldn't put it past the Huhsz to have set the whole thing up just to pocket a judge."

"My," Sharrow said, pulling a hand through her thick hair (Geis watched, eyes following those pale fingers as they plowed that black field). "What energy and enterprise those Huhsz boys display."

Geis nodded. "They've been lucky with their recruitment and investments recently, too," he said. "Highly fluid; probably the most profitable order on Golter just now. It's all helped them get their war chest together." His brows furrowed. "I'm sorry, Sharrow. I feel I've let you down."

She shrugged. "Had to happen sooner or later. You've done all you can. Thanks." She looked at him, then briefly put a hand out to touch his forearm. "I appreciate it, Geis."

"Let me hide you, Sharrow," he said suddenly.

She shook her head. "Geis—"

"I have interests they can't—"

"Geis, no; I—"

"No; listen—I've places nobody—"

"No, I—"

". . . safe houses; offices; whole estates that don't appear on any inventory, here and on other planets; cascade-owned companies my own chief execs don't know about . . ."

"I appreciate the offer, Geis, but—"

"Habitats; whole asteroids; mines on Fian and Speyr; island barges on Trontsephori—"

"Geis," she said, stopping and turning to him, taking his hands in hers for a moment. His thin face shone palely in the deepening red light. "Geis, I can't." She forced herself to smile. "You know they'd track me down eventually, and you'd only get into trouble for Harboring. They'll use the Passports. If they wanted to—if they had the excuse that they thought you were sheltering me—they could tear you apart, Geis."

"I can look after myself."

"I don't mean you personally, Geis; I mean this commercial empire you've been so busy constructing. I watch the news; the antitrust people are crawling all over you already."

Geis waved one hand. "Bureaucrats. I can deal with them."

"Not if the Huhsz use the Passports to open your data

banks and search your files. All these precious companies, all these . . . interests—you could lose them all."

Geis stood, staring at her. "I'd risk that," he said quietly.

She shook her head.

"I would," he insisted. "For you. If you'd let me, I'd do anything—"

"Geis, please," she said, turning from him and walking in the other direction, toward the distant shape of the ancient beachcombing machine. Geis paced after her.

"Sharrow, you know how I feel about you; just let—"

"*Geis!*" she said sharply, barely glancing back at him.

He stopped, looked down at his feet, then walked quickly after her.

"All right," he said when he was level with her again. "I'm sorry; I shouldn't have said anything. Didn't mean to embarrass you." He took a breath. "But I won't see you hounded like this. I can fight dirty, too. I have people in places you wouldn't expect; in places nobody expects. I won't let those religious maniacs get you."

"*I'm* not going to let them get me," she said. "Don't worry."

He gave a bitter laugh. "How can I not worry?"

She stopped and looked at him. "Just try. And don't do anything that's going to land both of us is even more trouble." She tipped her head to one side, staring at him.

Eventually he looked away. "All right," he said.

They resumed their walk.

"So," he said. "What will you do?"

She shrugged. "Run," she said. "They've only got a year. And—"

"A year and a day if we're going to be precise about it."

"Yes. Well, I'll just have to try to keep a step or two ahead of them for a year . . . and a day." She kicked at the glass surface beneath their feet. "And I suppose I have to try to find that last Lazy Gun. The one the Huhsz want. It's the only other way to end this."

"Will you get the team back together?" Geis asked, his voice neutral.

"I'll need them if I'm going to find that damn Gun," she told him. "And I'll have to try, anyway. If the Huhsz get hold of one of them ... it would make it easier to find me."

"Ah. Then it really doesn't wear off?"

"SNB? No, Geis, it doesn't wear off. Like certain exotic diseases, and unlike love, synchroneurobonding is for life."

Geis lowered his eyes. "You weren't always so cynical about love."

"As they say, ignorance pays."

Geis looked as though he were about to say something else, but then shook his head. "You'll need money, then," he said. "Let me—"

"I'm not destitute, Geis," she told him. "And who knows, perhaps there are still Antiquities contracts outstanding." She clasped her hands together, kneading them without realizing it. "If the family lore is right, the way to find the Lazy Gun is to find the *Universal Principles* first."

"Yes, *if* the lore is right," Geis said skeptically. "I've tried tracking that rumor down myself, and nobody knows how it started."

"It's all there is, Geis."

"Well, if you need any help finding the other people in the team ..."

"Last I heard, Miz was being entrepreneurial in the Log Jam, the Francks were raising sarflet litters in Regioner, and Cenuij had gone to ground somewhere in Caltasp Minor—Udeste, maybe. I'll find him."

Geis took a deep breath. "Well, according to my sources, yes, Cenuij Mu *is* in Caltasp, but it's a bit farther north than Udeste."

Sharrow cocked her head and raised an eyebrow. "Mm-hmm?"

Geis smiled sadly. "Looks like Lip City, cuz."

Sharrow nodded, gritting her teeth as she walked onward. She looked out to sea, where the last glow of the sun was vanishing fast on the bare curve of the horizon. "Oh, great," she said.

Geis studied the back of his hands. "I have a security concern with contracts for certain corporate clients' installations in Lip; it wouldn't be impossible for Mu to ... travel inadvertently to somewhere beyond the city limits. ..."

"No, Geis," she told him. "That won't work; kidnapping would just antagonize him. I'll find Cenuij. Maybe I can persuade my darling half sister to help; I think they're still in touch."

"Breyguhn?" Geis looked dubious. "She may not want to talk to you."

"It's worth a try." Sharrow looked thoughtful. "She *might* even have some idea about where the *Universal Principles* is."

Geis glanced at Sharrow. "That was what she was looking for in the Sea House, wasn't it?"

Sharrow nodded. "She sent me a letter last year with some garbled nonsense about finding out how to get the book."

Geis looked surprised. "She did?" he said.

Sharrow hoisted one eyebrow. "Yes, and claimed to have discovered the meaning of life as well, if I remember rightly."

"Ah," Geis said.

They stopped, not far from the dark bulk of the old beachcomber machine. She breathed deeply, looking around at the faint curve of beach; it was dark enough for the phosphorescence in the waves to show as ghostly green lines rippling on the shore. "So, Geis, any more good news for me, or is that it?"

"Oh, I think that's enough for now, don't you?" he said, a small, sad smile on his face.

"Well, I appreciate your telling me, Geis. But I'm going to have to move fairly rapidly from now on; it might be best for you and the rest of the family if you all kept out of my way for the next year. I'll need room to maneuver, know what I mean?"

"If you insist." He sounded hurt.

"It'll be all right," she told him, holding her hand out to his. He looked at her hand, then shook it. "Really, Geis, I'll be fine. I know what I'm doing. Thanks again." She leaned forward and quickly kissed his cheek.

She stepped back, releasing his hand. His smile was pale. He nodded, swallowing.

"I am, as ever, your faithful servant, cousin."

Geis managed to make the stilted statement sound both sad and sincere. He took a step back, closer to the water; a wave washed over one boot, and its spur terminal gave a little blue flash of light as it shorted. Geis flinched and stepped smartly away. Sharrow gave a small, involuntary laugh.

Geis smiled ruefully and scratched the side of his head. "Just can't get my dramatic exits right when you're around," he sighed. "Well, if ever you need me; if ever I can do anything . . . just call me."

"I shall. Good-bye."

"Farewell, Sharrow." He turned abruptly and walked quickly back to the bandamyion.

She watched him go, heading into the dunes. She heard him calling for the animal and laughed quietly when she saw him chasing the lolloping beast over the summit of a distant dune.

Finally she shook her head and turned away, toward the hydrofoil moored a hundred meters away along the deserted shore.

"Ah, hello there," said a voice right behind her.

She froze, then turned smoothly, left hand sliding into the pocket of her jacket.

There were a couple of tiny red lights high up on the front of the beachcombing machine ten meters away; the lights winked slowly, on and off. They hadn't been there a few seconds earlier.

"Yes?" she said.

"Am I addressing Lady Sharrow?" said the machine. Its voice was deep, with the distinctive chime at the start of each word which was supposed to ensure that people knew it was a machine doing the talking.

Her eyes narrowed. The machine sensed her left arm tensing. "I think," she said, "you know who I am."

"Well, indeed. Allow me to introduce myself. . . ." The machine made a whining noise and lurched toward her, the rubber treads on its left-side tracks splashing through the small waves.

She backed away, two quick, long steps. The machine stopped suddenly. "Oh, I beg your pardon. I didn't mean to startle you. Just a second . . ." The machine trundled back a couple of meters to where it had been. "There. As I was saying—allow me to introduce myself. I am a—"

"I don't care who you are; what are you doing spying on me and my cousin?"

"A necessary subterfuge, dear lady, to ensure that I had the relevant personages—namely yourself and Count Geis—correctly identified. Also, having unintentionally found myself in such close proximity to your conference, I thought it prudent and indeed only polite to delay making myself known to you until the said noble gentleman had bade you farewell, as—considerations of good manners apart—my instructions are to reveal myself to you and you alone, initially at any rate."

"You're hellish talkative for a beachcomber."

"Ah, dear lady, let not this rude appearance deceive you; beneath my tatterdemalion disguise lurk several brand-spanking-new components of a Suprotector (TradeMark) Personal Escort Suite, Mark Seventeen, Class Five, certified civil-space legal in all but a handful of jurisdictions, and battlefield limited in the remainder. And I—that is the aforesaid system, in full, combined with the services of various highly trained human operatives—am at your service, my lady, exclusively, for as long as you may desire."

"Really?" She sounded warily amused.

"Indeed," said the machine. "A mere beachcomber—for example—would not be able to tell you that the gun which you are currently holding in the left-hand pocket of your jacket, with your index finger on the trigger and your thumb ready to flick the safety catch, is a silenced FrintArms ten-millimeter HandCannon with eleven ten-seven coaxial depleted-uranium-casing mercury-core general-purpose rounds in the magazine plus one in the breach, and that you have another—double-ended—magazine in the opposite pocket, containing five armor-piercing and six wire-fléchette rounds."

Sharrow laughed out loud, taking her hand from her pocket and swiveling on her heel. She walked away down the beach. The machine lumbered after her, keeping a handful of paces behind.

"And I feel I must point out," the machine continued, "that FrintArms, Inc., strongly recommends that its hand-weapons are never carried with a round in the breach."

"The gun has," she said tartly, glancing behind as she walked, "a safety catch."

"Yes, but I think if you read the instruction manual—"

"So," she interrupted. "You're mine to command, are you?" she said.

". . . Absolutely."

"Wonderful. So who are you working for?"

"Why, you, mistress!"

"Yes, but who hired you?"

"Ah, dear lady, it is with the greatest embarrassment that I have to confess that in this matter I must—with a degree of anguish you may well find hard to credit—relinquish my absolute commitment to the fulfillment of your every whim. Put plainly, I am not at liberty to divulge that information. There, it is said. Let us quickly move on from this unfortunate quantum of dissonance to the ground state of accord that I trust will inform our future relationship."

"So you're not going to tell me." Sharrow nodded.

"My dear lady," the machine said, continuing to trundle after her. "Without saying so in so many words . . . correct."

"Right . . ."

"May I take it that you do wish my services?"

"Thanks, but I don't really need any help when it comes to looking after myself."

"Well," the machine chimed, with what sounded like amusement in its voice, "you *did* hire an escort unit the last time you visited the city of Arkosseur, and you *do* have a contract with a commercial army concern to guard your dwelling house on Jorve."

She glanced back at the machine. "Well, *aren't* we well informed."

"Thank you; I like to think so."

"So what's my favorite color?"

"Ultraviolet, you once told one of your tutors."

She stopped; so did the machine. She turned and looked up at the beachcomber's battered casing. She shook her head. "Shit, even *I'd* forgotten I said that." She looked down at the glass beach. "Ultraviolet, eh? Huh, so I did." She shrugged. "That's almost witty."

She turned and walked on, the beachcomber at her heel. "You seem to know me better than I do myself, machine," she said. "Anything else about me you think I should know? I mean, just in case I've forgotten."

"Your name is Sharrow—"

"No, I rarely forget that."

"—of the first house of Dascen Major, Golterian. You were born in 9965, in house Tzant, on the estate of the same name, since sold along with most of the rest of the Dascen Major fortune following the settlement required by the World Court after the dismemberment of your grandfather Gorko's—unhappily illegal—commercial network, rumored to be the greatest of its day."

"We've always thought big, as a family. Especially when it comes to disasters."

"Following the unfortunate death of your mother—"

"Murder, I think, is the technical term." She slowed her pace and clasped her hands behind her back.

"—murdered by Huhsz zealots, you were brought up by your father in a ... peripatetic existence, I think one might fairly say."

"When we weren't making a nuisance of ourselves at the homes of rich relations, it was equal parts casinos and courts; father had an obsession with screwing money out of one of them. Mostly they did it to him."

"You had ... various tutors—"

"Singularly lacking in a sense of humor, all of them."

"—and what might most charitably be called a check-ered school history."

"A lot of those records really shouldn't be trusted."

"Yes, there is a quite remarkable disparity between the written reports and most of the associated computer files. Several of the institutions you attended seemed to feel there might be a casual link between this phenomenon and your uncharacteristic keenness for the subject of computing."

"Coincidence; they couldn't prove a thing."

"Indeed, I don't think I've heard of anybody suing a school yearbook before."

"A matter of principle; family honor was at stake. And anyway, litigiousness runs in our family. Gorko issued a writ against his father for more pocket money when he was five, and Geis has almost sued himself several times."

"At your finishing schools in Claäv you developed an interest in politics and became ... popular with the local young men."

She shrugged. "I'd been a difficult child; I became an easy adolescent."

"To the surprise of everybody except, apparently, yourself, you won entrance to the diplomatic faculty of the university of Yadayeypon, but left after two years, on the outbreak of the Five Percent War."

"Another coincidence; the professor I was fucking to get good grades died on me, and I couldn't be bothered starting again from scratch."

"You crewed on an anti-Tax cruiser operating out of TP one-oh-five, a moon of Roaval, then—along with a group of seven other junior officers—became one of the first humans for three hundred years to take the then newly rereleased symbiovirus SNB-three. With you as leader, you and your fellow synchroneurobondees flew a squadron of single-seat modified excise clippers out of HomeAtLast, a military-commercial habitat stationed in near-Miykenns orbit, becoming the most successful squadron of the seventeen operating in the midsystem."

"Please—I'm blushing."

"Three of your team died in your last action, at the very end of the war while the surrender was being negotiated. Your own craft was seriously damaged, and you crash-landed on Nachtel's Ghost, suffering near-fatal injuries on top of the extreme irradiation and already serious wounds you had sustained during the original engagement."

"Nothing by halves; should be the family motto."

"You were cut from the wreck and treated under the war-internment regulations in the Tax-neutral hospital of a mining concern on Nachtel's Ghost—"

"Ghastly food."

"—where you lost the fetus of the child you were carrying by another of your team, Miz Gattse Ensil Kuma."

She stopped for a moment and looked up to see the hydrofoil twenty meters away. She pursed her lips, breathed deeply, and walked slowly on. "Yes! Terribly complicated way of going about getting an abortion. But then, I was sterilized at the same time, so it was practically a bargain."

"You spent the months immediately after the war in Tenaus prison hospital, Nachtel. You were liberated—on your twentieth birthday—under the terms of the Lunchbar Agreement; you and the four surviving members of your team formed a limited company and undertook occasionally legal commercial-surveillance and industrial-espionage work, then branched out into Antiquities research and retrieval, a profession you shared with your sister, Breyguhn."

"Half sister. And *we* never got caught."

"Your team's last successful contract was the location and disposal of what is believed to have been the second-last Lazy Gun, which resulted in the Gun's autoannihilation while under deconstruction in the physics department of Lip City university."

"Their methodology had been suspect for years."

"The resulting detonation destroyed approximately twenty percent of the city and resulted in the deaths of nearly half a million people."

She stopped walking. They had arrived at the piece of roughly cylindrical wreckage embedded in the fused silicate of the beach to which the hydrofoil was moored. She stared at the dark lump of half-melted metal.

"Your team split up immediately afterward," the machine went on. "You currently own one third of a tropical fish-breeding and retail business on the island of Jorve."

"Hmm," she said thoughtfully. "Sounds so banal, that last part. The approach of middle age; I'm losing my panache."

She shrugged and waded into the water, waves washing around her boots. She unlocked the hydrofoil's painter and let the rope reel back into its housing in the stem.

She looked at the beachcomber. "Well, thanks, but I don't think so," she said.

"You don't think what?"

She climbed onto the hydrofoil, slung her legs inside the footwell, and pulled the control wheel down. "I don't think I want your services, machine."

"Ah, now, wait a moment, Lady Sharrow . . ."

She flicked a few switches; the hydrofoil came to life, lights lighting, beepers beeping. "Thanks, but no."

"Just hold on, will you?" The machine sounded almost angry.

"Look," she said, starting the hydrofoil's engine and making it roar. She shouted, "Tell Geis thanks . . . but no thanks."

"Geis? Look, lady, you appear to be making certain assumptions about the identity of—"

"Oh, shut up and push me out here, will you?" She gunned the engine again, sending a froth of foam from the stern of the little boat. Its front foil levered down, knifing into the waves.

The beachcombing machine nudged the hydrofoil forward into the water. "Look, I have something to confess here—"

"That's enough." She smiled briefly at the beachcomber. "Thank you." She switched the boat's main lights on, creating a glittering pathway that swung across the waves.

"Wait! Will you just *wait*?"

Something in the machine's voice made her turn to look at it.

A section of the beachcomber's battered front casing swung up and back to reveal a red-glowing interior bright with screens and readouts. Sharrow frowned; her hand went to her jacket pocket as a man's head and shoulders appeared from the compartment.

He was young, muscular looking in a dark T-shirt, and quite bald; the red light threw dark shadows across his face and over eyes that looked gold in the half light. The skin on his smoothly reflecting head looked coppery.

"We have to—" he began, and she heard both the mechanized voice of the beachcomber and the man's own voice.

He plucked a tiny bead from his top lip.

"We have to talk," he said. There was a slick bassiness about his voice Sharrow knew she'd have found immensely attractive when she'd been younger.

"Who the hell are you?" she said, flicking a couple of switches in the hydrofoil's cockpit without taking her eyes off him, or her other hand from the gun in her pocket.

"Somebody who needs to talk to you," the young man said, baring his teeth in a winning smile. He gestured down at the casing of the beachcombing machine. "Sorry about the disguise," he said with a slightly embarrassed, deprecating gesture. "But it was felt—"

"No," she said, shaking her head. "No, I don't want to talk to you. Good-bye."

She tugged the controls, sending the hydrofoil nudging round on a pulse of foam, swamping the front of the beachcomber; water splashed over the hatch's lip into the beachcomber's interior.

"Careful!" the young man shouted, leaping back and glancing down. "But, Lady Sharrow!" he called desperately. "I have something to put to you—"

Sharrow pushed the throttle away from her; the 'foil's engine rasped, and the little boat surged out from the glass shore. "Really?" she shouted back. "Well, you can put it—"

But something obscene was lost to the thrashing water and the screaming exhausts. The craft roared out to sea, rose quickly onto its foils, and raced away.

2

The Chain
Gallery

Issier was the main island of the Midsea archipelago, lying
a thousand kilometers from any other land near the center of Phirar, Golter's third-largest ocean.

The little arrowhead hydrofoil swung out from the island's glass western shore and headed north, for Jorve, the
next island in the group. It docked half an hour later in a
marina just outside Place Issier II, the archipelago's largest
town and administrative capital.

Sharrow woke an apologetic guard in the marina office
and left a note for the harbor master telling him to put the
hydrofoil up for sale. She collected her bike, then took the
east-coast road north. She left her helmet off, driving in
plain goggles with the wind fierce in her hair; the cloud
overhead was fraying, letting moonlight and junklight spread
a gray-blue wash over the fields and orchards outside the
town.

She switched her bike's lights off, driving fast and leaning hard around the open, sweeping curves of the slowly
climbing road, its surface a faint snaking ribbon of steel blue
unwinding in front of her. Ravines beyond the crash barriers
gave brief glimpses of the rock-ragged coast beneath, where
the ocean swell terminated in glowing white lines of surf.
She put her lights on only when other traffic approached,
and thrilled each time to the heart-stopping sensation of to-

tal darkness in the instant after she killed the old bike's lights again.

An hour after she had stood on the glass shore of Issier, she arrived at the solitary, turreted house on the cliff where she lived.

"Sharrow, you can't do this!"

"You mean, You can't do this *to me*," she muttered.

"What?"

"Nothing." She took a camera the size of a little finger from a dressing-table drawer and clipped it into an interior pocket of the bag she'd packed.

"Sharrow!"

She frowned, turning away from the bag lying open on the big round bed in the big round bedroom that faced out to sea. "Hmm?" she said.

Jyr looked distraught; he had been crying. "How can you just leave?" He threw his arms wide. "I love you!"

She stared at him. The pale areas of his face looked reddened; the fashion on the island that summer had been for black-white skin like camouflage, and Jyr—convinced he suited the style—seemed determined to remain two-tone for the whole year.

She pushed past him, disappearing into her dressing room to reappear with a pair of long gloves, which she added to the pile of clothes in the overcrowded bag.

"Sharrow!" Jyr shouted behind her.

"What?" she said, frowning, one hand at her mouth tapping her teeth as she looked down at the bag, deep in thought. She had booked a ticket on a westbound flight leaving early the next morning, called her lawyer and her business partners to arrange a meeting, and contacted her bank to rearrange her finances. Still, she was sure she'd forgotten something.

"Don't go!" Jyr said. "Didn't you hear what I said? I love you!"

"Uh-huh," she said, kneeling on the bed to pull the bag closed.

"Sharrow," Jyr said quietly behind her, a catch in his voice. "Please . . ." He put his hands on her hips. She knocked his hands away, grunting as she struggled with the catches on the bag.

She forced the bag closed and stood up. Then she was

whirled around as Jyr grabbed her shoulders and shook her. "Stop doing this to me!" He shouted. "Stop ignoring me!"

"Well, stop shaking me!" she shouted.

He let her go and stood there, quivering, his eyes puffy. His hair, all white, looked disheveled. "At least explain," he said. "Why are you doing this? *Why* do you just have to go?"

"It's a long story."

"*Tell* me!"

"All right!" she snapped. "Because," she said, talking quickly, "once upon a time, long ago and far away, there was a young girl who'd been promised to a great temple by her parents. She met a man—a duke—and they fell in love. They swore nothing would separate them, but they were tricked, and she was taken to the temple after all.

"The duke came to rescue the girl; she escaped and brought with her the temple's greatest treasure. They married and she bore the duke twins—a boy and a girl. In an attempt to get the treasure back, agents of the faith killed the duke and his son.

"The treasure was hidden—no one knows where—and the duchess swore she'd avenge the deaths of her husband and child in any way she could, and to oppose the faith at every turn. She swore the surviving twin, a daughter, and all *her* descendants to the same oath.

"The faith responded in kind; a prophet had a vision and decided that the Messiah couldn't be born until the faithful had their treasure back, or the female line of the family had died out, whichever came first. And however it worked, it had to happen by the time of the decamillenium."

She studied Jyr's tearful, uncomprehending face for a moment, then shook her head. "Well," she said, exasperated, "you did ask."

"Take me with you," Jyr whispered.

"What? No."

"Take me with you," he repeated, taking one of her hands in his. "I'll do anything for you. Please."

She pulled her hand away. "Jyr," she said, looking levelly into his eyes. "It was a good summer and I had a lot of fun; I hope you did, too. But now I've got to go. Stay in the house until the lease runs out, if you want."

He slapped her.

She stared at him, her ears ringing, the impact of the

slap like an echo on her face. He'd never hit her before. She didn't know what she found more amazing: the fact he'd managed to surprise her, or that he'd even thought of trying to hit her in the first place.

He stood in front of her, his eyes wide.

She shook her head, smiled brightly, and said, "Oh, boy," then punched him hard in the jaw. Jyr's head snapped back; he fell crashing into the dressing table behind, scattering bottles, pots, jars, and brushes. He slid to the floor; perfumes and lotions spilled from smashed bottles and made dark stains on the tiles around him.

She turned, picked up her bag, and slung it over her shoulder. She hoisted a small satchel from the side of the bed and put it over her other shoulder. Jyr moaned, lying face down on the floor. The room began to reek of expensive perfume.

She inspected the knuckles on her left hand, frowning. "Get out of my house, now," she said. "Phone?" she spoke to the room.

"Ready," chimed a voice.

"Stand by," she said.

"Standing by."

She tapped Jyr on the backside with one boot. "You've got two minutes before I call the police and report an intruder."

"Oh gods, my jaw," Jyr whimpered, getting to his knees and holding his chin. The back of his head was bleeding. Bits of broken glass fell from him as he stood, shakily. She took a couple of steps away from him, watching him carefully. He almost fell again, then put one hand out to the dressing table to steady himself. "You've broken my jaw!"

"I don't think so," she said. "Not with an uppercut." She glanced at the bedside clock. "That's you down to about a minute and a half now, I'd say."

He looked at her. "You fucking heartless bitch." His voice was quite steady.

She shook her head. "No, Jyr, I never liked it when you talked dirty." She looked away from him. "Phone?"

". . . Standing by."

"Please call the local p—"

"All right!" Jyr roared, then winced and held his jaw as he stumbled for the door. "I'm going! I'm going! And I'm never coming *back*!" He hauled the bedroom door open and slammed it shut behind him; she listened to his feet hammering down the stairs, then heard the front door crash shut; the turret shook around her. A final slam was his car door, followed by the noise of the engine, whining away into the night.

She stood very still for a while, then her shoulders dropped a little, and her eyes closed.

She swayed slightly, swallowed, then breathed out as she opened her eyes again, sniffing. She wiped her eyes, took another deep breath, and walked away from the bed. She stopped briefly at the dressing table, setting a couple of bottles upright again.

". . . Standing by," said the room.

She looked at her reflection in the table's mirror. "Cancel," she said, then drew one finger through a thick pool of perfume on the table's wooden surface and dabbed the scent behind her ears as she walked toward the door.

She drove the bike back into town, helmet on, night-sight activated and all lights blazing.

She arrived at the tall town house that was the home of the Bassidges', the couple who owned the other two thirds of the tropical-fish business. Her lawyer was already there; she signed the necessary papers selling her share in the shop to them. She'd left her personal phone in the cliff house, knowing it would make her too easy to trace. After her lawyer had returned home and the Bassidges had gone to bed, she sat down at the house's antique desk-terminal and stayed there until dawn, taking a couple of zing-tabs to keep herself awake as she attempted to catch up on eight years of Antiquities news and data-gossip.

There were numerous outstanding contracts for the *Universal Principles;* several from universities, several more from big Corps known to invest in high-value Antiquities, a few from wealthy individual collectors who specialized in lost Unique books, and one anonymous contract. The latter offered the best financial advance, though only for Antiquities investigators with acceptable track records. She was almost tempted to draft a tender and mail it to the anonymous box number, but there was too much to settle first.

She suspected she'd end up looking for the book one way or the other. According to one of the more pervasive rumors that had circulated within the Dascen family and its attendant septs in the chaotic aftermath of her grandfather Gorko's fall, the whereabouts of the last Lazy Gun—the one stolen from the Huhsz by the duchess seven generations earlier and hidden after the duke's death—had been discovered by Gorko's agents and its location somehow recorded in the Unique book named the *Universal Principles*, which itself had been missing for a lot longer.

To Sharrow, the rumor had always seemed just mad enough to be true, though how you could leave a message in something that everybody agreed had vanished centuries earlier, she understood no better than anybody else.

At appropriate times during the night, to allow for the time differences involved, she phoned the Francks in Regioner, left a message for Miz in the Log Jam, failed to track down anybody by the name of Cenuij Mu in what passed for a city data base in Lip City, and filed a visitation request with the Truth Dissemination Service of the Sad Brothers of the Kept Weight, in the Sea House, Udeste province, Caltasp.

She checked on the last Lazy Gun's official Antiquities status too, just for the hell of it. There was, of course, only the one contract extant, from the World Court, offering a graded reward schedule for information leading to the weapon's safe apprehension and an equally impressive sliding scale of steep fines and grisly punishments for anybody harboring such information and not releasing it to the Court.

Nine years earlier there had been tens of contracts—a unique one from the Huhsz that specifically wanted the Gun taken from them by Sharrow's family over two hundred years earlier, and all the rest, which just wanted a Lazy Gun. She and the rest of the team had taken up one of the most lucrative anonymous contracts that required the capture or destruction of either Gun. They had fulfilled the contract, but to this day none of them knew who had paid them (or paid all but one of them; Cenuij Mu had refused his share after the Gun wiped a large part of Lip City off the map).

Shortly after the Lip City explosion, the World Court had legislated to forbid anybody else taking possession of the last remaining Gun, though of course every Antiquities specialist and team in the system knew damn well that the Huhsz—despite being prevented from saying so officially—would attempt to top any reward the World Court might offer for the fabled weapon.

She scrolled through the irreversible mutilations the World Court threatened to inflict on anybody obstructing the lawful sequestration of the last Gun, then clicked out of Antiquities contracts to try another way of tracking down Cenuij Mu in Lip City, once more without success.

Tansil Bassidge rose early and made breakfast; the two women ate together in front of the kitchen screen, watching the all-hours news service; then Tansil took her to the airport for the dawn stratocruiser.

She napped during the flight, landing at Udeste City Intercontinental a couple of hours later, still just ahead of the dawn.

The region of Udeste lay just inside Golter's southern temperate zone, jutting east into Phirar and west into Farvel, Golter's largest ocean. Bounded to the north by the Seproh plateau, its southern boundary was the narrow strip of the Security Franchise, which guarded the forests and fjords of the Embargoed Areas and—beyond—the mountains, tundra, and cold-desert of the historically rebellious province of Lantskaar, which stretched all the way down to the pack ice.

The Sea House lay at the very end of the final promontory of the Farvel Bight, a gulf that stretched in an almost unbroken curve nearly two thousand kilometers from the Areas to the House.

She hired a car and took the autotoll past and around the city-states, bishoprics, Corpslands, enclaves, and family estates of Inner Udeste, then joined an interroute through the villages and farmlands of Outer Udeste's western marches, across the moors toward the coast. The weather deteriorated continuously throughout the journey, increasing cloud compensating for the rising sun so that she seemed to drive forever in a gray-brown half light. Rain came and went in squalls. At the House limits the one entrance in the great chain-mesh fence straddled the small road in a clutter of ramshackle guard buildings on one side and a motley profusion of old, sad-looking tents on the other. A thunderstorm played over the broken hills to the north, and low clouds blanketed the sandy bluffs rising beyond the gate.

There was a short queue at the gate—the usual hopeful petitioners. She drove to the head of the column, sounding the car's Klaxon to shift the gaunt, hollow-eyed men and women out of the way. A scowling contract guard in a dripping camouflage cape walked up and pointed a carbine at her.

"Okay, what's your *name*?" he said, sounding disgusted. He looked up and down the length of the rain-gleaming turbiner.

"Sharrow," she told him.

"*Full* name," he sneered.

"Sharrow," she repeated, smiling. "I believe I'm expected."

The guard looked uncertain. He took a step back.

"Wait here," he said, then added, "ma'am." He disappeared into the guard cabin.

Moments later a captain appeared, fastening his tunic and settling a cap on his head; the guard she'd talked to first held an umbrella over the captain, who wrung his hands as he bent to look in through the window at her. "My lady, we see so few nobles here.... I'm so sorry ... single names take us by surprise ... all the riffraff we have to deal with ... Ah, might one ask for identification? Ah, of course, a noble-house passport ... thank you, thank you. Excellent, thank you, thank you. An honor, if I may say so...."

"Well, don't just stand there, trooper. The gate!"

Traversing the bluff, and dropping back beneath the clouds to the downlands with their ruined and empty towns and then to the canal-sectioned levels before the gravel beach and the great bay, took another half hour. The weather improved unaccountably when she reached the end of the road, where the creamy ribbon broadened out to become a spatulate apron whose seaward edge had disintegrated into rotten chunks of corroded concrete scattered like thick leaves across the sandy soil. Beyond lay Gravel Bay, a rough semicircle bisected by the shallow curve of the great stone causeway and half-filled by the vast bulk of the Sea House. The bay's upper slopes were brown and cream on gray, where decaying seaweed and a scum of windblown surf froth lay tattered and strewn like rags across the gray gravel.

She got out of the car, carrying her satchel; a cold wind tugged at her hair and made her culottes flap. She buttoned the old riding jacket and pulled on her long gloves.

At the end of the causeway stood two tall granite obelisks stationed on either side of the House's artificial isthmus; stretched between them was an enormous rusted iron chain that would have blocked further automotive progress, anyway, even if the concrete apron had connected with the ancient, time-polished flagstones of the causeway. A cold gust of wind brought the stench of rotting seaweed and raw sewage to her, almost making her gag.

She looked up. A little catchfire lightning played about the highest towers, turrets, and aerials of the Sea House. The cloud base, dark gray and solid looking, hung immediately above. She had been here only twice before, and on neither occasion had the rain and mist permitted her to see more than the first fifty meters or so of the Sea House's towering bulk. Today all three hundred meters of it was visible, soaring dimly up toward the overcast.

She pushed a nosegay-scarf up over her mouth and nose, hoisted her satchel onto her shoulder, picked her way through the stumps of decaying concrete, stepped over the great iron chain, and—limping slightly, but walking quickly nevertheless—started down the rutted, cambered surface of the causeway.

At least, she told herself, the rain had stopped.

The Sea House was probably as old as civilization on Golter; somewhere near its long-buried core it reputedly rested on the remains of an ancient castle or temple predating even the zero-year of the First War. Over the millennia the building had grown, accreting about itself new walls, courtyards, turrets, parapets, halls, towers, hangars, barracks, docks, and chimneys.

The history of the planet, even of the system, was written on its tiered burden of ancient stones; here the age had demanded defense, leaving battlements and ramparts; here the emphasis was on the glory of gods, producing helical inscript columns, mutilated idols, and a hundred other religious symbols fashioned in stone and wrought from metal, most of them meaningless for centuries; here the House's occupants had thought fit to honor political benefactors, resulting in statues, relief columns, and triumphal arches over walled-off roadways; at another place trade had been the order of the day, depositing cranes and jetties, graving docks, landing pads, and launch gantries like flotsam around the outskirts of the House's layered walls; on occasion information and communication had ruled, leaving a litter of rusting aerials, broken dishes, and punctured shell domes crusting the scattered summits of the vast structure.

The current incumbents of the Sea House—who claimed despite a wealth of evidence to the contrary that they had inhabited it from the beginning, but who had certainly ruled there for the last five hundred years or so— were the Sad Brothers of the Kept Weight, one of Golter's multitudinous ancient and arcane religious orders. They were exclusively male and claimed to believe in abstinence, continence, and acquiescence to the will of God.

By Golter standards they were cooperative and outgoing, to the extent of permitting secular scholars to study in the many libraries, archives, and depositories the House had accrued over the millennia. A veneer of ecumenicalism allowed visits by monks from other orders, and numerous prisoners from all over the system convicted under a variety of religious laws were held in the House. Other visitors were discouraged.

Sharrow was accepted at the House because six years earlier her half sister Breyguhn had smuggled herself into the structure in an attempt to find and steal the *Universal Principles*, one of the system's many fabled lost Unique books. Breyguhn had failed in her quest; she had been caught and imprisoned in the Sea House, and it was because she was her closest relation that Sharrow was allowed in to visit her.

With what was—arguably—a rare exhibition of an underlying sense of irony, the Sad Brothers had made the recovery of the *Universal Principles* the condition for Breyguhn's release. Whether this implied they did not possess the book but wished to, or that they already did and so knew the task was impossible, was a matter for conjecture.

At the far end of the causeway the stone-flagged road inclined upward to a huge, crumbling central gatehouse, which was the only landward aperture in the House's blank curtain wall of seaweed-hemmed granite. The gateway's deeply machicolated summit hung like a set of gigantic discolored teeth over a throat blocked by a rusting, ten-meter-square door of solid iron. The massive door—and the whole gatehouse—leaned out over the causeway's end in a manner that indicated either serious subsidence, or a desire to intimidate.

She picked a rock up from the fractured surface of the

wheel-grooved causeway and slammed it several times as hard as she could against the ungiving iron of the door. The noise was flat and dull. Rock dust and rust flakes drifted away on the breeze. She dropped the stone, her arm sore from the series of impacts.

After a minute or so she heard metallic sliding, scraping noises coming from the door. Then they faded. After another minute she hissed through her teeth in exasperation, picked up the stone again and slammed it against the door a few more times. She rubbed her arm and looked up into the dark arches of the stonework, searching for faces, cameras, or windows. After a while, the clanking noises returned.

Suddenly a grille opened in the door at chest height; more flakes of rust fell away. She bent down.

"Yes?" said a high, scratchy voice.

"Let me in," she said to the darkness behind the iron-framed hole.

"Ho! 'Let me in,' is it? What's your name, woman?"

She pushed her scarf down from her mouth. "Sharrow."

"*Full* na—"

"That *is* my full name, I'm a fucking aristo. Now let me in, creep."

"*What?*" the voice screeched. She stood back, putting her hands in her pockets while the grille slammed shut and a grinding, creaking noise seemed to shake the whole door. Finally the outline of a much smaller entrance appeared under the flakes of rust, and with a crunch a door swung open, large enough for a human to enter bowed. A small man in a filthy cowled cassock glared out at her. She held her passport in her right hand and shook it in front of his gray, unhealthy-looking face before he could say anything. He stared at the document.

"Cut the crap," she said. "I went through it all last time. I want to speak to Seigneur Jalistre."

"Do you, now? Well, you'll just have to wait. He—" the small monk began, swinging the door shut with one mana-cled hand.

She stepped forward, planting a boot in the doorway.

The brother looked down, eyes wide.

"Get . . . your . . . filthy . . . *female* foot out of my d—" he said, raising his gaze to find that he was looking down the barrel of a large handgun. She pressed his nose with it. His eyes crossed, focusing on the stubby silencer.

He swung the door open slowly, his chain rattling. "Come in," he croaked.

The silencer muzzle left a little white circle imprinted on the gray flesh at the tip of his nose.

"But, sire! She threatened me!"

"I'm sure. However, little brother, you are uninjured—a state subject to amendment, should you ever speak back to me like that again. You will take the Lady Sharrow's weapon, issue a receipt, then escort our guest to the Chain Gallery and equip her with a visitor's chain. At once." The holo image of Seigneur Jalistre's head, bright in the dim and musty gatekeeper's cell, turned to her. The Seigneur's broad, oiled face smiled thinly.

"Lady Sharrow, your sister will receive you in the Hall Dolorous. She had been expecting you."

"Half sister. Thanks," Sharrow said. The holo faded.

She turned and handed her gun to the furiously scowling gatekeeper. He took it, dropped it into a drawer, scribbled quickly on a slip of plastic, threw it at her, and whirled away. "This way, woman," he snarled. "We'll find you a nice *heavy* chain, I think. Oh yes." He scuttled off, muttering; his own chain rattled along the wall-tracks to the doorway as she followed.

The monk snapped the manacle over her right wrist and rattled the heavy iron chain vigorously, snapping it taut against the wall a few times, jerking her arm.

"There," he sneered. "That should keep you on the right track eh, my *lady*?"

She looked calmly at the heavy blue-black manacle and ran her fingers lightly over the rough links of her chain. "You know," she said, dropping her voice and smiling at him, "some people pay good money for this sort of treatment." She arched an eyebrow.

His eyes went wide; he clutched at each side of his cowl, pulling it down over his eyes, then with one skinny, shaking hand pointed to the far end of the long, dimly lit gallery. "Out! Get out of my sight! To the Hall Dolorous and much good may it do you!"

The Sea House was a prison without doors. It was a prison within and around all its other functions.

Everyone in the Sea House, from its most senior abbots and seigneurs to its most constrained and punished prisoners, was manacled and chained. Each chain ended in a miniature bogey—a set of four linked wheels that ran along flanged rails set into the stones of every corridor, room, and external space. These tracks, usually sunk into walls, often embedded in floors, sometimes crossing ceilings, and occasionally—supported on little gantries like banisters and rails—traversing large open spaces, constituted the skeleton of the chain system.

The deepest track was narrower than a finger; it connected the senior Brothers to the House by means of intricately jeweled movements and fine chains spun from a choice of precious metals, the exact element used indicating further subdivisions of rank.

The outermost track was used for visitors a well as lay and honored prisoners; it held a heavy steel chassis attached to an iron chain made from links thicker than a thumb.

The tracks in between provided for two grades of less senior Brothers, the House novices and their servants. Prisoners subject to harsher regimes wore drag-chains attached to their ankles and running on other, still more secure tracks; the lowest of the low were simply chained to dungeon walls. Legend also had it that there were secret places—deep and ancient, or high and (by Sea House standards) relatively modern places—where the chain system did not run, and the Order's senior officers led lives of unparalleled debauchery behind supposedly nonexistent doors . . . but the Sea House, and the chain system itself, did not encourage the investigation of such rumors.

Sharrow's chain-guide wheels clinked as she followed a dark corridor that memory told her ascended to the great Hall.

She encountered one other person on the way: a servant carrying a bulging laundry bundle and heading toward her, using the same wall-track as she. He stopped by a passing-circuit in the wall, flicked his own chain-guide through a set of ceramic points into the higher of the two tracks and waited—foot tapping impatiently—until she was almost level with him; then, as she ducked, he swung his chain over her head, down onto the track's main line, and continued on his way, muttering.

A grubby sock lay fallen on the floor of the corridor; she

turned to say something to the monk, but he had already disappeared into the shadows.

The Hall Dolorous was vast, dark, and unechoing. Its ceiling lost in darkness, its walls shrouded in great dull flags and faded banners that vanished into a hazy distance, the enormous space felt bitter-cold and smelled of charnel smoke. Sharrow shivered and held her scented scarf up to her nose again as she crossed the Hall's width, her chain clicking along the floor-track with a chittering sound like a monstrous insect.

Breyguhn sat in a high-backed stone chair at a massive granite table that looked capable of supporting a small house. A similar chair was stationed on the far side of the table from her, seven meters away. Above Breyguhn, a slab of crystal larger than the table loomed out of the shadows, hiding the Hall's ceiling. The streaked, canted window shed a rheumy yellow light down onto the surface of the great granite platform.

Breyguhn's severe face looked even paler than Sharrow remembered; her hair was tightly bunned, and she wore a loose slate-gray shift made from some coarse, thick material.

Sharrow sat in the vacant stone chair, legs dangling. Breyguhn's dark eyes regarded her.

"Sharrow," she said, her voice flat and faint, seemingly smothered by the pervasive silence of the Hall.

"Breyguhn," Sharrow nodded. "How are you?"

"I am *here*."

"Apart from that," she said levelly.

"There is no apart from that."

Breyguhn brought her hands up from her lap to lay her forearms on the cold, polished surface of the table, palms up. "What is it you want again? I think they told me, but I've forgotten."

Breyguhn was two years younger than Sharrow. She was broader built and a little shorter, with eyes deep set in a face that had once given the impression of strength but now looked pinched and worn.

"I need to find Cenuij," Sharrow told her. "And . . . you might be able to help me look for something—an Antiquity."

"What do you want from Cenuij?" Breyguhn sounded wary.

"The Huhsz have been granted their Passports; they're about to start hunting me. I need Cenuij on my side."

Breyguhn sneered. "You'll be lucky."

"If he won't come with me voluntarily, the Huhsz will force him to work with them. They'll use him to find me."

Breyguhn's eyes went wide. "Maybe he'd *like* that."

Sharrow shrugged. "Maybe," she said. "Maybe not, but at the very least, I have to warn him that when the Huhsz find I've gone, they might come looking for him." Sharrow nodded at Breyguhn. "You're the only person who seems to know exactly where he is."

Breyguhn shrugged. "I haven't seen Cenuij for six years," she said. "They don't allow visits from loved ones here. They allow only visitors whom one doesn't want to see; visitors guaranteed to torment one." Her mouth twisted humorlessly.

"But you're in contact with him," Sharrow said. "He writes."

Breyguhn smiled as if with difficulty, out of practice. "Yes, he writes—real letters, on paper. So much more romantic . . ." Her grin broadened, and Sharrow felt her skin crawl. "They come from Lip City."

"But does he live there?"

"Yes. I thought you knew."

"Whereabouts in the city?"

"Isn't he registered with City Hall?" Breyguhn smiled.

Sharrow frowned. "The place is a barrio, Brey. You know damn well. There are quarters that don't even have electricity."

Breyguhn's smile was wintery. "And whose fault is that, Sharrow?"

"Just tell me where Cenuij is, Brey."

Breyguhn shrugged. "I have no idea. I have to send my letters post restante." She looked down at the tabletop. Her smile faded quickly. "He sounds lonely," she said in a small voice. "I think he has other loves now, but he sounds lonely."

"Isn't there anything in any of his letters—"

Breyguhn looked up, gaze sharp. "Echo Street," she said suddenly.

"Echo Street."

"Don't tell him I told you."

"All right."

Breyguhn shivered. She drew her arms off the surface
of the granite table and let her hands fall to her lap again.
She looked uncertain for a moment. "What else was there?"

"Information on an Antiquity."

"Had you a particular one in mind?"

"The *U.P.*"

Breyguhn put her head back and laughed; a faint echo
of the noise came back, seconds later, from overhead. She
frowned and put one hand over her mouth. "Oh, dear. I'll
pay for that later." She squinted at Sharrow. "You want to go
after the *Universal Principles?*"

"Yes."

"Why," Breyguhn said. "That's the price the Brothers
have set for my release; are you doing this for me,
Sharrow?" she asked, her voice heavy with sarcasm. "How
sweet."

"It's for both of us," Sharrow said. She found herself
dropping her voice, even though she knew that it made no
difference if the Sea House's masters were listening in. "I
need the bit of . . . incidental information, the directions the
work is supposed to contain. Once I have that, I guarantee
I'll give the book to the Sad Brothers. You'll be free to leave
here."

Breyguhn put one hand fanned across her chest and
fluttered her eyelids dramatically. "And why do you think I
can help?" she asked, her voice artificially high.

Sharrow gritted her teeth. "Because," she said, "the last
time I was here you told me they let you use the libraries.
You thought you were on the trail at last. And—"

"*Yes.*" Breyguhn's eyes narrowed. "*And* I sent you," she
hissed, "a *letter.*" She glanced around, then leaned closer. "I
told you I had found the way," she whispered. "The *means*
to discover . . . that book."

Sharrow sighed. She remembered the letter from
Breyguhn; handwritten, barely legible, confused, and full of
wild accusations, bizarre, rambling political tirades and
screeds of incomprehensible pseudo-religious rantings.
Breyguhn's claim in the course of it that she knew how to
find the lost book had been mentioned almost as an aside in
the midst of a manically passionate attack on the legal-
political system in general and the World Court in particular. Sharrow had dismissed it at the time as literally

incredible. "Yes, Brey," she said. "And I wrote back to tell you I wasn't in the Antiquities business anymore."

"But I told you only *you* could find it!" Breyguhn spat the words out.

Sharrow nodded slowly, looking away. "Indeed you did."

"And you didn't believe me."

Sharrow shrugged. "You were the one who thought the book was *here*."

"Maybe it is," Breyguhn said, eyes narrowing. "Maybe they're all here: the *U.P.*, the *Gnost*, the *Analysis of Major Journeys;* all of them. Every damn book Golter's ever had and then lost in ten thousand years and more. They might all be here; a million Uniques, a million treasures, all buried here, lost, thrown away to rot on the dung pile this place is." She directed a small, thin smile at Sharrow. "I haven't found them, but they might be here. Even the Brothers themselves don't know. The House has secrets even they haven't guessed at."

"I'm sure," Sharrow said, tapping her fingers on the granite table. "Now—"

Breyguhn's eyes narrowed. "We both know what the book's supposed to lead to. What are you going to do with *that*?"

"Give it to the Huhsz," Sharrow said. She gave a small laugh, glancing around the vast shadows around them. "We both have . . . eccentric cults to pay off." She settled her gaze on Breyguhn again. "So. What have you got? What is it you know that—?"

"Blood fealty," Breyguhn said suddenly.

Sharrow frowned. "What?"

"Blood fealty," Breyguhn repeated. "Grandfather's inner circle of aides and servants were under genetic thrall to him; he'd had behavioral patterns programmed into them."

"I know; it was one of the reasons the World Court fell on him from the height it did."

"Huh," Breyguhn sighed, eyes bright for a moment. "Yes. If he'd got to a couple of their judges, or Corp. chief execs with that sort of power . . ." She shook her head.

Sharrow sighed. "So it's outlawed."

"Indeed. Outlawed." Breyguhn nodded. "Complete embargo; even in a war they won't release it." She talked quickly now, words spilling over each other. "But the old raptor hid information that way." Her eyes glittered. "When he knew those death-kites of the World Court were closing in on him, he had the most precious things hidden where only his descendants could find them! He did! He did it! I know—I've seen the records of the family laboratories; they're here!"

She sat forward in the great seat, resting her arms on the table surface. She lowered her voice to a whisper. "The Brothers scavenged much of what our grandfather built up, Sharrow—like filcher birds, on instinct. They don't do anything *with* it, they don't seem to care about the outside world; they just gather for gathering's sake ... but it's been lying moldering here for fifty years, and only *my* researches have unearthed it!"

Sharrow leaned forward. *"What?"* she said, trying to remain calm.

"The secret! All the secrets! All the things he'd found, all the Antiquities; ones he'd collected, ones he'd simply tracked down but not yet gathered to him! Locations programmed into his servants, to be played back by *us!*"

Sharrow sat back. "You're sure?"

"Certain!" Breyguhn's sallow, grimacing face was lowered almost to the surface of the table. Her hands were fists, beating the polished granite for emphasis, making her iron chain rattle and clink. " 'The female line' can access these secrets," she hissed. "That's all I know, and I don't know if it includes me; I was born after he was brought down, while he was awaiting trial, and he probably wasn't able to issue the instructions to his clinicians, but you must have inherited the access genes from your mother ... if they weren't scrambled by all that radiation or your precious SNB."

Sharrow waved her hand, dismissing this. "Not a problem. But what do I have to *do?*"

Breyguhn looked suddenly wary, sitting up and back and looking around quickly. "You promise you'll turn the book over to the Brothers once you have what you want from it?"

"Yes."

"You really promise? I'll tell Cenuij you promised."

Sharrow raised one hand. "Look, I promise."

Breyguhn leaned forward, her chin touching the granite table, her eyes wide. "For the *U.P.?*" she whispered. "Bencil Dornay."

"What?" Sharrow said, hardly catching the name. "Tansil . . . ?"

"No! Not Tansil! A man—Bencil, Bencil Dornay, of Vernasayal."

"All right," Sharrow said, nodding. "So do I just ask him, or what?"

Breyguhn giggled suddenly and put her unmanacled hand over her mouth in an unsettlingly girlish gesture. "No, Sharrow," she said, smirking. "No you can't just ask him."

"What then?"

"You have to exchange body fluids."

"What?" Sharrow said, sitting back.

Breyguhn giggled again, glancing around nervously as she did so. "Oh," Breyguhn waved one hand, her smirk subsiding. "A kiss will do, though you'd have to bite him. Or scratch him with fresh saliva under your fingernail. Anything that draws blood—infects him." She suppressed another giggle. "And I *think* the implication is you're supposed to do it in public, too. Isn't that *too* delicious?"

Sharrow looked suspicious. "Are you serious?"

Breyguhn shrugged, her eyes wide. "Perfectly; but then what have you got to lose, Sharrow? You used to love a bit of rough voyeurism with the servant classes, didn't you?"

"Hell, yes—or their pets."

"Bencil Dornay," Breyguhn hissed. "Don't forget!"

"I swear. On my much-donated honor."

"Sharrow! It's not funny. Don't you see what the world needs? Don't you know what this family has been working toward for generations? What Gorko achieved; what Geis might, if he was given the space, the chance?"

Sharrow closed her eyes.

"You selfish clown, Sharrow! You can't see it! You're like all the others—ears on the grass, waiting harvest. How long must we go on like this? These eternal cycles—boom and slump, poverty and frivolity while the death-hand of the Corps and the Colleges and Churches and Court turns the handle. What's the point? Stagnation! Meaninglessness!" Breyguhn shouted. "Our destiny is beyond! We *need* Antiquities, as banners, as rallying points, as bribes if need be; weapons if that's what they are! Break out of the cycle! We need soldiers, not lawyers! One strong man or strong woman with the *will*, not pandering to the lowest common denominator with endless petty compromises!"

"Breyguhn . . . ," Sharrow said, opening her eyes and feeling suddenly very tired.

"How long have we had space travel?" Breyguhn shouted, smacking her fist into the table surface; the chain whipped down, scattering chips of granite. Breyguhn didn't seem to notice. "Seven thousand years! Seven thousand years!" she roared, standing, throwing her arms wide, voice echoing from above. Sharrow heard a bell ringing somewhere.

"Seventy centuries, Sharrow! Seven millennia of footling about in the one miserable system, crawling from rock to rock, losing the gift *twice*, and after all this time half of what we once achieved is like magic to us now!"

Flecks of spittle made little arcs in the air from Breyguhn's lips; they shone in the thin yellow light, then fell to spot the broad surface of the huge table. "Evolution has stopped! The weak and the halt breed, diluting the species; they drag us all down into the mire. We must cut ourselves free!"

Sharrow glimpsed movement in the distance behind the other woman and heard a quick jingling noise.

"Brey—" she said, making a calming, sit-down motion with one hand.

"Can't you *see*? The nebulae should be ours, but we are left with the dust! Sweep it away!" Breyguhn screamed. "Sweep it all away! The slate is full; wipe it out and start again! The decamillenium approaches! Burn the chaff!"

Sharrow stood up as two burly monks dressed in grubby white habits appeared behind her half sister; the first monk took one end of Breyguhn's chain and with a practiced flick looped it over her head and around her arms, encircling her; he pulled tight, jerking her away from the great stone seat—her eyes closed, an expression of sudden joy on her pallid face—while the second monk threw a glittering bag over her head. There was a noise like a sigh, the bag ballooned, then collapsed, then was pulled from Breyguhn's head just as she too collapsed, limp and slack into the arms of the first brother. They zipped her into a straightcoat the shape of a thin, much be-strapped sleeping bag, then dragged her away along the floor, chains rattling.

The whole operation had taken place in less than a dozen heartbeats, and without the pair of monks even glancing at Sharrow.

She watched them go, feeling numb.

The trio disappeared into the shadows, and the rattling of their chains faded until all she could hear was a faint moaning noise of the wind in some flue, high above. She shivered, picked up her satchel, and started back across the empty breadth of the dark hall.

Seigneur Jalistre smiled brightly from the holo screen in the dullness of the gatekeeper's office. "Hmm. The *Universal Principles* for your reasonable expenses, and the freedom of your sister . . ."

"Half sister."

"Indeed, indeed," the Seigneur said, slowly stroking his smoothly fat chin. "Well, I shall put your proposal to my brethren, Lady Sharrow."

"Thank you," she said.

"Of course, you must understand that it is anything but a foregone conclusion that we shall accept your suggestion—we are not normally given to financing Antiquities contracts, and what with the upkeep of this magnificent but ancient building, we are far from being a rich Order, as I'm sure you appreciate. But I feel certain your proposition will be treated seriously. Doubtless we shall be in touch."

"It might be better if I call you," she told the holo image.

"As you wish. Might I suggest you give us a few days to consider your proposal?"

"I'll call in three or four days. Will that be all right?"

"That will be perfect, Lady Sharrow. I am only sorry your need for haste precluded a personal meeting."

"Some other time, perhaps."

"Indeed, indeed." The Seigneur nodded slowly. "Hmm. Well, good day then, Lady Sharrow. Pray tell brother gatekeeper he may resume possession of his office."

"Certainly. Good-bye."

She opened the door; the small gatekeeper stood outside by the postern in the main gate, scowling, the HandCannon held by the barrel in one grimy hand. The office holo screen grayed as she descended the steps to where the small monk waited. She handed him the small plastic slip he'd given her earlier.

"Receipt," she said.

"Gun," replied the gatekeeper. "Take it and get out."

The little monk swung open the postern and gestured to the outside world; a gust of rain and wind blew in, making his habit flap. "Hurry up, woman; get your filthy cloven body out of here!"

She took a step toward the door, then stopped and looked at the little monk. "You know," she said, "for a greeter, your attitude is somewhat suspect; I shall be sending a stiff note to the Udesten Hotel Guide."

"Stuff your smart remarks where only a woman can, trollop."

"And there *really* isn't any need for that sort of language."

"Out, menstruator!"

She stood on the threshold of the door. She shook her head. "I'm not menstruating." She smiled brightly. "Are you a castrato?"

The gatekeeper's eyes went wide. "No!" he barked.

She swung one foot, kicking him in the crotch through the weight of the thick black cassock; he doubled up and fell to the courtyard flagstones, wheezing, his chain clattering around him.

"No," she said, stepping out through the small door to the cold and the rain. "I didn't think so, somehow."

She walked away down the broad gray curve of the causeway, the rain spattering her face while the evil-smelling wind whipped her hair, and realized with some surprise that after nearly eight years of peaceful banality, that made two men she'd hit in less than twenty hours.

Life was becoming interesting again.

3

Echo Street

R oughly ten percent of the land area of Golter was autonomous state—countries in the accepted sense. The
rest was technically Free Land in the form of city-states;
beltland; commercial and industrial parks; farming collectives; ecclesiastical dependencies; bank franchises; sept res-
ervations; leased and freeheld familial estates; Antiquarian
societies' digs; contract diplomatic services' ambassadorial
domains; pressure-group protectorates; charity parklands;
union sanatoria; time-share zones; canal, rail, and road corridors and protected drove-ways; United World enclaves of
a score of different persuasions; hospital, school, and college
grounds; private and public army-training counties; and
land-parcels—usually squatted on—the subject of centuries-
old legal disputes which were effectively owned by the
courts concerned.

The inhabitants of these multifarious territories owed
their allegiance not to any geographically defined authority
or administration, but to the guilds, orders, scientific disci-
plines, linguistic groups, Corporations, clans, and other or-
ganizations that administered them.

The result was that while a physical map of Golter was
a relatively simple depiction of the planet's varied but unre-
markable geography, political maps tended to resemble

something plucked from the wreckage after an explosion in a paint factory.

So, although Udeste was a recognized area, and the city of the same name was the province's effective service capital, there was no necessary proprietorial, administrative, or jurisdictional link between the city and the surrounding countryside. Similarly, the province of Udeste owed no tribute to any bodies representing the continent of Caltasp Minor or even Entire, save that of the Continental Turnpike Authority.

The CTA maintained an impressive, if expensive, network of toll roads extending from the Security Franchise in the south to Pole City in the north. On her way back from the Sea House, Sharrow used the turbiner's head-up display to check on the bid prices for seats on the afternoon and evening strats from Udeste Transcontinental to Capitaller, six thousand kilometers to the northeast, and decided to hang onto the hired car.

Roundly cursing a heinously complex legal dispute that had grounded all charter aircraft in southern Caltasp for the past month; the CTA, for having won the battle against the railroads two millennia earlier; junketeers in general and lawyers heading for conferences in particular, Sharrow took Route Five out of Udeste City.

The turnpike skirted the edge of the Seproh plateau for eighteen hundred kilometers, lanes increasing in number as road trains, buses, and private cars joined from the cities on Caltasp's eastern seaboard and as the curtain-wall cliffs to the north decreased in height from nine kilometers to two.

She left the car on automatic and used its terminal to tap into data bases all over the system, catching up on news and searching out all she could on the fortunes of the Huhsz and the whereabouts of the scattered remnants of Gorko's legacy. She dozed for an hour to some quiet music, and watched the screen for a while.

She rendezvoused with a rest-mobile, ramping up into the echoing parking hold of the Air Cushion Vehicle and leaving the car for refueling while she stretched her legs. She stood on a glassed-in walkway high in the side of the ACV, watching the distant countryside move slowly past and the northbound traffic overtaking; road trains slowly, private vehicles as though the towering hovercraft was standing still.

Back on the road, she put the automobile on manual every now and again, taking the controls and spinning the engine up to maximum while the car boomed and the cloud shadows on the road flashed underneath the turbiner's wheels.

It was late afternoon when the turnpike bunched and swung into the Seproh Tunnel. The two-hour journey was midday bright; when the road exited to the Waist rain forests, it was already dark. She signaled ahead to another restmobile to book a cabin and caught up with the ACV an hour later, maneuvering the car toward it up the canyon formed by two of the parked road trains it was towing.

Just a little too tired to accept the attentions of a prettily handsome road-train driver she met in the bar, she slept soundly and alone in a small, quietly humming outside cabin.

She watched desert roll past while she breakfasted. Linear clouds disappeared into the blue distance above the turnpike's route, like sections of vapor trail.

Beyond the desert and the Callis Range came scrub, then irrigated farms; by the Big Bight the land was lush again. Late afternoon brought her to the colorful, tire-scuffed road signs welcoming her to Regioner.

Regioner—like its capital, Capitaller—owed its stunningly unimaginative name to a particularly bloody interlingual dispute that had taken place so long ago, one language had changed out of all recognition and the other had died entirely, outside of university language-department data bases.

She left the turnpike at sunset and took a laser-straight two-laner through prairies now ripe for their second harvest, sweeping through the warm darkness of the head-heavy crops with the radio loud, singing along at the top of her lungs while the foothills of the Coastal Range rose above the plain ahead.

An hour of hill climbing on intestinally convoluted roads, through dark tunnels and across narrow bridges, past laden orchards and around numerous towns and smaller settlements, brought her to a small, prettily color-washed but otherwise nondescript hill-village a couple of valleys away from Capitaller.

•   •   •

Zefla Franck, once described by Miz Gattse Kuma as nearly two meters of utter voluptuousness with a brain, strolled from the coach stop along the lane between the low white-painted houses near the summit of the hill, her long golden hair undone and straggling to the waist of her slinky dress, her shoes off and held over one shoulder. Her head was tipped back, her long neck curved.

The night was warm. The faint breeze rising from the orchards in the valley below smelled sweet.

She whistled and watched the sparkling sky, where Maidservant—Golter's second moon—shone blue-gray and bounteous near the horizon—a great stone-and-silver ship escorted and surrounded by a school of flickering, glittering lights: habitats and factories, satellites and mirrors, and departing and arriving ships.

The ships were quick, sharp points, sometimes leaving trails; the close-orbit satellites and habitats moved smoothly, some moderately quickly, some very slowly, giving the impression that they were flecks of brightness fixed to a concentric set of clear, revolving spheres; the great mirrors and most far-flung industrial and settlement orbiters hung stationary, fixed lights against the darkness.

It was, thought Zefla, really quite beautiful, and the light cast by all the various satellites, both natural and human-made, seemed soft, seductive, and even—despite its icy, polar-blue pallor—somehow warm. Moonlight and junklight. Junklight. Such a callous, mean-spirited name for something so beautiful—and not even accurate. No single piece of junk was big enough to be seen from the ground, and there was little enough real junk left, anyway; it had been tidied away, swept up, captured, slowed down, dropped in, and burnt off.

She watched a winking satellite move with a perfect, steady stateliness across the vault. She followed its progress as it crossed above her to vanish behind the eaves of a house on the west side of the lane, where soft lights glowed behind pastel shades and music played quietly. She recognized the tune and whistled along as she climbed some steps to a higher level of the lane. She kept her head down to make sure she didn't trip.

She hiccuped suddenly. "Shit!" she said.

Maybe it was looking downward that did it. She looked back up at the sky and hiccuped again. "Shit shit shit!"

She found another slowly moving satellite and determined to ignore the stupid hiccups and concentrate on tracking the little light across the sky. Another hiccup. "Shit!"

She was nearly home, and she hated going into the house with the hiccups; Dloan always made fun of her.

Another hiccup. She growled and fixed all her attention on the satellite.

Her shin hit something hard. "Aow, *fuck*!"

Zefla hopped around on one foot, clutching her shin. "Ow ow ow!" she said. She glared at what she'd bumped into; the moonlight, the junklight, and the warm glow from the leaves of the luminous shrubs at the door of the house revealed a huge pale car almost filling the narrow lane outside the house. Zefla glared at the insect-spattered snout of the auto and muttered.

The shoes she'd been carrying dropped from her fingers to the cobblestones; she hopped on top of the shoes, lost her footing, and fell with a yelp into the luminous bushes.

She lay in the shrubbery, cradled on her back by the creaking branches and surrounded by gently glowing leaves. Disturbed insects buzzed around her head and tickled her bare legs and forearms.

"Oh, sodomy," Zefla sighed as the door opened and her brother looked out. Another head poked out of the door, swiveling; the gaze glanced her way, then away, then back.

"Zef?" said a female voice.

"Hell's caries," Zefla groaned. "I might have known. I suppose this is your car?"

"Good to see you, too, Zefla," Sharrow said, smiling, as Dloan Franck came out of the doorway and offered his sister a hand. Zefla took hold and was pulled upright to stand, swaying hardly at all in front of Sharrow, who folded her arms and grinned at her.

Zefla felt Dloan dust her down and pull a few luminous leaves out of her tangled blond hair.

"Nice car," she said to Sharrow, as Dloan fussed and tutted, pulling a twig from the sleeve of her dress. She stood one-legged, leaning on her brother and rubbing at her bruised shin. "Thought they had collision-avoidance radar."

"It's switched off," Sharrow said, stooping to retrieve Zefla's shoes from the cobbles.

Zefla sighed. "Mine, too."

Sharrow offered her the shoes, but she knocked them gently aside and took the other woman in her arms.

"Sorry about your leg," Sharrow told Zefla, hugging her. "Never mind. It cured my—*hic!*— ... aw, shit ..."

Showered, dried, powdered, and perfumed, Zefla Franck lounged magnificently on a relaxer, her red-brown skin gleaming where her bath sheet didn't cover; another towel kept her hair piled high over her head. She drank a restorative from a long glass and looked out over the junklit valley and the lights of distant villages and houses; the glass of the old conservatory reflected her image and those of Sharrow and Dloan.

Sharrow stood by the glass wall, a drink in her hand, looking out.

Dloan sat in a hanging chair, his hands deep in the neck fur of a sarflet, ruffling the animal's tawny pelt while it sat there with an expression of sleepy bliss on its broad, black-snouted face.

Zefla shook her head. "I don't think so, Shar; they could start trying to trash Geis with the Passports, but it'd eat time; your cuz has lawyers the way other people have freckles, and he can afford *wizards*—grade-one legal slicks with minds like writ-grenades. Toss a few of those boys into the fray, and they could stall the Huhsz for decades; get them so entangled, they won't be able to take a piss without applying for a court order ..." Zefla hiccuped. "Damn!" She gulped. "Excuse me; more sober juice."

She drank deeply from the tall glass again. "... Shit," she continued, "even if they got blanket discovery, Geis could keep ahead of them just generating new companies; dance their grubby little asses through the tax-loop Labyrinth of No Return, shuffling liability, using anonymous proxies, cascading ownership. ... It would take them months to sort out what he's already *got,* never mind what he could create if he wanted to put up a smoke screen. The point to remember is, they've only got a year; with that sort of cast-iron limitation, even Geis's public exposure won't suffer more than a—*hic!* shit—blip when the shareholders realize it's just a glorified nuisance action that's going to evaporate like a fart in a hurricane when the clock stops."

Zefla drank again, then said, "What are you grinning at?"

Sharrow had turned away from the view while Zefla had been talking. She stood, smiling down at the other woman. "I've missed you, Zef."

"Thank you very much," Zefla said, holding one long leg out in front of her and looking at the bruise. "Wish I could say the same for your car."

Sharrow looked down and ran her finger around the top of her glass. "So are you saying I should just go to Geis?"

"Hell, no. I'm just saying that *if* you ever did have to—especially as a last resort after you've run the Huhsz around in circles for a few months and aren't getting any closer to the Gun—you needn't worry about hurting him."

"Even so," Sharrow said, frowning at her drink. "But just because of that . . . maybe I should take him up on his offer now."

"You—*hic!*—want to?" Zefla said, her eyebrows rising.

"No," Sharrow admitted, glancing at her.

"Then," said a deep, rumbling, reasonable voice from the other side of the conservatory, "don't."

Sharrow looked at Dloan. He was even taller than Zefla, and much broader. He had precise, short-cropped blond hair that merged smoothly into an equally carefully trimmed blond beard; he lounged in a crumpled sweat suit, exuding fitness. He kept on tickling the sarflet and looked up only momentarily at Sharrow, smiling as though shyly, then looking away again.

"And let's not forget the law is just one way of the Huhsz getting what they want," Zefla told Sharrow. "I'd guess what Geis would really have to worry about if he sheltered you wouldn't be a legal maneuver, it'd be simple betrayal. One disgruntled employee, one spy, one Huhsz convert in the right place, and all the law in the system wouldn't make any difference—they'd get you and destroy Geis."

Sharrow nodded. "All right, but the alternative is to take to the trail again and ask you guys to come with me."

"Shar, kid," Zefla said. "We never wanted to give it up."

"But I feel I'm being selfish; especially if I could just run to Geis and everything would be all right."

Zefla sighed exasperatedly. "Geis is a pain, Sharrow; the guy has a kind of charming facade, but basically he's a social inadequate whose real place in life is out mugging pensioners and cheating and beating on his girlfriends, and if he had three more names and been raised in a rookery in The Meg rather than the nursery at house Tzant, that's exactly what he would be doing. Instead he jumps out of the commercial equivalent of dark alleys, strips companies, and fucks their employees. He's got no idea how real people work, so he plays the market instead; he's a rich kid who thinks the banks and courts and Corps are his construction set, and he doesn't want anybody else to play. He wants you the way he wants a sexy company, as a bauble, a scalp, something to display. *Never* get beholden to people like that—they'll piss on you and then charge irrigation fees. You crawl under that scumball's skirts, and I'll never talk to you again."

Sharrow grinned and sat on a small chair by the glass wall. "So do we go back on the road?"

Zefla drank, nodded. "Just point us to the on-ramp, girl."

"You're sure?"

Zefla made a pained expression. "Shar, I've been lecturing law at Capitaller for the last five years; I've said all I'm ever going to say, and I keep hearing the same old fucking questions; a really smart student comes along now and again, but it's getting harder and harder to wait during the fallow times in between. An exciting day is when a hunky student bends over or one of the male staff starts growing a beard. My brain's atrophying. I need some excitement."

Sharrow looked at Dloan, who was sitting back in the gently swaying hanging chair and sipping at his drink, the sarflet snoring at his feet. "Dloan?" she said.

Dloan sat looking at her for a while. Eventually he took a long, deep breath, and said, "I was watching some screen a few days ago." He cleared his throat. "Some adventure series. The bad guys were firing bi-propellant HE rounds from FA three hundreds, fitted with silencers."

Dloan fell silent.

Sharrow looked at Zefla, who rolled her eyes.

"I'm holding my breath here, Dloan," Sharrow said.

Dloan looked down at the animal at his feet. "Well, obviously there's no point fitting a silencer when you're firing bi-propellants; the rocket stage makes . . . lots of noise."

"Oh, yes," Sharrow said. "Of course."

"Come on, Dlo," Zefla said. "That sort of stuff always annoyed you. So what?"

"Yes," Dloan said, "but it was the third act before I realized." He sucked his lips in and shook his head.

Zefla and Sharrow exchanged looks. Dloan reached down to stroke the sleeping sarflet.

"I think," Zefla said, "he means he's get—*hic!*—ting disgustingly rusty, and it's time he saw some action before he forgets which end of a gun goes against your shoulder."

Sharrow looked back to Dloan, who just sat there being blond and nodding wisely.

"Fine," Sharrow said.

Zefla drank again. "So—via the Book to the Gun. Think the Huhsz really will call off the hunt if you get them the Lazy Gun first?"

"So It Is Written," Sharrow said with sarcastically emphatic pronunciation.

"And Breyguhn's clue—whatever it is—is it going to work?"

"It sounds semiplausible," Sharrow said, shrugging. "These days that's about the best I have to go on."

"The *Universal Principles*," Zefla breathed. She looked thoughtful. "Supposed to be somewhere midsystem, if you can believe thousand-year-old rumors. This just an excuse to put some vacuum between you and the Huhsz?"

Sharrow shook her head. "Like I say, I have a lead." She glanced at Dloan, who was stroking the sarflet. "Gory details to follow," she told Zefla.

"Can't wait," Zefla said, waggling her dark-blond brows and flexing her perfect toes.

Sharrow raised her glass. "Think team," she said.

Zefla raised her glass. "Yo to that."

Dloan raised his glass. "Team," he said.

Zefla frowned at her glass as though it contained something disgusting. "This calls for something stronger," she said. "And I'm getting too sober anyway." She put the glass down under her seat, felt around, and pulled out an inhalant tube with a look of victorious anticipation on her face. "Let's get into something *mind-bending!*"

She stood in the doorway and looked out, shivering, at the night. It was raining, and the wind was hurrying down the dimly lit street, filling the air with paper scraps like a flock of palely fluttering injured birds. The water in the gutters was thick and black and smelled rancid, washed from some of the hillside tip-mines farther up the hill.

She was average height and dressed cheaply but gaudily: high heels, a micro skirt, and a figure-hugging top. She clutched a small, shiny black fake-hide purse, and wore a little pillbox hat with a black lace veil, which even with the heavy makeup couldn't quite hide the mass of ridged, twisted scar tissue that covered the left side of her face. She held a little transparent plastic parasol over herself, but some of its spokes were broken, and the wind kept gusting, sending rain spraying into her face every now and again. It smelled like somebody had used the doorway as a urinal earlier in the evening.

The street was fairly quiet for this time of night. The occasional car crawled past, windows mirrored. A variety of civilians splashed along the pavement, huddled under cloaks or umbrellas. There were few punters. The ones that were around mostly knew her already; you could always tell the new ones because they'd pass by the doorway she was standing in, do a double take—or just stare—then come forward, looking her up and down and grinning that big grin that said, My lucky night!

It was only when they looked beneath the veil that they backed off, embarrassed, apologizing, as though the Incident had somehow been their fault. . . . But there had been only a couple of those this evening.

The wind shook the scrawny wires strung between the low tenements, producing a whistling noise and making the dim yellow street lamps sway and flicker.

A trolley car went clanking up the street, its skinny whip-mast scratching at the wires above, producing crackling blue sparks. Two boys were hitching a late-night ride on the back fender; they had to keep quiet in case the conductor heard them, but when the blue flashes revealed a girl standing in a doorway, or up an alley with a client, they pointed and waved and made thrusting motions with their groins.

She hoped the trolley wouldn't make a spark when it went past her, but it did. She flinched at the harsh burst of light and the sizzle of noise. She waited for the boys to make some obscene gesture at her, but they were looking at somebody standing in the alleyway directly across from her. The trolley's power line flashed again, and she caught another glimpse of the figure in the alley opposite. Somebody in a long dark coat. For a moment she had the impression she was being watched. Her heart started to beat faster; oh, not police, not tonight!

Then the figure—medium height, face hidden by a hat and a filter mask—left the alleyway and walked down the pavement on the far side of the street, walking slightly oddly, stiff-legged, like somebody trying to disguise a limp.

Just then two uniformed policemen walked past her doorway, their long capes dripping. She shrank back, but they weren't on a roundup, not tonight. Probably they were intent on getting back to the precinct station and hitting the canteen. She relaxed again.

Suddenly the figure was in front of her.

She drew her breath in.

"Hi," the man said, pulling his mask down.

She relaxed. It wasn't the person from the other side of the street; it was a regular, the one she'd been hoping would turn up. He wore a short pale cape and a broad hat. He was a smallish, thin man with muddy-looking skin and intensely blue eyes you couldn't look at for too long.

"Oh," she said, and smiled. She had slightly prominent teeth, already spotted with decay. "Hi, sweetie."

"Sweetie . . . ," he said, sounding amused. He stood in the doorway with her and gently put his hand up underneath the lace veil to her face and stroked the rough surface of the old radiation burn. His fingers were delicate and slim. She tried not to flinch.

"You smell different this evening," he said. His voice was like his eyes, sharp and demanding.

"New perfume. Like it?"

"It'll do," he said. He withdrew his hand from her ruined face and sighed. "Shall we go?"

"Okay."

They left the doorway and walked down the street together, not touching; she had to walk quickly, teetering on her high heels, to keep up with him. A couple of times, glancing at their reflections in shop windows, she thought she saw the figure she'd seen earlier in the alleyway, following them with that odd stiff-legged gait.

•　　•　　•

"Here," he said, entering a narrow alley. It was dark, and she almost tripped on rubbish left on the dark, uneven bricks underfoot.

"But, doll," she said, following him down the alley and wondering what was going on. "This isn't your—"

"Shut up," he told her. He started up a flight of rickety wooden steps. She looked back and saw the stiff-legged figure enter the alleyway behind them, silhouetting against the marginally brighter street behind, then disappearing into the shadows. "Hurry up!" her client hissed from the top of the steps. She glanced back at the darkness where the figure had vanished, and then ran as fast as her high heels would allow, up the creaking wooden steps.

There was a broad wooden gantry at the top of the steps, dotted with small sheds and ladders; it stretched along the side of the dank, bow-sided tenement. She couldn't see him, but then a hand came out of the shadows and pulled her into the shelter of a small lean-to. A hand went over her mouth, and she let him pull her against him, his breath warm on the back of her neck. Something glinted in his other hand, pointing out to the deck of the wooden gantry. Her eyes were wide and her heart thudded. She clutched the little black purse to her chest, as though hoping it would protect her.

She heard a creaking noise, then slow footsteps. The hand over her mouth clamped tighter.

The figure in the long dark coat came into view, still walking lopsidedly, then stopping and standing directly opposite them. The figure reached in through the coat, and from what must have been a leg holster, pulled out a very long gun with a slim sight on top of the barrel. The man holding her tensed.

A creaking noise came from behind and beneath her.

The figure spun toward them, the gun coming up.

The man behind her shouted something; his gun fired, a burst of light and sound that lit up every grubby cranny of the alley and filled its length with a terrible barking noise. The figure with the rifle was blown back, folding in two; the great long gun made a quiet roar, and something flashed overhead as the figure went straight through the hand rail at the edge of the wooden gantry to fall flaming to the stones of the alleyway.

She looked up. Above the wooden gantry a small net

swung from a piece of broken guttering. The net swayed in the wind, making a fizzing, sputtering noise and glowing with a strange green light.

The man followed her gaze.

"Prophet's blood, it was only a stun-net," he whispered.

She tottered to the broken rail and looked down to see the figure lying torn almost in half and burning among the packing cases and trash against the wall of the tenement opposite. A smell of roasted flesh wafted up from the body, making her feel sick.

The man grabbed her hand. "Come on!" he said. They ran.

"God help me, I almost enjoyed that," he said, stumbling into the service entrance of the quiet apartment block. He took out his key, then paused, breathing hard, looking at her. "You're still keen, I hope, yes?"

"Never say no to a man with a gun," she said, trying to get out of the bright light shining near the laundry baskets.

He smiled and took off his short cloak with a flourish. "Let's take the service lift."

She busied herself with her makeup in the lift, turning to the corner and squinting into the little mirror, leaving the veil down while one hand worked behind it. She caught a glimpse of his face; he looked amused.

They entered his apartment. It was surprisingly plush, lit by subdued but expensive wall panels, full of ancient artworks and pieces of fancy-looking equipment. The rug in the main room—patterned after the fashion of an early electronic chip—had a deep, luxuriant pile. He lit a cheroot and sat down in a big couch. "Strip," he told her.

She stood just in front of him and—still determinedly holding the little purse—slowly pulled her veil away and let it fall to the floor. The radiation burn looked livid and raw, even under the makeup. The man on the couch swallowed, breathing deeply. He drew on the cheroot, then left it in his mouth as he folded his arms.

She took hold of the pillbox hat and removed it, too. Her hair had been gathered up under the hat; now it fell out, spilling down her back.

He looked surprised. "When did you—?" he began, frowning.

She held one hand up flat toward him and shook her

head, then put the same hand to the side of her face. She gripped the top edge of the radiation scar and slowly pulled it down, tearing it away from her cheek with a glutinous, sucking noise.

His eyes widened and his jaw dropped. The cheroot fell from his mouth onto the chest of his shirt.

She dropped the black purse from her other hand, which now held a small stubby pistol with no muzzle aperture. She spat out the fake teeth; they bounced on the printed-circuit rug.

"Hello, Cenuij," she said.

"Sha—!" he had time to gasp, before the gun in her hand buzzed, his eyes closed, and he went limp, sliding slowly off the couch onto the floor.

She sniffed, wondering what was burning, then took two quick steps toward him and removed the cheroot from the hole in his shirt before it burned any more of his chest hair.

He woke to the sound of spattering rain; he was sitting slumped in the rear seat of a tall All Terrain, and it was dark outside. Sharrow sat opposite him. His whole body was tingling, his head was sore, and he didn't think it wise to try speaking for a while. He looked around groggily.

Through rain-streaked glass to the right, he could see a giant open-cast mine lit by dotted lights. The mine had eaten away half of an enormous conical hill and was continuing to shave away the other half. Looking carefully, he could make out a motley collection of trucks, draglines, and lines of people with shovels, all working the canted gray face of the floodlit, sectioned hill. At least he wasn't having trouble focusing.

"Cenuij?" she said.

He looked at her. He decided to try speaking.

"What?" he said. His mouth seemed to be working all right. Good sign. He flexed the tingling muscles in his face.

Sharrow frowned. "Are you okay?"

"She fries my synapses with a neurostunner whose insurance warranty ran out around the time of the Skytube, then she asks if I'm okay," he said, attempting to laugh but coughing instead.

Sharrow poured something brown and fragrant from a flask into a cup; he took it and smelled spirit; he sipped at it, then knocked it back, smacking his lips. He almost threw it up again immediately, but held it down and felt it warm him.

"You once told me," she said, "that if you had to be knocked unconscious, that's the way you'd like it done, with one of those."

"I remember," he said. "It was the morning after Miz nearly rammed that Tax destroyer. We were in a tavern in Malishu, and you were whining about your hangover; you wore a low-cut green scoop-neck, and Miz had left a line of love bites like footprints leading down your left tit. But I didn't think you'd treat an innocent observation as a definite request."

"As you see," Sharrow grinned, "the stunner has totally scrambled that perfect memory."

"Just testing," Cenuij said.

He stretched. He didn't seem to be tied up in any way, and Sharrow wasn't holding the stun gun.

"Anyway," she said, "I'm sorry."

"Indeed. I can see contrition oozing from your every pore."

She nodded toward the open-cast mine. "Know where we are?"

"Mine Seven, a little west of the city perimeter road." He rubbed at his leg muscles; they still felt tingly and weak.

"We're right on the city limits," Sharrow said. She nodded. "I step out that door, and I'm outside the jurisdiction; you step out your side, and you're back in Lip City."

"What are you trying to do, Sharrow? Impress me with your navigational skills?"

"I'm giving you a choice, asking you to come with me . . . but if you won't, I'm letting you go."

"You kidnap me first, *then* you ask me?" Cenuij shook his head. "Retirement's addled your brains."

"Dammit, Cenuij! I didn't mean to snatch you; I just wanted to *get* to you. But that enthusiast with the stun-net rattled me. I wanted to get us both out of there."

"Well, congratulations," he said. "What a spiffing plan."

"All right," she said, raising her voice. "What was I supposed to do?" She got her voice under control again. "Would you have listened to me? If I'd tried to contact you, would you have given me the time to say anything?"

"No. I'd have switched off the instant I knew it was you."

"And if I'd written?"

"Same. Switched the screen off or torn the letter up, accordingly." He nodded quickly. "And if you'd approached me in the street, I'd have walked away, run away, hailed a cab, jumped on a trolley, told a policeman who you were—anything. In fact, all the things I intend to do right now, or at least as soon as my legs feel like they'll work again."

"So what was I supposed to do, you awkward bastard?" Sharrow shouted, leaning forward at him.

"Leave me a-fucking-lone, that's what!" he roared back into her face.

They glowered at each other, nose to nose. Then she sat back in the seat, looking out at the darkness on the other side of the car. He sat back, too.

"The Huhsz are after me," she said quietly, not looking at him. "Or they will be, very soon. With a hunting Passport. A legal execution warrant—"

"I know what a hunting Passport is," he snapped.

"They might try using you to get to me, Cenuij."

"Sharrow, can't you get it through those artfully wanton black curls that I want nothing to do with you? I won't indulge in some pathetic, nostalgic attempt to get us all back together again and be pals and pretend nothing bad ever happened—just in case that's what's on your mind—but equally I assure you I have no interest whatsoever trying to help the Huhsz second-guess your every action; that would be almost as bad as actually being in your company."

Sharrow looked as if she were trying to control herself, then suddenly sat forward again. "Nothing to do with me? So why are you fucking the only whore in Lip City who could pass for my clone?"

"I don't *fuck* her, Sharrow," Cenuij said, looking genuinely surprised. "I just enjoy *humiliating* her!" He laughed. "And anyway, she's rather better looking than you are." He smiled. "Apart from that unfortunate eight-year-old radiation burn. I wonder how the poor girl got *that*?"

"Cenuij—"

"And where's *she*? The real girl? What have you done with her?"

Sharrow waved one hand. "Teel's fine; she's spaced on

Zonk watching screen from the whirlbath in a hotel suite. *She's* having a great night."

"She'd better be," Cenuij said.

"Oh! You enjoy humiliating her, but now you're all concerned for her well-being." She sneered back. "Make sense, Cenuij."

He smiled. "I am. But you wouldn't understand."

"And what sort of weird kick do you get from humiliating her, anyway?"

Cenuij shrugged languidly. "Call it revenge."

Sharrow sat back again, shaking her head. "Shit, you're sick."

"*I'm* sick?" Cenuij laughed. He crossed his arms and gazed up at the car's ceiling lining. "She murders four hundred and sixty-eight thousand people, and she calls *me* sick!"

"Oh, for the last fucking time," she shouted. "I didn't know they were going to start hacking the gun to bits in the goddamn *city*!"

"You should have known!" he shouted back. "That's where their labs were! That's where they *announced* they were going to dismantle the damn thing!"

"I thought they meant the lab in the desert! I didn't know they'd do it in the city!"

"You should have *guessed*!"

"I couldn't believe anybody would be that stupid!"

"When have they ever been anything *else*?" Cenuij roared. "You *should* have guessed!"

"Well, I just fucking didn't!" Sharrow yelled. She sat back, sniffing mightily.

Cenuij sat silently, massaging his legs.

Eventually Sharrow said, "That was probably some contract hunter with the net-gun tonight. If they'd succeeded, you'd be in a Huhsz satrapy by dawn, all wired and juiced up so you'd have no fucking *choice* but to tell them what I was going to do next."

"So I'll stop talking to strangers," Cenuij said. He tested one leg, flexing it. He sat forward suddenly. "Where are my shoes?" he demanded.

Sharrow dug under her seat, threw them over to him. He slipped them on and fastened them.

"Have you heard from Breyguhn recently?" she asked.

He stopped tightening a heel strap and glanced at her.

"No. The good Brothers have what one might call a playful attitude toward mail. I expect I'll get another letter in a month or so."

"I saw her four days ago."

Cenuij looked wary. "Mm-hmm," he said, sitting back. "And how . . . how is she?"

Sharrow looked away. "Not too good. I mean, surviving physically, but . . ."

"She didn't give you . . . a letter or anything for me?" Cenuij asked.

"No." Sharrow shook her head. "Look," she said. "If we find the *Universal Principles*, we can get her out. I only need the message in it; we can give the Brothers the book itself."

Cenuij looked troubled, then sat back, sneering. "You say," he said. His cloak lay on the seat beside him; he put it over his shoulders and fastened it, laughing. "Some piece of utterly unattributable Dascen family folklore has it that your grandpa somehow left a message in a book nobody's set eyes on for a millennia, and of which there is no indication he even started to look for, and you *believe* it?" He shook his head.

"Dammit, Cenuij, it's the best we've got to go on."

"And what if this rumor is—by some miracle—only half-wrong and you do need the book itself?" Cenuij asked.

"We'll do all we can," Sharrow said, sighing. "I promised."

"You promised." Cenuij sat still for a while. He flexed both legs. "Okay," he said. "I'll think about it." He put one hand to the door of the vehicle.

Sharrow put her hand over his. He looked into her eyes, but she wouldn't take her hand away. "Cenuij," she said. "Please, come now. They'll take you if you try to stay. I'm telling the truth, I swear."

He looked at her hand. She took it away. He opened the door and climbed down out of the All Terrain. He stood holding the door for a moment, checking that his legs were going to hold him when he tried to walk.

"Sharrow," he said, looking up at her. "I'm only just starting to think that maybe you really are telling the truth about what happened to the Lazy Gun and Lip City." He gave a sort of half laugh. "But that's taken eight years; let's not rush things, shall we?"

She leaned forward, imploring. "Cenuij, we need you. *Please* . . . in the name of . . ." Her voice died away.

"Yes, Sharrow," he smiled. "In the name of what?" She just stared at him. He shook his head. "There's not really anything you respect or care about enough to use as an oath, is there?" He smiled. "Except perhaps yourself, and that wouldn't sound right, would it?" He took a step backward, letting go of the door. "Like I said, I'll think about it." He pulled his cloak closed. "Where can I contact you?"

She closed her eyes with a look of despair. "The Log Jam, with Miz," she said.

"Ah, of course." He turned to go, facing the giant open-cast mine on the dark hillside. Then he stopped and turned back, the rain blowing about him. He nodded behind him at the mine. "See that, Sharrow? The open-cast? Mining an ancient spoil heap; sifting the already discarded, looking for treasure in what was rubbish . . . maybe not even for the first time, either. We live in the dust of our forebears, insects crawling in their dung. Splendid, isn't it?"

He turned and walked away along the bank of an old tailings pond. He'd gone another few paces when he turned once more and called out, "By the way—you *were* very convincing about one thing . . . until you took the radiation scar off."

He laughed and strode off toward the half-consumed spoil heap.

4

Log Jam

Like a lot of Golterian oddities, the Log Jam was basically a tax dodge.

Jonolrey, Golter's second-largest continent, lay across Phirar from Caltasp. The same root word in a long-lost language that had provided the name for the ocean of Phirar had also given the region of Piphram its name. Once Piphram had been a powerful state, the greatest trading nation on the planet, practically running the world's entire merchant marine. But that had been long ago; now it was just another entangledly autonomous patchwork Free Area, no less prosperous or gaudy than any other part of the world.

The administrative capital of Piphram, which by sheer coincidence happened actually to lie within the area its contract covered, was the Log Jam.

Sunlit land slid under the small jet, flowing green and brown beneath its forward-veed wings as it throttled back and adjusted its position in the center of the conical glidepath.

Sharrow watched Dloan at the plane's controls; he sat in the pilot's seat of the hired aircraft, studying its instrument screens. He'd flown the plane manually for takeoff and ascent from Regioner and had wanted to land it, too, but the

Log Jam had had too many bad experiences with people trying to land on Carrier Field and so insisted on autolandings. Dloan was going to make sure it went all right.

Zefla, in a seat across from Sharrow, was fiddling with the small cabin's screen controls; channel-hopping to produce a confused succession of images and background sound bursts.

Sharrow looked out of the window, at the cloud-dappled land moving smoothly underneath.

"—alked to Doctor Fretis Braäst, moderator of the Huhsz college at Yadayeypon Ecclesiastical School."

"Well, *yes*," Zefla said, turning up the sound. Sharrow glanced up at the screen to see a well-groomed male presenter talking to camera; behind him, on the studio wall, was a gigantic, slightly grainy holograph of her own face. "You're a star, kid," Zefla said, smiling dazzlingly. Dloan turned around to watch.

Sharrow scowled at the screen. "Is that the best photo they could get? Must be ten years old; look at my hair. Ugh."

The blowup of Sharrow's face was replaced by a live holo of a trim-looking elderly man with white hair and a white beard. He had twinkly eyes and an understanding smile. He was dressed in a light-gray academic gown with discreet but numerous qualification ribbons decorating one side of the collar.

"Doctor Braäst," said the presenter, "this is a terrible thing, isn't it? Here we are, about to start the second decamillenium, and your faith wants to hunt down and kill—preferably put to death ceremonially, in fact—a woman who has never been convicted of anything and whose only crime appears to be having been born, and being born female."

Doctor Braäst smiled briefly. "Well, Keldon, I think you'll find that the Lady Sharrow *does* have a string of convictions for a variety of crimes in Malishu, Miykenns, dating—"

"Doctor Braäst," the presenter gave a pained smile and glanced down at a screenboard balanced on his knee. "Those were minor public order offenses; I don't think you can use fifteen-year-old fines for brawling and insulting a police officer as an excuse for—"

"I beg your pardon, Keldon," the white-haired man smiled. "I was just trying to keep things totally accurate."

"Well, fine, but to return to—"

"And I'd remind you that the whole issue of the use of such Passports is not a Huhsz tenet. This is a civil process with a pedigree over two millennia old; what we are told—and what we have to accept—is that this is a civilized response to the problem of assassination and the potential for disruption it implies."

"Well, I believe a lot of people would say that all assassination ought to be illegal—"

"Perhaps so, but it was found that its codification caused less disruption than extralegal actions."

"Well, well. We aren't here to discuss the history of legal . . . legal history, Doctor; we're talking about the fate of one woman you seem determined to persecute and hound to death with all the influence and resources your—extremely wealthy—faith can muster."

"Well, I agree that on the face of it this might seem terribly unfortunate for the lady—"

"I suspect most people would put it rather stronger than that—"

"Although this is a lady associated with the Accident in Lip City eight years—"

"This is all rumor, though, isn't it, Doctor Braäst? Smear tactics. She hasn't been convicted of anything. . . . In fact, she successfully sued two screen services that implicated her in the Lip City Accident—"

"I can understand you're frightened of her doing the same to you. . . ."

"But none of this alters the fact that you want this woman dead, Doctor Braäst. Why?"

(*"That's* more like it," Zefla said, nodding.)

"Keldon, this is an unfortunate matter going back many generations, to an act of desecration, violence, and rape carried out by one of the lady's ancestors—"

"A version of events that has always been vigorously denied by—"

"Of course it's been denied, Keldon," the small doctor said, looking exasperated. "If you'll just let me finish . . ."

"I beg your pardon; go on."

"In which a young temple virgin was abducted, several of our Order were seriously injured, and numerous acts of violently destructive desecration, some of them of an obscene and depraved nature I can't repeat here, were committed by troops of the Dascen clan—"

"Again, this is all denied—"

"Please let me finish. This unfortunate child was then raped, despoiled by Duke Chlea, forced to marry him and to bear children. When this poor, defiled, and frightened creature attempted to return herself and her twins to the safety and security of the temple she had known since she was an infant—"

"Now, really, Doctor Braäst, history is quite clear on this. The Huhsz . . . Huhsz supporters, I should say, simply attacked—"

"History is people and records and the human memory and therefore not infallible, Keldon; *we* have divine guidance in this, which *is*."

"But Doctor Braäst, surely no matter whose version of this tragic story you believe, there is no reason to carry this blood feud on into the present."

"But *we* did not," the white-haired man said reasonably. "This confused and unfortunate woman swore eternal antipathy to our faith; swore, indeed, that she would murder the next Prophet Incarnate, should he appear in her lifetime, and furthermore bound all her line to the same oath. That she had been raped, and then indoctrinated, by the Dascen tribe in an atmosphere of hatred and atheist lies might help to explain such an abomination, but it cannot excuse it.

"Our Patriarch was at first determined to ignore this outrage, but God himself, in a visitation of a kind that occurs less than once in a generation, spoke to him and told the blessed Patriarch that he had but one course of action: blood had to be met with blood. By all means meet tolerance with tolerance, but equally one must meet intolerance with intolerance.

"The Messiah *cannot* be born until the threat has been lifted or the desecration ameliorated. The oath has been made, the vendetta instituted, and all by the Dascen female line. They might think that they can rescind their rash and sacrilegious curse—indeed I perfectly understand that they want to do so now—but I'm afraid God's word is not to be so trifled with. What must be done must be done. Even if we *don't* get the Passports—though I am confident we shall—this is not a matter for compromise."

"Of course, Doctor Braäst, cynics might say that the real object of all this is to secure the return of what is now the very last Lazy Gun, which was the chief treasure taken from—"

"The exact nature of the treasure is irrelevant, Keldon, but it was as an act of mercy that God, through the Patriarch, allowed that the return of this device—never at any time used by the Huhsz, I might point out, and of purely ceremonial value—would signal an end to this tragic feud, from our side at least."

"But, Doctor, what it all boils down to is this: can *any* amount of this sort of reasoning, historical or otherwise, really justify this sort of barbaric practice in this day and age? Briefly, please."

"Barbarism is always with us, Keldon. Lip City suffered an act of unparalleled barbarity eight years ago. What we have been forced to do is not barbaric; it is the will and the mercy of God. We can no more ignore this duty than we can neglect the adoration of Him. The Lady Sharrow—though we may feel sorry for her on a human level—represents a living insult for all those of the True and Blessed Belief. Her fate is not a matter for debate. She is the last of her line—a sad, barren, and disabled figure whose misery has gone on too long. Her spirit, when it is finally released, will sing for joy that we were the ones who rescued her from her torment. I look forward to the eternal instant when her voice joins those of the Blessed whose conversion occurs after death; hers will be a muted exaltation, but it will be exaltation, nevertheless, and eternal. Surely we should all wish her that."

"Doctor Braäst, we're out of time. Thank you for those words."

"Thank you, Keldon."

"Well," the presenter said, turning to face the camera again with his eyebrows raised and just the suggestion of a shake of his head. "The war in Imthaid, now—"

Zefla switched the screen off. Dloan turned back to the jet's controls. The Log Jam was a vast metallic ice crystal, glittering in the distance at the margin of the land and sea.

Zefla turned to Sharrow, slinging one long leg over her seat. "Buncha religious fuckwits." She shook her head, blond hair swinging. "You're going to be a fucking heroine at the end of this, Shar, and they're going to look like the humorless hysterical dickshits they are."

Sharrow looked disconsolately at the darkened screen, nodding. "Only if they don't get me," she said, turning away and looking out the window, where the outlying sections of the Log Jam rose toward the dropping plane like a set of enormous, gleaming fingers.

The plane landed without incident on Carrier Field.

When the state of Piphram had been on the way downhill after its era of grandeur and wealth centuries earlier, many of the seaships of its merchant fleet had been sold, many more had been scrapped, and hundreds had been mothballed. The mothballed ships—everything from megatonne bulk carriers to the most delicate and exquisite repossessed private yacht—had mostly been brought home, to lie in a broad lagoon on the coast of Piphram's Phirarian province and await better trading conditions.

Subsequently a modest land boom on the nearby coastal strip, between the Snowy Mountains and the lagoon-dotted coast, pushed property prices up, and Piphram's historically punitive real-estate taxes exaggerated the effect. Then somebody—spotting a loophole in the Tax status of the lagoons—thought of using a couple of old car ferries as temporary floating dormitories.

The two down-at-stern ferries, or rather their marginal situation, had proved to be a seed-point; within the chaos of Golter's furiously complicated economic ecology, finance—along with its relevant material manifestations—tended to concentrate and crystallize almost instantaneously around any region where the conditions for profit making were even one shade more promising than elsewhere.

Thus, the Log Jam had grown from a few rusty hulks to a fully fledged city in less than a hundred years. At first the ships were moored together in clumps and people moved between them on small craft, then later the vessels were joined together. Some were welded to each other and some had secondary housing, office and factory units built upon and between them until the individual identity of the majority of the ships began to disappear in the emerging topology of the conglomerative city.

The Log Jam now comprised many thousands of ships, and a new one was added every few weeks; it had spread to the limits of the first lagoon, then spread out to sea and taken over three other lagoons along the coast, to become home to over two million people. Its main airport—which could be moved as one unit so that it was always on the outskirts of the city—was composed of forty old oil tankers joined side by side, their decks stripped, smoothed, and strengthened to take the strats and transport aircraft. Its largely mothballed space port was a collection of ancient oil production platforms, towering at the southernmost end of the city; its docks were a few dozen dry docks, crane-carrying bulk carriers, and militarily obsolete fleet auxiliary vessels.

Eight old aircraft carriers, remnants of a commercial navy, jointly made up Carrier Field, where the V-winged executive jet landed.

The little plane was quickly towed away and downlifted to be stored in the bowels of one of the adjoining ex-supertankers which now served as supplementary hangars to the antique carriers.

Sharrow, Zefla, and Dloan looked around the deck of the old ship while a tall, stooped steward with a full beard loaded their baggage onto a whining trolley. The weather was warm and humid and the sun high in a slightly hazy sky.

"Mornin' t'yez," wheezed the steward, nodding to them. "This your first time t'the Jam, hn?"

"No," said Sharrow, scowling.

"It is mine," Zefla said brightly.

"Almost a crime, lovely lady like yerself not visitin the Jam till now, if ye don't mind me sayin so, ma'am," the steward told Zefla. He took the control stick at the front of the cart and started to walk away, the cart whining behind him. "Been a good few years an more since we ad the priv'lidge of welcomin two such beautiful ladies such as yourselves to the old Jam. Makes the day a better one just seein two such enchantin 'zamples of the fair sex, it do, an it were a pretty fine day t'begin with. But made the better now with your presence, lovely ladies, like I says. An no mistake."

"You are too kind," Zefla laughed.

"And talkative," muttered Sharrow.

"Wha's that, ma'am?"

"Nothing," Sharrow said.

They followed the tall steward across the deck of the field toward the superstructure that had been one of the old carriers' command islands and was now the Arrivals hall. A line of laden baggage carts blocked their way. Dloan was looking at them suspiciously.

Zefla looked around, frowning. "I thought Miz said he'd—"

A brassy, sonorous musical chord burst from beyond the baggage trolleys; a flock of white seabirds, undisturbed by the jet's arrival, flew squawking from the superstructure as the sound echoed across the deck. The baggage trolleys jerked into motion as a small tractor unit at one end pulled them away, revealing a twenty-strong ceremonial band sitting behind, all dressed in bright red-and-gold uniforms and blowing on glittering and extremely noisy instruments.

Sharrow recognized the tune but couldn't remember the name. She looked at Zefla, who shrugged. Dloan was kneeling, a large pistol in his hands, though it was pointed at the deck for the moment as he looked around. The band stood up and started walking toward them, still playing. Dloan had switched his attention to the tall, bearded steward, who was now no longer stooped, and who was taking off his jacket. He threw his hat away, ripped the beard off.

He stepped forward, went down on one knee in front of Sharrow, and took her hand in his.

"My lady! Our leader!" he exclaimed, and kissed her hand.

The band members were surging around and past them, instruments swinging to and fro, up and down. Dloan had stood and was holstering his pistol. Zefla laughed, her hands over her ears. Sharrow smiled and shook her head as Miz reached into his shirt, produced a bunch of flowers, and presented them to her. She accepted them, putting the blossoms to her nose while Miz jumped to his feet.

He was tall, loose-limbed, and his pale brown face—framed by long, straight fair hair—looked younger than it deserved to, and almost determinedly carefree. He had sparkling eyes cratered in a network of fine lines, a thin hook of a nose, and a great, grinning mouth with generous lips and uneven teeth.

"Idiot!" she shouted at him, laughing; the band blared and circled around them.

He put his arms out, a questioning look on his face. She put the flower stems in her mouth, holding them with her teeth, then went to him, embracing him.

"Hiya, beautiful!" he shouted over the noise of the band, and lifted her off her feet. He whirled her around once, winking broadly at Zefla and Dloan in turn as he did so. His smile sparkled in the sunlight and seemed to rival the carrier's deck in extent.

He set Sharrow back on her feet, still holding her. She pushed her head forward to deposit the flowers on his shoulder, in a curiously animallike gesture that brought a brief tremor to his face; a sudden expression of something between desire and despair. It was gone in an instant, and only Zefla saw it. The flowers fell between Miz and Sharrow, nestling against their chests.

"Good to see ya, youngster!" he shouted.

"Not so young anymore," Sharrow told him.

"I knew you'd say that."

"Well, I never could hide much from you."

"There was a lot you never wanted to," he leered. He waggled his eyebrows.

"Oh," she tutted, pushing him away. The flowers fell toward the deck; he scooped them up easily and with a look of pretended hurt clutched them to his chest. His eyes closed, then he swiveled to bow very formally to Zefla and present them to her instead. Zefla took them and threw them to Sharrow, and while Miz was still watching their trajectory, stepped forward and hugged him, lifting him off his feet and whirling him around, all in the middle of the bellowing, glittering, encircling band.

"Waaaa!" Miz wailed, as Zefla spun faster.

Dloan smiled; Sharrow laughed.

"Ah, Lady Sharrow."

"Brother Seigneur."

"Doubtless you wish to know the result of our deliberations concerning your proposal."

"Yes, please."

"I am happy to say that the Brethren have agreed. When the property is delivered, your sister will be released."

"Half sister. And the expenses?"

"On what is called commercial Scale Two, I believe. Will that be acceptable?"

"I suppose so."

"We shall have a business agency draw up the contract

itself; they will sort out the details with you or your lawyer. Their number will be tagged to this message record."

"Thank you. I'll call them now."

"Indeed. Your servant, my lady."

The broad face in the holo smiled insincerely.

A fresh warm wind blew, making the lines of bunting flutter and rustle in gay lines across the shock of cloudless blue sky. The sea quivered, spangling, and across the sharp, glittering creases of the waves the small yachts came skimming like flat stones, their sails bosoming out and flourishing vivid stripes and bright patterns at the massed spectators. The crowd lining the rails of the ships or seated on the choicer barges roared into the breeze and waved hats and scarves; they threw streamers and let off noisy fireworks.

The yachts rounded the stand-turn buoy, heeling until their gunwales touched the water, then righted, reset their sails for the new reach, and raced off toward the next buoy with the wind directly behind them. Spinnakers blossomed, one by one, snapping and filling like the chests of exotic displaying birds. A few of the yacht crews found time to wave back at the crowd; the people roared again, as though trying to fill the gaudy sails with their breath.

Miz guided Sharrow through the groups of chattering people on the barge, nodding to faces he recognized and occasionally exchanging greetings but not stopping to make introductions. He was dressed in achingly bright shorts and a short-sleeved shirt only a fraction quieter than the cheers of the crowds on the spectator barges. Sharrow wore a long gauzy dress of pale green; she sported dark glasses and held a parasol. Miz carried her satchel for her.

Several of the people they passed turned and looked after them, wondering who Miz's new companion was. Nobody seemed to know, though a few thought she looked vaguely familiar. Miz lifted a couple of drinks from a waiter's tray, leaving a coin behind, then he nodded toward a pontoon bar where little shell-boats were moored like buds on branches, paid for one, and strode down the ramp to the floating deck—again nodding to the parties filling some of the other shell-boats—and set the drinks down on the central table of the boat. He helped Sharrow aboard.

They sat watching all the bustle of the regatta for a while, drinking their drinks and sampling the sweetmeats and savories the waiters brought around; freshmenters in cat-canoes and sampans glided among the shell-boats, selling their own wares.

She had outlined the situation over dinner at his hotel the previous night, asking him to sleep on it. They and the Francks had dined in the circular funnel restaurant of the old cruise ship, watching the lights of the Log Jam as they seemed to revolve beneath them.

They had danced, gone for a last few drinks and inhalants in Miz's impressively large suite looking out over a floodlit marina; then while the Francks went for a walk on deck, he had walked her to her room, kissing her cheek and leaving, backing off, blowing kisses. She had half expected him to try to stay or ask her to come back to his suite, but he hadn't.

Sharrow looked from the gaudy regatta to Miz's tanned, grinning face and twirled her parasol.

"So what have you decided, Miz? Will you come with us?"

"Yes," he told her, nodding quickly. He adjusted the shell-boat's sunshade, then took off his own dark glasses. "I *do* have a little business to attend to here first, however." He smiled widely, steel-blue eyes scintillating.

She laughed at his expression; it was so childishly roguish.

He looked young and healthy and handsome as ever, she thought. There was an energy in him, as though his life held a momentum greater than that of others'; the poor kid from the barrios of Speyr come up from nothing and heading higher still, brimming with ideas and schemes and general mischief.

"What sort of business? Will it take long?" she asked, twirling her parasol to watch the pattern of light and shade it cast on his open, eager face.

He bit his lips, put one hand over the side of the little shell-boat, and dabbled his fingers in the water. "It's just a little lifting operation," he said, glancing at her. "Actually, I might be able to expedite it, now that you lot are here—bring it forward a bit, if you'll help."

She frowned at the water where his hand trailed. "A lifting operation?" she said. "You've gone into the marine salvage business?" She sounded confused.

He laughed. "No, not that sort of lifting," he said, and sounded almost embarrassed.

She nodded. "Oh . . . *that* sort of lifting."

"Yes," he said.

"What is it you're going for?"

He slid along the circular seat to her side, making the shell-boat list. He put his chin on her shoulder and spoke softly into her ear, which was revealed under the mass of swept-back black hair. He breathed her perfume in, closing his eyes, then sensed her moving away from him. He sighed and opened his eyes. She was angled away from him, staring at him over the top of her dark glasses, her huge eyes wide.

"Say that again," she said. He looked beyond where she sat, then mouthed the words without actually speaking them.

She mouthed the words back, and he watched her lips.

The Crownstar Addendum? her lips said. Her eyes became wider still. He nodded. Sharrow pointed at his chest and mouthed: You Are Fucking Crazy.

He shrugged and sat back.

She dropped the parasol to the seat and set the dark glasses on the table, then put one hand under her armpit and the other over her eyes. "This must be the silly season for Antiquities," she breathed.

"Don't you admire my ambition?" Miz laughed.

She looked at him. "I thought *we* were going for something difficult. I thought the . . . article you're talking about was supposed to be unstealable."

"Whisper when you say that last word," he said quietly, looking around the other shell-boats. "It's only applied to one thing around here."

"What are you going to do with it once you've got it?"

"Well, it started when I was contacted by an anonymous buyer," Miz said breezily. "But I think I'll ransom it back to the relevant authorities. That might be safer."

"Safer!" she laughed. He looked hurt. "Why?" she asked. "Why are you doing this? I thought you were doing all right here."

"I am," he said, looking insulted. He waved around. "I'm rich. I don't *need* to do it."

"So don't!" she said through her teeth.

"It's too late to back out now," he told her. "I have a

tame official who's going to help; he's terribly excited about it all."

"Oh, good grief," she groaned.

"It's so *easy*," he said, leaning close to her again. "I thought it was crazy, too, when it was first suggested, but the more I looked into it and found out the truth of where and how it's stored, the easier I realized it was going to be. It'd be crazy *not* to do it."

"In other words," she said, "you got bored."

"Na," he said, waving with one hand and looking flattered.

"So," she said. "How do you propose to set about this probably suicidal task?"

"Hey, kid," he said, beaming a smile at her and putting his arms wide. "Am I the Tech King, or not?"

"You are, after all, the Tech King, Miz, of course," she said, a dubious expression on her face. "But—"

"Look, it's all set up." He dropped his voice again and sat closer. "The technical part of it's over, really; it's just putting the final human bits of it together that I've been working on." He looked at her carefully, to see how he was doing. "Look," he said, putting on his most winning smile, "it'll be fine. I'm serious. There won't even be a fuss, dammit. They won't even know the thing's actually *gone* until I tell them; this is a totally beautiful plan I have here, and you'll thank me later for letting you become a part of what is not so much a theft but more of a work of art in itself, really. Honestly. And like I say, I can even bring it forward now that you guys are here, so it'll all be over by the time we have to start outrunning the Huhsz. *If* you'll help. Will you help?"

She looked deeply suspicious. "If you can convince me this plan's viable and we won't all spend the rest of our lives on the hand pumps in some prison-hulk eating plankton, yes."

"Ah," Miz laughed, slapping her knee. "No danger of that."

"No?"

"Na." He shook his head adamantly. "They'd *kill* us three and turn you over to the Huhsz for the reward."

"Oh, thanks."

He looked instantly stricken with contrition. "Wo, sorry. That wasn't very funny, was it?"

"Am I laughing?" She put her dark glasses back on and sipped her drink.

Miz pursed his lips. "This stuff about the Huhsz," he said. "There no other way out?"

"I stay ahead of them for a year, or get them their Lazy Gun." She shrugged. "That's it."

"They can't be bought off?"

"Certainly they can—by giving them the Gun."

"But not with, like, money?"

"No, Miz. It's a matter of dogma—faith."

"Yeah," he said. "So?" He looked genuinely puzzled.

"The answer is no," Sharrow said patiently. "They can't be bought off."

"Anyway," Miz said, and tapped her on the shoulder with one finger, a knowing look on his face. "The Tech King has thought up a way of slowing the bad guys down." He winked at her.

"Oh yes?"

"Ever been to the K'lel desert?"

She shook her head.

"Or Aïs city?" Miz asked, grinning.

"Too arid for my taste," Sharrow smiled, rubbing her fingers up and down the stem of her glass. "I'm a moist kind of girl really, deep down."

Miz crossed his eyes for a moment. "Please," he said, sighing theatrically. He cleared his throat. "I'm serious." He leaned close again. "These Passports are the World Court extra-specials, aren't they? The unlosable ones with this weird sort of warp-type hole thingy in them?"

She frowned. "You're losing me with all this technical jargon, Tech King."

He slapped her thigh gently. "You know what I mean. The nanoevent holes left over after the AIT Accident. Each Passport'll incorporate one of them, won't it?"

"Yes," she said.

"And they'll be coming out of Yada to be initiated at the Huhsz World Shrine?"

"I imagine so, but . . ."

He sat back, tapping the side of his head. "I have a fiendish plan, my leader," he said.

She shook her head, sighing. "And I thought you might have gotten sensible in your old age."

"Perish the thought." He grimaced. "And anyway, *you're*

the one wants to go looking for a book that hasn't been heard of for a millennium without even the benefit of a paying contract in the vague hope it'll somehow lead to a Lazy Gun."

"Yes," she said, dropping her voice and putting her face close to his. "But the book is only *lost*, not the most heavily guarded piece of jewelry on the fucking planet."

Miz waved this distinction away with one hand as though it were a bothersome fly. "Did you get your contract set up with the Sea House guys?"

"Spoke to them this morning. Scale Two exes."

"Huh. They handling it themselves?"

She shook her head. "Agency called The Keep."

"The Keep?" Miz frowned. "Never heard of them."

"Me neither. Must be new. Seem to know what they're talking about."

"What is this damn book, anyway?" Miz asked, sounding annoyed. "The *U.P.*—what's it about?"

Sharrow shrugged. "The only known part of the text is the dedication page. That gives a very rough idea, but the whole point of the fashion for noble houses commissioning Unique books was that the contents stayed a secret. For what it's worth, just going on the names involved, this Unique's meant to be the best of them."

"Hmm. Maybe I'll wait till they make the holo." He shrugged. "And anyway, how come you think you can track it down when nobody else has been able to?"

"Gorko," Sharrow said. "And Breyguhn."

"What, your grandpa?"

"Yes. According to Breyguhn, Gorko found out where the book was but didn't try to lift it. He's supposed to have left a record of where it is, or was. Breyguhn claims she knows how I can get hold of this information."

Miz thought about this, then said, "Shit, yes, the book. That's what she was after when she broke into the Sea House, wasn't it?"

"Yes. And she thinks she's on the trail now." Sharrow shrugged. "Or she could be having a joke at my expense."

"A joke?" Miz looked intrigued.

She shook her head. "Wait till you hear *how* I'm supposed to access the information Breyguhn's found."

"Tell me now. I hate being teased."

"No."

"Tell me!" he said, leaning closer and tickling her waist.
She stifled a shriek and tried to slide away, slapping his
hand. "Stop that! Behave yourself!" She held up her glass in
front of her. "Look at this. See—empty."

He stopped trying to tickle her and looked around for
a waiter, a wide grin on his face. His expression changed as
he looked back up the ramp to the barge. "Ah," he said.
"Somebody I'd like you to meet. Back in a trice." He sprang
from the shell-boat, leaving it rocking.

She watched him go as he paced up the pontoon, waving at some people calling from another shell-boat.

Sharrow sat back in the seat, staring into the middle
distance where another arm of the Log Jam sparkled in the
sunshine, light reflecting off a thousand windows of a floating apartment block. *The Crownstar Addendum,* she
thought. *Oh dear.* She had the unnerving feeling that they
were all going off the rails: Miz trying to stay young by getting involved with this preposterous scheme to snatch one of
the system's most secure treasures; Cenuij chasing scar-girls
in Lip; Zefla getting wasted every night, and Dloan becoming a screen-junkie. As for herself, she was just getting old,
mired in banality.

A waiter appeared with a drink on a tray. She looked
around to see Miz at the far end of the ramp, talking to a
tall, plump man in long ceremonial robes of blue and gold,
the Log Jam's colors. The two men walked down toward the
shell-boats, the tall official nodding his head tolerantly as
Miz made a joke. A small entourage of lesser officials followed behind. She sipped her drink as the group approached. The official made a small gesture with one gloved,
heavily ringed hand; his minions stopped a few meters back
on the pontoon and stood there in the sunlight trying to look
dignified while he and Miz walked to the shell-boat where
she sat.

"The Lady Sharrow," Miz said. "The honorable Vice Invigilator Ethce Lebmellin."

The official bowed slowly, with just that degree of care
that indicated he was not used to bowing. Sharrow nodded.

"My lady, this is indeed a pleasure," the Vice Invigilator
said. His voice was high and soft; his face was leaner than
the body beneath the long, formal robes suggested. His eyes
looked dark and cold.

"How do you do?" she said.

"May I welcome you to our humble city?"

"You may indeed," she said. "Will you join us, sir?"

"Nothing would give me greater pleasure, dear lady, but I regret affairs of state require my presence elsewhere. Perhaps another time."

"Perhaps," she said, and smiled.

"Mr. Kuma," Lebmellin said, turning to the other man.

"Triplicate, Mr. Lebmellin," Miz said quietly.

Sharrow frowned, wondering if she'd heard right. *Triplicate?* she thought. She wouldn't have heard the word at all but for the fact Miz pronounced it so carefully.

The robed official didn't look in the least confused; he just looked at the other man for a second, then said, "Triplicate," also very quietly. Miz smiled.

The official turned to her, bowing again, and returned along the pontoon to the barge, his entourage sweeping behind him like nestlings after their mother.

Miz sat back down in the shell-boat, looking quietly pleased with himself.

"That your tame official?" Sharrow said quietly.

Miz nodded. "Devious big fuck—wouldn't trust him farther than I could throw him. But he's the guy who can be in the right place at the right time, and he's hungry."

"You really are going ahead with this, aren't you?"

"Damn right I am."

"And the, ah . . . T-word just there—a password?"

Miz giggled. "Kind of." He glanced at her. "Tee-hee-hee," he said.

"You're mad," she told him.

"Nonsense. This'll work out fine."

"What boundless optimism you display, Miz," she said, shaking her head.

"Well," he said, shrugging, "why not?" Then a look of uncertainty crossed his face. "There is just one *slightly* worrying development recently. Well . . . over the last few weeks." He pulled at his lower lip with his fingers. "Not sure if it's actually a security leak as such, but kind of worrying."

"What?" she said.

He turned side-on to face her again. "You know they have those sial races, down in Tile?"

"Yes," she said. "They take the animals' own brains out and replace them with human ones."

"Yeah, criminals' brains, Tile being a bit uncivilized. Anyway." He coughed. "Somebody seems to be naming sials after my embarrassments."

"What?"

"For example, three weeks ago I had a shipment of, um . . . legally sensitive antique electronic circuitry being moved on a Land Car from Deblissav to Meridian. As the car was going through a pass in a mountain range called The Teeth, it was mined, attacked and looted. Bandits got clean away." He shrugged. "Two days later the winner at Tile Races was called Electric Toothache."

She considered this. "Kind of tenuous, though, isn't it?" she said, amused.

"There have been others," he said. He looked genuinely worried. "I've had my agent there look into it, but we can't work out how it's being done. The stables keep the names secret until the race and then decide on a name on the day. Supposed to help prevent cheating. Somebody's getting the owners to name their beasts after things that go wrong in my affairs. And I can't work out why."

She patted his shoulder. "You're working too hard, dear," she said.

"I should have known better than to tell you," he said, draining his glass. He nodded at hers. "Come on—take your drink and we'll go watch the race finish."

They abandoned the little boat, leaving it rocking on the waves. She twirled her parasol as they walked back toward the barge, the water under the pontoon making slapping, gulping noises on the slats and floats of the walkway and the circular hulls of the shell-boats.

Thrial was the sun. Rafe was little more than a molten blob, while M'hlyr was solid on its one ever-outward-facing side. Fian was sufficiently cold near its unwobbling poles for water ice to exist despite the fact most metals would run like water at its equator. Trontsephori was smaller than Golter—a clouded water world whose weather systems were so classically simple, they resembled a crude simulation. Speyr was almost as large as Golter, terraformed five millennia earlier. Then came Golter, with its three moons, followed by a belt of asteroids, then Miykenns, colonized even earlier than Speyr, followed by the system's giants: Roaval—ringed and mooned—and Phrastesis, shelled in still-settling debris after the enigmatic destruction of its moons during the Second War. After it came the small giant, Nachtel, with its cold, just-habitable moon, Nachtel's Ghost. Plesk, Vio, and Prenstaleraf made up the outer system, each one colder and rockier and tinier in turn, trailing off like something at the end of a sentence. Assorted debris and comets completed the system.

Thrial was a ring of pure white-gold inset with veins of platinum; it opened on a concealed hinge made from what appeared to be extruded diamond thirteen. The planets hung on loops of equally unlikely allotropic mercury and were each represented by a flawless example of the relevant birthstone according to the Piphramic Astrology, precisely graded to indicate planetary size on a logarithmic scale. Moons were red diamonds, the asteroids emerald dust, and the comets a tinily beaded fringe of dark carbon fibers, each tipped with a microscopic sphere of white gold. Distance from Thrial was represented by molecule-wide lines somehow etched into the ambivalent loops of mercury.

The Crownstar Addendum, as the necklace had been called for four or five thousand years, was beyond argument the single most precious piece of jewelry in the system, either extant or missing. All by itself, in its sheer pricelessness, the Crownstar Addendum provided the theoretical security for the Log Jam's currency, commercial guarantees, and insurance bonds. Its melted-down and split-up value alone would have kept an averagely extravagant noble family comfortably for a century or so, or even bought a minor house name, but that element of its value was insignificant compared to its intrinsic worth as something precious and mysterious that had somehow survived—and, to the extent that it could, had often been part of—Golter's frenetically embroiled and feverish history.

Exactly who or what had made it, for whom, and when, and how, nobody knew.

No more did they know what the Crownstar itself was, if there had ever been such a thing. On Golter the chances were about equal that if the Crownstar had existed it had been hidden, broken up, or just lost.

Whatever the Crownstar had been, and wherever it had ended up, there was no doubt concerning the location of its Addendum; it was kept deep in a special vault located inside a battleship near the center of the Log Jam. It was taken out—under intense security—only for very rare and special occasions; it was never, ever worn, and the impregnability of its vault—effectively a gigantic revolving safe made from three thousand tonnes of armor plate—had in recent years become almost as legendary as the fabled necklace itself.

Ethce Lebmellin watched from his plushly decorated seat in the reviewing stand as the two winning yachtsmen acknowledged the cheers of the crowd and started to ascend the steps toward him. The first prize was an ornate and ancient silver cup; it sat in front of him, gleaming in the reflected light striking off the waves. The gaily striped awning above flapped and snapped in the breeze.

Lebmellin looked at the prize-cup, studying his reflection on its curved, polished surface. A rather silly prize for a rather silly pastime, he thought. The sort of thing the middle orders tended to waste their lives over, imagining they had accomplished something.

A familiar feeling of self-disgust and bitterness welled up inside him. He felt used and reviled. He was like this cup—this decorative, overdecorated trinket. Like it, he was dragged out for certain ceremonial duties, briefly admired, made use of, then packed away again without as much as a second thought. They were both fussily ornamented, had little apparent practical use, and they were both hollow. Was this what he had worked for?

He had spent years in the diplomatic colleges of Yadayeypon, studying hard while the smart-ass lower-order kids made fun of his plodding progress, and the smoothly urbane scions of major houses—and minor houses better off than his own—sneered at his unfashionable clothes.

And what had he received, for all those late nights, all those given-up holidays, all those taunts and sly looks? An undistinguished qualification, while others had drunk and snorted and fornicated their way to outstanding success, and others had simply not cared, their positions in some family concern or Corp. guaranteed just by their name.

He doubted any of them even remembered him.

A sinecure; a post of utmost vapidity for a small, parochially eccentric city-state. It was probably no more than his brilliant contemporaries had expected of him.

He rose to present the cup to the two fresh, sweating faces. He let them touch his gloves and kiss his ceremonial rings, wanting to draw his hand away and wipe it, feeling that everybody was watching him and thinking what a fool he looked. He spoke a few predictable, meaningless words to them, then handed the two men their empty prize. They held it aloft, to more cheers. He looked around at the crowds, despising them.

You'll applaud me one day, he thought.

He realized he was smiling but decided it was only fitting, given the general rejoicing.

He thought of that upstart barrow-thief Miz Gattse Kuma and that snotty aristocrat with her laughing, dismissive eyes. *Want to use me to get our treasure?* he thought, still smiling, his heart beating faster. *Think you can buy just my robe and my cooperation without buying the man inside, with his own desires and ambitions and plans? Well,* he thought. *I have a little surprise for you, my friends!*

5

Lifting Party

T he Abyssal Plain Nodule Processing Plant Mobile Repair Module woke up at one second before midnight, its circuits and sensors quickly establishing its location, internal state, and external circumstances, as well as its programmed instructions.

It was on Golter, in a shallow lagoon off the coast of Piphram, under the floating city called the Log Jam; it was fully functional and recently overhauled, with all reservoirs, tanks, magazines, and batteries registering ninety-nine percent capacity or above; a subset of instructions refamiliarized it with the extra equipment and weaponry it had been fitted with, finding those fully ready too.

Its cupola sensor was at a true depth of 27.1 meters; its tracks, two meters lower, were sunk into soft mud to a depth of forty centimeters. Assuming its chronometer to be correct, the tide should be half-ebbed. The keel of a large stationary vessel lay eight meters above it. Light was scarce, seeping in from the occasional gap between distant ships, in shafts that barely illuminated the surrounding mud; the light signature indicated it was artificial. There was a faint current, only a few millimeters per second. The seabed was quiet; the water itself was filled with a distant, inchoate rumble of sound, an amalgam of noises coming from the ships that stretched for kilometers in all compass directions.

Water quality was brackish, oxygen poor, and moderately polluted with a broad spectrum of contaminants, though it was comparatively transparent. There was a confusing jumble of mostly metallic junk and wreckage lying under the surface of the mud at levels from nine meters down to barely submerged. Magnetic fields lay in static patterns all around; distant fluctuations were motors. Electrical activity was dispersed and ubiquitous in the ships above it.

Radiation was normal, for Golter.

Its instructions were clear. It readied itself, then adjusted its buoyancy by dropping two large weights from its flanks; they fell a few centimeters and embedded themselves in the mud, barely disturbing the surface. The mud still held it, but its motors would break that grip. It carried out the quietest possible start, flutter-feeding its motors so that it moved away at first much more slowly than the current, coming up and out of the mud as its buoyancy brought its tracks to the seabed's surface.

Using its tracks and impellers, it accelerated smoothly and almost silently to a slow crawl and began a wide turn that would take it toward the destination it could already sense: the keel of a long vessel whose girth—allied with the angle of taper from beam to stem and stern—as well as the depth of water the craft was drawing, indicated that it was, or had been, a large capital ship—probably a battleship.

High in the superstructure of a five-hundred-meter liner that had once plied the lucrative trade routes between Jonolrey and Caltasp, Ethce Lebmellin entered the state suite where the reception was in noisy full-swing. He was dressed in full ceremonial robes—cumbersomely sumptuous clothes of red, gold, and blue covered in designs of extinct or mythical sea creatures that made his every step a battle of colorful monsters.

Lebmellin's aides started introducing him to the guests. He heard himself making automatic replies as he went through the motions of greeting, inquiry, and ingratiation. Two decades of training for and taking part in receptions, banquets, and parties, at first in the academies and colleges of Yadayeypon and later in the Log Jam itself, had given Lebmellin ample reserves of exactly the sort of flawlessly unthinking politeness such occasions demanded.

He could see Kuma at the far side of the room, introducing people to the aristocrat and his other two new friends—the man called Dloan, as bulky and quiet as any bodyguard Lebmellin had ever seen, and his bewitchingly attractive sister.

People seemed pathetically anxious to meet the noblewoman, who—in perhaps only a few days' time—would be running for her life, trying to escape the Huhsz. The aristocrat, standing under the bright colored lights near the center of the reception room, had taken off her shoes; her naked feet were half-submerged in the thick pile of the room's richly patterned carpet. Lebmellin loathed such aristocratic affectation. He had to suppress a sneer as he shared a joke with a popular and influential courtesan it would have been foolish to antagonize.

He laughed lightly, putting his head back. Good; Kuma was just introducing the Franck woman to the Chief Invigilator.

A few minutes after midnight, routine repair work on a factory ship a couple of vessels away from what had once been the Imperial Tilian Navy's flagship *Devastator* resulted in a small explosion in the manufacturing vessel's bilges.

The Repair Module sensed the faintest of alterations to the dim hanging shape of a distant ship, then registered the shock wave as it passed through the attached hulls above, and finally heard and felt the explosion pulsing through the water around it as it trundled quietly and softly across the mud toward the old battleship.

The gas detonation fractured several of the factory ship's outer plates and ruptured the insulation of a main power cable, so that when the water rushed in through the gaps in the ship's hull, it shorted out the electricity supply for several dozen ships near the heart of the Log Jam. That part of the city sank into darkness.

The module sensed the electrical fields immediately around fade and die, leaving only the magnetic signatures of the fabric of the ships themselves.

Emergency lights burned on the ships for a few seconds until their standby generators took up the strain, so that, one by one, the vessels flickered into brightness again. The Log Jam's power-supply center—tapping the reactors of dozens of old submarines and four of the eight nuclear-powered carriers that made up Carrier Field—instituted checks to determine where the power line had shorted, before it started to reroute electricity to the affected area.

The power supply in the *Devastator* took a little longer to reestablish while its alarms were checked. When the old battleship's systems did fire up again, much of the emergency wiring—replaced only a few months earlier as part of the vessel's rolling refit program by an electrical company very distantly owned by Miz Gattse Kuma—promptly melted, starting numerous but small fires throughout the old ship. The system was shut down again. Duty engineers on the *Devastator*—who, after the guards, made up the bulk of the old battleship's fifty or so night staff—worked to reroute the generator supply while battery-powered firecontrol systems tackled the fires; most were put out within a few minutes.

The module half plowed, half floated gently on, approaching the dark space under the silent battleship, whose wide, flat bottom hung suspended just a handful of meters above the floor of soft black mud.

Lebmellin fought the desire to look at his timepiece or ask an aide the hour. He watched the Chief Invigilator as the older man fell under the spell of the golden-haired Franck woman. The aristocrat was quite outshone in her company. Zefla Franck glowed; she filled the space about her with life and beauty and an attraction you could almost taste.

The Sharrow woman had a sort of quiet, dark beauty, understated despite the strength of her features, and forbidding, even if one had not known she was from a major house; she was like a dark cloud-covered planet clothed in quiet, cold mystery.

But the Franck woman was like Thrial, like the sun—a radiance Lebmellin could feel on his face as she joshed and joked with his immediate superior. And the old fool was lapping it up, falling for it, falling for her.

Mine, thought Lebmellin, watching her as she talked and laughed, savoring the way she put her head back and the exquisite shape it gave that long, inviting neck. *Mine,* he told himself, fastening his gaze on her hand when it went out to touch the ornately embroidered material on the arm of the Chief Invigilator's robe.

You'll be mine, Lebmellin told her piled mass of shining golden hair and her wise-child laughing eyes and her perfect, agile, ever minutely swiveling and shifting figure and her luxurious, enveloping, softly welcoming voice and mouth. *Mine, when this is over, and I can have whatever I want.* Mine.

The Chief Invigilator offered to show the Francks the Log Jam from his yacht. She accepted; her brother declined gracefully, to the obvious relief of the Chief Invigilator. He swept off with her on his arm, taking only his two bodyguards, private secretary, butler, chef, and physician with him and leaving the rest of his entourage behind to look briefly uneasy, then to relax and enjoy themselves.

The main power was reconnected by a different route before the *Devastator*'s generator could be hooked into the circuit. When the battleship's circuits came alive again, many of the alarms went off. There were still dozens of small fires burning aboard, and though they, too, were extinguished shortly after the power returned, there was smoke in many of the ship's spaces, only gradually being sucked out of the vessel as its ventilation system rumbled back to life.

The alarms continued to sound, refusing to be reset without triggering again. The engineers and guard techs scratched their heads and ran various checks.

It was a few minutes before they realized that they weren't dealing with a set of persistent and interlinked false alarms, and that something really was wrong.

By that time the module had used a thermal lance to cut its way through the battleship's mine-armor just a little to port of the vessel's keel, directly under the Addendum Vault. It trundled back a little to let the three-meter disc of white-heat-edged metal thump onto the mud and disappear, then powered through the thick plume of disturbed mud until it was just underneath the hole. It reconfigured its tracks and motor chassis for minimum-cross-sectional shape and vertical large-bore pipe-working, then floated up into the flooded bilgespace.

The Crownstar Addendum lay in what had been the *Devastator*'s B-turret magazine. The magazine and the turret above had been designed to rotate as a unit to train the three forty-centimeter guns on their targets; it had been heavily armored to start with, and on its conversion from magazine to vault had been reinforced with extra titanium armor, as well as having all its entrances but one sealed up, so that once it had been swiveled away from the matching aperture in the magazine cylinder's sleeve, the only way in was through at least a meter of armor plate.

The module placed a shaped charge, rather larger than any projectile the *Devastator* had ever fired, under the base of the magazine vault, then crawled to one side of the flooded compartment, withdrew all its surface sensors into its armored carapace, and switched its listening devices off entirely.

The detonation shuddered through every single one of the *Devastator*'s sixty thousand tonnes. It raised eyebrows and clinked ice cubes in glasses on adjoining ships. Two senior technicians in the battleship's security-control room looked slowly at each other and then reached for the Maximum Alert panic button. Every alarm on the ship, that hadn't gone off already, proceeded to.

Lebmellin got the call about a third after midnight; he was waiting for it, so sensed his communications aide becoming still as she listened to something more important than the chatter of world news and Jam systems reports that usually spoke to her wired eardrum. She closed one eye, checking her lid-screen.

The Chief Invigilator's comm man was already talking into a brooch phone.

Lebmellin's aide tapped his elbow once and spoke the code he was expecting. "Sir, a Court representative has arrived unexpectedly. He's aboard the *Caltasp Princess*."

"Oh, dear," Lebmellin said. He turned back to the industrialist he'd been talking to, to make his apologies.

"It's on F deck!" the security chief said, slamming the console and looking around the smoke-misted atmosphere of the control room, where lights flashed from most surfaces and every seat was occupied with people punching buttons, talking quickly into phones, and thumbing through manuals. "Oh, sorry, Vice Invigilator," he said, standing quickly.

Lebmellin left his aides in the corridor and strode into the center of the room, his gaze sweeping around the boards and walls of flashing lights. "Well, now," he said in his best calm-but-determined voice. "What is going on, eh, chief?"

"Something's broken into the vault, sir. Straight up and

in after a power cut; it's only two bulkheads—fairly thin bulkheads—away from the central chamber now. The last-ditch stuff ought to activate, but as nothing else has stopped it . . ." He shrugged. "It's jammed the vault, sir, but it can't get away; we have two microsubs under the hole and four—soon six—crawler units standing by at the side of the hull, plus the duty submarine on its way to the nearest practicable space with divers ready, and all deck surfaces within two hundred meters under guard. We've informed the City Marines, and they have aircraft and more men standing by. The Chief Invigilator is—"

"Indisposed, I believe," Lebmellin said smoothly.

". . . yes, sir. Unavailable, sir, so we contacted you."

"Very good, chief," Lebmellin said. "Please return to your post."

The module broke through into the central vault in a cloud of smoke, its carapace glowing red hot. A machine gun opened up, sprinkling the module with fire; it lumbered on regardless, dragging a wrecked track behind it. One of its arms had been torn off, and its casing had been dented and scarred in various places.

Gas gushed into the circular space, filling it with unseen fumes that would have killed a human in seconds. The machine trundled and squeaked to the center of the chamber where a titanium sleeve had descended from the ceiling to cover the transparent crystal casing around the Addendum itself.

The module mortared a shaped-charge fusing pin at the point where the titanium sleeve disappeared into the ceiling, piercing the armor and jamming the sleeve in position. A pulse weapon fired, filling the hazy, gas-choked chamber with sparks but failing to scramble the module's photonic circuitry.

The machine extracted what looked like a very thick rug about a meter wide from an armored compartment under its carapace, wrapped the rug clumsily around the titanium column using its one functioning heavy arm, then sent the light pulse triggering the prepatterned close-cutter; the charge blasted four microscopically thin crevices through the metal, and a meter of the titanium sleeve fell apart to reveal the undamaged crystal dome within holding the Crownstar Addendum, like a seed cluster within a halved fruit.

The module loosed its most delicate arm from a slot on its side and reached toward the crystal dome, a hypersonic cutter humming on the end of the spindly arm. It made an incision around the base of the thick crystal dome, lifted it carefully off and placed it to one side, then reached in for the Addendum, lying on a neck-shaped slope of plain black cloth.

The three multijointed digits closed in on the necklace, swiveling and adjusting as they neared, as if uncertain how to pick it up.

Then they slowed, and stopped.

The module made a gasping, grinding noise and seemed to collapse on its tracks. The arm reaching for the Addendum sagged, lopsided, its metal and plastic fingers still a couple of centimeters away from its goal. The fingers trembled, flexed for one last time, then drooped.

Smoke leaked from the carapace of the module, joining the gas and the fumes and smoke already filling the chamber. A noise like a groan came from the battered machine.

It was a quarter of an hour before the emergency motors were able to grind and force the vault around so that its door and the magazine sleeve door were aligned, and before the central chamber was cool and gas free enough for Lebmellin, the security chief, and the other guards to enter.

They wore gas masks; they stepped in, over pieces of wreckage still glowing, and found the module where it had stopped, its thin metallic arm stretched out, grasping for the Addendum. The guards eyed it warily; their chief looked around the wrecked chamber with a look of disbelieving fury.

Lebmellin stepped gingerly over a lump of sliced titanium, holding his robes up off the debris-scattered deck. "Perhaps we ought to rename the ship the *Devastated*, eh, chief?" he said, and chuckled behind his mask.

The security chief gave him a bleak smile.

Lebmellin went to the necklace, staring intently at it without touching it.

"Best be careful, sir" the security chief said, his voice muffled by the mask. "We don't know that thing's really dead yet."

"Hm," Lebmellin said. He looked around, then nodded at the security chief, who motioned the guards out of the chamber.

The two men went to a metal fire-hose cabinet on the wall, and each inserted a small key into what looked like an ordinary, nonlocking handle. The dented mild steel cabinet swung open, and Lebmellin reached in under the remains of the ancient canvas hose for a thin package wrapped in clean rags.

Lebmellin peeled back the rags to reveal the real Crownstar Addendum, which of course was far too valuable to leave the vault or ever be left exactly where people thought it was. The two men took magnifiers from their pockets and stared at the necklace. They both sighed at the same time.

"Well, chief," Lebmellin said. He reached inside his robe with the hand not holding the Addendum and rubbed his chest. "It's here, but we are going to have to fill out an *awful* lot of forms, and probably in triplicate."

At exactly that point, the module made a noise like a shot and moved briefly on its tracks before falling silent again. The security chief spun around, eyes wide, a cry starting in his throat. After a moment he turned back. "Probably just cooling," he said, smiling shamefacedly.

The Vice Invigilator looked unimpressed. "Yes, chief." He covered the necklace in his hand with the rags and put it back in the fire-hose cupboard; they locked it together.

Lebmellin nodded at the machine. "Have the men force that thing back out the way it came," he said. "Let the units under the ship take it away. We don't want it doing anything awkward like self-destructing, now, do we?"

"No, sir." The security chief looked pained. "Of course, it may do just that if we try to move it."

Lebmellin looked meaningfully at the fire-hose cupboard. "Only the Chief Invigilator and five members of the City Board may move what's in there; for tonight, we have no choice. Dump that damned thing down the hole it came through and make sure this place is extremely well guarded."

"Yes, sir."

"Now, do let's leave; there's a terribly regrettable smell in here, even with this mask, and my hair is going to stink for absolutely *days*. Call the guards back in."

"Sir."

They supervised the removal of the necklace the module had been about to grasp; Lebmellin went with the fifty fully armed Marines who escorted two nervous-looking bank vice presidents to the Jam's second-most-secure vault, in the Log Jam branch of the First International Bank, on a purpose-built concrete barge modeled on an ancient oil-production platform.

Lebmellin left the bank on his official ACV with his aides. The security chief called from the *Devastator*. The module had been levered and hoisted back down through the ship without incident and was now being dragged away from beneath the hull by a Marine crawler.

"Very good," Lebmellin said, staring up through the cockpit canopy at the junklit clouds above. He smiled at his comm aide and official secretary, wondering which one was in Kuma's employ. Possibly both.

He took a deep breath, holding one hand over his chest as he did so, as though breathless. He smiled beatifically. "I believe Mr. Kuma was throwing a party after the reception; let's see what's left of it, shall we? You needn't stay; you may all then depart for some well-earned sleep."

"Sir."

Miz Gattse Kuma's party on the old mixed-traffic ferry was just starting to lose momentum. The upper-car deck of the ferry held a dance floor; the lower train deck held half a dozen train carriages fitted out with snug bars. The ferry was a recent acquisition moored on the outer fringe of the Log Jam, facing out to the lagoon sandbar and the sea beyond and attached to the rest of the city only by ordinary gangplanks. Using its stabilizers, the ship was able to rock itself from side to side and so simulate a moderate ocean swell, which all but the most sensitively constituted partygoers had thought highly amusing.

Lebmellin climbed to the bridge of the old ferry, ignoring the dispersing party and nodding to the burly men who made up Kuma's security team. His mouth was dry, and he found that he was trembling, partly in delayed response to the theft of the Addendum itself, and partly in anticipation of what was going to happen now.

The wide red-lit bridge was almost empty; much of the ferry's instrumentation had been removed. They were there;

the noblewoman, Kuma, and the Franck man. They all wore street clothes. The aristocrat carried a small shoulder satchel. He nodded to Kuma—relaxed and holding a drink—and moved to a pool of light over a chart table where a drinks tray sat, crystal goblets glittering.

"You have the piece, Mr. Lebmellin?" Kuma said.

"Here," he said, taking it out of his robe. He laid it on the chart table, opening the cloth. The three clustered around, staring at it.

He watched them while they gaped at the jewel. He tried to see what was different about them, how this SNB virus, this ancient piece of scientific wizardry, had changed them, infected them with each other somehow, made them—at times, the rumor went—better able to anticipate one another's reactions than identical twins. He had done his homework on Mr. Kuma; he knew his past, and how this viral drug had altered him—and these others—forever. But how did it show itself? Could you see it? Could you detect it in their voices? Were they reacting similarly now? Did they think the same things all the time? He frowned at them, trying to see something he knew could not be seen.

Whatever, he thought, suppressing a smile; for all their fabled powers, they were no more immune to the spell-casting attractions of the necklace than anybody else.

The Crownstar Addendum did not disappoint. It lay there gleaming, light sliding off its conventionally impossible mercury loops as though it were creating its own pure, clean brilliance; as though it were part of something even more fabulous from a finer plane of existence that had intruded into the mundane universe by accident.

Lebmellin looked around at them, smirking. Even the aristocrat had deigned to be impressed. Out of the corner of his eye he saw movement at the far end of the bridge and thought he heard a muffled thump from above. The Franck man, the one who looked like a bodyguard, looked up.

"It is beautiful," Sharrow said, her voice soft.

"But you might find these a little easier to spend," Kuma said, dropping a little hide bag onto the table beside the necklace. He drew the string, opening the bag and revealing a dozen medium-sized emeralds.

"Quite," Lebmellin said. He lifted the bag up and smiled at the green stones.

"This calls for a drink," Kuma said, lifting one of the

crystal decanters. He poured some gold-flecked Speyr-spirit for Lebmellin.

"Let me show you a salute from Yadayeypon, Mr. Kuma," Lebmellin said, putting the bag of emeralds in his robe. He took the other man's glass, poured its contents into his own glass—the flakes of gold leaf swirling in the light-blue liquid—then reversed the process and finally poured half back into his own glass again. He handed the tolerantly smiling Kuma his glass back.

"What's the toast?" Kuma inquired. "Absent poisoners?"

"Indeed," Lebmellin smiled.

The windows at either end of the bridge shattered and broke, just as the door to the bridge slammed open. Suddenly the bridge was full of black-fatigued men holding unlikely looking guns. Dloan Franck had started to go for his own pistol, but then stopped. He put his hands up slowly.

Lebmellin had his own gun out by then. Kuma turned to him, still holding his drink and looking slightly annoyed. "Lebmellin," he said. "Have you lost your fucking mind?"

"No, Mr. Kuma," Lebmellin said, taking the Addendum up and putting it back in his robes while his men relieved the three of their hand weapons. "Though you might be in danger of losing more than that."

One of the black-dressed men handed Lebmellin a crescent-shaped device like a tiara; Lebmellin put it on his head. The other men were doing likewise. Dloan Franck stared, frowning mightily, at the gun the man nearest to him was holding. A little red light winked on top of the gun's night scope.

"Lebmellin, old son," Kuma said, with what sounded like weary sorrow, "unless you've got an army out there, this could all end very messily indeed. Why don't you just put the piece back down on the table, and we'll forget this ever happened?"

Lebmellin smiled. He nodded to another of the black-dressed men, who held a plain metal cube, about thirty centimeters to a side. He set the box on the chart table; there was a big red button on its top.

"This," Lebmellin said, "is a Mind Bomb."

They didn't look very impressed. The aristocrat and Kuma both looked at Dloan Franck, who shrugged.

"This," Lebmellin went on, "will cause anybody within a fifty-meter radius to lose consciousness for half an hour—

unless they are wearing one of these." Lebmellin tapped his tiara.

Miz stared at Lebmellin, seemingly aghast. Dloan looked at Sharrow and shook his head slightly.

"Unpleasant dreams, my friends," Lebmellin said. He pushed the red button down hard.

Sharrow cleared her throat. Miz Gattse Kuma sniggered.

Dloan Franck was still looking at the gun Lebmellin's man held. The little red light on the sight had just gone off. The man was looking at the gun, too. He gulped.

Lebmellin stared at the three still-standing people around the chart table, then stepped forward and slammed the red button down again as hard as he could.

As though it were a signal, the woman and two men burst away from the table at the same instant, whirling around to respectively punch, kick, and head-butt the three men nearest them. Dloan and Sharrow overpowered the two men who'd taken their guns while they were still trying to get their own rifles to work. Miz made a grab for Lebmellin, but he had pushed himself away from the table and fell back, stumbling across the deck of the red-lit bridge.

Four black-clothed bodies lay on the floor around the chart table; everybody else seemed to be fighting. Another man fell to the deck; the aristocrat followed him down, straddling him and punching him and tearing something from his clothing. Lebmellin saw two of his men at the bridge doorway pointing their guns at the melee and shaking the rifles when they didn't work. Sharrow fired the gun she'd taken back, and one of the men at the door fell to the deck, screaming and clutching his thigh; the other threw his gun down and ran.

Lebmellin ran too. He got to the end of the bridge and hauled himself out of the shattered window. Somebody shouted behind him. He fell to the deck aft of the broken window, landing heavily.

Sharrow got up and ran after Lebmellin; she saw him hobbling along the deck outside. She jumped out of the window, landing on something small and hard lying on the metal deck, like a pebble. A big, sleek jet-engined power-boat was idling by the hull of the ferry. She leveled the HandCannon at Lebmellin, twenty meters away. Somebody shouted a challenge from the far end of the deck; the bulky figure of the Vice Invigilator skidded and stopped. Lebmellin glanced back at her, hesitated, then threw himself over the rail and fell through the darkness.

Sharrow watched him tumble. He hit the starboard engine nacelle of the powerboat below and bounced slackly into the black water. A second later a door gull-winged open halfway along the craft's cabin, and a figure threw itself out, also splashing into the waves.

"What's happening?" Miz said from the broken bridge window.

Sharrow glanced back at him and shrugged. "Lots," she said, and looked down at the deck to see what her foot was resting on. It was the Crownstar Addendum. "Oh," she said. "Found the piece." She picked it up carefully.

"Good," Miz said. The muffled engines of the powerboat below revved up; it started to drift forward, then its engines screamed and it pushed away across the small waves, spray billowing from its hull as it accelerated and rose up on two sets of A-shaped legs to reveal itself as a hydrofoil.

Miz and Dloan joined Sharrow at the rail; the black hydrofoil powered into the night, twin blue-pink cones of light pulsing from its engines. Dloan held the metal box Lebmellin had called a Mind Bomb—its top hinged back—and one of the guns the black-dressed men had carried.

"Look," he said to Miz, while Sharrow squinted at the dark water. Dloan opened up the stock of the rifle, pulling out some wires. "Ordinary synaptic stunners with a radio-controlled off switch." Dloan held up the Mind Bomb, which was empty save for a single tiny piece of electronic circuitry. "And a radio transmitter . . ."

Miz looked, mystified, from the empty box to Dloan's face.

"I think I can see somebody . . . ," Sharrow said, shading her eyes.

"Hello!" a faint, female voice said from the waves below.

"Zefla?" Dloan said, setting the gun and box on the deck.

A voice floated back sarcastically. "No, but I can take a message."

Sharrow thought she could just see Zefla, her blond head bobbing in the water. "What are you doing down there?" she called.

"Waiting for a *rope*, perhaps?"

"If you're going to be cheeky, you can look for Lebmellin. He's down there somewhere. Can you see him?"

"No. About that rope . . ."

Just before they lowered her a rope ladder, Lebmellin bumped into Zefla. His body went drifting past facedown, his distorted skull oozing blood.

Zefla held on to the corpse for a moment. Miz frowned, looking down. "What are you doing, Zef?" he called.

"Checking the double-crossing son of a bitch for the emeralds," Zef shouted back.

"Na, don't bother," Miz told her. "They were fakes, anyway."

Zefla made a growling noise. Sharrow gave Miz a hard look, and he beamed a broad smile at her.

"Isn't this great?" he said, sighing happily. "Just like the old days!"

Sharrow shook her head, secured the ladder, and threw the end down to Zefla.

They helped her over the rail; she was dressed in knickers and a short black underslip.

"You all right?" Sharrow asked her.

"Oh, fine," Zefla said, dripping. "Chief Invigilator's been killed, his yacht's sunk, and I was kidnapped." She started to wring her hair out. "How's your evening been?"

"Tell you later," Miz said, turning from one of his hired men. "Jam security and Marines on the way," he told Sharrow.

She shoved the Addendum into her satchel. "Let's go," she said.

Their route took them down into the bowels of the ship and past a couple of Miz's nervous-looking hired hands. He told the guards to stop anybody else from following them.

A gangplank just above sea level led from the stern of the ferry into a larger passenger ship. As they crossed, they heard shooting and the sound of helicopters. Miz kicked the end of the gangplank into the water after they'd passed.

They ran through the echoing, deserted space that had been the vessel's engine room. On the far side was a crudely welded-in doorway, half-burned paint still peeling from annealed metal near where the flame had burned.

A short corridor of large-bore pipe led to a similar door.

When Miz closed it behind them, they were at the bottom of a huge, tall, clangingly echoing space; naked metal walls towered into the darkness above. A single yellow bulb shone weakly, suspended at the end of a skinny wire descending from the shadows. The air smelled stale and metallic.

"Old oil tanker," Miz said breathlessly, leading the way across the water-puddled floor of the huge tank. Their shadows swung across the tank floor like the hands of a clock. "Boat's in a dock a few tanks along."

"Something fast, I hope," Zefla said.

"Nup," Miz said. "The hired hands have those; we've got an ancient sailboat with an electric motor. It'll take us to a marina on shore. Not what they'll be looking for at all."

"You hope," Sharrow said.

They jogged on, leaping the I beams that were the vessel's ribs and ducking through a couple of torch-burned doors through to other tanks.

A pain hit Sharrow in the lower ribs, making her gasp. She ran on, holding her side. "You okay?" Zefla asked.

Sharrow nodded, motioned the others on. "Just a stitch; keep going."

Then the lights went out. "Shit," Sharrow heard Miz say. The sound of footsteps in front of her slowed.

The faintest of glows came from ahead, light spilling from a couple of tanks beyond. "Probably just a fuse, not enemy action," Miz said. "Watch out for the I beams. Ouch!"

"Find one?" Zefla inquired.

There was a muffled explosion somewhere behind them, followed by a distant banging noise. "Oh *fuck*!" Miz shouted.

"Just one of those nights really, isn't it?" Zefla said.

"Yeah," Miz said. "I bet we get to Aïs City and it's raining. Well, come on."

They ran. The pain in Sharrow's abdomen got worse, and her legs started to hurt as well, stabbing pains piercing her with every step.

"Sharrow?" she heard Dloan say in the darkness, as the silhouette of Miz climbed through to another tank.

"Here," she gasped as she staggered. "Keep going, dammit. I'm here, I'm here."

The others drew farther ahead. They crossed another tank, stumbling up to the I beams and splashing through unseen puddles of water. Her legs burned with pain; she gritted her teeth, tears coming unbidden to her eyes. Zefla, then Dloan, made it through the door to the next tank. The pain was getting worse. She heard one of them asking her something.

"Keep *going!*" she yelled, fighting the urge to scream, terrified of what was happening to her but determined to fight it.

Suddenly it was as though her head were being crushed in a vise, and a wave of agony swept over her from shoulders to calves, as though she were being skinned alive. She staggered and stopped, tasting blood in her mouth.

There was a noise of metal sliding heavily over metal, then a sharp detonation of pain inside the back of her head. She crumpled up, falling to the cold steel deck, unconscious before she hit.

She knew she hadn't been out long, maybe a minute or two. There was a distant banging noise coming from somewhere, and she thought she heard somebody shouting her name. The pain had gone. She was hunched, fetal, on the metal, lying on her right side in a shallow puddle. The opened satchel lay in another puddle a meter away. Her knees and forehead ached, and it felt as if she'd bit her tongue. She had been sick; the vomit lay spreading quietly into the puddle in front of her. She groaned and wobbled upright, her hair flapping wetly against her face. She pulled the opened satchel out of its puddle, then spat and looked around. It was suddenly very bright in the tank; brighter than it had been before the lights went out.

She looked behind her. Sitting on a pair of gaudily colored deck chairs were two identical young men. They had fresh, scrubbed, pale, coppery-pink faces beneath entirely bald scalps, and they were dressed very plainly in tight gray suits. Their irises were yellow. One held what looked like a naked plastic doll. She had a vague feeling she recognized the two men. They smiled, together.

She looked away and closed her eyes, but when she looked back, they were still there. It had gone very quiet in the tank. A narrow metal stairway against one hull wall led up in a series of staggered flights toward the ship's deck level.

She looked at the tank's two doors; both were sealed by metal shutters attached to some sort of sliding mechanism.

What looked like a large pressurized gas cylinder lay on the floor of the tank by the side of the two young men; a hose snaked away toward the bulkhead leading to the tank she'd been heading for. She could hear a hissing noise. She gagged, doubling up and feeling in her jacket for her gun.

It wasn't there.

A stunning pain in her back and shoulders forced a scream from her and brought her arching back up. It was gone almost in the same instant. She fell back into the puddle, staring up at the harsh white lights beaming down from the top of the tank.

"Looking for your gun, Lady Sharrow?" one of the pleasant-looking young men said. His voice echoed around the tank.

She forced herself to sit up again. The two young men were smiling broadly, sitting with their legs crossed at exactly the same angle. The overhead lights reflected off their bald heads and made their golden eyes glow. One young man still held the doll, the other her gun.

She remembered now where she had seen one of them before: on the glass shore of Issier, in the vehicle disguised as a beachcomber.

They smiled once more, in unison. "Hello again," said the one with the gun. "Thank you for dropping by." He smiled broadly and made a stirring, circling motion with the gun. "You had to leave so precipitously on our last meeting, Lady Sharrow. I felt we didn't really get a chance to talk, so thought I'd arrange another get-together."

"Where are my friends?" she said hoarsely.

"In their little boat by now, I'd imagine," the man with the gun said. "Or alternatively, gassed and dead on the other side of that wall." He nodded, smiling, at the bulkhead.

"What do you want?" she said tiredly. The smell of her own sickness filled her nose for a moment, making her gag again.

The two young men glanced at each other; it was like watching somebody looking in a mirror. "What do we want?" the same one said again. "Gosh—nothing we haven't already got, in a sense, I suppose." He put her gun in an inside pocket of his plain gray jacket, drew out the Crownstar Addendum, smiled happily at the necklace, then slipped it back inside his jacket again. "Got the bauble, which is the main thing." He grinned. "And of course we have *you*, pretty lady." He nodded to his twin who held the doll; he poked the tiny figure sharply between the legs with one finger.

Incredible, impossible pain surged out of her groin and belly. She screamed, doubling up again and moaning as she quivered, convulsing across the deck.

The pain ebbed gradually.

She lay there, breathing hard, her heart thumping. Then she crawled around until she could see the two young men again. The one who'd been doing the talking was laughing silently.

"Bet that smarted, what?" He took a small kerchief from a breast pocket and wiped his eyes. He put it away and composed himself. "Now then, to business." He made a cylinder of his fist, put it to his mouth, and cleared his throat theatrically.

"The body is a code, my dear Lady Sharrow, and we have yours. We can do what my attractive assistant here has just done to you, anytime, anywhere." He cocked his head to one side. "And if you don't do as you're told, like a good little Sharrow, we'll have to spank you." He looked at the other young man. "Won't we?"

The other one nodded and flicked a finger at the rump of the doll.

"No, please—" she heard herself say before the pain hit.

It was as though she'd been whacked on the behind by the flat of a sword with a blow fit to break legs. She felt her mouth gape as she gagged again, her face down against the cool metal of the tank floor. Tears squeezed from her eyes.

"Thank you for the necklace," the young man said matter-of-factly. "We really do appreciate the efforts you and Mr. Kuma went to to secure it, I want you to know that. But we do feel you could do *even better*, you know? You see, we rather think you might be intending to look for another Antiquity. Can you guess what it is?"

She looked up, her breath quick and shallow. She had to blink hard to see them properly, still sitting there on their deck chairs in their severe gray suits, their legs crossed, their bald pates gleaming. She couldn't talk. She shook her head instead.

"Oh, come on, now—you must be able to," the young man chided. "I'll give you a clue: you've already found one, it's the last of its kind, and everybody but *everybody* who's anybody wants one. Come on, it's *easy!*"

She lowered her head to the tank floor again, nodding.

"It's also," the young man continued, "supposed to be the only weapon ever made with a semblance of a sense of humor."

She brought her head up. "The Lazy Gun," she said, her voice weak.

"That's right!" the young man said brightly. "The Lazy Gun!" He sat forward in the deck chair, smiling broadly. "Now, of course we recognize that you have your own reasons for wanting to find this remarkable—and now unique—weapon, and will probably want to turn the Gun over to our friends the Huhsz, in the hope that they'll stop trying to catch and kill you. An understandable desire on your part, of course, but one—sadly—that does somewhat conflict with the plans the interests that we represent have for the weapon.

"In brief, we would *far* prefer that you give the Gun to us. Now we'll be letting you know the details of this little scheme nearer the time, but that's given you the general idea. You give the Gun to us, or we'll be terribly upset, and we'll let you know it, too, via one of these small but perfectly formed mannequins." The young man waved one hand toward the doll. "Got that?"

She nodded, swallowing and then coughing. "Yes," she croaked.

"Oh, and may we counsel you *not* to run to that ghastly cousin of yours? Even the resourceful Geis won't be able to help you against the people we work for, or protect you well enough to prevent us getting in touch with you through the mannequin. Besides which, we do have plans for old Geisy as well, actually. So all in all we really do think you'd be best advised to stick with us. What do you say?"

He paused, then put one hand to his ear. "Sorry?" he said. "Didn't hear you there. . . ."

She nodded. "Yes," she said. "All right."

"Super. We'll be in touch again, Lady Sharrow," he told her. "Every now and again we'll make our presence felt. Just to keep you convinced this hasn't been a dream, and we are quite serious." He smiled and spread his arms wide. "I really would urge you to do your utmost to cooperate with us, Lady Sharrow. I mean, just think: supposing these started to fall into the hands of your enemies?" He looked at the doll lying in the hands of his twin, then gazed back into her eyes, shaking his head. "Life could become very unpleasant indeed, I'd imagine. You agree, I take it?"

She nodded.

"Jolly good!" The young man clapped his hands, then pulled the sleeve of his gray jacket up and looked at a wrist screen. He started to whistle as he watched the display for a while.

After a minute or so, he nodded a few times, then crossed his arms and smiled up at her again.

"There, my dear. That's probably given all of the above time to sink into your memory." He flashed his broad smile, then nodded to his image, who cradled the doll in both hands and carefully placed it on the metal deck between his booted feet.

"Twin," said the other young man, "the lights, please."

The one who hadn't spoken raised the heel of his right boot over the doll.

She had time to suck in air but not to scream before he brought his foot stamping down on the doll's head.

Something beyond pain detonated inside her skull.

She woke to a dim glow. The doorways to the adjoining tanks were still closed off by the metal shutters. There was no sign of the two young men, their deck chairs, or the gas cylinder. The naked plastic doll with the squashed, shattered head lay by her gun on the deck.

She drew herself up on her hands and stayed that way for a while, half lying, half supported by her arms.

She picked up the gun and the doll. The gun was still loaded. She put it in her jacket, then tested the doll, pressing it gingerly. It seemed to have stopped working. Circuitry foam sparkled dully inside the broken head.

She put the doll in her satchel and struggled to her feet, staggering. She reached into a pocket and pulled out the old heirloom timepiece. It had been smashed, the glass face broken. She shook it, then her head, then put the watch back in its pocket.

She rinsed her mouth in a puddle of relatively clean-looking water.

She couldn't find any way to open the shutters over the

doors, so she climbed the clanging metal stairway toward the tanker deck above, stopping to rest at each turn.

She hauled herself out onto the deck as the dawn broke pink and sharp above. She walked unsteadily along the deck, heading toward the tanker's distant superstructure, where a few lights burned. She breathed deeply and tried not to sway too much as she walked.

Then a man jumped out from behind a pipe cluster about ten meters in front of her. He was dressed like a refugee from the worst fancy-dress party in the history of the world, clad in a baggy suit of violently clashing red and green stripes. He lifted what looked like an artificial leg and pointed it at her, telling her to stop or he'd shoot.

She stared at him for a moment, then laughed loudly and told him where to stick his third leg.

He shot her.

6

Solo

C ontinual noise and constant vibration. But something
hushing, reassuring, comforting about these surrounding
sensations, as though they were the acceptable successors of
a womb-remembered external busy-ness, a comforting re-
minder that all was well and being attended to.

She became gradually aware that she was warm and
prone and—when she stirred her tired, tingling limbs—
naked under some smooth cloth. She tried to open her eyes
but could not. The drone of noise called her back to sleep;
the shaking all around her became a rocking, like the arms
of somebody she had never known.

Her fingers and hands tingled.

She had been playing in the snow in the grounds of
Tzant; she and Geis had been throwing snowballs at
Breyguhn and the Higres and the Frenstechow children, a
running battle that had gone on around the great maze and
down into the formal gardens. It had been a startlingly cold
winter that year; there were days when if you spat, you
could hear the spittle crack and freeze before it hit the
snow, and the huge house smelled of the tape the servants
had sealed the window frames with, to keep out drafts.

Geis was fifteen or sixteen then; she was eleven,
Breyguhn nine. Geis and she end up in the gazebo, fending
off the others as they closed in. Geis looks into her eyes, his

face glowing; a snowball whizzes over his head. To the death, cuz! he shouts, and she nods, and he tries to kiss her, but she giggles and pushes him away and quickly gathers more snow together, while Breyguhn screams imprecations in the distance and snowballs thud into the wooden boards of the gazebo.

She woke slowly, turning over in the narrow cot. There were voices talking somewhere beyond the wall. An antiseptic, hospital smell came off the sheets beneath her. She remembered something about a puddle and throwing up into it, but she felt all right now, just hungry and slightly queasy at the same time. There was a light behind her; that was what she had turned away from. Her hair, beneath her on the thin pillow, smelled washed. Her eyes insisted on closing again. She let them; the view had been hazy anyway. The voices outside her head went on.

The Lazy Gun came and talked to her in her sleep.

In her dream the Lazy Gun had legs and a little head, like a doll's. (She started to wake again, remembering the doll; she wanted her doll. She didn't try to open her eyes but felt around her for the doll—under the pillow, down the sides of her naked body where the sheets were tucked in, against the vibrating metal wall to one side and the metal bars of the cot on the other . . . but there was no doll. She gave up.)

The Gun was still there when she returned to the dream. It cocked its tiny doll-head to one side and asked her why she was going to look for it.

I can't remember, she told the gun.

It walked around for a while on its spindly legs making annoyed, clicking noises and then stopped and said, You shouldn't.

I shouldn't what, she said.

You shouldn't look for me, it told her. I bring nothing but trouble. Remember Lip City.

She got very angry and shouted something at it, and it disappeared.

There had been eight Lazy Guns. A Lazy Gun was a little over half a meter in length, about thirty centimeters in width and twenty centimeters in height. Its front was made up of two stubby cylinders that protruded from the smooth, matt silver main body. The cylinders ended in slightly bulged black glass lenses. A couple of hand controls sitting on stalks, an eyesight curving up on another extension, and a broad, adjustable metal strap all indicated that the weapons had been designed to be fired from the waist.

There were two controls, one on each hand grip: a zoom wheel and a trigger.

You looked through the sight, zoomed in until the target you had selected just filled your vision; then you pressed the trigger. The Lazy Gun did the rest instantaneously.

But you had no idea whatsoever exactly what was going to happen next.

If you had aimed at a person, a spear might suddenly materialize and pierce them through the chest, or some snake's spit fang might graze their neck, or a ship's anchor might appear falling above them, crushing them, or two enormous switch-electrodes would leap briefly into being on either side of the hapless target and vaporize him or her.

If you had aimed the gun at something larger, like a tank or a house, then it might implode, explode, collapse in a pile of dust, be struck by a section of a tidal wave or a lava flow, be turned inside out, or just disappear entirely, with or without a bang.

Increasing scale seemed to rob a Lazy Gun of its eccentric poesy; turn it on a city or a mountain, and it tended simply to drop an appropriately sized nuclear or thermonuclear explosion onto it. The only known exception had been when what was believed to have been a comet nucleus had destroyed a city-sized berg-barge on the water world of Trontsephori.

Rumor had it that some of the earlier Lazy Guns, at least, had shown what looked suspiciously like humor when they had been used: criminals saved from firing squads so that they could be the subjects of experiments had died under a hail of bullets, all hitting their hearts at the same time; an obsolete submarine had been straddled by depth charges; a mad king obsessed with metals had been smothered under a deluge of mercury.

The braver physicists—those who didn't try to deny the existence of Lazy Guns altogether—ventured that the weapons somehow accessed different dimensions: they monitored other continua and dipped into one to pluck out their chosen method of destruction and transfer it to this universe, where it carried out its destructive task, then promptly disappeared, only its effects remaining. Or they created whatever they desired to create from the ground-state of quantum fluctuation that invested the fabric of space. Or they were time machines.

Any one of these possibilities was so mind-boggling in its implications and ramifications—provided that one could understand or ever harness the technology involved—that the fact that a Lazy Gun was light but massy, and weighed exactly three times as much turned upside down as it did right side up, was almost trivial by comparison.

Unfortunately—for the cause of scientific advancement—when a Lazy Gun felt it was being interfered with, it destroyed itself. What appeared to be a matter/antimatter reaction took place, turning the parts of the gun not actually annihilated into plasma and causing a blast of the sort normally associated with a medium-yield fission device. It was this kind of explosion that had devastated Lip City, though most of the subsequent illnesses and deaths caused by radiation had resulted not directly from the initial detonation but from the scattering of fissile material from the cores of the City University physics department's research reactors.

(And she was there again distracted—from that sweetly succulent pummeling—to gaze at the line of desert hills beyond the softly billowing white curtains and the stone balustrade of the hotel-room balcony. She watched the faint crease of dawn-light above as it was suddenly swamped by the stuttering pulses of silent fire from beyond the horizon. She looked—dazed and dazzled and wondering, still in her shaken instant of ignorance and cresting bliss—from that distant eruption of light to Miz's face as he reared above her, eyes tightly closed, his mouth stretched open in a silent shout, the sheen of sweat on his hollowed cheek lit by the flickering light of annihilation, and as release came flooding—with knowledge, with realization, so that her squeezed, convulsing cry became a scream of terror—she experienced a grain of vanishing, collapsing ecstasy, immediately swept away and lost in a storm of guilt and self-disgust.)

The Lazy Guns had not had a happy history; they had turned up during the Interregnum following the Second

War, seemingly products of Halo, the vast Thrial-polar Machine Intelligence artifact/habitat destroyed by whatever mysterious weapon had been fired from—and which appeared to have obliterated—the moons of the gas giant planet Phrastesis. The Guns had floated like soap bubbles through the spasming chaos of the war-ravaged system in their drifting, otherwise empty, lifeboats, and one by one they had been captured, stolen, used, abused, hidden, lost, rediscovered, and used and abused again.

And one by one they had met their ends: one had been turned on Thrial by the insane theocrat into whose hands it had fallen; the weapon had refused, or been unable, to destroy the sun, and Gun and theocrat had simply vanished. Two Guns had annihilated themselves when people had tried to take them apart. One had taken a lucky hit during an air strike, another was believed to have been deliberately attacked by a suicidal assassin while in the armory of the noble family that had discovered it, and one—its lenses staring down a pair of electron microscopes—had created a series of nanobang matricial holes in the World Court's Anifrast Institute of Technology before whatever bizarre event had occurred that led to the institute, all it had contained (except for the twenty-three gently radiating holes) and a precise circle of land approximately thirteen hundred meters in diameter disappearing to be replaced by an attractive, perfectly hemispherical saltwater lake stocked with a variety of polar-oceanic plankton, fish, and mammals.

Perhaps it was simply bad luck, but despite the fact that the sheer capability of the Guns ought to have ensured their owner could effectively become ruler of the entire system, the weapons had invariably been the downfall of whoever had come into possession of them.

The Guns even had their own small, schismed cult; the Fellowship of the Gun believed the devices were the ambiguous, testing gifts from a superior alien civilization, and that when the final Gun was found and venerated—worshiped rather than used—the aliens would finally appear among the people of the system and lead them to paradise, while the The Free Fellowship of the Gun believed simply that the Guns were gods, and (now) that the one remaining Gun was *the* God.

The Huhsz faith regarded both these cults as idolatry in nature; as far as they were concerned, the Gun stolen from

them by Sharrow's ancestor had simply been a temple treasure, albeit the principal one. They wanted it back because
they regarded it as their property and because it had become an article of faith that unless it was recovered—or the
Dascen female line wiped out—their Messiah could not be
born on time, on or before the advent of the decamillenium.

She opened her eyes groggily, to focus on a man sitting less
than a meter away. He was dressed in a uniform that hurt
her eyes—bright violet and shining yellow. His face was
round and dark and very serious. "Who are you?" she whispered.

"I am God," he said, nodding politely.

She looked at him for a while, listening to the hum that
was all around her. The place they were in lurched.

"God?" she said.

The man nodded. "God," he said.

"I see," she said, drifting away again.

The hum became a lullaby.

She woke slowly, turning over in the narrow cot. There were
voices talking somewhere beyond the wall. An antiseptic,
hospital smell came off the sheets. She remembered being a
bubble, blown through the system on the blast-fronts of the
war's erupting energies. She was one of the team now. She
could remember what the doctor had told them, before they
became infected with it—every word. . . .

"You *won't* notice it most of the time," the doc told her/
them. "It's not telepathy, and it's not some doze-head feeling
of mystical oneness with you fellows; it's just the ability to
know how somebody'll react in a given situation. It's a short-
cut, a way of building up instant rapport without having to
wait for a few years—probably longer than the war—and
still never get there because the attrition rate's so high you
never achieve a stable combat unit.

"You want to know the truth? It's an anti-fuck-up agent.
Ever watched dumb-screen, where ops always go according
to plan, and nobody ever shoots their own people by mistake? That's what SNB helps make come true. It makes war
a little bit more like it's supposed to be: less entropic, less
chaotic—more tidy. I trust some of you are mature enough
to realize that this makes it a top-brass wet dream. . . ."

That's me, she whispered to herself. *I'm one of the team now. Eight of us.*

She woke up into a white space with no walls but a low ceiling; there was a Lazy Gun there. She couldn't tell which one.

Nothing but trouble, sang the Gun, dancing round her on its skinny, wobbly legs. Nothing but death and destruction and trouble. She grabbed at the Gun; it tried to dance away from her, giggling, but she caught it and held it and strapped it to her. A wall that was a mirror appeared as soon as she touched the weapon. The Lazy Gun's controls were as she remembered them—delicate, somehow, and beautiful. Its sides and top surface were covered in fabulously complicated scrollwork, incised into the silver casing. It was—she realized as she turned with it—a hunting gun. She pointed it at the mirror and smiled at herself as she pushed the trigger.

She woke up and looked around the small cabin; it was a cube barely two meters square. There was another bunk above hers, a light metal drawer unit with her clothes folded neatly inside, a plastic chair, a locked door with a single plastic hook on it, and an air vent. That was all. No window.

Whatever sort of vehicle she was in, it was still moving. She could hear what sounded like combustion engines, and something about the way the deck beneath her vibrated and the whole cabin moved now and again suggested that she was on an Air Cushion Vehicle. Her stomach growled.

She considered trying to go back to sleep, but she'd slept enough. She took out her clothes and looked in the pockets; they held nothing. Her satchel was nowhere to be seen, either.

She got out of the small bed, feeling stiff and hungry. She checked herself over; there were faint bruises on her knees, and she could feel a tiny ulcer on her tongue where she'd bit herself, but there were no other signs of damage. She dressed, then hammered on the door until somebody came.

"God?" she said to the man with the dark, round face she'd seen earlier in what she had assumed to be a dream. He shifted awkwardly on the small plastic seat and brushed imaginary dust from the thigh of his violently clashing yellow-and-violet uniform trousers. "Well," he said. "Technically, yes." A pained expression passed over his face.

"Right," she said. "I see."

"I used," the man offered, frowning, "to be called Elson Roa." He was tall and spindly, and he sat very still with a look of faint surprise on his face. His fair hair stuck up from his forehead, adding to the impression of slight bewilderment.

"Elson Roa," she repeated.

"But then I became God," he nodded. "Or rather realized that I always had been God. God in the monotheistic sense that I am all that really exists." He was silent for a moment. "I can see you are an apparence who is going to need an explanation."

"An explanation," she said. "Yes. That might be a good idea."

She ate the reconstituted E-rations from the heated aluminum tray as though they were the finest banquet ever set before woman. The girl who had brought the food was the same one who'd escorted her to the toilet; she was dressed in brown and yellow, and she sat in the cabin's little plastic seat, watching with fascination as Sharrow squeezed the last dregs from the sweet pouch, licked her lips and handed the tray back to her, and said, "Delicious. Could I have another one of those, please?"

The girl left to get some more food, locking the door behind her. The old hovercraft droned on, pitching rhythmically for a few moments as it traversed taller-than-average waves.

Sharrow had been captured by Solipsists.

They were a fifty-or-so-strong band of licensed privateers incorporated under the laws of Shaphet and dedicated to self-fulfillment, union-rate security provision, and—where possible—robbing the rich. Mostly, however, they were hired by insurance and finance companies to frighten reluctant clients and repossess unpaid-for material. Their ACV—a third-hand war-surplus marsh-patrol vessel from the Security Franchise—had itself been a repo job; the Solipsists had taken over the payments and renamed it the *Solo*.

Their attack on the fringe of the Log Jam had not been an unqualified success. They had heard there was a convention of circus performers taking place on a hotel-ship in the Jam, and so disguised themselves as a troop of three-legged mutants, with their guns inside their hollow legs—hence the artificial limb Sharrow had been shot with. But they'd got their dates wrong; the convention wasn't for another month.

They had attempted to gate-crash Miz's party on board the ferry but found there was too much security, so they'd split up and gone in search of stray guests wandering away from the party, hoping to surprise and rob them; instead, several of the Solipsists had been surprised and captured by the Jam's own security services after the fracas on the ferry, and a couple had been shot and wounded by Marines. The rest had only just got away, taking the big ACV charging along the lagoon sandbar in its own dawn-lit sandstorm while the Marines and Navy argued over who had jurisdiction to put a shot across their bows.

Apart from a few credit and debit cards, a handful of passports, and a small amount of jewelry, Sharrow had been their only real prize; they'd probably have left her, too, but for the fact she'd been carrying a major House Passport.

The Solipsists had let her see a newssheet that mentioned the deaths of the Log Jam's Vice and Chief Invigilators and a few security-personnel injuries, but which did not talk about finding any bodies gassed in the tanks of old oil tankers.

They wouldn't let her call anybody; they intended to take her far north, to the Free City and traditional hostage-transfer point of Ifagea on the Pilla Sea to see if they could ransom her back to her family from there.

"I don't have any immediate family," she told Roa.

"There must be somebody who would pay for you," Roa said, looking puzzled. "Or you must have your own money."

"Not much of that. I've a cousin who might pay a ransom. I don't know. . . ."

"Well, perhaps we can sort that out later," Roa said, staring at a fingernail.

"I know," Sharrow said. "Take me to Aïs, in Nasahapley, not Ifagea."

Roa's brows knitted. "Why?" he said.

"Well, I think I'm meeting some friends there. They'll bring some money."

Roa looked dubious. "How much?"

"How much do you want?" she asked.

"How much would you suggest?" Roa countered.

She looked at him. "I've no idea. Haven't you done this before?"

"Not as such," Roa admitted.

"How about a hundred Thrial?" she joked.

Roa considered this. He put one boot on the other knee and tried to dig mud out from between the grips. "There are forty-six other apparences aboard," he said, sounding embarrassed and refusing to meet her gaze. "Make it forty-six hundred . . . I mean, forty-seven."

She stared at him, then decided he was serious. The sum was less than the average yearly income on Golter.

"Oh, what the heck," she said. "Let's call it five *K*."

Roa shook his head. "That might cause difficulties."

"Just the forty-seven hundred?"

"Yes," Roa nodded emphatically.

"It's a deal," she said. "Net-call a chap called Miz Gattse Kuma and tell him I'll meet him in Aïs, soon as you can get there."

Roa mumbled something.

"Pardon?" she said.

"We'll have to think about that," Roa said, clearing his throat. "The last time we were in Aïs, we had some problems with certain—apparent—small craft that were damaged in the harbor."

"Well," Sharrow said. "See what you can do."

"I shall tell my apparences," Roa said, standing up and looking determined.

He left, locking the door. Sharrow lay back on the narrow cot, shaking her head.

At least Aïs was closer than Ifagea. She hoped they got there before the—apparently—not terribly well-informed Solipsists heard she would soon be fair game for the Huhsz hunting mission, and worth a lot more than forty-seven hundred.

The creaking, salt-encrusted, rust-streaked hovercraft *Solo* had headed north from the Log Jam up the coast of Piphram, its holed exhausts blattering, its route marked by twin lines of smoke from its alcohol-powered rotary engines, stirred into wide helices by its dented, vibrating propellers. It refueled from a commercial tanker in the Omequeth estuary and crossed the Shiyl peninsula over the Omequeth

Corridor, still heading north toward the savanna south of Nasahapley.

"But if you're God," Sharrow said to Elson Roa, "why do you need the others?"

"What others?" Roa said.

Sharrow looked exasperated. "Oh, come on."

Elson Roa shrugged. "My apparences? They are the sign that my will is not yet strong enough to support my existence without extraneous help. I am working on this." Roa coughed. "It is, indeed, in a very real sense, an encouraging sign that we lost six of our number at the Log Jam, as this indicates my will is becoming stronger."

"I see," Sharrow said, nodding thoughtfully. This was her third day aboard, the second after she'd woken up following her overenthusiastically applied nerve-blast on the deck of the Log Jam tanker. It was her third talk with the lanky, serious, very still and staidly eccentric Solipsist leader.

They were due to arrive in Aïs tomorrow.

The Solo's route north and west had been a circuitous one, determined by estuaries, land corridors, seas, lakes, and arguments among Roa and his apparences concerning the reality or otherwise of apparent obstacles such as islands and small craft. They were anyway making slow progress at least partly because the Solipsists seemed unable to work the ACV's major sensory and navigational apparatus, and so could not travel at night or in mist and fog.

"So," he said. "Are you immortal?"

Roa looked thoughtful. "I'm not sure," he said. "The idea may not be relevant; time itself may be a redundant concept. What do you think? I may have created you as a platform for part of just such an answer."

"I really have no idea," she confessed. She waved a hand toward the bulkhead behind her. "What about the others? Do they—the apparences—all call themselves God, too?" she asked.

"Apparently," Roa said, without the hint of a smile.

"Hmm." She bit her lip.

Roa looked awkward. He seemed to think of something and reached into a pocket in his violet-and-yellow tunic and pulled out a grubby piece of paper. "Ah," he said, clearing his throat. "Your friend Mr. Kuma sent a signal to say, um . . ." Roa squinted at the piece of paper, frowned, turned it upside down, and finally scrunched it away in his pocket again. "Well, it said he'd meet you in Aïs, at the, um, Continental Hotel. . . . He's paid the money into the account we asked him to, and, um . . . he wished you well."

"Oh," she said. "Good."

Roa looked suddenly confused. "Um, apart from one, who's an atheist," he said suddenly.

"I beg your pardon?"

"We all call ourselves God except for one apparence, who is an atheist.

"Ah-ha," she said, nodding slowly. "And what does this person call themself?"

" 'Me.' "

". . . uh-huh."

Roa cleared his throat, then closed his eyes and made a strange humming noise while rolling his head around on his neck for a few moments.

Then he opened his eyes. She smiled at him.

He looked displeased, got up, and walked out.

She suspected he'd been hoping that when he opened his eyes, she'd have disappeared.

The Gun came into her dreams again that night. It was reading one of the Huhsz Passports. The Passports looked like books, and she tried to read what the book said, but every time she looked over the Gun's shoulder it shied away, dipping and ducking on its skinny, bendy telescopic legs, and continued to read the Passports, laughing to itself now and again, and no matter what she did, she couldn't get to see what it was finding so funny, so she kicked at its legs the next time, and the Gun tripped and fell. She grabbed the Passport, but the Gun jumped up again, very angry, and shot her before she could open the book to see what it said.

She woke terrified in the small cot, palms sweating. They were heading for Aïs, near the Huhsz World Shrine. She and the Passports were going to be in the same place. She was mad; what was Miz thinking of? Probably they were all going to die.

Perhaps she should just give herself up. She stared into the darkness while the hovercraft whispered around her, tomb dark.

What could she do against the Passports? What could anybody do? Miz was mad, or setting up a trap. You couldn't destroy the Passports; they carried one of the nanobang holes left over from the AIT Accident, each one broadcasting a small amount of radiation and a vast quantity of neutrinos, making them impossible to hide. Even if you destroyed the fabric of the Passport, the hole would survive, and that was what the World Court recognized. *Mad, mad, mad,* she thought, twisting over and over in her cot, entangling herself in the thin sheet. The Huhsz could only hunt her; the World Court could order her arrest virtually anywhere if the Passports were destroyed (except what good would it do to destroy the fabric and leave the hole? What *was* Miz planning? What could he do? Put them on a fast ship and sling them at the sun? The World Court would commandeer a faster ship. . . . You couldn't hide them, you couldn't hold on to them, you couldn't destroy them. . . .)

She fell asleep again eventually, her thoughts still revolving and repeating and echoing in her skull, dancing graceless pirouettes of hopelessness and despair.

Apart from, apparently, some trouble with a group of peasant-squatters and an overhead power line, the *Solo*'s journey to Aïs was uneventful. Sharrow had been released from her cabin. Her passport and her satchel full of personal effects—including her gun, credit cards, and cash, rather surprisingly—had been returned. She had watched the latter part of the journey from the flight deck of the old ACV and talked to more of the Solipsists.

She discovered that the other Solipsists saw no contradiction in being part of a group of which they were not the leader; they all assumed they *were*, and Roa was just something they had imagined to deal with the boring parts of the job. There were still arguments, but the system of Roa being in charge appeared to work. (Democracy was out; they'd only vote for themselves again.)

Roa wisely did not name a second-in-command, in case this was taken as a sign that he was growing uncertain. This had happened before, and Roa had almost been murdered in his sleep by the person/figment concerned. Roa had dealt with the person sternly, hence at least one of the dents in the *Solo*'s stern starboard airscrew.

The old ACV powered along the coast of Nasahapley toward Aïs. An hour before they got there, she watched from the flight deck as they passed the territory's religious cantonment, the sprawling, walled settlement on the coastal floodplain dominated by the black-and-gold spires of the Huhsz World Shrine.

She waited for the regretful words, the apologetic explanation and the change of course that would take the hovercraft curving round toward the shrine, but it never happened.

The *Solo* was too large to be allowed to travel in Greater Aïs county, where they had rules about that sort of thing. Elson Roa and a couple of the others unloaded a small half-track from the ACV's garage deck and took her to the city in that, leaving the other apparences to argue with the harbor authorities about landing dues, mooring rates, and untreated sewage discharges.

The small half-track rumbled into the dusty main square of Aïs; ocher, colonnaded buildings sloped on all sides. They had driven part of the way down the central reservation of a boulevard, collecting a couple of small shrubs on the nudge bars and a traffic violation. The half-track's driver—a young albino originally called Keteo, who drove with more enthusiasm than skill and more speed than accuracy—skidded the half-track to a stop just before the square's central fountain and sat staring malevolently at the flower beds across the other side of the square.

It was a hot day; the sun was bright in the clear sky. The terminus of the Transcontinental Monorail stood just beyond the flower beds Keteo was staring at so intently. Sharrow looked around the square, where traffic—mostly buses—moved, and people—almost all totally nude—walked.

"Oh shit," Sharrow said. "Just my luck to arrive in Nudist Week."

Roa, who had been looking strangely tense until that point, relaxed and smiled. "Nudist Week," he said, sounding relieved. "Yes, they really are, aren't they? Of course."

Sharrow looked around the square again, wondering if Miz and the Francks were here yet.

"Well," Roa said to her. "Here we are. I have no idea whether I shall need you in the future, but I trust I imagine you well, if we do meet again." He fell silent and stared at his fingernails.

She looked from him to the other two Solipsists; the

man beside Roa was sitting with his eyes tightly closed. Keteo the driver was gunning the engine and muttering something as he glared at the distant flower bed. Roa looked away and closed his eyes. He made a humming noise and started to roll his head.

She got down out of the half-track and stood on the road. Buses grumbled past; people—mostly naked, many carrying briefcases—walked past.

Elson Roa opened his eyes. He looked briefly delighted, then saw her standing on the road surface and started. He frowned down at her.

"Oh," he said. "Politeness." He reached down with one hand. She shook it. "Good-bye," he said.

"Good-bye," she replied, and turned and walked away.

When she looked back, Roa and the other backseat Solipsist were arguing vehemently with the driver and gesticulating alternately at the flower beds and the boulevard.

She walked self-consciously to the monorail station. As she walked up the steps, the Solipsist half-track roared out of the square, just missing the flower beds and sending mostly naked pedestrians scattering in all directions as it bounced down the boulevard back toward the port.

She felt more and more awkward walking among the naked people in the station concourse, so she stopped to take her clothes off in a phone booth and was promptly arrested for stripping in public, an offense against common decency.

7

Operating Difficulties

T he K'lel desert was a few million square kilometers of
karst—eroded limestone devoid of topsoil. Karst forms
when carbon dioxide dissolved in rain reacts with porous
limestone as the moisture permeates it on its way to an underlying layer of impervious rock. Golter had had not one
but several ages when there had been widespread and
rather crude industrialization, and each time, one of the major centers had been downwind of K'lel, a lushly but shallowly forested area already vulnerable to the scouring effect
of the Belt winds. The succession of increased carbon-
dioxide levels and heavy acid rainfall in the past had gradually destroyed the forests and eroded the rock while the Belt
winds had produced a dust bowl from the remaining soil,
creating a change in the climate that only accelerated the
desertification.

Eventually only the rock had been left, frayed and
sculpted into spears and pinnacles of knife-sharp karst—a
forest of pitted stone blades stretching from horizon to horizon, baked in the heat of the equatorial sun and dotted with
collapsed caves where a few parched plants clung on in
dark, sunken oases, and striated by tattered ribbons of seemingly level ground where the karst's brittle corrugations
were on a scale of centimeters rather than kilometers.

There were always plans to revivify the dead heart of

the continent, but they never came to anything; even the seemingly promising scheme to replace the main spaceport for Golter's eastern hemisphere, Ikueshleng, with a new complex in the desert had failed. Apart from some ruins, a sprinkling of old waste silos, a few vast, automated solar-energy farms, and the Transcontinental Monorail—also sun powered—the K'lel was empty.

She squatted on her haunches in the shadow of the monorail support, holding her rifle butt down on the dusty ripples of stone, clenching the gun between her knees while she adjusted the scarf around her head, tucking one end into the collar of her light jacket.

It was midmorning; the high cirrus clouds were poised like feathery arches over the warming expanse of karst, and the still air sucked sweat from exposed skin with an enthusiasm bordering on kleptomania. She slipped the mask up over her mouth and nose and reseated the dark visor over her eyes, then sat back, holding the gun, her fingers tapping on the barrel. She took a drink from her water bottle and glanced at her watch. She looked over at Dloan, crouching at the other leg of the monorail, rifle slung over his back, wires from his head scarf leading into an opened junction box in the support leg. He looked up at her and shook his head.

Sharrow leaned back against the already uncomfortably warm support leg. She shifted her satchel so that it was between her back and the hot metal of the monorail support. She looked at the time again. She hated waiting.

They met up again in the Continental Hotel in Aïs, after Sharrow had bailed herself out of Aïs's vice-squad pound and bribed the desk sergeant to lose the record of her arrest.

She finally arrived at the hotel—clothed again, and veiled, even if it did attract attention—but there was nobody there registered as Kuma or any other name she could imagine the others might be using.

She stood, tapping her fingers on the cool surface of the reception desk while the smiling and quite naked clerk scratched delicately under one armpit with a pen. She wondered whether to ask if there were any messages for her; she was starting to worry about giving her location away to the Huhsz. She'd think about it. She bought a newssheet to see if the Huhsz had their Passports yet and headed for the bar.

The first person she saw was a fully clothed Cenuij Mu.

"My watch says the damn thing should be visible by now," Miz said, tight-beaming from the top of the monorail line, two kilometers away around the shallow curve the twinned tracks took to avoid a region of collapsed caves.

"Mine, too," Sharrow said into the mask. She squinted into the distance, trying to make out the tiny dot that was Miz, sitting on the baking top-surface of the monorail; the last time she'd looked, she'd been able to see him and the lump on the ground beneath him, which was the camouflaged-netted All Terrain, but the heat had increased sufficiently in just the last ten minutes for it to be impossible to see either now; with the naked eye the white line of the rail writhed and shimmered, smearing any detail. She tried adjusting the magnification and the polarization of the visor but gave up after a while.

"Nothing on the phones?" she asked.

"Just expansion noises," Miz replied.

She looked at her watch again.

"So what changed your mind?" she asked Cenuij, in the elevator to the floor where the others were waiting.

He sighed and pulled back the left sleeve of his shirt.

She bent forward, looking. "Nasty. Laser?"

"I believe so," he said, pulling down his sleeve again. "There were three this time. They wrecked my apartment. Last I heard—before I had to run away—my insurance company was refusing to pay out." Cenuij made a sniffing noise and leaned back against the wall of the lift, arms crossed. "When all this is over, I shall ask you to cover that loss."

"I promise," Sharrow said, holding up one hand.

"Hmm," Cenuij said as the elevator slowed. "Meanwhile, Miz appears to think there's some point in staging . . ." Cenuij looked around the elevator, then shrugged. "A train robbery."

Sharrow raised her eyebrows. The elevator stopped.

"For . . . artifacts," Cenuij said, as the doors opened and they left, "that are indestructible, can't be hidden, and it would be suicide to hold on to." He shook his head as they walked down the wide corridor. "Does the Log Jam turn everybody's brains to mush?"

"It does when you head-butt a hydrofoil from twenty meters up," she told him.

She pulled her mask down; the air was a hot blast at the back of her throat. She waved at Dloan. He took the plugs out of his ears, cocked his head.

"Aren't you getting anything?" she asked.

He shrugged. "Just the carrier signal; nothing about the train being late or being on this section of track yet."

She turned back, frowning. "Shit," she said, and flicked a grain of dust off the muzzle of the hunting rifle. She put the mask back up.

Miz stood looking out of the hotel-room window, glaring at Aïs's dusty eastern suburbs. He glanced at Cenuij, who was taking the doll apart on the table, a magnifier clipped over his eyes.

"I was set up," Miz said incredulously. He flapped his arms as he turned back to look at the others. "Some bastard had *me* steal the fucking necklace and let Lebmellin think he was going to double-cross me, but they had it all worked out; fucking Mind Bomb shit and the guns it switched off. And the setup in the tanker—it was all done that day; I checked that route myself during the morning. . . ." His voice trailed off as he sat heavily in the couch beside Sharrow. "And look at this!" He reached out to the low table in front of the couch and snatched up the newssheet Sharrow had brought with her. "Repurloined Jewel wins the first race in Tile yesterday! Bastards!"

"Hey," Sharrow said, putting her arm on his shoulders.

"Anyway," he said, "enough. You had a worse time." He squinted at her. "Two *identical* guys?" he said.

"Completely identical." Sharrow nodded, taking her arm away. "Clone identical."

"Or android identical," Cenuij said from the table, putting down the magnifier.

"You think so?" she asked.

Cenuij stood, stretching. "Just a thought."

"I thought androids came kind of expensive," Sharrow said, swirling her drink. "I mean, when the hell do you ever see an android these days?"

"Oh, I don't know. I think I've dated a few," Zefla grunted, going to the room's bar for a drink.

"They tend to stay in Vembyr, certainly," Cenuij agreed. "But they travel occasionally, and like everybody else"— Cenuij smiled frostily at Sharrow—"they each have their price."

"Dloan was in Vembyr once," Zefla said, turning from the flasks and bottles displayed in the cooler. "Weren't you, Dlo?"

Dloan nodded. "Arms auction."

"What's it like?" Miz asked him.

Dloan looked thoughtful, then nodded and said, "Quiet."

"Anyway," Zefla said, taking a bottle from the cooler, "fuck the androids. What about that doll?"

Cenuij looked at it lying spread out on the table. "Could have been made anywhere," he told them. "PVC body with strain gauges and an optical wiring loom; battery pack and a chunk of mostly redundant circuitry foam, plus an electronic coder-transmitter working at the long-wave limit of normal net frequencies." Cenuij looked to Dloan. "Could the doll have been linked to some form of nerve-gun to do what she's described?"

Dloan nodded. "Modified stunner can produce those effects. Illegal, most places."

"I didn't see any gun," Sharrow said, trying to remember. "There were the two guys, the two chairs, the gas cylinder . . ."

"Chlorine!" Miz said, slapping both knees and jumping up from the couch to go to the window again, running one hand through his hair. "Fucking *chlorine*! Sons of bitches."

"The gun could have been anywhere in the tank," Cenuij said, glancing at Dloan, who nodded. "Possibly with the master unit controlling the androids, if that's what they were. Or," Cenuij added, nodding at Sharrow, "the doll could have been transmitting directly."

Nobody said anything.

Sharrow cleared her throat. "You mean there might be something inside *me* picking up the signals from the doll?"

"Possible," Cenuij said, gathering the bits and pieces of the doll together. "This long-wave transmitter isn't how you'd normally slave a gun to a remote. It's . . . strange."

"But how could there be something in me?" Sharrow said. "Inside my head . . . ?"

Cenuij shoved the remains of the doll into a disposal bag. "Had any brain surgery recently?" he asked, smiling humorlessly.

"No." Sharrow shook her head. "I haven't been near a doctor for . . . fourteen, fifteen years?"

Cenuij scraped the last few bits of the doll into the bag. "Not since Nachtel's Ghost, in fact, after the crash," he said. He sealed the disposal bag. "So it was a nerve-gun."

"I hope so," Sharrow said, staring toward the window where Miz was standing again, looking out over the dusty city.

"You want this?" Cenuij asked her, holding up the bag with the doll's remains in it.

She shook her head and crossed her arms, as though cold.

They booked a private compartment on the dawn-hour Aïs—Yadayeypon Limited. Three hours into the journey the train left behind the last vestiges of Outer Jonolrey's prairies and decelerated across the first jagged outcrops of karst for its last stop before the eastern seaboard. They completed their breakfast and watched the pale gray, intermittently spired landscape below start to dot with houses, solar arrays, and fenced compounds.

They were the only people who got off. The straggled town felt like frontier territory, lazy and open and half-finished. The local vehicle dealer had the six-wheel All Terrain waiting in the station car park; Miz signed the papers, they collected a last few supplies from a general hardware store, and then set off into the karst along a bumpy, dusty solar-farm road that roughly paralleled the widely spaced fence of inverted U's supporting the thin white lines of the monorails.

Sharrow looked up as something moved above her on the monorail. Cenuij looked down, his scarf-enfolded head showing over the edge of the rail eight meters above.

"What exactly is going on?" he said.

She shrugged. "No idea." She looked at Dloan, still listening to the monorail's circuits, then along to the next support leg, where Zefla was sitting in the shade, her head bowed.

"Well, that's fine," Cenuij said tetchily. "I'll just stay up here and get heatstroke, shall I?" He disappeared again.

"What an excellent idea," Sharrow muttered, then tight-beamed to the point on the rail two kilometers away where Miz was. "Miz?"

"Yeah?" Miz's voice said.

"Still nothing?"

"Still nothing."

"How long till the next one's through in the other direction?"

"Twenty minutes."

"Miz, you are absolutely sure—" she began.

"Look, kid," Miz said, sounding annoyed. "It's the regular fucking express, the Passports were issued yesterday, and my agent in Yada says a Huhsz front-company hired a private carriage on this train, today, about five minutes after the Passports hearing broke up. How does it all sound to you?"

"All right, all—" she began.

"Whoa," Miz said. There was silence for a few moments, then Miz's voice returned, suddenly urgent. "Got something on the phones . . . definite vibration . . . should be it. All ready?"

She glanced at Dloan, who was holding one hand to his ear. He looked up at her and nodded. "Here it comes," he said.

"Ready," Sharrow told Miz. She whistled to Cenuij, who stuck his head over the top again. "It's on its way," she told him.

"About time."

"Got the other foil ready?"

"Of course; putting the gunge on now." He shook his head. "Stopping a monorail with glue—how do I get into these situations?" His head disappeared.

Sharrow looked at the squatting figure a hundred meters up the line. "Zef?"

Zefla jerked. Her head came up; she looked around and waved. "Business?" her sleepy voice said in Sharrow's ears.

"Yes, business. *Try* to stay awake, Zef."

"Oh, all right, then."

Dloan shut the junction box in the monorail leg and started climbing up the handholds toward the top of the rail.

Sharrow felt her heart start to race. She checked the rifle again. She brought out the HandCannon and checked it too. They were undergunned for an operation like this, but they hadn't had time to get together all the gear they'd wanted.

The morning after she'd been dropped in Aïs by the Solipsists and met up with the others, they heard the Passports would be issued within the next twenty hours.

Miz told them his plan; Cenuij told him he was crazy. Zefla's considered opinion on its legal implications was that it was "cheeky."

They had just enough time to set up the All Terrain purchase for the next day and storm through Aïs in a variety of taxis, buying up desert gear, bits of comm equipment, and the heaviest automatic hunting rifles and ammunition the Aïs county laws would allow them to have. Just another day or so and Miz could have had heavier weaponry flown in and cleared through one of his front companies, but the Passports were issued on time that day and they had no choice but to make their move.

Their final purchases had been three large discs of coated heavy-duty aluminum foil—spare parts for a portable solar furnace—and some glue. While Dloan and Miz had been buying those, Sharrow had been in the hotel, placing a call to a descendant of one of the Dascen family's servants, a man rich enough to have a butler and a private secretary, both of whom Sharrow had to go through first before she got to Bencil Dornay, who cordially and graciously invited her to his mountain house, along with her friends.

"—ast!" Sharrow heard Miz say.

"What?" she sent back, rattled by the tone of his voice. There was no reply. She stared into the distance, where the white line of the monorail disappeared into the desert shimmer.

"I can see it!" Cenuij shouted from above.

An infinitesimal silent line appeared on the liquid horizon, barely visible through the trembling air. The tiny bright line lengthened; sun burst off it briefly, flickering, then blinked out again.

Sharrow stood up and clicked the visor magnification to twenty. It was like looking at a toy train set reflected in a pool of wobbling mercury. The train was still a couple of kilometers away from where Miz was lying on the top of the monorail. She watched the shadows of the support legs flicking across the train's nose as it raced along under the rail, a tearing silver line curving through the heat.

She counted.

"Shit," she heard herself say. The shadows were strobing across the train's aircraft-sleek snout at almost three per second. The supports were spaced every hundred meters, and the expresses normally ran at about two-twenty meters per second; that was the speed they'd based their calculations on. She drew a breath, to tell Miz to throw the foil over early, when she saw a flash under the monorail.

"Foil's down!" she heard Miz yell.

If Miz's plan was going to work, the train's needle radar should now be picking up the echo of the foil screen and slamming the emergency brakes on.

"It's going too fast," she beamed to Zefla. "It'll overshoot."

"On my way," Zefla sent back, and started running toward Sharrow.

A roaring, screaming noise came through the tightbeam; Miz was just audible above the racket, shouting, "Feels like it's braking. Here it comes!"

"Start running!" Cenuij called down to Sharrow.

"I'm running, I'm running," she muttered, sprinting across the corrugated karst toward the next support leg.

Two kilometers away, Miz lay on the top of the monorail, his cheek held just off the burning surface. The vibration and the noise bored through him; the humming from beneath built into a teeth-aching buzz that seemed to threaten to jolt him right off the rail. He spread himself out, trying to clamp himself to the rail with his hands and feet. Beneath him the circle of foil he'd dropped into the path of the train vibrated gently on its plastic stays, its coated surface reflecting the train's radar. The noise and vibration rose to a crescendo as the furiously braking train screamed past underneath.

"Shi-i-i-i-t!" Miz said, his teeth chattering, every bone in his body seeming to judder. The vortex of air swept up and over him, lashing at his clothes.

The bullet nose of the decelerating train hit the circle of foil, ripping through it instantly and sending the shredded pieces fluttering through the air like a flock of falling silver birds.

The train roared away, still braking. Miz jumped up. "I'd put that second foil down now, kids!" he tight-beamed, then ran to the support leg and started climbing down toward the All Terrain.

Sharrow slowed, looking back down the curving line of support legs; light and shade flickered at their limit. She ran on through the parched air, still slowing, and waited for the second circle of foil to drop above her. She could hear the train now, a distant roar.

"Going fast, eh?" Zefla grinned, dashing past.

The second foil reflector dropped and spread ten meters ahead of Sharrow. She stopped, breathing hard, a furnace in the back of her throat. Zefla jogged on, fifty meters in front of her. Sharrow looked back; the train came on, still slowing. The noise stayed almost constant as the slipstream ebbed and the wail of protesting superconductors gradually faded as the train drew closer.

Then it was above her, the carriages flicking past just a couple of meters over her head; the train's sleek nose hit the second foil screen and held it, tearing it from its stays so that the glistening membrane wrapped around the snout of the front carriage, snapping and cracking around it until the train drew to a stop.

She was just behind the rear of the last carriage; it hung, swinging slightly from the white line of track. She ran on, jumping ridges in the limestone and following Zefla, her gun out ready in front of her. Zefla glanced back.

Suddenly something dropped out of the train from the second-last carriage, between Sharrow and Zefla. In the same instant that it came fluttering down from the still-swinging hatch, she recognized the gold-and-black shape as a Huhsz uniform. Sharrow knew Zefla would dive for cover just *there*. Sharrow went in the same direction, dropping into the cover of a corrugation in the karst, her gun tracking the falling uniform.

The Huhsz officer's cape hit the ground as empty as it had been when it left the train. Dust rose. She aimed at the opened highway. A handgun and face appeared. She waited. Handgun and face withdrew again.

A movement to her right made her heart race briefly before she realized it was the shadow of the train on a long ridge of karst by the track-side; she was seeing what must be Dloan and Cenuij's shadows as they got into position above the train.

Sharrow shifted her position a few meters along the shallow trench into better cover.

Something else fell from the train, at its nose; the foil screen flashed and glittered, rustling to the ground.

"Shit," Sharrow breathed. She touched the side of her mask. "Foil's fallen off," she broadcast. "Break something."

"Right," Dloan's voice said.

They'd smeared the second foil with glue so that it would stick to the front of the train, but obviously it hadn't held; now the railway's technicians and controllers back in Yadayeypon would be looking at their screens and readouts and seeing a clear view in front of the train and probably no indications of damage. Soon they would start thinking about letting the train continue on its way again.

There was a pause, then a loud bang from above. Sharrow relaxed a little; that ought to be Dloan and Cenuij doing something terminal to the train's power supply. A brief grinding noise overhead, and the sight of the second-last carriage, settling down a little lower and sitting very still while the other carriages swayed slightly, confirmed that its superconductors were no longer holding it up inside the monorail; the train was trapped.

She glanced back, down to the end of the train and beyond. A line of dust a kilometer or so away was Miz in the All Terrain. She looked back to the hatch. A larger gun appeared, and a face; the gun sparkled.

The ridge of karst Sharrow had been crouched behind earlier dissolved in an erupting cloud of dust and a rasping bellow of noise as a thousand tiny explosions tore through the brittle, eroded rock. Sharrow was too close to do anything but curl up and try to shield herself from the shrapnel slivers of stone whirling away from the devastation. Debris pattered against her back; a couple of the impacts stung like needles. She tried to roll farther away, then, when the noise stopped but she could hear rifle shots, leapt up, firing.

Bullets sparked around the empty hatch; the hatch cover itself clanged and jerked and swayed as Zefla's fire hit and pierced it from the other side.

There was a percussive thump form the hatch; something flashed into the ground and exploded. The air was filled by a crackling noise, and the ground under the hatch leapt and danced with tiny explosions, all raising dust about the initial impact site. There was an impression of blurring, buzzing, furious movement in the air.

Sharrow ducked down, cursing. She pulled a small flare from her satchel, lit it, and lobbed it to one side of the spreading ripple of explosions.

They'd fired a flea-cluster round. The individual microgrenades each had twelve random, explosive bounces to find the heat signature of a human being nearby, then they would blow up anyway. Properly used, they were devastating, but the canister was designed to be lobbed, not fired straight down into the ground. She guessed less than half the microgrenades had survived the initial shock.

Sharrow kept down, waiting for one of the deadly little pebbles to land at her feet, doubting that any of them would be distracted by the burning flare. Then a stuttered ripple of noise announced the tiny grenades had self-destructed. She peeked up, gun ready.

A head appeared looking down from the hatchway. She shot it. The man's head jerked once, as though nodding at something; then it hung there, and a limp arm flopped out of the hatch. Blood started to fall toward the dark cape lying on the karst. The arm and head were pulled away inside. She fired the rest of the magazine, watching most of the bullets spark and ricochet off the train's underside.

"Fuck this," Sharrow said. She kept the rifle trained on the hatch one-handed, reloaded it, then pulled the HandCannon out of her pocket, put it to her mouth, and sprang the magazine, catching it in her teeth. She turned it around with the hand holding the pistol, pushing the magazine home again. She tight-beamed to where she thought Zefla was. "Zef?"

Nothing.

"Zef?" she broadcast.

"Morning," Zefla drawled, almost lazily.

"Cover."

"Okay."

Zefla started firing at the hatch door again. Sharrow fired, too, then scrambled out of the karst trench and ran, leaping over the corrugations, toward the small crater where the flea-cluster round had landed. She got almost under-neath the hatch; Zefla stopped firing. Sharrow aimed the ri-fle at the underbelly of the train carriage just in front of the hatch, then fired a dozen rounds into the metal. Some rico-cheted; one whined past her left shoulder. She took out the HandCannon and fired into the same area, the recoil punch-ing back into her hand and shaking her whole arm as the gun bellowed. The A-P rounds left neat little holes in the carriage skin.

Something moved in the hatchway; she loosed the rest of the pistol's rounds into the hatchway itself, the noise changing from the sharp crack of the Armor Piercing shells to the whine of the fléchette rounds. Then she ran, back and to one side, out from under the train. She rolled into cover, crying out as a sharp edge of karst sliced through her jacket and cut her shoulder. She sat up, quickly rubbed her shoul-der, then reloaded while Miz pulled up the All Terrain di-rectly under the train's last carriage.

From here she could see the top of the train and the monorail itself. Dloan and Cenuij had disappeared; there was a hint of an opened section on the roof of the last car-riage.

Suddenly the Huhsz carriage shook; its windows shat-tered and burst, spraying out. There was a sharp, manic buzz of noise she recognized, and a series of popping, crack-ling noises. A couple of the flea rounds jumped out of the shattered carriage and leapt around like tiny firecrackers on the karst surface for a few seconds, then they detonated. The wrecked Huhsz carriage stayed silent; gray smoke drifted from it.

"What the fuck was *that*?" Miz broadcast from the All Terrain.

"Flea-cluster," Sharrow said. "Cenuij? Dloan?" she called urgently.

"Here," Cenuij sighed.

"You guys all right?" Zefla's voice said.

"Both fine. They tried to roll a flea-cluster at us. Our large friend rolled it straight back in at them and closed the door. He's just gone in for a look around."

"Yeah, Dloan!" Zefla whooped.

"This might be them," Dloan said. Sharrow saw him at one of the blown-out windows in the Huhsz carriage. He was fiddling with something.

"What are you doing now?" Sharrow said, puzzled.

"Tying a bit of string to this briefcase," Dloan said, as though it should be obvious. "Nobody underneath this carriage?"

"All clear," Sharrow told him. Dloan threw the large briefcase out of the smashed window. It jerked open as the string tied inside the carriage came taut. There was a crack and the whine of fléchettes; the briefcase bounced into the air on a cloud of smoke, then fell back, swaying on the end of the string. A series of what looked like large black books tumbled out of it and thumped dustily to the karst.

"Ah-*ha*," said Sharrow.

She stood on top of the waste silo—a dusty yellow mound on the side of a dusty yellow hill with the karst desert behind them, a field of pale, frozen flames in the fierce glare of the afternoon sun. Miz sat in the All Terrain, talking on the transceiver. The silo's valve-heads were protected by a small blockhouse covered in ancient, fading radiation symbols and death's-heads. Dloan attached a thermal charge to the door's lock; the charge burned brighter than the noon sun, and Dloan kicked the door open.

The interior of the blockhouse was black after the glare of the burning charge and the blinding sunlight; it was roastingly hot, too. Sharrow held the five Passports. They were solid and heavy, even though they were fashioned largely from titanium and woven carbon fiber. The external text, addressed to officials and responsible individuals everywhere, commanding their complete cooperation under the laws of the World Court, and threatening untold punishments for anybody who tried to destroy the Passports, was engraved on thin flat sheets of diamond secured to the covers. The matricial holes were blue carbuncles embedded in one corner of each of the solid documents; a sequence of recessed buttons along their spines controlled the Passports' circuitry, which could produce a hologram of the World Court judges and a recording of their voices, also commanding complete cooperation from all and sundry before going into the details of their pan-political authority and legal provenance.

Cenuij swung the meter-long, bullet-shaped slug away from the top of the silo's access shaft. The radiation monitor cuff on his wrist whined quietly.

Cenuij and Dloan together heaved the shaft lock open; the massive shutter made a protesting, creaking noise, and the radiation cuff sirened louder. Sharrow approached the dark well of the shaft.

"Well," Cenuij said to her, "don't stand there admiring the damn things; chuck them down before we all get fried."

Sharrow dropped the Passports into the shaft. They made a vanishing, clunking noise. She helped Cenuij hold the shutter. Dloan primed the bundle of explosive, thermal charge and assorted ammunition rounds, sealed it inside the inspection slug, and then maneuvered the bullet-shaped slug into place above the shaft while Cenuij's radiation monitor warbled away.

The slug slid into place, securing the shutter; they let it go and it disappeared down the shaft, cable unwinding from a reel in the ceiling.

"Okay," Dloan said, heading for the door.

They got back into the cool interior of the All Terrain. Miz grinned at Sharrow. "Done it?"

"Yes," Sharrow said, wiping sweat from her face.

"Great," Miz said, pulling on the car's controls to take them away from the silo. They bumped off its domed top and back onto the track leading into the hills.

"Is that plane on the way yet?" Cenuij demanded from the rear of the bouncing All Terrain.

"Pilot had a problem with customs in Hapley City," Miz said. "Sorted out now; meeting us two klicks north of here. She'll be keeping low to stay out of surface radar. There's a bit of fuss about the train."

"What about satellites?" Cenuij said.

"By the time they process what they've got, we'll be away," Miz said. "Worst happens, the plane's impounded." He shrugged. "We're leaving it at Chanasteria Field, anyway."

"Five seconds," Dloan said. Miz stopped the All Terrain on the track just before it entered a shallow canyon; they all watched the bulge of the waste silo.

There was an impression of noise, an almost subsonic concussion in the air and from the ground. A little dust drifted from the door of the blockhouse.

"That ought to slow the bastards down," Miz said, restarting the vehicle.

Sharrow nodded. "With any luck."

"I hope it was worth it," Cenuij said.

"Well, yahoo for us," Zefla yawned. "This calls for a drink."

"Maybe Bencil Dornay'll fix you a cocktail if you ask him nicely," Miz told her, gunning the All Terrain's engine as they rumbled into the canyon.

Sharrow looked out the window at the drifting dust.

8

The Mortal
Message

S he swam above the landscape. The water was a quiet
milky-blue; the landscape below glowed green. Diving
toward it, she could see tiny roads and houses, glittering
lakes and patches of dark forest. She touched the cool crystal, her naked limbs pulsing, forcing, keeping her down; her
black hair floated around her head, a slow cloud of darkness,
swirling languidly.

She stilled her arms and legs and rose gently upward
through the warm water.

On the surface she rolled over and lay floating, watching the vague shadow her body cast on the pale-pink tiles of
the ceiling. She shifted her limbs this way and that, watching the fuzzy figure on the ceiling respond. Then she kicked
out for the side, pulled herself out, and took a towel from a
table. She went to the parapet, where a breeze from the valley blew in, bringing a scent of late-summer richness. The
cool air flowed over the parapet and around her wet body,
making her shiver. She put her arms on the wooden rail of
the glass-fronted parapet and watched the hairs on her forearms unstick themselves from the beads of moisture there
and rise, each on its own tiny mound of flesh.

The view led across the valley to evergreen forests and
high summer pasture. The mountains above held no trace of
snow yet, though farther on, beyond the horizon, the center

of the range held peaks with permanent snowfields and small glaciers. Beyond the lip of rock above, high streaks of clouds and vapor trails crossed the pale-blue vault like spindrift.

She put the towel around her shoulders and walked to the edge of the pool, looking down into the gradually calming, green-glowing waters. The landscape below trembled and shook, as though convulsing in the throes of some terrible quake.

The house of Bencil Dornay was built under an overhang on a great mountain in the Morspe range overlooking the Vernasayal valley, three and a half thousand kilometers south of Yadayeypon, almost within sight of Jonolrey's western coast and the rollers of Southern, Golter's fourth ocean. The house clung beneath an undercut buttress like a particularly stubborn sea crustacean determined to stay clamped to its rock even though the tide had gone out long ago. The house's most unsettling feature was its swimming pool, which was on the very lowest of the dwelling's five floors, and which was glass-bottomed.

Faced with the green glow rising from the pool and the dim but otherwise unobstructed view it offered of the valley far below, people of a nervous disposition being shown around for the first time had been known to turn a remarkably similar shade. Hardier, more adventurous guests willing to display their trust in modern building techniques rarely missed an opportunity to take a dip in the pool, even if it was just to say they'd done it.

Sharrow stood there and waited for some time, until the water beading her skin had mostly dried and the chopping water in the pool had stilled completely, so that the view of the valley five hundred meters below was clear and distinct and heart stopping; then she dived gracefully back in.

The pain came while she was swimming back to the side, just under her ribs, then in her legs. She felt it and tried to ignore it, swimming on, gritting her teeth. She got to the pool-side, put her hands on the ridged tiles, tensing her arms. Not again. It couldn't happen again.

The pain slammed into her ears like a pair of white-hot swords; she heard herself gasp. She tried to clutch at the pool-side as the next wave hit, searing her from shoulders to calves. She cried out, falling back in the water, coughing and choking as she tried to swim and to curl up at the same time. Not all of it again. What came next? What did she have to prepare for now? The pain ebbed; she grabbed at the pool-side again. She was suddenly weak, unable to pull herself out; she felt to one side with her foot, seeking the steps. Her right hand found a handle recessed in the tiles. She gripped it, knowing what would happen now. Her body convulsed as the agony tore through her, as if her body was a socket and the pain some huge, obscene plug, transmitting a vast and terrible current of agony.

She doubled up in the water, concentrating on her grip on the tile handle, terrified of letting go. She felt her face go under water and tried to hold her breath while the pain went on and on and a low moan escaped her lips in a string of bubbles. She wanted to breathe, but she couldn't uncurl herself from the fetal position she'd assumed. A roaring noise grew in her ears.

Then the pain eased, evaporating.

Spluttering, coughing, spitting water, she pulled on the tile handle and felt her head bump into the pool-side. She surfaced, breathing at last, and put out her other hand, found the handle, found both handles. One foot slotted into an underwater step. She kept her eyes closed and dragged herself upward with the dregs of her strength. She felt the edge of the pool against her belly and collapsed onto the warm plastic tiles there, her legs still floating in the water.

Then strong hands were pulling her, lifting her, holding her, arms enfolding her. She opened her eyes long enough to see the worried faces of Zefla and Miz and started to say something to them, to tell them not to worry; then the great sword smashed into her backside, and she spasmed, collapsing. They held her again, taking her weight, and she felt herself lifted, one toe sliding over the tiles, and then she was laid down on something soft, and they held her, warm against her, whispering to her, and were still there when the last brief instant of agony burst again inside her head, ending everything.

She woke to the sound of bird-song. She was still lying by the pool-side, covered by towels. Zefla lay beside her, cradling her head, gently rocking her. A bird chirped and she looked around for it.

"Sharrow?" Zefla said quietly.

The bluebird sat on the wooden parapet of the pool terrace. Sharrow watched it watching her, then turned to Zefla. "Hello," she said. Her voice sounded small.

"You okay?" Zefla asked.

The bluebird flew away. Miz appeared, dressed in trunks, squatting down. "Called the—" he started to say to Zefla, then saw Sharrow's eyes were open. "Well, hi," he said softly, putting one hand out to her face and touching her cheek. "Back with us again, are you?" he asked, smiling.

"I'm all right," she said, rolling over and trying to sit up. Zefla put an arm to her back, helping her. She shivered, and Miz wrapped a towel around her shoulders.

"All that wasn't what you'd call natural, was it?" Zefla said.

She shook her head. "It was the same as the last time. In the tank. Exactly the same. A recording." She tried to laugh. "They did say they'd be in touch."

Miz looked over to the pool. "Could be a nerve gun or something down there, in the valley. Beaming straight up."

"Or something in the house," Zefla said, patting at Sharrow's hair with a towel.

"Maybe," Sharrow said. "Maybe."

"If I ever get my hands on whoever's doing this," Miz said quietly. "I'm going to kill them, but I'm—"

Sharrow put her hand out, held Miz's arm, squeezing it. "Ssh, ssh," she whispered.

Miz sighed and stood. "Well, I'm going to take a look around the house, starting with the next floor up. I'll get Dlo or Cen to take a look down in the valley." He reached down, put his hand on Sharrow's head for a moment. "You going to be all right?"

"I'll be fine," she said.

"Good girl." Miz walked quickly away.

"Girl," Sharrow muttered, shaking her head.

"Let's get you to bed, eh?" Zefla said.

Sharrow used Zefla's shoulder to help her get up. Eventually she stood, supported by the other woman. "No. I was having a swim. It's gone now; I feel fine."

"You're crazy," Zefla said, but let Sharrow shrug off the towel she was holding around her shoulders and walked with her to the side of the pool. Sharrow stood there for a moment, composing herself, drawing herself upright and flexing her shoulders. She dived into the water; it was a rather ragged dive, but then she surfaced and struck out strongly for the far side.

Zefla sat down on the side of the pool, her dark red-brown legs dangling in the water. She grinned at the pale, lithe figure forcing its way through the lime-glowing water to the far side and shook her head.

"How's our patient, Doctor Clave?" Bencil Dornay asked.

"Fit and healthy, it would seem," the elderly clinician said, entering the lounge with Sharrow at his side.

Bencil Dornay was a compact, clipped man of late middle years with small green eyes set in a pale olive face; he had a neatly trimmed beard and perfectly manicured hands. He dressed casually, almost carelessly, in clothes that were of the very best quality, if not the last word in fashion. His father had left the employ of Gorko, Sharrow's grandfather, when the World Court had ordered the dissolution of the old man's estate. Dornay senior had gone into business and been highly successful, and bought himself a shorter name. Bencil had been even more successful than his father, reducing his own names from three to two. He had no children, but he had applied to the relevant authorities to be allowed to clone himself and hoped the succeeding version of himself might be able to afford the next step, shedding one more name to instigate a minor noble house.

"Fit enough to dance, perhaps, Doctor Clave?" Dornay asked, eyes twinkling as he glanced at Sharrow, who smiled. "I was planning a small party in the lady's honor tomorrow evening. This little dizzy spell won't prevent her from dancing, will it?"

"Certainly not," Doctor Clave said. He was rotund and heavily bearded and had an air of amiable distraction about him. He seemed so much like how Sharrow remembered doctors were supposed to be that she wondered just how much was an act. "Though I'd—" The doctor cleared his throat. "Advise having medical attention on hand at this party, naturally."

Bencil Dornay smiled. "Why, Doctor, you didn't imagine I would dare conduct a soiree without you in attendance, did you?"

"I should think not." The doctor looked at a small clipboard. "Well, I'd better see if those lazy techs have got all that stuff back in the plane. . . ."

"Let me see you out," Bencil Dornay offered. "Lady Sharrow," he said. She nodded. He and the clinician walked to the elevator. She watched them go.

Sharrow could just remember Bencil Dornay's father from a single one of those seasons when she had visited the great house of Tzant while the estate had still technically belonged to the Dascen family, yet its administration—and fate—had been in the hands of the Court.

Dornay senior had left Gorko's employ twenty years earlier, and had already become a rich trader; it had been his particular pleasure to revisit as an honored guest the house he had served in as domum-secretary. He had been a stooped, kindly man Sharrow remembered as seeming very old (but then, she had been very young) with a perfect memory for every item in the vast, half-empty, and mostly unused pile that had been house Tzant. She and the other children had played games with him, asking him what was in a particular drawer or cupboard in some long-neglected room of some distant wing, and found that he was almost invariably correct, down to the last spoon, the last button and toothpick.

Breyguhn had said she thought he was a wizard and had had every last grain of dust numbered and filed. She delighted in moving things from drawer to drawer and cupboard to cupboard and room to room, trying to confuse him when the others came running back, breathless with the news that he was wrong.

Sharrow couldn't honestly claim that she remembered Bencil Dornay himself; he had been sent to collage before she was born, and if they had ever met, she had quite forgotten the occasion.

Dornay senior must have been in Gorko's genetic thrall for over four decades by then. The code that would—according to Breyguhn—tell Sharrow where the *Universal Principles* was had been added to the message in his cells shortly before Gorko had fallen. Just by the very act of fathering him, Dornay senior had passed that message on to his son, where it waited now—if Breyguhn was right—half a century later.

And all it needed—she thought, with a kind of bitterness—was a kiss.

Sharrow turned and walked to the far end of the

lounge, where a glassed-in terrace looked out onto an ocean of cloud. The others sat watching a holoscreen.

"Well?" Miz said, attempting to guide her into a chair. She gave an exasperated tut, waving his arm away, and sat in another seat.

"What's the news?" She nodded at the screen, where a map showed what looked like a schematic of a war.

"The Huhsz are playing things down," Cenuij said. "They've apologized for the accident on the train—said some munitions went off accidentally, denying there was any attack. They say the Passports will be initiated in a few days' time, after a period of mourning for the Blessed Ones killed on the train."

"Hey," Zefla said to Sharrow. "We saw that house you had on the island. It looked really nice."

"Thanks," Sharrow said. "Still standing, was it?"

"Dammit, Sharrow, what did the doctor say?" Miz said.

She shrugged, looking at the war-map in the screen. "There is something in there." She tapped her head. "In here."

"Oh no," Zefla breathed.

"What, exactly?" Cenuij said, sitting forward.

"Some crystal-virus, probably," Sharrow said, looking around them. "Just a molecule thick, most places, growing round and into my brain stem. One thread disappears down my spine and ends up in my right foot. The rest branch"— she shrugged—"into the rest of my skull."

"Gods, Sharrow," Zefla breathed.

"A *crystal-virus*," Cenuij said, eyes wide. "That's war-tech." He glanced at the corridor leading to the elevator. "How did that old duffer know—?"

"That old duffer knows what he's talking about," Sharrow said. "And he's got all the best gear. He medicked for the Free Traders' navy on Trontsephori during the Barge War, and he volunteered to help metaplegics after the Five Percent. He didn't know what he was looking for—I don't know he even believed me—but he kept looking, and it showed up on an NMR scan. The doc wants me to visit a specialist hospital for more tests; I said I'd think about it."

"Will they be able to take it out?" Miz asked, looking worried. "Operate or . . . something?"

Sharrow shook her head.

"Not that stuff," Cenuij said, obviously impressed. "It

grows less than a centimeter a month, but once it's in, it's in. To take it out, you'd need the original virus, and that'll be locked back up in a Court compound in some military habitat. If there's another war the Court thinks justifies the escalation, you might see it again. Not until."

"Couldn't we steal it?" Miz said.

"Are you mad?" Cenuij asked him.

Dloan shook his head. "Tricky," he said.

Zefla put one hand to her mouth, staring at Sharrow, her eyes bright.

"So *that's* what was picking up the long-wave signal from the doll," Cenuij said, staring straight ahead and nodding. "A crystal-virus." He gave a small laugh and looked at Sharrow. "Shit, yes, that's all you'd need. If it was put in while you were in hospital on the Ghost, it's had long enough to grow right down the length of your body. The strand into your foot must be the aerial. The lattice could itself sit there forever and you'd never notice. Probably pulls less power than an iris; then the right code comes along, and zap!"

"'Ouch' might be a better description," Sharrow said.

"And using the long-wave," Cenuij said. "Perfect—you don't need much definition, and it'll penetrate. . . ."

"So these signals come from the comm net," Zefla said. "Satellites and shit?" Cenuij didn't reply; he was staring out at the carpet of cloud beyond the sun-bright terrace outside. Sharrow nodded. Zefla spread her hands. "Can't we find out who's sending the signals?"

"You'll be lucky," Dloan said.

"Out of the question," Cenuij said, dismissing the idea with a wave of the hand.

"Well, how the hell do we stop it?" Miz said loudly. "We can't let that happen again!"

"Live in a mine shaft, maybe," Cenuij suggested. "Or find somewhere off-net. Though even off-net, if somebody knew where you were, they could beam a signal at you. That doll they had in the tanker was just a close-range transmitter. . . ."

"How about a pain-disruptor collar?" Zefla asked.

"Forget it," Cenuij said. He made a tutting noise. "Damn, I'd like to have talked to that old doc." He pulled his phone from his pocket. "Wonder if I should call him."

"Ask him tomorrow night," Sharrow told him. "He's coming to the party."

"That still on?" Miz asked.

"Why not?" Sharrow shrugged, looking at where Bencil Dornay had escorted the doctor toward the elevator. "He's only inviting people he trusts, and he isn't telling anybody we're here." She smiled at Miz. "He really wanted to throw a party in our honor; I couldn't refuse."

Miz looked skeptical.

"Will you do it, then?" Cenuij asked her with a strange, unsettling smile.

She looked at his thin, inquiring face. "Yes, Cenuij; I'll do it then."

Zefla got out of her seat and knelt by Sharrow's, hugging her. "You poor kid; you're in the wars, aren't you?"

Sharrow put a hand through Zefla's ringleted hair, fingertips touching her scalp. "Actually, a war sounds like just what I need right now."

She stood in her room, facing the mirror, her underclothes and dress lying on the bed behind her, the lights on full. She gazed at herself. There was still some slight bruising on her knees from when she'd fallen in the tank in the Log Jam, though the hint of discoloration on her forehead from the same fall had gone. There was a cut on her shoulder, from the karst, and two broken nails where her hand had gripped the handhold in the pool that morning.

She put her arms above her head, watching her breasts rise, then lower, as she dropped her arms again. She turned side-on, relaxing, and frowned at the bulge of her belly. She stared at her thighs in the mirror, then looked down at them, wondering if they were getting lumpy yet. She couldn't see anything. Maybe her eyesight was going.

She had never undergone any type of alteration—apart from orthodontic work when she was a child—and never used any antigeriatric drug, legal or otherwise. She had sworn she never would. But now, even before there were any obvious signs of age on her body, she thought she knew how older people must feel: that desire not to change, not to deteriorate. Was it simply that she wanted to remain attractive? She gazed into her own eyes.

Mostly, she thought, *I want to remain attractive to myself. If no man ever saw me again, I'd still want to look good*

*to me. I'd trade five, ten years of life to look like this until the
end.*

She shook her head at herself, a small frown on her
face.

"So die young, narcissist," she whispered to herself.

At least the Huhsz might ensure she never grew old.

She turned to dress.

The body is a code, she thought, reaching for her slip.
And froze, thinking of where she had heard that phrase, and
of what she was supposed to discover from Bencil Dornay
this evening, and how.

In the curving corridor, by one window looking out into a
gulf of darkness strung and beaded with the necklace lights
of distant roads and the clustered jewels of towns and villages, opposite the wide staircase that led to the house reception floor, its lit depths already bustling with talk and
music and laughter, she found Cenuij Mu sitting on a couch,
dressed in a formal black robe and reading what looked like
a letter.

He looked up when she approached. He inspected her,
then nodded. "Very elegant," he told her. He looked down at
the letter, folded it, and put it away in the black robe.

She checked her reflection in the windows, severe in
court-formal black. Her dress was floor-length and long-
sleeved, decorated with plain platinum jewelery worn
around her high-collared neck and on her gloved hands. A
black net held her hair, constellated with diamonds. "Court-
prophylactic," she said, turning to check her profile. "Prissy,
constipated style," she told him. She shook her head at her
reflection. "Damn shame I look so drop-dead stunning in
it."

She expected a reply to that, but Cenuij didn't seem to
be listening. He was staring into the middle distance.

She sat beside him on the couch, the dress and collar
forcing her to sit very erect, her head up. "Was that a letter
from Breyguhn?" she asked him.

He nodded, still staring away around the curve of corridor. "Yes. Just delivered."

"How is she?"

Cenuij shook his head, then shrugged. "She mentioned
you," he said.

"Ah," Sharrow said. "Did she mention anything about this message I'm supposed to get from Dornay?"

Cenuij shrugged again. He looked tired. "Nothing directly," he said.

"Can't help wondering what form it's going to take," Sharrow admitted. The music and chattering from the floor below swelled briefly, then ebbed again before Cenuij replied.

"If it's the sort of thing I think she's talking about," he said, "it could be expressed in a variety of ways. He might not simply say whatever it is he knows; it might be encoded as a drawing, some body-pose from a sign-dance, a whistled tune. It could even vary according to the circumstances he's in when the programming takes over."

"I'd no idea this was one of your areas of expertise, Cenuij."

"Merely a smattering," he said, seeming to collect himself. "Breyguhn knows more."

"We'll get her out," Sharrow told him.

He looked annoyed. "Why *do* you two hate each other so much?" he asked.

She stared at him for a moment, then shrugged. "Partly your standard sibling rivalry," she told him. "And the rest is . . . ." She shook her head. "Too long a story. Brey'll tell you in her own time, I expect." Sharrow held one of Cenuij's hands. "Soon, Cenny; she'll tell you soon. This nonsense with Dornay should put us on the track of the book; we'll find it. She'll be out soon."

Cenuij looked down, and his hand moved, as though about to take the letter out again. "That's all I want," he whispered.

She put her arm around him.

"And you, Sharrow?" he said, twisting away from her to look her in the eyes. "What do you want? What do you *really* want? Do you know?"

She gazed levelly at him. "To live, I suppose," she said, with what she hoped sounded like sarcasm.

"No good; too common. What else?"

She wanted to look away from his intense, narrow gaze, but forced herself to meet it. "You really want to know?" she asked.

"Of course! I asked you, didn't I?"

She shrugged. She pursed her lips and looked deliberately away, out into the darkness beyond the windows. "Not to be alone," she said, looking at him and lifting her chin just a little, as if in defiance. "And not to let people down."

He gave a harsh laugh and got up from the couch. He stood above her, straightening his robe. "Such a humorist, our little Sharrow," he said. Then he smiled broadly and put his arm out toward her. "Shall we?"

She smiled without warmth, took his arm, and they descended to the party.

There were perhaps a hundred guests. The band was entirely acoustic and by that measure extremely up-to-date; Bencil Dornay's own kitchen staff had prepared the tables of delicacies themselves. Dornay took her around his guests, introducing them. They were business colleagues, senior staff in his trading firm, a few local dignitaries and worthies, rich friends from nearby houses, and some local artists. Sharrow entertained the idea that Bencil Dornay's guests just happened to be uniformly polite, but guessed that they had been told not to ask any embarrassing questions on the lines, of How does it feel to be hunted by the Huhsz?

"You are very brave, Lady Sharrow," Dornay said to her. They stood by one of the food-laden tables, watching a juggling troupe perform on a small stage raised in the middle of the reception hall's dance floor. People had left a discreet clearing around the host and his guest.

"Brave, Mr. Dornay?" she said. He had dressed in pure white.

"My lady," Dornay said, looking into her eyes. "I have requested my guests say nothing about the unfortunate circumstances you find yourself in. Nor shall I, but let me say only that your composure would astonish me, had I not known the family you come from."

She smiled. "You think old Gorko would be proud of me?"

"It was my misfortune only to meet that great man once," Dornay said. "A bird cannot land once on a great tree and claim to know it. But I imagine that he would, yes."

She watched the spinning wands of the jugglers as they flashed to and fro beneath the spotlights. "We believe the Passports my . . . pursuers require are safe, for now."

"Thank the gods," Dornay said. "They appear not to have been initiated, but I feared a trick, and we are not so

far from their scrofulous World Shrine. I have taken every
precaution, of course, but ... well, perhaps I should have
canceled this evening."

"Ah, now, Mr. Dornay, I believe I forbade you ..."

"Indeed," Bencil Dornay laughed lightly. "Indeed.
What was I to do? My family no longer exists to serve yours,
dear lady, but I am your servant nevertheless."

"You are too kind. As I say, I believe I am safe for now.
And I'm grateful for your hospitality."

"My house is yours, dear lady; I am yours to command."

She looked at him then, as the jugglers drew gasps with
their complicated closing routine.

"Do you mean that, Mr. Dornay?" she asked him,
searching his eyes.

"Oh, absolutely, dear lady," he said, eyes shining. "I am
not merely being polite; I mean these things literally. It
would be my pleasure and an honor to serve you in any way
I can."

She looked away for a moment. "Well," she said, and
smiled waveringly at him. The lights came up as the jugglers
finished their display to decorously wild applause. "I ... I
do have a favor to ask you." She had to raise her voice a little to make herself heard.

Dornay looked delighted, but from the corner of her
eye she could see guests—released from the spell of the juggling troupe—moving a little closer to her and Dornay and
looking expectantly at the two of them. She let him see her
gaze flick around the people. "Perhaps later," she said, smiling.

She stood on the terrace, a drink in her hand, the darkness
at her back as she leaned against the shoulder-high parapet,
the reception room like a giant bright screen in front of her.
People were dancing inside. Clouds hid the junklight.

Miz came out, wandering across the terrace, smoking
something sweet smelling from a little cup-kettle. He leant
back beside her and offered her the gently fuming cup, but
she shook her head.

"Haven't seen you up dancing yet," he said, breathing
deeply.

"That's right."

"You used to dance so well," he said, glancing at her. "*We* used to dance so well."

"I remember."

"Remember that dance competition in Malishu? The endurance one where the prize was to go to dinner with the brave and heroic pilots of the Clipper Squadrons?" He laughed at the memory.

"Yes," she said. "I remember."

"Hell," he said, turning around to look out over the dark valley. "We'd have won, too, if the MPs hadn't arrived looking for us."

"We were AWOL; taught me never to trust you with dates again."

"I got confused. We'd crossed the dateline during the party the night before." Miz looked bewildered and squinted up at the dark clouds. "Several times, actually, I think."

"Hmm," she said.

"Anyway," he said, "want to try it again?" He nodded back at the hall and the dancing people. "This lot look feeble; give them a couple of hours, and they'll be falling like raindrops."

She shook her head. "I don't think so," she said. "Not right now."

He sighed and turned around, taking another snort from the cup-kettle. "Well, if it comes to the end of the night," he said, pretending snootiness, "and you don't get offered a lift home, don't come crying to me." He nodded once, primly emphatic, and headed back to the reception hall, practicing his dance steps on the way, drink held out in one hand, the fuming cup-kettle in the other. She watched him go.

She had been remembering a ball in Geis's father's house, in Siynscen, when she'd been fifteen or sixteen. Breyguhn had fallen in love with Geis that summer—or thought she had, at least—when they had all stayed at the estate. Sharrow had told her she was silly, and far too young; Geis was almost twenty. What would he want with a child like her? And anyway, Geis was an altogether tiresome person—an awkward, overeager fool with funny eyes and a plump behind. In fact, she herself was quite fed up with him wanting to dance with her at these sorts of functions, and wanting to kiss her and give her stupid presents.

Nevertheless, Breyguhn was determined she would declare her undying love for Geis at the ball, stubbornly maintaining that Geis was kind and dashing and poetic and clever. Sharrow had poured scorn on all this, but then, when she had stood in their dressing room, all fussed around by servants (and enjoying the attention and the luxury of it, because their father had lost a lot of money that year and had dismissed all their own staff save his android butler), and seen her half sister in her first ball gown (albeit borrowed, like her own, from a better-off second cousin), with her hair piled up like a woman's, her budding breasts pushed by the bodice to form a cleavage, and her eyes, made up, glowing with confidence and a kind of power, Sharrow had thought, with some amusement and only a hint of jealousy, that perhaps dear, tedious old Geis might just find Brey attractive after all.

She'd watched Geis as he and some of his officer-cadet friends entered the party. They were in the uniform of the Alliance Navy; the ball itself was a fund-raising event for the Tax Alliance, and Geis had been into space for a couple of months on an Alliance warship.

She realized then that she hadn't really looked at Geis for a year or two, not properly *looked* at him.

She had never liked uniforms, but Geis looked almost handsome in his. He moved less awkwardly, he sported a dark, trimmed beard that quite suited him and made him look older, and he had lost the puppy fat he'd carried through his midteens. She had drifted close to him, unseen, early on in the evening before the ball properly started, hearing him laughing lustily with his friends and hearing them laughing at what he said, and—perhaps, she told herself later, in the spell of those gales of male laughter—had determined then not to treat Geis with her usual disdain, should he ask her for a dance. She would see what happened, she thought, walking away from the young men. She would do nothing so petty and low as to try to entrap her cousin just to prove something to her foolish little half sister, but if he really had improved so, and if he did, at some point, maybe, ask her for a dance . . .

He asked her for the first dance. For the rest of the evening they hardly left each other's side between dances, or each other's arms during them.

She watched as she stepped and moved and was held and turned and displayed and admired on the dance floor: Breyguhn's eyes took on a look of surprise at first; then that slowly became hurt, until hurt was replaced by scorn and what she must have thought was recognition, upon which her eyes filled with tears, and finally with hate.

She danced on, exulting, not caring. Geis looked as dashing and handsome as Breyguhn had said. He had changed, he had more to talk about, had become more like a man than a boy. Even his remaining goucheness seemed like enthusiasm—gusto, indeed. She listened to him and looked at him and danced with him and thought about him, and decided that had she not been exactly who she was, had she been just a little more like everybody else and just a little less difficult to please, she could almost have fallen for her cousin.

Breyguhn left the ball early with their father and his mistress, in a storm of tears. A duenna was left to wait for Sharrow. She and Geis danced until they were the last couple left on the dance floor and the band was making deliberate mistakes and taking long pauses between numbers. She even let Geis kiss her—though she didn't respond— when they went out to the dawn-lit garden for some fresh air (her chaperone coughing delicately from a nearby bower). Then she'd had herself taken home.

She had seen Geis face-to-face only twice in the two years after that. She had been away at finishing school, then started at Yadayeypon University, in both places discovering the fresh, unexpected, and surprising pleasures of sex, and the power her looks and her birthright (judiciously deployed) gave her over young—and not so young—men, who were vastly more moodily interesting and intellectually stimulating than cousin Geis, the part-time Navy goon and geekiskly successful *businessman*.

The following year, at her father's funeral, they'd exchanged a few words (though she'd overheard rather more), and when she did finally agree to meet him properly—at the launch of an airship (which he had named after her! The embarrassment!)—she had been rather curt with him, claiming she had been too busy to answer his letters and just hated talking on the phone. He had looked hurt, and she'd felt a terrible, cruel urge to laugh.

She'd seen him once more before the war, a few months later, at a new-year party he'd thrown in a villa in the Blue Hills, in Piphram.

Then the Five Percent War had finally broken out, and she had joined the anti-Tax forces, partly because theirs seemed the more romantic cause, partly because she considered them the more politically progressive side, and partly as a kind of revenge.

And if it had done nothing else—she thought, as she drained her glass and smiled ruefully at the great wide screen that was the window into Bencil Dornay's party—the war had finally signaled the end of her willfully extended and determinedly wanton girlhood.

And more, she thought, smiling sadly at the dancing, happy people on the other side of the windows, remembering that last engagement, frantic and terrible and pitiless in the cold and the silence of the dark seconds of space between Nachtel and Nachtel's Ghost.

And more.

She made to finish her drink, but the glass was already dry.

A little later she returned to the party.

"Your grandfather was a truly great man, my lady. The great are always seen as a threat by the lesser; they can't help it. It's not just jealousy, though there was much of that in your grandfather's case. It is an instinctive reaction. They know (without knowing that they know) that there is something awesome in their midst, and they must make way for it. That is cause for resentment—an ignoble and small-minded emotion, like jealousy, and just as endemic. Your grandfather was brought down by a great mass of small people, dear lady. They were worms; he was a raptor. He had the vision to look out of our furrow, and the courage to do what had to be done, but the worms fear change; they think worm thoughts, ever burrowing and recycling, never raising their heads from the loam. You know, your grandfather could have lived the life of a great duke; he could have maintained the worth of the house and made it gradually greater still, he could have encouraged science, the arts, built great buildings, endowed foundations, become a World Counselor, helped control the Court—and no doubt have enjoyed what personal happiness was ever to be his. Instead he gambled it all, the way the truly great must if they are not to lie on their deathbed and know that they have wasted their talents, that the life they have lived has been one many a lesser man could have lived. We call what transpired failure, but I tell you it cannot fail to inspire those of us who keep his memory. He lives on, in our hearts, and he will receive the respect he deserves one day, when the world and the system have changed to become a temple fit for his memory to be venerated within."

Sharrow stood before the giant portrait of her grandfather in a private room of the overhang house. Bencil Dornay had offered to show her his personal shrine while a group of mime artists were performing in the reception room.

Gorko was depicted in the painting as a giant of a man with a huge, carved face and great bristling whiskers; his body looked exaggeratedly muscled under a tight riding tunic, and the bandamyion mount beside him looked out of scale. Something like fire shone from Gorko's staring eyes. The portrait was at one end of the narrow room, draped in plush hangings. Apart from the painting, the room was empty.

"Hmm," Sharrow said. "Fate preserve us from greatness."

Dornay shook his head. "Dear lady, don't let the mean-of-spirit infect you." He glanced at the tall portrait. "Greatness is his legacy, and our hope."

"Do we really need greatness, Mr. Dornay?" she asked him.

He turned slowly and walked toward the doors at the far end of the room, and she followed him. "We must need it, my lady. It is all that leads us onward. With it we may dream. Without it, we merely subsist."

"But so often," she said, "the people we call great seem to lead us to destruction."

"Their own, indeed," Dornay said, opening the doors and ushering her into a small hallway. "And those around them, I daresay. But destruction can be a positive act, too: the clearing out of rot, the excising of diseased tissue, the brushing away of the old to make room for the new. We are all so loath to offend, to cause any pain. The great have the vision to see beyond such pettiness. Do we curse the doctor for some small pain when it saves us a greater one? Does any worthwhile adult blame his parents for the occasional slap as a child?"

They descended by elevator to the party. "Your rhetorical questions disarm me," Sharrow told him.

"You were to ask me something, I believe, good lady," Dornay said, as they walked into the dimly lit rear of the hall. In the center a complicated formal dance was in progress; people walked and skipped in knots that tied and untied across the floor. Sharrow thought the band looked bored.

"Yes," she said. She stopped and looked at him. His eyes twinkled and he blinked rapidly. There was nobody nearby. She took a breath. "My grandfather left some information with your father; he passed it on to you."

Dornay looked uncertain. "To me?" he asked.

"By blood-fealty," she said.

He was silent for a few moments. Then his eyes widened. He took a deep breath. "In me!" he gasped. "In me, dear lady!" His eyes stared into hers. "How? What do I—? But, dear lady, this is a privilege! A singular honor! Tell me—tell me what I must do!"

She looked down for a second, wondering how to put it. All the lines she'd rehearsed for this moment sounded wrong.

Then Dornay made a gulping noise. "Of course! Dear lady . . ."

She looked up to see him biting his lower lip. Blood welled. He drew a white handkerchief from his robe, offered it to her. "If you will, my lady." He nodded delicately, looking at her lips.

She understood, and put the handkerchief in her mouth, wetting the end. When the end of the handkerchief was heavy with her saliva, she handed it back to him. He put it quickly to the cut. She wanted to look away but found herself gritting her teeth instead. Dornay sucked on the handkerchief for a while, then dabbed at his lip with it until the blood stopped flowing.

"Whatever I have to tell, I shall tell only you, dear lady," he told her. He took a few deep breaths. "Now, shall we . . . ?"

The guests were stretched round the circular dance floor like the membrane of a bubble; she and Dornay were motioned forward so that they could see the dancers clearly.

They watched the dance develop for a minute or so. Dornay looked around as though searching for something, seeming to grow increasingly agitated. Finally he said, "Dear lady, shall we dance?" and took her hand.

"What?" she said. "But—"

He pulled her out from the line of people facing the groups of dancers; he drew her to him, taking hold of her waist. She put her hands to his neck almost automatically. There was a strange sheen about his face, and a look of emptiness in his eyes. She felt herself shudder.

He stepped back and began to move into and through the formal dancing groups, bumping into people, oblivious, drawing the start of protests from dancers whose backs he connected with, until they realized it was their host they were about to berate.

He moved on, pulling and pushing and maneuvering her with him while she did her best to follow with her flawed, limp-hesitant step. They swept away across the wide floor, disrupting and destroying the carefully worked-out patterns of the ancient dance they had invaded.

Pushed and pulled, twirled and swayed this way and that, and trying to keep her feet out from under his, Sharrow had little chance to notice anybody else's reactions as together she and Dornay brought the rest of the dancers to a staring, bewildered, incredulous halt. The band faltered, the tune stopped. Bencil Dornay danced on, around this way, back that. The bandleader watched them, trying to nod in time somehow; then she had the band attempt some suitable tune. A few of the watching people started to form pairs and began to dance as well.

Sharrow looked into Bencil Dornay's sweating, blank-eyed face and felt a wave of revulsion course through her that almost made her gag.

Their course became a spiral, tightening gradually as Dornay turned and turned and turned in a closing, whorling twist of motion. They reached the coiled center of their figure, and stopped. Then suddenly Dornay let go of her, spun around once, his white robe belling out, and dropped to the floor as though felled with an ax. His head hit the hardwood with a crack; she felt the impact through her feet and the bones of her legs. Somebody screamed.

She stood there openmouthed, pushed back as people

flooded forward to the white body lying under the dance-floor lights. She stared, shaking her head.

"Excuse me—" Doctor Clave said, threading between the people.

Sharrow looked at her hands.

Miz came up to her, pulled her away. "Sharrow, are you all right? Sharrow?"

The guests continued to rush in from every side, packing and swirling around the huddle of people as though caught in a vortex.

"What?" she said. "What?"

"What happened? Are you all right?" His face swam in front of her, open and concerned.

"I'm . . . I'm . . ."

There were gasps from the crowd of people. She saw some of them glance at her and look away. Miz pulled her farther back. Dloan appeared suddenly between her and the crowd. Zefla was at her other side, putting an arm around her.

She saw one person work his way out of the knot of people pressing around the center of the dance floor and walk toward her. It was Cenuij; he seemed to be writing in a small notebook.

He came up to where she stood, flanked by Zefla and Miz. He made a final emphatic dot in the notebook, clipped the pen back in, snapped it shut, and put it in his robe. He glanced back at the crowd and shrugged. "Dead," he told them. He pulled a cheroot from his robe and lit it. "Told us what we needed to know, though." He looked past Zefla. "Oh look." He nodded. "The bar's free." He walked away.

2.

THE SIGNALS OF DECAY, THE WEAPONRY OF DECEIT

9

Reunions

The viewing gallery was built like a steeply raked auditorium. Scattered throughout its thousand or so seats were only a few dozen people, most of them asleep. She sat alone.

Her field of view was almost filled by the giant screen; the giant screen was almost filled by Golter. The great globe turned with a smooth and stately inevitability, a silent thunder implicit in the monumental graduation of the changing, revolving face it presented to the darkness, and something of its immense scale apparent in the linearity of that vast unhurriedness.

It shone: a gigantic disc of blue and white and ocher and green, god-fabulous in extent and more beautiful than love.

She sat looking at it. She was muscularly slim and of about average height, perhaps a little more. She was quite bald; beneath her blond eyebrows her blue eyes were held in tear-drop shapes by small folds in the outside corners; her nose was broad and her nostrils flared. She wore dark overalls and clutched a small satchel to her chest as she sat watching the planet on the huge screen.

The local police chief had been very understanding. He had known Mr. Dornay personally, and only an urgent professional engagement had prevented him from attending the party himself. It must have been a terrible experience for her; he quite understood. An inquest would be held at a later date, but a simple recorded statement from her would almost certainly be quite sufficient. Doctor Clave had already determined the cause of death to be a massive brain hemorrhage—unusual, these days, but not unknown. She must not blame herself. Of course she was free to go; he perfectly comprehended her desire not to stay any longer than she had to in a place that now held such tragic memories for her. Anyway, he had no desire to detain her when she was the officially sanctioned quarry of the legally authorized but surely woefully misguided and arguably rather inhumane sect pursuing her; it would give him no pleasure whatsoever to have this horrible event occur within his jurisdiction. He was sure she understood.

Dornay's private secretary was next to be interviewed. She left the police chief in Bencil Dornay's study and joined the others in the house library, where Cenuij was making excited noises over a desk-screen.

"Okay?" Miz said, coming to meet her.

"Nothing to worry about," she said, "but I've been told to get out of town." She nodded to Zefla and Dloan, who stood by Cenuij's shoulder.

"That's it!" Cenuij said, pressing a button to take a copy of the display. He tapped the screen with a finger. The glyphs shown there were all roughly the same: variations on an elaborate, whorled, crisscrossed shape formed from a single line. On the desk beside Cenuij sat the notebook he'd been drawing in just after Dornay had died; its small screen displayed a shape similar to those on the desk-screen. "That's the one," he said excitedly. He tapped the notebook and one of the glyphs in turn. "Miykenns Capital, in Cevese script, Ladyr dynasty."

Sharrow stared at the pattern drawn on the notebook screen, seeing the single line leading into the complex glyph, its spiraled structure, and its central, tightening coil ending in a dot.

"That was what we . . . traced?" she said.

Zefla heard the catch in Sharrow's voice and put her arm around her.

"Yup," Cenuij said, tearing the print from the desk-screen slot and grinning at it. "Shaky brushwork. A Cevese script scholar would have a fit—"

"Oh, Cenny, for goodness sake . . . ," Zefla said.

"—but that's it," Cenuij said, smacking the printout with the backs of his fingers. "Could contain a mistake of course, in the circumstances, but at the very least it's Miykenns Darkside, almost certainly Miykenns Capital, and if these epicycles are right"—he pointed at two small circles on one spiral—"it's in the time of the Ladyr dynasty."

"So, Malishu?" Miz said.

Cenuij shook his head. "Doubt it, not then. Next, we have to look back to see where the capital was during the Ladyr dynasty." His lip curled slightly. "Could be anywhere. Knowing the Ladyrs, they sold it to the highest bidder." He turned back to the desk-screen. "Library: Miykenns; history; Ladyr dynasty. Display; the capital of Miykenns."

The screen halved into text and a multilayered holo map.

Miz peered. *"Pharpech?"* he said. "Never heard of it."

"I have," Zefla said.

"Congratulations," Cenuij told her, zooming the bewildering structured map, then swooping the view back again. "You probably form part of a small and very exclusive club."

"Yeah," Zefla said, staring at the ceiling with a look of intense concentration on her face. "One of my lecturers used it as an example of a degenerated . . . something or other."

"Well," Cenuij said, "it was supposedly capital of Miykenns under the Ladyrs eight hundred years ago." He scanned the text. "And hasn't looked forward since. Last entry in the encyclopedia is—ye gods—twenty years ago. The coronation of King Tard the Seventeenth. Prophet's blood!" Cenuij sat back in surprise. " 'No pictures available.' "

"A *king*?" Miz laughed.

"Retro suburb," Zefla breathed.

"The latest of the"—Cenuij scrolled the screen, then laughed—"Useless Kings," he said. "Well, how disarmingly honest."

"How far is this place from Malishu?" Sharrow asked.

Cenuij checked. "About as far away as you can get. Nearest rail line is . . . ha! I don't believe it; it says two days' *march* away!" He looked around at the others. "This sounds like the place they invented the phrase 'time warp' to cover."

Zefla nudged Sharrow with her hip. "Nice and far from the Huhsz."

"Hmm," Sharrow said, unconvinced. "Does it say what their religion is?"

Cenuij scrolled the text. "Basically homegrown. Monarch worship and theophobia."

"Theophobia?" Miz said.

"They hate gods," Zefla said.

"Fair enough," Miz said, nodding. "If I lived somewhere not even within hailing distance of the outskirts of the back-end-of-nowhere, I'd want somebody in authority to blame, too."

Miz booked tickets for them all, to Miykenns. A series of cross-routed phone calls ensured that a trusted exec in one of Miz's holding companies in The Meg had his sister's best friend book another ticket, in the name of Ysul Demri, for the water-world of Trontsephori.

Zefla shaved Sharrow's hair off and spread a thin film of depilatory oil over her scalp. Miz sat on the bed behind them and pretended to cry. Sharrow inserted the contacts, used dabs of skinweld to alter the shape of her eyes, spray-bleached her eyebrows, and inserted small plugs into her nostrils, lifting them and flaring them.

She looked at her ears in the dressing-table mirror. "My ears stick out," she said, frowning. She looked up at Zefla, standing behind her. "Do you think my ears stick out?"

Zefla shrugged. Miz shook his head. Sharrow decided her ears stuck out and used skinweld on them, too.

Dloan sat on the bed beside Miz with Sharrow's satchel turned inside out on his lap. He unpicked the stitching, then reached in and withdrew her new identity papers, handing them to her. She looked at her holo in her ID while Zefla carefully removed the depilatory film.

" 'Ysul Demri,' eh?" Zefla said, glancing at the name on Sharrow's new ID as she crumpled the stubble-studded film and threw it into a bin. She squinted at the holo. "Totally convincing. Always fancy being a bald, did you?" She started to spread hair-preventing cream over Sharrow's scalp.

Sharrow nodded. "They're supposed to have more fun."

Zefla's hands glided over her soft skin, gently rubbing the cream in. Miz made sensuous grunting noises in the background.

• • •

"Geis?"

"Sharrow. I hope you don't mind my calling you ... Can't we get vision on this?"

"No. I'm dressing at the moment."

"I beg your pardon. Shall I call back?"

"No, it's all right. It's ... good to hear from you, Geis, but do you mind my asking how you found me?"

"Not at all. I've had my comm people scanning all the public data bases for your name. I thought I might be able to warn you if it looked like the Huhsz were closing in. I hope you don't mind. . . ."

"I suppose not. My life seems to be pretty public-domain these days."

"I don't want to alarm you—we're pretty certain the Huhsz haven't got access to this sort of hacking power. But there's a report on the local contract-police data base that there was some sort of incident at a party at this guy's house last night. Didn't he work for the family once?"

"That was his father. But, yes, there was an incident."

"The police aren't holding you, are they?"

"No. It's been cleared up. I'll be on my way soon."

"I see. Anyway, Sharrow, I was calling for a couple of reasons. There are a lot of confused reports coming out of the Log Jam at the moment. I won't ask you about that ... but I did hear about what happened to that monorail in the K'lel, and my satellite people tell me there's a lot of Huhsz activity around an old nuclear-waste silo on the edge of the desert. I just wanted to say ... well, I'd better not say too much, even over this channel, though it is pretty secure. . . . But I did want to say congratulations. It took one of my best AIs *seconds* to come up with the same scheme, even after it was pointed in the right direction. It was brilliant."

"Thanks. It was Miz's idea, actually."

"Oh. Still, it was good. But of course it won't delay them for very long. I understand the holes in the Passports might continue to radiate for quite a while, but the Huhsz have placed orders for portable magnetic inclusion chambers with Continental Fusion, Inc.—and, well, it'll make thing difficult for them, I suppose, having to cart gear that size around with them, but I just wanted to say that my offer stands: I'll do all I can—*everything* I can—to protect you, if you'll just give me the chance."

"And I still appreciate it, Geis, but I'll try to dodge them for a while longer."

"I think you're very brave. Please remember: if you need any help at all, I am yours to command."

"The last person who said that . . ."

"Sorry?"

"Nothing. Yes, thanks. I'll remember."

She left the viewing gallery and in the double doors between the auditorium and the main corridor bumped into a man just on his way in. She started to apologize, then saw his bright smile, his bald head. He looked at her bald scalp and smiled even more broadly as the doors behind her opened and somebody else entered the narrow space between the two sets of doors and put what felt like a gun to the nape of her neck.

"Oh, Lady Sharrow," the first young man said, sounding perfectly delighted and still gazing at her bald head. "You didn't need to go to all that trouble just for us!"

They traveled separately to Ikueshleng, the spaceport for Golter's eastern hemisphere. The others had already gone when she got there. She paid cash for a standby to Stager. She watched some screen while she waited, feeling nervous but trying not to look it. Golter had had some bad experiences with crashing spacecraft over the millennia, and as a result one of the few things that was strictly controlled about the planet was space traffic. The vast majority of commercial traffic was restricted to two ports serving a hemisphere each, and both the resulting bottlenecks, though Free Ports and so not closely bureaucratically controlled, were inevitably dangerous places for people on the run.

She survived unchallenged and caught a shuttle around noon; half an hour later she was in Stager, the kilometer-diameter, five-wheel space station that was the traveler's usual next port of call after Ikueshleng.

She found a midsystem discount-ticket shop in wheel five and bought a high bounce-factor single to Phrastesis Habitats via Miykenns/Malishu-station. She watched the clerk put her credit card into the reader and tried not to look relieved when the transaction went through. She had to sign an insurance disclaimer and scribbled something that might just have passed for *Ysul Demri* if you'd had a good imagination. She bought a disposable phone with a hundred thrials of credit embedded, a basic-model wrist-screen, and a newssheet and ate a light lunch in a small, overpriced café; then she walked around the curve of the wheel's outer rim to the viewing gallery.

She sat between them, in the very back row of the gallery. She stared at the screen. The one on her right did the talking.

"Three baldies in a row!" he sniggered. "What a laugh, eh?"

The one on her left sat watching the screen with a jacket over his lap. He held the gun underneath the jacket, pointed into her side just below her ribs. Guns tended not to be terribly popular baggage items with the people who ran space stations—she had reluctantly abandoned her HandCannon to a left-luggage agency in Ikueshleng—and she was almost tempted to believe the gun poking into her ribs was a fake, but she thought better of doing anything that would ensure she'd find out.

She looked at the profile of the silent man holding the gun. He was identical to the one on her right. She could see no sign that either of them was an android.

"I said, what a laugh, eh?" The one on her right poked her with one finger. Her right hand flicked out, grabbed his hand; she glared into his eyes. His mouth made an O. He looked amused. The gun under her left ribs prodded briefly.

She let go of his hand. It had been warm; it had felt like a human hand.

"My, we're touchy," the young man on her right said. "I almost wish we'd brought one of our mannequins along." He pulled at the collar of his tight gray businesslike jacket, adjusting his cuffs. "I take it you had your little flashback two days ago, did you?"

She watched the planet for a moment, looking down on what must be noon on Issier (there: white fluffs of cloud in the center of Phirar, covering the archipelago) and nodded slowly.

"I believe I felt something at one point," she said.

"Just to let you know we haven't forgotten you," the young man said. "I hear you were seeing an old friend of the family; terrible shame about old Bencil Dornay. What a shock that must have been for you."

She sought southern Caltasp under its own speckled cover of cloud and identified the huge smooth curve of Farvel Bight, its northern limit hidden under the clouds that reputedly never broke above the Sea House.

"Our family likes its old servants to know we haven't forgotten them," she told the young man. "Or their children."

"Indeed," the young man said. "So now you're on your way to Miykenns, aren't you, Lady Sharrow. . . ?" He paused. "Except you missed the ship you were booked on, and which the rest of your team took."

She looked up, tracing again the route she'd taken to the Francks' home, then on to Lip City.

"Did I?" she said. "Damn. I hate it when that happens."

"And instead you're off to Trontsephori, isn't that right?"

She looked down the long coast of Piphram, straining to make out the lagoons and the dot that was the Log Jam.

"Am I?" she said.

"No, Ysul," the young man said almost gently. "No, you're not." He sighed. "You're Phrastesis bound, according to your ticket. But somehow I don't think you'll make it all the way there."

She looked from the burning bright heart of Jonolrey's K'lel desert into his eyes.

"You're very well-informed for a messenger boy," she said. "You should be in the travel business."

He smiled coldly at her. "Don't be unpleasant, Lady Sharrow," he said. He put out his hand and stroked her upper arm with one finger. "We can be so much more unpleasant to you than you can be to us."

She looked down at the slowly stroking finger, then back to his eyes. He watched his finger, too, as though it didn't belong to him. "Not *even*," he said quietly, "that greasy little overachiever of a cousin of yours will be able to help you, if we decide to be really unpleasant to you . . . Lady Sharrow."

She reached out to take hold of his stroking finger, but he took it away, folding his arms.

"You know," she said, "I'm really getting a little fed up with you and all your attentions." She frowned at him. "Just who are you? Why are you doing this? What sort of weird enjoyment do you get from it? Or do you just do whatever you're told?"

He smiled tolerantly. "Let me give you a word of advice—"

"No," she said. "Let *me* give *you* a word of advice." She leaned toward him, away from the gun. "Stop doing this, or I'll hurt you—if you can be hurt—or I'll kill you. Kill or destroy both of you—"

The young man was pretending to look frightened; he was pulling faces at his twin sitting on her other side. The gun was stuck harder under her ribs. She ignored the gun and reached out with her left hand and took the other young man's chin in her hand.

"No, listen to me," she said, gripping his chin hard, feeling the warm smoothness of it and forcing one finger into the side of his neck, to touch the beat of blood beneath his skin. He smelled of cheap scent. He looked at her and tried to smirk, but the way she was holding his chin made it difficult. The gun was a sharp pain under her ribs, but she couldn't really care just at that point. She shook his chin a little.

"I'll do whatever I can to both of you," she said. "And I don't give a flying fuck what you or your employers do to me. I've never liked being treated the way you miserable little pricks have been treating me, and I don't respond well to that sort of persuasion, understand? You getting all this?"

She made a play of searching his eyes. "Are you? Whoever I'm talking to in there? Comprehend? You've made your point and you'll get your Gun. Now just *fuck off;* or we'll all suffer." She smiled bleakly. "Yes, I'll suffer most, I don't doubt." The bleak smile faded. "But at least I won't be alone."

She let go of his chin slowly, pushing his head away a little with her last touch.

The young man smoothed a hand over his scalp and readjusted his jacket collar. He cleared his throat, glancing at his image on her other side. "Your talent for destruction extends to yourself I see, Lady Sharrow," he said. "How democratic in one so noble."

She got up slowly, holding her satchel. "Eat my shit, you puppet," she told him. She paused as she moved past the one with the gun, looking into his eyes and then glancing at his lap. "I trust the rest of your weaponry is rather more intimidating."

She walked, trying not to limp, along the aisle toward

the gangway, the back of her naked scalp and the area between her shoulder blades itching and tingling, waiting for
the shot that would kill her, or just the start of the pain
again, but she made it to the end of the aisle, then down the
steps, then through the double doors without anything happening.

In the corridor outside she collapsed back against the
wall, swallowing, breathing heavily, and putting her head
back against the soft bulkhead. She closed her eyes for a
moment.

Then she made her eyes go as wide as they could, blew
her cheeks out, and with a slight shake of her head, walked
away.

She landed on Miykenns three days later. The shuttle bellied down onto the wide, calm waters of Lake Malishu, its
still hot hull creating bursts of steam with each skimming
kiss so that its progress was marked by a series of small, distinct clouds, each curling around itself like a gauzy leaf and
rising into the warm, still air while the craft whizzed on, finally settling onto the lake's mirror-surface in a long
unzipping trail of white.

Beyond the early-morning coastal mists, the Entraxrln
towered distantly on all sides, as though the lake existed in
the eye of some vast purple storm.

She stepped lightly onto the jetty on Embarkation Island. Miykenns's gravity was barely seventy percent of
Golter's; the ship she'd journeyed on had maintained one
Golter-g during acceleration and deceleration, and so
Miykenns gave her the delicious feeling that she was about
to float away all the time. It was a sensation that had led to
more than a few broken limbs and heads over the time that
people from Golter had been landing on Miykenns and suddenly feeling as though they could leap tall buildings.

She looked around and breathed deeply. The heady,
fruity air filled her instantly with a careless, dizzy optimism, and an aching nostalgia that was sweet and poignant
at once.

She and her fellow passengers were presented with
flowers by tall, smiling Tourist Agency youngsters and
shown the way to the maglev terminal. Malishu's usual in-
formality manifested itself in a total lack of any visible officials between the shuttle jetty and the maglev platform; its

renowned organizational prowess manifested itself in the fact that an empty train had departed just before the passengers got there.

People stood on the open platform watching the winking light at the rear of the train as it disappeared down the causeway heading across the misty lake for the city.

Then groans turned to cheers as it became obvious the slowly flashing light had stopped and was coming nearer. Applause greeted the returning train.

She sat in the nose of the observation car, a huge smile on her face as she watched the great towers and sheet-membranes of the Entraxrln draw nearer while flocks of birds drifted across the lake on either side like huge clouds of lazy snowflakes under the clearing morning mists.

The Entraxrln was a couple of kilometers tall around the lake; by the time the city became evident—nestled, packed, and crusted around and inside its vast dark trunks and cables—she had to lean forward in her seat and crane her neck to see the pale reaches of the topmost spindles and the slowly swell-waving membranes of the vast structure.

She sat back in her seat, still smiling. "Welcome to Embarkation Island," said a recorded voice as they hurtled, slowing, into Malishu Central Rail Station. It shouldn't have been that funny, but she found herself laughing along with everybody else.

The Entraxrln of Miykenns had fascinated astronomers on Golter for millennia before people ever set foot on the globe. Observatory records written on clay tablets thirteen thousand years earlier—which by some miracle had survived all of Golter's frenetic history in between and even remained translatable—spoke of the several theories attempting to account for Miykenns's strange appearance: white and blue swirls on one side, and a strange, dark, slowly changing aspect on the other, rarely obscured by the white marks that always dotted what was assumed to be the ocean, and on which—with a good telescope on a high mountain on a calm night—distinct and swirling patterns could just be made out, like drips of pale-hued paints dropped onto the surface of a darker tint, and stirred into thin lines and creamy whorls.

It had been five millennia from the season that tablet

had been fired to the day when people finally set foot on
Miykenns and discovered the truth.

The Entraxrln was a plant—a single vast vegetable that
must have been growing on Miykenns for at least two million years. It was, by several orders of magnitude, both the
oldest and the largest living thing in the entire system.

It covered three continents, two oceans, five sizable
seas, and thousands of islands. It controlled the weather, it
withstood tsunami, it tamed volcanoes, it diverted glaciers, it
mined minerals, it irrigated the desert, it drained seas, and
it leveled mountains. It grew up to three kilometers tall on
land and had covered mountains eight thousand meters
high; its tendrils had been found buried in volcanic vents in
the deepest ocean trenches.

Its roots, trunks, leaf-membranes, and anchor-cables
covered the land beneath like an enormous, airy mat, producing something that looked vaguely like a forest—with
trunks and layers of canopy—but built on the scale of a
planet-wide weather system. Consequently, a physical map
of Miykenns was as bafflingly complex as a political chart of
Golter.

Humanity had been colonizing the Entraxrln's great do-
matium for seven thousand years, spreading out among its
mountainous trunks and beneath its dim, diminishing layers,
heading away from the clearings where they had landed to
inhabit the plant's bounteous commonwealth of levels and
carve and work its trunks for dwellings and artifacts, and to
trap or farm its various parasitic and symbiotic fauna and
flora for food. Malishu, favored by the great lake the
Entraxrln had left uncovered for its own mysterious
reasons—and by its almost central position in the vast
plant—had been the planet's capital for most of those seven
millennia.

She hired a tri-shaw with a breezily prolix driver and found
a small pension in the Artists' Quarter, at the base of one of
the city's eleven great composite trunks. The fluted slope of
the helically netted column rose into the haze and mists
above, the houses and narrow, zigzagging streets and
bridges petering out as the gradient grew steeper.

She screened the city news channel before she went
out; it held nothing about her or the Huhsz.

She walked toward the inner city through the lunchtime crowds inundating the markets and marquee art galleries; her nose was assaulted by smells she'd forgotten she knew—of the fruits, bulbs, flowers, and tubers of the various plants that coexisted with the Entraxrln; of the rainbow-skinned fish and spike-mouth crustaceans from the lake; and of the cooked meats and potages made from the animals that lived within the great plant: jelly-birds, glide-monkeys, bell-mouths, cable-runners, trap-blossoms, tunnel-slugs, and a hundred others. Painters and sculptors, silhouettists and aurists, scentifiers and holo artists, called out to her from their stalls and tents, telling her—as they told everybody—that she had an interesting profile or skull or aura or scent.

A few stares and a couple of shouts convinced her that baldness wasn't a major fashion feature in Malishu this season, so she found a drugstore and bought a wig and some eyebrow spray, then continued.

She grew tired after a while and paid a few coins for the one-way hire of a bike into the inner city, riding a little shakily and trying not to be too touristically distracted by the gradually heightening buildings and the cloudy canopies of Entraxrln membranes fifteen hundred meters above while the half-kilometer-wide trunk column around which the inner city had grown up—like dolls' houses at the base of a great tree—drew slowly closer.

"You just walked out?" Zefla giggled, a hand over her mouth. They were sitting in a lunch bar at the foot of a Corp. tower in Malishu's central business district.

Sharrow shrugged. "Oh, I was just getting fed up with it all. I don't even know what they were supposed to tell me." She stirred her salty soup. "Maybe they just wanted to show me how clever they were, that we hadn't fooled them."

"But no more of those pains?" Zefla said.

"Not so far."

Zefla nodded. She had dressed as soberly as she could, in a dark two-piece. Her height didn't attract attention in Malishu, where most people were around two meters tall. She'd tied her hair up and wore a rather dowdy hat. "You got a gun yet?"

"That's next," Sharrow said. "How's the Central?"

"Comfortable." Zefla smiled. "Been done out since, but the Bole bar is still the same." Zefla's smile widened. "Hey, Grappsle's still there. He remembered us. Asked after you."

Sharrow grinned. "That was good of him."

"Yeah. We told him you were on the run." Zefla bit into her sandwich.

"Oh, thanks."

"Obviously hadn't heard the news," Zefla continued, chewing. "He just seemed to assume it was a jealous wife." She shrugged. "Men, eh?"

"Hmm." Sharrow sipped her soup. "And where are the boys?"

"Cenny marched Miz and Dlo down to the City Library before they could unpack properly. They're trying to find out more about this Pharpech place. A lot of stuff's available only on nonstandard format DBs, and some of it's on flimsies and *paper*, for Fate's sake." Zefla shook her head at such incontinent archaicism and tore another bite from her sandwich. "Probably hit the university stacks tomorrow," she mumbled through a mouthful of food.

Sharrow sipped her soup until Zefla swallowed, then said, "Had a chance to screen the legal situation?"

Zefla shook her head. "Got all I'm ever going to get from the public data bases in about five minutes. Under System law the Kingdom of Pharpech doesn't exist. The area around it's still theoretically Settlement Territory under the auspices of the (First) Colonial Settlement Board, Defunct. That takes us back to the thirty-three hundreds, and it's got *much* more complicated since. There are at least fifteen competing and mutually aggravational land-title disputes, all dormant for way over a century, so technically moribund— but there are just *bound* to be loopholes. I can smell them.

"Going as far back as it's *sensible* to go, the Kingdom was created as a Dukedom by the Ladyrs in return for tap-mining rights on the territory outskirts. It was declared capital when the Ladyrs needed a casting vote on the Planetary Board and the burgers of Malishu weren't being cooperative. The then duke declared himself king when the Ladyr dynasty collapsed. The Conglomerate that fell heir to the tap-mining rights got a Title by Use deed over their patch, which seems to have been the only bit anyone really cared about—and which has been closed down for three hundred years, anyway—and . . . well, apart from removing its status as planetary capital, nobody ever got around to sorting out Pharpech's legal status.

"If you want an opinion, with eight cents of de facto existence, the Kingdom's been going so long, a decent gang of greased-up legal hot shots could swing Full Diplomatic Acceptance and even a seat on the Miykenns World Council under Common Law in under a year. But in the meantime," Zefla said, "it's in Nowhere Territory." She smiled happily and waved her arms. "Just one of those little legal oxbows on the great floodplain of System law. There are zillions."

"You got all that in five minutes?" Sharrow grinned.

"Maybe ten. I lose track when I'm enjoying myself." Zefla shrugged. "Anyway, I'll be heading for the Uni legal faculty myself soon. See if there's anything the public DBs have missed."

"You don't think there's anything we'll be able to use?"

"No," Zefla said. "Buying some defunct mining claim, forging docs, and pretending to the throne . . ." She shook her head. "Pharpech's complexities all seem to be in the distant past; there's no confusion recent enough to exploit. Unless I can dig up something very unexpected indeed, we aren't going to crack this one via the legal route. I'll keep looking, though."

"Okay," Sharrow said. "I'll check out the travel possibilities, but assuming that doesn't take long, let me know if I can help you or the boys." She reached into her satchel. "Here, I got this phone . . ."

"Right." Zefla tapped the code for Sharrow's disposable phone into her own. "How's your hotel?"

"Comfortable. In the Artists' Quarter."

"What's *it* like these days?"

"Full of artists."

"No improvement, then."

"Even more twee, if anything."

"And the hunkies?"

"I have a horrible feeling nothing's changed there, either; the good-looking ones are gay, and the interesting ones turn out to be mad."

"Hard times," Zefla agreed.

"Hmm." Sharrow nodded, a pained expression on her face. "It's been too long," she said. "I hear words like 'hard,' and I'm in danger of sliding off my seat." She looked out at the gentle, filtered light of afternoon. "Doesn't help having all these huge fucking towering columns rearing up all over the place here, either. . . ." She sighed. "I may be forced to

desperate measures. I haven't seen one for so long, I'm starting to forget what they look like."

"Well, hey," Zefla said, looking amused. "There's always
Miz. He'd be up for it."

She shook her head. "I know. But . . ." She looked away.

"Old wounds, eh?" Zefla said, washing her sandwich
down with some wine.

Sharrow gazed away with a lost expression Zefla knew
from over a decade and a half earlier. "Yeah, old wounds,"
she said quietly.

"Good afternoon, madam. How may I help you?"

"Good afternoon. I'd like a FrintArms HandCannon,
please."

"A—? Oh, now, that's an awfully big gun for such a
lovely lady. I mean, not everybody thinks ladies should carry
guns at all, though I say they have a right to. But I think . . .
I might . . . Let's have a look down here. I might have just
the thing for you. Yes, here we are! Look at that, isn't it
neat? Now, that is a FrintArms product as well, but it's
what's called a laser—a light-pistol some people call them.
Very small, as you see; fits easily into a pocket or bag; won't
spoil the line of a jacket, and you won't feel you're lugging
half a tonne of iron around with you. We do a range of
matching accessories, including—if I may say so—a rather
saucy garter holster. Wish I got to do the fitting for that!
Ha—just my little joke. And there's *even* . . . here we are—
this special presentation pack: gun, charged battery, charging unit, beautiful glider-hide shoulder holster with
adjustable fitting and contrast stitching, and a discount on
your next battery. Full instructions, of course, and a voucher
for free lessons at your local gun club or range. Or there's
the *special* presentation pack; it has all the other one's got
but with *two* charged batteries and a night-sight, too. Here,
feel that—don't worry; it's a dummy battery—isn't it neat?
Feel how light it is? Smooth, see? No bits to stick out and
catch on your clothes, *and* beautifully balanced. And of
course the beauty of a laser is, there's no recoil. Because it's
shooting light, you see? Beautiful gun, beautiful gun; my
wife has one. Really. That's not a line, she really has. Now,
I can do you that one—with a battery and a free charge—for
ninety-five; or the presentation pack on a special offer for

one-nineteen; or this, the special presentation pack, for one-forty-nine."

"I'll take the special."

"Sound choice, madam, *sound* choice. Now, do—?"

"And a HandCannon, with the eighty-mill silencer, five GP clips, three six-five AP/wire-fléchettes clips, two bipropellant HE clips, two incendiary clips, and a Special Projectile Pack if you have one—the one with the embedding homing rounds, not the signalers. I assume the night-sight on this toy is compatible."

"Aah . . . yes. And how does madam wish to pay?"

She slapped her credit card on the counter. "Eventually."

She walked away from the gun shop, the satchel heavy on her shoulder. She bought a newssheet and read it on the open-top deck of the tram she took back to the Artists' Quarter.

She scanned the flimsy, thumbing through its stored pages on fast-forward and stopping to look closely at something only once.

She'd glanced at the race results from Tile.

One of the runners-up the day before had been *Dance of Death*.

10

Just
A
Concept

"**M** mm. Hello?"

"Hiya, doll. Oh . . . 'doll.' That wasn't very . . . Shit."

"Get on with it, Zef."

"Sorry. Meet me at the Crying Statue in an hour—how's that?"

"Too damn succinct for a lawyer."

"I'm out of practice."

"I know the feeling. The Crying Statue, in an hour."

"See you there, doll . . . Shit."

Two women made their way from the Crying Statue in Malishu's Tourist Quarter across the carved-open arc of Tube Bridge to the University Precincts. Above them the midmorning mists were lifting into the air among the stalk towers and stay-cables of the Entraxrln, obscuring the distant, under-ocean view of the highest membrane layers.

They walked quickly along pavements still damp from the morning smir. Sharrow, in a long dark dress and jacket and the high-heeled boots she tended to favor when going anywhere with Zefla, strode determinedly with her head up, a severe, slightly forbidding look on her face, discouraging contact. The striking, sternly poised face, dramatic auburn hair, and precise, upright carriage almost disguised the fact that every second step was a slight fall, a tiny flaw in the pattern, a misplaced beat in the rhythm of her body.

Zefla strolled—long-stepped in culottes and a light coat-shirt—with an almost disjointed looseness, head moving from side to side, smiling at everyone and no one, walking with a kind of easy familiarity as though she belonged here, knew these people, made this walk every day.

Heads turned as they crossed the bridge over the trickle-throated bed of the Ishumin river and entered the partially walled warren of the university: merchants at stalls lost the thread of their sales pitch, people using phones forgot what they were talking about, passengers at tram stops neglected to press the call-button for the next tram so that it rushed clanking past them. At least two men, looking back over their shoulders, bumped into other people.

Sharrow started to get uneasy as they passed through Apophyge Gate into the dark clutter of the literature faculty prefecture. "You *sure* you weren't followed?" she asked Zefla.

Zefla looked mildly incredulous. "Of *course* I was *followed*," she said scornfully. "But never by anybody with anything lethal in mind." She put her arm through Sharrow's and looked quietly smug. "Quite the opposite, I imagine."

"I'd forgotten we could be conspicuous," Sharrow admitted, but seemed to relax a little. She lifted her gaze from the cramped cobble-barks of Metonymy Street to the airy sweep of stay-cables describing elegant arcs above the distant grid of the mathematics faculty. She began to whistle.

They walked on, still arm in arm. Zefla looked thoughtful for a while, then smiled; a youth crossing the street in front of them with an armful of ancient books, caught unintentionally in the beam of that smile, promptly dropped the tomes. Zefla went, "Whoops," as she stepped over the crouching student's head, then gazed at Sharrow.

"Whistling . . . ," Zefla said.

"Hmm?" Sharrow looked at her.

They stopped at a street corner to study a faculties map. Zefla bent, hands clasped behind her back, inspecting the map.

"Whistling," she repeated. "Well, it *used* to mean only one thing."

Sharrow had an uncharacteristically broad smile on her face when Zefla turned back to her. Sharrow shrugged and

cleared her throat as they turned to head up a steep side
street toward the history faculty. "Damn, am I that transparent?"

"You look tired, too."

Sharrow rubbed under her eyes gently. "Worth every
bag and line."

"Who was the lucky fellow?"

"Musician."

"Strings? Wind? Keyboard? Composition?" Zefla inquired.

Sharrow grinned at her, brown eyebrows flexing. "Per-
cussion," she said huskily.

Zefla sniggered, then assumed a serious expression,
lifting her head up and enunciating clearly. "Don't brag,
dear; it's unbecoming."

"Ah, war is hell," Miz Gattse Ensil Kuma said, sitting back
luxuriantly in the perfumed pillows of the small canal-boat.
He lifted the stemmed glass of slushed trax spirit from the
boat's table and sipped at it delicately, watching the gently
glowing lanterns as they floated past them. The boat's own
lantern shone softly, creaking on the end of a bowed, spindly
branch above them. People in fancy dress passed on the canal walkway a few meters away, trailing streamers and
laughing, their faces hidden by grotesque and fabulous
masks. Above, over the dark city, fireworks blazed distantly,
their flashes lighting up the layers of Entraxrln membrane
and sometimes silhouetting the open weave-work of the
composite trunks. The boat whirred quietly on along the
raised, open section of canal.

Sharrow—actually, at that moment, Commander Sharrow of the anti-Tax League Irregular Forces Eleventh Clipper Squadron—sat across the little table from him. For the
first time since they'd met almost a year ago, she was out of
uniform and not dressed in ease-fatigues or street sloppies.
She wore a rainbow-mirrored half mask that just covered
her eyes and the bridge of her nose. It was topped by a cap
of white- and green-dyed lake-bird feathers; her dress was
bright green, short, low-cut and clinging, and her legs, in
the fashion of the day, were sheathed in a transparent covering of polymerised perfume-oil. She had long, perfectly
shaped legs, and they gleamed, they glistened, they glinted

under the suspended lanterns that swung on bowed stalks over the dark canal.

He could hardly keep his eyes off those long, slinkily muscular legs. He knew the dry, slick touch of perfume-oil, the smooth, blissful feel of that slowly evaporating, few-molecules thick covering; he had experienced it many times on other women, and it was no longer quite so freshly erotic an experience as it had been once. But sitting here, alone with her in this little purring, gently bumping boat on the last night of the festival, he wanted to touch her, hold her, stroke and kiss her more than he could remember ever wanting any woman. The urge, the need was as scarifying and intense as he remembered from just before he'd first gotten laid; it burned in him, infested him, ran brilliant and urgent in his blood.

It was suddenly irrelevant to him that she was his commanding officer and an aristo—things that had, in some kind of piqued, invertedly snobbish way in the past prevented him from ever thinking of her as a woman (and a beautiful, attractive, intelligent one, at that; the kind he would normally know just from the first glance, the first word, that he would want to bed if he could) rather than his tactically brilliant but curt and scathingly sarcastic CO, or an arrogant overprivileged brat from Golter who had drop-dead looks and knew it.

"A toast," Sharrow said, uncrossing her gauzily shining legs and sitting forward. She raised her glass.

"What to?" Miz asked, looking at the colorfully distorted reflection of his face in her rainbow-mirror mask. His own mask lay on his chest, looped around his neck.

"Iphrenil toast," she said. "The secret toast; we each toast what we choose to."

"Stupid custom." He sighed. "Okay."

They clinked glasses. Masked figures dressed as deep-country bandits ran along the canal, whooping and firing popguns. He ignored them and looked into her eyes as he drank from his glass. *Here's to getting you into bed, my commander,* he thought to himself.

Her dark, mocking eyes looked back at him from behind the mask. A small smile creased her lips.

A flower grenade landed between them in the well of the little boat. She laughed a dark brown laugh, electrifying him. She kicked the grenade over to him; he kicked it back;

the perfumed fuse burned smokily. She trapped the fist-sized ball beneath her naked foot, watching it (and he could feel the SNB kicking in, this becoming a tactical situation for both of them, Slowdown coming on, and he knew the possibilities and the potential courses she would be evaluating right then. He waited, in that lengthened instant, to see what she would do), then just as the fuse seemed to go out, she kicked the grenade over to him; he laughed, outlucked, and tried to kick the ball out of the way.

The flower grenade burst with a loud pop, scattering a cloud of color all around him, surrounding him in a thousand tiny, expanding blooms. Some stuck to him; others were so small and dry, they went up his nose and made him sneeze; the scent reeked.

He coughed and sneezed and tried to wave the flowers away, distantly aware of her clapping her hands and laughing uproariously. People on shore cheered and whistled.

He sat, wiping his nose on a handkerchief and brushing the sticky flowers off his dress jacket. Some of the blooms had landed in his glass. He wrinkled his nose, threw the scent-contaminated spirit overboard.

"Streme Tunnel!" shouted a ceremonially robed official sitting on a high seat on the canal path. "Streme Tunnel! Fifty meters!" He nodded to them as they acknowledged, waving.

Miz turned, looking forward over the bows of the small boat. Ahead, the tube-canal entered a wide basin where most people were decanting from their boats.

The circular canal—twenty kilometers long and one of two girdling what had once been the outer city—was really just an Entraxrln root-transport tube with the top half cut off. The section they were approaching now had not been sliced open, and soon disappeared into a dark mass of Entraxrln mat the size of a small range of hills and covered with the houses and tenements of Streme prefecture. Streme Tunnel was five kilometers long and took over an hour for the average boat to negotiate. Most people not asleep or amorously inclined tended to get out here.

He turned back to her, sighing and shrugging.

"Well," he said, trying to put just the right note of regret into his voice, "it would appear to be de-boating time, up ahead."

She set her mouth in a line, an expression he knew was

not neutral, but which he still could not fully interpret. It might be annoyance or merely acceptance. Still, something in his chest seemed to release like a spring. *Maybe*, he thought.

She drank from her glass, frowning.

He sat back, deliberately relaxed, and crossed his arms. He thought quickly, Do I want to do this? Yes. But it's breaking the code we've all followed without ever discussing or agreeing to it; no sex between neurobondees. With people from other groups, yes; with anybody else in the military habitats where they were based ninety percent of the time, yes. But not in-group. Too many people thought it would upset the delicate web of anticipation and response that existed between the teams when they flew combat missions together.

I know, he thought, and I don't fucking care. She's the commander; let her decide. I *want* her.

So he uncrossed his arms and glanced back at the tunnel mouth as they entered the basin and the canal fluted out, broadening around them. He looked back into her eyes and said calmly, not too loudly, "So what shall we do? Get out or go through?"

Her gaze slid from his eyes to the tunnel ahead, then back again. She took a breath.

She's mine, he thought. Oh, don't let me be wrong!

"What do you want to do?" she asked him.

He shrugged, adjusted a pillow at his side. "Well, I'm comfortable here. . . ."

"You want to go through," she said, the mirror-mask rising as she tipped her head back, as if daring him.

He just shrugged.

She looked at the people on the shore, and up at the sporadic bursts of fireworks above the city's dark twinkle of lights. "I don't know," she said, looking back at him. And suddenly she was all haughty Golter noble, nose in the air, imperious and straight-backed, her voice commanding: "Persuade me."

He smiled. A year ago that would have been it; he'd have bridled at that arrogance, and laughed and said, Na, it'd be boring in the tunnel; let's rejoin the others and have some real fun (and would secretly have hoped that she *had* wanted to go through, and so would be hurt that he'd said it would be boring) . . . but now he was a little older and a lot wiser, and he knew her better, too, and he was fairly sure now that he knew what it meant that she should suddenly revert to the behavior of her earlier life.

And even then, even in that instant when he knew he was on the tremulous brink of something he wanted more desperately than he'd ever wanted anything before, and knew that it was going to break new and dangerous ground, and maybe endanger him, her, and the others, and knew that he knew, and *didn't care*, because life was there to be lived just this one time, and that meant gambling, seizing each and every chance for happiness and advancement— even then he found time to think, to be struck by the realization: How old we have become.

Not one of us over twenty; she—this stunning, glorious creature in front of him—only just nineteen. And yet in the last year we have become ancient, from children to cynical, war-worn, half-careless, half-uncaring veterans who will take their enemies when and where they can in the darkness and the single-ship loneliness of the battle, coupling with them across microseconds of space, tussling and teasing and tangling with them until only one was left . . . and took their pleasures cut from the same template—total, intense and furiously concentrated involvement, immediately followed by utter indifference.

Persuade you, he thought. "Okay," he said, smiling at her. "Come on through the tunnel and I promise I'll tell you what I toasted to."

She made a funny expression, drawing both ends of her mouth down, the tendons in her neck standing out. It was an expression he'd never seen on her before. He smiled despite himself, thinking how suddenly young she had looked.

"I don't know," she said, the mirror-mask looking down at her glass. "Then I'd have to tell you what *I* toasted to. . . ."

She looked up into his eyes, and he wondered if it was possible to give a come-hither look from behind a mask. He settled back in the plushness of the cushions. Something sang in his soul. The tunnel entrance drifted closer.

Boat marshals called to them, reminding them this was their last chance to decant. People on shore made knowing, lowing noises and shouted ribald advice. He scarcely heard them.

"You're persuaded?" he said.

She nodded. "I'm persuaded."

He sat very still.

She reached up and took off the rainbow-mirror mask, just as the tunnel mouth came up to swallow them.

"This is it," Zefla said. "31/3 Little Grant Terrace."

The three-story structure was even more darkly ramshackle than its neighbors. It was Malishu-vernacular in style, sculpted from bluey-purple layer-mat supported by fire-hardened beams of brown stalk-timber. It looked out over a narrow-railinged, bark-cobbled street to a view of the steeply raked roofs—some tented, some bark-tiled—of the modern history department, and out toward the city's northern suburbs.

The place looked dead. The ground floor had no windows and the tall windows in the two upper floors were dark and dirty. The door, made from poorly cured bark that had warped and split over the years, hung crooked over a nailed-on extra sill. Zefla pulled on a string handle. They couldn't hear any sound from the interior. Zefla tested the door, but it was either locked or badly stuck.

Sharrow looked up at the guttering; a section hung loose, dripping water despite the fact that the roof and street had now dried after the early-morning drizzle. She kicked fragments of a fallen roof tile into a weed-ruffed hole in the pavement, wrinkling her nose in distaste. "I take it being the world authority on the Kingdom of the Pharpech doesn't attract major funding."

Zefla pulled harder on the string door-pull and stood back. "Maybe it does," she said. "But the guy feels closer to the place living in an antiquated ruin like this."

"Method scholarship?" Sharrow said skeptically. "More likely this is Cenuij's idea of a joke."

Zefla shook her head earnestly. "Oh, no. I can tell, he was genuine. I think he wanted to come himself, but he reckons your man here would be more receptive to us."

"Huh," Sharrow said, frowning at the skeleton of a tiny animal lying just inside the doorway's recess. "*That* description could cover a tankful of shit."

A window creaked open on the third floor, and a small, gray-haired, bearded man stuck his head out and looked down at them.

"Hello?" he said.

"Hello," Zefla called. "We're looking for a gentleman called Ivexton Travapeth."

"Yes," said the little man.

Zefla paused, then said, "You're not him, then?"

"No."

"Right. Do you know where we can find him?"

"Yes."

Zefla looked at Sharrow, who started whistling.

"Could you tell us where he is?" Zefla said.

"Yes," the little man said, blinking.

"Wrong department," Sharrow muttered, folding her arms and turning to look back out over the city. "It's the Formal Logic building, and they're working to rule."

"Where is he?" Zefla asked, trying not to giggle.

"Oh, here," the man nodded.

"May we see him?" Zefla said.

"Oh, yes."

"Keep going," Sharrow told Zefla quietly. "The Passports only last a year."

"Good," Zefla said. "Thank you. We'd have phoned or screened, but Mr. Travapeth seems to discourage that sort of contact."

"Yes."

"Yes. Could you let us in?"

"Yes, yes," the small man nodded.

Sharrow started to make loud snoring noises.

Zefla nudged her. "Please come down and let us in," she said, smiling at the little man.

"Very well," the gray-bearded man said, and disappeared. A window banged shut.

Sharrow's head thumped onto Zefla's shoulder. She yawned. "Wake me when the door opens or the universe ends, whichever's sooner."

Zefla patted her auburn locks.

The door opened, creaking. Sharrow turned to look. The small gray-bearded man peeked out, looked up and down the street, then opened the door wide. He was pulling on a pair of floppy trousers with attached soft-shoes; he tied the cord and tucked his shirt into his trousers as he stood there, grinning at the two women. He was tiny, even smaller than he'd looked at the window. Zefla thought he looked cuddly.

"Good morning," she said.

"Yes," he replied, and beckoned them to enter. Zefla and Sharrow stepped over the high sill into a dull but not dark space looking onto a small courtyard, partially shielded from them by a sheet hanging from the floor above. The air smelled of sweat and cooked fats. A grunting, wheezing male-sounding noise came from the other side of the grubby sheet. Zefla glanced at Sharrow, who shrugged.

"I hope you're hearing that, too," she told Zefla, "or I'm more tired than I thought and flashing back to last night."

The gray-bearded man went on before them, still hitching up his trousers and tucking in the last few folds of his creased shirt as he bustled forward around the edge of the hanging sheet. They followed. The courtyard was small and cluttered; balconies ran around the two floors above, giving access to other rooms. A light covering of membrane made a gauzy roof above.

The floor of the atrium was covered with carpets and mats, on which stood half a dozen overstuffed bookshelves and a couple of tables covered with layers and rolls of paper. Exercise equipment in the shape of dumbbells, weights, heavy clubs, and flexible bars lay strewn among the stuff of ancient scholarship.

In the center of it all stood the tallish, gaunt figure of an almost naked elderly man with a white mat of hair on his chest and a shock of thick black hair on his head. He was clad in a grubby loincloth and clutched a pair of hand-weights, which he was raising alternately, breathing heavily and grunting with each lift. There was sweat on his lined, tanned face. Zefla reckoned he was seventy at least, though his figure was relatively youthful; only the white chest-hair and a certain slackness around his belly revealed his age. "Ha—good morning lovely ladies!" he said in a deep voice. "Ivexton Travapeth at your service."

He thumped the hand-weights down on a massive book that seemed to be holding down one corner of an age-brown chart, raising dust and making the table beneath shudder. "And how may this humble and undeserving scholar help two such radiantly pulchritudinous gentle-ladies?" He stood, arms crossed, biceps bulging, on the balls of his feet, facing them, still breathing heavily. His expression was somewhere between mischievous and lecherous.

"Good morning, Mr. Travapeth," Zefla said, nodding as

she stepped forward and put out her hand. They shook. "My name is Ms. Franck; this is my assistant, Ms. Demri."

Sharrow nodded as Travapeth glanced, smiling, at her. "We're researchers for an independent screen production company, MGK Productions. Our card." Zefla handed him a card from one of Miz's many front companies.

Travapeth squinted at the card. "Ah, you are from Golter. I thought so from your accent, of course. How may Travapeth help you, my saxicolous damsels?"

Zefla smiled. "We'd like to talk to you about a place called Pharpech."

Ivexton Travapeth rocked back on his heels a little. "Indeed?" he said.

At that point the little man rushed out of the shadows behind the scholar, holding open a long gray gown. He jumped and tried to put the gown over the tall man's shoulders. He failed and tried several more times while Travapeth boomed:

"Pharpech! Ah, dear, belovable lady, you utter a word—an almost magical word—that summons up such a welter of emotion in this well-traveled breast"—there was a hollow thud as Travapeth struck his white-haired chest with one fist—"I scarcely know where or how to begin to respond."

The little man put the gown over one forearm and pulled a chair from beneath a table, stationing it behind Travapeth. He climbed up onto the chair and went to put the gown over the scholar's shoulders just as Travapeth moved away toward a chest-high wooden stand holding a set of dumbbells. The little gray-haired man fell to the floor with a squeal.

Travapeth lifted the dumbbells from the stand, grunting.

"You say a *screen* production company?" he said, straining to lift the dumbbells to his chin. The little man picked himself up and dusted himself down, retrieved the gown from the carpet, and looked sulkily at Travapeth. Sharrow had her lips tightly closed.

"That's right." Zefla smiled.

The little gray-haired man scowled at Travapeth, then left the gown draped over the chair and returned to the shadows, muttering incoherently and shaking his head.

"Hmm," Travapeth said, finally heaving the dumbbells level with the top of his shoulders and standing there panting for a moment. He swallowed. "I happen to know His Majesty King Tard the Seventeenth rather well," he boomed. He smiled at the two women with a sort of radiant humility. "I was present at his coronation, you know, back when you two beautiful ladies were still suckling at the generous globes of your mothers' breasts, I imagine." He sighed contemplatively, perhaps sadly, then looked more serious as he strained at the dumbbells, and after a while relaxed. "And I have to say," he panted, "His Majesty has shown . . . a consistent reluctance . . . to allow any sort of pictographic record . . . to be taken of his realm . . . which the modern world seems to regard as . . . bordering on the pathological."

"We understand that," Zefla said. "Nevertheless, Pharpech appears to be a fascinating and even romantic place, from what one reads about it, and we do feel that it would be worth some time and effort—by an experienced and highly talented team of individuals widely respected in their respective fields—to produce a true, factual, and faithful account of life in what represents one of the last vestiges of a time gone by, miraculously still surviving into the present day."

Travapeth seemed to strain again. Then he grunted; he put the dumbbells back on their stand and reached with a shaking hand for a stained towel lying crumpled on top of a bookcase.

"Quite so," he said, shaking the towel until it uncrumpled. "But try explaining that to His Majesty."

"Let me be candid," Zefla said as Travapeth wiped under his armpits, and then his face. (Sharrow looked away.) "Our intention is to go there initially without any equipment—without even still cameras, if that's what it takes—and perhaps, with your good offices, if that proves agreeable to you, establish some sort of understanding with whatever authorities control the sort of very limited access rights we require for the extremely respectful and tasteful prestige documentary production we have in mind."

Travapeth nodded, blew his nose noisily into the towel, and put it back on top of the bookcase. Sharrow coughed and studied the upper balcony. Zefla glided smoothly on. "We do of course recognize the difficulties involved, and we hope that—as a highly respected scholar and the foremost expert on Pharpech in the entire system—you would agree to act as our historical and anthropological consultant."

Travapeth's brows knitted together as he flexed his shoulders and went to a sit-up bench, lying on it and jamming his feet under the bars.

"Yes, I see," he said, clasping his hands behind his neck.

"Should you agree to this," Zefla continued, "we would of course credit you on screen."

"Mm-hmm," Travapeth said, grunting as he did a sit-up.

"And, naturally," Zefla said, "there would be a substantial fee involved, reflecting both the added academic weight your involvement in this prestigious project would contribute and the worth of your valuable time."

Travapeth sat back on the narrow padding of the sit-up bench with a sigh. He stared up at the courtyard's membrane ceiling.

"Of course," he said, "financial matters are hardly my first concern."

"Of course," Zefla agreed. "I can well imagine."

"But—just to give me a rough idea . . . ?" He performed another sit-up, then twisted, touching both elbows off his knees in turn.

"Might we suggest ten thousand, inclusive?" Zefla said.

The scholar paused, touching elbow to knee.

"Four immediately," Zefla said, "should you be prepared to help us, then three on the first day of principal photography and three on transmission."

"Repeat fees?" Travapeth grunted, still swinging from side to side.

"Industry Prestige Documentary Production standard."

"Single screen credit?"

"Same size, half the duration of the director's."

"Call it fifteen."

Zefla sucked in her breath and sounded apologetic. "I'm not really authorized to exceed twelve thousand for any single individual."

Travapeth sat back, panting heavily. "Butler!" he shouted into the air, his voice resounding around the atrium. His sweat-streaked face looked upside down at Zefla. "My dear girl," he breathed, "you won't *need* any other individual. I am all that you require; all that you could possibly ask for." He leered.

From the corner of her eye Zefla caught Sharrow turning away with a hand stuffed in her mouth, just as the little man appeared from the shadows again, struggling to carry a huge bucket full of water.

"Fifteen," Travapeth repeated, closing his eyes. "Six, five, four."

Zefla looked down, shaking her head and rubbing her chin.

"Well, then," Travapeth sighed. "In three equal tranches; can't say fairer than that."

The little man grabbed the chair with the gown draped over it and dragged it with him as he staggered up to where Travapeth lay panting on the sit-up bench; he climbed up onto the chair, heaved the bucket up level with his chest, then dumped the water over Travapeth's deep-breathing, nine-tenths naked frame. Zefla stepped back quickly from the splash.

The scholar shuddered mightily as the water poured off him onto the mat beneath. He spluttered and blinked his eyes as the butler climbed down from the seat and walked away.

Travapeth smiled wetly at Zefla. "Do we have a deal, dear girl?"

Zefla glanced at Sharrow, who nodded almost imperceptibly.

"Ugh! Fate! Did you see his loincloth going clingy and see-through after the little guy poured the water over him? Yech!"

"Thankfully, my eyes were averted at that point."

"And that stuff about 'the generous globes of your mother's breasts'!" Zefla said in a booming voice, then squealed, hand over her mouth as they walked laughing down Imagery Lane through units and packs of students moving between lectures.

"I thought I was going to throw up," Sharrow said.

"Well, you shouldn't have tried to put your whole hand into your mouth," Zefla told her.

"It was that or howl."

"Still, at least he seems to know what he's talking about."

"Hmm," Sharrow said. "So far, so plausible; we'll see if Cenuij is impressed." She nodded down the street to their right. "Let's go down here. There's a place I remember."

"Okay," Zefla said. They turned down Structuralist Street.

"Down here somewhere," Sharrow said, looking around. The street was busy and edged with cafés and esta-minets.

"Actually," Zefla said, putting her arm through Sharrow's again, and looking up at the high membrane waving slowly two kilometers above. "Now I think about it, maybe I do kind of admire his brazenness."

Sharrow glared at Zefla. "You really can't hate anybody for more than about three seconds, can you?"

Zefla smiled guiltily. "Ah, he wasn't that bad." She shrugged. "He's a character."

"Let's hope he stays a minor one," Sharrow muttered.

Zefla laughed. "What's the aim of this sentimental journey, anyway?" She looked along the crowded street. "Where are we heading for now?"

"The Bistro Onomatopoeia," Sharrow told her.

"Oh, I remember that place," Zefla said. She peered into the distance, a pretend frown on her face. "How do you spell it again?" she asked.

"*Oh,*" they chanted together, "*just the way it sounds.*"

She kept her cap down over her eyes and her boots on the rickety seat opposite. Her uniform jacket hung over the back of her own chair.

"Schlotch." She said, and took another drink of the trax spirit.

"Schlotch?" Miz asked.

"Schlotch," she confirmed.

"Mud scraped off a boot," Dloan said, tapping her boot with the toe of his own.

She shook her head slowly, looking down at her hands where they were clasped between her uniformed thighs. She belched. "Nup," she said.

Next round the table was Cenuij.

"A turd dropping into a toilet bowl," he suggested, his gaze shining out from two black eyes he'd collected a couple of nights earlier. "From ten thousand meters."

"Close," she said, then giggled, waving one hand as the others started to heckle. "Na—na, not close at all. I lied. I lied. Ha ha ha."

"The noise a—hic! shit—sockful of pickled jelly-bird

brains makes when swung vigorously against an Excise Clipper escape hatch by a dwarf wearing a jump-girdle on his head."

Sharrow glanced up at Zefla and shook her head quickly. "Too prosaic."

Zefla shrugged. "Fair enough."

Cara cleared his throat carefully. "The noise a speckle bug makes—" he began patiently.

They all pulled off their caps and started throwing them at him and shouting, "No!" "Choose another track!" "No, no, no!" "Fuck this goddamn speckle bug!" "Think of something else!"

Cara flinched, grinning under the barrage of caps, putting his arms out over the table so that his drink wasn't spilled. "But," he said, sounding reasonable, "it's got to be right eventually. . . ."

"Nar, wrong again," Sharrow said. She took some more trax. She felt drunker than she ought to feel. Could it be because she was drinking on an empty stomach? They'd come to the Onomatopoeia for hangover cures and lunch, but somehow—it being their last day before another tour unless peace broke out—it had turned all too easily into another drinking bout.

Had she had breakfast? She accepted her cap back from somebody and put it over her crew-cut scalp. No, she couldn't remember whether she'd had breakfast or not.

She drained the trax, said, "Next!" quite loudly, and put her glass down and pointed at Miz at the same time. Somebody refilled her glass.

Miz looked thoughtful. Then his thin, bright face lit up. "A Tax cruiser hitting *another* asteroid at half the speed of—"

They all started shouting and throwing their caps at him.

"This is getting too silly," Froterin said, as Miz bent to retrieve the caps. Froterin looked massively around at them all. "Everybody's starting to repeat themselves."

"What was that?" "Pardon?" "Eh?"

Froterin stood shakily, his seat scraping back across the pavement, teetering and almost falling into the street. He put his hand onto his broad chest, over his heart. "But now," he rumbled, "I think it's time for a little song. . . ." He started to sing: "Oh, Caltasp, oh Caaaltasp . . ."

"Oh, Fate . . ." "My cap!" "Give me my cap!" "Mine first, I'm less drunk and I aim better anyway!" "Throw something else!" "I know!" "Not *my* drink, you cretin—use *his*!"

"Oh CAAALtasp, oh CAAALtasp—"

"My ears! My ears!" "It's no good, sir; caps just bounce off it!" "Oh no! His glass is empty!"

Vleit got out of her seat and tip-toed around to Sharrow while the rest tried to stop Froterin from singing. Vleit had a wicked grin on her face, and when she got to Sharrow, she crouched down and whispered in her ear.

Sharrow nodded vigorously, and they both dissolved into a fit of giggles and then throaty, coughing laughter. "Yes!" Sharrow nodded, crying with laughter. "Yes!"

"Oh CAAAALtasp, oh CAAAAAAALtasp, oh thank you very much," Froterin said, and sat down with the mug of mullbeer Miz had brought him. He sat supping happily.

"She got it! Vleit—hic! shit—got it!"

"What?" "What was it?" "Come on!"

Sharrow sat shaking her head and drying her eyes on her shirtsleeve while Vleit got up from the café pavement, holding her stomach and still laughing.

"What!" "That's cheating!" "What was the answer?"

"Not telling," Sharrow laughed.

"You got to tell," Miz protested. "Otherwise how do we know Vleit's really won?"

Sharrow put her cap back on again and glanced at Vleit; they both started giggling again, then guffawing. "You want to tell them?" Sharrow said.

"Not me, commander." Vleit shook her head, still giggling. "You tell them. Rank Has Its Problems—remember?"

"Yeah!" "What was it?" "Yeah; come on; tell us!"

"All right, all right," Sharrow said, sitting up properly in her seat. Then, suddenly, she looked worried; her smooth brow furrowed. "Shit," she said. "I've forgotten what the fucking word was." She shook her head.

She put her head down on the table and pretended to cry. At least two caps bounced off her before Cenuij roared, "Schlotch."

Sharrow looked up quickly. "You sure?"

"Positive," Cenuij said precisely.

Sharrow sighed. "Yeah—schlotch."

"So?" Miz said, arms wide. "What's *schlotch* onomato-poeic for or with or whatever?"

"It's the sound," Sharrow said, leaning conspiratorially over the table, and glancing up and down the street. "Of . . ." She shook her head. "It's no good," she said with feigned regret. "I'm just not drunk enough yet to tell you."

"*What?*" "Sharrow!" "Oh, come on . . ." "Don't be ridiculous." "Vleit—what the hell was it?" "Sharrow—you said you'd tell. What is it?"

Sharrow grinned, fended off a flung cap, then put her head back and laughed loudly while the others protested.

A timid-looking waiter approached from out of the bistro, holding a tray nervously to his chest as though it were a shield. He came up to Sharrow; she smiled at the young waiter and adjusted her cap.

The waiter coughed. "Um, Commander Sharrow?" he said.

"You read a good name tag, kid," Miz said, winking at him.

"Yeah," Cenuij said. "Stick with us, we'll make you a waiter. Oh. You *are* a—"

Sharrow waved them both to be quiet. "Yes," she said, staring rather blearily at the youth.

"Phone call for you, Commander. Military." The young waiter scurried back into the bistro.

Sharrow looked puzzled. She put her hand into the pocket of her uniform jacket, which was hanging over the back of her seat. She winced and grimaced, then brought her hand out covered in red goo. "What miserable scumbag put ghrettis sauce all over my fucking comm set?" she roared, standing and letting the red sauce drip onto the pavement.

"Shit," Miz said in a small voice. "I thought I did that to Dloan's jacket, back at the inn."

"Dloan's?" Sharrow shouted at him. She pointed at Dloan's uniform. "How many bars on his jacket? One! How many on mine? Two!" she yelled, pointing at them with her other hand.

Miz shrugged, smiling. "I thought I was seeing double."

"Fucking double guard duties," Sharrow muttered as she strode past him toward the bistro interior. "Get that shit out of my pocket—now!"

"Must be strong stuff, that ghrettis sauce," she heard

Dloan musing. "Mil comm set's supposed to be waterproof to a pressure of . . ."

Inside the bistro it was quiet and dark; only the staff were there. "Thanks, Vol," she said to the proprietor as she took the phone.

"Commander Sharrow here," she said, nodding appreciatively to Vol when he handed her a cloth for her hand.

She closed her eyes as she listened. After a while she said, "Comm set broke down, sir. No idea why, sir." Her eyes screwed tighter. "Possibly enemy action, sir."

She wiped her hand and nodded again to Vol, who went to sit at the far end of the bistro with the rest of the staff.

She glanced back through the bistro's windows to the street at the group, who were trying to sort out whose cap was whose. She smiled, watching them, then returned her attention to the phone. "Yes, sir! On our way, sir," she said, and made to put the phone down. "I beg your pardon, sir?" She frowned at her reflection on the other side of the bar, visible through the glasses and between the upended barrels. "The doc? I mean, surgeon-commander . . . of course, sir."

She looked at her reflection again, shrugged at herself.

"Yes," she said into the phone. "Hi, Doc. What's the problem?" She leaned on the bar, pushing her cap up and rubbing her face. "What—? Oh, the checkups." She grinned at her reflection. "What is it? Somebody taken a rad-blast, or are we talking exotic diseases?"

She listened for half a minute or so.

She watched the reflection of her face in the mirror go pale.

After a while she cleared her throat and said, "Yes, I'll do that, Doc. Of course." She started to put the phone down again, then stopped and said, "Thanks, Doc," into it, and only then put it back behind the counter.

She stood there for a moment, staring at her image in the mirror. She glanced down at her shirt. "Shit," she whispered, looking back up to her reflection. "And you're pickling the little fucker."

Vol came back around the other side of the bar with a tray full of dirty glasses. She started when she saw him, then leaned over, beckoning.

"Vol. Vol!" she whispered.

The aproned proprietor, burly-fit and placid as ever, leaned over to her and whispered back, "Yes, commander?"

"Vol, you got anything'll make me sick as a lubber?"

"Sick as a lubber?" he said, looking puzzled.

"Yes!" she whispered, glancing out at the others. "Filthy, gut-grenaded, throat-scouring, turned-inside-out sick!"

Vol shrugged. "Too much drink usually does the trick," he said.

"No!" she hissed. "No, something else!"

"Stick your fingers down your throat?"

She shook her head quickly. "Tried that as a kid; got it to work on my half sister, but never on me. What else?" She glanced at the others again. "Quickly!"

"Very salty water," Vol said, spreading his hands.

She slapped him on the shoulder. "Fix me enough for two."

She turned and walked toward the door, hesitated, then bit her lip and put her hand into a trouser pocket. She pulled out a coin and clutched it in her hand as she went out to the others. They looked up at her. Miz was still scraping her jacket pocket clean of sauce; the comm set lay on the table covered in red, like something butchered.

She spread her arms. "Well, they still haven't sorted out the situation, guys," she told them. There were various mutters, mostly of disapproval. "They're still talking," she said. "But meanwhile the festivities continue; looks like another tour at least. We're overdue at Embarkation Asshole now." She sighed. "I'll go phone a truck." She hesitated, then went up to Miz and presented the coin in her hand to him. "Toss that," she told him.

Miz looked around at the others. He shrugged, tossed the coin. She looked at how it landed on the table. She nodded and turned to go.

"*Yes?*" Miz said pointedly.

"Tell you later," she told him, and went back into the bistro.

"Thanks, Vol," she said, taking the glass of cloudy water from him and heading for the toilet. "Phone us a military truck, will you?" she called. She took a preparatory sip of the salted water. "Yech!"

"Commander Sharrow!" Vol called after her. "You said make enough for two—is that all for you?"

She shook her head. "Not exactly."

• • •

"Bleurghch! Aauullleurch! Hooowwerchresst-t-t!" she
shouted down the toilet hole, and for a few moments, as her
stomach clenched again (and she thought, *Hell, maybe* this's
*doing the little bastard more harm than the booze would
have*), she listened to the noises she was making, and remembered the game they'd been playing, and actually found
it all ridiculously funny.

Zefla watched Sharrow looking at the facade of what had
been the Bistro Onomatopoeia, and which was now an antique bookshop.

Sharrow shook her head.

"Oh well," she said. She looked down at a coin she held
in her hand. "Guess that proves it." She put the coin back
in her pocket. "You never can go back." She turned and
walked away.

Zefla looked a moment longer at the bookshop sign,
then hurried after Sharrow.

"Hey," she said. "Look on the bright side—we're looking for a book, and what do we find in one of our old drinking haunts? A bookshop!" She slapped Sharrow across the
shoulders. "It's a good omen, really."

Sharrow turned to Zefla as they walked. "Zef," she said,
tiredly. "Shut up."

11

Deep Country

S he sat at the window of the gently rocking train, watching the Extraxrln roll past outside, the airily tangled,
cable-curved vastness of it and the sheer size of the twisting,
fluted nets of the composite trunks making her feel tinier
than a doll—a model soldier in a train set laid out on the
floor of a quiet, dark forest that went on forever.

Here the Extraxrln seemed much more mysterious and
alien than it did in Malishu; it imposed itself, it seemed to
exist in another plane of being from mere people, forever
separated from them by the titanic, crushing slowness of its
inexorably patient metabolism.

From this window she had watched hours of it pass
slowly by; she had seen distant clouds and small rainstorms,
she had watched herds of tramplers bound away across the
floor-membrane, she had gazed at trawler-balloons and their
attendant feaster birds cruising the high membranes, she
had caught sight of the high, dark freckles on the lofted
membranes that were glide-monkey troupes, peered dubiously at herds of wild jemers loping across open spaces with
a strange, stiff-legged gait, knowing that they would be riding the tamed version of the awkward-looking animals, and
she had seen a single great stom—black, somehow ferocious
even as little more than a speck, and with a wingspan great
as a small plane—wheeling around far above, effortlessly

weaving its way between the hanging strings and ropes of growing cables.

Zefla sat opposite Sharrow, one elbow on the opened window ledge, a hand supporting her head. The warm breeze blew in, disturbing the blond fall of her hair. Her other hand held a portable screen. Her head rocked slightly from side to side in time with the creaking, flexing carriage.

The compartment door opened squeakily and Cenuij looked in.

"Welcome to nowhere," he said, smiling brightly. "We just left the comm net." He withdrew and closed the door.

Zefla looked vaguely surprised, then went back to her novel. Sharrow pulled out her little disposable phone. Its display flashed Transception Problem. She clicked a few buttons experimentally, then shrugged and put the phone away in her satchel.

Sharrow glanced at her watch. Another four hours on this train, another day on a second train, then two days after that they might just be in Pharpech if all went according to plan.

She looked out the window again.

"And this is the view from the back of the castle; that's looking south. No, north. Well, more northeast, I suppose. I think." Travapeth handed the holo print to Zefla, who glanced at it and smiled again.

"Enchanting," she said. Zefla passed the print across the conference table to Sharrow, who hardly bothered to glance at it.

"Hmm," she said, stifling a yawn. She passed the print to Cenuij, sitting around the table from her. He looked at it. There was a sour, disgusted look on his face. He studied the holo as if trying to decide whether to tear it up, spit on it, or set it on fire. Eventually he put it facedown on a large pile of prints lying on the table.

They had hired a small office in a modern block in the city center; Travapeth—clad in an ancient and grubby professorial robe that had probably once been maroon—had visited two days in a row, drinking large amounts of trax wine on each occasion and holding forth at some length—and with gradually increasing volume—on any and every aspect of the Kingdom of Pharpech that Zefla, Sharrow, or Cenuij could think of.

Miz and Dloan, meanwhile, were tracking down any further information they could find on the Kingdom in data bases and publications; they were also completing the travel arrangements.

Zefla and Sharrow had been worried Cenuij would take exception to Travapeth's bombastic demeanor; with Cenuij, things could always go either way when he met people who had as high an opinion of themselves as he did of himself. They had waited until Cenuij was in a particularly good mood before they introduced the two men to each other. It had worked; Cenuij seemed almost to have warmed to the old scholar, but today, after lunch in a private booth in a nearby restaurant, Travapeth had insisted on showing them the flat and holo photographs he had taken on his visits to the Kingdom, from the first time he'd gone there as a student fifty years earlier, up to his last visit, five years ago.

"Ah," Travapeth said. He brought another carton of prints up from the floor at his side, depositing the carton on the table and delving inside. "Now, these are especially interesting," he said, plonking the thick wad of prints on the polished bark table. Dust puffed out from between the holos. Sharrow sighed. Cenuij, a look of horror on his face, glanced beneath the table to see how many more cartons Travapeth had down there.

"These date from twenty years ago," Travapeth said, helping himself to a blister-fruit from the bowl.

Something small and red wriggled out from a hole in the bottom of the carton the prints had been in; it ran fast and eight-legged across the table toward the edge. Travapeth brought his hand holding the blister-fruit crunching down on the insect as he said, "These date from the time of His Majesty's coronation."

Zefla stared at the old scholar's hand as he rolled it back and forth, making sure the insect was fully squashed.

"As I say," Travapeth went on, absently wiping his red-stained hand on a different-colored stain already decorating the thigh of his robe, "I was personally invited to the coronation by His Majesty." He polished the blister-fruit on roughly the same part of the robe he'd wiped the insect on, and then bit into the fruit, talking through the resulting yellowish mush and waving the dripping fruit around. "I shink thish shirst one ish a short of zheneral zhiew . . ."

Sharrow put one hand under her armpit and her other hand to her brow.

"Enchanting," Zefla said, passing the print to Sharrow. It was sticky. Sharrow gave it to Cenuij.

"Ah," Travapeth said, swallowing. "Now—still the coronation day, but here we have the ceremony of the holy book being brought out of the vault."

Sharrow looked up.

"Holy book?" Zefla said brightly. She accepted the print from the scholar's thin, age-spotted hand.

"Yes," Travapeth said, frowning at the holo. "The monarch has to be sitting on the book, on the throne in the cathedral when he is crowned." He handed the print of Zefla, a leery smile on his face. ". . . Sitting on it with fundament bared, I may add," he added. "The monarch has to bare his nether regions to the skin cover of the book." The elderly scholar took another deep bite from the blister-fruit and sat smiling at Zefla as he masticated.

"Fascinating," Zefla said, glancing at the print and passing it on. Sharrow looked at it. She sensed Cenuij waiting, tense, in the other seat.

The slightly blurred holo showed a crowd of serious-looking but colorfully attired men holding the poles supporting an opened palanquin in which something light-brown and about the size of a briefcase sat, resting on a white cushion. The by-now-familiar ramshackle bulk of Pharpech Castle rose in the background, at the end of the small city's main square. She quickly turned the holo from side to side and up and down, but the image of the book in the palanquin didn't reveal any more from other angles.

"What sort of holy book is it?" Sharrow asked. "Which one?" She pretended to stifle another yawn and smiled apologetically at Travapeth as she did so. She handed the holo to Cenuij, who looked at it, then put it down. He jotted something in his notebook.

"I have to confess, dear girl, that I don't know," Travapeth admitted, frowning. He took another bite from the fruit. "Shome short of ancient tome shuppposhed to have been a gisht shrom"—he swallowed—"the Ladyr Emperor to the first of the Useless Kings." Travapeth waved the dripping fruit around. Zefla flinched, then calmly wiped her eye. "I of course offered to inspect the book for His Majesty, to determine its identity, provenance, and importance, but in this was refused, unusually." Travapeth shrugged. "All I know is that it's an encased book, some sort of precious metal, probably silver. It's about as thick as your hand, as long as your forearm, and its breadth is roughly twenty-eight and a half centimeters."

Cenuij sat back in his seat, fingers drumming on the table. Sharrow felt herself evaluating the scene, trying to gauge just how much interest they appeared to be showing. Too little might look as suspicious as too much.

Travapeth crunched into the core of the blister-fruit, frowned, and spat a few seeds into the carton the holos had come from. "The book's never been opened," he said. "Rumor is it's booby-trapped, but anyway, it's locked, and *naturally* there's no key. I might have at least been able to establish the work's identity had the old king not had it recovered—or rather additionally covered—in the skin of some revolutionary peasant leader some years before I first traveled to the Kingdom." Travapeth sighed.

"It's a very colorful ceremony, the coronation, isn't it?" Zefla said, turning to Sharrow and Cenuij and tapping her notebook stylo on the table's polished surface. Sharrow nodded (thinking *good girl*), as Zefla turned back to Travapeth, who was taking aim at the office's litter bin, stationed beneath a window near one corner of the room. He threw the core of the blister-fruit; it thumped soggily against the wall above and fell behind the bin. Travapeth shook his head.

"It would make very good screen," Zefla said to him. She glanced around at Sharrow and Cenuij. "I'd just *adore* to record something like that ceremony," she said (Sharrow and Cenuij both nodded). "So ethnic," Zefla said to Travapeth, her hands out in front of her as though supporting two large invisible spheres. "So . . . so *real*."

Travapeth looked wise.

"I don't suppose," Zefla said, "the current king is thinking of resigning or anything, is he?"

Travapeth wiped his hands on the front of his robe and shook his head. "I believe not, dear girl. The present king's grandfather did abdicate; he took himself off to a monastery to pursue a life of holy despisal. But King Tard . . . well, he's not really the religious type." Travapeth frowned. "He does believe in their god, of course, but I don't believe it would be inaccurate to term his religious observances perfunctory rather than assiduous."

"They don't ever reenact——?" Zefla began. But Travapeth boomed on.

"Of course, sudden conversions to extreme holiness have been known to occur in the present royal family, usually following traumatic events in the life of the noble person concerned——involvement in an unsuccessful coup, being discovered with somebody else's spouse or one's own mount, finding one has been made general of an army being sent to root out guerrillas and revolutionaries in deep country——that sort of thing. But for a monarch to take up holy orders is relatively rare; they tend to die in harness." Travapeth's eyebrows rose. "Literally so in the case of the king's great-grandfather, who accidentally strangled himself to death in a *very* unlikely position while suspended from the ceiling of a room in a house of less than spotless reputation." The old scholar gave a sort of grunting laugh and grimaced dubiously at Zefla as he took a drink from a goblet of trax wine, and gargled with it before swallowing.

"Well," Zefla said. "Perhaps we might be able to catch some other ceremony. If we do get permission to work there."

"Certainly," Travapeth said, belching. "There's the annual rededication of the cathedral, the maledictions before the annual glide-monkey hunt——that's quite colorful, and the hunt itself is exciting. . . . Well, they call it a hunt; it's more of a spectator sport. Then there's the new-year mass-executions day, the debtors' flogging festival . . . and there are always events celebrating the birth of a new royal baby or the king's acquisition of some new piece of technology."

"Yes," Zefla said, tapping the stylo on the conference table again. "These pieces of modern technology that the kings purchase every now and again——I take it they have purely symbolic value?"

Travapeth shook his head. "Not even that, sweet lady; they are bought merely to remove any monetary surplus from the country's economy. This, ah, apparently strange behavior is designed to keep the kingdom stable by soaking up profit that might otherwise lead to progress and therefore instability. This is the very reason that Pharpech is also known as the Court of the Useless Kings." Travapeth frowned and gestured with his hands. "This might strike us as a rather eccentric way to run a state, but I think we have to respect the Pharpechians' right to run their country the way they want, and certainly one cannot deny that it works; there has been no progress whatsoever in Pharpech for nearly eight hundred years. In its own way, that's quite an achievement."

Cenuij made an almost inaudible noise and jotted something in his notebook.

"Of course," Travapeth sighed, "this practice can be taken too far; I was present in the kingdom when His Majesty the present King took delivery of his radio telescope."

"I thought the area was radio opaque," Cenuij said.

"Oh, absolutely," Travapeth said. "And of course there's no break in the canopy for hundreds of kilometers. But you miss the point, my dear sir. The telescope was not bought to be used; there was nobody in the realm able to operate it and no electricity supply available anyway. As I have related, modern technology—with the partial exception of the guards' and the army's weapons—is effectively banned in the Kingdom."

The old scholar suddenly looked quite sad and dropped his voice a little. "Even my own modest camera fell foul of this rule after the unfortunate business of the king being thrown from his mount while performing the annual capital boundary riding, during my last visit. . . ." Travapeth seemed to collect himself, sitting straight in his seat and raising his voice again. "No, sir. The King bought the telescope because it cost exactly the amount of money the treasury had to spend and because it was totally useless. Although I believe he did enjoy sliding around inside the bowl for a while, which goes against the letter but not the spirit of the Uselessness creed. . . . But no," Travapeth said, and came close to scowling. "My complaint is with the site the king chose for his telescope, which was the old castle library; he had the library torn down and all the books burned." Travapeth shook his head. "Disgraceful behavior," he muttered into his wine goblet.

Sharrow stared at him, then made a small note in her own notebook, just to be doing something. *Oh shit,* she thought.

Zefla was shaking her head, making noises of polite outrage.

Cenuij had stiffened. "*All* the books?" he said, voice hoarse. "Burned?"

Travapeth looked up, eyebrows raised. "I'm afraid so,"

he said, nodding sadly. "They went into the castle furnace; coated the whole city in ash and black, half-burned pages." The old scholar shook his head. "Tragedy, really."

"Terrible," Zefla agreed.

"And for the townspeople, of course," Travapeth said. "As I've said, Pharpech experiences rain only rarely, and the roof-Tax tends to discourage people from covering the top-most floor of their dwellings, so all that ash made a quite terrible mess."

"Were any very valuable books destroyed?" Cenuij said. He gave a small smile. "I'm something of an antiquarian book collector in my spare time. I'd hate to think . . ."

"To be honest, I doubt it," Travapeth said, nodding to Zefla as she refilled his goblet with wine. "Thank you, dear girl." He looked at Cenuij. "Pharpech is something of a des-ert for bibliophiles, dear sir. There is no literary tradition as such; only a very few of the top officials in the Kingdom, a couple of family tutors, and sometimes the monarch can read at all. Though, as one might expect, this has led to a rich oral culture. But no, sir; the library was a Useless pur-chase, bought a few hundred years ago from an auction house here in Malishu; it had belonged to a noble family fallen on hard times.

"All the rare and valuable books had already been sold individually; what the king destroyed was merely the stan-dard collected classics most noble families favor instead of wallpaper to line one room of their mansions, though usually the wallpaper is in more danger of being read. Its purchase as a Useless article was arguably a change of circumstance of only a very limited degree. I very much doubt that the system bibliocontinua lost anything irreplaceable in the vandalistic conflagration. But dammit, sir, it's the *principle* involved!" Travapeth said loudly, banging his goblet down on the table and spilling wine over the holos and the patch of table in front of him.

"I couldn't agree more," Cenuij said. He made another note.

"As a result," the old scholar said, dabbing at a patch of spilled wine on the table with the cuff of his robe, "the only book left in the whole castle is probably the one the monarch sits on during the coronation. Whatever *it* is."

"Hmm," Sharrow said, nodding.

"Right," Zefla said, laying her stylo down. "Tell me some more about these festivals, Ivexton. Which ones would you say are the most vibrant, the most *colorful* . . . ?"

"So what do you think?" Sharrow asked.

Cenuij shrugged and stirred spice into his mullbeer. "I suppose it could be what we're looking for," he said.

They sat, all five, in a private booth in a café near the rented office. Miz and Dloan had their route organized; it would involve taking a flying boat from Malishu to Long Strand, a maglev express to LiveInHope, then two slow trains to the Pharpech outlands border, where there was a small settlement they could hire guides and buy mounts in. They hadn't yet booked any tickets.

"I thought the book had been lost for a lot more than the eight cents since the Ladyrs," Miz said.

"Anything up to two millennia, depending whose account you trust." Cenuij nodded. "But that's just since anybody *admitted* to owning it. Maybe the Ladyrs stumbled on it when they were dispossessing an uncooperative family or sacking a Corp. that hadn't paid its protection money quickly enough. Maybe it had never really been truly lost. Maybe they didn't know what it was they had—just another old unopened book that might come in handy one day." Cenuij shrugged. "Anyway, sending it to a coprolite like Pharpech when the antiimperial heat was on must have seemed like a neat idea at the time." He supped his ale. "It worked, after all; nobody's found it, though obviously old Gorko had his nose to the trail."

"So do we go?" Zefla asked. She sucked on an inhalant.

"Well," Sharrow said, "I don't see how Breyguhn or anybody else could have set up what happened to Bencil Dornay; the pattern he traced was pretty unambiguous, and it sounds like there is exactly one book in the castle at Pharpech." She spread her hands. "I think we go."

"Keeps you out of the way of the Huhsz, too," Miz said, rolling trax spirit around in his glass. "Caught a recent news report? They're saying *two* heavyweight missions left Golter yesterday, one bound for Tront and the other headed this way."

"I heard," she said. "At least they sound confused. Any more interesting race winners in Tile?"

Miz shook his head. "Nothing since *Dance of Death*."

"How we doing for funds?" Zefla inquired, apparently trying to hold her breath and talk at the same time.

"Fluid," Sharrow said. "Barely used a third of our allowance. The only drawback is response-time—shuffling the credit trail so it's difficult to follow. But that shouldn't be a problem unless we need a lot of cash very quickly."

Miz held his small glass of trax spirit up to the light, frowning at it. "What sort of funds are we taking to Pharpech?" he asked.

"Cash, gold, diamonds, and trinkets," Sharrow said.

("This looks cloudy," Miz said, nudging Dloan and nodding at the trax glass. "D'you think it's cloudy?")

"Getting past the border guards might swallow a fair amount," Sharrow said to Zefla. "But once we're in, everything's supposed to be cheaper than dirty water."

"Which is probably about all they have to sell," Cenuij said.

"Think that's what's in this glass," Miz muttered, squinting at the trax glass. He held it in front of Cenuij's nose. "That look cloudy to you?"

"We'll have to play it by ear regarding the gear we can take in," Sharrow said. "Apparently it'll depend on what sort of mood the border guards are in."

"No other way into this place?" Miz said, sniffing at the glass. "Struck me we're doing all this horribly *officially*. I mean, I was standing in a holiday agent's today talking about travel insurance. I mean, *travel insurance*! Have we really come to this?" He held the trax up to the light again, then waved it in front of Sharrow's face. "Cloudy/not cloudy— what do you think?" he asked her.

"There are lots of other ways in," Sharrow said, pushing Miz's glass out of the way. "But they're all even more complicated, too dangerous, and involve walking or riding enormous distances in the company of people who kill, capture, or rob other people as a way of life. The border guards sound like nursery wardens in comparison."

"I still say a decent pilot could take a chopper or a VTOL in through—" Miz began, still frowning at his glass.

"Well, *you* try finding a plane," Sharrow said, "anywhere on Miykenns. Flying boats or nothing—that's your choice."

"Yes, Miz," Cenuij smiled. "I think you'll find a lot of people felt the same way earlier in Miykenns's history; that's why there's so little cable and membrane clutter around Malishu, and why the extensive Pilot's Cemetery is such a poignant feature on the sightseeing circuit."

"I bet I could—" Miz began.

"Something else," Zefla said quickly, slapping the table. "We are *not* taking Travapeth."

"He might come in useful," Cenuij said.

"Yeah," Zefla said. "So's a broken leg if you want to kick yourself in the back of the head."

"No Travapeth," Sharrow said, then frowned at Miz, who had taken a small torch out of his jacket pocket and was shining it through the glass of trax spirit.

Zefla sighed. "The old guy's going to be awfully upset when we don't make the documentary," she said. "He was talking about a book tie-in. And he could use the money."

"He doesn't think we're going to get to make the thing, anyway," Sharrow said, brows furrowing as she watched Miz sniff at the trax glass again. "He's got five grand," she told Zefla, "for three days of sitting pontificating, flirting like a gigolo, and having wine and food poured down him. Easiest money *he's* ever going to make."

Miz made a tutting noise and put the trax glass to his ear. He flicked its rim gently with one finger, an expression of deep concentration on his face.

"Oh, give me that!" Sharrow said, exasperated. She took the glass from his fingers before he could protest, put it to her lips, and drained it.

Then her face creased into a sour expression, and she turned and spat the trax out behind her, onto the age-stained planks of the booth. She wiped her mouth with her sleeve. "What did you do—piss in it?" she asked Miz. "That was horrible!"

"Hell, I *knew* that," he said, looking annoyed. "But was it cloudy?" He nodded at the stain on the planks. "We'll never know now."

"Oh, stop farting about and go and get us a bottle," she told him.

"Not if you're just going to spit it all over the floor," he said primly, turning sideways in his seat and crossing his arms and legs.

"*I'll* get us a bottle," Zefla said, rising.
"Filthy peacemaker," Sharrow said.
"Hey, Zef—make sure it's not cloudy. . . ."

The Entraxrln deep country was sinking into an early-evening purple gloom. The layers of membrane here grew closer and thicker, and the trunks and stalks were thinner but far more numerous; cables looped and curved and hung everywhere, strung with great tattered lengths and folds of wind-torn leaf-membrane. There was no longer any real sense of there being ground underfoot, although the undulating landscape resembled a purple downland, it was a landscape in which great holes had been cut and huge suspended skeins of material added; some of the holes lengthened to tunnels and dropped into deeper, darker layers farther down, while others narrowed and doubled back, and throughout this bewildering three-dimensional maze, great roots and tubes ran, undulating across the maroon layers like huge blood vessels standing out on the skin of some enormous sleeping animal.

The captain stood in the doorway of the guard cabin and watched the group of riders and their pack animals as they plodded off into the slowly gathering darkness along the track to the capital.

The captain pulled on his pipe a few times, surrounding his head with a cloud of smoke.

The guard sergeant struggled up the steps toward the captain, holding two sacks.

"Claim they're not tourists, sir," the sergeant said. "Say they're Travelers." He deposited the two sacks at the captain's feet. "Not a sect I'd heard of, sir, must confess." He opened the sacks up. "Least one of them's dressed proper for a holy man. Order of the Book, he said—wants to try to give the king some books, sir. I told him the king didn't hold with books, but he didn't seem bothered."

The captain stirred some of their booty with his foot. Bottles clinked; he could see the usual collection of cameras, a couple of sets of magnifiers, a civilian night-sight, and some cash.

"Two of them were ladies, sir; veiled, they were. None of them fitted any descriptions of undesirables. Guides were known to us—regular fellows."

The captain squatted down, boots creaking. He poked

at a piece of mysterious-looking equipment with the stem of his pipe. The piece of equipment started to play music. He poked it again and it went quiet. He lifted it and put it inside his shirt.

"Quite generous they were, really. It's all here, sir, naturally."

The captain reached into a sack and pulled out a bottle, putting the pipe back in his mouth as he weighed the trax spirit bottle in his hand.

"Oh, dear; I wouldn't touch that one, sir. Looks a bit cloudy if you ask me."

She woke in the night. Her backside was sore. The room was very dark, the bed felt strange, and the place smelled odd. There was somebody in here with her; she could sense breathing. A rippling blue-gray light flashed, jarring a confusing image of the room across her eyes. She remembered. This was the inn called The Broken Neck on the square beneath the castle: a haven after the long ride on the swaying, cantankerous, and rank-smelling jemers and two nights in rough, communal guest houses in the dark deep-country. Cenuij had gained entrance to the monastery hospitale while they had come here, to the two best rooms in the inn and suspiciously spicy food and strong wine, which had made her fall asleep over the table. Zefla had put her to bed; it was she who was sleeping in the other lumpy bed across the chamber.

Of course, she thought, as another silent burst of lightning flickered through the windows, and she calmed.

I am in Pharpech.

She got out of the massive, creaking, bowed bed with its pile of coarse blankets and two slightly softer sheets, waited for another flash, then with the memory of the room's image held in her eyes, crossed to the tall windows. They had a balcony; she hadn't thought it looked very safe when they'd first taken the room, but she would trust it. The window creaked a little when she opened it. She stepped outside, closed the window, and moved sideways along the bark-clad wall to the cable-branch railing.

The darkness outside made her dizzy. She could feel, even somehow hear, that she was in the open air, but there was no light anywhere; nothing from the sky, where the membrane cut out any celestial light, and nothing from—she couldn't think of this place as a city—the town, either. Her fingers felt for the thin railing and found it, gripped it. Like being blind, she thought.

The air was a little colder than it had been earlier; she wore an extremely modest nightdress, and only her neck and ankles felt the breeze. She stood there, waiting for another flash of lightning, frightened of the balcony and the three-story drop to the alley beneath.

The lightning was there, far off in the distance, seemingly half-above and half-beneath the higher membranes. The light revealed part of the four- or five-kilometer-wide semiclearing around Pharpech town, and the nearby composite trunks. The town itself was a half-glimpsed jumble of geometric shapes curving away beneath her.

And there had been something else, half-glimpsed to her right, level with her, only a few meters away. A figure, a person. Her heart jumped.

"Sharrow?" she heard Miz whisper, uncertain.

She smiled into the darkness. "No," she whispered. "Ysul."

"Oh, yeah." Miz coughed quietly. "Your dinner repeating on you, too?"

"No," she whispered, wanting to laugh. "The lightning."

"Oh."

She looked over, trying to see him. Eventually the lightning flared again. He was standing facing her, looking toward her the way she was looking toward him. She suppressed a giggle. "Forgot your jim-jams, huh?"

"Hey," he said, his whisper close in the utter darkness. "These balconies aren't that far apart. I bet I could get over there." He sounded innocently delighted, like a small boy.

"Don't you dare!" she whispered. She thought she could hear him moving—skin on thin, heat-cured cable.

She stared at where she knew he was, as if trying to force her eyes to see by sheer force of will. Then she looked deliberately away, hoping to see him from the side of her eye. She couldn't.

"Miz!" she whispered. "Don't! You'll kill yourself. It's three sto—"

The lightning came again, and there was Miz, standing on the outside of the balcony, holding on to its railing with one hand while reaching out toward her with the other. She had time to see the expression on his face, eager, happy, and mischievous; then as the blue light disappeared, she heard his breath and felt the draft of air as he leapt over to her balcony. She reached out and grabbed him, fastening her arms around him.

"Madman!" she hissed into his ear.

He chuckled, swung over the railing, and hugged her.

"Isn't this romantic?" he sighed happily. He smelled of sweet male sweat and smoke and—faintly—of scent.

"Get back to your room!" she told him, squirming in his embrace. "And use the doors!"

He moved sensuously against her, working her back against the bark-clad wall; he nuzzled her neck, smoothed his hands down her flanks to her thighs and behind. "Mmm, you feel *good*."

"Miz!" she said, pushing his arms down and away from her, taking his wrists in her hands. He made a plaintive noise and licked at her neck.

Then he just broke her grip on his wrists and took her face in his hands, kissing her.

She let him for a while, and let his tongue explore her mouth, but then (seeing again, without wishing to, the billowing curtains and the stone balustrade of another hotel bedroom, light-minutes and eight years away from here, and his face above her, beautiful and ecstatic and lit by the stuttering spasms of annihilation light swamping the dawn above Lip City) gradually she calmed the tempo of the kiss down and guided his hands behind her shoulders and put her arms around him, and moved her head to one side of his, and rested her cheek on his shoulder, and patted his back.

She felt him heave a deep sigh.

"What's a chap got to do to get to you these days, Sha— Ysul?" he said, sounding sad and a little bewildered.

She hugged him tighter and shrugged, shook her head, knowing he could feel each movement.

The Entraxrln sky above them lit up again as the lightning moved closer.

"Hey," he said, raising his head. "Remember that time in the inn in Malishu, in the top story, with the fireworks and all that stuff?"

She nodded her head.

"That was fun, eh?" he said softly.

"Yes," she said. "Yes, it was."

She kept hold of him and he kept hold of her, and she looked out to where the lightning played, and saw another couple of flashes, and even heard a little distant rumbling, and then eventually he shivered in her arms and kissed her forehead and let go of her. "I'd better get back and make sure Dloan's still snoring," he whispered.

"Come by the door, then," she said, taking his arm and trying to pull him toward the open windows. He resisted, staying where he was.

"Can't," he said. "Our door's locked. Either I go back the way I came or I sleep with you."

"Or on the floor," she told him.

"Or with Zef," he whispered brightly. "Hey, or *both* of you!"

"You have my bed," she said. "*I'll* sleep with Zef."

"You did that once before," he said, sounding unconvincingly hurt, "and I was *very* upset."

"Only because we wouldn't let you watch."

"True," he agreed. "Is that supposed to make it better?"

"Are you going in through this window or not?"

"Not. I'm going back the way I came. Dloan's snoring needs me."

"Miz—" But he had already slung one leg over the balcony; she felt the wind on her cheek as he swung the other one over too. "Maniac!" she whispered. "Be care—"

The lightning came and he made his leap: he gasped, then she heard the skin-on-railing noise again, and he whispered triumphantly, "There. Almost too easy."

"You're insane, Kuma."

"Never denied it. But I'm *so* graceful. Good night, my lady."

"Good night, madman."

She heard him blow a kiss, then move away. She waited. A moment later there was a muffled thud, and she heard him say, "Ouch!"

She smiled into the darkness, quite sure that he had bumped into something deliberately just for a laugh, just for her.

The lightning swept above, flooding the enclosed landscape with a quick, sharp, monochrome light that seemed to be over before it had fully begun, and—in providing such vanishingly brief instants of contrast—somehow only intensified the darkness.

12

Snow Fall

T hey had been lovers for a few months. It was only the second time they had been back to Miykenns since the perfume festival and their ride in the little canal-boat through the long, dark, scented vein of the canal. They delighted in their luck; Malishu was celebrating again when they returned, just entering a huge retro binge of ancient costumes and sporadically cheap food and drugs as people celebrated the 7021st Founding Week.

They had dined and danced and drank, they had taken a short ride in a canal-boat and watched vivid holos flicker and pulse in the air above the city, depicting the arrival of the first explorers, scientists, and settlers seven millennia earlier. The holos went on to display a brief history of Miykenns, which they both watched as they strolled hand in hand down the narrow streets back to their inn beneath the bare hill near the city Signaling Museum.

The last part of the holo display was made up of edited highlights of the current war. They stood on the threshold of the inn, watching. Above the city they saw darkly shining fleets of liberated excise clippers flying in formation; the bombardment of the laser pits on the Phrastesis-Nachtel asteroid bases; rioting miners on Nachtel's Ghost; and a Tax cruiser blowing up. "Hey," Miz said, as the blossoming light of the cruiser's death faded slowly above Malishu. "Wasn't that the one *we* got, out past the Ghost?"

She watched the secondary detonations burst like sparkling flowers within the sphere of glowing wreckage that had been the Tax cruiser. "Yes," she said, cuddling closer to him, fitting herself around him. "One of ours, indeed." She rubbed one hand over the chest of his uniform jacket. "Anyway, let's get back to the room, eh?" She turned away, taking a grip of his shoulder and trying to pull him in through the door.

"Hell," he said, allowing himself to be pulled. "*We* took those pix; shouldn't we get royalties or something?"

Their room was on the top floor, a tall, wide space roofed with translucent woven Entraxrln membrane, bowed like a loose tent over the supporting poles and beams.

They made love sitting on the end of the bed, facing a wall of mirrors; he beneath her and she on his lap, facing the same way so that they could see themselves in the dim city-light filtering down through the translucent roof as he put his arms up underneath hers, gripping her shoulders, holding her breasts, rubbing her flat belly, sliding down to the tight curls of hair and moist cleft beneath while her head kept turning to one side, then the other, kissing him as her hands moved up and down his sides and thighs, holding his balls as he flexed slowly under her and she moved, clenching and loosening, up and down on him.

They were panting, straining, watching each other, gaze fastened to the same place on the surface of the mirror, watching with a kind of eager, ravenous solemnity as they concentrated, wrapped up in the approaching moment, conscious only of themselves and each other; the whole world, the entire system and universe shrunk to this pulsed, focused joining with nothing else, nowhere else, no-when else mattering, when the fireworks burst overhead.

The light was furious, shocking. They both stopped moving to gaze openmouthed at the membrane fabric above. Then, as the noise cracked and thundered down into the room, they looked back into the mirror together and started laughing. They fell back onto the bed, giggling under the multicolored lights inundating the soft roof above them.

"What lousy timing," she said, laughing so hard, she laughed him out of her. "Shit."

"Corn-screen would have had it happen just as we

came," he agreed. He shifted underneath her and she rolled off.

She lay on the bed beside him, gently bit one of his nipples. "You're not giving up *now* are you?"

"Hell, no, I don't *want* to!" he said, gesturing at the roof, where red and green lights strobed and noise like gunfire rattled. "But this is fucking distracting!"

She was still for a second, then bounced off the bed.

"I've had an idea," she told him.

She stopped his ears with little bits of tissue she soaked with her own spittle, and then she did the same to her own ears. The noise of the fireworks was lessened, deadened.

Then she picked up her knickers, lying on the floor at the side of the bed, held them with both hands, and ripped them.

"Hey," she heard him protest, voice booming dully. "I bought you those. . . ."

She put a finger to her mouth and shook her head.

She tore the delicate, perfumed material into two strips. She put one black band over his eyes, tying it behind his head so that he was made quite blind, and then she did the same to herself, so that in that shared but separate, self-created darkness, and surrounded by that distanced, heavy, undersea sound, they made love with only touch as their guide.

She was blind. Blind and surrounded by mushy, roaring noises, and she knew there were lights exploding all around. Some part of her wanted to find this funny, because she'd been in just this situation before not all that long ago, but she couldn't laugh.

Anyway, she couldn't indulge herself, she had the others to worry about. Worrying for all of them—that was her job.

Somebody was calling to her, quietly screaming her name.

Iron taste in mouth. Smell of burning. She felt another part of herself start bawling at her to wake up: Burning! Fire! Run! The roaring noise filled her head. Run!

But there wasn't anywhere to run to. She knew that.

There was something else to worry about, too, but apart from knowing it was important, she couldn't remember what it was.

The voice in her ears shouted her name. Why couldn't

they leave her in peace? Her head tipped forward; it felt terribly heavy and large. Still a smell of burning, acrid and sharp.

Her nose itched. She reached to scratch it, and her left arm suddenly turned into a pipe full of acid, gushing pain into her. She tried to cry out, but somehow she couldn't. She was choking.

She struggled to put her head back. Her helmet clunked hard against something that shouldn't have been there. Of course; she was wearing a helmet. But it didn't feel right.

"Sharrow!" screamed a tiny voice through the roaring.

"Yes, yes," she muttered, coughing and spitting. She accidentally tried to make a *be quiet* motion with her left arm, and the pain tore through her. This time she was able to shout.

She spat again. Noises tinkled and whined in her ears above the continual roaring and the voices shouting her name. At least she thought it was her name.

"Sharrow?" she heard herself say.

"Sharrow! Come in!—Was that her? Keep—! Miz!—debris!—from this range!—only water!—Are you crazy?"

What a lot of babbling, she said to herself, and could feel her brow furrowing as she thought, *Miz?* Didn't she have something she was supposed to tell him, some secret?

She tried to open her eyes. But she shouldn't even need to do that, should she?

She was exhausted. Her left arm wouldn't move, she felt incredibly heavy and cold, and there were lots of other pains and discomforts clamoring for her attention now, too.

"Sharrow! Fate, Shar. *Please* answer—wake up!"

Shut up, she told them. *Can't get any peace these days.* . . .

. . . They sailed through a tunnel. It was dark, but a little paper lantern glowed above them, and the air was sweet. He had joined her on the pillows, lean and hard and eager and gentle. They had lain together for a long time later, listening to the warm water gurgle beneath them and the tiny hum of the ship. . . .

The ship! Where was the ship? It should be here, all around her. She tried to shift in the hard, uncomfortable seat, but the pain in her arm came back. She heard herself cry out.

"Sharrow!" a voice said quite distinctly in her ears.

"Miz?" she said. It was his voice. She wondered why she was blind and the ship wasn't talking to her.

"Sharrow? Can you hear me?"

"Miz?" she said louder. Her mouth felt funny. The roaring in her ears pulsated away, heavy and insistent, like some too-quick surf pounding into her ears.

"Sharrow, *talk* to me!"

"All right!" she shouted angrily. Was the man deaf?

"Thank Fate! Listen, kid—what's your status?"

"Status?" she said, confused. "Don't know. What do you—?"

"Shit. Okay, you're spinning. First we've got to stop that. You've got to keep awake and stop the spin."

"Spin," she said. Spin? Was that something to do with the secret she'd been keeping from him? She made a determined effort to open her eyes. She thought they were open, but she still couldn't see anything.

She brought her right arm up; it was incredibly heavy. She tried to bring it to her face, but the arm wouldn't move very far. It fell back, crashing into something and hurting her.

She started to cry.

"Sharrow!" the voice said. "Keep it together, girl!"

"Don't call me *girl!*"

"I'll call you anything I fucking want until you get that ship leveled."

"Prick," she muttered. She pushed her head as far forward as she could and rammed her right arm up. Heavily gloved fingers thumped into her faceplate. It felt wrong: wrong shape, wrong place. Her nose hurt. Her arm was quivering with the effort of keeping it there against her helmet. She felt down to the helmet rim, took a deep breath, then pushed up.

Snap. She cried out with pain. Her nose burned; blood filled her mouth. Her arm crashed down into her lap.

But the ship was back; it was there around her. The lid-screens swam into focus while the ship's systems whispered and tingled and swarmed through her, filtering down through her awareness as the transceiver in her helmet spoke to the wafer-unit buried in the back of her skull. She felt around, looked at the lid-screens, and listened to the music of systems status, the roaring in her ears reduced to dull background.

She was a force at the core of sensation. It was like floating in the center of a huge sphere of color and movement and displayed symbols; a sphere made of in-holo'd screens, like windows to other dimensions, each one giving a summary of its state and singing a single note of song. She only had to look at one of those windows and will *shift* to be there, looking down onto the details of that landscape—itself often composed of more subwindows—all the rest of the screens reduced to a smear of color on the outskirts of her vision, where a flash of movement or an associated change in their harmonics would signal something needing her attention.

She floated in the middle of it all, taking stock.

"Fucking hell," she said. "What a mess."

"What?" Miz said in her ears.

"Got status," she said, looking around. The ship was a wreck. "Good fucking grief." What to do first?

"Reduce spin or you'll black out again," Miz said urgently.

"Oh, yes," she said. The spin was insane; she looked to the main tanks, but they were empty. The bow thrusts had some water left. She woke the motor up, swung it to operating temperature, and pushed the fuel through. Nothing happened.

Why wasn't the burn working?

Spinning too much. Wrong route. She closed off one valve, opened another; water hit the reaction chamber and plasma went bursting out from the ship's nose. Miz was shouting something, but she couldn't hear what he was saying. The weight got worse, and the roaring came back and became a noise like darkness.

She felt something snap.

Wrong way! she thought, vectoring the thrust right around.

The worst of the weight lifted slowly; the roaring went back to what it had been before and then gradually faded. Her body started to lift in the seat, pulling out of the squashed, crumpled attitude it had taken up. Give it ten more seconds. She opened her eyes. The inside of the faceplate was smeared with blood. She closed her eyes, sought out the suit-view in the lid-screen display, and shifted down into it.

The emergency controls gleamed in the backup lighting. No holos. The flattie status screens were blown or pulsing red.

She turned her head to the left.

The port instrument bulkhead had come to pay her couch a visit. It felt like the port-rear ceiling had had the same idea. That was what was stopping her head from going right back; probably what had nearly ripped her helmet off, too. Her seat had been half torn from its mountings by the impact, which had caught her left arm between the bulkhead and the armrest.

She stared. Could that really be her arm disappearing into all that mangled-up shit? She ignored the memory of the pain and pulled hard.

It was as though she'd slammed an ax into herself. Her head jerked around inside the helmet; she fought the scream, but it forced its way out of her throat anyway.

She blinked tears away. Her arm remained pinned.

So much for that idea.

She moved her head. Looked like her right arm wasn't in terribly good shape anymore, either. She tried to move it, but it wouldn't cooperate. Numb. "*Be* like that, then," she muttered, trying to sound unconcerned.

Physically brave, she told herself. *Physically brave.* That was the one accurate phrase she remembered from when she'd hacked into her service file (though it had been embedded among a load of nonsense about her being impatient and arrogant. How *dare* they?). *Physically brave.* Remember that.

She shifted out of helmet-view. The ship's bow tank drained, the pipes emptied, and the motor cut out. She reached to the main tanks, but of course, there was nothing there. The back-up tanks were dry, too. The ship was still spinning, but only once every eight seconds.

"You did it!" Miz shouted. Broadcasting on radio; the comm laser was dead.

She attempted to sort some sense out of the nav gear's gibberish and tried the ship's external sensors, but they came up fuzz-gray. The backups were out, too, apart from one nonholo camera in the bow, fixed staring straight ahead. All it showed were lots of nebulae, a glimpse of a white disc ahead with a reddish-golden disc behind it, then nebulae again, then the white-disc/red-gold disc combination again, and so on.

"Where the hell am I?" she said.

"Can't read you," Miz said. "Open the data channel."

"Only got input," she said. "It's open."

"Shit," he said. "Okay, here's what I have."

The nav gear started acting sensibly again. She was still on the Outside of Nachtel's Ghost, about a quarter second Inward from the engagement position, tumbling and twisting toward the moon.

"Right," she said. "Just let me get my bearings here. . . ."

The external view she had now—flagged as thousand magnification—showed a wrecked excise clipper spinning slowly in front of her, its black hull flayed and pitted, its rear end gone, ruptured plates fluting tumorously from the craft's waist to shred away to nothing from about three quarters of the way back, ending in a glinting mess of shining metal.

There was something biological, even sexual about the ruined ship, its matt black skin like dull clothes ripped apart to reveal the flesh beneath, exposed and open. She'd never seen a ship so badly damaged.

She thought, *Poor fucker—lift that driver's chow-bucket off its hook and send it back to Stores* . . . then realized that this was the view from Miz's ship; he was following her, and what she was looking at was her own craft. She was the unfortunate pilot she'd been consigning to oblivion.

She selected trajectory forecast while she looked at the doc window. The medical unit seemed to have given up on her. Then she remembered where the doc's tubes plugged into her. She shifted back to helmet-view, staring at where her left forearm disappeared between the bulging instrument bulkhead and the seat armrest; the gap was about three centimeters. *Hmm*, she thought.

She shifted back to nav; she was heading straight for Nachtel's Ghost. The icy little world was still nearly a tenth of a light-second away, and it would take her the best part of an hour to get there, but she was going to go right down the throat of the gravity well. Even if she could miss Nachtel's Ghost, she'd be pointing at Nachtel itself, with no way to miss it; seen from its barely habitable moon, the gas giant filled half the sky. She'd have to slingshot.

Instinctively, she reached again for the main tanks.

"Shit," she said.

She glanced at the group-status holo, which had been part of the squirt Miz had sent. "Miz!" she shouted. "The others!"

"Vleit and Frot are dead," Miz said quickly. "Zef's chasing Cara but getting no reply. Kid, there's nothing you can—"

"You've got damage, too!" she said.

"Yeah, some laser-work from the cruiser and ice abrasion from that water-screen you left behind when you got zapped—"

"Miz," she whispered, "are—?"

"I'm sure, Sharrow," Miz said, his voice thick. "Dead and gone. Probably never knew what hit them."

"How did they *do* this to us?" she said.

"I don't know," Miz said wearily. "Cenuij wants to call War Crime on that engagement; says nobody reacts that fast and there must have been an AI in charge. I think we just got outlucked. Cruiser took some damage and flared home—now *forget about the engagement*! Have you any reaction mass? We have to get you into orbit around the Ghost."

She'd shifted into life support. "No point," she said. "The recycler's wrecked, and I'm losing gas. I've enough to breathe for about . . . two hours, then that's it."

"That suit or cabin?"

"Suit. Cabin's got less; pressure leak."

"Shit," Miz said. She could almost hear him thinking. "The doc," he said. "It could floor your metabolism and—"

"The doc," she said, "is fucked."

"Damn," he said. It was such a mild curse, she almost laughed. "Could you bail out?" he asked her. "I could match with you. You could zap across . . . or I could get over to you. . . ."

"I don't think there's quite the time," she said. She glanced into suit-view and looked briefly at her one trapped and one . . . broken? dislocated? arm. "There might be other problems with that approach, anyhow."

"What about reaction mass?"

She glanced around. "Nothing."

"Come on! There must be something! Check!"

She initiated a checking routine and looked carefully at

each tank glyph in turn. The check routine said zero everywhere and staying that way. Her own senses told her the same thing. She tried blipping the feed from each tank in turn, just in case there was water there and it was a sensor or display fault.

"Nothing," she said. "Displaying empty, acting empty."

"Think think think," she heard Miz mutter. She suspected he hadn't meant her to hear that, or had simply been unaware he was speaking. Suddenly she wanted to hold him and started to cry again. She did it quietly, so he wouldn't hear.

"This might sound mad," he said. "But I could use my laser. Hit you in the right place, get some reaction that way. . . ."

"It does sound mad," she said.

"There's got to be something!" She could hear the desperation in his voice.

"Hey," she said. "Want to hear another crazy idea?"

"Anything."

"Crash-land on the Ghost."

"What?"

"Cruise in and crash-land, like a plane."

"You haven't got any wings!"

"I've got a shape that looks vaguely aerodynamic; bit like the end of a spiked gun. And there's the snowfields."

"*What?*"

"The snowfields," she said. "They're hundreds of meters deep on the Ghost, in places—lo-grav. And there's *air.*"

"Pretty thin air."

"Getting thinner all the time," she agreed. "Unbreathable in another thousand years; crap terraforming . . . but it's there."

"But how you going to *fly?*"

"Oh, I can't," she said, taking another look around the ship's systems from the highest level. What a total fucking mess. If this was a simulation, she'd be clicking out now and hitting Replay to go back to just before it had all gone so horribly wrong, and try again.

"It was just an idea," she told him. "I used to wake up in the night and try to think up ways out of horrible situations to get me back to sleep, and one idea I had was using the Ghost's snowfields to crash-land on." She sighed. "But I always imagined I'd have some control as I went in."

She shook her head at the unsavable mess around her and swooped back into close-range nav view. "I think I'm dead, Miz." She listened to her own voice and was amazed at how cool she sounded. *Physically brave.*

"Forget it. I'll run that idea of the crash-land past the machine; see what it thinks."

"Aw, don't spoil my fun," she said. "I never even ran it through mine. . . ."

"Fucking hell," she heard him say after a while. "My machine's as crazy as you."

"It says it'll work?"

"Um, three-quarters empty mass . . . drag . . . need details of the snow compression; depth it becomes ice . . . depends on the angle . . . no; the machine's not quite as crazy as you. And you'd need some fine-tuning, in-atmosphere, at the start anyway. . . ."

"Run an insertion past the machine, anyway," she said.

"Running it."

"At least it'd be spectacular," she said. "Burning up in the atmosphere or slamming into the snow. Better than hazing out from oxygen starvation."

"Don't talk like that! . . . *Shit*, there must be something . . ."

She had remembered some time ago what the secret was. "Hey," she said gently. "Miz?"

"What?"

"Pick a number between one and two."

"*What?*"

"Pick a whole number between one and two. Please."

"Oh . . . one," he said. She smiled sadly. "*Well?*" he said.

He said it the way he had when she'd got him to toss the coin outside the Bistro Onomatopoeia, a week earlier.

She shook her head, even though it hurt and he couldn't see.

"Nothing," she said. "Tell you later." She shifted back to the doc, down into the external readouts. Cabin cold, external air poor, and pressure falling. Aggregate radiation dosage . . . Oh, well. She felt herself shrug and grimaced as her left arm protested. She was going to die, anyway; she wouldn't live long enough to experience the radiation sickness. *And I'd have made a lousy mother anyway*, she told herself.

She kept wanting to press Replay, to snap out of this disastrous simulation and start again, or just break the link and go for a drink with the guys. It didn't feel right that she was trapped in this situation as firmly as she was trapped in the seat, pinned there by the weight of circumstance and chance.

At first, when she'd joined up, she'd thought she could never be one of the dead ones. She told herself they must have made a mistake, and she just wasn't going to.

Later she'd started to get scared sometimes, when pilots she'd thought even better than she had died. Had she been wrong about how good they were, or wrong about skill saving you every time? Maybe it didn't. Maybe luck did come into it. And that made it frightening, because nobody knew how to train for that. You carried a lucky tooth or a special letter or always made sure you were last out of the mess; she'd known people who did that sort of thing. . . . A lot of them were dead, too.

"Look," Miz said, "I'm still catching up with you; I'll match velocities. I'll get over to you. It can't take—"

"Miz," she said, quieting him. "No." She let out a long, ragged sigh. "I'm trapped in here. I'd have to be cut out."

"Oh, shit," he groaned.

The way he said it, she knew he was talking about something else. "What?" she said.

"You don't need that much to take you into the Ghost's atmosphere at the right angle," he said. "Just a nudge, a few seconds' burst . . . Hey!" His voice brightened again. "*I'll* nudge you! I'll just fly alongside and—"

"Forget it—you'll just break your own ship."

"Look, if we can't think of anything—"

"Wait," she said.

"What?"

She reached into the ship's plumbing, found no readout for the relevant section of pipe, but the record of valves shut . . .

"Hey," she said. "You know I put the thrust the wrong way at first, made the spin worse?"

"Yeah?"

"I got confused because before that I tried sending the water around the loop against the spin."

"So?"

"So there might be water in the closed section of loop."

"Isn't it showing?"

"No readout."

"Shit," he said. "There *might* be some in there."

"Yes, and it might be frozen," she said, shifting into the ship's patchy temperature map.

"Hold on," he said. "I'll run it through. . . ." His voice went away. She was left alone for a few moments.

She'd always expected to be reliving her life at this point, but it didn't seem to be happening. She felt cold and battered and tired. This combat flying lark was supposed to have been just a little exotic incident in her life, something to tell people about when she was old. It had never been meant to get this important, never been planned to be this crucial and ghastly and hopeless. It *certainly* wasn't supposed to be the end of everything. It *couldn't* all just end, could it?

Yes it could, she thought. Somehow she'd never really thought about it before, but yes; of course it could. She didn't just accept it now; she *knew* it now. What a time to learn that particular lesson.

"Yeah!" Miz hollered. "If it's there, there's enough!"

"Well," she said. "We won't know until we try."

"But you've got reaction mass!" he yelled. "You can do it!"

"Two minutes ago you were telling me I was crazy to even think about this; now suddenly it's a great idea."

"It's a chance, kid," he said, quieter. There was something else in his voice, too: the equivalent of one arm holding some surprise behind his back, and a sly smile on his face.

"And?" she said.

"I just ran a routine for your in-atmosphere control."

"Using your astonishing powers of laser control, you will fashion a pair of crude but serviceable wings from—"

"Quiet, smart-ass. Dig down to the clip's nonmil suite."

"Pardon? Oh, all right." She shifted down the systems root to the clipper's full display. What was this heap of civilian shit meant to do? Was he just trying to distract her?

"See the gyros?"

"*Gyros?* No."

"Labeled FTU-one and -two—Fine Trimming Units."

"Yes," she said. "Well, the bow cluster, anyway. Shit, I thought those were stripped when these boats were militarized."

"They never got around to it," Miz told her. "Now, can you get power to that bow cluster?"

"Yes. But wouldn't it be better—?"

"No. It doesn't matter that you're tumbling on insertion if we get the burn timed right, and you might need all the maneuvering power in those gyros."

"All right, all right," she said. "They're taking power."

"Okay!" he yelled. "We'll rework the figures when we're closer. Now, I'm going to try to match velocities; that should make things more accurate. Get ready for some *incredibly* skillful flying on the part of the Tech King, and then be ready to read out lots and lots of exciting numbers once I'm alongside, unless you can get the output comm link sorted."

"Can't wait," she said, the tiredness tingling through her. She just wanted to sleep. She forgot about her left arm for a second and tried to stretch.

She cut off the shout of pain as fast as she could.

"What?" Miz's voice said quickly.

She breathed hard a couple of times.

"I just remembered I paid my mess bill yesterday," she lied.

"Wow." Miz laughed. "You really *do* tempt fate, don't you?"

"Yes," she said. "It must be male."

"That's more like it," he said. "Okay—let's see if I can get this thing spinning and twisting like yours. . . ."

"Okay," he said, and she could hear the fear in his voice. "Here we go, kid."

They had talked it through for the last half hour; she'd given him all the data she could, he'd run it past his machine dozens of times, and every time it came out Maybe. She'd got the gyros up to speed, braked each one in turn, and the ship had responded. She'd settled on a routine that would let her use the gyros to control the ship during its descent through the atmosphere of Nachtel's Ghost.

They'd done a tenth-second burst from the pipes into the reaction chamber and got power; there was water in the pipe, and it wasn't frozen. They'd got a recent snowfield map of the Ghost from their base via Dloan, who was escorting Cenuij's damaged craft back there; they'd selected a big snowfield on the equator. Miz had shown her the view he had of her ship, perfectly parallel with his own and slowly rolling while the rest of the system revolved around it. She'd complimented him on his flying and tried not to look too closely at the damage.

But now he had to move away, and she had to make that last burn, hoping the water in the pipe-work would be enough, and it hadn't frozen somewhere farther up the duct, and that the pump would work, and that the power didn't fail, or even fluctuate.

"You take care now," she said.

"Don't worry," he told her. "Thirty seconds."

"Me, worry?" she said, trying not to let him hear the fear and pain in her voice. She was finding it more of a strain now. Her arm was hurting really badly, and she was frightened. She wanted to tell Miz that there was a precedent for all this, that when she'd been five years old she'd been saved by a fall into the snow, but she had never been able to tell him that full story, and he had never pressed her for it. She wanted to tell him she loved him and she was pregnant by him, but she couldn't tell him any of that, either.

"Look, ah . . . kid," he said (and she just knew he'd be grimacing now, and that if he hadn't had the helmet on, he'd be scratching the side of his head). "I know there's . . . you know—things we haven't said during the last few months. I mean, me and you, since we've been, you know, well, together, but—"

"You're making a complete mess of this, Miz," she told him, her voice matter-of-fact while her eyes filled with tears. "Don't say anything else now. Tell me later. Ten seconds."

He was silent for six of them.

Eventually he said, "Good luck, Sharrow."

She was still thinking what to say in reply when she opened the valve, the motor roared in the distance, and she had to devote all her attention to the attitude and heading readings. She shifted to the view through the one little flat-tie camera in the craft's nose.

The planet came up to meet her, a curved white wall. The ship encountered the atmosphere's outer layers. She tried the radio and heard interference. "Miz?" she said.

". . . ust hear y—"

She shouted, "If this goes badly and I make a *crater*, I want it named after *me*!"

If he replied, she never heard him.

The falling ship plowed deeper into the planet's atmosphere and began to judder and moan.

The five of them sat on the tavern terrace a little outside Pharpech city, she with her memories.

The others watched the huge stom as it wheeled and banked above the deep country a kilometer east of the tavern, beating back up toward the middle layer of Entraxrln membrane it had cruised down from earlier. The monkeyeater birds mobbed it, stooping at its back and head in great plummeting circles, turning quickly this way and that, zigzagging erratically, unpredictably, wings like jagged hooks in the air. The stom, four times the size of the monkey-eaters, moved with a ponderous grace that approached dignity, as it ducked its massive reptilian head and took what ponderous, almost gentle evasive action it was able to.

"Come on, baby," Zefla said. Sharrow had handed her the binoculars; Miz watched through another pair of field glasses.

"Put some effort in there," Miz muttered.

Sparrow looked at Dłoan, squinting in the same direction. His hands gripped the bark rail of the tavern porch, squeezing and releasing unconsciously.

She watched the stom as it struggled higher in the air, still beset by the scrappy, mobbing shapes of the monkeyeaters.

One of them was still falling.

The four of them had come out here for dinner at an inn called The Pulled Nail on the outskirts of the town after a day spent sight-seeing. Cenuij hadn't been in touch since they'd left him at the door of the monastery hospitale the night before; he was supposed to be trying to get an audience with the king. He would leave word at the inn if he had anything to report.

Pharpech in daylight hadn't looked so bad. The people seemed friendly enough, though their accent was difficult to understand, and they had decided halfway through the day that they'd buy local clothes tomorrow; theirs made them too conspicuous, and people tended to ask them—in those strange accents, and with a hint of incredulity—what had possessed them to come to a place like Pharpech.

One of the things she'd found it hard to get used to was how difficult it was to access information. All it really meant, most of the time, was that you had to resort to rather obvious methods like asking people directions, or what a certain building was; nevertheless, it was unsettling, and despite all her supposed maturity and sophistication, she had the unnerving feeling that she was a child again, trapped in a baffling world of mysterious intent and arcane significance, forever making guesses at how it all worked but never knowing exactly the right questions to ask.

The first thing they'd done, on the advice of their two guides who were setting off back to the border that morning, was take their jemer mounts to a stable on the outskirts of town, where they sold the creatures—after much haggling on Miz's part—for slightly more than they'd paid for them. Then they became tourists for the day.

They had seen the great square in daylight, its flat, mostly unroofed buildings crowded around the sloped paving stones like a strange rectangular crowd of people, all squashed up shoulder to shoulder, grimly determined not to miss whatever was going on in the square (and yet most of them were gaily painted and awninged, hiding little workshops and stalls like shiny shoes peeking out from under the just-raised skirts of their canopies).

They had found the people fairly fascinating, too. A few of them rode on jemers, though most were on foot like them, the crowding majority of them colorfully if simply dressed, but—apart from their almost invariably pale skin—far more physically varied than they were used to: very fat people, unhealthily gaunt people, people in dirty rags, people with deformities . . .

They had viewed the castle from the outside: three stone stories that looked planned and passing symmetrical, topped by a ramshackle excrescence of Entraxrln timber stacked and tacked and piled and leaning to produce a vertical warren of apartments, halls, and the occasional grudged-looking concession to defense in the shape of gawky, teetering towers and forlorn stretches of battlement, all of it dotted randomly with windows and protrusions and capped by a few creaky towers pointing uncertainly toward the layers of leaf-membrane above as though in puzzled inquiry.

The rest of the town had been confusing, repetitive, occasionally riotous. The cathedral was small and disappointing; even its bell, which rang out each hour, sounded flat. The only really interesting feature the cathedral possessed was a stone statue of the Pharpechian God on the outside of the building, having various unpleasant things done to Him by small, fiendishly grinning Pharpechian figures armed with farming implements and instruments of torture.

They had walked the narrow streets, tramping up and down narrow lanes and twisting alleys, dodging water thrown from upstairs windows, treading in rotting vegetables and worse. They had continually found themselves back where they had started and often been followed by crowds of children—so many children!—and sometimes adults, many of whom seemed to want to take them home or show them around personally. Zefla smiled generously at the more persistent protoguides and talked quickly in High Judicial Caltaspian to them, usually leaving them bobbing in her wake, looking beatifically bemused.

By lunchtime they were exhausted. They returned to the inn, then kept to the outskirts of the town in the afternoon, passing the high walls of various monasteries and prisons, a school, and a hospital. The monastery hospitale where Cenuij had been given a bed for the night looked closed and deserted, though they could hear muted curse-singing over the high walls.

They found the royal zoo; a sad moldering of cages and pits where sick animals paced to and fro or threw themselves at fire-hardened bars, snarling. A glide-monkey troupe huddled in a corner of their net-roofed pit, their connective limb membranes wrapped around them like cloaks, their large eyes peeking out fearfully. A tangle-tooth paced back and forward in a small cage, head down, its emaciated body containing in its movements only an echo of the animal's lithe power. One huge, bare cage contained a full-grown stom, sitting crouched by one wall, its wings tied and splinted, its snout and legs scarred and cut. Even while they watched, appalled at the size of the animal and the painful squalidness of its situation, the beast raised its meter-long head and hit it off the wall a few times, drawing dark purple blood.

"Why is its wing splinted?" Zefla asked a zookeeper.

"Not exactly splinted, lady—more tied up," the keeper replied. He carried a bucket full of something bloody and gently steaming. Sharrow wrinkled her nose and moved up wind. The keeper shook his head and looked serious. "See, she just roars and beats her wings against the bars of the cage all day if you don't tie her up."

They didn't stay long in the royal zoo.

The town became farmland quite suddenly, the streets leading past the various walled institutions straight into fields, where the membrane-beds stretched like neat lines of straked, fresh wounds into the distance and the serried plants of the Entraxrln's secondary or tertiary ecology sat troughed and still. A field-guard recommended the tavern, a kilometer away along one of the raised, scar-tissue roads.

They sat on the terrace of The Pulled Nail, eating surprisingly subtly cooked meats and vegetables; then Dloan pointed out the stom as it flew down the dulling light of the evening from a distant gap in the second-highest membrane level; the beast turned, carving the air, heading for a composite trunk and the specks of a glide-monkey troupe. But the monkey-eater birds roosting farther up the trunk-space had seen the reptile and stooped, their cries faint but furious through the still air, and began to mob the single black giant. It had turned, something resigned but almost amused about its delicately lumbering, slow-motion movements, a calm core of stolidity set among the jerky whizzings of the monkey-eaters, electrons to its weighty nucleus.

She supposed they were what people saw as noble beasts, something of their perceived authority evident in the fact that they were one of the few species of Miykennsian fauna that had an original name, rather than a Golterian fix-up.

She could feel the others wanting the stom to escape unharmed, as it surely would, but only she, she thought, had seen the tiny gray-green scrap of one monkey-eater fly too close to the head of the stom; she'd had Zefla's binoculars, and seen the bird skim daringly close to that huge head, and had a fleeting impression of the snapping jaws closing on it, wounding it, winging it as the bird was pulled off course across the air before escaping in a small, brief cloud of gray-green and starting to fall.

It was falling still.

She could still just see it, naked-eyed now.

It was spiraling quickly down, five hundred meters beneath where it had been savaged, still trying to fly but only managing a half-braked helical dive toward the ground below.

Above it, just behind it, matching its hopeless, graceless, desperate tumble with a more controlled and smooth spiral of its own, another bird was keeping close station, refusing to leave its fellow.

She followed them both. The two dots were soon lost in the groundscape of undulating membrane matting in the distance. When she looked up again, the stom had made it back through the gap in the leaf-membrane a kilometer above. The other monkey-eaters gave up the chase, and Miz, Zef, and Dlo made appreciative noises and sat down to their meal again.

She sat down, too, after a while.

She ate her meal slowly, not joining in the conversation, often glancing at the region where the two birds had disappeared, and only took a drink of her wine when one bird reappeared, flying slowly, as though tired, flapping effortfully upward, toward the columnar colony that was its home, alone.

13

At the Court
of the
Useless Kings

His Majesty King Tard the Seventeenth, Lord of Despite, Seventy-fourth of the Useless Kings, Lord Pro-
tector and Master of Pharpech, its Dominions, Citizens,
Lower Classes, Animals and Women, Prime Detester of God
the Infernal Wizard, Exchequer of the Mean, and Guardian
of the Imperial Charter, sat on the Stom Throne in the castle's Great Hall, squinting narrow-eyed at the skinny, suspiciously clever-looking monk kneeling on the throne steps in
front of him.

The throne room was a dark and smoky place. It was
devoid of windows so that God couldn't see in, and it stank
of cloying scents emanating from smoking censers because
that kept His unquiet spirit entering. The throne was at one
end of the room, and the king's dozen or so courtiers and
secretaries sat on small stools stationed on the steps of the
throne's square dais, their stature and significance expressed
by how far up the dais steps and how close to the royal presence they were allowed to sit.

The Stom Throne—carved in the shape of one of the
great flying reptiles, its wings forming the sides of the
throne, its back and seat, and its bowed head functioning as
a footrest—swung gently in the air above the dais, hanging
by wires from the incense-blackened barrel-ceiling of the

room and held just a few centimeters off the time-dulled and threadbare carpet spread across the top of the dais.

His courtiers said the throne was suspended like this to symbolize his authority and elevation above the common herd, but he just liked the way you could make the throne swing if you rocked back and forward a lot. Two very large, quiet Royal Guardsmen stood on the broad tail of the Stom Throne, armed with laser carbines disguised as muskets; sometimes he'd get them to join in the swinging. If you got people to kneel close to the throne and then started to swing while they were talking, you could get the big carved beak of the Stom Throne to thump them in the chest or head and make them retreat off the dais, where officially he didn't have to listen to them. He was thinking about doing that to this monk.

It was unusual for this sort of person to be presented to him; usually his courtiers kept them out. He always got suspicious of his courtiers when they did something out of character. He knew that—naturally—they feared and respected him, but sometimes he thought they wouldn't be beyond talking behind his back or having little plans of their own.

Anyway, he didn't like the monk's face. There was something too narrow and sharp and penetrating about it, and there was a look of amused contempt about his expression that suggested he found the king or his Kingdom ridiculous. He distrusted the monk instantly. People had died for less. A lot less.

One of his courtiers mumbled into his ear about the monk's mission. The king was mildly surprised by what he was told, but still suspicious.

"So," he said to the monk, "you are of an Order which also despises the Great Infernal Wizard."

"Indeed, Your Gracious Majesty," the monk said, looking down modestly at the carpet. His voice sounded respectful. "Our Belief—perhaps not so dissimilar from your own more venerable and more widely followed creed—is that God is a Mad Scientist and we His experimental subjects, doomed forever to run the Maze of Life through apparently random and unjust punishments for meaningless and paltry rewards and no discernible good reason save His evil pleasure."

The king stared at the skinny monk. The man's accent

was off-putting and his language complicated, but he had the odd impression that the monk had actually been complimentary just there. He leaned forward in the gently swinging throne.

"D'you hate God, too?" he said, wrinkling his nose and frowning.

The skinny monk, clad in a black cassock embellished only with a small metal box tied on a thong around his neck, smiled in an odd way and said, "Yes, Your Majesty. We do, with a vengeance."

"Good," the king said. He sat back and studied the skinny monk. The monk glanced at the courtier who'd briefed the king, but the courtier kept shaking his head. One did not speak to the king until one was spoken to.

The king prided himself on being something of a statesman; he knew the value of having allies, even though the kingdom itself was quite self-sufficient and under no immediate external threat. There were bandits and rebels in the deep country, as ever, and the usual closet reformers in the Kingdom and even the court, but the king knew how to deal with them: you asked a courtier and got him to check how they'd been dealt with in the past. Still, times changed on the outside even if they didn't change here, and it never did any harm to have people in the world beyond who sympathized with Pharpech, and it had always annoyed the king that so few people out there seemed to have heard of his realm.

He'd quiz this monk. "How many of there are you?"

"Here in your realm, Your Majesty? Only myself, of our Order—"

He shook his head. "No, everywhere. How many of you altogether?"

The skinny monk looked sad. "We number only a few thousand at the moment, Your Majesty," he admitted. "Though many of us are in positions of some power where we must, of course, keep our beliefs secret."

"Hmm," said the king. "Who's your leader?"

"Majesty," the monk said, looking troubled, "we have no leader. We have a parliament, a gathering of equals in which each man is his own high priest, and in that lies our problem." The skinny monk looked up and smiled with more warmth. "You see, Your Majesty, I have come humbly, on behalf of all my fellows, to petition you to become our spiritual leader."

Petitions petitions petitions. The king was heartily sick of petitions. But at least this one was from outside the Kingdom, from people who didn't owe him everything, anyway, and so had a damn cheek petitioning him for anything. . . . No, this came from people who were doing it because of their respect for him and what he represented. He rather liked the idea.

"Spiritual leader?" he said, trying not to sound too taken with the title.

"Yes, Your Majesty," said the skinny monk. "We seek your approval of our humble creed because you are the head of a like-minded faith that has survived for many centuries, and so gives us hope. We wish to ask for your blessing, and—if you would be so kind as to grant it—for the ultimate blessing of you becoming head of our church. We would undertake to do nothing to disgrace your name, and to do everything to help honor the name of yourself and the Kingdom of Pharpech." The monk looked touchingly modest. "Majesty, please believe we do not wish to impose upon your renowned good nature and generosity, but such is our heartfelt respect for you, and so great is our desire to gain your approval—undeserving wretches though we may be— that we felt we would be derelict in our duties to our faith if we did not approach you."

The king looked confused. He didn't want to give his blessing to people who were undeserving wretches. He had enough of those already.

"What?" he said. "You're saying *you're* undeserving wretches?"

The skinny monk looked uncertain for a second, then bowed his head. "Only compared to you, Your Majesty. Compared to the unbelievers, we are the deserving and enlightened. As the saying has it, modesty is most effective when it is uncalled for." The skinny monk smiled up at him again. His eyes looked moist.

The king didn't quite understand that last remark— probably due to the skinny monk's odd accent—but he knew the little fellow thought he'd said something mildly witty, and so made a little polite laughing noise and looked around at his courtiers, nodding at them, so that they laughed and nodded at each other too. The king prided himself on being able to put people at their ease in this manner.

"Good monk," he said, sitting back in the Stom Throne and adjusting his day-robe around him as the great throne swung gently, "I am minded to accept your humble request." The king smiled. "We shall talk further, I think." He put on his wise expression, and the skinny monk looked almost pathetically pleased. He wiped his eyes with the backs of his hands.

How touching! the king thought.

He waved one hand graciously to the side, making a curl in the thick incense smoke. He indicated a couple of clerks standing to one side, holding cushions on which sat large flattish objects, ornate metal boxes. "Now, I understand you have brought Us some *presents*. . . ."

"Indeed, Your Majesty," the skinny monk said, glancing around as the clerks came shuffling forward. They stood in a line at his side. He took the box from the first of the clerks and held it up to the king. It looked like a larger version of the little box on the thong around his neck. "It is a book, Your Majesty." He fiddled with the lock on the metallic box.

"A *book*?" the king said. He sat forward in the throne, gripping the edges of the Stom's wings. He *hated* books. "A *book*?" he roared. His courtiers knew he hated books! How could they let this simpering cur come before him if they knew he'd come bearing *books*? He looked furiously at the nearest courtiers. Their expressions changed instantly from smirking satisfaction to shocked outrage.

"But it is God's book, Your Majesty!" the skinny monk whined, jaw trembling as his thin hands struggled to open the book's jeweled metal casing.

"*God's* book?" the king bellowed, standing up in the Stom Throne. This was . . . what was it called? Sacrilege! The great throne swung to and fro while the king glared down at the hapless monk. "Did you say *God's book*?" he shouted. He raised his hand to order the heretical . . . heretic be taken away.

"Yes, Your Majesty," the monk said, suddenly pulling the book apart, pages riffling. "Because it is *blank*!"

He held the book up before him like a shield, face turned away from the king's wrath, while the flittering white pages fell fanning apart.

The king glanced around at his courtiers. They looked surprised and angry. He was aware that he was standing up in the swinging throne, in a position that might make a lesser man look a fool.

He thought quickly. Then he realized that it was quite funny. He started to laugh. He sat down in his throne, laughing, and looked around at his courtiers, until they started to laugh, too.

"What, good monk? Are they *all* blank?"

"Yes, Your Majesty!" the skinny monk said, gulping, laying the first book down and taking up the next from the second clerk. "See!" He put that one down, lifted the next and the next and the last. "See, Your Majesty! See, see—all blank! And look: the pages themselves are too slick and shiny to be written upon; no ink pen will write, and even lasers will simply reflect. They cannot even be used as blank notebooks. They are truly Useless books!"

"What?" shouted the king. He put his head back and roared with laughter. "Useless!" he shouted, lying back in the Stom Throne and laughing so much that his sides ached. "Useless!"

He laughed until he started to cough. He waved away a courtier holding a glass of wine and sat forward in the throne, smiling kindly down at the monk.

"You are a good fellow, little monk, and a credit to your Order. You may stay as Our guest, and we shall have more to say to each other." Intensely pleased at having successfully completed such an elegant speech, the king snapped his fingers at a secretary, who scurried forward, pen and pad at the ready, his head bowed. "See Our little monk is made welcome," the king told him. "Find good apartments for him."

"Yes, Your Majesty."

The secretary led the relieved monk away. The king inspected the shiny-paged books. He chuckled and ordered them to be put with the smaller Useless items in the castle's trophy gallery.

"Shit," said Cenuij, sitting on the bed in Miz and Dloan's room, staring at the little stick-on screen Miz had unrolled onto the covers. It showed a ghostly view of a glass display cabinet containing a collection of old-fashioned electrical goods.

"Looks like a shop-window display from a historical drama," Miz said. He rotated the night-sight view that the fake jewel on the cover of the book was seeing, but all it showed was more useless kitchen hardware.

"Safe to broadcast this?" Dloan said, peering at the screen.

Miz shrugged. "It's pseudo-directional after the initiating squirt and the transmitter's freq-hopping. I doubt they have stuff to pick this up, even if they're not quite as lo-tech as they pretend to be."

"I trust this works on the same principle," Cenuij said, holding up the miniature book on the thong around his neck. Beneath the rags he'd worn to make his way to The Broken Neck, he wore the plain black habit he'd dressed in since they'd entered the kingdom.

"Yeah," Miz said, "but don't use it except in an emergency, just in case." He tried the sonic display from another jewel set into the cover of the bugged book in the castle, but all it showed in the screen was a mono holo of the interior of a small display case. The last fake jewel, an electrical field sensor, registered nothing, not even any activity in the electrical gear around it. Obviously any backup power sources they'd ever had had run out long ago.

"Nothing," Miz said, clicking the screen off.

"I thought he'd put them in with the one other book he had," Cenuij admitted. He shrugged. "Oh well, they got me into the castle. And His Majesty's confidence."

"Fun in there?" Zefla asked, pouring herself and the others a drink.

Cenuij waved one arm. "Stacked to the rafters with treasure, trash, petty jealousies, pathetic plots, superstition, and suspicion," he said.

"You must feel at home, Cenuij," Sharrow said.

"Absolutely," he agreed. "I'm not missing you at all."

"Had a chance to look for the book yet?" Miz asked.

"Give me time," Cenuij said, annoyed. "I've only been there two days; it's a little early to start inquiring about the castle treasures. So far I've met the king once, the queen and a couple of *extremely* unpleasant children far too often already, and I've had to hang out with a bunch of vapidly vicious courtiers and cretinously religious functionaries. The unholy life in Pharpech appears to consist largely of rising at an extremely early hour and chanting curses to God in drafty chapels between profoundly uninspiring meals and bouts of gossip whose mind-boggling pettiness is rivaled only by its poisonous malevolence.

"So far all I've discovered about the castle vaults is their approximate location. I suspect they're higher-tech than the rest of this squalid retro theme park, but I don't know any more yet." Cenuij drank quickly from his wine mug. "So what have you tourists been up to, while I've been infiltrating the very heart of the kingdom and winning the confidence of its most powerful inhabitant, at no small risk to myself?"

"Oh, just farting around." Miz grinned.

"We checked the weapons and stuff," Dloan said.

"We burned the extra hollow pages from the Useless books," Zefla said, "eventually."

"Miz has identified the place the local criminal fraternity whiles away those long hours between acts of villainy," Sharrow said. "Dloan is planning a journey into the deep country to make contact with the rebels, and Zefla and I are making discreet inquiries about the various artisan, merchant-class, and women's-rights reform movements."

"Oh well, at least you're keeping yourselves *busy*," Cenuij said. He smiled.

"It passes the time while you're doing all the work, Cenny," Sharrow told him.

The cathedral clock chimed flatly in the distance. Cenuij drained his wine mug. "Quite. Well, that's the hour for evensong; time to go and sing God's hatreds. I'd better get back and carry on doing all that work, hadn't I?" He handed Sharrow the mug. "Thanks for the wine."

"Don't mention it."

The thief swung into the booth, through the floor-length dirty curtains and down into the trestle bench across from Miz. The noise of the smoky inn abated only slightly as the heavy curtains swung back. A couple of yellow-glowing candles, one on each of the narrow booth's side walls, flickered in the draft.

The thief was small for a Miykennsian. Dressed in dark, undistinguished clothes, he had a beard, several facial scars on his pale skin, and greasy hair. His nose was wide, the nostrils flared above lips set in a sneer. His eyes were deepset, hidden.

"You wanted to see me, Golter-man?" His voice was quiet and hoarse, but there was a strange smoothness about it that reminded Miz of a razor applied to flesh—the way it slipped in, without pain at first, almost unnoticed.

Miz sat back, holding his tankard of mullbeer. "Yes," he said. He nodded at the table. "Would you like a drink?"

The thief's lips briefly shaped themselves into a smile. "I've one coming; why don't you pay for it?"

"All right." Miz sipped at his drink, saw the thief watching him with his contemptuous sneer, then opened his throat, sank about half the beer, and set the tankard down with a thump on the rough wooden table. He wiped his lips with his sleeve for good measure.

The man sitting on the other side of the table didn't look impressed. The curtain opened behind him; he turned and grabbed the wrist of the serving girl who came through, grinning at her as she put the bottle and cup down on the table. She smiled nervously back.

The thief turned to Miz. "Well, pay the girl."

Miz dug into the pocket of his jerkin and handed the girl some coins. She gaped at what he'd given her, then tried to close her hand and turn quickly away.

The thief still held her wrist; he yanked her so that she fell back against the table. She gave a small cry of pain. The thief pried open her fingers and lifted out the money Miz had given her. He looked at the coins and seemed surprised. He took two of them, reached up and slipped them both down the girl's bodice, then pushed her upright and slapped her behind as he propelled her out of the booth. He bit on a coin, then put it and the rest away in his dark tunic.

"You overtipped," he said, breaking the seal on the bottle and pouring some of the trax spirit into the little bark cup.

"Yeah," Miz said. "What with that and this old-fashioned courtesy displayed to womenfolk, I'm finding it really hard to fit in here."

The thief drank from the cup, watching Miz over the rim. His throat moved as he swallowed. He refilled the cup. "I heard Golter men hand their women their cocks to keep when they take up with them."

"Only the lucky ones," Miz said. The thief looked levelly at him. Miz shrugged, spread his hands. "You didn't hear *where* they keep them."

The thief drank the second cup of trax, then flicked the last of the spirit out onto the rough tabletop. He spat into the little cup, wiped around the bowl with the hem of his hide waistcoat, then leaned across the table to Miz, holding up the cup in his hands as though it were some jewel. "Drink?" he said, putting his other hand on the bottle.

Miz shoved the tankard over to the other man, took the bark cup, and let the other man fill it. Miz knocked the trax back in one go. It was rough; he tried not to cough. The thief drained the tankard, then leaned back, stuck his head out through the curtain, and shouted something.

The serving girl came back through the curtain with another cup and two tankards full of beer. She looked at the thief, who looked at Miz.

Miz said, "Oh, no, please, allow *me*," and dug for more coins in his jerkin.

He paid the girl roughly what the thief had let her keep the last time. She still looked pleased.

Miz supped his beer. "I might be interested in exporting some ethnic artifacts," he told the thief.

"Apply to the castle," the thief told him.

Miz shrugged. "The ethnic artifacts I'm interested in"— Miz put his head to one side, looking up at the ceiling beyond the open-roofed booth—"aren't actually for sale. But I'd pay a good price to somebody who might help me come into possession of them."

The thief swirled his beer around in his tankard. "What things are you talking about? Where are they?"

"Could be almost anything," Miz said. "Some of them"—he imitated the thief, swirling his beer around in his tankard—"might be in the castle."

The thief looked into his eyes for a while. "The castle?" he said, flatly.

Miz nodded. "Yes. How practical do you think it might be to have something from the castle fall into one's hands?"

The thief nodded, seeming to look away. He stood slowly, holding the tankard. "Wait here," he said. "I have somebody who might be able to help you." He backed out of the booth through the dull, heavy curtains.

Miz sat alone for a moment. He drank his beer. He looked around the grubby booth. The place reeked of sweat, spilled drink, possibly spilled blood, and something Miz suspected was beer gone badly off. The Eye and Poker—he'd heard more inspiring names for inns. This one was in the less reputable part of Pharpech town, down the steep side of the hill from the castle and out to the east in an area of creakily tumbledown tenements that housed stinking tanneries and bonemeal works. Even with a gun in his pocket and a viblade in his boot, he'd felt vulnerable walking in here.

He looked up at the top edge of the booth wall, a meter above his head and a meter below the yellow-stained ceiling of the bar. He was sure he could see little brown stalactites on the ceiling.

He turned his attention to the bark wall behind him. Now that he looked carefully, there was a distinct line of greasy blackness at about scalp height, where countless unwashed heads of probably inhabited hair had left their mark over the years. Miz tutted, disgusted, and felt the back of his head. He altered his position in the seat, lifting his feet up and sitting sideways on the bench, his head against the side wall of the booth.

The noise from the bar seemed to have faded. He turned his head, frowning.

The heavy curtains jerked. Three crossbow bolts thudded into the bark at the back of the booth, neatly into the lower part of the greasy line he'd looked at a few seconds earlier, where his head had been.

He stared at them. Then he pulled his gun from his pocket and pushed the beer tankard over so that it spilled beer across the table and down spattering onto the stained floor; the puddle spread to the hem of the booth's curtains, where it would be visible from the bar outside.

Miz got up on his knees and swung quickly and silently across to the trestle bench on the other side of the table. He sat on the table, feet on the bench, to one side of the booth. It was still very quiet outside; just a few whispers and the noise of a chair or two being scraped across uneven floorboards. There were three little tears in the heavy curtains where the quarrels had entered. The holes let in tiny beams of smoky light.

He waited, gun ready, heart pounding.

The curtain moved millimetrically; the light from one of the three holes blinked out.

He thrust an arm through the divide in the curtains and grabbed the man outside by the neck as he threw himself forward and out. He landed crouching, his back to the narrow bark divide between two booths, his arm tight around the neck of the man he'd grabbed, who thudded sitting onto the floor. It was the thief he'd first spoken to; Miz rammed his gun just under the man's right ear.

The bar had cleared almost entirely; only a haze of smoke and a few unfinished drinks on the tables showed that the place had been packed a few minutes earlier. Standing with their backs to the bar itself were three men holding crossbows. One of them had reloaded, one was about to fit the bolt into its groove, and the other had frozen in the act of pulling the crossbow taut again.

The one with the loaded crossbow was pointing it at him. Miz forced the thief's head to one side with the barrel of the laser. The thief smelled rancid; he struggled a little, but Miz pulled his arm tighter around his neck, never taking his eyes off the man with the crossbow. The thief went still. He wheezed as he breathed.

There were a couple of other men still in the bar, near the doorway; they both held heavy-looking pistols, but they seemed to be backing off toward the doors. Miz was more worried about the booth next to his. He thought he glimpsed its curtain move out of the corner of his eye. He shifted across the floor so that his back was to the curtains of the booth he'd been in.

"Now, boys," Miz said, grinning at the man with the crossbow. "Let's just take this sensibly and nobody'll get hurt." He stood up slowly, keeping the thief between himself and the three men with the crossbows. "What do you say?"

Nobody said anything. The thief in his arm went on wheezing. Miz could feel the man trying to swallow. He loosened his grip just a little. "Perhaps our friend here has something he'd like to contribute."

The two men near the door slipped outside. Miz prodded the thief with the gun again. "Say something calming, *dummy*."

"Let him go," gasped the thief. Still no reaction.

These bozos are waiting on something, Miz thought. He heard a noise somewhere behind him in the booth. They'd gone over the top! There was a squelching noise from the floor behind him. He whirled around, taking the thief with him. A long, thin blade flashed out of the curtains and thudded into the thief's torso just under the sternum, and glistening point appearing out of his back through the hide of his tunic. He made a grunting noise.

Miz had already ducked, dropping and turning. The crossbow bolt smacked into the back of the thief's skull, sending his body jackknifing forward through the curtains and into the man holding the knife, forcing him to fall backward over the table.

Miz's gun made a crackling, spitting noise. The man who'd fired the crossbow shook as the beams hit his chest, flames licking around the edges of the little craters on his jacket. He dropped the crossbow and hung his head. He stood like that for a moment, while Miz moved away from the booth where the man with the knife was still trying to extricate himself from the curtains and the body of the thief. Then the crossbow man fell slowly back, whacking his head off the bar and crumpling to the floor. Blood sizzled against the flames flickering on his jacket.

The other two crossbow men looked at each other. The one who had now loaded his quarrel smiled nervously at Miz. He nodded at Miz's gun, swallowing.

"We didn't realize you was from the castle," he said, and very carefully took the quarrel back out of its groove. The other man released the tension in his bow and let it fall to the ground. They both glanced at the dead man lying on the floor.

The man in the booth got the thief's body off him and from behind the curtains shouted, "Me neither, sire!" A terrified bearded face poked slowly from behind the booth's curtains.

Miz looked warily around. He smiled insincerely at the two crossbow men and the knife-wielder. "Boys, you're going to see me out of this rather rough neighborhood." He glanced at the man in the booth. "You go to the front door and get the heroes out there to give you their guns."

The bearded man gulped. He came out from behind the curtains, leaving the thief's body lying half-in and half-out of the booth. He walked to the door. He opened it gently and called out. There was some conversation, which became heated, and then the sound of running footsteps. The bearded man smiled at Miz in a sickly fashion. "They ran away, sire," he said.

"Why don't you do the same?"

The man needed no more prompting; he was out the

door in an instant. Miz turned to the other two. "Chaps, you and I are going to go out the back way."

The two men looked at each other.

Miz frowned mightily. "There *must* be a back way."

"Yes, sire," one of the men said, "but it's through the tannery."

Miz sniffed the air. "Is *that* what it is?" he said. "I thought the beer was off."

"You stink."

"Blame the tannery," Miz said as Zefla dried his hair.

Sharrow poked at one of Miz's locally made boots with the toe of her own. "These are falling apart," she said. "I thought you bought them only two days ago."

Miz shrugged beneath his towel as Dloan handed him a glass of wine. "Yeah. Don't know what the hell I stepped in."

"So," Sharrow said, "the local ruffians don't want to play." She sat down in the one comfortable easy chair in Miz and Dloan's room.

"Apart from playing Let's Perforate Miz's Head, correct," Miz agreed. He looked at Sharrow as Zefla finished drying his hair. "I'm worried. Cenuij talked about the king having spies and informers. What if word of this gets back to the castle?"

Sharrow shrugged. "What can we do?"

Miz nodded at Dloan. "Why don't we all go with Dlo tomorrow? We can call it a safari—get out of town for a few days, camp somewhere near deep country, let Dlo—maybe me, too—head in, try to contact these revolutionaries."

"Cenuij doesn't think much of the idea," Zefla said, tossing Miz a scent spray.

"Thanks," Miz said. "Yeah, well, he wouldn't, would he? I think it's worth doing just to get away for a while."

"You really think we might be in danger after tonight?" Sharrow asked.

"It's possible," Miz said, spraying under his arms.

"What about Cenuij?" Dloan said.

"He's not in trouble." Sharrow waved one hand. "We can leave a message for him with the innkeeper; it's not worth the risk of using the comm gear." Sharrow nodded, looking thoughtful. "Okay, we'll go."

"Camping out in the bush for a few nights," Zefla said, crossing her eyes. "Oh, the utter joy of it."

The airship drifted over the sunlit jungle, a blue-white bubble against the blue-white skies of tropical Caltasp after the rainy season. The canopy slid slowly by underneath, the tops of the highest trees only five meters or so beneath the keel of the open gondola, where she, Geis, Breyguhn, and Geis's martialer knelt, their long guns poking over the gunwales of the boat-shaped basket.

The smells and sounds of the jungle wrapped around them, mysterious and exciting and a little frightening.

"We're on a perfect heading," Geis said, talking very quietly to her and Breyguhn. "The wind's taking us over one of the best areas, and our shadow's trailing us." He looked at the martialer, a small, rotund, perpetually smiling man from Speyr who looked more like a comedy actor than a combat tutor. "Is that not so, martialer?"

"Indeed, sire," the martialer smiled. "A perfect heading."

When Geis had first introduced the martialer to her and Breyguhn, in the arbor of the Autumn Palace, he had asked him to prove his skills as he saw fit. The fat little fellow had smiled even more broadly and—suddenly flourishing a stiletto—whirled and thrown. A white-wing, fluttering past a trellis ten meters away, was suddenly pinned to the wood. Sharrow had been impressed and Geis delighted. Breyguhn had been shocked. "What did you do that for?" she'd said, almost in tears, but the little man had held up one finger, padded to the trellis, and removed the knife with barely any effort. The white-wing, which had only just been held by one wing, had flown away. . . .

"There!" Sharrow said, pointing to the forest floor.

They looked down as they passed slowly to one side of a clearing. There was a water hole, and on the dusty ground near it a large animal with smooth green skin lay dead, its guts spilled onto the ground. Another animal—smaller, but powerful looking—stood in the pool of intestines, biting and tugging at something inside the fallen herbivore's belly cavity. The predator raised its head to look at the balloon, its golden-red snout covered in green blood.

"A *rox*!" Geis whispered. "Wonderful!"

"Ugh," Breyguhn said, watching from the other side of the gondola.

The martialer took the airship's control box from his pocket and flicked a switch. The drifting vessel hummed almost inaudibly above them, coming to a stop. The rox, its broad jaws still working as it chewed on its kill, looked up at them, unworried. It put its head to one side, still chewing.

"Cousin?" Geis said to her.

Sharrow shook her head. "No," she said. "You."

Geis looked delighted. He turned and sighted along the long powder gun.

Sharrow watched Breyguhn grimace, looking over the edge of the gondola but not really enjoying what she was seeing. Sharrow turned to look, too.

"You become one with the gun and the line and the target," Geis whispered, aiming (the martialer sat nodding wisely). "Damn—he's gone back inside the guts of the thing."

"Yeaurk," Breyguhn said, sitting down on the other side of the gondola.

"Don't rock us!" Geis whispered urgently.

The martialer put the airship controls down, raised both hands above his head, and clapped them loudly together. Sharrow laughed; the rox's head came up, freshly green, and looked at them again.

"Got you," whispered Geis. The gun roared. Geis bumped backward in the gondola; a cloud of smoke drifted down the wind. The rox had stopped chewing. It collapsed to the ground, front knees thumping into the dust; dark-red blood pumped from its head as it fell over, kicked once, and was still.

"Yes!"

"Well done."

"Fine shot, sire."

"Ugh. Is it over? Have you done it? Is there a lot of blood?"

"Take us over there, martialer; I want to get down and cut a couple of trophies."

"Sire."

"Poor animal. What chance did it have?" Breyguhn said, peeking over the gondola at the two corpses lying side by side.

"The chance of not being seen," Geis said happily, and shrugged.

"It was quick," Sharrow told Breyguhn, trying to ally herself with Geis's maturity rather than with her half sister's youth, even though she was closer in age to Brey, who was only twelve.

"Yes," Geis said, preparing the rope ladder as the martialer guided the airship through the warm air toward the clearing. "It wouldn't know what hit it."

"It still seems cruel to me," Breyguhn said, crossing her arms.

"Not at all," Geis said. "It killed that heuskyn down there; I killed it."

"It's the law of the jungle," Sharrow told Breyguhn.

Geis laughed. "Literally," he said. "And it didn't suffer the way the heuskyn must have." A puzzled, exasperated look appeared on his face. "I've often thought, you know, that that's what matters—suffering. Not death, not actually killing. If you die instantly—really instantly, with no warning whatsoever—what are you missing? Your life might be terrible from then on until when you were going to die, anyway. Of course, it might have been great fun, instead, but the point is that at any given moment you just don't know which. I don't think there should be any penalty for killing somebody instantaneously."

"But what about the people left behind, their family and friends?" Breyguhn protested.

Geis shrugged again, glancing over the side of the gondola as they drew slowly to a stop. "The law doesn't pretend we prosecute murderers because of the effect on the murdered person's nearest and dearest."

He and the martialer hauled the rope ladder to the gunwale.

"But then," Sharrow said, "if people knew they could be killed at any time, and their murderer would get away with it, everybody would be frightened all the time. No matter who you killed, they'd always have suffered." She spread her hands.

Geis looked at her, face creased in a frown. "Hmm," he said, his lips taut. "Yes, that's a point. I hadn't thought of that." He looked at the martialer, who smiled at him. Geis shrugged, handed the martialer his gun, and said, "Oh, well. Back to the drawing board on that idea."

He took his knife from its sheath, held it between his teeth, then lowered himself over the side of the gondola and down the rope ladder.

Sharrow watched him descend. He climbed down out of the shadow of the airship; the sunlight glinted on the blade of the knife in his mouth. She leaned out farther, aiming her gun down at the crown of his head as it nodded its way down the ladder toward the ground.

"Excuse me, lady." The martialer took the gun from her with a regretful smile.

She sat back in the seat. Breyguhn smirked. She tried not to blush. "I wasn't *actually* going to fire it, martialer."

"I know, Lady Sharrow," he nodded, taking a round from the breach and handing her the gun back, "but it is dangerous to point guns at people."

"I know," she said. "But the safety catch was on, and I'm very sorry. You won't tell Geis, will you?" She smiled her most winning smile.

"I doubt that will be required, lady," the martialer said.

"*He* might not . . . ," Breyguhn said, smirking at Sharrow.

"Oh, he doesn't believe anything you tell him anyway, Brey," Sharrow said, dismissing the girl with a wave. She smiled again at the martialer, who smiled back. Breyguhn scowled.

"Hey, girls!" shouted a faint, taunting voice from below. "Any particular *part* of this beast you'd like?"

They camped on a low rise at the edge of what was probably a range of small jagged hills the Entraxrln had grown over long before, leaving clogged canyons and deep, dark caves leading up steep V-sided ravines; tall spires, splayed and spread over the landscape in a way that looked geological rather than vegetable, were probably rocky pinnacles, wrapped in the Entraxrln's intimate embrace and now acting as anchor-points for membrane cables. The landscape in the hills and beyond them was even more dark and choked than it had been in the three days since they'd left the town. They had passed a few little towns and villages, and seen a couple of small castles in the distance, homes of lesser nobles, but had encountered few other travelers.

Leeskever, their guide—a lean, garrulously knowledgable and spectacularly ugly hide-trapper they'd met in the

Broken Neck, and who sported an eye patch Zefla thought most dashing—said that if the gentlemen wanted to see any savages or outlaws, they'd be in there somewhere, but he wasn't going to lead them any farther. This was bandit country.

Miz decided that his place was looking after the ladies. Dloan went in alone, on foot.

They left the jemer mounts to graze and passed the next two days walking near the camp and climbing the more gently sloped cables with loop-guides, while Leeskever talked about the thousands of animals he'd killed and the half dozen or so buddies he'd lost to stom, tangle-teeth, other assorted wild animals, and the effects of gravity when people fell off cables—all of them in country much like this.

Sharrow slipped out of the camp a couple of times when Leeskever wouldn't notice, tramping half a klick into the Entraxrln undergrowth to do some target practice. She used the silencer on the HandCannon and set up some blister-fruits ten, twenty, and forty meters away.

On her second visit to her private shooting gallery, she heard something move above and behind her just as she was changing from one magazine to another; she slammed the clip home, stepped to one side, and turned. She had the impression of something diving toward her, and fired.

The clip she'd just loaded was wire-fléchette. She checked the magazine later; four rounds had fired.

She wasn't sure how many hit whatever it was trying to jump her, but it disappeared in an exploding cloud of purple blood she had to jump away to avoid. When she went back to stir the warm, gentle steaming debris with her boot, she couldn't tell what it had been, except that it had had fur rather than skin or feathers. The biggest bit of chewed-looking bone left was smaller than her little finger.

She decided she didn't need any more target practice.

They sat, secured by ropes to hard-bark spikes stuck into the three-meter broad cable above them. They ate lunch, feeling a warm, sappy-smelling tunnel-wind blow about them, looking down the hundred meters or so to the ground. The rise holding their camp was visible a kilometer away across the grotesquely deformed landscape of the Entraxrln.

Leeskever shoved the tap-spike into a veinlike bulge on the surface of the cable. Clear water seeped through the membrane over the end of the hollow spike and started to fill a little cup hanging under its handle. He sniffed the wind. "That'll bring the king's stom, that wind," he said.

They all looked at him.

"Glide-monkeys," he said. "Stom come for the annual migration; there's one male troupe that's half-tamed. They roost in the trunk north of the town."

"They don't actually *ride* them, do they?" Zefla said.

Leeskever laughed. "Na! And never did, neither. Don't you believe what people tell you. Stom'd sooner eat you than smell you. Just legend, all that stuff about flying them." He sipped water from the small cup, then passed it to Zefla. "The king and his court go up to one of the male roosts in the trunk and stand looking at the beasts, choose one as their own, tippy-toe up to it, waft some sleepy-gas at it, and spray a mark on it. Coward courtiers and ministers have their aides do it; the rest pretend they're brave." Leeskever accepted the cup back from Zefla and hung it under the dripping tap-spike. "Then the dignitaries sit in their viewing gallery, watch the stom take monkeys and cheer on their particular beast. Highly civilized spectacle."

"Sounds it," Miz said.

"What's *that*?" Zefla said, pointing down.

"Eh?" said Leeskever. "Ah—now that is one of those tangle-teeth I was telling you about."

"This the beast that has a taste for your companions?" Zefla asked him.

"Might even be the same one, for all I know," Leeskever said.

They watched the long striped back of the tangle-tooth as the quadruped padded slowly through the jungled confusion of roots, stalks, and long tatters of fallen membrane on the level below.

Sharrow remembered the airship, and the animal Geis had killed. When he'd returned, blooded, to the gondola, he'd presented her and Breyguhn with nothing more nocuous and shocking than the animal's ears.

She had accepted her still-warm gift gracefully. Breyguhn couldn't bear to touch the blood-matted thing. Still, while Sharrow had thrown hers away the day they left the Autumn Palace estates to return to their respective schools, Breyguhn had kept her trophy for years.

•   •   •

Dloan came out of the deep country the following morning, morose and unsuccessful. He'd had to shoot two inept bandits, but apart from that he hadn't seen anybody. There might well be rebels and the like in the deep-country, but they'd kept well out of his way.

They set off back to the town that afternoon with the wind soft behind them. Several troupes of stom flew over them a kilometer up, heading in the same direction. Leeskever nodded wisely.

They paid him at the same inn on the outskirts of the town they'd eaten at the day after they'd first arrived. Miz went in to town alone, disguised. Their rooms were still being kept for them; a beggar had asked after them, and the innkeeper had given him the note they'd left for him. Nobody else had inquired about them.

"A decent bed and hot water!" Zefla said, marching into her and Sharrow's room. "Fucking luxury!"

She slept well at first, then woke during the depths of the night wondering what was happening, and thought there was something long and cold crawling over her skin at her throat.

She sat up, whimpering and pulling at her nightdress, then felt to the skin at the top of her chest, and with her hands there, looking into the utter darkness, hearing Zefla stir and make a fading, still-asleep huh-ing noise, she realized what was happening.

It was their way of saying they were still in touch, even here. So much for being off-net.

The feeling was like a cold finger drawn across her skin, right around the base of her neck, like an executioner sketching where the ax will fall. Then another line, then another and another, each one farther out than the last.

The shape of the Crownstar Addendum was traced out on her skin, to the last strand, the last planet of the system.

The long looping orbit of Prensteleraf was drawn around her neck and down over the tops of her breasts. After a while, when no more happened, she lay down in the soft, sagging bed again.

The final signal, a few moments later, was a surprise: a

single heavy but not painful line drawn around her scalp, about where would sit the rim of a hat, or a crown.

This was not a dream, she told herself before she fell asleep again.

But still, in the morning, she was not sure.

14

Vegetable Plot

"I can't believe I'm doing this," Miz whispered.

Dloan shrugged. He scratched his head, looking down at the great broad tail lying on the dust of the reeking cage. He lifted the tail, then put it back down again. "I need something to hold it up," he whispered.

"Well don't look at me!" Miz hissed, crouching at the stom's snout with a tank of gas. He pumped the handle a few times and pulled the trigger again, squirting the gas toward the beast's nostrils. Miz put his kerchief up over his mouth and coughed.

Dloan looked around.

"Hurry up!" Miz said. "This stuff is making *me* sleepy!"

Dloan took his knife and went to the stom's side; he reached up and started cutting the ropes holding the animal's left wing into its body.

"Dlo!" Miz said, eyes wide. "Are you crazy?"

Dloan said nothing; he let the ropes fall to the stinking floor of the cage. The stom's great black wing unfolded gently like a collapsing tent. The beast stirred a little. Miz flinched back, gulping, then came forward again, spraying the gas quickly into the stom's snout. "Shh!" he told the sleeping animal. "Shh! There, there . . ."

Dloan removed one of the planks that had held the wing straight, took it to the rear of the beast, and by prop-ping it between the wall and the cage floor, used it to keep the stom's tail up off the dust. Then he disappeared underneath the tail.

Miz glanced at the front of the cage. Even with the intensifier glasses on, the night was appallingly dark. Zefla was watching the zoo night-watchman's hut, but Miz felt horribly vulnerable stuck in this cage crouched centimeters from the snout of an animal that looked as if it could swallow him whole.

Not that he was sure he'd have swapped with Dloan. He watched Dloan's feet kick on the floor of the cage as he pushed himself farther in underneath the stom. Miz looked away.

He looked up at the barred ceiling of the cage. Of all the things he could ever have imagined doing in his life, squatting in a stinking cage surrounded by the rotted, half-eaten corpses of glide-monkeys in the middle of the night in the remotest, most backward part of the Entraxrln of Miykenns, drugging an animal the size of a light aircraft while an accomplice interfered with the beast's genitals, would not really have been the first to leap to mind.

The stom made a deep, sighing noise. Miz pumped more gas at it. Dloan wriggled out from underneath its rump.

"Got it?" Miz asked. Dloan nodded. Miz patted the animal's snout gently. "Poor bitch; probably the most fun she's had in years, and she slept through it."

Dloan stood there, holding a wooden scraper and a small sealed pot, his trousers and jerkin stained. He had an odd expression on his face.

Miz squirted one last burst of gas at the animal, then stood up. "Right. Let's get going before she starts screaming rape."

"No," Dloan said, coming toward him.

"*No?*" Miz said, letting Dloan take the gas canister from his hand. Dloan put the scraper and pot down on the floor and crouched at the animal's snout; he pumped the canister, spraying the gas into its nostrils. "Dloan!" Miz said, incredulous. "What are you doing?"

"Trying to kill it," Dloan said. He kept pumping and kept spraying, while Miz shook his head and walked around in a circle, head in his hands, muttering.

Dloan pumped until the canister was empty and a dew

of evaporating droplets lay around the animal's nostrils. Little rivulets ran down its snout and fell spotting to the dust. Dloan swayed as he crouched there, mechanically spraying from an empty tank; Miz went over and grabbed him, choking on the cloud of gas. He pulled on Dloan's massive shoulders and finally got him to move; they collapsed back on the floor of the cage. Dloan came to, shaking his head.

"Oof!" Miz wheezed. "Get off me!"

Dloan stood unsteadily, shaking his head. He swayed, looking at the silent animal, then retrieved the pot and the wooden scraper and stumbled for the rear of the cage. Miz followed him, scrubbing out their tracks in the dust as he went.

They relocked the door with a piece of bent wire, collected Zefla from her lookout position near the watchman's hut, and rendezvoused with Cenuij at a postern in an unlit section of the the castle precincts.

"You stink," he said as Miz handed him the sealed pot.

"Oh, shut up," Miz told him.

Lines of bunting hung above the main square of Pharpech town; stalls, traders, and entertainers provided foci for the swirling, milling crowds of people celebrating the annual migration of the glide-monkeys and the return of the stom, and especially the Royal Troupe.

Noise blared from the castle end of the square, where a group of men pretending to be stom danced around in a cleared arena in front of the royal reviewing stand. The stom-dancers held their arms out, displaying giant black wings made from dyed membrane and springy bark strips as they ran at and turned around each other, making unconvincing roaring noises. Priests and monks sitting in the higher levels of the reviewing stand and dressed in ceremonial robes kept up a running cantillation describing the proceedings.

The king sat with the queen, trying not to fall asleep.

Sharrow nibbled at a blister-fruit sorbet as she and Miz walked through the crowds, refusing offered bargains and brandished foods.

"No, I think it's just that he's finally cracked," she said. "The vaginal secretions of a female stom." She shook her head. "He probably doesn't need the stuff at all; I bet he just did it as a joke on you and Dlo."

"He'd better not have," Miz said, eyes narrowing. "Or he'll find some unpleasant things being done to *him* as he sleeps."

A great cry went up; children dressed as glide-monkeys ran into the arena in front of the reviewing stand and scampered squealing and giggling before the great black swooping shapes of the stom-dancers.

The king jumped, woken from a daydream. He clapped dutifully as the children overacted, pretending to die, flapping and jerking on the cobbles of the arena to sound of further cheers.

Deep in the castle, in the apothecary's workshop, a long trestle table held a collection of beaten metal canisters, each with a detachable top holding a pump handle and a trigger. A pair of mud-colored, slimly fingered hands gently lifted the most ornately decorated of the canisters on the table— the one with the royal crest on it—opened it up, smeared a clear, greasy gel around the bottom of the pressure vessel, and carefully replaced it.

The male stom nest-space, hollowed out of a huge trunk six hundred meters above the ground-layer three kilometers north of the town, was a dark and rank-smelling cavern of a place. The way up to it was by hoist-cage and internal ladders rising through narrow, blocked-off rainwater downchannels. There was an antechamber to the roost itself where the king, his courtiers, other members of the royal family, nobles, and their hangers-on all assembled, crowding into the dark, springily floored, candle-lit space, talking in hushed voices while royal guards checked that the male stom there in the nest-space were quiet and restive and generally looked as though they were settling down for the night.

The atmosphere was unsurprisingly tense; Cenuij felt it affect even him. The air was warm and stank of male stom and sweating nobles. He slid through the crowd of men with their canisters of tagging-paint and their guns and swords. He stood behind the king's archimpietist as the priest exorcised the gas canisters of any divine influence. Then he slipped away to the hide at the end of the nest-space itself, to try to find a vantage point.

There was still a little light left from the dusk outside.

Cenuij crouched down and peeked out of a vertical slit cut out of the back of the roost cavern, surrounded by the boots and legs of men peering through horizontal slits higher up. It was like being blind. Miykennsians were supposed to have rather better night-vision than Golterians, but he wondered how any of them could see anything in this gloom.

"Here we are," the scratchy, nasal voice of the queen said, and Cenuij felt somebody bump into him. He looked around.

The queen—a blousy creature with far too much makeup, zero dress sense, and apparently so incapable of ever deciding what jewelery to wear each morning that she simply threw on all of it—ushered her eldest son forward.

"Daddy's new choirboy will look after you," she whispered. She smiled toothily at Cenuij. "Won't you?"

Cenuij looked at the child: six or seven, fat, all gums and gapped teeth, grinning idiotically, and holding a model stom in his hand. There was some sort of sweet-smelling sticky stuff around his mouth.

Cenuij smiled insincerely up at the queen.

"Of course," he said. The boy handed him the model stom, climbed over him, leaving a trail of stickiness, and plonked himself down in Cenuij's lap, hogging the view through the slit and forcing a gasp of breath from Cenuij, who had to lift the child up for a moment to sit him in a position where he wasn't crushing his testicles.

"Make sure he keeps quiet!" the queen whispered.

The boy stuck his nose into the viewing slit, wiping his hands on Cenuij's cassock. Cenuij stared at the back of the child's grubby neck and thought of several different ways of complying with the queen's request.

The first few noblemen and courtiers were those brave enough to choose or unlucky enough to be landed with stom at the far end of the roost, near the mouth-shaped exit. They crept up through the center of the chewed-out cavern, past the dozing forms of hunkered-down stom, one or two of which watched them go past and made deep, rumbling noises that made their neighbors restless; but otherwise the stom did not react.

It was difficult for Cenuij, with so low a vantage point and a fat, sticky child in front of him, to see much of what was going on, even though his eyes had adjusted to the gloom, but he knew that what was supposed to be happening was that the man concerned approached his selected stom, gently sprayed the sleeping gas into its snout, then sprayed a patch or two of paint onto the side of its barrel chest, just below and forward of the wing root. Judging by the general mutters of approval and the reappearance of each of the men concerned—looks of considerable relief on their faces—everything was going according to plan.

It came to the king's turn. He had opted for one of the stom near the middle of the cavern: a large, middle-aged beast he'd seemingly chosen for a couple of years running because it had an excellent record at taking glide-monkeys. Cenuij ignored the sickly-sweet smell of the child in his lap and edged closer to look out over the boy's grease-slicked hair. He watched the dark-clothed figure crouch down and walk between the rows of snoring, rumbling animals.

The king approached the stom he'd selected. Cenuij could just see him giving his gas canister a final couple of pumps. Then he aimed it at the snout of the huge sleeping animal, spraying it for a couple of seconds.

The stom didn't react for a moment. The king crept forward toward it, spray can held out in front of him.

The stom shook itself; its great long head came up. The king stopped, then stepped back. The people around Cenuij went very still. The stom opened its mouth and made a yawning motion. The king sprayed gas at its head for five, ten seconds. The stom shook its head, then opened its mouth and roared. It reared up on its legs until it almost touched the top of the cavern, unfolding its wings as its bellow echoed through the nest; stom throughout the roost stirred and came awake; two on either side of the king woke up, too, their snouts waving in the air.

People started to shout and scream. The boy on his lap tried to force his head up into Cenuij's chin so he could see better; he rammed the boy's head back down, fastening himself to the slit.

"Run!" people shouted. "Run, Your Majesty!" The stom in front of the king wobbled and staggered forward; he raised the gas canister and squirted more gas at it; the beast reared upright again and stood swaying. The two stom on either side rose up, too; others at the back of the cavern lumbered off their nest-bowls, shuffling forward, necks craning, trying to move down to the middle of the roost and blocking the view from the rear of the cave.

"Guards!" somebody shouted. Cenuij felt a delicious thrill in his guts. The boy on his lap started to cry. The king's stom—just visible above the heads of the other animals—fell slowly forward and disappeared. There was a scream from the middle of the cavern. The floor shuddered. People screamed and shouted all around Cenuij. He clenched his fists. The boy squirmed out from his lap and ran away through the forest of legs.

Royal Guardsmen ran into the roost chamber, guns drawn. They fired at the animals nearest them, guns roaring and snapping; bullets and laser bolts burst among the crowded animals, producing screams and roars and clouds of smoke and vaporized skin. The three rearmost stom whirled around and charged the guardsmen, who kept on firing but had to retreat. Two stom fell howling to the ground, heads ruptured, pumping blood; one crushed a guardsman under it, another wounded animal grabbed one of the men, picked him up, and tossed him against the curved wall of the chamber with one blurring shake of its head. A fusillade of shots tore open its chest, and it fell. Behind it, the push toward the cavern mouth became a rush, then a stampede; the floor vibrated to the thudding, thumping steps of the giant beasts, and the air was filled with their cries and the noise of the guards' guns as they advanced again.

The people around Cenuij yelled and shouted and stamped their feet. He pushed his face against the slit, trying to hide his smile.

The firing went on, flat-sounding in the soft-walled roost. Three more stom fell as they crowded around the far end of the cavern, calling and screaming as they piled up there, trying to escape.

"The king! The king!" people cried as the guardsmen fought their way across the fallen bodies of the stom to the center of the cavern.

"The blockhead's dead, you brainless toadies," Cenuij whispered.

The last few of the stom able to escape did so, launching themselves from the cavern mouth into the late dusk light. Dead and dying animals lay bleeding or struggling to move on the floor of the roost. The guardsmen reached the middle of the cavern.

Cenuij composed his face into an expression of abject

grief and got ready to look away from the slit. He breathed deeply, closing his eyes for a moment.

"Look!" a voice cried. He opened his eyes again.

Something moved above the guardsmen, on the wall of the nest-space near the roof. A tiny figure, waving.

"The king!" somebody shouted. "Hurrah!"

A great cheer went up.

Cenuij stared, appalled.

The tomb was a part-buried black granite cube that had been placed, on Gorko's instructions, on a hill beyond the formal gardens of house Tzant.

She remembered when the tomb had first been emplaced; one of the old servants had taken her back out after the ceremony so that she could see it again without everybody else around. The duenna told her that the tomb was important and that grandfather Gorko had wanted her to see it like this. Neither Sharrow nor the duenna could guess why. Then they had gone back to the house, for cakes.

The other children had always been frightened of the black sarcophagus, because halfway up one side there was a small smoke-glass window, and if you got a torch, you could shine it in and see the embalmed corpse of old grandpa Gorko sitting in his best scuffed ballistic hides on his favorite motorbike, crouched over the handlebars as though still alive, his black helmet and mirrored visor reflecting the torchlight and seeming to stare back out at you.

Most of the children her age ran away shrieking when they saw the old man's cadaver, but she recalled thinking it was nice that Gorko had been put in a place where the little smoke-glass window showed the valleys and hills of the house parklands, so that grandfather could still have a pleasant view, even in death. And she never forgot that grandfather Gorko had wanted her to see the tomb specially, even if she still didn't understand why.

When—as happened every season or two—her father's chasing pack of debtors drew too close to his heels and he had to leave the latest hotel in the middle of the night and head for the temporary sanctuary of Tzant, she'd always liked to visit the tomb on the hill. She'd climb up one of the nearby trees, pull herself along an overreaching limb, and drop down to sit on top of the sarcophagus, listening to the trees in the wind and looking out in the same direction as her grandfather.

In the shade of the trees, the black granite was cool to the touch on all but the sunniest days, and sometimes she would lie or sit there for hours, just thinking. There was a sentence—just three words—engraved on top of the tomb; it said THINGS WILL CHANGE in hand-sized letters cut a finger deep into the granite. People were a little puzzled by the words; it was neither a recognized saying nor a maxim of Gorko's. But it was what he had wanted for his epitaph, and so there it was.

Every now and again she would clear the fallen leaves, broken twigs, and dead insects from the little water-filled trenches of the tomb's inscription. One winter she had pried the letter-shaped lumps of ice out of those trenches and thrown them one by one at Breyguhn, who was chucking snowballs up at her from the ground; one of the thrown letters had gashed Breyguhn's cheek, and she had run off screaming back to the house.

She lay back on the cool stone, her head cushioned by her coat. She hadn't been up here for years. She looked up at the pattern of darkness the coppery leaves made against the blue-green sky, feeling the warm breeze move across her arms and face. She closed her eyes, remembering the first time she'd made love in the open air, a few months earlier in a bower in a shady, out-of-the way courtyard buried in Yada's sprawling history faculty. That had been one evening during Fresher's Week, she thought. She tried to remember the young man's name but couldn't.

She put a hand out to feel the chiseled letters of the cube's strange inscription.

There was talk of the tomb being moved when the World Court sold house Tzant next year. She hoped it would be allowed to stay where it was. Probably some other noble family would buy the estate, or some newly rich person or big company, but she couldn't see why they would object to letting her grandpa rest peacefully in his chosen tomb, looking out over a favorite view. She could understand somebody wanting to make the place their own if they moved in, but would they really grudge one small corner of the estate for the remains of the man who'd built it?

She closed her eyes. Yes, she supposed they might. The size of the tomb and the fact that it was out of the way were both irrelevant details; it was a symbol, and it didn't really matter much what size they were—it was the thought that mattered.

Today hadn't gone too badly so far, despite all her fears. She had managed to avoid both Geis and Breyguhn at the funeral; Geis had arrived late, anyway, lucky to have got compassionate leave at all for somebody who hadn't been a close relation, and Breyguhn had been as concerned to keep out of Sharrow's way as Sharrow had been to ignore her.

Sharrow hadn't seen Geis since the ball in his father's house at Siynscon over a year earlier. He'd called her numerous times since then, especially since she'd gone to university, but she'd always found ways of avoiding meeting him face-to-face. She told herself that this was for his own good; if he had become infatuated with her at the ball, then—given that she had no intention of taking things further—it was as well that he had time to forget about her and find somebody else. She still occasionally felt herself flush when she thought about that night.

She didn't regret having let Geis dance with her and still did not believe she had done anything wrong, but to somebody watching, it might have looked as though she were throwing herself at her cousin, and that really was embarrassing. As for the thought that it might have appeared she was only setting out to beguile him to thwart Breyguhn—that was worse.

Lying there on the polished black rock of the sarcophagus, Sharrow rubbed at one leg, remembering that shock of cold pain two seasons earlier.

She hadn't seen Breyguhn since the northern winter and that mean-spirited attack in the skidder rink. Brey had gone to finishing school, and her father had continued to gamble, working himself further and further into debt and despair; both of them were people she felt happy to ignore.

She heard the voices as though part of a dream.

It was Geis and Breyguhn.

". . . sure it won't come to a war," Geis was saying. "Everyone has too much to lose."

Breyguhn said something that ended with, ". . . dying?"

Geis laughed quietly. "Of course," he said. "Everybody is. You have to be a little afraid of it just to give your best."

The voices came from the left edge of the tomb, where the path came up from the overgrown little valley that lay between the hill the tomb stood on and the terrace bordering the house's lawns and formal gardens. Sharrow rolled quietly over on her front.

"But you . . . you should never *act* afraid of it," Geis said.

Sharrow heard what might have been a hand slapping stone.

"This fellow, old Gorko. He might have had nightmares about dying every time he fell asleep for all we know, but he acted like he wasn't scared of anything. He knew what he wanted and he went out to get it, and even though he knew it was dangerous, he didn't hesitate for a second." There was a pause. "He was a great man. A very, very great man. We could learn a lot from him."

Another pause. Then, "Shall we sit? You look a bit tired."

"All right."

"Here—we'll sit on this."

Sharrow heard something flap, then a rustle. She wondered whether she should make herself known, or creep over to the edge and look down on her cousin and half sister. She lay there, undecided.

"You're so dashing these days," Breyguhn said with a small laugh.

"Ah," Geis laughed, too. "It's the uniform."

"No it isn't; I'm sure a slob in a uniform is still a slob." (Sharrow gritted her teeth; she had said exactly that to Breyguhn a year ago. Breyguhn had disagreed, of course.)

Geis laughed gently again. "Well," he said. "There are chaps in the service who could certainly do with a lesson in grooming, I'll give you that. Some fellows can look untidy the instant after their man's dressed them to parade spec. Mind if I smoke?"

"Of course not. Is that something else they do in the Navy?"

"Well, it's not a regulation." Geis laughed.

Sharrow heard a click, then smelled shoan smoke; the mild narcotic was banned in Yada and illegal in parts of Caltasp. She wasn't a great fan of the stuff herself; it didn't deliver much of a hit, and it smelled overly sweet.

"What is that?"

"This? It's shoan—from Speyr. Harmless stuff. Gives you a bit of a buzz, you know."

"Could I try some?"

"Well, I'm not sure your . . ."

"What?"

"I'm not sure that your old—"

"You were going to say that daddy wouldn't approve, weren't you?"

". . . Yes. Yes, I was."

"Well, that doesn't apply now, does it?"

There was another pause, and what might have been a sigh or a sniff.

"Brey . . . ," Geis said.

"Oh, give me that."

After a while Breyguhn coughed, then stopped.

"You sure—" Geis said.

Breyguhn coughed again. "Woo," she said after a few moments.

"You all right?"

"Fine."

"Look, I haven't really had a chance to say properly how sorry—"

"Oh, Geis, stop it."

"I just wanted to say—"

"Don't! Don't!" Breyguhn sobbed, and then there was another rustling sound, and Breyguhn said something else, but suddenly it sounded muffled.

"There there," Geis said gently, so quietly Sharrow could hardly hear.

"Oh, Geis," Breyguhn said. "You've always . . . I've . . . Ever . . ." She broke down, sobbing. The sobs became muffled again.

"Brey, Brey . . . ," Geis said softly.

There was silence, then some sounds that Sharrow wasn't sure were from Geis and Breyguhn or from the grass and bushes and leaves around her, moving in the breeze. Then a noise like a moan.

"Brey," Geis said, something chiding in his voice.

"Oh, Geis, please, please . . . I want to . . . so much. . . ."

What? thought Sharrow. She pulled herself to the edge of the sarcophagus, where she could see the valley path and the bushes on the side of the hill. She glanced over the edge of the tomb.

Geis and Breyguhn were embracing and kissing, both kneeling on Geis's Alliance Navy uniform cape, spread out

on the grass at the side of the tomb. As Sharrow watched,
Breyguhn's hands pulled Geis's shirt out of his trousers and
then disappeared inside them. One of Geis's hands moved
to Breyguhn's skirted leg and slid slowly upward as he laid
her down on the cape.

Sharrow stared amazed at Breyguhn's face for a second,
then pulled herself away when she realized Brey only had to
open her eyes to see her looking down at her.

Sharrow lay near the edge of the black cube, listening
to Breyguhn and Geis as their breathing became heavier
and more labored; she heard the rustling noise of clothes
being moved over skin and other clothes. The breathing became louder still and started to sound like moans. Breyguhn
shouted out at one point, and Geis mumbled something, but
Brey whispered quickly, and soon they were moaning together again, and Sharrow lay there, feeling herself blush
despite herself, her eyes wide, her mouth closed round her
right wrist, teeth biting her own flesh so that she wouldn't
laugh or cry out and let them know she was there.

"*Sharrow!*" Geis shouted.

Sharrow froze, skin pimpling. The black surface of the
sarcophagus roof seemed suddenly very cold.

Had he seen her? How could he have known . . . ?

Then she realized, and relaxed.

She smiled, feeling smug, then frowned, unsure
whether it was a compliment or an insult.

She listened to Geis breathing hard as he said, "Brey,
Brey, I'm sorry. . . . I don't know what—"

Breyguhn howled. Sharrow's flesh crawled. Breyguhn
sobbed something, but she couldn't make out what it was.
There was some more rustling, hurried and urgent.

"Brey, please. I meant—"

"Leave me alone!" shrieked Breyguhn, and then
Sharrow heard footsteps on the grassed path, and one last
moan from Geis. Breyguhn appeared where Sharrow could
see her, forcing her way through the bushes growing over
the path. Sharrow started to edge away from the side of the
tomb in case Brey turned and saw her, but Breyguhn didn't
look back; she disappeared sobbing into the undergrowth,
heading toward the house.

Sharrow lay there for another ten minutes, not daring to
move. She listened to Geis dressing, then smelled another

shoan cheroot. She thought she heard Geis sit down again and give a small laugh.

Eventually she heard him rise and then saw him, too, head back down the path.

She lay there a while longer before she dropped down where they had been. The flattened grass by the side of the tomb looked sordid somehow, she thought. You could tell exactly what had gone on here just by looking at it. She smiled to herself and stooped to pick up a half-smoked shoan stub. She sniffed it, considered keeping it for later. Then she thought of Geis's lips on it, and Breyguhn's, and of his lips on hers. . . .

"Yuk," she said to herself, and let the stub drop to the grass.

She slipped her formal gray shoes back on and draped the ash-colored coat over her shoulders. She took a slightly circuitous route back to the house, where the reception following her father's funeral was going quietly ahead without her.

"Oh, cheer up, Cenuij," Zefla said. She poured him some more wine.

"I will not cheer up," he said, slurring his words.

They had gone back out to The Pulled Nail that evening; Cenuij had left the festivities at the castle as soon as decently possible and joined them.

He drank from his goblet. "I can't believe that dunderbrained bumpkin survived," he said, slowly shaking his head. "Climbed up the wall. You'd have thought any self-respecting stom would have plucked him off like a blisterfruit, but the brainless little shit survived!" He drank deeply from the goblet again. "Fucking *ridiculous!*" he said.

"What was that last comment?" Sharrow said, coming back into the private room they'd hired and sitting down at the table. "A self-critical assessment of your recent ideas, Cenuij?"

He looked at her, eyes watery. He pointed at her with the hand holding the goblet. "That . . . ," he said, narrowing his eyes. He looked at her for a moment. Then he sighed and shook his head sadly. "That is actually almost a fair comment," he conceded, putting the goblet down and placing his head on his hands. He stared at the table surface.

"Hey," Zefla said, patting his back. "You've tried, Cen. Twice."

"Twice!" Cenuij said, holding his opened hands out and staring at the ceiling as though appealing to it. "Prophet's blood, twice!"

"Not to worry," Zefla said.

"We'll think of something else," Miz said, rocking back in his chair.

"It'll be all right in the end," Dloan agreed, nodding.

Cenuij fixed Zefla, Miz, and Dloan in turn with a bleary look. "Sorry, could you all be a bit more *vague*? I hate being bombarded with details."

Miz grinned and shook his head. Dloan was expressionless.

"Oh, Cenuij . . . ," Zefla said, putting her arm around him.

" 'Oh, Cenuij,' " he muttered, trying to imitate her. He shrugged her arm off and stood up. "Call of nature," he said, heading wavily for the door.

As he opened the door, the noise of the inn's main bar—where people were dutifully celebrating the fact that the king was still alive—swelled to a roar, then sank back to a murmur again as the door swung to.

Miz shrugged. He reached into his jerkin and took out an inhalant tube. "Well, I was saving this until we'd got the damn book, but—"

"Yeah," Zefla said, face brightening dramatically. "But what the hell, eh?"

Miz cracked the inhalant. They each took a few breaths.

"Anyway," Sharrow said, after she'd let her breath out. "Maybe this vault isn't as impregnable as Cenuij thinks."

"Yeah," Miz said, coughing. "Fucking hell—we took out the one they kept the *C.A.* in; compared to that, anything else should be easy."

"Just getting the equipment might be a problem," Dloan said.

"Think team," Zefla said, grinning broadly. She handed the tube back to Miz, who was looking at the door of the room and frowning deeply. "What's the matter?" she asked him.

He nodded toward the door as his hand went to his pocket. "Gone very quiet down there all of a sudden," he said.

The others listened. The background buzz of noise from the bar below had disappeared.

Miz rocked forward in his seat and took out his gun. "Personal experience," he said, getting up and padding to the door, "has taught me it's a very bad sign when Pharpechian bars go this quiet." He looked at Dloan and nodded sideways to the door. "You go and check it out, Dlo."

Dloan got up silently.

Miz grinned. "Hey, I was only kidding. . . ."

Dloan held up one hand. "No, I'll go," he said.

Miz looked up at the expression on the big man's face. "Yeah," he said. "You go."

As Dloan opened the door, there was a scream from downstairs, then a terrible wailing and crying. Sharrow looked around at the others. Dloan went out. Miz watched him walk along to the stairs leading down to the bar. The wailing got louder. He closed the door.

"What the hell's *that*?" Zefla breathed.

"Cenuij just told a joke?" Sharrow suggested. She reached into her jacket pocket and took out the HandCannon.

The wailing kept going. Dloan came back unharmed after a couple of minutes, closing the door behind him and sitting in his seat.

"Well?" Sharrow said.

Dloan looked at her. "The king is dead," he told her.

"*What*?" Miz said, coming over to the table.

Dloan explained it as he'd heard it.

The king had been demonstrating to the banquet guests how he'd escaped from the stom that evening. He'd climbed all the way up a large tapestry hanging against one wall of the banqueting hall and stood on the rafters, waving his wine goblet around as he described his strength, dexterity, bravery, and sureness of foot. He had slipped and fallen, hit the heavy banqueting table with his head and spattered a surprisingly large amount of brains over the tenth course, a sweet.

"Yeah!" Zefla said, not too loudly, and then immediately covered her hand with her mouth. She looked around guiltily.

Miz took a last suck on the inhalant. "The king is dead," he said, passing the tube to Zefla.

"At least this might cheer Cenuij up," Sharrow said.

Miz looked at the door. "Yeah, where's he got—?"

Cenuij opened the door and came in. He locked the door and crossed to and opened the window, then kicked a nearby stool underneath it; he climbed up on the stool and looked out. He turned back and smiled unconvincingly at them.

They were all staring at him.

"Cenuij?" Zefla said. "You okay?"

"Fine," he said, voice hoarse. There was a sheen of sweat on his face. He nodded at the window. "Let's go."

"What?" Miz said, putting his gun away in his jerkin.

"Don't put that away, we might need it," Cenuij said. "Come on, let's go. Just leave the money on the table."

"Cenuij," Sharrow said. "Have you heard? The king is dead."

He nodded quickly, looking exasperated. "Yes, yes, I know," he said. He nodded at the door he'd locked. "But a load of monks just turned up and asked for lodgings here."

"So?" Sharrow said.

Cenuij swallowed. "They're Huhsz."

15

Escape Clause

Miz dumped a load of coins on the table and went out along the landing to check if Cenuij was right. Zefla lifted the two remaining bottles of trax spirit. Sharrow shoved the inhalant tube into a pocket; she was surprised to find that her hands were shaking. Cenuij was persuaded that the drop from the window was a little too great; Dloan checked along the corridor outside and found some back stairs.

Miz came back from looking down into the hall of the inn.

"Yeah," he whispered. "It's the Huhsz."

A minute later they were gone, quitting the inn's rear courtyard and heading out onto a small track that looped around through a field to the road for the town.

They had hired torch-carriers to escort them from the town to the inn, but didn't want to wait for the youths to rouse themselves from the inn's kitchens, or attract the Huhsz's attention with lights. They'd all brought night-glasses with them except for Zefla, who held on to Dloan's hand as they walked quickly up the road. They looked back to see a tall carriage surrounded by dark figures being maneuvered through the archway into the inn's main courtyard.

"Sons of bitches," Miz breathed. "I saw ten—how about you?" he asked Cenuij.

"Twenty, maybe more," Cenuij said.

"Shit," Miz said. He looked at Sharrow, a pale ghost striding alongside, unknowingly disguising her limp as she did so. "Now what?"

"Forget the book," she said. "We run."

"I have a better idea," Cenuij said. He smiled at Sharrow as she looked back at him. "We hobble the Huhsz first, *then* we run."

"How?" she asked.

"A word in the right ears in the castle ought to do it," Cenuij said. "I'll tell the archdispietist I've heard the Huhsz are here and that they're God-worshiping republicans. That should put the fear of God into the Pharpechian religious authorities. Especially at the moment."

"Well, don't take too long," Sharrow said. "We're going to get the fastest mounts we can find and set off for the railway."

"It might be best if we didn't split up," Zefla said. "What if Cenuij is expected to stay in the castle, to join in the mourning or something?"

"Yes," Sharrow said, looking at Cenuij. "What if?"

"Don't worry," he told her. "You arrange the transport; I'll delay the Huhsz and get out in time."

"Fate, feels like free-fall."

Geis smiled. "Watch," he said. He took a pen from the pocket of his Navy dress jacket, held it front of him, then let it go. The pen fell slowly toward the floor of the elevator. Geis retrieved the pen when it was about level with his polished knee boots and put it back in his pocket.

Sharrow jumped lightly and floated towards the ceiling, then pressed herself back down with her fingers, laughing.

"You're not supposed to do that," Geis said, grinning as he watched her pull her dress down from where it had ridden up her legs.

"I see why you said we had to finish our drinks," Sharrow said, steadying herself against the wall by the grab-handles. Geis still held both their glasses from the party, but he'd insisted they drink up before they took the elevator to inspect the gallery.

The air whistled around the lift like a distant scream.

Geis glanced at the depth display. "Should start braking

now," he said. The elevator shook slightly, the screaming noise altered in pitch, and weight gradually returned.

"What was this anyway?" Sharrow asked.

"Old gold mine," Geis said as the lift slowed further and they felt their weight increase. The scream died to a moan.

"Feels like we're almost through the crust," Sharrow said, flexing her legs.

"Hardly," Geis said. "But we are very deep—deep enough to need refrigeration to keep the tunnels comfortable." The lift came smoothly to a stop, and the doors opened.

"Where the hell *is* he?" Sharrow looked up at where the first hint of the slow dawn was turning the membrane sky a faint, streaky blue.

They had quit The Broken Neck almost as fast as they had The Pulled Nail. They returned to the stable on the other side of town where they'd sold the jemers they'd ridden in on. There hadn't been any need to hammer at the door to get the proprietors up; like most people in Pharpech town, they had been awake all night, first celebrating the king's miraculous escape, then mourning his tragic demise. Cenuij was supposed to meet them there, but they'd already waited two hours.

The stable had gone quiet behind them, the owner and his family finally gone to bed. They waited on the road outside. Zefla lay curled up asleep among their baggage, her head resting against a shallow bark crate full of empty beer jugs the stable had left out for collection by the local brewery. Dloan sat near her, looking down the road the way Cenuij ought to come, while Miz paced up and down and Sharrow alternated standing with her arms folded, foot tapping, and also pacing up and down. Their five mounts and two pack jemers snored and snorted fitfully, lying sleeping at the side of the road.

"Let me call him," Miz said to Sharrow, coming up to her and waving the transceiver.

She shook her head. "He'll call us as soon as he can."

"Well, let me go in and find out what's happening!" Miz pleaded, pointing to the low, dark lump that was the town, barely outlined against the lighter darkness behind it.

"No, Miz," she said.

Miz held his hands up in a gesture of desperation. "So what do we do? Wait here forever? Leave without him?"

"Wait till he comes. We can't leave him here for the Huhsz. Anyway," she said, "he's probably the only one who remembers the route back to the railway. . . ." Her voice trailed off as the transceiver in Miz's hand buzzed.

Miz glanced at the dark, windowless wall of the stable behind him, turned away from it, then clicked the communicator on. "Yes?" he said quietly.

"Miz." It was Cenuij's voice. "You have the animals?"

"Yeah, we gave you the ugly one. What's keeping you?"

"Desecrations. Listen—meet me behind the cathedral as soon as you can."

"*What?*" Miz said, glancing at Sharrow.

"Behind the cathedral. Ride in. Bring my mount. And something the same size as the book."

"The same—?" Miz began.

Sharrow took hold of his hand, talking into the transceiver. "Cenuij, what about the Huhsz?"

"Taken care of. I have to go now—"

"Cenuij!" Sharrow said. "Reassure me."

"Eh?" They could hear the note of impatience in his voice. "Oh . . . it's all a Huhsz trick. Flee for your lives. Happy?"

"No," she said. "Get out of there."

"Absolutely not. Behind the cathedral; bring a book. Out."

The transceiver chimed once and went silent.

"Call him back," Sharrow said.

Miz tried. "Switched off." He shrugged.

Sharrow glared at the transceiver. "Bastard," she said.

Miz put it back in his pocket and held his arms out. "Now what?"

The tunnel revealed beyond the elevator doors was four meters across and gently lit. The air in the tunnel was as warm as the evening breeze had been on the terrace of the villa five kilometers above on the shoulder of one of the Blue Hills of Piphram, where the new-year party was still in full swing. Geis showed her into a small electric buggy. He took a small bottle from his jacket and filled both their glasses with the echirn spirit. They clinked glasses solemnly; then he took the buggy's controls, and the vehicle jerked into motion, spilling a little of her drink on the yoke of her dress.

"Eek," she said, and burped decorously.

"Whoops." Geis grinned and handed her a handkerchief. "Sorry," he said.

"That's quite all right," she told him, dabbing at her dress. The lights of the corridor moved smoothly past as they drove toward a set of steel-blue doors filling the tunnel ahead. She looked back toward the lift. "Hope they're not missing you at the party."

"Let them," Geis said. He took a pack of cheroots from his jacket. "Smoke?" he asked as he slowed down for the doors.

"Shoan, right?"

"How'd you guess?"

"I'm a genius."

Geis just grinned as the buggy halted; he jumped out, went to the tall doors, pressing his hand to a panel, and stepped back. The meter-thick doors swung outward slowly and silently, revealing a short stretch of narrower tunnel beyond and then a similar set of doors.

"Geis," Sharrow said, hiccuping once as she drew on the cheroot, lighting it. "You're collecting doors. Your art collection consists of several sets of nuke-proof doors."

Geis swung back into the buggy and started it moving.

"Come to think of it," he said, "they *are* antiques. I hadn't thought of that."

She stuck the cheroot between her lips and put her hand out toward him as they slowed for the second set of doors. "I demand my Finders Fee," she said.

He took her hand and kissed it. "Later," he said. He jumped out of the buggy and went to the doors ahead.

She frowned, looking at her hand, then turned to look back at the first set of doors; they had closed.

"Hey, Zef?"

"Mmm?"

"Up, girl. We need your pillow."

"What?"

The gallery was a long cavern alcoved with short tunnels, each fitted with its own blast door; the gallery's gray ceiling was half-hidden by cable runs, pipes, and ducting. Geis turned all the lights on and had the alcove doors swing open. Each alcove held a few paintings, statues, full bookcases, or a piece of ancient technology.

She drank from her glass and smoked the shoan cheroot, walking with him from alcove to alcove, surveying the collected treasures, some belonging to Geis's branch of the family, some the property of the Dascen house itself and not claimed by the World Court, and some the investments of Geis's family's companies.

She made a show of looking around. "You didn't rescue old Gorko's tomb when they removed it from Tzant, did you?" she asked, smiling at him.

He shook his head. "I couldn't. It's still under Court jurisdiction." If Geis connected the tomb with his enjoyment of Breyguhn that afternoon of the funeral, it didn't show on his face. "Ended up in a warehouse in Vembyr," he told her, "if I remember correctly. I'll bid for it, of course, if and when it . . ." He paused, looking puzzled. "Why are you grinning like that?"

"Nothing," she said, looking away. "You don't *really* think any of this stuff's going to be at risk, do you?" she asked, drawing her light wrap over her bare shoulders as they moved beneath the chill down-draft of a ventilation grille.

"Oh, it's just a precaution," Geis said, glancing at her. "Are you cold?" he asked. "Here, have my jacket."

"Don't be silly," she told him, pushing his offered jacket away.

He slung his jacket over his shoulder. "I don't think there will be a war. Even if there is, it'll probably be over quickly, and probably just be a space war; but you can't be sure. I thought it best to get this stuff to safety while there was a threat. It might look like overreaction, but these things are priceless, irreplaceable. And they are my responsibility." He grinned at her. "I wouldn't expect a *student* to understand, though. You lot all support the anti-Tax side anyway, don't you?"

She snorted. "The ones who aren't on establishment scholarships, or too deep in their studies to care, or permanently zonked, yes," she told him.

He stopped in front of an alcove where a glisteningly polished marble statue showed two naked lovers embracing. He refilled her glass.

"Well," he said. "I have some sympathies with the anti-Tax side, too, but——"

"You're in the Alliance *Navy,* cuz," she reminded him.

"In logistics liaison, on a sporadic commission," he said. "I'm not likely to be fighting space battles."

"So *what*?" she said scornfully.

"I believe I have a duty to be there," he said reasonably. "To represent the family's best interests. But I don't want to be put in a position of actually . . ."

"Fighting."

". . . making a mistake that would cost lives," he said, smiling.

She ground the stub of the cheroot under one heel. "Very convincing," she said.

She walked on. Geis stopped to swivel his boot over the cheroot stub as well.

They left Zefla at the stables with her mount and the two pack animals and rode into the town. Cenuij met them in a narrow cobbled street between the cathedral and a tall, teetering tenement.

It was still very dark; they didn't see Cenuij until he appeared out of the shadows beneath an overhanging story above a shop-front.

Sharrow jumped down and grabbed the throat of his cassock with one hand. She held the HandCannon in the other.

"This had better be good, Mu."

"It is!" he whispered, as Miz and Dloan joined them. Cenuij pointed at the cathedral with one shaking hand. "The book is in there! In the cathedral! Now! And it's practically unguarded!"

Miz bent forward, eyes narrowing. "Define 'practically.'"

"Two guards?" Cenuij said.

Miz straightened and looked around at the dark bulk of the cathedral. "Hmm," he said.

"Did you bring something the same size as the book?" Cenuij asked as Sharrow let go of his habit.

"Yes," she said.

"Perfect." Cenuij rubbed his hands together.

"The small matter of the Huhsz, Cenuij . . . ," Sharrow said.

Cenuij waved one hand. "A detachment of Royal Guardsmen went out to surround the inn over an hour ago. The Huhsz will be spending some time in custody; certainly they won't be seeing daylight until the prince is crowned king next week."

"So why's the book in the cathedral now if the coronation's not till next week?" Miz asked.

Cenuij's smile showed up in the darkness. "The terms of the late king's will dictated that when he lay in state in the cathedral, it should be with his feet lying on the book. It's a position of disgrace usually reserved for enemies' skulls and unfaithful mistresses. His Majesty's bibliophobia to the rescue." Cenuij adjusted his habit and drew himself up and said primly, "I thought it too good an opportunity to miss."

"You'd better be right about the Huhsz," she told him. "Where exactly is the book?"

"Follow me."

"I didn't really have any choice, Sharrow," Geis said wearily, following her past the softly lit alcoves. "I had to join the Navy, for my own self-respect and because, when you have this sort of power, this responsibility, you can't choose not to have it when the decisions become tough. You can't afford to prevaricate or delegate; you have to be engaged. You can't stay neutral; you can *say* you're neutral, and try to act as though you are, but that neutrality will always help one side more than the other. That's just the way power works ... the leverage it exerts." He shrugged. "Anyway, it's mealymouthed, dishonorable, even, to shy away from something like this. One side has to be more right than the other, has to be better for ... for us, and I have a responsibility to try to work out which, and then to act on that evaluation. One has to declare for one side or the other." He smiled ruefully. "I know it's tough at the bottom, too, and maybe in worse ways, but it really isn't that easy being at the top. There's less freedom than people think."

"If you say so." She shrugged.

They came to an alcove where a giant plastic packing case a couple of meters square sat on a couple of low trestles.

"Latest arrival," Geis said, patting the case. "Shall we open it?"

"Why not?"

He unclipped the catches, swung a lever up, and stepped back. The front of the case split, opening outward like the blast doors earlier; a white tidal wave of tiny foam squares flooded from the interior of the case, spilling out over Geis and submerging him up to the waist. She gave a little yelp and stepped back, laughing as the white avalanche swept around her, the level of tickling squares rising to her knees before the flood subsided.

Geis had turned back to look at her, laughing and brushing foam squares out of his hair. Behind him in the packing case, still secured by straps and lapped by white foam squares, was another life-size statue of two lovers. The statue looked like part of a series; it seemed the two lovers were no longer merely embracing, but actually copulating.

Geis spread his hands. "The tide of history," he laughed. She smiled. He waded through the wash of foam squares to her and stood in front of her, studying her. "You are so beautiful," he said softly.

He let his jacket drop behind him.

"Geis," she said.

"Sharrow . . ." He put one hand behind her neck and pulled her to him, kissing her. She put one hand against his chest and tried to push him away. His lips covered hers, his tongue trying to force its way between. He came closer, putting his other arm around her, pulling her to him.

She forced her head to one side for a moment, gulping. "Geis," she said, laughing nervously.

He pulled her back and kissed her neck and ears and face, muttering things she could never remember later, and while she tried to push him away, still half laughing, he ran his hands down her back, under her wrap, and up between that and her thin dress. His lips found hers again as she started to speak his name, and his tongue slipped into her mouth. She almost choked, straining to pull her head back as he bent over her; she dropped her glass to push him away with both hands.

"G—" she managed, before they tumbled over backward into the slope of white foam.

There were two guards in the cathedral sacristy, left there to look after the hated and possibly holy book while the nave of the cathedral was hurriedly prepared to accept the late king's body, the head of which was currently being packed and stitched into something approaching physiological acceptability in the castle surgery.

One of the guards opened the door when Cenuij knocked.

"My son, I have come to exorcise the book," he told him.

The guard frowned but opened the door. Cenuij entered. The guard stuck his head out into the cloister to look around. Miz put his gun gently against the guard's head, just behind his ear, and the man went very still. Cenuij drew his own gun as the other guard was standing up and reaching for his carbine.

Geis straddled her, still kissing her, then suddenly pulled his face away, breathing hard, his hands parting her wrap and running down over her dress, over her breasts and belly.

"It's all right," he said breathlessly, smiling down at her. "It's all right."

She pushed her pelvis upward, trying to heave him off; her arms foundered in the soft depths of foamy squares. "It is *not* all right," she gasped.

He pulled his shirt open, buttons popping. "Don't worry," he said. He grabbed her dress around her stockinged thighs and pushed it up.

"Geis!"

He fell back on top of her, his head moving quickly from side to side as he tried to kiss her again. He grabbed her arms with his hands, then held both her wrists with one hand and started to undo his trousers. "It's all *right*, Sharrow," he said breathlessly.

"Geis!" she screamed. *"No!"*

"Don't worry, I love you." He fumbled with her underclothes.

She went limp.

"It's perfectly simple," Miz said, addressing the two guards who were sitting on the floor of the sacristy. Cenuij stood by the locked door. Sharrow and Dloan lifted the book out of its palanquin and put it on a long, low vestment chest. Dloan slit the stitching on the book's skin cover with a viblade. The guards watched, eyes wide.

"We're going to take this actually quite worthless book

away with us," Miz told them, "and replace it with this rather attractive crate of empty beer jugs." Miz pointed at the squat beer crate. The guards looked at it, then back at him. "And you aren't going to say anything, because if you do, and we're caught, we'll destroy the book. So the choice is: raise the alarm and have to admit you let us take this supposedly incredibly precious article without really putting up a fight, or say nothing." Miz spread his hands, smiling happily. "*And* live to spend these small tokens of our appreciation for your cooperation." He counted out some silver coins and slipped them into the guards' pockets.

Sharrow held the skin cover while Dloan slid the book out. The case revealed was made of stainless steel embedded with smooth stones of jacinth, sard, chrysoberyl, and tourmaline and inlaid with whorls of soft gold. Dloan checked the lock mechanism. He smiled.

Cenuij pushed him out of the way and put his hands on the book's case, gently turning it on its side. There was a single glyph on what looked like the spine of the metal box. It wasn't a script that any of the others recognized, but Cenuij's face radiated joy when he saw it.

"Yes," he whispered, stroking the surface of the casing.

"This is it?" Miz asked quietly.

Cenuij glanced at the two guards, then went, smiling, back to his position at the door.

Sharrow lifted the beer crate up onto the vestment chest. She shook the crate, rattling it, then crouched down to the lowest of the shallow, two-meter-long drawers in the chest, sliding it out and lifting the elaborately embroidered robe within. She sliced off part of its train with the viblade, then tore the material into strips and stuffed those between the dumpy beer jugs. She shook the crate again, seemed satisfied with its silence, put the top on, and slid it into the skin-book cover as she kicked the vestment drawer closed again.

Dloan had found some needles and thread. "How's your invisible stitching?" he asked Sharrow.

She shook her head. "Not so much invisible as nonexistent."

Dloan shrugged. "Allow me," he said modestly, sucking the end of the thread.

· · ·

"I love you, I love you," Geis mumbled, trying to push his hand inside her knickers.

She remained limp. "Geis," she said, very quietly and meekly.

"What?" he panted. His flushed face looked down at hers, concerned.

"Get *off* me!" she roared, bringing her head up to crack his nose while one knee came up between his legs.

Her knee couldn't connect because Geis's trousers were in the way, but her forehead thumped into Geis's nose and mouth. He gasped. She pulled her hands free from his and wriggled around, turning underneath him and forcing her arms and legs through the depth of foam squares. She found the floor beneath and half crawled, half swam away, then staggered out to a wall, hauling herself upright.

Geis sat in the middle of the wedge of white foam. He touched the end of his nose, glaring at her and breathing hard.

"That wasn't very nice, cuz," he said. His voice was soft and flat. There was an expression of predatory appraisal in his eyes that sent a chill through her. For the first time in her life she felt frightened of a man. Her bottom lip started to tremble, and she clamped her jaw shut, raising her head and glaring right back at him. They held each other's gaze for a while.

He glanced toward the ceiling. "It's an awful long way back to the surface," he said quietly. "We're very alone." He started to slide through the hill of white foam toward her.

She swallowed. "Forget it, Geis," she said, and was relieved, even in her terror, that her voice sounded level and calm. "Lay a finger on me, and I swear I'll bite your fucking throat out." She wasn't sure she didn't mean it entirely literally, but the way it came out, it sounded absurd and pathetic in her ears. Her heart pounded and she couldn't breathe.

Geis stopped moving. He stared at her a moment longer, that same expression of raptorial calculation like a mask across his eyes.

She gulped a breath and tried to swallow again, her throat dry.

Then Geis gave a small laugh, relaxed, and looked bashful. He sniffed, inspected his fingers for blood, and attempted to waggle his two front teeth.

"Well, cuz," he said. "I take it the answer's no." He grinned.

She pulled the wrap back across her shoulders. "That wasn't funny, Geis," she said.

He laughed. "It wasn't meant to be *funny,*" he said. "Fun, yes, but not funny."

"Well it wasn't either," she said, slipping one shoe back on and looking around for the other one. "Find my shoe and take me back to the party."

"Yes, sir," Geis said, sighing.

They returned to the new-year party via the buggy and the tunnel and the elevator. Geis joked and was charming and apologized offhandedly for what had happened. He offered her a drink from the echirn bottle and another shoan cheroot; she stared at the lift wall, monosyllabic. Geis laughed at her for being such a poor sport.

She joined the anti-Tax forces a few months later.

"I never really intended to pursue a life of crime," Miz told the two guards, glancing at his watch. The others had been gone five minutes. He was giving them ten minutes' start. The guards still sat on the floor, watching him. He'd taken the magazines out of their projectile carbines and was walking around the sacristy with the clips in one hand and his gun in the other.

He glanced up at a tall wardrobe, then looked back at the guards. "But I fell in with a bad crowd when I was young. . . ." He climbed up on a solid-looking desk at the side of the wardrobe, keeping his gun trained on the guards all the time. "My family."

He peeked quickly at the top of the wardrobe, then put the magazines up there and jumped down. "Of course," he said. "Society was to blame. . . ."

They sat together under the furs in the rear of the open sleigh as it charged between the steep banks of snow. The sleighman cracked his whip over the heads of the twin sials straining in their jingling traces; a breeze stirred the treetops overhead, dislodging powdery snow and making the road lights swing on their wires.

"I *did* see a VTOL," Miz said to her as the hotel came into view around the side of the hill. The hotel and the other buildings in the small village were speckled with lights creating pools of amber, yellow, and white on the snow, and behind the hotel, on the uncovered handball court, glittered the sleek silver shape of a private jet. Traditional music thudded from the hotel ballroom and mingled with modern sounds from the open windows of the bar, the combined cacophony echoing off the cliffs behind the village.

People in furs and ski clothes were sitting drinking steaming bowls of winter wine on the hotel's front steps; the sials' breath blew out in great white clouds as the sleigh drew up.

Sharrow looked at the svelte body of the private jet and frowned.

They were waiting five kilometers out of town, where the road crested a ridge and a series of root-tubes were carried diagonally over the track on enormous bark trestles, leaving about enough room for a rider to pass underneath without ducking.

Dloan climbed to the top of one of the tubes and watched the road leading back toward the town. He saw the single rider approaching. There was nobody following.

"Okay?" Sharrow asked him as Miz reined the jemer in.

He shook his head. "Hell no," he said, rubbing his behind. "These things *really* give you a sore bum when they gallop, don't they?"

"Sharrow—cuz! Hello!"

The bar of the hotel was packed; Geis had to fight his way through the crowds to her and shout above the music thundering from the speakers to make himself heard. He was dressed in shorts and a light summer shirt that looked odd among the ski suits and heavy winter clothes everybody else was wearing. He was tanned and looked fitter and better proportioned than Sharrow remembered.

"Hello, Geis. Geis; Miz," Sharrow said, nodding from one man to the other. She saw Breyguhn moving through the press of people toward them. "Shit," Sharrow breathed, looking away as she took her coat off. It was two years to the day since she'd last seen Geis, that night in the gold mine turned vault, deep under the Blue Hills of Piphram. The last time she'd seen Brey had been even longer ago, at their father's funeral.

"Mr. Kuma," Geis was saying, smiling thinly and drawing himself up. He nodded.

"Delighted," Miz said.

"Sharrow," Geis said, pushing between her and Miz. "Season's greetings!" She turned her head, letting him kiss her cheek. "Great party!" he shouted. "Yours?"

"No," she said. "Just the hotel's."

Geis gestured to Breyguhn as she approached, then turned to Sharrow. "Haven't seen you since before the war," he bellowed. "Had us sick with worry when we heard you'd been hurt. Why didn't you answer my calls?"

"We were on opposite sides, Geis," she reminded him.

"Well," Geis laughed. "That's all forgotten now. . . ."

"Hello, Sharrow."

"Brey—hi. How are you?"

"Fine. Enjoying yourself here?" Breyguhn wore a filmy white summer dress; her hair was up and artfully wisped and curled. She was carefully made-up, and her face looked elegantly narrow. Sharrow wondered if she'd had surgery, or some gray-area genetic treatment.

"Yes," Sharrow told her. "It's been a good holiday. What brings you here?"

Breyguhn shrugged. "Oh," she said, "a whim." She glanced at Geis, who was smiling broadly at Miz while gesturing at the bar. "Not my idea," Brey continued. "There was a family party in Piph, and Geis suddenly decided it would be amusing to drop in on you and your friends and wish you Happy New Year. Nobody else wanted to come, but I thought I'd keep Geis company." She shrugged. "It was a *very* boring party."

"Piphram." Sharrow nodded. "So that's why you're in your summer threads."

"Like I say, it was all very spur-of-the—"

"Ordered some drinks," Geis shouted, moving to shepherd them toward one corner of the packed bar. "Should be a booth over here for us. . . ."

Breyguhn looked Sharrow down and up as best she could in the crush. "Anyway, you look well. Fully recovered from your war wounds?"

"Near as dammit." Sharrow nodded.

"And how is the Antiquities business?" Breyguhn asked Sharrow as they moved among the merry, jostling warmth of the revelers.

"Pays the bills, Brey," Sharrow said. They came to a booth being held vacant for them by a very large man in a formal suit and mirrored nightglasses, who bowed to Geis and stood to one side. Miz winked at the bodyguard. They sat in the booth.

"Should be space for another three," Geis said. "Your other teammates are here, aren't they?" he asked Sharrow, pouring from a huge pitcher of wine.

"They're around," Sharrow said, putting her coat, gloves, and hat on the bench beside her. "Zef's probably dancing. I'll go find her."

"No, really," Geis said. "There's no—"

Sharrow slid out of the booth, past the bodyguard and away through the crowds toward the ballroom.

"Oh," Sharrow said. She stared down at the message in the dust.

Miz looked, too. "Very droll," he said. He crossed the hotel room to the bar; he opened the cooler and surveyed the contents. "Very fucking droll indeed."

Cenuij had gone pale. Sweat glistened among the hairs on his top lip. His hands shook as he touched the interior of the casing. "No!" he whispered hoarsely. He put one hand into the dust, stirring it as though searching for something else underneath, then raised the same quivering hand to his brow and stared at the words engraved on the shining stainless steel. He shook his head. Zefla took his shoulders as he backed away and sat down, collapsing into a seat. He stared straight ahead. Zefla squatted at his side, patting his shoulders. He put his still shaking hands down into his lap. The dust left a mark on his temple.

Dloan shrugged and started packing away the equipment he and Miz had used to check and then open the lock on the book's casing.

Sharrow turned back the frontispieces and the inside cover of the casing.

The Universal Principles,

said the engraved legend on the titanium-foil cover in an antique version of Golter Standard script.

By The Command Of The Widow Empress Echenestria, The Blessed Of Jonolri And Golter, To The Greater Glory Of The True God Thrial, This Solar Year Six Thousand Three

*Hundred And Thirty Seven, This Book Is Offered, Being The
Collected Dispositions Of The First And Second Post-
Schismatic Intervarsital Convocations (Historical,
Philosophical, Theological, Cosmological), Also The Last
Summation By The Condemned Un-Godly Machine*
Parsemius, *The Life-Elegies Of The Esteemed Imperial Poets
Folldar And Creeäsunn The Younger, And The Presiding
Commentary Of The Court Sage System.*

*By Court Decree Maximal Made Perpetually Unique
In The Image Of The Single God-Head, These Are
The Universal Principles.*

The engravings on the four following pages of diamond leaf
showed, firstly, a symmetrically spotted Thrial, followed by
a diagram of the whole system, then a magnified nebula,
and finally a view of thin, bubblelike filaments and membranes—lines of tiny pits freckling the smooth hard sheet of
cold diamond. Sharrow ran her fingers over the scratches of
the second page.

"It might still be here," she said. "Somewhere. Recorded somehow."

Cenuij was silent.

Miz shook his head as he took a bottle from the cooler.
"I doubt it, somehow."

"Yes." Sharrow sighed. "Actually," she said, putting her
hand into the book's empty casing and lifting a little of the
paper-dust in the bottom, "so do I." She let the dust run
through her fingers.

"What about the message Gorko's supposed to have
left?" Zefla asked quietly, stroking Cenuij's shoulder. "Has
that gone, too, if it was ever there?"

Sharrow shifted her focus from the lines her fingers
made against the gray-brown dust to the three engraved
words beneath.

"Oh, it's here," she said, staring at the sentence. "It was
always here. It just wasn't a message until Gorko used it somewhere else. But I think I know where he's pointing us now."

"You do?" Miz asked, looking surprised and pleased.
"Where?"

"Vembyr," she said. "The city where the androids are."
She let the case slam shut.

• • •

Zefla and Dloan were both involved in a complicated group-dance in the ballroom; Sharrow left them to it. She found Cenuij at the bar and steered him toward the booth.

Cenuij stumbled and almost fell over a table as they squeezed through the crowd. He laughed cruelly and told the people at the table it shouldn't be where it was; how dare they move a table? Who gave them authority? So what if it was bolted to the floor?

She dragged him away. "You got drunk fast," she said.

"Tell you the secret if you buy me a drink."

"We have an early start tomorrow, remember?"

"But that's why I started early this evening!" Cenuij said, gesturing wildly and knocking somebody's drink. "Do you *mind*?" he snarled at the woman he'd bumped into. "People have to *clean* this floor, you know!"

"Sorry," Sharrow said to the woman with a smile, pushing Cenuij onward and then following him.

"Get me a drink," Cenuij told her.

"Later. Come and meet my ghastly relations."

"You mean there's *worse* than *you*?" Cenuij said, horrified.

They arrived at the booth; she introduced Geis and Breyguhn.

The two men exchanged formal greetings, then Cenuij turned to Breyguhn.

"Ms. Dascen," he said carefully. He took Breyguhn's hand and kissed it. Cenuij knew that technically Brey wasn't a full Dascen at all; Sharrow guessed that addressing her as such was done more to annoy her than to flatter Breyguhn.

"Why, Mr. Mu," Breyguhn said, smiling at Cenuij and then glancing at Sharrow.

Cenuij breathed deeply and seemed to collect himself. "Your sister has told me so much about you," he said. Sharrow found herself gritting her teeth to stop herself from saying anything. "I of course believed every word," he went on, "and have always wanted to meet you." Cenuij smiled. He was still holding Breyguhn's hand. "I would consider it an honor if you would grant me the next dance." He gestured grandly in the very general direction of the ballroom.

Breyguhn laughed and stood. "Delighted." She smiled at Sharrow as she and Cenuij made their way back through the shouting, laughing crowd.

Sharrow watched them go, eyes narrowed.

• • •

TEXTBEGIN UNSOURCED HOMING MESSAGE MIYKENNS/GOLTER ANON/TKEEP. COMMERCIAL MAXENCRYPT.
Ref.: COntracT #0083347100232(TKEEP).
Please be advised Contract only partially fulfilled. Item now in our possession but only casing and already-known dedication still extant. Rest of text printed on paper that has rotted to dust over past twelve centuries. Nature of time lock on case and chemical composition of paper dust indicates this may have been intentional. Detailed examination of case and remaining contents reveals no other storage medium save (naked-eye visible) message engraved in rear of case, quote THINGS WILL CHANGE. unquote. Case believed to be late Terhama'a (Golterian) Limited, comprising precious and semiprecious stones and gold on steel, plus four diamond-leaf engravings frontis. Total estimated value conservatively 10MnT. Please advise.
Reply CME to one-shot homing dest. #MS94473.3449.1[1]
TEXTEND

TEXTBEGIN HOMING MESSAGE GOLTER/MIYKENNS TKEEP/ANON. COMMERCIAL MAXENCRYPT.
Ref.: OSHD #MS94473.3449.1[0]
Extant remains acceptable under Contract clause 37.1. Kindly deliver via Vessel "Victory," Mine Seven Subsurface Crawler Base, Equatorial Region, NG, soonest.
TEXTEND

TEXTBEGIN UNSOURCED HOMING MESSAGE MIYKENNS/GOLTER ANON/HOUSE (S. JALISTRE) COMMERCIAL MAXENCRYPT.
Ref.: COntracT #0083347100232(TKEEP).
Seigneur, please see attached message from agency. Confirm property to be delivered to Nachtel's Ghost.
Reply CME to one-shot homing dest. #MS97821.7702.1[1]
TEXTEND

TEXTBEGIN HOMING MESSAGE GOLTER/MIYKENNS HOUSE/ANON. COMMERCIAL MAXENCRYPT.
Ref.: OSHD #MS97821.7702.1[0] Destination confirmed. Please deliver to our agents on NG as advised.
TEXTEND

• • •

She walked back from the hire-bureau through the morning rush hour of bicycles, trams, and cars. The streets were busy. Unlike Malishu, SkyView didn't actually ban private transport, though it did discourage it.

The city was perched on a plateau that stuck half a kilometer above the surrounding sea of undulating Entraxrln canopy like a vast wart on pale skin. It was a chill, raw place even though it was only a couple of thousand kilometers from the equator, and less than two thousand meters above sea level. Denied the Entraxrln's relatively balmy autoclimate, SkyView relied entirely on Thrial for its warmth, and the sun was noticeably smaller in the sky than it was seen from the surface of Golter.

The hire-bureau was near the main funicular station where they'd first arrived in the city three days earlier, rising from the purple gloom of the Entraxrln evening to the wide glory of a Miykenns sunset in brilliant cerise. Now commuters who had just made the same trip swept her along with them through the cool, crisp, cloudless morning.

She had sent her first message early last night and received its reply after supper. She'd asked for the confirmation from the Sea House within minutes but hadn't waited for a reply; there was a three-hour round-trip signal delay, and it was then very early morning on Golter. She doubted the Seigneur was an early riser.

She read the two replies again, waiting on a traffic island while cars whirred and trams clanked past. She raised her face to the sunlight, seeking the weak warmth with a kind of hunger after the weeks in Pharpech's perpetual gloom. The light shone down the canyon of city streets, reflecting off high glass-fronted buildings on either side, pouring onto the river of traffic and the crowds of people. *NG, soonest*, she read once more, and then stuffed the pieces of flimsy into a pocket.

"Why there?" she said to herself. Her breath smoked in front of her face. She pulled on her gloves and fastened her jacket as the traffic stopped and she crossed the road in the midst of the crowd.

She watched a big seaplane roar overhead; it banked above the city as it started its approach. The plateau lake must still be ice free. She watched the aircraft disappear behind the buildings with an expression on her face somewhere between wistfulness and bitterness.

Nachtel's Ghost. They wanted her to deliver the book to Nachtel's Ghost—outward to the limits of the system, not inward, not toward Golter, where the Sea House was. She walked back to the hotel, stopping and looking in shops and displays, making sure she wasn't being followed. Her reflection, seen in one window, had a pinched, pale look about it. She inspected her face and saw again the message in the dust that was all that was left of the *Universal Principles:* THINGS WILL CHANGE.

She drew her jacket tighter still, recalling the chill granite surface of her grandfather's tomb when it had still been at Tzant, and the freezing cold of the Ghost—the remembered fall in the remembered fall. She shivered.

16

The Ghost

Physically brave, she thought as the hired ship shuddered its way into the thin, cold, evaporating atmosphere of Nachtel's Ghost. *Physically brave.*

She had left the others in SkyView. They would wait there until she had finished in Nachtel's Ghost and decide where to rendezvous later. They'd had news from Golter; all Miz's assets had been frozen while the Log Jam attempted to have a warrant issued for his arrest in connection with an unspecified offense within its jurisdiction. Miz had lawyers working on the case, and anyway, had emergency funds he could access, but not until he was actually present on Golter. Sharrow had used up most of the rest of the contract-expenses allowance chartering a private spacecraft to take her from SkyView to Nachtel's Ghost; comm net gossip and news reports both had it that the Huhsz were waiting at Embarkation Island, and she'd been traveling as Ysul Demri long enough for there to be an even chance they knew her pseudonym.

She had not been back to the Ghost since the crash-landing that had both saved her and almost killed her. The crippled ex-excise clipper had fallen like a meteorite through the wasted air of the small planet-moon, slowing and slewing as it spun and wobbled and disintegrated on its long arcing plunge toward the planet's snow-covered surface. She couldn't remember anything after she'd shouted to Miz about wanting any crater she made being named after her. Miz hadn't heard her, anyway.

The crash report later concluded she'd probably run out of gyro-maneuvering power ten kilometers up, while the craft was still traveling at over a kilometer a second. It had started to tumble and tear itself to pieces immediately afterward, and only luck had saved her after that. The central section of the ship—containing the combat-pressure hull, life-support systems, and central plasma-power plant—had stayed relatively intact, reduced to a jagged, roughly spherical shape that had continued to slow as it somersaulted and shed further small pieces of wreckage like burning shrapnel through the air.

She could recall nothing of those final minutes, and nothing of the crash itself, as the piece of wreckage containing her buried itself inside a snow-wave, one of the thousands migrating across the surface of the planet's equatorial snow fields like sand dunes across a desert.

A crawler carrying mining supplies had been within a couple of kilometers. The crew had found her, a few minutes before it would have been too late, crushed and folded inside the steaming, radiation-contaminated wreckage of the ship, buried two hundred meters under the surface of the snow-wave at the end of a collapsed tunnel of ice and snow.

The crawler's crew had cut her out; the medics at First Cut mine had treated the physical injuries, while specialist war-embargoed systems were brought in from Trench City, the planet's capital, to treat the radiation sickness that had brought her even closer to death.

It had been two months before they'd even thought it worthwhile restoring her to consciousness. When she awoke, the war had been over for a month, and the military-standard interface wafer buried at the back of her skull had been removed. The effects of the synchroneurobonding virus were irreversible, while the nanotechnology and tissue-cloning techniques that repaired the ravages of the radiation pulse were withdrawn only after the course of treatment had finished.

And—perhaps—something else had been added: the crystal virus that had grown over the years and then lain dormant within her skull until a few weeks ago, when she'd been running with the others through the dried-up tank of the ancient oil-carrier, in the Log Jam.

Her memories of the hospital in the mine complex were hazy. She remembered the Tenaus military prison hospital much better; gradually recovering, waiting for the final peace deal to be worked out, beginning to exercise her body in the gym to restore her lost fitness, and exercising her brain whenever she could, remembering—obsessively, the prison psychologist had worried—every detail she could dredge from her memory from the age of five onward, because she'd been terrified that the treatment had altered her, made her somebody different by destroying some of her memories.

She wanted to recall everything and to try to assess if the memories she found buried in herself were the ones she could remember from before; it seemed like a check on the kind of alteration she feared that the act of recalling a memory itself left a memory, and that that could be compared with the experience of remembering in the present.

In the end there was no sure way of telling, but she found no obvious holes in her memory. When she'd been allowed to send and receive communications, the people who wrote to her seemed to relate to her the way she remembered. Nobody seemed to notice any change; certainly they didn't mention any.

They had to write to her because visits were not allowed, and the light-delay from Tenaus Habitat to almost anywhere else was too long for real-time conversations. She had had one phone call with Miz, calling from HomeAtLast, in orbit above Miykenns. In a way it had been the best phone conversation of her life; the minutes-long gaps while the signal carrying the words you had just spoken traveled to their destination meant that you just had to sit there looking at the screen and the other person. Calling anybody else, she'd have watched screen or read something in between, but with Miz she just sat and stared at his face. They'd had an hour; it had only really been ten minutes and had seemed like one.

Had they put the crystal-virus into her there, in Tenaus? Nachtel's Ghost seemed like the more obvious place, while she'd been hovering close to death in a state more like suspended animation than anything else, beyond stimulus, sensation, or dreams . . . but perhaps it had been done in Tenaus. Why would a Tax-neutral mining company want to implant a transceiver virus in a near-dead crashed military pilot?

But then, she thought, why would somebody in a military prison hospital want to do that, either?

Why would anybody?

A cold, keen wind cut out of a sky the color of verdigris. The sun dangled like a hopeless bauble dispensing thin amounts of light. Leeward, the dark train of a departing storm trailed its snowy skirts high into the swiveling tides of light. The snow-cliff at her back reared like an enormous wave, poised ready to break on the sloped black beach of the shield volcano's flanks.

The crawler that had brought her here rumbled back on its tracks, over the clinker and the wind-drifted ramps of ash, reversing into the snow tunnel. She watched its glinting metal carapace and maser-nostriled snout slide back into the base of the snow-cliff and trundle back and up until the slope of the tunnel removed it from her view.

She turned and looked up the barely discernible slope of the volcano through veils of lifting steam and vapor toward the tumbled remains of the old geothermal station buildings, a set of fractured concrete blocks strewn haphazardly across the darkly gleaming lava field. Snow-covered pools dotted depressions in the lava, and in the distance—maybe twenty kilometers away—the latest of the volcano's vents piled white steam and smoke into the sky. She looked straight up. Overhead, the gas giant Nachtel hung hemispheric, pale gold and hazy orange in the sky, filling a quarter of it.

She pulled the hood of her jacket tighter against the thin, freezing wind and set off across the fractured, gray-black lava field toward the ruined concrete buildings up the slope, clutching the empty book to her chest.

She was breathing hard when she got to the smashed blockhouses; the atmosphere was desperately thin, even though comparatively little effort was required to walk in the Ghost's weak gravity. Agoraphobia was endemic in visitors to the planet-moon who ventured into the open; the air felt so thin and Nachtel could loom so huge above that it seemed each floating step must send the walker bounding away from the surface altogether, swept away into the green, subliming sky.

"Hello?" she called.

Her voice echoed around the concrete walls of the first collapsed concrete building. Quakes had left all the thick-walled, windowless structures canted and listing, and the concrete apron they had been built upon had split and sundered, leaving jagged chunks of material sticking up like broken teeth, their rusted reinforcing rods tangling or torn out like failed brace-work.

She held the book to her chest and walked over the tilted slabs of concrete from building to building, having to stoop and use her free hand in places where the fractured geography of the ruins made walking, even in that low gravity, impossible.

The building farthest up-slope was the largest in the complex; she stepped over the fallen lintel of its broad doorway.

Though the structure's walls were intact, its roof had folded in the middle, then caved in and fallen to produce a shallow V of concrete that slanted down into an ice-rimmed pool of standing water, which—perhaps still connected to the network of abandoned thermal pipe-work buried in the volcano—was warm enough to produce lazy strokes of steam in the calm, subzero air.

There was a narrow beach of black clinker gathered in one corner of the ruin, against the far wall.

There were two men there. She recognized them.

They were dressed only in swimming trunks and sat in the same two deck chairs she remembered from the tanker. A flowery parasol stuck at a jaunty angle out of the black beach behind them, and between their seats there was a small folding table holding bottles and glasses.

The one on the right stood up and waved to her.

"Delighted you could join us!" he called, then took a couple of steps forward to the water and dived lithely in with barely a splash. The waves looked tall and odd as they moved across the pool.

She stuck her left hand in her pocket and walked along the gentle slope of the collapsed roof. The young bald-headed man who'd dived into the water swam past her, grinning and waving. The other was drinking from a tall glass. He watched his companion as he reached the far end of the pool, where the doorway was, and then turned and started on his way back.

"Have a seat, doll," the young man said pleasantly, pointing at the deck chair his twin had vacated. She looked at it, then looked around and sat. She kept her left hand in her pocket. The book was on her lap. She pushed the jacket's hood back.

"Ah, red," the young man said, smiling at her hair. "Very attractive; it suits you."

His pale body looked trim and well-muscled. She couldn't see any cold bumps. His trunks were opticloth, and showed a few seconds of a tropical beach scene: golden sand, a single big roller, and one graceful surfer, forever climbing up onto her board and riding into a curling blue tunnel in the wave.

The other young man rose dripping out of the water and strolled up the beach, his skin steaming. His trunks showed somebody heli-diving, throwing themselves from a helicopter into a great fissure on some rocky coast, just as a huge pulse of surf surged frothing up the channel.

The surfer-trunked man reached under his deck chair and threw his companion a towel. He dabbed at himself, then sat cross-legged on the dark clinker of the beach in front of them with the towel draped over his shoulders. He grinned at the other man.

"A pleasant journey here, I trust, Lady Sharrow?" the one in the deck chair said.

She nodded slowly. "Acceptable," she told him.

"I'm sorry," he said, tapping his forehead. He lifted a glass from the tray of spirit bottles on the table between him and her. "May I offer you a drink?"

"No, thank you," she said.

"May I . . . ?" the other one said, leaning forward and nodding at the book on her lap.

She tipped the thick book in her lap so that she could hold it with one gloved hand and then handed it to him. He smiled tolerantly and accepted it.

"It's all right, Lady Sharrow," he said, opening the book's metal casing. "You won't be needing your gun."

She left her hand in her pocket, anyway, gripping the HandCannon. The one sitting on the beach looked briefly at the interior of the book, studying the title page and the diamond-leaf plates for a couple of seconds each. He smiled as he read the words engraved in the back of the casing and held the book up so that his companion in the deck chair could read the inscription, too. They both laughed lightly.

"Terrible, isn't it?" the one in the deck chair said to her. "Such a waste. Ah, well."

The one holding the book tipped it upside down so that the paper-dust fell out and drifted down to coat the black beach with a single swirled streak of gray.

"We are so careless with our treasures," he said. He closed the book and set it to one side.

"We mistake the priceless for the worthless," agreed the one in the deck chair, topping up his glass from a bottle of trax spirit.

"I must say," the one on the beach said, "you don't seem terribly surprised to find us here, Lady Sharrow." He sounded disappointed. He accepted a tall glass from his twin, then drank and smiled up at her. "We'd rather hoped you might be."

She shrugged.

"Typical, isn't it?" said the one in the chair to his twin. "Women go quiet only when you'd actually quite like to hear what they have to say."

The other one looked at her and shook his head sadly.

"Anyway," the man in the deck chair said, "on behalf of the agency and our clients—the Sad Brothers, in this case— thank you for the book. But now, as you can probably guess, we want you to look for the final Lazy Gun, if you don't mind."

She looked at him.

"No questions?" he asked her. She shook her head. He laughed lightly. "And we thought you'd have so many. Ah, well." He smiled broadly, waving his glass. "Oh, by the way, you did get our message, back in . . . ?" He frowned, looked at the other young man.

"Pharpech," the one on the beach provided.

"Ah yes, Pharpech," the young man said, pronouncing the word with exaggerated care and a sort of conspiratorial grimace. "Was our signal received?"

She thought before answering. "The necklace?" she said. "Yes."

The young man in the chair looked happy.

"Super," he said. "Just so you didn't think that being off-net meant being out of touch with us." He put his drink down and lay back in the chair, hands behind his head. His underarms were bare and smooth. The hairs on the rest of his body looked thin and white; only his blond eyebrows held any hint of color. She looked at the one on the beach. Sunlight gleamed on the dome of his skull. He didn't seem to have any cold bumps, either.

"Well, don't let us detain you, Lady Sharrow," he said. He patted the book. "Thank you for delivering the piece, as per contract. We'll be in touch, perhaps. Perhaps not."

"Try not to take too long," the one in the deck chair said, still lying back soaking up the sparse sunlight, eyes closed.

"And don't get caught," the other one chipped in.

She rose slowly to her feet. The one with the girl surfing on his trunks lay there, hands behind his naked scalp, eyes closed, legs slightly spread. The one sitting cross-legged on the beach leaned forward, whistling, and started trying to build a little tower of black clinker, but it kept falling apart.

"Bon voyage," the one on the deck chair said without opening his eyes.

She walked away for five steps, then turned. They were as they had been. She drew the HandCannon out and pointed it at the one with the heli-diving scene, which was playing across the stretched rear of his trunks just as it had been across the crumpled front.

She stood like that for nearly half a minute. Eventually the one she was aiming at glanced around at her, did a double take and swiveled to face her.

He shaded his eyes, looking up at her. "Yes, Lady Sharrow?"

The one on the deck chair opened his eyes, blinking and looking mildly surprised.

She said, "I was thinking of finding out the messy way whether you're both androids."

The two young men looked at each other. The one on the chair shrugged and said, "Androids? Why should it matter whether *either* of us is an android?"

She pointed the gun at him. "Call it simple curiosity," she said. "Or revenge for what happened in the tanker, and in Bencil Dornay's house."

"But we only *hurt* you," the one on the deck chair protested.

"Yes, and you were *so* rude to us in Stager," the beach one said, frowning tight-lipped at her and nodding emphatically. "All we'd been going to tell you was that we'd acquired the contract from the Sad Brothers and you'd be seeing us here if you got the book, but you were so horrible to us, we didn't."

She kept the gun pointing at the one in the chair, then lowered it.

She aimed deliberately at the book, slowly closing one eye.

The man on the beach threw himself in front of the metal casing. The one in the chair leapt up, arms out toward her and his hands spread. He stepped over his twin, lying hunched up over the book.

"Now, now, Lady Sharrow," he said. "There's no need to turn vandal." He smiled nervously.

She took a deep breath, then pocketed the gun.

"I really can't work you people out at all," she said.

The one standing facing her, trunks repeating the surfing scene, looked puzzled and pleased at the same time. She turned on her heel and walked away across the flaking concrete, back to the doorway.

Her skull and back tingled the whole way there, again waiting for a shot, or for the pain, but when she turned around in the doorway, they were still in the same positions: one curled up, fetal, around the book-casing, the other standing in front of his twin, watching her.

She walked down through the shattered ramps of concrete and the wilderness of fractured lava, back to the snow-cliff and the tunnel where the crawler was waiting.

The crawler took her back to Mine Seven; the weather stayed clear enough for her to take a flight to Trench City, where the hired spacecraft was waiting. She used its terminal to get in touch with the others. She couldn't contact them directly, but there was a filed message from Zefla reporting all was well in SkyView. She left an entry in the personal columns of the *Net Gazette* letting them know she had made the delivery. Thinking of cryptic messages, she checked up on the Tile race results for the past week.

There had been one winner called Hollow Book, three days earlier, the day she'd left from Miykenns.

She scanned the other mounts mentioned, wondering if it could just all be coincidence. Shy Dancer? Wonder Thing? Little Resheril Goes North? Sundry Floozies? Borrowed Sunset? Molgarin's Keep? Right Way Round? Mash That Meat? Scrap The Whole Thing? Crush That Butt? Bip!? . . . None of the other names seemed to mean anything. Unless Shy Dancer was another reference to Bencil Dornay, of course . . . and Wonder Thing could refer to the Lazy Gun, and . . . She gave up; if you thought hard enough, there could be significance in every name or none, and there was no way of knowing where to draw the line.

She kept thinking about the crash and the time she'd spent in the mining hospital. She tried hacking into the relevant data banks from Trench, but the wartime records weren't accessible from outside the mining complex where they were held. She left the meter running on the hired spacecraft *Wheeler Dealer* (and left its two-woman crew, Tenel and Choss Esrup, to lose more money in Trench's casinos and game-bars) and took a tube train to the First Cut mine, where she'd been hospitalized originally, after the crash.

The First Cut mine had been the first large-scale mining operation to be set up on the Ghost. The supply of heavy metals in its immediate area had been mostly worked out millennia earlier, and the big companies had moved to lusher pastures, leaving smaller concerns to work the thin veins of ores still left. First Cut's accommodation warrens had been largely abandoned, an underground city reduced to the population of a town.

"Ysul Demri," she said, sitting in the seat the clerk indicated. "I'm interested in the part the Ghost played in the Five Percent War, and I'd like access to the complex records for the time."

The clerk was a big, blotchily skinned woman who ran her section of the First Cut warren's administrative affairs from a booth in a small, steamy café in Drag Three, one of the warren's main hall-streets. People walked past outside, some pushing trolleys and stalls; in the center of the street, small cars hummed past, warners chiming. The clerk watched her with one eye; the other was kept closed while she lid-screened.

"Only abstracts and interpretations available in the city archives," she said.

A plumbing loom of eight small-bore pipes ran from the counter samovar-cisterns around the café's walls to the various booths and over the ceiling to loop down to the central tables. The clerk put her cup under one of the small brass taps on the wall and poured herself a measure of something sweet-smelling.

"I know," Sharrow said. She had bought her own cup and filled it from the same tap the clerk had used. "I was really hoping to get to the raw stuff."

The clerk was silent for a couple of seconds, then she drank from her cup. "You want the Foundation," she told Sharrow. "They took over the DBs when the hospital moved to new quarters, just after the war. The hospital leases back what it needs from them, like us."

Sharrow sipped the warm, bittersweet liquid. "The Foundation?" she asked.

"Commonwealth Foundation," the clerk said, opening both eyes for a second and looking surprised. "The People. Haven't you heard of them?"

"I'm sorry, no," Sharrow said.

The clerk closed both eyes for a moment. "I guess not. We tend to forget, out here," she said. She opened one eye. "Level Seven on down, any shaft. I'll tell them you're coming."

"Thank you," Sharrow said.

"But they don't part with stuff without a good reason, usually. Best of luck."

"To sum up: the history of Golter, and of the system, is one of a continual search for stability. It is a search that has itself consistently helped destroy the quality it was instigated to discover. Arguably, every conceivable system of political power management has now been tried; none survive conceptually with any degree of credibility, and even the last full-scale bid to impose central authority in the shape of the Ladyr dynasty was more of a retrofashion pastiche of previous imperial eras—which even the participants themselves found it difficult to take seriously—than a serious attempt to establish a lasting hegemony over the power functions of the system.

"The current stalemate between progressive and re-

gressive forces has given us seven hundred years of bureau-
cratic constipation in the shape of the World Court and the
associated but largely symbolic Council. Power today rests
in the hands of the lawyers. Those whose function it ought
to be merely to help regulate have come instead—following
the failure of nerve in those with the rightful claim and historical provenance required for leadership—to legislate. By
their very nature, they will ensure that having taken the
reins of power into their hands, they cannot legally be
wrested from them.

"What must be remembered by those who care for the
future as well as the history of our species is that law is no
more than an abstraction of justice, an expression of a society's political will and philosophical conceptions. Truth,
right, and justice are processes, not states. They are dynamic
functions that can be expressed and understood only
through *action*. . . . And arguably the time for action is fast
approaching. Thank you."

The young lecturer executed a small bow to the packed
theater and started boxing his paper-written notes. The hall
erupted, startling her. She stood at the back of the lecture
theater, clutching her satchel and looking around at the two
thousand or so people crammed into the space. They were
all on their feet, clapping and cheering and stamping their
feet.

Lectures in Yadayeypon had never been like this, she
thought. The lecturer—a slim, medium-tall young man with
dark curls and darker eyes—was escorted from the foot of
the theater by a shield of efficient-looking security guards in
white uniforms who had taken up the first row of seats in
the auditorium. The guards had to keep a hundred or so
people back from the door the young man had exited
through; the besieging crowd waved notebooks and cameras
and recorders, pleading with the blank-faced guards to let
them through.

She stood for a while, sporadically jostled by the departing crowds of mostly young and very polite people filing
out of the lecture theater. She was trying to recall witnessing
a more charismatic speaker, but could not. There had been
a startling buzz of emotion crackling through the whole theater throughout the hour of the lecture she'd caught, even
though the things the young man had actually been saying
weren't particularly original or dramatic. Nevertheless, the

feeling was infectious and undeniable. She'd had the same feeling of excitement, of *impendingness* that she got sometimes when she heard an especially talented new band or singer, or read some particularly promising poet, or saw some screen or stage prodigy for the first time. It was something akin to the first, lustful stage of obsessive love.

She shook herself out of it and checked the time. There was another tube back to Trench in an hour. She very much doubted she was going to have any luck getting to see this fellow who seemed to control access to everything, including fifteen-year-old hospital records, but she had to see the authorities, anyway, to get her gun back; they'd taken it from her when she'd gone into the lecture theater.

The Commonwealth Foundation appeared to be part charity, part Irregular University, and part political party. It seemed to have taken over most of First Cut's largely deserted lower warren, and this young man, Girmeyn, gave every appearance of being its leader, even though nobody ever quite addressed him as such.

"Girmeyn will see you now, Ms. Demri," the white-uniformed guard said.

She had been watching screen, sitting in the draftily warm cave of a waiting room with about two hundred other people who were petitioning to see the man.

She looked up, surprised. She'd given up any hope of seeing Girmeyn when she'd seen the crowd. All she wanted now was to retrieve the HandCannon.

"He *will*?" she said. People sitting nearby stared at her.

"Please follow me," the guard said.

She followed the white-uniformed guard as he led her to the end of the waiting room and into a corridor. The corridor ended in a long, comfortably furnished chamber looking down into a huge cavern.

The cavern was walled in naked black rock. Its smooth floor was covered with ancient, glittering machinery that towered twenty meters into the space, almost level with the windows of the gallery. The complicated, indecipherable machines—so ambiguous in their convoluted design, they could have been turbines, generators, nuclear or chemical reactors, or agents of a hundred other processes—glittered under bright overhead lights. Huge pale stalactites fluted pendulously from the roof of the cavern in moist folds of deposited rock, counterpointed by stalagmites on the cavern floor beneath. Where the machinery got in the way, the deposits had merged, the never less than meter-thick columns conjoined to and mingling intimately with the silent machines.

She stared at the scene for a few seconds, made dizzy by the sheer weight of time implicit in the slumped topology of the palely gleaming, technology-enfolding pillars.

"Ms. Demri?" an elderly white-uniformed man said.

She looked around. "Yes?"

"This way." He held out his hand. Girmeyn sat behind a large desk at the far end of the room, surrounded by a variety of people with yoke screens, hand screens, brow projectors, patch screens, and, judging by the one-eyed aspect of a couple of them, lid-screens. She was shown into a large seat to one side of the desk, across a smaller table from a similar seat and just by the windows looking out into the cavern.

She sat still for a few minutes, watching what looked remarkably like a prince conducting the affairs of state, before the young man stood up behind his desk, bowed to the people, and walked over to join her. The men and women surrounding the desk mostly stood where they were; some sat down on seats and some on the floor. Sharrow stood up to shake his hand. His grip was strong and warm.

"Ms. Demri," he said. His voice was deeper than she'd expected. He bowed to her and sat in the other seat. He was dressed as he had been in the lecture theater half an hour earlier, in a conservative black academic gown. He was even younger than she'd thought—early rather than midtwenties. His exquisitely tangled medium-length hair was blue-black, his pale brown, depilated skin was smooth and unblemished. His lips were full and expressive beneath a long, delicate nose. His jaw was strong, and he had a dimple on his chin. He sat relaxed but formal in the seat, his dark eyes inspecting her.

"It's very kind of you to see me," she said, "but I really only want access to some fifteen-year-old hospital records." She glanced behind her. "There are so many people waiting out there, I feel positively unworthy."

"Are you a student of the Five Percent War, Ms. Demri?" he asked. There was a practiced ease about his voice that belonged in somebody of immense experience and authority three times his age. His voice poured over her.

"Yes," she said. "I am."

"May I ask where?"

"Well, I did attend Yadayeypon some time ago. But I'm independent now; it's almost more of a hobby. . . ."

He smiled, revealing perfect teeth. "I must have led an even more sheltered life than I thought, Ms. Demri, if students have to carry such large pieces of ordnance around with them." He glanced around to the desk and made a motion with one hand. The elderly guard who'd first greeted her brought the HandCannon over.

"It is safe to handle, sir," he said, presenting the gun to Girmeyn, who inspected it.

From the way he held it, she knew he had probably never held a gun in his life.

The elderly guard stooped toward her; he held the gun's magazine in one hand, and in the other, between two fingers, a General Purpose HandCannon round. She looked up at it and then him.

"You shouldn't keep a round in the breach like that, ma'am," he told her. "It's dangerous."

"So I'm told," she said, sighing. The guard went back to the desk. Girmeyn passed the HandCannon to her just as the elderly guard had to him. She put it in her pocket.

"Thank you," she said. He seemed to be expecting something more. She shrugged. "The competition for research grants is unusually fierce this year."

He smiled. "You think these old hospital records will help you in your studies?"

She was starting to wonder. She had a feeling—somehow quite distinct but utterly vague at the same time—that there was something important going on here, but she had no clue whatsoever what it might be. "They might," she said. "I can't help thinking this is all getting out of proportion. It's not an especially important request, I'd have thought, and you're obviously so busy. . . ." She waved one hand.

"Details matter, though, don't you think?" he said. "Sometimes what appear to be utterly inconsequential actions have the most enormous results. Chance makes the casual momentous. It is the fulcrum upon which the levers of action rest."

She chanced a small laugh. "Do you always speak in epigrams, Mr. Girmeyn?"

He smiled broadly, dazzlingly. "Occupational hazard," he said, spreading his hands. "Allow me to attenuate my portentousness for you."

She grinned, looked down. "I heard the latter half of your lecture," she said. "It was very impressive."

"In content or delivery?" he asked, slinging an arm over the back of his chair.

"In delivery, absolutely," she told him. "In content . . ." She shrugged. "To employ a phrase you might take issue with, the jury's still out on that."

"Hmm," he said, frowning and smiling at the same time. "The usual answer to that question is 'both.'"

She glanced around at the people around the desk, most of whom were pretending not to look at Girmeyn and her. "I'm sure it is," she told him.

"My arguments didn't touch you, then?" He looked sad. She had a brief, vertiginous, revelatory feeling that she could very easily fall in love with this man, and that not only had hundreds, perhaps thousands of people already done so, but that many more might yet.

She cleared her throat. "They worry me. They sound so much like what so many people want to hear, what they believe they would say if they were sufficiently articulate."

"Using your chosen terminology," he said quietly, "I would have to plead guilty. And enter a special defense of being right, and the current law wrong." He smiled.

"I think," she said carefully, "that perhaps too many people want things to be simple when they are not and cannot be. Encouraging that desire is seductive and rewarding, but also dangerous."

He looked away a little, as if inspecting something far in the distance over her left shoulder. He nodded slowly for a few moments. "I think power has always been like that," he said, his voice low.

"I have a . . . relation," she said, "who I think has become, largely because of her environment, quite thoroughly deranged over the last few years." She met Girmeyn's gaze and looked into the darkness there. "I have the disquieting feeling that she wouldn't have disagreed with a single word you said today."

He shrugged with exaggerated slowness. "Still, don't be

alarmed, Ms. Demri," he said. "I am just a humble function- ary. Indeed, technically I am still a student." He smiled, still holding her gaze. "Two years ago they asked me to lecture; last year they began to call me professor, and now people come to me and ask for my help, and some invite me to visit them and advise them ... oh, all over the Ghost." He smiled. "But I am still a student, still learning."

"Next year, the system?"

He looked puzzled, then favored her with another broad, ravishing smile. "At least!" he laughed.

She couldn't help laughing, too, still gazing at him.

He wouldn't look away. She held his gaze, drinking it in.

Eventually she started to consider being the one to break off because otherwise they might sit here like this for the rest of the day. Then the elderly guard approached again. He stood to one side and coughed.

"Yes?" Girmeyn said, laughing a little as he looked at the other man.

"I'm sorry, sir," the elderly guard said, glancing at her. "The dinner this evening—the train is waiting."

Girmeyn looked genuinely annoyed. He held his hands palms up toward her. "I must go, Ms. Demri. Can I per- suade you to accompany me? Or wait for me here? I would love to talk longer with you."

"I think it would be best if I left," she said. "I have to leave the Ghost very soon." There was a voice inside her screaming, *Yes! Yes! Say yes, you idiot!* But she ignored it.

He sighed. "That's unfortunate," he said, rising. She got up, too. They shook hands. He held her hand while he said, "I hope we shall meet again."

"So do I," she said. She smiled, still holding his hand. "I don't know why I'm saying this," she said, feeling her face, neck, and chest go warm. "But I think you're the most remarkable person I've ever met."

He made a small, snorting laugh and looked down. She let his hand go, and he put them both behind his back. He looked up at her again. "And you are the first person to make me blush in about ten years." He bowed formally. "Till the next time, Ms. Demri," he said.

She nodded. "Till then."

He started to turn away, then said, "Oh, you may have your records."

"Thank you."

He turned and began to walk away. She watched him stop, a couple of steps away. He turned back to look at her, his hands still clasped behind his back. "Why did you *really* come here, Ms. Demri?" he asked.

She shrugged. "Something I just couldn't get out of my head," she told him.

He considered this, then shook his head once and walked away through a door set in the wall behind the desk, followed by his functionaries and attendants.

She stood there for a while, wondering exactly what it was she was feeling. Then the elderly guard approached, handed her a data chip, the HandCannon's magazine and extra round, and saw her to the exit. As she walked toward the doors, she looked out at the silent, glittering cavern on the far side of the glass.

For a few minutes she had quite forgotten it existed.

She caught the next tube to Trench City and sat on the train with a big grin on her face, awash with a strange, exhilarating feeling that she had just experienced something consummately important whose meaning was still hidden from her, but growing. It took an act of will to run the data chip she'd been given through her wrist screen.

The records told her nothing. If there had been anything exceptional about the hospital where she'd been treated, or its staff or systems, she couldn't find it. The First Cut mine itself had been just another mining complex, owned by the usual anonymous Corp. which rented the shafts and remaining deposits out to the smaller cooperatives, collectives, and entrepreneurs.

She gave up on the chip and just sat there, thinking of that enormous cavern and its mysterious, time-encrusted machines, the dark subniveal space they inhabited resonating in her like some awesome chord.

She dragged her all-girl ship crew out of an all-boy sex show joint in Trench and left for Golter that evening.

"Hi, doll. Just replying to your message. Sure got us beat. We've made some inquiries into this Keep agency and got precisely nowhere. Looks brand new; no previous jobs, contracts ... nothing. Best set of commercial references you've ever seen, but no pattern to them. Rumor is they put in a loss-leader tender for the book contract; had the other agencies changing their underwear on the hour, but nothing's been heard of them since. No physical address and no record of who's working for them, either. How the grisly twins you met in the tanker came to be on the payroll, we can't work out. Can't see any reason why you *shouldn't* ask the Sad Brothers why they employed that particular agency, as you suggested, but something tells me you won't get any joy there. Whole thing stinks. Much like the Sea House, come to think of it.

"None of us had heard of this Girmeyn guy or the Commonwealth Foundation. The public-access records all look innocuous enough. I've started a legal look-see, but so far it's coming drier than a bar in Temperance City.

"The info chip they gave you: if it's that data-dense and unsorted, the only thing we can think of is to hand it over to an AI. Hire one or ask your cousin for a favor . . . though I guess you'd have to tell them what you're looking for, which might not be so smart. Suppose you've already thought of that, though.

"Sorry this is all so unhelpful. Umm . . . We're all fine; there doesn't seem to be any monklike activity nearby. We'll be leaving soon. See you at the arranged place. Love from all. Well, apart from Cenny, maybe. Ah, shit . . ." Zefla made a pained face, then shook her head. "Just call me Ms. Tactful. What the hell—have a safe voyage. See ya, doll."

The image faded inside the holo screen. Sharrow realized she'd tensed up a little as she'd watched the signal. She let go of the seat's arms, letting her body float within the chair.

The control and data screens of the Charter Space Ship *Wheeler Dealer* glowed gently around her. The bridge, like the rest of the ship, was unusually quiet; the vessel was just past the midpoint of its journey to Golter, in free-fall a couple of hours before it would turn its engines back on to begin braking. Equally conducive to the relative hush was the fact that the ship's two crew-women, who favored heavy-duty industro-thrash music, were both soundly asleep in their bunks.

Sharrow stared into the unreal gray depths of the holo screen for a while, then sighed.

"Ship?"

"Ready, client Lady Sharrow," the computer toned.

"*You're* not an AI, are you?"

"I am not an Artificial Intelligence. I am a semi—"

"Never mind. Okay, thanks. I'm finished here."

3.

A
TROPHY
OF
A
PAST
DISPUTE

17

Conscience
of
Prisoners

A warm rain fell on Ikueshleng. The private spacecraft *Wheeler Dealer* buttoned down through the darkness of Outer Jonolrey toward the fifty-kilometer diameter patch of sunlight that presided over the port. The ship lanced through the encircling clouds of drizzle, its dull-red glowing hull leaving a trail of steam behind it in the dark air, then glinting watery gold as it entered the cloud-filtered shaft of reflected sunlight beamed down onto the enclave from the orbiting mirrors.

The craft puffed vapor as it adjusted its fall and flexed stubby legs. It thumped onto and rolled along a concrete runway on the outskirts of the port. It braked and turned, trundling toward a slowly pulsing holo showing continually descending red and green horizontal lines, stopping when it was in the center of the holo.

The square of concrete beneath dropped slowly away, taking the ship with it.

"Shit," Tenel said, glancing at the screen beside the lock door. "Spot check."

Sharrow checked the screen. In the hangar space they'd been shuffled to, there was a tired male official in Port Inspection overalls holding a clipboard.

"Aw, penetration, man," Choss said. "Ain't payin the Ik's

fuckin import dues on this spit." She started fishing bottles of trax spirit out of her kitbag and leaving them in the corridor by the lock door.

Sharrow watched as the official in the hangar outside yawned and then spoke to his clipboard; his voice came out of the screen. "Hello, persons on the vessel *Wheeler Dealer,*" he said. "Transport Standards and Customs check; please have your vehicle documentation ready and baggage prepared for inspection."

"Yeah, yeah," Tenel said, finger on the screen transmit button. "On our way."

"One at a time, please," the official said, sounding bored. "Crew first."

Tenel flicked a data chip out of the screen slot and, shaking her head, stepped into the lock; the door slid open. The air lock was a standard single-aperture rotating-cylinder design that meant you couldn't have both doors open at once. The door rolled closed again, and they heard the inner sleeve and the outer door rotate together.

Sharrow and Choss watched the official nod to Tenel when she stepped off the external-access ramp, take the data chip and stick it onto his clipboard, then inspect her kitbag and wave the clipboard up and down her body a couple of times. He tapped an entry on the clipboard. "Next," he said.

"Loada shit, man," Choss muttered. She made a farting noise with her mouth and stepped into the lock. Sharrow was looking at the HandCannon, trying to recall if Ikueshleng required that one have a license for bringing weaponry in. She couldn't remember, and she wasn't sure that going to pick up the gun she'd deposited with Left Luggage here was such a good idea. She shrugged. The worst that could happen would be they'd confiscate it. She stuck it back in her satchel.

"Next, please," the man's voice said. The lock door opened; she stepped in. The lock half rotated, then stopped.

She stood there, trapped in the meter-diameter space. She pressed the control patches. Nothing happened. She got the gun out of her satchel, slung the satchel over her head, and crouched down.

She thought she heard something, then the lock started to rotate very slowly. The craft's hull metal came into view at the leading edge of the lock's aperture. The lock stopped again. She aimed the gun at the edge of the door.

The lock shifted suddenly, opening a gap about ten centimeters wide to the outside. She glimpsed a vertical sliver of unoccupied hangar.

The gas grenade came in from the top of the door, hitting the deck to her right as the lock rotated back, trapping her.

She stared, horror-struck and paralyzed, at the grenade clicking away on the floor.

For an instant she was five years old again.

A warm rain fell on Ikueshleng. Ships came and went, flying in on wings or relying on the shape of their bodies for lift, or landing vertically, engines screaming. Other sporadic roars were ships taking off, while every now and again a near-subsonic pulse of sound followed by a great whoop of noise and then a distant bellow of igniting engines announced an induction tube hurling a craft into the atmosphere.

Near one edge of the port's artificial plateau, a long rectangle of concrete hinged down, producing a shallow ramp into a brightly lit space. Rumbling up from the port's depths and out onto the rain-slicked surface apron came a tall, boxy vehicle running on four three-meter-high wheels; it was joined to another that followed it up into the drizzle, leading another carriage behind it, and another and another.

The twenty-section Land Car started to turn before the final carriages had risen onto the concrete surface. The vehicle's front wheels ran through puddles on the apron, sending waves washing out to the edges of the shallow depressions. The grimy water surged back in as the wheels passed, only to be pushed out again and again as tire after tire of the accelerating car rolled its intersecting tread over exactly the same path its predecessors had taken.

The Land Car came to the edge of the concrete, where a gate in Ikueshleng's perimeter fence gave access to the bedraggled scrub beyond. The drop was two meters or more, but the car didn't pause; its front section described a graceful arc as it drooped toward the damp ground, the links with the section behind tensing to support it. Its wheels met the ground and took the section's weight again as the rest of the car followed, each carriage bumping gently down in a ripple of movement that swept back along the vehicle's two-hundred-meter length like a snake moving from one branch

to another. The vehicle rumbled off through the fine veils of
rain toward the line of darkness a kilometer away, where the
artificial noon of the port gave way to the predawn gloom of
a cloudy tropical morning.

Sharrow watched the rain collect on the window of her
cell, beyond the plastic-covered steel bars. The raindrops
became little slanted rivulets as the car increased speed.
The landscape beyond the thick glass and slip-streamed
moisture was flat, covered in scrappy bushes and patches of
flail-grass that looked as though they could use the rain. She
looked down at the paper note the warder had slipped
through the food-hatch in her door.

*Heard you're aboard too. Court Police picked us up in
Stager on some nonsense about assassinating Invigilators.
Next stop Yada, apparently. Who got you?*

Love and kisses, Miz and the gang.

She had nothing to write with. She crumpled the note
in her hand. Outside, the reflected sunlight disappeared as
though switched off. The Land Car rumbled through the
dark beyond.

The hunters who'd caught her were a mother-and-son team;
the son had worked for the Ikueshleng Port Authority and
had contacts in Trench City's space port. The Huhsz had
leaked the fact she was traveling as Ysul Demri into a data-
base used by contract security personnel, licensed assassins,
bodyguards, and bounty hunters. Finding out which craft
she was on and arranging to borrow the relevant uniform
had been comparatively easy.

The vehicle she was on was one of a fleet of World
Court–licensed Secure Goods and Detained Persons' Surface Transporters, though everybody just called them Land
Cars. This one, the *Lesson Learned*, made regular runs between Ikueshleng and Yadayeypon with goods and people
the airlines, rail services, road authorities, and insurance
companies preferred not to handle.

The *Lesson Learned* was run by the Sons of Depletion,
one of an increasing number of secular Wounded Orders
that seemed to be part of a new Golter metafashion. Each of
the Land Car's crew had voluntarily been made deaf and
mute. Several of the warders she'd seen had gone even further and had their mouths sewn up; Sharrow assumed they
had to be drip fed or have a tube put down their nose.

Others had had one eye sewn up, too, and one man, an officer by his uniform, had had his mouth and both his eyes surgically closed. He had to be led around the car by a sighted helper, and his only mode of communication was through the Order's private touch-code, the sender's fingertips playing over the back of the receiver's hand as though on a fleshy keyboard.

A Land Car. She remembered Miz mentioning he'd had some cargo stolen from one, but that had been on Speyr, in bandit country. This was Golter, and nobody attacked a Court-licensed vehicle unless they were suicidal or mad. Even Geis couldn't help her now.

The bounty-hunter son came to see her after dawn. Close up, he was a pasty-faced, unhealthy-looking individual. He grimaced as he sat down on the fold-down seat across the soft-floored padded cell from her. He kept a stun-pistol pointed at her. She sat cross-legged on the bunk, dressed in the Land Car's prison overalls. She still had a headache, caused by whatever gas they'd used in the grenade.

"I just wanted you to know there's nothing personal in this," the man told her, grinning feebly. He was in his late twenties, maybe, thin and clean-shaven.

"Oh," she said, "thanks." She didn't bother attempting to disguise the bitterness in her voice.

"I know all about you," the man said, coughing. "I always read up all I can on our marks, and I kinda admire you, really."

"This is all making me feel a lot better," she told him. "If you admire me so fucking much, let me go."

He shook his head. "Can't do that," he said. "Too much at stake. Told the Huhsz we have you; they're expecting to trade at Yada. If we don't turn up with you, they're going to be awwwful peeved." He grinned.

She looked at him, drawing her head back a little. "Get out of here, you cretin."

"You can't talk to me like that, lady," he said, scowling. "I can stay and I can talk all I want. I could use this gun," he said, gesturing with the stun-pistol. He glanced at the door, then back at her. "I could gas you again; I could do anything I *wanted* to you."

"Try it, fuckwit," she said.

The man sneered. He stood up. "Yeah, proud aristo,

eh?" He held his hands out. The skin on them was angry and blistered. "I held the Passports in my hands, lady. I seen them. I seen what's going to kill you. I'll be thinking of you and all that pride when they put you to death—slowly, I hope."

She was frowning.

The man buzzed the door. It opened. "Good long journey to Yadayeypon, *lady*," he said.

"Wait," she said, holding up one hand.

He ignored her. "Plenty of time to think about what them Huhsz'll do to you when they get you."

"Wait!" she said as he went out of the door. She jumped off the bunk. "Did you say—?"

" 'Bye," the bounty hunter said, as the deaf-mute Son of Depletion outside closed the door again.

The *Lesson Learned* rolled across the savannah of the Chey Nar peninsula all day, heading north on ancient drove-ways between the crop fields. By the evening the Land Car had reached the foothills of the Cathrivacian Mountains and started the long detour around them that avoided a heavily tolled pass, heading up through the light forests of Undalt and Lower Tazdecttedy, rising on its suspension to brush the tops of the small trees with its underbody as it climbed through the clouds for the plateau of High Marden.

Traffic stopped on the Shruprov-Takandra turnpike the following morning while the car passed over it, each set of wheels raising themselves above the turnpike fence and then setting down again to rumble over the road itself.

Somebody in the halted traffic—there was usually at least one—decided to have some sport by jumping the lights and driving underneath the Land Car, timing their approach so that they passed between the sets of wheels. The driver on this occasion failed; his small car caught the edge of one of the *Lesson Learned*'s nearside tires and spun, bouncing off the inside of the wheels on the other side and ending up underneath the edge of the Land Car; the *Lesson Learned*'s tires rolled on over the automobile, crushing and compressing it into a half-meter-high sandwich of junk.

The Land Car didn't stop or even slow down; the Order had indemnities against that sort of thing.

It forded the Vounti River near Ca-Blay in a rainstorm and turned southwest, setting a course that would take it across the plateau toward Mar Scarp and the downs and valleys of Marden County on the borders of Yadayeypon Province.

They brought her meals on trenchers or disposable plates. She tried to get the guards to bring her something to write with but failed; she made ink from some nuts that had garnished a meal and used one of her bite-sharpened nails to write on the other side of Miz's note, then put it in the door slot just before that evening's meal. It was still there when her meal appeared. She buzzed the door, but nobody answered. She checked every part of the cell; there didn't seem to be any way out without help or equipment. There was no screen. She spent a lot of time just looking out the small window.

The bounty hunter had said he'd held the Passports in his hands. And he had looked ill. She had known for some time what the symptoms of radiation sickness were; it had been one of the first things the doc had told them about when they'd joined the anti-Tax Navy.

There had been a fashion, millennia ago, for assassination by plutonium among the governing classes of the system—pens, medals, and articles of clothing had been the favored delivery systems—and for centuries nobody in a position of power would ever be without a personal radiation monitor, but the practice had been abandoned—banned and outlawed in that order long ago—and only a few Corps, administrations, and old Houses with long memories still bothered with such precautions.

It had not even occurred to her, Miz, or any of the others that the Huhsz would simply ignore the fact that the Passports had been irradiated. She hadn't thought to tell anybody.

No wonder the Huhsz missions had been able to move so swiftly. They hadn't bothered with any containment mechanism; they had simply taken the Passports around as normal, and let the energy-broadcasting Holes they contained infect whoever came into range with their soaked tribute of ancient poison.

But why hadn't Geis noticed? He seemed to have been following all that had gone on pretty closely; why hadn't he spotted what was going on? She couldn't understand. He must have known. . . .

It didn't matter. Whatever had happened, it came back to her. She had done it again. She had caused—was causing—people to die of radiation. Again. Eight years after Lip City and the Lazy Gun's self-destruction.

"Cursed," she whispered, when she realized. She thought—hoped—she had probably spoken too softly for the cell's microphone to pick up.

Cursed, she thought, shaking her head and turning to the tiny barred window again, refusing to re-live that instant of realization in the dawn-lit hotel room eight years ago, when bliss had been forever contaminated by guilt.

The Land Car moved more slowly in High Marden, where the landscape was cut and parceled into small units. The countryside was littered with villages and towns, and there were many detours to be made around both those and estates and enclaves that would charge the car a toll.

The *Lesson Learned* was continually crossing walls in Marden. When the walls were especially high, the big wheels underneath her cell were lifted so far up, they blocked her view.

The villages and hamlets passed by; houses were white and colored dots speckling the green hillsides. The Land Car took to rivers twice, bumping and twisting down their courses, ducking under bridges, splashing through shallows and bridging over the deeper pools, rigid links between the carriages supporting each one in turn.

In the evening light the car passed along the shore of the Scodde Sea, over gravel fields and open meadows where a variety of grazing animals fled from it, bouncing and leaping across the grasslands in bleating, bellowing herds. As the car turned a corner around a farm wall, she saw the *Lesson Learned*'s leading carriage and caught a glimpse of some brown shapes running underneath, between the vehicle's first two sets of giant wheels.

She had heard that some animals ran on just in front or underneath Land Cars for hours at a time, until their strength or their hearts gave out and they fell.

She looked away.

She rose on the last day she would spend in the car. A line of white piled clouds ahead marked the Airthit Mountains; beyond lay Yadayeypon. The hills and forests thickened out of the arable land of Marden County as the *Lesson Learned* started to gain height again. She had given up trying to get them to take messages; they still hadn't answered the door buzzer.

She watched the trees thin and disappear; when the wind-torn clouds parted above, it was to reveal distant peaks, sharp and brilliant white. The air in the cell became cold, and her breathing became labored. Then they were through the pass and descending into trees again. The *Lesson Learned* had entered Yadayeypon Province.

She sat in the steeply tipped cell, swallowing and yawning now and again to clear her ears as the air pressure increased, and thought of how she might kill herself.

But she could not see suicide as a way of cheating them; rather, it would feel like giving in. It was probably the sensible thing to do, but it would be ignominious. She thought she understood now the old warrior codes which held that when every other choice and freedom had been removed from one, it was still possible to confound the enemy by dying well, no matter how terrified one felt. Certainly she had not felt so without hope since her ship had been tumbling powerless toward Nachtel's Ghost, fifteen years earlier, but she had survived that. At a cost, perhaps, but she had survived.

She hadn't slept well during the night, as every revolution of these great wheels brought her closer to Yadayeypon, and the fear and despair grew inside her. She sat cross-legged on the bunk, trying to cheer herself up, until the very desperation of her attempts became pathetic, and she wept.

After a while she fell asleep again, wan and exhausted, against the slope of trembling bulkhead behind her narrow cot.

She woke suddenly and didn't dare hope it was what she thought it might be. An explosion shook the cell, jarring her teeth; she passed through fear, elation, and back to fear again in a second.

A jolt sent her flying off the bunk; she landed on all fours on the floor. She could hear gunfire. The cell tipped as the carriage rattled and bounced along an incline, jarring her and everything in it. She struggled up the slope to the bunk and grabbed the window bars, trying to see outside.

The Land Car's tall shadow was flung up a steep, grassy hillside toward a distant line of trees; the vehicle was crashing over and through what looked like dry stone walls. A smoky trail appeared suddenly from underneath the carriage in front, crossed a small field, and detonated against a wall in a dirty fountain of earth and stone. A ripple shook the cell and vibrated through the bars in her hands as a part of the *Lesson Learned*'s shadow five or six carriages along was suddenly obscured in a dark, blossoming cloud. There was a flash of light from one end of the stand of trees. Something burst from the carriage in front of her, spraying wreckage; the cell leapt around her. A light tank in dazzle camouflage appeared from the trees, tearing down the hillside toward the Land Car; earth exploded into the air in front of it.

There was a terrific crash from behind her, she had a brief impression of the front of the Land Car's shadow twisting and of the light tank firing again; then the cell whipped and heaved around her, shaking her like dice in a cup.

The carriage rolled right over six times. She was conscious through it all. She fought the urge to brace herself and just went limp, crashing around the cell with the cot's mattress and sleeping bag flopping and falling continually around her; it was like being trapped in a tumble drier. She had time to reflect that there was something to be said for padded cells, and that you could tell each time the wheels hit the ground because the bounce was slightly different.

It stopped; she was weightless for a moment, then slammed into the padded cell door, hurting her left shoulder.

The mattress and sleeping bag fell on top of her.

Another massive crash shook the whole carriage.

There was silence.

She stood awkwardly, rubbing her shoulder and feeling her head, looking for bruises or blood. Gunfire sounded in the distance.

She tried to climb up to the bunk, but there was nothing to hold on to. She jumped, caught the window bars, and pulled herself up, ignoring the pain in her shoulder, but all she could see was dark-blue evening sky. She dropped to the canted floor that the cell door and corridor wall had become. More firing. It went on for a while; a couple of thudding detonations shook the carriage.

She tried the door buzzer, but it didn't seem to be working.

After a while she heard movement outside the cell, then the lock buzzed. She drew to one side, away from the door. Voices.

"Blow it," she heard a man say.

She buried herself under the cot mattress and stuck her fingers in her ears; the explosion clanged around the cell, leaving her ears ringing.

She looked up into a gray haze. The door had disappeared. She started coughing in the acrid fumes of the blast. A gun and a man's face appeared where the door had been.

The man wore an armored helmet painted in a hallucinatory purple-and-green design. He wore matt-black multisights over his eyes and had a little roundel painted on his forehead with the words AIM HERE printed underneath, and an arrow. He frowned at her.

"Haven't we met?" he said.

She coughed, then laughed. "I was wondering who could be crazy enough to attack a Land Car."

Another man appeared. He had a dark round face and was bare-headed apart from a bright yellow bandanna with the word REAL smeared on it in what looked like dried blood. He frowned strenuously.

She waved. "Politeness," she said.

"Politeness," Elson Roa replied, nodding.

It was warm and humid in the late-afternoon air; they were in the tropics, and the altitude was less than five hundred meters, though the prevailing winds—spilling down from the glaciers of the continent's core—kept the temperature moderate.

She stood on what had been the side of one of the *Lesson Learned*'s cell-block sections; another carriage lay upended against its roof. The thin prison overalls flapped in the warm breeze, and she could feel the air moving over her naked scalp. She looked around, smiling, watching Thrial disappear over the mountain ridge to the west. . . .

Segments of the smashed Land Car lay strewn around the bottom of a dry, steep-sided valley like pieces of a toy after a child's tantrum. Some carriages had turned on their backs, their suspension components looking naked and vulnerable, and their wheels pointing pathetically upward to the patchily clouded sky. Smoke and steam drifted down the valley on the wind.

Solipsists in gaudy uniforms crawled all over the tangled necklace of torn-open boxes that was the *Lesson Learned*. A couple of light tanks and five half-tracks sat tilted on the grassy banks around the central valley, engines idling noisily.

A group of stunned Sons of Depletion sat on the grass, hands clasped at their necks, guarded by two Solipsists who appeared to be naked apart from skin paint. Bodies lay near one of the still-smoking carriages.

Roa's head appeared from a smashed window; she reached down and helped pull him out. He carried a small briefcase and her satchel.

"This is yours," he said, handing the satchel to her.

"Thank you," she said, putting the strap over her head.

Roa and the other Solipsist who had rescued her stood looking around the scene, then Roa shrugged.

"Let us go," he said.

They climbed down through the carriage's suspension components to the ground. All around, men in gaudy uniforms and body paint were staggering from the wreck to their own vehicles, loaded with booty.

She followed Roa as he ducked under one of the Land Car's buckled connecting corridors to the other side of the wreck, where a big open half-track was waiting; a radar unit revolved on a thin mast above the vehicle. A blond face grinned down from the rear of the vehicle as Sharrow approached.

"Okay, I believe you about the Solipsists now," Zefla called.

"Hey, kid!" Miz shouted, turning around.

"These are your apparences?" Elson Roa asked as he climbed into the half-track behind her. Sharrow was hugging Zefla; the others were dressed as she was, in dark prison overalls. Miz blew her a kiss; Cenuij tutted and patted at a cut forehead with a handkerchief, and Dloan sat massively, grinning at her.

Keteo, the driver who'd taken her and Roa into Aïs City a month earlier, was sitting in the vehicle's central seat, clutching the wheel. He turned around, saw her, and closed his eyes, making a humming noise from beneath his magenta-and-white-painted steel hat. His combat jacket was bright pink. A body-painted Solipsist—naked except for a beret—sat to Keteo's left, clutching a microphone.

"Yes," she said, smiling at Roa and still holding Zefla. "They're my apparences."

"Oh, thanks," Cenuij muttered.

"Then we'd better take them, too," Roa said, frowning.

Keteo turned around, looking annoyed.

"Molgarin didn't say anything about—" he began.

Roa slapped him on the top of his armored hat. "Drive," he said.

Miz stood up from the half-track's rear seat, wanting to hug Sharrow, too, but was forced to sit back down as the half-track lurched off across the grass. Sharrow and Zefla were thrown back onto the seat, laughing. Roa clutched at the half-track's roll-bar, which held a small holo screen, a pair of heavy machine guns, and an empty, soot-smeared rocket launcher.

The half-track thumped and crashed over the uneven ground, heading down the valley toward some trees. Roa studied the holo screen, then tapped the body-painted Solipsist in the front seat.

"Tell everybody there are aircraft coming," he told the shivering man.

"Attention *everybody!*" the body-painted man shouted into the microphone. He paused. "*Watch the skies!*" he screamed, then he threw himself down into the footwell, leaving the microphone on the seat.

Roa shook his head.

A Solipsist dressed in violet and lime, dragging a long black box, ran toward them, waving. Roa banged Keteo's tin hat again; the half-track skidded to a stop, plowing turf with its tracks and sending everybody sliding out of their seats. Roa went, "Oof!" as he was thrown against the roll-bar. He glared at the back of Keteo's tin hat, then reached down to pull the long black box into the half-track. He tapped Keteo's helmet again and hung on grimly as the half-track leapt away.

Sharrow hung onto the radar mast behind the seat, looking back to watch the Solipsists run from the wrecked

Land Car and tumble into their half-tracks. The two garishly painted light tanks were already bouncing across the grass, following Roa's vehicle.

"You all right?" Miz shouted to her over the noise of the machine's engine.

"Yes," Sharrow said.

An aircraft screamed overhead. She ducked instinctively. They all watched the sleek gray shape disappear over the sunset-rouged summits of the hills to their right. Another three planes flashed across the valley, higher up.

"Oh shit," Cenuij said.

Roa readied the twin machine guns.

The half-track skidded off the grass onto a narrow wheel-grooved track leading down through a small forest. Dust tumbled into the air behind them.

They heard the noise of the jets again, then a series of flat, crumping sounds. The half-track's radio made squawking, screeching noises.

The track steepened and started to twist as it followed a rocky gully downward. Keteo avoided a large boulder lying at the side of the track by a centimeter or so, skidded, and almost sent the machine over the edge of the ravine, then hauled it straight again and gunned the engine.

Roa turned around and looked back up the track to where the first light tank had appeared in its own cloud of dust. A series of sharp explosions came from behind it. Keteo drove off the track and along a stretch of grassy bank to avoid a dead bird lying in the road.

"Interesting driving technique," Miz shouted to Sharrow, nodding approvingly.

Cenuij closed his eyes. "I felt safer in the fucking Land Car."

Behind them, smoke rose into the dark-blue sky above the trees. The track left the forest and ran along the side of a wide grassy valley crossed by stone walls and bisected by a stream that appeared from a small side valley. The end of the valley was about half a kilometer away.

"Uh-oh," Dloan said, turning to look behind them.

Cenuij was looking suspiciously at the long black box by Roa's feet.

Roa reached under the roll-bar and lifted the microphone off the front seat. "Hello, *Solo*—" he said.

A great roar of noise slapped down on them; they all ducked again. Sharrow saw the jet tear overhead. Roa threw the mike down, grabbed the machine guns, and fired at the already-distant aircraft, scattering cartridge cases into the rear footwell.

"Where are the missiles?" Roa yelled.

"Under the seat!" Keteo yelled.

The air filled with a humming noise. Sharrow glanced at Dloan; he'd put his hands over his eyes.

There was a flash of light from behind them. Sharrow half heard, half saw a blur of movement to one side as something fell into the grass by the side of the track. Then the half-track's long hood exploded.

Everything stopped. Silence, as the wreckage tumbled out of the sky around them and what was left of the half-track plowed into the track in a wave of dust and small stones.

Sound came back slowly; her ears began ringing. There were several other muffled explosions in the confusion as the broken half-track crashed to a stop. She was in the footwell, picking herself up; Roa was above her, looking stunned, his face bloody.

Smoke everywhere.

She saw Miz; he pulled her to her feet, shouting something at her. Dloan helped Zefla down from the vehicle. Cenuij sat, blinking, looking surprised.

Then she was out on the grass, staggering and running. She thought she'd left the satchel behind, but it was there, flapping against her hip. She followed Dloan and Zef; Miz ran at her side. Farther back up the track the two light tanks burned fiercely, pools of bright-orange fire beneath bulb-headed columns of smoke.

Another plane screamed overhead. Explosions crackled throughout the valley. She kept her head down, hearing shrapnel zizz through the air and plunk into the grass.

They ran toward a small stone animal pen by the side of the stream. Dloan and Zefla dived over the pen's stone wall. Cenuij vaulted; she jumped, falling into the grass circle within. She looked over, back to the wreck of the blazing half-track. Miz was helping Keteo carry a long, heavy-looking kitbag. She wiped sweat from her eyes and looked up.

In the sky above the hills, a large plane flew in front of red, sunlit clouds. A line of ruby-tinged shapes fell from the rear of the plane, becoming dark as they fell into the shadow of the hill, and blossoming into parachutes before they were hidden by the hills themselves.

"Definitely safer in the Land Car," Cenuij muttered.

"Excellent response time," Dloan murmured.

"Recognize them?" Zefla said.

"No," Dloan said as Miz and Keteo—limping heavily, face covered with blood—heaved the kitbag over the wall of the pen and then collapsed over it.

"Who we dealing with here?" Miz said, breathing hard.

"Just saying," Dloan said. "Contract army; couldn't recognize them."

"Where's Roa?" Keteo asked, wiping blood from his eyes.

Zefla looked over the top of the stones toward the wrecked half-track. "Can't see him," she said. She looked back at Keteo. "What about the radio guy?" she asked.

Keteo shook his head. "No more," he said, then knelt, looking over the stone parapet. Miz was tearing the kitbag open, between glancing up and around.

"What hit us?" Sharrow said.

"Down!" Miz shouted. The scream of a jet came almost instantly. The ground pulsed beneath them, and rocks tumbled off the pen wall. They waited for the pattering debris to stop falling, then looked up. A crater had been blasted in the river bed twenty meters upstream; water was pooling into the steaming, smoke-shrouded hole.

"Shit," Cenuij said, holding his leg.

"Debris?" Zefla asked him, sliding over to him.

Cenuij grimaced. He lifted his leg up, flexed his ankle. "I'll survive."

"Tank sensors . . . ," Dloan said, his voice trailing off as he watched Miz pull a large gun out of the kitbag. Keteo went over and pulled another tube-shaped weapon out. Dloan joined them, eyes wide.

Sharrow shook herself; she opened her satchel and saw the HandCannon. She pulled the gun out and searched through the spare clips in the bottom of the bag. Her redhead wig was down there, too, but she ignored it.

"Shit, here's another one," Cenuij said.

The plane swooped, barreling straight toward them. Miz lifted the gun he'd found, trying and failing to make it fire. Sharrow found the HandCannon's bipropellant clip, but it was too late. Something fell from the plane, tumbling. She fired up, anyway, as the plane tore overhead, the gun thud-thudding in her hand as the jet swept over. Something whistled through the air, just ahead of the zooming jet's roar.

She hugged the ground. Detonations rippled through the earth and grass; a noise like a million firecrackers burst overhead. The debris was tiny and sounded metallic. She raised her head first. More detonations crackled downstream.

"Terrible aiming," Dloan said by her side as he took up a large gun. He pulled a magazine out of the kitbag, then another and another.

"Cluster bombs!" Cenuij said, gulping as he looked at where a last few explosions were flashing and cracking down the valley. "Are they *legal*?"

Keteo banged the side of the tube-weapon he held, muttering.

"They become legal," Zefla said. "When you do something like attack a Court-licensed Land Car."

Sharrow threw the empty clip away and emplaced the bipropellant magazine. "Think they'll stop bombing?" she said, digging for the other rocket clip in the satchel. "Those paras must be pretty close."

Miz checked the gun he had. "You'll be lucky," he said.

"These rounds are all the wrong caliber," Dloan said, digging through the kitbag. He sounded disappointed.

"Two more," Zefla said, looking up the valley.

Two sharp, dark shapes turned against the fading evening light, then seemed to hover there, growing larger.

"We should have taken that box," Cenuij said. "That black box. The Court—"

"*Solo!*" Keteo yelled. He pointed down the valley.

Sharrow saw two flashing lights; they rose into the air on two masts above a large dark shape. More lights glittered, and the dark shape became a large ACV, two—then, as it slewed briefly, four—large propellers visible above it.

Keteo whooped.

Dloan stared at the hovercraft. "How did they get *that* up *here*?" he asked.

"Rivers!" Keteo said cockily.

Sharrow looked back to the two approaching jets as they bellied down, each leaving two thin gray tubes of vapor behind them, curling from their wingtips in the humid evening air. Miz tried to fire at the planes, but the gun wouldn't work.

"Shit," he said. "This thing needs a fucking power pack. . . ."

Dloan turned to look at the jets and put down the gun he was holding, watching the aircraft as a third shape turned in the air above the valley head and started on the same bombing run. He shook his head.

"No matter," he said softly.

The planes floated closer. Sharrow held the Hand-Cannon in both hands, ready. Two black shapes hung under each of the planes' wings. The canisters detached and started to fall, tumbling through the air toward them.

"Aw, fuck . . . ," she heard Miz say.

" 'Bye," Dloan said softly.

Then both planes became cerise spheres. The falling canisters pulsed bright pink in the same instant.

The light was too bright. Sharrow closed her eyes, not comprehending. Dloan shouted something, then he thudded into her, on top of her, putting the light out. The world pulsed and quivered, shock waves hammering into her already-ringing ears.

The weight on her lifted. She opened her eyes. Dloan was standing above her, eyes bulging, mouth hanging open.

"Dloan!" she shouted. "Get down!"

Dloan swiveled, mouth still hanging open. Keteo stood up beside him, his mouth open, too. He was staring back toward the half-track. Sharrow got up on her knees beside Dloan.

The two jets had disappeared. Tiny glowing bits of wreckage were falling all about, landing smoking in the surrounding grass, hissing in the water and clunking into the stones of the animal pen like some bizarre hail. Zefla yelped and brushed one red-hot shard off her arm. Echoes rumbled around the valley. There was a long smoking crater on the flank of the hill across from them, tattered wriggles of smoke guttered from a scatter of small fires downstream from the pen, and from the dip beyond, a dark black cloud was rising on a shaft of smoke and flame, partially obscuring the view down the valley toward the *Solo*.

The third jet swept overhead, climbing and turning hard. It, too, became a vivid ball of light: the explosion shook the ground, and the wreckage fell gracefully to the hill in a thousand fiery pieces, trailing black smoke like some vast firework gone wrong.

Keteo leapt into the air. "Roa!" he yelled, flourishing the unused weapon tube.

Sharrow went to the downhill parapet of the animal pen. They seemed to be surrounded by pillars of smoke. Beyond the rising column left by one of the crashed planes, the *Solo* was visible, stationary a few hundred meters down the valley, engines droning.

The half-track sat, still burning in the gloom beneath the dark hill. Violet light sparkled just behind it. She turned and looked above the hillside where the wreckage burned. A dot in the distant sky burst with light.

"Roa!" Keteo yelled again. He grinned down at Sharrow, then looked slightly embarrassed, and shrugged. "Me, really," he said.

She shook her head.

"Wow!" Dloan said, looking around at them all. "Wow!"

"*That's* what was in that box," Cenuij said crisply. He snorted. "The wonders of ancient technology."

"Oh, boy," Zefla said. "Is that bozo Roa in trouble now."

Light ridged the hilltop above the flaming wreckage of the third plane. Ricochets whined off the stones of a nearby wall as the sound cracked over them.

"Paras are here," Dloan said, as they all ducked down again.

"I can see Roa moving," Zefla said, peeking out of a hole in the wall.

Answering fire from the ACV echoed around the valley. More gunfire came from the ridge of the hill, pattering around them.

Miz was crouched down beside Keteo. "Got a communicator?" he asked the youth.

"Yeah!" he said.

"How about using it to tell your pals in the ACV we're on our way?"

"Good idea!" Keteo said. He pulled a small device from his pink combat jacket. "*Solo?*" he said.

Miz sidled over to Sharrow, who was taking aim at the hill summit. "Down the stream?" he asked her.

Keteo chattered excitedly to somebody on the *Solo*.

"Yes," she said. "Down the stream. Anytime you like." She rose up just enough to fire at the hillside. Some careless soldier skylined, and so died in silhouette. Sharrow ducked back, changing magazines.

"Okay?" Miz asked Keteo, over the sound of bullets thudding into the ground and stones around them.

"Okay!" the boy yelled. "They're waiting."

"Let's go," Miz said. "Down the stream bed." He nodded at Keteo's pink combat jacket, which even in the gathering darkness looked very pale. "That jacket makes you kind of conspicuous, kid; you might want to ditch it."

Keteo looked at Miz as though he were mad.

Sharrow declipped the bipropellants.

Miz watched her, scratching his head. "Will you stop fiddling and *fire* that damn thing?" he said.

She glared at him. "These are B-Ps," she said. "No better against infantry and too easy to back-trace."

"Oh, my mistake," Miz said, watching her shove a different magazine home. A small explosion threw soil into the air ten meters upstream.

"Rifle grenade," Dloan said.

She was ready to fire. She glanced at the others.

"Go!" she yelled. She started firing. Zefla and Dloan—quickly followed by Keteo and then Cenuij—jumped over the stream-side wall of the animal pen.

Sharrow ducked down again. She changed clips again, her ears ringing, her wrists aching. Miz was sitting a meter away, his face just visible, grinning at her.

"Get!" she yelled at him.

"You get," he told her. He held his hand out for the gun.

"No," she said.

She turned and started firing. Something dropped into the animal pen a couple of meters away; Miz dived, grabbed, and threw the rifle grenade away toward the road. It exploded in midair.

She looked around; shrapnel tinkled against the far wall. Bullets sang off the stones they were crouched behind.

"Let's both get," Miz suggested.

They leapt the wall, stumbled down across the grass to the shallow river, and staggered in, then waded downstream, heads bowed, slipping on submerged rocks, bullets whizzing above.

The *Solo* was invisible, hidden by the hollow where one of the downed planes had crashed. The ACV's flashing lights lit up rising smoke in front of them and the grass on either side of the stream ahead. An underwater pulse almost threw them off their feet; a grenade made a white exploding shape in the stream, back near the animal pen.

They came to the lip of a small waterfall and struggled out onto the grass, running down into the hollow where the wreckage of the aircraft burned in cratered patches and the *Solo* waited, its slab-sided stern turned to them, rear ramp closed but a small door open above a mesh ladder. Elson Roa was climbing the ladder over the bulge of the hovercraft's man-high skirt. The Francks were right behind him. Keteo was helping Cenuij, who was limping.

Sharrow and Miz ran down through the big ACV's prop wash. "Wish they'd put those fucking lights out," Miz gasped.

They splashed through the stream again as Zefla climbed to the door. Tall splashes in the water announced bullets falling among them, and sparks burst off the rear of the hovercraft; air whistled out of small, ragged punctures in its skirt. Dloan waited for Keteo, then picked him up and threw the boy halfway up the ladder. He scrambled the rest.

Cenuij was next, hauling himself hand over hand.

Sharrow and Miz reached the black curve of the ACV's skirt. Dloan made to help her up, but she nodded him to go next. He paused on the way up as something pulled at the dark cloth covering his right leg, then he continued.

"Ah!" Miz said, and whirled around. Sharrow looked back to see him glance at one hand and then stick it behind his back and look at her. "Nothing," he shouted above the noise of the engines, grinning. Blood dripped into the water behind him. He nodded at the ladder. "After you," he yelled.

She stuck the gun in her mouth, gripped the ladder, and climbed. Miz was right beneath her.

Cenuij was in the door, reaching down to her. He looked furious.

"Can you believe it?" he said, grasping her hand. "He threw it away! Thought it had stopped working, so he threw it away!"

Cenuij pulled her toward him. Roa was farther in, yelling into a communicator. Dloan sat on the floor inside, holding his leg. The ACV was moving. Shots thumped around the opened door.

Sharrow hauled herself into the doorway and turned to reach down for Miz.

At first she thought Cenuij was doing the same thing, then he slumped heavily on top of her and tumbled out the door.

She grabbed at him but missed; he fell past Miz, bounced off the ACV's skirt, and landed slackly on the grassy bank of the stream, limbs flopping spread around him.

Miz hesitated, looking down and back as spray burst from beneath the hovercraft's skirt.

Cenuij lay on the grass, staring up at the sky, eyes open, blood pouring from each side of his head.

The ACV moved away and picked up speed, puffing up great shrouding clouds of spray into the hollow in front of the waterfall and punching huge rolling holes in the smoke from the burning wreckage, all lit by the flames and the hovercraft's flickering lights. Roa was still shouting. Hands came and held Sharrow's shoulders.

She saw Miz tense as he looked down at Cenuij, getting ready to leap off the ladder.

"Miz!" she shouted. He looked up at her. The spray rose about him as the ACV accelerated, engines barking and clattering.

Cenuij lay still, ten, then twenty meters away as the pulsing light faded around him. Then the hovercraft's lights finally flicked off.

"Miz!" she screamed into the shadows.

She reached down, felt his hand, and pulled him up. She and Zefla hauled him in through the door.

The small waterfall reflected the fading flames of the plane wreck; the hollow became a bowl of shadows as the *Solo* drew away.

Cenuij's body lay motionless on the ground, a dark X like something pinned out, sacrificed to the encroaching darkness.

18

The Dark City

The android crossed the central plaza and walked along the quiet street through skeins and patches of ground mist and past the shells of tall, roofless buildings filled with watery morning sunlight. The android was slender and a little below the height of the average Golter male; its outer substance was formed from metal and plastic, and it wore no clothes. Its body had been sculpted to vaguely resemble a rather idealized male figure, though without genitalia. Its chest was usually said to remind people of the breastplate from a suit of ancient armor. Its head held two ear-shaped microphones, two eyes like round sunglass lenses, a flat nose with two sensory nostril slits, and a small loudspeaker shaped like a pair of slightly open lips.

Where the buildings gave way to a small park, the android turned and descended a wide set of curving steps, past arcades edged by tattered, faded awnings, down toward the mist-strewn waters of the silent harbor. On the esplanade it turned and made for the Guest's Quarter. Sunlight threw its long, thin shadow behind it, across paving stones that were clean and without litter but cracked and holed.

The android carried a slim plastic folder in one hand; the plastic went slap-slap against its plastic-covered thigh for a few steps as the light breeze caught it; then the tall fig-

ure shifted its arm slightly, holding the folder farther away
from its leg. The noise stopped.

Vembyr was a city of many towers and spires and fine,
ancient buildings that curved around a picturesque bay
backed by tall forested hills in southwest Jonolrey. It had
been abandoned by humans five millennia earlier after a nuclear power plant farther down the coast had blown up and
the winds had been blowing from that direction. The fall-out
had covered the city, forcing its evacuation. It had lain abandoned for centuries, slowly falling into disrepair and visited
only by scientists or their remotes monitoring the slowly de-
creasing radiation levels, until the androids had
finally won their legal battle for civil rights and started looking for a homeland on Golter.

The android separatist faction took out a ten-thousand-
year lease on the whole city for a sum little more than
nominal.

On the other side of the harbor, the android left the esplanade and climbed another broad curved set of steps,
through a slowly rising cloud of mist. About halfway up it
stopped to watch another android who was walking along a
single step with a halting, shuffling gait, crossing from one
side of the tall flight to the other. The android walking along
the steps passed a meter away from the other; it gave no
sign of noticing it, but continued its hesitant walk to the far
edge of the steps, then turned and walked slowly back the
way it had come. The first android watched it pass again,
then continued up the flight. A shallow groove had been
worn in the step's white marble a centimeter or so deep.

The android with the plastic folder walked away along
the deserted arcade at the top and disappeared into the silent mist.

In the street that housed the Irregular Embassy, a group of
androids of various model-types were dismantling a shining
metal tube that crossed the street ten meters up, between
two ornately decorated stone buildings that had been recently restored. A couple of large dump trucks sat in the
middle of the street, their cranes lifting sections of the
transit-system tube away as the pieces were freed. An android with a welding arm was cutting at the tube's shiny
surface, producing a waterfall of sparks that descended

through the light, golden mist at the end of the street like pieces of splashing, fading sunlight.

The android entered the embassy. Its client was waiting in the courtyard garden.

She sat on a small stone bench by a tinkling fountain. She was artificially bald, a little over average height, and sat more erect than most humans did. She wore heavy boots, a thick, dark-green pleated skirt, a pale hide riding jacket, and a white shirt. A fur hat lay on the stone bench at her side with a pair of hide gloves on top of it.

She rose to meet it when it entered the courtyard.

"Lady Sharrow," it said. It caught the hint of movement in her arm and duly extended its own, to shake hands with her. "My name is Feril," it said. "I am to represent you. Pleased to meet you."

"How do you do," she said, nodding. They sat on the stone bench. The fountain played with a quiet, pattering noise. In the misty light the small garden seemed to glow around them; they sat surrounded by a precise profusion of tiny, brightly colored flowers.

"I have news of your friends," Feril told her. "Their court hearing seems to be going well."

She smiled. Her face showed traces of having been altered recently; there were hints of inflammation in the corner of her eyes, where the skin had been stuck down, and her blond eyebrows showed a fraction of a millimeter of dark growth at their roots. The android had seen a picture of her on the city news service when she had arrived a week earlier, and it thought her nose looked different, too.

"Is it?" she said. "Good."

"Yes. Ms. Franck is an able advocate, and Mr. Kuma was allowed to use his extensive personal wealth to employ some fine legal brains. The nature of the witnesses will be their greatest asset, I believe, as courts are not often inclined to trust the evidence of hired security personnel. The trial has been fixed for Bihelion next year."

The woman looked surprised. "Taking their time, aren't they?"

"I believe that is because you are also indicted, but cannot be brought to trial until the Huhsz Passports have run out."

She laughed lightly, putting her head back and looking

up past the gleaming slates of the embassy roof to the gauzy bright sky above. "That's very sporting of them." She looked back at it. "Will the trial be in the Jam, or Yada?"

"Ms. Franck is attempting to have the venue moved to Yadayeypon."

She smiled. "Judges named?"

"A number have been suggested."

"All male and elderly?"

"I believe so."

She made a clicking noise with the side of her mouth and winked. "Good old Zef," she said.

"There will doubtless be wrangling over the venue, but your friends ought to be able to return within the next four or five days."

"Good." She sighed and put her clasped hands onto her lap. "And what of the Passports?"

"They have been impounded in the quarantine terminal at Ikueshleng and are themselves the subject of a complex legal dispute concerning radioactive contamination, but they are still operative." It paused to give her time to say something, then it volunteered, "I should say that it would be a fortnight or so before the city of Vembyr would have to release you to the Huhsz."

"But in the meantime I'm free to go?" she said. She looked from one of its eyes to the other the way humans often did, as though searching for something.

It nodded. "Yes. I have left the release papers with the embassy here. The terms of your visa require that you inform me of your movements within the city boundary, but you may leave those at any time."

"Hmm. May I pay a visit to some of the Court-impounded material stored here?" she asked. The android was silent. When it didn't react, she went on, "My grandfather, Gorko; there's some of his stuff stored here, I think. May I see it?"

"Oh, yes," the android said, and nodded. "We have charge of some goods that used to belong to your family; once certain legal complications have been resolved, the material that the Court has established jurisdiction over will be auctioned. I believe I can arrange for you to inspect the trove, if you wish."

"Yes, thank you," she nodded, looking away.

"It may take a few days to gain permission. Might I ask how long you intend to stay in Vembyr?"

"A few days," she said with a faint smile. "It might be convenient to meet my friends here. Would that be all right?"

"Well, as I trust you have been made aware, humans are advised to stay no longer than forty days in Vembyr, anyway, to avoid too great an exposure to radioactive contamination, but I have been asked to inform you that while every reasonable precaution will be taken, the city administration feels unable to guarantee your safety should you desire to stay here for any length of time. As well as the hunting Passports themselves, there is a substantial bounty on your life, and while it is unlikely any android would wish such remuneration, it is possible some outside agency could attempt to kidnap or attack you here."

"Well, no change there."

"I should also point out in that regard that in four days' time we shall have the monthly auction, which always brings an influx of people. As this month's sale is of mainly military and gray-tech goods, the parties we may expect to play host to could well include the sort of person who might wish you harm."

"Are you saying I ought to leave before then?" the woman asked.

Feril thought she sounded tired. "Not necessarily. There are secure apartments within the old Jeraight fortress in Chine District," it told her. "You might wish to stay there."

She rose and walked slowly to the fountain. She looked down at the splashing pool, then dipped her hand into the water and held some of the fluid in her hand. She shook her head.

"I know," she said. She moved her head to indicate the embassy building behind her. "They showed me." She stood up. "Too much like a prison," she said, brushing water from her hand. "Is there a hotel? Apartments?"

"The City Hotel has politely declined to house you, I regret to say."

She gave a small, snorting laugh. "Can't say I blame them," she said.

"But if security is not your absolute priority, there are many vacant apartments," it told her. "There is one in my own building; as your legal representative and custodian, I suggest that it might be convenient for you to live there."

She smiled oddly, a hint of a frown on her upper face. "You don't mind?" she asked. "As you say, I tend to attract a deal of unwelcome attention these days."

"I do not mind. Your past life intrigues and interests me, as does the character it reveals." It paused. She was looking even more amused. It continued. "We seem to get on well enough, from this initial impression." It made a shrug. "It would be pleasant."

"Pleasant," she repeated, smiling. "Very well then, Feril."

The *Solo* had charged down the valley through the darkness, over walls and roads, demolishing farm outbuildings, wrecking a barn, causing several car crashes and terrifying hundreds of animals, especially the ones it rolled right over. It had taken an hour to get to the Yallam river, where it crashed onto the waves from a bank three or four meters high, only its speed saving it from tipping over into the swirling black water. It roared away downstream. Its radar indicated several aircraft following it, but none approached nearer than ten kilometers.

Dloan had shaken his head when Elson Roa admitted he had thrown away whatever fabulous weapon had brought down two planes and their already-launched ordnance in one discharge. The Solipsist leader had attempted to use the weapon against the ground troops on the other side of the valley, and determined when it didn't work that the weapon had had only a limited number of shots in it to start with, and he had used them all up.

Dloan bit his tongue on the subject of ancient weaponry occasionally being more intelligent than the people who came to use it. Cenuij, Dloan thought, would not have been so tactful, and the realization was more painful than the trifling wound in his leg.

Zefla couldn't stop shivering, though it was not cold inside the big ACV. There were only about twenty Solipsists left on board. Nobody else had made it back to the *Solo* from the attack on the Land Car, though some of the others were believed to have been captured rather than killed. Zefla could not understand how Roa could be so phlegmatic, either about the loss of most of his force and the inevitable loss of the *Solo*, too, or the fact that—by using the embargoed antiaircraft weapon as well as attacking the Court-protected Land Car—he had done not one but two things for either of which the World Court would pursue him to the ends of the system and imprison him for life, at least.

Miz sat in the ACV's medic cabin, watching Sharrow treat the wound in his hand. The bullet had gone right through the muscle at the base of his thumb; he still had about fifty percent of its use, and it would be a hundred percent in a month or so. It was the sort of million-Thrial wound conscripts in unpopular wars dreamt about. He tried to joke with Sharrow about it, but later in the heads he found some blood in his hair that was probably Cenuij's and promptly threw up.

Sharrow felt Cenuij fall against her and watched his body tumble from the door and bounce on the hovercraft's skirt a hundred times that night, as the big ACV rumbled down the Yallam.

Disaster came at Eph, where the river flowed past and around the city in a narrow gorge. Heavy rains upstream a few days earlier meant the river had risen a couple of meters since the Solipsists had come upstream, and the *Solo* lost all four of its propellers under the first railway bridge.

They drifted downriver, engines still roaring as Roa's helmsman tried to use the stumps of the shattered propeller blades to keep some way on the craft. It didn't work; the *Solo* bumped into barges, bridge supports, and wharves all the way around the city, watched by townspeople and tracked by a small flotilla of brightly lit pleasure craft held back by a couple of police boats.

"*Why?*" Sharrow asked Roa when he came staggering down the steps into the ACV's echoing garage space.

"Why what?" he shouted above the noise of the screaming engines, looking tired and confused.

"Why did you attack the Land Car?" she yelled, steadying herself against the bulkhead as the hovercraft lurched. "What was the point?"

"We were hired to," Roa shouted, frowning, as though it should have been obvious.

"By whom?"

"I don't know," Roa said quietly, so that she saw rather than heard the words. The Solipsist leader closed his eyes and started to hum. The ACV lurched again, and he was thrown against the bulkhead. Roa braced himself with one arm, then said, "Excuse me," and disappeared back up the stairs to the flight deck.

Roa didn't object when they proposed buying one of a couple of assault inflatables they'd found in the hovercraft's garage.

He took a check.

They took to the waves as they were passing the lagoon of the Stramph-Veddick Circus Lands and made it into the enclave despite a black-body, almost silent and armed-looking heli-drone coming down to take a long, hard look at them as they bounced over the chopping dark waters toward the fabulous lights of the circus.

The *Solo* sailed forlornly on into the night. The Solipsists had switched its lights back on, and the last they saw of it, the old hovercraft was scraping under some trees on its way downriver, losing what remained of its propellers against the overhanging branches in a distant, explosive clattering.

Miz had business contacts in the circus; he talked them out of some money, and the team onto a tourist charter flight out of the theme park that morning. He picked up money from one of his office managers when they landed in Bo-Chen in southern Jonolrey and hired an auto car. They slept fitfully most of the way to Vembyr, and when Zefla woke, it was with the opinion that having slept on it, with the exception of Sharrow, probably the best thing they could do was go to Yadayeypon voluntarily and answer their indictments after all.

Miz had taken a few days to be convinced.

"I am sorry you lost your friend," Feril said.

"Friend," she repeated, frowning a little. "I'm not sure Cenuij was ever a *friend*," she said. "But"—she gave a strange, small laugh—"we were very close."

She stood on an old tarpaulin spattered with tiny flecks of dried plaster. A single naked electric bulb burned brightly in the middle of the room, shedding a fierce yellow-white light throughout the room and casting a deep shadow across the floor behind her. She was thinking about going for a walk. There was something inexplicably soothing about watching the android work, but there was also something about the harshness of the light that made her uncomfortable.

The tall, wide windows looked out into darkness.

"Have you many happy memories of him?" Feril asked. The android was perched on a stepladder, holding a small bucket in one hand and a trowel in the other.

"Not many," she said, trying to remember. "Well, yes—some." She sounded exasperated as she said, "We argued a lot . . . but I've never objected to a good argument."

"You said he was your team classicist. Will you have to get another?"

She shook her head. "It doesn't work that way."

"Oh," Feril said. It scooped a glistening lump of plaster from the bucket onto the trowel blade, then set the bucket down on the top step of the ladder.

"May I ask a favor of you?" she said.

"Yes," Feril said. An ornate plaster frieze shaped like a long, flower-filled trellis filled the angle between the wall and the ceiling of half the room, starting in the corner by the door and ending where the android stood on the ladder. It carefully applied the plaster to the end of the frieze.

"I'd like to find out if there have been any androids who've suddenly left Vembyr and disappeared recently; especially pairs of androids. Androids who could pass for human at very close range."

The android was silent for a couple of seconds, patiently using the trowel to keep the drooping lump of plaster in place. Then it said, "No, none have been reported leaving the city for the last nine years."

"Hmm. Before that?"

The machine paused only briefly. "The city records go back five millennia," the machine said, sounding regretful. "During that time the android population of Vembyr has remained roughly static at twenty-three thousand, with perhaps a tenth of that number at large in the rest of the system. Only a few hundred androids have ever been constructed who might pass for human. None live in the city, and some—about forty or so—are officially missing, untraced. Indeed, the majority of missing androids are human simulacra. They are believed to have been taken unwillingly, probably by rich individuals, and used for . . . a variety of acts, all of which are illegal when perpetrated against humans."

"I'll bet," she said. She put one hand under her armpit and the other to her mouth, tapping her teeth with her fingers. "Does anyone still *make* androids?"

"Oh, no," the machine said, turning to look at her. "That has been prohibited for the last twelve hundred years. Even we may only repair existing examples, though we believe the World Court will grant us permission to manufacture a hundred or so androids from currently available spare parts sometime before the end of the next century."

It turned back to the plaster and—over the next few minutes, as the plaster began to set—it gradually worked the still soft folds of the material into the shape of a delicate white flower, backed by a section of trellis.

Sometime before the end of the next century, she thought. Certainly that was only a hundred and one years away, but it was still strange to realize the scales the androids thought on. It was as though, with their ability to think a thousand thoughts in the time it would take a human to think one, and yet to exist effectively indefinitely, the androids had abandoned what humanity thought of as the normal calibrations of time, to exist on, at what was—again, to the human mind, unless one was a scientist used to working in nanoseconds or billions of years—the extremities of temporality.

Feril paused, inspecting its handiwork. It glanced down at her for a moment, then took another scoop of plaster from the bucket it held and applied that to the frieze.

"Do you actually enjoy doing this, Feril?" she asked.

"This?" it said, dabbing at the plaster with its hands. "Restoring the plaster-work?"

"Restoring everything."

"Yes," it said, "it is pleasant. I do literally what humans talk about figuratively; I switch parts of my mind off. Sometimes, rather than do that, I think about something else: often when plastering, I replay old human adventure yarns, reexperiencing them in old books, or ancient flat-screen works, or more modern pieces."

"Adventure yarns?" she grinned.

"Indeed," the android said, patting the drying plaster in such a way as to produce a stipple effect on the surface of a rough-skinned, globular fruit it had just sculpted. "It is satisfying in the extreme to have done plastering work, or inlaying, or wood-carving; it is hugely enjoyable to drive a vehicle one has rebuilt, or to walk around, or just look at a building one has brought from a shell to habitability, but the processes involved are rarely directly rewarding at the time, and to divert oneself with adventures of derring-do is a nice counterpoint, I believe." It turned and looked back at her. "Your own life will be an adventure story one day, I don't doubt, Lady Sharrow. I—" It broke off, turning smoothly and resuming its task.

She frowned, then gave a small smile and looked at the floorboards for a moment.

"Not all humans grudge androids their longevity just because we've found we cannot afford to grant ourselves that gift, Feril," she said. "I am flattered you think my life might ever be worth your perusal, when I am long dead and you are still alive."

The android paused, then turned to her again. "I beg your pardon nevertheless, Lady Sharrow," it said. "We were, and I was, made in the image of humanity, and in the enthusiasm of the moment I exhibited what was at least a lack of thought and could have been construed as cruelty. We have always regarded it as our duty to reflect what is best in humankind, given that we are the work of your intellects rather than the processes of blind evolution, however purposeful in that blindness nature may be, and however noble and sophisticated its results. I am guilty of falling beneath both the standards we set ourselves and those humanity has the right to expect of us, and I apologize."

She looked up at the machine, poised with perfect stillness on top of the ladder, its body spotted with lumps of plaster. There was a small smile on her face. She might have shaken her head just a fraction.

"Contrition so elegant," she said after a pause, "needs not the parent of hurt to merit its existence, and what was intended to soothe harm just as fitly pleases contentment."

The android looked at her for a moment. "Vitrelian," it said. "*The Trials of a Patient man;* Act Five, Scene Three. Lady Sharrow; I have admired the excitements of your life and even envied you in a way, but now I find you are learned, too." It made a show of shaking its head. "I am lost in admiration."

She laughed. "Feril," she said, "it's just as well you're not a man; you would break a thousand hearts, if you had the mind to."

Feril waved its hand expressively as it turned back to its work. "I believe there are various glands and other append-ages that would have to be involved, too; the coordination required would baffle my humble personality."

"Dissembler," she said, and laughed. The noise, echoing in the bare room, sounded strange. She felt a pang of guilt at having so forgotten Cenuij's death, however briefly.

She stood up and stretched, watching her shadow move about the room, limbs lengthened and magnified. "I think," she said, "I shall go for a walk."

"Please take care," the android said, glancing at her again.

"Don't worry about me," she said, patting the pocket of her jacket where the HandCannon was.

She walked through the dark city for an hour or more, along towpaths and through tunnels, past dark ruins and lit build-ings, along deserted roads and boulevards and across tall bridges and aqueducts. She met very few androids and no humans at all. One team of androids was cleaning the face of a tall stone building in the darkness; another group was lifting an old barge from a canal, using a creaking iron and hawser boat-lift, all lit by floodlights.

She walked, hardly seeing the city. In her mind she re-played the destruction of the *Lesson Learned* and the events following it, trying to remember everything but sure that she was failing, that there was something in there that was very important and she had missed it.

She had not deliberately recalled the Land Car attack since it had happened; it had been enough to know that each time she slept, she would replay those last seconds in the rear door of the old hovercraft, feeling Cenuij slip and fall past her, trying to grab him, calling on Miz, seeing Cenuij's body lying there in the flickering orange light, and then—even while she knew it was a dream—living it again and again, with Miz falling past her, shot and dying, or Miz and Cenuij somehow changing places as one fell past the other, and looking out from the door to see that although it had been Cenuij who'd fallen past her, it was Miz lying there on the grass. A few times—sufficient to wake her up without fail, brow damp, pulse racing—the body lying by the little waterfall had been hers, and she had looked from the retreating ACV at her own blank face, staring blind and dead into the fiery darkness of the sky.

Vembyr's galleries and arcades echoed to her footsteps like the entrances to dark mines in the city's mountainous geography.

She used a small torch to light her way in places, and all the time tried to work out what it was that was nagging at her: some detail, some tiny observed incident or throwaway remark that had meant nothing at the time, but which was shouting now from the depths of her memory, insistent and important.

But she could not remember and returned no wiser than she had left, to a message from Breyguhn that a plaster-spotted Feril handed her without comment.

It was ink-printed on perforated paper.

From the House of the Sad Brothers of the Kept Weight.
YOU KILLED HIM. I AM STAYING HERE.
                                                BREYGUHN.

For the girl's fifteenth birthday, Breyguhn's father had a traveling circus come to the parklands of the family's old Summer Palace in the Zault hills, where the wealthier Dascens and their guests tended to spend the hot season, if they happened to be in Golter's northern hemisphere at the time.

Breyguhn had just finished junior college and in the autumn would be going—assuming her father could afford it—to finishing school. Sharrow had narrowed the choice of institution somewhat by being thrown out of the three best, all of which were in Claäv, and all of which had expelled her in circumstances of such apparent (but mysterious) turpitude that the schools concerned refused even to countenance accepting another girl from the same family, even if she shared only one parent.

This, which Breyguhn saw as a grievous, shaming, and even maliciously intended limitation on her freedom and prospects, had done nothing to endear Sharrow to her; however, the two had been sworn by their father, one tearful night a few weeks earlier after he had lost the last of Sharrow's late mother's jewels in a bones game, at least to attempt to get along with each other.

On his return from this disaster he had been handed

two envelopes by the hotel receptionist: one containing a final demand from the hotel management, the other a message from Breyguhn's mother—from whom he had been separated for five years—intimating that she had fallen in love again and wanted a divorce.

He had brandished a loaded pistol and wept, and talked of suicide, and thus suitably terrified both girls and ensured their acquiescence to his demands for a peace agreement.

The visit to the Summer Palace would be the first long-term test of this pact.

Their father had been lucky in the casinos earlier that month, and although the gesture of chartering the circus for a few days used up most of his funds and left his many debts still unpaid, he had convinced himself that his fortunes had changed in some strategic manner with that series of wins, and that lavishing money on his younger daughter was so far from being an extravagance as to be an investment; it would *ensure* that fate continue to smile upon him. Like a sacrifice, in a way.

Sharrow, who too well remembered the straitened circumstances of her own fifteenth birthday when, rather than being showered with presents, she had received nothing but apologies and a request that she give her father the jeweled, platinum-cloth gown that was the last unhocked or unsold possession her mother had left her so that he could pay off an urgent gambling debt, had not been conspicuously enthusiastic in conveying birthday good wishes to her half sister.

Sharrow found solace in the fact that Breyguhn obviously thought the hired circus would have been a suitable gift for a younger child, not the woman she was so proud of having become (though she was equally obviously determined to enjoy the gift to the utmost). She was also happy not to have to stay very long at the Summer Palace after enduring Breyguhn's birthday celebrations; she had been invited to go skiing in Throsse with the family of a young man she had met during an open day at her last finishing school.

He was the brother of one of the other girls, the son of a commercial army owner, and Sharrow thought he was quite wonderfully fine. She had *almost* lain with him that first day; only their discovery in the cupboard by a couple of other girls had prevented them requiting their tryst. It would probably have meant another expulsion if she hadn't

successfully bribed the two girls later. Since then she had
written to him and he to her, and she had been just *con-
sumed* with bliss when she'd received the invitation to join
his family at their chalet.

Skiing was not something she really enjoyed, though—
grimly determined—she had set about becoming proficient
at it while in Claäv; but to be with this particular young
man, she would gladly have undertaken any trial, undergone
any torment. Her father had linked his approval of the skiing trip to her attendance at Breyguhn's birthday, but suffering her half sister for a couple of days was a small price to
pay for the expected ecstasy awaiting her in Throsse. (Compared to that, even her feelings of victorious joy at having
been granted a scholarship to go to Yadayeypon University
for the coming semester shrank into insignificance.)

"If you're so utterly wonderful with computers, Shar, why
don't you hack into a bank and make daddy rich again?"

"Because they're practically impregnable unless you
work in one, that's why," she replied scornfully. "Any idiot
knows that."

"Well, you do, anyway."

"Oh, I'm sorry—was that supposed to be funny?"

"I don't believe you could hack into a . . . a calculator."

"Oh, don't you? How interesting."

The sunlit rolling hills of the estate blued away to the
horizon, softly ruffled green and yellow waves of fragrant
vegetation under a cloudless blue sky. Lakes glinted in the
distance.

They sat together in a gently swaying carousal circling
around a giant fairground wheel. A number of the children
and adults resident at the house for the summer sat in other
carousels. What with them and the servants and their
children—happily invited to share in the fun by Breyguhn's
father, though Brey herself had been silently chagrined at
the idea—the temporary fairground on the grass-ball lawn
was almost busy.

"Girls? Hello, girls?"

They both turned around with smiles fixed on their
faces to look back and up at their father, who was in the
carousel behind. His android butler, Skave, sat at his side,
incongruous in the formal servant's suit their father liked it

to wear. A round black butler's hat sat on its naked metal head.

Skave stared into the distance, its metal hands gripping the safety barrier. The tubular metal barrier looked slightly dented under Skave's hands, though this probably indicated a minor malfunction rather than some android analog of fear; the machine was elderly, dating from the first Golterian era that had thought fit—and had the ability—to create androids. Their father's debts meant it hadn't been properly maintained for the last few years, and recently its coordination and movements had become erratic.

"What, Daddy?"

"Having fun?"

"Pardon?"

"Having fun?"

"Oh, yes."

"Oh, incredible fun—unbelievable."

"Jolly good! They're having fun; isn't that excellent, Skave?"

"Indeed, sir."

"Do you remember that old merry-go-round in the ballroom? Sharrow?"

Breyguhn dug her in the ribs. Sharrow sighed exasperatedly and turned around to look back at her father, shaking her head as she tapped one ear. "Can't hear you," she shouted.

When the ride finished, the big wheel reversed to let the people off; their father and Skave were first out of their carousel and onto the boardwalk, then it was their turn to step down. Father took Breyguhn's hand; Skave took Sharrow's.

Sharrow screamed as the android's metal fingers crushed hers.

The old machine let go immediately and wobbled as though it were about to fall over, its head shaking in its collar. Sharrow bent double over her aching fingers. "You stupid machine!" she wailed. "You've broken my fingers!"

"Mistress, mistress, mistress . . . ," the android said plaintively, still shaking. It looked at its own hand, as if confused.

Breyguhn took a step back, watching it all.

Her father held Sharrow by the shoulders, then gently took her hand and kissed it, teasing her fingers out. "There," he said. "They're not broken, my love. They're all right, see? They're fine, they're perfect, beautiful fingers. Mmm. Just made to kiss. Mmm. What fingers. There, how kissable. You see? Silly old Skave. I must oil him, or whatever one does. Look at him; he's quivering, silly old sap. Skave, say sorry."

"Mistress," the old android said, its voice quivering. "I am most terribly sorry. Terribly, terribly sorry."

Blinking through her tears, she looked at the machine, conscious of Breyguhn watching her. She tried not to sob. "You *idiot!*" she told it.

The android vibrated again, hands shaking.

"Oh, my love, my little love; why, silly old Skave didn't mean it. Here—another kiss . . ."

"Right," Sharrow said, swinging into Breyguhn's room while she was combing her long brown hair before the mirror. Breyguhn watched as Sharrow plumped herself down on the bed and unrolled a simple stick-on computer. She flicked her hair back and woke the machine up with a couple of keystrokes. "You wanted to see some hacking; I'll show you some hacking."

Breyguhn finished doing her hair and tied it up, then joined the older girl on the bed. She looked at the screen. It was all figures and letters.

"Very exciting, I'm sure. What exactly are you trying to do, Shar?"

Sharrow used her right hand to click across the worn-looking surface of the keyboard. Her left hand still hurt, but she used it for the occasional shift stroke.

"Hacking into Skave's homeboard. I'm going to give the incompetent old wreck a nightmare."

"Really?" Breyguhn said, rolling over on the bed, her nightgown wrapping itself around her. The screen was still boring.

"Yes," Sharrow said. "Skave is so ancient, they programmed something like sleep into it so it can assimilate what happened during the day and amend its own programs. It's so old and hidebound, it doesn't really need to do it anymore, but it's become a habit. I'm going to shift its snoozing ass into a Nightmare game." Her fingers performed a ballet across the board.

"What?" Breyguhn said, looking interested as she sidled

closer across the bedclothes. "One of those things people dream into, to see how long they can last?"

"That's the idea," Sharrow said, watching a complexly folded holo of a deepframe data base's architecture spring up like a polychromatic mountain range from the stick-on's screen. She touched it, sliding her fingers into the image, shifting parts of that landscape and tutting to herself as her still sore left hand manipulated the wrong bits and had to correct. Finally she was satisfied and Entered the hologlyph code.

The folded shape disappeared to be replaced immediately by an infinite corridor that disappeared into the screen. She smiled and reached in with one hand while her other thumb kept Exponential Shift depressed.

"We're going to give old Skave a night to remember," she said, selecting a section in the forward-scrolling corridor and stopping there. "Only for him it'll last for a thousand nights, and he can't wake up out of it."

"A *thousand* nights?" Breyguhn said, trying to see further into the image.

Sharrow rolled her eyes. "That's how much *faster* than *us* they think, you doughball," she said. She keyed Auto Load; she already had the estate's smart but nonsentient system well mapped and primed. Glyphs surged and sank, figure-screens race-scrolled and flickered.

"There," she said after the screen went still.

"Is that it?" Breyguhn said, looking disappointed.

Sharrow looked at her. "Girlie, what I just did was interrupt the system of a 'droid that's been around for seven thousand years." She snapped the stick-on shut. "Watch for it at breakfast tomorrow morning, and don't order anything hot unless you enjoy eating off your lap."

She put her hand into Breyguhn's hair and ruffled it vigorously, shaking the other girl's head.

Breyguhn put her hand up and forced Sharrow's away.

Their father was distraught. "Skave!" he said. "Skave!" he still had his napkin tucked in his shirt as he paced around the breakfast room, kneading his hands. "After all these years! I can't forgive myself. I should have kept him in better repair. It's all my fault!"

He went to the window again. Outside, two bulkily powerful androids and a man in tech overalls were just closing the doors of the secure van that would take the inert body of Skave away.

The android had been discovered still locked into its download collar in the house's Mechanicals cellar, its eyes wide and staring, its head vibrating from side to side. A diagnostic scan revealed that its personality had effectively been wiped out, along with much of its intrinsicised programming and even some of its supposedly hard-wired functions-suite.

The android/AI management and leasing company that had been called in to help had advised that only some bizarre and—especially after all these millennia—unlikely nanophysical fault could have caused the fugue, or (rather more likely in their experience) somebody had hacked into the android's home data base and deliberately fried its geriatric brains.

Sharrow sat looking upset but feeling determinedly smug while her father wrung his hands and paced up and down the room, refusing to be comforted by his relations. She felt the buddings of guilt when she thought about what had happened to Skave, but squashed them with the sheer totality of her success in having proved her hacking skills to Breyguhn—*that* ought to put the fear of Fate into her—and with the harshly comforting idea that Skave had been old and becoming useless, and hence long overdue for retirement, or whatever happened to outmoded robots.

She put her hands beneath the table and squeezed her left hand in her right, to take her mind off what she had done, and to remind herself of part of the reason why she had thought of it in the first place. She watched her father knead his hands as he paced and felt the stabs of pain go up her own arms. She squeezed harder, keeping her face straight, until her eyes threatened to water, then she stopped.

Breyguhn seemed genuinely shocked. Sharrow watched glances of delicious complicity alternate with something like horror as they sat at the breakfast table with the rest of the family, listening to their father fret and mourn.

"Lost to us! Lost to us, after all these years! In the family for a millennia and lost to us in *my* stewardship! Our last asset! The shame!"

Sharrow collected herself, shook her head sadly, and

helped herself to icebread from the table cooler. Breyguhn sat looking at her, eyes wide.

Sharrow accessed the house system and saw the report the people who'd taken Skave away had sent to her father. They were sending the report by personal letter, too. She had no way of intercepting *that*.

To her relief, it didn't implicate her or anybody else in the household; the android management/leasing company reckoned somebody had hacked in from outside (they strongly advised a thorough up-grade of the estate's systems, which they would be honored to quote for at most reasonable rates). She was briefly proud of their judgment that whoever had done the job was quite possibly a professional, they had covered their tracks so well.

The report concluded that the android required a new brain, and as such had to be regarded as a total loss unless there was a major and extremely unlikely change in the law. As all owned androids were extremely valuable regardless of condition, they assumed a substantial claim on the android's insurance would be the next step, and would retain the machine in their vaults if required, and cooperate with any insurance assessor.

Sharrow put her head in her hands when she read that part. She knew her father no longer had any insurance on Skave—why pay a premium on something that hadn't gone wrong in seven thousand years, when the same money could win a million in the right bones game? Why, it would be a waste.

She switched off the stick-on and let it roll itself up.

"That stupid machine was part of our inheritance!" Breyguhn hissed. They were in the skidder rink, waiting between rides while the other adults and children gave up their small cars and walked over the rink's floor of compacted snow to the side barriers, to be replaced by new drivers. Beyond the shallow bowl of the refrigerated rink, the weather was hot and sunny, and every now and again a soft, warm gust of wind would bring a smell of flowers and greenery rolling across the chill of the rink's own sharply wintery scent.

Breyguhn had taken great delight in charging Sharrow's skidder several times during the last ride. Sharrow's preferred method of skidder driving was to avoid all collisions, so as a technique for annoying her, these constant crashes were more successful than most of the stratagems Breyguhn employed.

"Oh, so what?" Sharrow said, glancing around to make sure there was nobody to overhear her. "The old fool would only have sold Skave; we were never going to see any of the money it was worth."

"We *might* have!" Breyguhn insisted, as the last few people found cars and the Klaxon sounded, warning that the signal was about to be transmitted that would switch each skidder's engine on again.

"Might!" Sharrow laughed. "Not in a million chances, child. He'd have hocked Skave the next time he lost heavily. He'd sell anything to get stake money. He'd sell *us* to get stake money." Sharrow made a show of looking her half sister up and down. "Well, he might get a good price for me, anyway."

"He *loved* Skave," Breyguhn said. "He'd never have sold him."

"Rubbish," Sharrow said with prodigious disdain.

"You don't know!"

"All I know," Sharrow said coolly as the Klaxon sounded and the skidders came alive again, "is that you're a pain and I can't wait to get the hell away from here and go"—she flicked her eyebrows and made a thrusting motion with her pelvis—"skiing."

She twirled her car away over the white surface, avoiding Breyguhn's crude lunge at her and showering her with icy spray as she raced off around the oval track.

Sharrow's car stripped its track a minute later, leaving the broad metal bracelet laid out on the snow behind it like the train of some strange dress. Sharrow kicked at the accelerator, but the skidder's automatics had shut the engine off. She thumped her hands off the wheel, grimacing as her sore hand protested by jabbing pain along her arm; then she stood up in the car and waited for a break in the traffic of hurtling skidders and happily shouting, shrieking people, and made her way carefully but quickly across the white surface to the side.

Breyguhn claimed later she had turned back against the flow of traffic to see if she could help Sharrow, after noticing that her skidder had stopped. She knew it was against the rules, but she just hadn't thought. Then her accelerator had jammed and she must have panicked. She felt terrible about hitting Sharrow and crushing her against the barrier and breaking her leg.

Especially as it stopped her going on her skiing holiday.

Sharrow sat up in the bed, surrounded by cushions. Her father held her in his arms, patting her back.

"I know, I know, my love. Everything's against us just now, isn't it? Poor Skave taken from us; you with your naughty leg going and breaking itself, poor Brey hardly sleeping because she feels it was her fault, and me with two such unhappy daughters."

He patted the back of Sharrow's head as she rested her chin on his shoulder and looked at Breyguhn, who sat in a small seat near the door. Breyguhn crossed her eyes and shook her head quickly from side to side when their father mentioned Skave, made a silent scream, and held her thigh when he talked about Sharrow's leg, and then closed her eyes and tilted her head to one side as though peacefully asleep when he mentioned her.

"But we'll be all right, won't we, my pet? The medics will have that silly old leg sorted in no time, won't they?"

Breyguhn mimed a limp, crooked leg suddenly becoming straight; she waggled it around.

"Of course they will. It'll be as though it never happened, eh, won't it? You'll soon forget all about it, won't you?"

Breyguhn mimed sudden forgetfulness with a finger to her lips and a series of stagily puzzled expressions.

Sharrow smiled thinly as her father patted her back. She looked at Breyguhn and slowly shook her head.

Breyguhn crossed her arms and sat there, sneering.

Sharrow bedded one of the younger medics while she still had the cast on and got him to make sure that her leg would never be perfect again; she would always walk with a slight limp and so never forget.

Her father couldn't understand why his daughter was still lame. He threatened to sue the family medical franchise, but couldn't afford to.

At university Sharrow's limp became a trademark, a talisman, her insignia—like an eye patch or a dueling scar.

She always did refuse to have any further treatment. Her father just couldn't understand it at all.

19

Spoiling Bid

T he android and the woman stood beside an old-
fashioned automobile on a weed-strewn quay in the old
docks, looking out to sea. The antique car hissed every now
and again and leaked steam. Behind it, beyond the shells of
the ruined warehouses, mists rose perpetually from the
warm waters of the inlet, climbing and reclimbing the frost-
gray planes of a lifeless sky. Thrial was a red fruit wrapped
in tissues of mist. Buildings in the distance wavered on the
boundary of visibility.

The helicopter came swinging around the peninsula, its
engine voice rattling like drumfire off the cliffs and buildings looming through the mist. The machine slowed as it
crossed the harbor mole, then swiveled in the air and
landed quickly and gracefully in a swirling bowl of curling
mist and a small storm of tiny stones and dead, windblown
leaves.

She rocked on her feet. The android stood stock still.

Miz jumped down from the pilot's seat, unclipping the
control stalk from his ear and handing the instrument to a
uniformed man who was sliding into the seat he had vacated. Miz looked pleased with himself. His right hand was
lightly bandaged. Zefla and Dloan appeared from the far
side of the helicopter; Dloan limped a little.

Zefla smiled when she saw Sharrow. "It's Yada, end of next year, with three old cuties," she said when they hugged.

"I heard. Hi, Dloan."

"Good landing, eh?"

"Wonderful, Miz. This is Feril, my legalist and custodian while we're here."

"Hello to you all," the android said. It pointed to the ancient, hissing steam car as it donned a set of driver's goggles. "Allow me to take you to the Lady Sharrow's apartments.

Miz looked out over the misty city. The jet-faced sandstone apartment block sat halfway up a built-up hill looking out over an old canal basin connected by a flight of locks and an inclined plane to the city's inner harbor. Sharrow's rooms were on the top floor, one story above the apartment Feril lived in. The android had only recently moved out of the top-floor apartment after renovating it.

It was the androids' stated intention to return the city of Vembyr to a state resembling its condition during the time of the Lizard Court, when by general agreement the city had been at its most culturally vibrant and architecturally coherent. As well as rebuilding the ancient steam-powered automobile it had used to transport them from the docks, Feril had restored two other apartment blocks over the past few decades; this was its third.

All the rooms were tall. Wood paneling carved with intricate abstract patterns climbed from floors of polished wood to agate and marble dados, from which plain white plaster walls rose to fabulously complicated plaster friezes composed of leaves and vines and little peeking lizard faces. The room they were in was sparsely furnished with black wood-and-hide furniture that looked both severely formal and strangely organic.

"*How* much?" Sharrow said.

"Ten million," Zefla said, nodding. She was standing by a paneled wall, running her hand over it.

Miz spread his arms as he turned from the window. He stood there, silhouetted. "The guy didn't even look surprised!" he exclaimed.

"Judge did," Zefla said, peering intently at the paneling. "You could see she'd thought it was just a formality, setting bail that high. She had to consult the Court AI right then, in front of everybody, probably asking if she could reset the bail beyond *anybody's* reach, but the rules say no. So Roa walked free."

"Who'd *risk* ten mill on somebody that crazy?" Miz said.

"No clues, I take it?" Sharrow asked.

Zefla left the paneling and came to sit with Sharrow on a long couch. She shrugged. "Bail company. Had the money there in a cash-good clip within the hour. No idea who's behind it."

"Maybe it's the same son-of-a-bitch named the noon race winner *Minus A Fifth* in Tile yesterday," Miz said, leaning back against the window sill.

"Oh, Miz," Zefla said, frowning at him.

"Yeah," he said, "I know. I'm being paranoid."

Sharrow felt the nagging sensation return—that feeling there was something she'd missed, something important.

"Miz?" she said.

"Hmm?"

"Come away from the window, will you?"

"What?" Miz said, frowning and looking around behind him. He eased forward, taking his weight off the glass and stepping away.

Sharrow was aware they were all looking at her. Miz glanced back at the city beyond the window again. She found herself looking around the room for Cenuij. She made a half-exasperated, half-despairing gesture with her arms. "I'm sorry. It's me who's paranoid." She pointed at the window and told Miz, "I'm sure there isn't a sniper out there, and the glass won't give way behind you."

Miz smiled uncertainly at first, then sat down on a pale hide chair.

"Anyway," Dloan said, flexing his wounded leg a little, "we're here. What is it we've come to see?"

"Something Gorko left behind," Sharrow told him. She looked around at the others, feeling something was wrong, and realized that she was looking for Cenuij again, to catch his gaze. "We go to the warehouse tonight," she said.

"A warehouse?" Miz said.

"A lot of family possessions are stored here, courtesy of the World Court," Sharrow said.

"The storage rates are cheap," Zefla explained to Miz, who was still looking puzzled.

"Some of the stuff's Gorko's," Sharrow told him, "but they haven't been able to dispose of it yet, and some of it's still disputed; the Court says it's theirs, my family says it's ours."

"Which category does whatever we've come to look at fall into?" Zefla asked.

"The latter," Sharrow said. "It's Gorko's tomb."

"His *tomb*?" Miz said.

Sharrow nodded.

Zefla looked mystified. "How did the book lead to the tomb?"

Sharrow looked around the wide, white room, her eyes narrowing. "Tell you somewhere else," she said.

"Don't you trust your new friend?" Miz inquired.

"Oh, I trust it," Sharrow said, looking at the delicate leaves, fronds, stems, and flowers described in the patterned plaster filling the angle between wall and ceiling. "But who knows . . . ?"

There was silence in the room for a while. Then Zefla clapped her hands together and said, "There anywhere a girl can get a drink around here?"

"Good idea," Sharrow said, rising. "Let's try the City Hotel; we need to get you lot booked in, anyway. They won't let me stay there, but I don't think I'm banned from the bar."

The warehouse extended into the distance: section after section, aisle after aisle, shelf after shelf. Sharrow stood with the others at the entrance, while Feril and the warehouse's caretaker android turned all the lights on from a great board full of switches, slowly filling the cavern with yellow pools of illumination.

"Sheech," Zefla said, leaning one elbow on Sharrow's shoulder. "This Gorko's shit?"

"Yes," Sharrow said.

"What, *all* of it?"

Sharrow looked slowly around as the last few lights flicked on in the distance. "This is just one house," she said.

"Wow," Miz said.

"Lady Sharrow," Feril said. "You wished to see your late grandfather's tomb?"

"Please," she nodded.

"This way."

• • •

They walked through the dusty debris of her family's past, among the piled crates and past the stacked boxes and faded labels and yellowing lists tied and pinned to the assorted containers. The items that weren't boxed were covered in translucent plastic wrapping secured by World Court code-seals.

After a short walk they came to a section of the warehouse dominated by a large plastic-sheeted cube about four meters square, standing on a metal pallet and surrounded by crates, boxes, and a variety of loose items also shrouded with the translucent sheeting.

"That is the tomb," Feril said, pointing at the dark cube.

"Oh," Miz said. He sounded disappointed. "I'd kind of thought it'd be bigger."

"That's all there is," Sharrow told him.

Feril found a way through to the cube; they trailed after it. "I shall take the wrapping off," it told them. It found the plastic sheet's Court seal and ran its fingers over the input surface. The plastic sheet parted around the sarcophagus, and Feril and Dloan pulled it off, revealing the black mirror-surface of the tomb's polished granite. Sharrow pulled a crate over and stood on it to look through the little smoke-glass window halfway up one black wall.

She put one hand to the side of her face to screen out the light from the warehouse, then took a small torch from her pocket and shone it through the window.

She looked down at the others. "It's empty," she said, trying not to sound shocked.

"Your grandfather's body is in the Noble's Temple in Yadayeypon," Feril said. "It was felt that a warehouse was not a fit place for human remains."

"Same could be said for Yada," muttered Miz.

"I didn't know," Sharrow admitted. She squinted in through the smoke-glass window again.

"The World Court did not publicize the removal of your grandfather's remains," Feril said.

"They take his bike to Yada, too?" she asked.

"His bike?" Feril said. "Ah, the vehicle in the tomb with him. No. That is ... here," the android said, turning and pointing at a long translucent bundle.

"Ah, well," Sharrow said, clicking off the torch and stepping down from the pallet. She looked around. "I really wanted to pay my respects to the old man, but . . ."

"I'm sorry," Feril said, "I should have realized. You asked to see the tomb and . . ." Its dull mirror-eyes gazed levelly at her, reflecting the black stone tomb behind. "How silly of me. I do apologize."

"That's all right." Sharrow sighed, looking around at the other boxes. She shrugged. "Would you mind if I have a look at some of this other stuff? I knew house Tzant well. . . ."

"By all means," the android said. It opened the seals on a variety of nearby crates and packages while Dloan and Miz pulled the wrappings off.

"That's fine," Sharrow said, after the android had opened twenty or so of the plastic bundles and—far from showing any sign of stopping—actually seemed to be speeding up.

Feril, bent over to de-seal a tall crate, stood immediately, bowed to Sharrow, and said, "Please, look at your leisure. Unless you need me for anything else, I shall be at or near the door."

"Thank you," she said.

The android walked away, disappearing between the stacked cases.

"Never seen an android *embarrassed* before," Zefla said after a little while.

"Idiot," Miz said, sitting on a low sideboard constructed from blackwood and seagrain and edged with brushed platinum studded with opals.

"Oh, well," Dloan said. "At least some of this stuff looks interesting. . . ." He gazed around at the opened packages.

"I take it this fouls up the plan," Miz said.

"Hmm," Sharrow said, frowning. She stroked a heavy fur cloak of silver inlaid within black, which lay draped over a huge crystal bowl crusted with jewels and strung with loops of precious metals; they both sat on a mirror-rug covering an antique holotank.

Zefla strolled toward a huge, intricately carved wooden cupboard and opened a door. "Whee!" she said, and pulled out a bottle. "A stand-up wine cellar." She sat up on the sideboard with Miz.

"Look what I found," she said.

"Amazing," Miz said, shaking his head and looking

closely at Zefla. "Is there anywhere you *can't* find a drink, Zef?"

"I sincerely hope not." Zefla waved the dusty bottle at Sharrow. "Fancy depleting the inventory?"

"Is it legal?" Sharrow asked.

Zefla shook her head emphatically. "Not even arguably."

"All right, then," Sharrow said, as Zefla took a knife from her pocket and started opening the bottle.

"Let them sue us," Miz said.

"I know a good lawyer," Zefla told him.

They drank the wine from the bottle. Dloan inspected a presentation set of hunting rifles. Miz calculated the break-up value of the sideboard he was sitting on. Zefla donned the fur cloak, dragging its meter-long hem across the dusty warehouse floor.

"Fate, it's heavy," she said, shucking the cloak and hoisting it back on top of the ceremonial bowl. "They actually *wear* stuff like that?" She shook her head. "The weight of tradition."

Sharrow sat side-saddle on the unwrapped motor bike, looking glum.

"Hey," Zefla said. "Any more news about Breyguhn?"

"Still staying where she is," Sharrow said.

"Crazy," Miz said.

Sharrow nodded. "I tried to call her; the Brothers said she's there now as a willing guest. They said she wouldn't talk to me."

Zefla shook her head. "You think that's the truth?"

Sharrow shrugged. "I don't know. They might be lying, or Breyguhn might really want to stay. The way she was when I saw her last, it's just about believable."

"Think hearing about Cenuij could have flipped her over the edge?" Zefla asked.

"If she wasn't long gone already," Sharrow said. She got off the bike and walked toward the black cube of the tomb, squinting up at it. "Dloan," she said. "Think you could give me a punt up there?"

"Surely." Dloan put one of the hunting rifles back in its case, stepped to the side of the tomb, and made a stirrup with his hands. Sharrow was lifted toward the top of the sarcophagus and pulled herself up.

"You be careful up there," Miz called.

"Yes, of course," Sharrow said, gazing at the top surface

of the black granite cube. "I wonder if we can get this thing ope . . ." Her voice trailed off as she looked down at the bike she had been sitting on.

"Shar?" Zefla frowned.

Sharrow glanced around the warehouse. She sat on the edge of the black cube, turned, and lowered herself on her hands, then let herself drop to the warehouse floor.

She walked over to the bike, a strange expression on her face. The others looked baffled. Sharrow put her hand on the bike's front faring and stared at the machine.

The bike was long and low-slung and had a single deeply contoured seat aft off a bulging gas tank and above a shiny V4 hydrogen engine. Its two wheels were dark tori of flex-metal, trenched by carved grip-curves so that they looked like giant gears.

Above the curve of the front wheel's splash-guard, what appeared to be the bike's light cluster and instrument binnacle was a solid, bulky mass covered with a thin aerodynamic faring. Two stubby cylinders protruded from the matt silver of the main casing, ending in a pair of darkly bulbous lenses. A couple of oddly impractical stalks protruded from the casing, a strap with no apparent purpose lay draped across the gas tank, and the two main instrument dials at the rear of the binnacle looked tacked on.

Sharrow knelt down by the tipped front wheel, patting the roughened silver surface over the two dark lenses.

Miz shrugged. Dloan continued to look puzzled. Zefla took another swig from the bottle. Then her expression changed suddenly from incomprehension to amazement. She sputtered wine and pointed. "Is that the Lazy Gu—?" She coughed, then patted her chest.

"*What?*" Miz said loudly, then looked around guiltily.

Dloan looked puzzled for a moment longer, then smiled and nodded slowly.

Sharrow shook her head, rising and inspecting the point where the two instrument dials disappeared into holes cut in the binnacle. "No," she said, inserting a fingernail into the gap, then sliding it back and forth. "The real thing wouldn't let you cut these holes in it." She stepped back and folded her arms, looking the bike up and down. "But somebody's gone to some trouble to make it look like one."

The others crowded around the bike.

Miz peered closely at the instruments. "Maybe you get

on, fire it up, and it takes you to where the real thing's stashed," he said.

"Like a pair of magic shoes in a fairy tale." Zefla nodded.

"Maybe," Sharrow said.

Dloan leaned closer, inspecting the instruments. He frowned, then tapped both main read-outs. They were old-fashioned electromechanical dials with slim plastic needles pointing to numbers printed around the edges of the instrument faces.

"Hmm," Dloan said, gripping the dials and shaking them; they moved in the binnacle.

"What?" Zefla said.

"According to these instruments," Dloan said, straightening, "this thing's doing fifty klicks an hour and it's revving at sixty a second."

"Never trust a Lazy Gun," Zefla muttered.

"Really?" Sharrow said. "Let's see . . ." She put a hand on each of the two dials and pulled.

"Hey, careful—" Zefla said, stepping back.

The dials clicked out of the binnacle, coming cleanly away. There were no wires trailing from them. Sharrow turned them over; the instruments had no obvious connections anywhere on their stainless-steel surface.

"One needle's moving," Dloan said quietly.

Sharrow held the instruments in front of her. The speedometer needle swung a little, then steadied. The tachometer needle stayed steady. Dloan reached out, altered the orientation of the instrument cluster so that it was lying flat, then, while Sharrow still held them, turned the dials around ninety degrees and back. The speedometer needle shifted around the dial, but kept pointing in the same direction, toward one wall of the warehouse.

Sharrow nodded in the direction the needle was indicating. "Then let's walk that way, shall we?"

They bumped into Feril while they were walking down the aisle, intent on the two instruments. Sharrow smiled awkwardly and turned the dials' faces to her chest. The android just stood there.

"May I help?" it said.

Sharrow smiled. "May we borrow your car for a while?"

"The vehicle is a little temperamental," Feril told them,

sounding apologetic. "Might I suggest I drive you wherever you wish to go?"

Sharrow and the others exchanged looks. Feril looked up at the ceiling and said, "I know it wouldn't even cross your mind, but just supposing you were thinking of taking something from the trove. It would be wise not to let the caretaker observe you doing so. I myself am quite neutral in the matter."

Sharrow opened her jacket and concealed the bulky dials inside as best she could. "We'll accept your offer of the lift, Feril, thank you."

"My pleasure," the android said.

Gray waves dashed themselves against black boulders; spray flew up, sunset lit, to blow across the tumble of boulders in quick veils of gray-pink mist, dropping and whirling into the crannies between the rocks.

The wind blew into her face, strong and cool and damp. The sunset was a wide stain of red at the ocean's edge. She turned and looked up the grassy slope to the road, where the car sat hissing quietly. Strands of steam leaked from beneath the vehicle and were torn away on the curling wind. There was a light on in the automobile's rear compartment, and through the open door she could see Miz and Dloan peering at a screen they'd unfurled over the floor of the car.

Feril and Zefla sat on a couple of boulders at the side of the road about fifty meters away, looking out to sea, talking.

Miz got out of the car and walked down to her. He stood by her side, making a show of breathing in the brine-laced air.

"Well?" Sharrow asked him.

"I'll tell you if you'll tell me how the book led to the tomb," Miz said, smiling faintly.

Sharrow shrugged. "The message in the casing," she said.

Miz frowned for a moment. "What? 'Things Will Change'?"

Sharrow nodded. "That's the inscription on Gorko's tomb."

"But the tomb's only ... what?"

"Fifty years old," she said. "And the book was missing for twelve centuries." She smiled thinly at the sunset.

"Gorko must have found out what was in the casing, even if he never got to the book itself. Maybe it was just good Antiquities research; maybe one of his agents was able to inspect the book, or remote-scan it while it was in Pharpech. But somehow he found out what the inscription was and had it duplicated on his tomb."

Miz looked vaguely disappointed. "Huh," he said.

She looked up at Miz, who was nodding slowly. "So," she said, "where do the dials point?"

Miz pursed his lips and nodded out across the ocean. "Over the sea and far away," he said.

"Caltasp?" she asked.

"Sort of," he said. He glanced at her. "The Areas," he added.

She closed her eyes for a moment. "Are you sure?"

"Come and see."

They walked back to the car. She stood at the opened door, one hand resting on the car's slatted wooden roof.

The flex-screen lying on the floor displayed a flat map of Golter's southern hemisphere, distorted to show true direction. They both watched as Dloan traced a line from a compass-rosed point in southern Jonolrey across the Phirar to the region between Caltasp and Lantskaar.

"Depends how accurate these gauges are," Dloan said, tapping numbers into the calculator display at the side of the map. "And on whether the direction display is working on the GPS or magnetic. But if the speedo shows true direction and the rev counter is kilometers times one hundred, then it's the Embargoed Areas."

"Oh, shit," Sharrow breathed.

They had driven eighty kilometers out of Vembyr along the pitted surface of the deserted coastal highway, heading south and west. They had passed the entombed ruins of the ancient reactor a couple of kilometers back, just before the cut-off for the point. They were about fifty kilometers farther west than they had been in the city, and the needle on the bike's fake tachometer had moved one half of a division on its scale, indicating fifty-nine and a half revolutions per second rather than the sixty it had shown in the warehouse.

"We can get a more accurate fix with a better map," Dloan said, laying the static-stiffened screen over the dials, then turning it briefly transparent. "And maybe triangulate if we can get a reading from a good way north of the city."

"I'll get the copter back," Miz told Sharrow, nodding.

"That should narrow it down pretty well," Dloan said, tapping out more figures and studying the result. "But just going on this, if it isn't under the ocean, it's somewhere in the fjords, in the Areas."

Sharrow looked up the road at Zefla and Feril. The two were standing now; Zefla was pointing out to sea, her long blond hair blown cloud-ragged by the wind. Red light reflected from the polished surfaces of the android's head and body.

A gust rocked Sharrow on her feet. Her skirt whipped at her boots, and she stuck her hands in her jacket pockets, feeling the cold weight of the gun against her left hand.

She saw Zefla glance toward the car and waved at her. The woman and the android began walking back to the car.

That night she did not dream of Cenuij, but instead dreamt that her arm died; her left arm became paralyzed and numb, then began to wither and shrink, but somehow remained the same size it had always been, but was still dead, and so she had to find somebody who would bury it for her, and wandered around a city that seemed to be crowded but where she could only find people who looked just like her but weren't, and nobody would bury the arm for her.

Eventually she tried to make a box, a coffin, for the arm, to carry it around in, but it was difficult to make it with just one arm.

She woke in the middle of the night, in the wide white bed in the shadows of the tall white room in the apartment block Feril was renovating. She was lying on her left arm, which had gone to sleep. She got up and sat in a seat by the side of the bed for a while, drinking a glass of water and massaging her tingling arm as blood and feeling returned to it.

She thought she would be awake for the rest of the night, but then fell asleep there, to wake up stiff and sore in the morning, her right hand still clutching the other arm as though comforting it.

The monthly auction started the next day. Aircraft arrived from all over Golter, filling the City Hotel with mercenary chiefs, arms dealers, militaria collectors, weapon-fund managers, contract army reps, and a scattering of specialist media people. The auction hall itself was an old conference center three blocks from the warehouse where the Tzant trove was stored.

Sharrow had refused to hide away while the auction was held, and she and Zefla, both wearing veiled hats and dull, loose-fitting suits, sat in a small drinks lounge attached to the conference facility, watching the people come and go.

Miz and Dloan had left the city to travel up the coast in one of Miz's company helicopters, getting another fix on the position the bike dials were indicating. If the triangulation confirmed the dials were pointing where they seemed to be, Dloan would attend the auction's second and final day so he could buy the sort of gear they'd need if they were to mount an expedition to the Areas.

"You're mad," Zefla said quietly, lifting her veil to drink from her glass as she leaned closer to Sharrow. "You should be hiding." She sipped her drink, finishing it. "I'm mad, too, for letting you talk me into this. I should have told Dloan, or Miz, or just locked you up. You talk me into the most insane things."

"Oh, stop whining and go and get us another drink," Sharrow whispered. Zefla sat back sharply, then made a grunting noise and started to get up.

"Good grief," Sharrow said, taking Zefla's arm. "Look who's here."

Elson Roa stood at the bar. He was dressed in a sober business robe and carried a sensible hat. A similarly garbed young woman they didn't recognize stood at Roa's side, toting a briefcase.

"Wonder what he's come for," Zefla said.

"Yes," Sharrow said, slipping her glass under her veil to sip at her drink. "I wonder."

They watched the auction through the afternoon, strolling from the lounge to the main hall and back again, keeping track of the events on the center's closed-circuit screens.

The multifarious items came up for sale and were knocked down; all the items easily made their reserve price, which meant—according to a media person they overheard filing a report—that the pessimistic large-scale conflict forecasts that various analysts had been making recently were being confirmed by the traders. Weapons futures rose another point that afternoon.

Elson Roa didn't appear to buy anything, but he and his

assistant seemed to be watching everybody just as carefully as were Sharrow and Zefla.

The first day's selling ended late in the evening. Sharrow and Zefla strolled past the docks and then sat on a pair of bollards as though soaking up the late-evening sun, watching the people who had come for the auction as they departed in their various craft for yachts offshore, or hotels in nearby regions, where the radiation level was what Golter considered normal.

They watched Elson Roa and his assistant approach a chartered VTOL jet, then Sharrow shook her head.

"What *is* he doing?" she said, then turned to Zefla. "Cover," she said. She stood up, ignoring Zefla's protests, and walked over to intercept the Solipsist leader.

"Politeness," she said, putting her veil back.

Elson Roa looked at her strangely as though not recognizing her at first, then bowed slightly and said, "Yes, hello."

"Congratulations on your bail," she said, searching his expression. He looked mildly surprised. "I believe you've set a new record. You must have rich friends."

Roa shook his head emphatically. "A strong will," he said, raising his voice to counter the noise of a jet taking off. "I think I am beginning to alter reality."

"I think you must be," she agreed. "Does your alteration to reality have a name?"

"I do not believe it needs one," the tall Solipsist said coolly.

"Perhaps not," she said. She smiled. "So, what brings you to the auction?"

Roa looked puzzled and pointed to the VTOL. "That," he said.

Sharrow looked levelly at him. She had the depressing feeling that Roa didn't realize it was a joke most people got out of their system in junior high.

She shook her head. "Never mind." She glanced at the female assistant at Roa's side, not sure if she recognized the woman. "How is Keteo? I don't see him here."

Roa's brows furrowed. "He is gone from me; he proved to be only a temporary apparance."

"Oh? What appeared to happen to him?"

"He appeared to become religious and join some decamillennialist faith. A section of my personality I am best rid of, I think."

"Ah-hah," she said.

Roa looked at his assistant, then at the waiting jet. "I must go now. Good-bye." He bowed.

She raised one hand. "Pleasant journey. Watch out for low bridges."

Roa ignored this as he walked for the plane.

She rejoined Zefla.

"Anything?" Zefla said.

"Nothing," Sharrow told her.

Roa's plane rolled toward the take-off pad and was gone a few minutes later.

They met up with Miz and Dloan at the hotel and had dinner in their suite. The men had worked out the position the bike dials were indicating to a ten-kilometer circle near the head of a ninety-kilometer-long fjord deep in the Embargoed Areas. They discussed the options for getting safely into and out of the Areas.

Later Sharrow took the service stairs out of the packed, noisy hotel and walked back to her apartments through the dark city. She got slightly lost but then saw Feril's steam car parked on the street in a pool of light cast from the brightly lit lobby of the apartment block. The lights were on in the apartment Feril was renovating just below her own.

She stood in the lobby waiting for the lift, whistling quietly to herself. She thought she heard the clack-clack of android footsteps on the stairwell at one point and looked up the steps around the side of the lift shaft waiting for Feril to appear, but they stopped somewhere above.

The elevator appeared and she took it to her floor. She was about to open the door to her apartment when she heard a door open on the floor below.

"Lady Sharrow?" she heard Feril call.

She looked down the stairwell. Feril's head poked around the side of the lift shaft. "Yes, Feril?"

"I think there was somebody here to see you," the android told her. It sounded puzzled. "But it was strange."

"How?" she said.

"The person looked like an android, but it was actually a human dressed to resemble an android; they didn't respond to my transceiver and a simple EM scan—"

"Did they go in here?" Sharrow said quickly, jabbing her thumb toward her apartment.

"I believe so," Feril said. "I thought perhaps it was somebody you knew."

She looked back at the door to her apartment. "Wait here," she said. She pressed the button for the lift and heard it rumbling in its shaft.

She looked back down at the android. "On second thought," she said, "don't wait here. Just to be on the safe side—get out of the building."

The lift doors hissed open. "Do you think—?" she heard Feril say as she swung into the elevator and pressed the button for the first floor. The lift descended. She checked the HandCannon.

There was nobody on the first floor, or in the lobby. She kept against the wall and went to the doors; there was no way she could get out to the street without it being obvious. She sidled back to the rear of the lobby and made her way out of a dusty office and a short corridor into a dark side street.

She walked quickly to the corner building, keeping her boot heels off the pavement so they wouldn't make a noise. She looked out. Light from the apartment block lobby cast a soft glow for a half block in each direction. After a few seconds Sharrow made out a pale figure crouched in the shadows diagonally across the street, in an awninged doorway under another building. The figure—it did look like a rather bulky android—was looking up toward the top of the apartment block and seemed to be holding something in both hands.

Sharrow sensed movement to her left, at the apartment-block doors; she saw the figure in the doorway look quickly down from the top of the building to the doors.

Sharrow glanced to her left, to see Feril come out of the lobby doors and stand on the pavement between the doors and the silent bulk of the antique steam car. Feril looked diagonally across the street toward the figure crouching in the doorway, then raised one hand.

The figure brought a hand gun up and fired at Feril. The android flicked its head to one side; light flared on the stonework immediately behind it as a crackle of noise burst across the street. Feril dropped to the paving stones. Sharrow aimed the HandCannon as the figure raised its other hand and seemed to shake something. She fired the HandCannon.

Light flickered above her an instant before it burst from the muzzle of the gun. The wall beside Sharrow rippled as the gun roared. A mighty thump came through the soles of her boots and then a crushing, numbing pulse of sound rolled down over her, dwarfing the percussive bark of the gun.

She half fell, half dropped to the ground, then rolled across the pavement toward the building and under the cover of a broad window sill as the blast echoed and re-echoed off nearby buildings and merged with a terrible, tearing noise. Chunks of masonry and huge long shards of glass began to fall and shatter on the street and pavement.

Dust choked her nostrils; the roaring noise filled her ears through an insistent, cacophonous ringing.

When all but the ringing stopped, she stood up, brushing dust and flakes of stone from her jacket and skirt.

She looked up through a cloud of gray, moonlit dust. The top half of the apartment block had disappeared. Most of it had fallen into the street in front, entirely blocking it and burying the lobby doors and the ancient steam car under a ten-meter-high pile of dust-clouded rubble; there was no sign of Feril.

She tried going back the way she had come, but rubble filled the dark corridor, blocking the way to the office; her little torch made a white cone in the dry, throat-coating dust. She went back out, coughing and choking, and clambered over the rubble toward the doorway where the figure had been crouching.

Whoever it had been, her shot had killed them; the metal and plastic chest bore only a small puncture mark near its center, but there was a sticky red mess a meter up the wall behind where the person had been crouching, and a slowly advancing puddle of deep, dark red was making its glistening way across the dust and debris-strewn floor of the doorway, its thickly gleaming surface picking up little particles of drifting, coating dust as it moved.

She kicked aside pieces of rubble and pulled at the figure's head.

The head/helmet came away after she gave it a half twist.

A man. At first, with an odd sense of relief, she thought that she didn't recognize him.

But then she took another look at that youthful but now

slack face, and with a feeling of sadness that became anger and then a kind of despair, she recognized Keteo.

She was unsure whether she wanted to cry or to punch that smooth, boyish, dead face. Then just as she was about to shove the android-head helmet back over the young ex-Solipsist's head, she saw something glint at the collar of the olive T-shirt he wore.

She drew the thin chain out.

On the end of it hung a small planet-and-single-moon locket, the symbol of an intern-grade Huhsz Lay Novice.

She looked into the youth's dead eyes again, then let the trinket drop back to his chest. She stood up and let the hollow android head fall beside him in the doorway.

A large truck drew up in the street behind her, wheels skidding through the glass and stone wreckage in front of the main rubble heap. The truck's lights picked out the dust-shrouded remains of the building. Two androids jumped out of the vehicle and stood looking at the pile, then moved to a section of it and quickly started to pick up lumps of the fallen masonry and throw it behind them, excavating a trench in the debris.

Sharrow left Keteo lying in the doorway and walked over to the two toiling androids, keeping out of the way of the bits of rubble they were sending flying back behind them. Another truck appeared at the end of the street and roared toward the wreckage. One of the androids stopped working when it saw her.

"You must be Lady Sharrow," it said. It paused. "I have told Feril you are alive and apparently well."

"You mean it's *alive* in there?" she said incredulously, pointing at the huge pile of rubble as the second truck stopped and half a dozen androids jumped out holding construction equipment.

"Yes," the android told her as it stepped aside to let two larger androids get at where it had been excavating. "Feril is under the car, between the axles, and although trapped and a little dented, is in no obvious immediate danger."

She looked up through the clearing dust at what was left of the apartment block; dark, glassless windows revealed only a shell behind. The top four stories had either fallen into the street or collapsed down inside the rest of the building. Timbers stuck out of the rubble like broken bones. One white chunk of plaster lay near her foot, its flowers and trellis-work all cracked and coated gray. One of the androids working at the wreckage threw away something that might have been a piece of the old steam car's slatted roof. She shook her head.

"Tell Feril," she said to the android who was still standing, looking at her, "that . . ." She shrugged and shook her head and then sat down on the dusty rubble and put her shaking hands over her head as she half said, half moaned, "I'm sorry. . . ."

"Sharrow! Thank the gods you're alive. You have no idea how difficult it is getting reliable information out of that city. Are you all right?"

"Just fine. How are you, Geis?"

"I'm well."

"So?" she said. "You left a message; what is it?"

"Yes I did, and thanks for calling back." The flat image on the old wall-phone in what had once been Vembyr's Central Post Office waved a hand dismissively. "But dammit, Sharrow, I'm concerned for you. For the last time, *please* let me help you. I'm still at your service."

"And I still appreciate it, Geis," she told him, looking at the walls of the old curtained booth to escape the intensity of those staring eyes. "But I still have ideas of my own I want to pursue."

Geis looked uncertain. "But, Sharrow, whatever your plans might be, can they be more dependable, any safer than accepting my help?"

She shrugged. "Who can say, Geis?"

A pained look passed over his face. "I was sorry to hear about Cenuij Mu, but at least the others are still alive. If not for yourself, then for their sake, reconsider."

"We've thought it all through, Geis. We know what we're doing."

Geis sat back, shaking his head. He sighed, fiddling with something on the desk in front of him. "Well, I don't know; now we have Breyguhn refusing to leave the Sea House." He looked up. "If you want, I might be able to have her taken from there, get her away from its influence to somewhere they can try to make her well again." He sounded eager. "Shall I do that?"

Sharrow shook her head. "Not on my account. If she's happy, let her stay."

Geis almost looked amused for a moment. "'Happy'?" he said. "In that place?"

"I believe it's always been a relative term." She shrugged. "And maybe that's where she feels she can best come to terms with Cenuij's death. Anyway, as far as I understand it, it wasn't a once-only offer by the Sad Brothers; she's free to go at any time."

"Oh, yes," Geis said, playing with the pen on his desk. "But it can't do her any good, stuck in there."

"It's her choice, Geis."

Geis looked at her levelly for a while. He seemed sad and tired. "Choice," he said heavily. A small smile disturbed his face. "We all think we have so much of that, don't we?"

She looked away for a moment. "Yes. Terrible old world, isn't it?" She glanced at the time display. "Look, Geis, I have to go. I'm meeting the others. I appreciate your offer, I really do, but let us try to do this the way we know best."

He gazed out of the screen at her for a while, his eyes moving about her image as though trying to fix it in his mind. Then his shoulders drooped a little, and he nodded. "Yes. You were always so determined, so hard, weren't you?" He smiled and took a deep breath. "Good luck, Sharrow," he said.

"Thanks, Geis. And to you."

He opened his mouth to say something, then just nodded. He reached out. The screen in front of her went gray, leaving her alone in the darkened booth.

In the grand ballroom of the east wing of house Tzant that winter there was a merry-go-round. It sat in the center of the huge room's ancient wooden map-floor, rotundly magnificent, gaily painted, flag-bedecked, and glitteringly competitive with the extravagantly carved gilt mirrors and enormous sparkling chandeliers of the ballroom. The most splendid chandelier of all, which normally hung like an incandescent inverted fountain in the center of the room, had been removed to one of the stables to make room for the merry-go-round. The fair-ground ride ran on electricity and made a rich humming noise as it revolved. Sharrow liked that noise more than the music of the organ, which usually played as the merry-go-round spun.

There were eighty different animals on the ride, all life-size and mythical or extinct. She usually rode on the trafe, a fierce-looking extinct flightless bird nearly three meters high with a serrated bill and huge claw-feet.

She was alone on the ride that day, hugging the neck of the trafe as the ride spun around, silent save for the room-filling boom of the electric motor. She watched her reflection sweep past in each of the tall gilt-framed mirrors in turn. The motor-hum seemed to buzz up through the wooden body of the long-extinct bird and resonate through her, intense and numbing and reassuring. Sometimes she fell asleep on the fabulous bird, and traveled for a long time through the warm air of the ballroom, between the enormous mirrors on one wall and the closed curtains of the windows facing them on the other.

She preferred the curtains closed because it was winter and outside lay the snow, blank and cold and soft.

The back of the trafe on the spinning merry-go-round was the only place she knew she could sleep safely. If she did dream while she rode the great bird, she dreamt good dreams, of warmth and coziness and being hugged; she dreamt of her mother lifting her from her bath, of being dried in huge, delicately scented towels and carried to her bed while her mother sang softly to her.

Too often, in her bed in the room they had given her next to her father's, she could feel the white of the sheets and see that cold absence even once the lights were out, and—falling asleep within that plump whiteness—she'd have the nightmare; the cold tumbling nightmare as she emptied her lungs at the sight of her mother lying on the floor of the cable-car, blood pouring from her torn body, arm coming up into her chest and pushing her away, out into the cold and down to the snow, falling away still screaming, eyes wide, seeing the cable-car above her burst apart in a bright cracking pulse of sound, an instant before she thudded into the freezing grip of the snow.

"Sharrow?"

She sat up on the bird's back, seeing her father approaching from the far end of the ballroom. He held the hand of a little girl, perhaps a couple of years younger than she. The girl looked shy and not very pretty. Sharrow turned her head to keep looking at them as the merry-go-round whirled her around, then lost sight of them.

"Skave!" she heard her father shout. "Turn that thing off."

The old android, standing in the center of the ride, cut the power and applied the brakes.

Sharrow watched her father and the little girl as they came closer, walking across the map-floor, over the seagrain of Golter's oceans and the native woods of its continents.

The merry-go-round came slowly to a stop and was silent. The bird she was riding ended up on the far side of the ride from her father and the little girl. Sharrow waited for them to walk around to her. When they did, her father smiled and glanced down at the child whose hand he held.

"Look, my darling," he said to Sharrow. "This is the surprise I promised you: a little sister!"

Sharrow looked down at the other girl. Her father stooped and caught the child under the arms, lifting her up so that her head was above his.

"Isn't she lovely?" he asked Sharrow, his eager, puffy face peeking out from the little girl's skirts. The girl turned her face away from Sharrow. "Her name is Breyguhn," her father told her. "Breyguhn," he said, lowering her a little so that her head was level with his, "this is Sharrow. She's your big sister." He looked at Sharrow again. "You're going to be the best of friends, aren't you?"

Sharrow looked at the other child, who hid her face behind her father's head.

"Who's her mummy?" Sharrow asked eventually.

Her father looked dismayed, then cheerful. "Her mummy's going to be *your* new mummy," he said. "She's an old friend of mine . . . of your mummy's and mine, and . . ." He smiled broadly, swallowing. "She's very nice. So is Breyguhn, aren't you, Brey? Hmm? Oh, don't cry; what's to cry about? Come on, say hello to your big sister. Sharrow, say hello to—Sharrow?"

She'd got down off the trafe bird and walked around to the ride's controls. She glared up at Skave and pushed him out of the way.

"Now, now, Miss Sharrow . . . ," the old android said, stepping back awkwardly and almost falling.

She'd seen the android work the controls. She pushed the brake lever up and swung the power handle across. The merry-go-round buzzed and hummed and started to move.

"Sharrow?" her father said, walking into sight, still holding the crying child.

"Now, now, Miss Sharrow," Skave said as she pushed it

farther back through the assorted weyr-beasts, monsters, and extinct animals of Golter's real and imagined past. The old android's hands fluttered in front of its chest as she kept on pushing it. "Now, now, Miss Sharrow. Now, now—ah!"

Skave fell off the edge of the ride, twisted with bewildering speed, and landed safely on all fours, looking surprised.

"Sharrow!" her father shouted. "Sharrow! What do you think you're doing? Come back here! Sharrow!"

The ride buzzed up to full speed, humming deeply like an ancient spinning top.

"Sharrow! *Sharrow!*"

She clambered back up onto the neck of the trafe bird and closed her eyes.

She stood on the piazza, leaning on the marble balustrade and looking down at the old blow-stone merry-go-round on the terrace below. The androids restoring the ride were trying to start its ancient hydraulic motors for the first time in centuries; mostly they were finding where all its leaks and inadequately secured seals and joints were, each attempted start resulting in a fresh burst of water from some new part of the furiously complicated, gaudily decorated old fairground ride. The terrace around it was covered with water.

She watched as one more creaking, groaning half revolution of the antique roundabout culminated in another wet explosion and a hissing fountain arcing into the air.

She glanced at the others sitting, bored, in the pavement section of a cosmetically restored but closed café on the other side of the piazza; then she turned to Feril.

"We are going to the Embargoed Areas," she told the android, "to try to find the last Lazy Gun."

Feril looked down. "You did not need to tell me that."

"I suspected you had already guessed."

"Indeed," Feril said, "I must admit that I had."

She cleared her throat. "Feril, I've talked this over with the others, and we'd like you to come along with us, if you want."

Feril looked silently at her for what seemed like a long time. "I see," it said. It looked down at the old roundabout on the terrace beneath, watching its fellows swarm over it, making adjustments. "Why?" it said.

"Because we feel you could be useful," she said, "and

because we feel we need another person along, and because I think you might benefit from the experience, and because . . . we like you." She looked away for a moment. "Though it will be dangerous." She cocked an eyebrow. "Maybe if we *really* liked you, the last thing we'd do would be to invite you along quite possibly to get killed."

Feril made a shrugging motion. "If I accompanied you, I would save my current personality with the city," it said. "Should I be destroyed, I would lose only the memories of the experiences after I left here. I would continue to exist as an entity within the city AI cluster, and I would obtain a guarantee that I would live again when the next batch of androids is allowed to be built."

She was silent, watching it.

"You are sure," it said, "that the others in your team would not object to my presence?"

She glanced at Zefla, Miz, and Dloan again. Dloan and Zefla were talking. Miz was watching her, chin on his uninjured hand.

"They trust who I trust," she told the machine. "Any one of them could have vetoed the idea. *We* want you to come with us."

The android tapped one steel-and-plastic finger on the marble, then nodded as it turned to her. "Thank you. I accept. I shall come with you."

She put her hand out to the machine. "I hope you will not have cause to regret this," she said, smiling.

It gripped her hand gently. "Regret is for humans," it said.

She laughed. "Really?"

The machine shrugged and let go of her hand. "Oh, no. It's just something we tell ourselves."

20

The Quiet
Shore

T rees stood in dense, dark-massed profusion from moun-
taintop to tideline. The ocean lay flat, black, and still
against the silent shore like something fallen under the
heavy green spell of the forest. A bird flew slowly across the
water parallel with the land, like a pale sliver of the soft gray
clouds cast out of the sky and searching for a way back.

Half a kilometer out from the fjord mouth, the surface
of the ocean swirled and frothed, then swelled and spilled
from three dark, bulbous shapes.

The tri-hull submarine surfaced and floated stationary
for a moment, water streaming from its fins and stubby central tower. Then a series of dull clanging noises chimed out
across the water, and with a swirl of wash churning round its
smooth black flanks, the central section and starboard hull
slid slowly astern, leaving the port hull floating alone and
facing the shore.

When it had dropped just behind the single hull, the
submarine's went ahead again, using delicate surging pulses
of power from its bow to snick its rounded snout into the
hull's stern. A great slow stream of water washed out behind
the submarine as it drove quietly for the shore, pushing the
hull ahead of it.

The leading hull grounded in the shallows of a small
sandy beach on the southern edge of the fjord's mouth, its

hemispherical black nose rising as it pushed a broad, bulging wave across the few meters of water toward the crescent's pale slope. Surf washed up the beach and along the
rocks on either side.

"I do hope you understand; I have *of course* given much
thought to this, but in the end I have the safety of my ship
and crew to consider. Of course, this is covered in our
contract—"

"Of course."

"—but it really would be asking for trouble to take you
any farther in. The fjord is quite deep—though there are
underwater ridges in places according to our deep scan—
but it's just so *narrow;* a ship this size just wouldn't be able
to maneuver at all. With the obvious danger of hostile action, it would be foolhardy to venture farther. As I say, I
have my crew to think about. Now, if I could just have your
signature . . . I mean, many of them have families. . . ."

"Indeed."

"I'm so glad you understand. Our underwriters have
been blowing *very* cool in this last financial year, I can tell
you, and even switching the log-graph off is going to make
them suspicious. You can turn that trick only so many times,
believe me. Ah . . . here and here . . ."

The captain held his clipboard up for her to sign the release papers. She took off one glove, picked up the stylo,
and scribbled her name. She was dressed in insulated combat fatigues and knee boots; a warm, ballisticized fur cap
covered her head, the ear pads clipped up. She and the captain were standing on deck near the bow of the grounded
port hull; its single hemi-door had swung open, and a ramp
had been extended from the interior to the shallows. The
first of the two big six-wheel All Terrain trucks fired into life
and rumbled slowly out of the hull, down the ramp, through
the water, and up onto the white-sand beach. The deck beneath them shifted as the vehicle's weight was transferred
from hull to land.

The AT's gray-and-green camouflage flickered uncertainly for a few moments as it adjusted, then settled to a
suitably nondescript set of interleaved shades that exactly
matched the color of the sand and the shadows under trees.
A heavy stub-nosed cannon sat stowed above one of the two
cab hatches.

The captain turned over a couple of pages. "And here and here, please," he said. He shook his head and made a clicking noise with his tongue. "If only the fjord was a *little* wider!" He stared concernedly at the mouth of the fjord, as though willing the ridge-straked slopes of the mountains to draw back from the dark waters. He sighed, his breath smoking in the cold, still air.

"Yes, well," Sharrow said.

The second All Terrain lumbered out of the front hull section and onto the beach, making the hull bob again. Zefla waved from one of the vehicle's roof hatches.

"And one last one here . . . ," the captain said, folding the flimsies back over the clipboard and pointing. Sharrow signed again.

"There," she said.

"Thank you, Lady Sharrow," the captain said, smiling. He put his gloves back on and bowed deeply. The sunglasses he hadn't needed when they'd surfaced fell out of a pocket in his quilted jacket. He stooped to retrieve them, his gloves making the operation difficult.

He straightened to find her smiling bleakly at him, holding her hand out. He stuck the sunglasses in his mouth, the clipboard under his armpit, and took one glove off again. He shook her hand. "A pleasure, Lady Sharrow," he told her. "And let me wish you all the best in"—his gaze flicked around the quiet forests and the tall mountains—"whatever you may be undertaking."

"Thank you."

"Well, see you in four days' time, unless we hear from you," he said, grinning.

"Right," she said, turning away. "Until then."

"Good hunting!" he called.

Sharrow made her way down a thin metal ladder to the hull's interior, where the sub's deck crew were getting ready to retract the ramp and close the door again. She checked that there was nothing left behind, then walked down the ramp to the shore, her boots sinking into the sand.

Just as she turned to look back at the gaping round mouth of the hull, a white jet of steam flew up into the air behind it from the submarine's conning tower. The shriek of the vessel's emergency siren shook the air above the beach, then cut off as the white feather of the steam plume stood, just beginning to drift in the air. The men in the mouth of the opened hull section froze. A voice boomed out above them: the captain's, breathless and panicky. "Air alert!" he shouted through the speakers. "Aircraft coming! Abandon the hull!"

"Shit!" Sharrow said, spinning on her heel.

The men in the hull swarmed up the ladder to the deck; Sharrow clambered into the cab of the second AT. Zefla, also dressed in camouflage fatigues, was standing on her seat, her head and torso sticking out of the hatch above, watching the seaward skies through a pair of high-power field-glasses. Feril was at the vehicle's wheel, poised and delicate among the AT's chunkily businesslike controls.

"Fucking hell," Miz's voice said over the com, "that was quick. Thought they didn't bother much with the surv-sats these days."

"Maybe we were misinformed," Sharrow said, buckling herself into her seat. She glanced at the android as the AT in front sprayed sand from its six big tires and lumbered up the beach for the rocks bordering the thin scrub at the edge of the forest. "Follow Miz," she told Feril. The android nodded and slipped the vehicle into drive.

The six-wheeler lurched forward, following the leading AT toward the trees. Sharrow watched the last few crewmen jump from the sub's front hull section to the main hull, then saw the water froth around the rear of the fat central section as the vessel abandoned both hulls and powered astern, surrounding itself with foam. The small figures sprinted along the hull and disappeared down a hatch, swinging it shut. The submarine swam back through its own wake, starting to turn and submerge at the same time; the grounded hull section bobbed in the wash while the jettisoned starboard hull rolled back and forward, gently rising and falling in the waves.

"There's no fucking way into these trees!" Miz yelled.

"Make one," Sharrow said. "Zef?" she said, glancing up. "Zef?" she shouted.

Zefla ducked down, shaking her head, her hair gathered up inside a combat cap. "Nothing yet," she said, and grabbed an intercom stalk and clipped it to her ear.

The AT in front of them bounced over the rocks and charged over the grass at the trees, thumping into them and breaking branches. "Shit!' Miz's voice said as the vehicle bounced back again, tires gouging scooped trenches in the

grass and spraying earth back at them. Clods thumped into
the sloped chin and screen of their AT.

"Wait a moment," they heard Dloan say. He appeared
out of the hatch beside the roof-mounted cannon and tore
the cover off the gun.

Sharrow glanced back; the submarine was submerged
save for its tower, sinking rapidly into the swirling water as
it continued to swing out astern from the shore.

"Back," Dloan said, swinging the cannon around on its
ring so that it was right in front of him and aimed at the
trees. The AT reversed. Feril pulled their own vehicle back.
"Steady her," Dloan said. The front AT stopped.

"Got it," Zefla said through the intercom. "Single plane.
Low—looks big . . . fairly slow."

Dloan fired; the cannon pulsed flame ahead and smoke
into the air on either side. The trees immediately in front of
the AT exploded near the ground in a flicker of fire and a
welter of brown and green and torn white wood; limbs and
branches fell in all directions, tearing into other trees as
they fell. Dloan advanced the fire into the forest, striking
other trees and flinging more debris into the air.

Even in the cab the noise was deafening. Sharrow
reached behind and grabbed a long black canvas bag with a
crude aircraft symbol scrawled on it. She pulled a long tube
from the bag as the two ATs advanced into the smoking
breach in the forest. The cannon fell silent.

Clunking noises came from above Sharrow; the AT
creaked and waddled as it climbed its way over the wrecked
trees.

"Ouch!" Zefla said. "Fucking raining tree out here . . .
shit—smoke trail!" Her voice was suddenly urgent. "Flash—
smoke trail. Another one, headed straight. Three-four klicks
out, closing."

Their second vehicle was hardly into the break in the
forest. Sharrow readied the antiaircraft weapon. Miz was
turning his vehicle into a small clearing to their right.
Sharrow stood up on the seat, swinging the hatch back and
sticking her head and shoulders through.

The plane was a lumpy line at the end of two dull
smudges of smoke capped by sparks. Where the sub had
been, there was just a patch of disturbed water near the
abandoned floating hull. The plane's image enlarged in the

missile launcher's sight, went briefly fuzzy, then came sharp; she flicked the safety off.

"Heading for that hull," Zefla said.

The first missile slammed into the jettisoned starboard hull in a brief flash of flame and a fountain of white spray; the second missile waved up and down through the air toward them, while the plane behind, still a couple of kilometers off, gradually banked away.

Sharrow watched its silhouette tilt and thicken in the missile-launcher sight. It was a flying boat, about the size of an ancient heavy bomber: pairs of engines high on each wing root, and a V-strutted float near the tip of each wing. Six small missiles remaining, under the wings. It disappeared behind the trees.

The second missile vanished behind the rear of the grounded port hull an instant before there was a flash of light inside the hull, and a gout of smoke burst into the sky at its stern; an echoing bellow of noise preceded a weak puff of smoke from the wide mouth of the hull.

Sharrow listened to the sound of the plane's jets as they echoed off the mountains. She put the missile-launcher back to stand-by.

"Where'd it go?" Miz said.

"Think it went down the fjord," Dloan said. Sharrow turned to see Dloan in the hatch of the stationary leading AT, its nose stuck into the trees. He was pointing the cannon over their heads at where the plane had been.

"See any markings?" Sharrow asked Zefla.

Zefla shook her head. "Didn't look like a Franchise ship to me."

"I think I *saw* one of those old things in Quay Beagh," Dloan said. "While we were negotiating for the sub."

"Think it could be another private operator?" Miz asked. They heard him grunt as the leading AT rocked back, reversing, then attempted to plow forward again, only to be resisted once more by the flexing trunks of the trees. "Now that's what I call contempt for the Areas Laws," he said, sounding almost amused. "Barreling right in with an antique that belongs in a museum of flight. Shit, we could have used ACVs after all."

"Whatever," Sharrow said, "it might be back. We're sitting targets here; let's head along the coast and find somewhere to hole up."

"Sound thinking," Zefla said.

They reversed the two ATs out of the track they had gouged in the forest. The wreck of the grounded submarine hull had settled by the stern, its rear under water, leaking smoke into the calm air. The jettisoned starboard hull had rolled right over onto its back, rocking back and forth as it settled slowly in the water.

The two All Terrains picked their way along the jumbled rock and tattered grass line between the water and the trees.

The plane had left a faint line of exhaust smoke a hundred meters or so above the center of the broad fjord. Zefla stayed on watch; Sharrow sat back in her seat with the missile-launcher on her lap. She looked over at Feril, sitting with apparent unconcern as it guided their AT after Miz and Dloan's.

"Sorry about all this," she said.

"Please don't be," the android said, turning its head to her for a moment. "This is highly exciting."

Sharrow shook her head, smiling. "Could be more exciting yet if we can't find a place to hide."

They had gone less than a kilometer down the side of the fjord and found no breaks in the trees, no fallen boulders large enough to hide behind and no other form of cover, when Zefla shouted.

"It's back!"

The flying boat appeared, a gray dot against the dark mountains toward the head of the fjord.

"Hell's teeth," Miz growled.

Sharrow watched the flying boat tilt and turn until it was heading straight toward them. She shook her head. "This is no good—"

"Firing!" yelled Zefla. Two bursts of smoke curled from under the wing roots of the plane.

"Stop!" Sharrow told the android. She grabbed her satchel from beneath the seat. "All out!"

"Shit," Miz said. Both ATs skidded to a stop.

"Head for the fucking trees," Zefla muttered, dropping from the hatch, bouncing on her seat, and kicking the door open. She jumped to the ground holding a small back-pack, followed by Feril. Sharrow jumped from the other door. Miz leapt from the AT in front and ran for the trees as well.

"Out, Dloan!" Sharrow yelled. She was heading for

some large rocks near the water's edge. She clicked the safety off the missile-launcher.

Dloan stood in the hatch of the front AT, sighting the cannon at the plane; the two missiles were bright points at the end of smoky trails, racing closer over the black, still water. "Dloan!" she yelled. She threw herself down between two rocks and sighted the missile-launcher.

The missiles zipped in; they missed the two ATs and screamed overhead, detonating in the forest fifty meters behind them. Dloan started firing the cannon; she could see each tracered eighth shell arcing up and out across the water, falling a hundred meters short of the plane in distant, tiny white splashes. She fired the missile; there was a bang as the tube juddered against her shoulder, then a flash and a clap of noise when the missile ignited and a whoosh as it raced away.

The plane flew lazily on up the center of the fjord, maybe two thousand meters away now; the missile lanced out of an intercept course.

Dloan had stopped firing the cannon.

The missile was a kilometer away, then five hundred meters.

"Oh well," Sharrow said to herself. "Just ignore it, then, assholes."

Light glittered around the nose of the flying boat.

The missile blew up; it flashed and disintegrated in the air, creating a thick black paw of smoke from which dozens of little dark claws trailed out and down, falling into the water in a flurry of tall splashes.

"Son of a bitch," Sharrow breathed. The plane tipped toward them once more.

Dloan fired the cannon again, sparks arcing high toward the plane. The plane flew through the rising bulb of smoke left by their intercepted missile. It fired another two of its own.

Sharrow glanced at the AT. "*Dloan!*" she screamed. She saw him crouch down a little behind the cannon. He fired a last burst of shells, then sprang out of the hatch and ran along the top of the AT's roof. Sharrow could have sworn he had a great big smile on his face.

Dloan jumped the three meters to the ground, rolled and dived into light cover a half second before the pair of missiles screamed into the ATs and blew them both to smithereens.

She must have ducked. She lifted her head to the smoke and the flame. Both vehicles had been obliterated. Hers lay on its back, burning fiercely. The other AT still seemed to be the right way up, but its body had been torn half-off, lifted so that the three engines lay exposed between the flayed, burning tires. What was left of it shook, crackling with secondary detonations; she ducked down again and watched the flying boat fly past a half-kilometer out and curving away from them again.

A line of black smoke curled from its starboard engine. It was losing height, and it sounded rough and clattery. Somebody whooped from the trees.

She looked at her left hand, resting on the ground. It hurt. She pulled it away, peering at the blood, then shook it, cleaning earth away from the cut. It didn't look serious.

"Yee-ha!" whooped the same voice from the trees. Dloan.

The flying boat labored on through the air for another kilometer, gaining height; then it tipped and banked, turning and heading back down the fjord again, this time angling for the far shore as the black smoke behind it thickened and it dropped closer and closer to the water.

The air cracked and rang as more explosions sounded in the two wrecked ATs; smoke piled into the sky.

"Sharrow?" Miz shouted during a lull.

"Here!" she shouted. "I'm all right."

The flying boat hit the water, bounced in a double curtain of spray and hit again, stopping quickly and slewing around as it came to rest facing them, fifteen hundred meters away.

She slung the satchel onto her back and crawled away from the shore-side rocks, staying in the cover of some smaller boulders until she was near the trees; then she got up and ran in a crouch to where the others were lying just inside the cover, watching the ATs burn and the flying boat near the far shore sink. Its glassy, complicated nose was already raised in the air; one wing float was canted out of the water, the other submerged.

She dropped down beside them.

"Okay?" Zefla asked her.

"Yes. Nice shooting, Dloan," she said, wiping her bloody hand on the trousers of her fatigues.

"Thanks," Dloan grinned. "Fancy missile-intercepting laser couldn't deal with old-fashioned cannon shells." He sighed massively, looking happy.

"Yeah, but now what do we do?" Miz said, looking at her. "Swim the rest of the way?"

"Oh," Feril said, "look. What unorthodox camouflage." Sharrow looked.

Zefla squinted through the field glasses. She groaned.

"I don't fucking believe it," she said. She handed the binoculars to Sharrow. "No, that's not true." She shook her head. "I do believe it."

Sharrow watched through glasses; the faceted nose of the flying boat was tipped high up now, pointing at the sky. From doors just under the wing roots she could see perhaps three dozen or so small figures clambering into what she guessed were inflatable boats. It all looked a little confused.

Sharrow could make the figures out easily because they were dressed in shocking pinks, lime greens, blood reds, loud violets, and bright yellows that were even more vibrant and obvious than the orange boats they were packing into. She put the glasses down.

"They really are mad," she said, more to herself than anybody else. "It's Elson Roa and his gang."

"*That* maniac?" Miz said, eyes wide. He gestured at the sinking plane, its fuselage now vertical to the sky and submerged almost to the wings. Two bright clusters of color were just visible to the naked eye, heading slowly away from the sinking aircraft toward the thick green blanket of trees on the far shore. "That's him?" Miz said. "Again?"

Sharrow nodded slowly, setting the field glasses down on the ground. "Yes," she said. "Again."

The ammunition in the burning ATs continued to explode for a few minutes, then the fires began to die and the detonations ceased. They ventured out from the trees and searched the wreckage scattered around the remains of the two ATs until they heard a series of quiet phutting noises and saw thin fountains in the water nearby.

"Machine gun," Dloan said, looking toward the far side of the fjord. The air cracked and whined; little clouds of dust jumped off rocks around them. They retreated quickly into the forest.

They had one light emergency tent and survival rations in a small back-pack Zefla had rescued; Sharrow had her satchel, which contained the HandCannon, the two dials from the old bike, and a first-aid kit. Miz had rescued a medium machine gun and a single antiaircraft missile. They'd found some clothes and a few more ration packs while they'd searched the wreckage. Apart from that, all they had was what they stood in: fatigues or hiking gear, a pistol each, a couple of knives, one small medical kit and whatever else had happened to be in their pockets.

"I should have thought," Sharrow said, banging the heel of her hands off her temples. She winced as her left hand hit; she had washed the wound in a stream and put a plaster on it, but it still hurt. Miz still wore a small bandage on his hand, too, and Dloan limped a little, just as she did.

We are coming to reflect each other, she thought.

They sat in a small hollow, around a smoky, feeble fire they had finally lasered alight. The late afternoon was made evening by the tall trees rising around them.

"I should have thought," she repeated. "We could have got more stuff together to take out of the ATs while we were looking for a place to hole up." She shook her head.

"Look," Miz said. "We're all alive; we have a tent, some food, and we have guns; we can shoot what we need to eat." He gestured at the forest around them. "There must be plenty of game in here. Or there's fish." He patted one pocket in his fancy, much be-pocketed hiking jacket. "I've got hooks and some line; we can make a rod."

Sharrow looked dubious. "Yes. Meanwhile, we've got four days to walk two hundred klicks," she said, "for a rendezvous our brave captain probably isn't even going to try to make."

"We could leave somebody here," Zefla said. She held her combat cap out on a stick in front of the fire, drying it. She sat loosely cross-legged, at her ease. Dloan had his injured leg out in front of him. Miz had rolled up a rock to sit on; the android squatted on its haunches, looking skeletally sharp and angled. "Some of us could go on to the end of the fjord," Zefla continued, "while somebody stays behind to meet the sub and tell them to come back later."

"We've nothing to signal with," Sharrow said, taking her

pocket phone out of her jacket. "The dedicated comm stuff was in the ATs, and these won't work here."

"Well," Dloan said, "technically they do, but the calls get transferred to the Security Franchise, and they come to investigate the source."

"Yes, Dloan," Sharrow said. "Thank you."

"I could signal the submarine," Feril said. It tapped its chest. "I have a communicator; it's not long range, but it need not utilize the phone frequencies. I could communicate with the submarine even when it is under water, if it comes within a few kilometers."

"Could you get in touch with it now?" Miz asked.

"I suspect not," the android admitted.

"What about the Solipsists?" Dloan said. "Maybe they don't realize who we are." He looked at Sharrow. "We could try radioing them."

She shook her head. "Somehow, I think they know exactly who we are," she said. "Anyway, it's not worth breaking silence."

"Oh, come on," Miz said, poking at the fire with a branch. "The Franchise people can't have missed *that* performance." He nodded in the direction of the wrecked ATs, smoldering on the shore a hundred meters away through the trees. "They're probably on their way in now to pick us up."

"Of course," Dloan said, "they might just nuke us instead."

Sharrow glared at him.

"So do we hike to whatever's at the end of the fjord, or what?" Zefla said.

Sharrow nodded. "We'd better, or Elson and his boys'll get there first."

She took the two bike dials from her satchel. "Still pointing that way; range is down to just under a hundred klicks. If the maps were right and these are accurate, whatever they're pointing at is at the head of the fjord." She put the dials away again. "Or was."

"Pity we lost the maps," Dloan said, flexing his leg.

"Actually," Feril said, holding up one hand tentatively. "I have remembered the map of the area."

"Oh, yeah?" Miz looked skeptically at the android. "So how far is it to the end of the fjord?"

"Hugging the coast, approximately eighty-nine kilometers," the android told them. "Though there are a couple of sizable rivers to be forded."

"Two days in and two back," Dloan said.

"If I may say," the android began. They looked at it. "I could perhaps get there and back in about twenty hours." It looked around at them, then made an almost bashful shrugging motion.

"So Feril could scout ahead," Zefla said. "But what do we do when the rest of us get there?"

"If we find the Lazy Gun," Sharrow said, "we just make a phone call. When the Franchise forces come in to investigate, we take whatever they arrived in—aircraft probably."

"Just like that?" Zefla said.

"We *will* have a Lazy Gun," Miz said, grinning.

"And if the gun is not there?" Feril asked.

Sharrow looked at the android. "Then we think again." She picked up a length of branch and threw it into the smoking heart of the fire.

They kept near the edge of the trees as far as possible, ten meters or so from the shore. The interior of the forest was very quiet. The only noise they heard over those first few hours, while the early-winter light faded gradually around them, was that of rushing water in the tumbling, rock-strewn streams they crossed, and the sound of branches and twigs breaking underfoot.

The floor of the forest was covered with old trees and rotting trunks; trees were tilted and canted at various angles, producing tangles they had to walk around. Clearings made by fallen trees bristled with new growth and afforded them glimpses of the gray and darkening sky.

"Kind of disorganized, isn't it?" Miz said to Sharrow, ducking under a fallen trunk raised off the ground by the bowed trees nearby. "I thought forests were just trunks and a nice soft carpet of—shit!" The hood on his jacket snagged on a branch and almost pulled him off his feet. He released it and glared at Sharrow before continuing. "Trunks and a nice soft carpet of needles."

She ducked under the trunk. "Those were plantations, Miz," she told him. "This is forest—the real thing."

"Well, it's damn messy," he said, brushing rotten wood out of his jacket hood. "Might as well be back in the fucking Entraxrln." He looked around. "We'd have had a hard time getting through this lot with the ATs, anyway; might have had to stick to the shore, sats or not." He slipped on a root hidden in the ground cover of needles and fallen twigs and staggered. He shook his head. "Fucking Solipsists."

Sharrow smiled.

They camped when the light got too dim for them to see properly; they had two sets of night-sight glasses, but two people would still have to have gone without, and they couldn't have traveled very quickly. They were anyway tired after only a couple of hours walking; they found a level area next to a stream, hidden from the other side of the fjord by the bank, and decided to stop there.

Sharrow changed the dressing on her cut hand. Dloan worked out how to pitch the thin emergency tent. Zefla looked for wood to make a fire. Miz sat on a stone and started unlacing his boots. His feet were sore; he'd been hobbling for the last half hour.

Feril put wood down by the circle of stones it had set in place, then attempted to help Dloan with the tent until the man shooed it away. It came and squatted near Miz.

"Damn boots," Miz said, struggling to untie the laces. They seemed to have become tighter after they'd got wet. He'd thought the boots looked great in the store in Quay Beagh; really chunky and rugged and outdoorsy, in hide and with real laces, like something out of an ancient photograph; but now he was starting to wish he'd gone for a more modern pair with memory-foam inserts, heater elements, and quick-release buckles. Of course, he hadn't chosen his boots thinking he was actually going to be doing much *walking* in them.

"Don't suppose you have this problem," Miz grunted, glancing at the android as he pulled at his laces.

"Not really," Feril said. "Though I do have pads on my feet that have to be replaced every few years." It looked at its feet.

"What a fucking Fate-forsaken place," Miz breathed, looking around the dark enclosure of trees.

Feril looked around. "Oh, I don't know," it said. "I think it's rather beautiful."

"Yeah," Miz said, trying to tease one lace out from under another. "Well, maybe you see things differently."

"Yes," the android said. "I suppose I do." It watched

Zefla dump a load of wood onto the ground by the fire and then heap pieces into the center of the stone circle. She used her laser pistol on low power and wide beam to dry and then ignite the twigs; they burned smokily.

"Hey," Miz said to the android, looking embarrassed. "My fingers are getting cold. Could you give me a hand here?"

Feril said nothing as it came over to kneel before Miz and untie his bootlaces.

They sat around the fire in the black darkness of a deep forest under thick overcast, four hundred kilometers from the nearest sunlight-mirror footprint, streetlight, or headlamp. They chewed on emergency army rations. They had enough for two more meals each.

"We'll catch something tomorrow," Miz said, chomping on a foodslab, looking around at the others. Their faces seemed to move oddly in the flickering orange firelight. He nodded. "Tomorrow we'll shoot something big and have a proper roast, real meat."

"Yuk," said Zefla.

"We haven't seen a damn thing so far," Sharrow told him.

"Yeah," Miz said, wagging the half-eaten foodslab at her. "But there must be all sorts of big game in these mountains. We'll find something."

"Excuse me," Feril said from the top of the riverbank, a couple of meters above them. Its metal-and-plastic face looked down at them, glinting in the firelight. It had volunteered to keep watch while they ate.

"Yes, Feril?" Sharrow said.

"What I believe is an inflatable boat has just left the far shore; it is heading this way."

Dloan reached for the machine gun and stood up. He slipped on a pair of night-sight glasses.

"How far away is it?" Sharrow asked.

"A hundred meters or so out from the far shore," Feril said.

"Let's take a look," Sharrow said.

They trooped down to the trees facing the shore, Dloan leading Zefla, and Sharrow leading Miz, who tripped a couple of times on his undone laces. They lay on the ground; with the night sights zoomed on infrared, Sharrow and

Dloan could just see the heat signature of the people in the inflatable.

Dloan found a boulder and rested the machine gun on it, its barrel pointing at nearly forty-five degrees.

"Should just about have the range," he said. "Better get back," he told the others, "just in case they have something that can home in on this."

They fell back a little into the trees.

Dloan fired a dozen or so rounds, filling the night with sound and light; Sharrow had to turn the sights away, the fire was so bright. There were no tracers in the shells, but when she looked back, she could see the tiny sparks of the bullets in the night-sights for about half their arcing journey over the fjord. As they cooled, they disappeared.

"Just over them and to the left," Feril called out.

Dloan adjusted his aim, then fired again. They heard the sound of the gun echoing off mountains and cliffs far away. A clatter and a snicking sound announced Dloan was changing magazines.

"Still a little to the left," Feril said.

Dloan fired once more. Sharrow saw no alteration in the furry-looking image in the sight.

"Yes!" Feril said.

Dloan paused, fired again. "Right! To the right!" Feril shouted as Dloan fired. The gun fell silent.

"I believe they are in difficulties," Feril said.

Sharrow watched the hazy image in the night sight change; it grew smaller, and eventually, after a minute or so, there was just the hint of a few tiny heat sources in the water.

"Their craft has sunk," Feril announced. "They appear to be swimming back to shore."

"Good shooting again," Sharrow told Dloan.

"Hmm," he said, sounding satisfied.

He came back up from the shore. Sharrow turned to go as Dloan passed them, then saw the android still staring at the far side of the fjord. She checked the glasses, but all they showed were the same few indistinct heat-glows against the gray clutter of the fjord's cold waters.

She watched the android for a few moments. It didn't seem to notice her. "Feril?" she said.

It turned to her. "Yes?"

"What is it?" she asked.

Miz made a tutting noise and took Zefla's hand, to follow her following Dloan back to their camp.

"Oh," the android said, after the briefest of pauses. It glanced back out to the dark waters. "I was just thinking: given that there appeared to be eight or nine people in the inflatable, and only seven are swimming back to shore, and what could well be one or two bodies are floating where the boat went down"—it turned to face her again—"I believe I have just been party to a murder—two murders, perhaps."

She was silent. The android looked back out to the water again, then back at her.

"How do you feel about that?" she asked.

It made a shrug. "I am not sure yet," it said, sounding puzzled. "I shall have to think about it."

She inspected its image in the night sight.

This close up, people in a night-sight glowed vibrant and gaudy and obvious. The android was a vague light-sketch in comparison, its body only fractionally warmer than its surroundings.

"I'm sorry," she said eventually.

"What for?" it asked her.

"Involving you in all this."

"I was delighted to be asked," it reminded her.

"I know," she said, "but still."

"Please, don't be," it told her. "This is all ... extremely interesting for me. I am recording much of what has been happening recently at maximum saturation for later replay, enjoyment, and analysis. I get to do that very rarely. It is novel. I am having fun." It made a human gesture with its hands, lifting them briefly, palms up, from the sides of its body.

"Fun," she said, smiling slightly.

"In a sense," Feril said.

She shook her head, looking down at the faint, seeping warmth of the forest floor.

"Shall I make my reconnoitering expedition?" the android asked. "Shall I go to the head of the fjord?"

"Not yet," she said. She turned to look at the weak, almost transparent signature of their fire's column of rising smoke, thirty meters away in the forest. "I'd like you to keep watch tonight, if you don't mind."

"Of course not," it said. Feril turned to look back at the fjord again. "You are worried that they still have a boat and may try to repeat the apparent attack we have just thwarted."

"Exactly," she smiled. "Spoken like one of the team." She laughed lightly. "Well, sort of."

Feril drew itself back a little. "Thank you," it said. It nodded up the slope. "I shall keep watch from there, where I can see the fjord and the immediate vicinity."

They walked that way. The android turned and sank down on its haunches at the point it determined gave it the best sight lines. "Ah-ha," it said.

She looked, too.

There were two fires burning on the other side of the fjord; two tiny, hard yellow specks vibrating in the granular darkness. She took the night-sights off and could still just see them from the side of her eyes.

She put the sights back on. "They've made more distance than we have," she said.

"About three kilometers," Feril said.

"Hmm," she said. "We still have one heat-seeking missile left. We could give them an unpleasant good-night present."

"Indeed," Feril said. "Though the fires could be decoys."

She watched the distant fires. "How far have *they* got to walk to the end of the fjord?"

"One hundred and nine kilometers," Feril said. "There are two small fjords off the main one on their side."

"Though they probably still have an inflatable."

"Yes. They could use that to ferry themselves across the mouths of the side-fjords, though it might be vulnerable to attack with the machine gun."

"Hmm," she said, and yawned. "Oh well. Speaking personally, it's time for bed." She looked down into the hollow where the small tent lay inflated. It was supposedly comfortably two-person and could take three at a pinch. It was fit for four only if everybody was on very friendly terms indeed.

"Oh," she said. "Would you like a gun while you're on guard?"

"I think not." Feril watched her yawn again. "Good night, Lady Sharrow," it said. It sounded very formal.

"Good night," she said.

· · ·

Cenuij sat in the burning truck, looking baleful and sighing a lot. The flames and the exploding ammunition didn't seem to harm him. He was cradling something in his arms wrapped in a shawl. She recognized the shawl; it was one of the family's birthing shawls. She had been wrapped in that when she'd been a baby, as had her own mother, and hers before her. . . . She wondered where Cenuij had got it, and worried that the baby inside the shawl might be harmed by the flames of the burning truck.

She shouted to Cenuij, but he didn't seem to hear her.

When she tried to move around the burning truck to look into the shawl and see who the baby was, Cenuij moved as well, swiveling and hunching up so that his shoulder hid the infant.

She threw something at him; it bounced off his head and he turned angrily; he threw the shawl and what it held straight at her, and she put out her arms to catch it as the shawl unwrapped itself from the flying bundle and fell to the flames. It was the Lazy Gun she caught.

The shawl burned brightly in the wreckage, then lifted and rose flagrantly into the sky like a lasered bird.

She rocked the Gun in her arms, singing quietly.

She awoke to the stale, half-repellent, half-comforting smell of human bodies. She sat up and the dream faded from her memory. She felt stiff and tired; the seemingly soft ground under the tent had concealed rocks or roots or something that had made lying down uncomfortable, no matter what position she had assumed. Every time she had rolled over, she had woken up, and—packed in among the others, sleeping equally lightly—she had probably woken them up each time, too, just as they had her. She was cold on the side facing the flank of the tent; the single blanket they had between them had disappeared from over her early on in the night. She made a mental note in the future to accept the boys' offer to take the two outside positions. The plaster-covered wound on her hand throbbed dully.

She clambered over the others and opened the tent to a bitterly cold morning and the sound of wind roaring in the treetops. She stretched and grunted, feeling hungry and wondering what the hell they were going to use for toilet paper. Feril waved from its position at the top of the bank.

She replaced the plaster on her hand and poured more

antiseptic over it, aware that she was using up the supplies in the medical kit faster than she'd have liked.

It seemed to take a long time to get everybody up and moving and ready to set off; she had the dispiriting impression that the Solipsists, for all their martial eccentricity, would have been up at dawn and long since set out on their march—singing soldierly songs and beating drums, in her imagination.

They struck camp at last and headed away through the forest beneath the swaying, roaring tops of the trees. Their bellies rumbled. Breakfast had been a quarter of a foodslab each; they had seven of the bland but filling bars left.

The fjord was a wind-ruffled, sometimes white-flecked expanse of gray through the dark trunks to their right.

They walked through the day. It rained once for an hour, spattering light, torn drops through breaks in the canopy above. Miz wanted to stop and shelter, but they kept on going. They took turns to walk near the edge of the trees, keeping watch on the far shore, but didn't see anything. They had spied a few birds, glimpsed movements high in tree branches and heard plenty of quick, tiny rustles in the undergrowth, but encountered no large animals.

Lunch was half a foodslab each, and all the icy stream water they could stomach. They had to drink from their cupped hands; Sharrow felt hers going numb after the second scoop. By the time she had finished drinking, the only thing she could feel was the cut in her left hand, still throbbing.

The android sat patiently by the stream. Zefla was down at the shore; Dloan had disappeared into the woods, and Miz sat on an exposed root, retying his boots and grumbling.

She sat beside the android. Her feet were aching. "How far have we traveled so far, Feril?"

"Seventeen kilometers," it replied.

"Seventy-two to go," she said wearily. "Too slow. How long would it take you to get to the end of the fjord and back now?"

"I estimate about sixteen hours," it said.

She sat there, feeling hungry and dirty, itchy and footsore, her hand wound nagging at her like a toothache. The android looked just as it always had—at once delicate and powerful, smooth and hard. A few tree needles stuck to its lower legs, but otherwise its metal-and-plastic skin seemed unmarked.

"If you go," she said, "you'd best take a gun."

"If you think I ought to, I shall."

"I think you ought to."

"You will keep guard yourselves tonight?"

"We'll set up some sort of rota."

She talked to the others about Feril going on ahead. Miz was reluctant to part with a gun and thought it risky giving the android the bike dials, too, but it was agreed.

"Do be careful," she told the android, presenting it with the dials. "We don't know what's up there, but whatever it is, it'll probably be well guarded."

"Yeah," said Miz. "Old automatics can end up getting pretty trigger-happy."

"I shall be careful, believe me," the android said.

Sharrow put her good hand on its shoulder. The plastic-covered metal was cold to the touch. "Good luck."

"Thank you," it said. "I shall see you tomorrow." It turned and set off, the dials and a small laser pistol clutched to its chest. It ran quickly and gracefully away between the tree trunks, the pale pads on its feet dully flashing in the forest gloom. It disappeared.

"Hope we really can trust that thing," Miz said.

"It could have murdered us all in our sleep last night if it had wanted to," Zefla told him.

"It's not that simple, though, is it?" Miz said, looking at Sharrow, who shrugged.

"It's become simpler since the vehicles were destroyed," she said. "We'll see what Feril finds up there."

"If he comes back," Miz said, hoisting the small backpack.

"Oh, stop whining," Sharrow said, turning to follow the android. "Come on."

She fell asleep during her watch that night, waking from a dream of fire and death in which she and Cenuij walked hand in hand through a terrible silent pitch darkness to the noise of thunder and the flickering pulse of lightning among the clouds and summits on the far side of the fjord.

Cold rain, which had been warm blood in her dream, spattered her face. The tree she was leaning against creaked and groaned in the wind, lusty and furious in the canopy above.

She shivered and stood up, feeling stiff and sore. A headache pounded dully over her eyes. She looked around to check that all was well. The fjord was a rough, wind-whipped surface visible between the marginally cooler tree trunks. At least the weather made another water-borne attack by the Solipsists unlikely.

The tent, behind her in a little dip in the ground, glowed with a soft, enveloping warmth. She looked at the time display in the night-sight. Still an hour before she could wake Miz and claim her place between the other two sleepers.

She walked around a little, trying to keep awake and warm. Her swollen hand pulsed regular messages of pain up her arm. The rain tumbled through the branches in great gathered drops, plopping onto her cap and shoulders and wetting her face. The camouflaged fatigues were waterproof, but dribbles had sneaked down her neck, perhaps while she'd been asleep; she could feel them insinuating their way down her back and between her breasts with a cold, unwelcome intimacy.

She sat on a fallen trunk, looking out at the spray-shredded surface of the fjord and listening to the gusting wind charging out of the dark, thick-clouded night. The rain cleared for a while, revealing details on the far side of the fjord, so that she was able to look out to where the Solipsists' fires had burned that night. That pair of fierce specks had glittered through the evening like baleful eyes from the depths of an ancient myth, and—despite the fact that the shore the Solipsists were traveling on had looked more rugged and indented than their own had been that day—they had burned still farther ahead than they had the night before.

A great gust of wind shook the trees above her, dislodging drops that struck her face. She wiped them from the night-sight lenses with the heel of her good hand.

Where the Solipsists' twin fires had blazed against the steep dark mat of forest, there was only one faint image left now; a last dying memory of warmth in the loud, surrounding night, like one of those eyes slowly closing, the life within it going out.

She watched that hazy, uncertain image and—for all

that it was the product and symbol of people who had, for no good reason she could discern, suddenly become her enemies—she willed that distant, ember memory to prevail against the leaching cold that made her teeth ache and her body shiver, and against the laws that ran the universe and the system and the world and every thing and body within it—the laws of decay, consumption, exhaustion, and death.

Then the rain came again, brushing its way up the fjord in tall sheets, and by that interposing sweep extinguished—if not the fading embers themselves—the projected image of that fire in her eyes.

21

A Short
Walk

"**B** ut what's he *like*?"

"Oh ... attractive, I suppose."

"What? Tallish, darkish, handsomish? Hunkish?"

"All of the above. Well, maybe not hunkish ... But that's not it; it's his ... manner. When you hear him, it sounds like something between philosophy and politics, and even if you don't agree with what he's saying, you can't help being impressed by the way he says it. It's as though he knows even more than he's saying, knows everything, but still really needs your approval, your agreement for it to be true, and you just can't help but give it. You feel flattered, privileged ... seduced.

"It looked like there was a big but vague organization there—something that had grown up organically around him. And even though most of the people I saw were young, there were plenty of older people there, too, and I got the impression he was talking to the establishment on the Ghost, maybe beyond. But he was just an amazing person."

"Obviously," Zefla said, smiling at her as they walked.

It was cold. The weather had turned just before dawn, the heavy rain clouds blowing away before a chill, clear sky that had shed moonlight and sparse junklight on the forested mountains of the fjord, coating them in silent silver.

Then Thrial had risen, casting a rich glow like pink-gold down the fjord.

After a miserably small breakfast that had left them all hungry, and with only a quarter of a foodslab left each, Miz and Dloan had decided to make a serious effort to kill something edible for lunch. The two men had set off uphill when they broke camp that morning, hoping to find game in the higher forest.

Sharrow and Zefla walked through patches of frost and puddles skinned with brittle crusts of thin, glass-clear ice. Their breath smoked in the air.

Sharrow felt spacey and vague and slightly numb; she kept shivering, even though she didn't really feel cold. She put it down to lack of food. She felt ashamed at how pampered she had become; she hadn't realized how much simple things like toilet paper and a toothbrush meant to her, and felt demeaned that their absence could assume such significance.

Her hand throbbed dully inside her glove; she had taken some painkillers. She hadn't changed the plaster that morning because the hand had swelled up during the night, and it hurt too much when she'd tried taking the glove off. She'd decided just to let it be; perhaps it would get better of its own accord.

"Probably end up as one of those sordid cult leaders," Zefla said after a while as they plodded into a bare area of the forest where a fire had left thousands of tree trunks standing upright and bare, black posts already surrounded by slender young trees forcing their way toward the sky around them. "You know, peddling some weird concoction of retread gibberish and living in a palace while their followers sleep shifts and work the streets and give you this big flatline smile when you tell them where to stuff their tracts."

"No," Sharrow said, shaking her head (and felt dizzy when she did that, and stumbled on a blackened branch crusted with white). "No, I don't think so. I don't think that's what's going to happen to this guy, not at all."

Zefla looked at Sharrow as they walked, an expression of concern on her face. "You all right?" she asked.

"Hungry!" Sharrow laughed. She nodded to herself, breathing deeply in the chill air and staring up at the blue expanse above. "How about you?"

"Never better," Zefla said, scratching through her

gathered-up hair to her itchy scalp. "Could use a shower, though." She took another look at Sharrow as she stumbled again. "Maybe we'll take another rest soon."

"Yes," Sharrow said, shaking her head briefly as though trying to clear it. "Why not?"

They tramped among the fresh young trees and the burned dead.

Sharrow and Zefla stopped in a small clearing near the shore to eat the last of their food, then waited for Miz and Dloan to rejoin them. Sharrow continued to deny there was anything wrong with her, then fell fast asleep, propped against a tree trunk. Zefla was worried; she thought Sharrow looked ill. Her gray, drawn face twitched as Zefla watched, and her lips worked.

Zefla looked up at the mountain slopes. She was surprised they hadn't heard any shots. She left Sharrow to sleep and went down to the shingle beach. She left her little backpack there, so that Miz and Dloan wouldn't walk past them. Then she went back to sit with Sharrow.

The men arrived an hour later. They were both limping—Dloan from the bullet wound he'd received the night Cenuij had died, Miz from the combination of hard boots and soft feet.

They were empty-handed. Zefla thought they had brought something, but it was only the back-pack she'd left on the shingle. They had shot at a few birds with their laser pistols and killed one, but it had been crawling with parasites when they'd picked it up, and they hadn't thought it worth eating. They still hadn't seen any large animals, though they had heard impressive bellowing noises from still farther up-slope.

"Fish," Miz said, as he and Dloan tore into the last of their foodslabs and Sharrow looked sleepily at them, frowning and rubbing her left glove. "We'll do some fishing." He grinned at the others. "Fish—we'll eat fish tonight." He patted the pocket of his fancy hunting jacket that held the fishing gear.

They heard what sounded like gunfire just as they were setting off again: a distance-dulled crackle that seemed to come from farther down the fjord in the direction they were heading.

They ran to the shore and stood there, gazing down the fjord.

"Shit," Miz said. "Wonder what *that* means."

Nobody suggesting anything.

They had been walking for about an hour when they saw Feril jogging toward them through the trees.

"Welcome back," Zefla said. Sharrow just stood there, smiling at the android.

"Thank you," Feril said. It still had the dials and the laser they had given it; it presented both to Zefla.

"So?" Miz asked it.

"I have been to the end of the fjord," the android began.

"Let's walk and listen at the same time, eh?" Zefla said.

They hiked on; Feril walked backward in front of them without once putting a foot wrong, which was an unsettling but also rather impressive sight.

"The ground between here and the end of the fjord," it told them, "is similar to that you have already traversed. There are two sizable streams to be crossed, one of which has a fallen tree across it and so is quite easy, the second of which is more difficult and has to be waded. There is a place where one must either cross a very exposed beach only a kilometer or so from a point on the far side, or make a four- or five-kilometer detour around some cliffs."

"What did you do?" Zefla asked.

"On my outward journey," Feril told her. "I crossed the beach without incident; on my return, I again started to cross the beach. But then I was fired upon." Its upper body did a quarter turn to show a bullet graze on one shoulder. It kept on walking. "I returned fire with the laser pistol but then decided that my position was too exposed and entered the water. I completed that part of the journey crawling along just under the fjord's surface."

Zefla smiled. Miz shook his head. Dloan looked vaguely impressed. Sharrow just blinked and said, "Hmm."

"Where is this beach?" Dloan asked.

"About ten kilometers from here."

Dloan nodded. "We heard the gunfire."

"So they're that much farther ahead?" Zefla said.

"I believe only a sniper has been left on the point opposite the beach," Feril said. "I think I saw the main body of the Solipsists earlier, about another three kilometers farther down the fjord, ferrying themselves across the mouth of a side-fjord in an inflatable boat. I attempted to fire on the boat, but the range was approximately four kilometers, and I was not able to observe any effect."

Dloan shook his head understandingly.

"So," Miz said, "what have we got to look forward to apart from finding the Solipsists there first?"

"There are no more major obstacles after the beach I mentioned, though there is a small hill to be climbed, avoiding a cliff that is sheer to the water. The end of the fjord has many small islands and rocks, starting from about ten kilometers or so from its head; I believe these are why the flying boat did not simply land immediately. The end of the fjord is quite sudden; there is no significant narrowing, just the islands and then an almost straight length of shore in front of a marshy plain, which looks as though it is the result of land reclamation.

"The gun is, I believe, in a stone tower. The tower is approximately fifteen meters high and seven meters in diameter and topped with a hemispherical black dome of indeterminate substance. It stands in the center of a stone square about fifty meters to a side; the square has a circular wall half a meter high built upon it, which just touches the midpoint of each edge of the square, and four-meter-high stone posts at each corner. A small river delta forms the far boundary of the square; on this side there is a field of tall rushes.

"The stone tower is surrounded by numerous human bodies, pieces of equipment, and debris; these are mostly within the circular stone wall. From the state of decay involved, I would estimate that some of the bodies and pieces of debris have been there for many decades. The most recent bodies in the vicinity appear to be those of two young men I took to be Solipsists by their uniforms. Both bodies were attached to parachutes; one lay against the inside of the circular wall, his parachute snagged on a small tree just outside the square; the other parachutist appeared to have been dragged for some distance through the rushes before being stopped by rocks, and I was able to determine that he had been killed by some form of laser device that had removed his head. It had also left a hole in his chest and another in his groin, consistent with a sixty-millimeter beam. I deduced that the dome on top of the tower housed such a device, perhaps along with the concomitant detection and tracking equipment it would require."

"Amazing deduction," muttered Miz. He glanced at Sharrow, but she didn't seem to have heard.

"I noticed," Feril continued, "that the few birds that overflew the area are kept well away from the tower, though there were avian bodies of various species distributed around it, along with those of numerous small animals. Insects appeared to be tolerated. I conducted a brief experiment with pieces of wood and found that anything moving within fifty meters of the center of the tower with a frontal area greater than approximately two square centimeters will be attacked by the tower's defenses. I believe this to be a powerful X-ray laser, though the beam used on the pieces of wood I threw into this zone was considerably smaller than those that had killed the two Solipsist parachutists. I also noticed that when the dead parachutist resting against the inside of the wall moved—when his parachute was caught by a gust of wind—the beam that hit him was narrow and attenuated, and one of several dozen or so that had seemingly hit him after his death while he was presumably in the same state of morbid mobility."

"Well," Sharrow said, "sounds good news and bad." She looked distracted, grimacing as she rubbed at her left glove. "Let's assume whatever's in the tower is . . . intact, but—"

"But how the hell do we get in when nobody else has?" Miz said, kicking at a rotten branch in his way.

"Ah," the android said. It held up one finger. "I mentioned the stone posts at each corner of the square."

"Yes?" Zefla said.

"Beneath a cover on the top of each post," Feril said, "there is a hand-lock plate, a security device in the shape of a double-thumbed hand. From their construction I would say that they are designed to react to some chemical or genetic trigger rather than the more usual handprint pattern. At least two of these posts appear to be operational, the other two having been partially dismantled. All four bear the legend, 'Female line.' "

Sharrow stopped; they all did.

Zefla looked at her. "Sounds like Gorko again," she said. "Might just switch the thing off for you, eh, kid?"

Sharrow was staring at her feet. Then she looked up at Zefla and seemed to shake, and then smiled and nodded.

"Yes," she said. She gazed at her left hand, holding it awkwardly. "Yes, it might."

"So even if the Solipsists do get there first," Miz said, "they won't be able to do anything."

"Yeah," Zefla said. "But if they do get there before we do, they can make it impossible for us to do anything, either."

Sharrow swayed, blinking, trying to think. There was something else, too. So hard to think.

Zefla looked at Feril. "When will you have to set off if you're to rendezvous with the sub?"

(*Yes, that's it,* Sharrow thought.)

"In about thirty hours," Feril said.

Zefla nodded, looking at Sharrow. "Onward?" she asked.

Sharrow swallowed. "Onward," she said.

Her hand hurt. She felt hungry and nauseous at the same time. She recalled Miz talking about eating fish, and suddenly her mouth filled with saliva as she remembered the taste of spiced, blackened fish. That had been in Shouxaine, in Tile, many years ago. She had sat at the rough wooden tables with the others, beneath the lanterns and the firecracker strings and the glow-ropes. They had eaten fish caught in the lake that afternoon and drunk a lot of wine; then she and Miz had gone to bed, and then, while they were making love, the firecrackers had gone off, and she was there again, in the hotel of Malishu, on the bed under the membrane roof in front of the tall mirrors, but even as she thought about that, something dragged her further onward, transported her forward and back at the same time, to that quiet hotel in the mountains, with the view over the hills and the windows opened to the cool breeze that blew the gauzy white curtains softly in and made her skin tingle and dried her sweat and gave Miz cold bumps, and her hands stroked him, fingers stroked him, smoothing the skin on his back and his flanks and shoulders and behind and chest, urging him, controlling him, moving him, and he was a beautiful gray shape above her in the first hint of dawn, and a slowly pulsing presence inside her, a soft-hard rocking nudging her closer and closer to an edge like the edge of the balcony, gray-pink stone through the haze of curtains, shoving and nuzzling and pressing her closer and closer, his

breath and her breath like the noise of surf, so that she remembered building sand castles on the shore once when
she was young.

Breyguhn and she: they had each built a castle and
made it as high and as strong as they could, right alongside
each other; they had each put a paper flag on top of the tallest tower of their castles and waited to see whose castle
would collapse first; the two-moon tide had come in strong
and fast, and the waves beat at the walls they had each built,
and she had seen her own castle start to crumble at the
edges, but knew she had built better and had really been
watching Breyguhn's, willing the waves to hit the base of
that sea-facing wall, and watched wave after wave after wave
hit the sand, bringing the wall to the point of crumbling but
not quite undermining it sufficiently, and slowly an incredible sensation of expectation and frustration had built up in
her chest and belly, along with a fury that the sea could so
nearly hand her victory but then hold back—as the power
and strength of the waves seemed to ebb briefly, and no
more damage was done—and started to believe that it was
never going to happen, that neither castle was ever going to
fall, but then seen the waves come strongly in again, breaking and surging and sucking at the castles' walls, and then
finally, finally, finally, with a sudden last pulsed rush of
waves—waves that went on and on, piling into the sand
when the thing was done and the contest decided—the
whole wall of Breyguhn's castle collapsed and fell, tipping
out and breaking in the air and disintegrating into the
waves, turning them golden-brown as the surf fell tumbling
over the wreckage and burst against the rough vulnerability
of the sand revealed inside, and smoothed that and slipped
back and surged forward again and smoothed and slipped
and smoothed and slipped and smoothed, tumbling
Breyguhn's tower and flag into the water.

But then the light had flared, beautiful and terrifying,
sublime and sickening, erupting over the beach and the
mountains as the burst, glittering ship spun end over end toward the cold planet where she fell forever to the snow, a
snowflake amid the fall.

There had been another night when she slept badly, trying
to curl up around her injured hand, holding the thing to her
like a treasure and trying to will the pain to stop and let her

sleep until eventually she fell into a kind of coma from sheer exhaustion, a semisleep in which she dreamt of the distant sparks of the two fires on the other side of the fjord, so far in front of them now that they could only just be glimpsed with the naked eye, flickering through the trees. She had thought she'd heard Cenuij calling to them from the trees ahead, but at least he hadn't actually appeared in her dream.

Then she was woken with the others to the freezing cold of another day when the floor of gray flat water and the ceiling of gray flat clouds were shackled together by chains of sleet, and in the clear spells between the hail and the sleet showers they could see that the mountaintops were covered in white.

She marched on, talking with the others and to herself and getting hungrier and thinking about food and wishing her hand would stop hurting, and telling the others she was fine even though she wasn't. They took the detour the android had suggested, around the beach in front of the cliff, near the point on the other side of the fjord, then crossed the first of the two large streams the android had warned them about by going across a fallen tree. Miz cut some branches off it with a laser to make the traverse easier, but still she almost fell.

The forest was a cold, dark, damp place, and she hated it. She hated her hand for hurting and her belly for being empty and her head for being dizzy and sore and her anus and vagina for itching and her eyes for not focusing and her brain for not working properly.

The android carried her across the second stream, the cold water washing around its chest.

They walked on as the weather cleared a little, then got even colder while dark, tall clouds built up to windward and started toward them. Sometime about then she began to forget which day this was and where exactly they were and what they were looking for and why they were looking for it.

Plodding on became everything; her being became centered on the in-out ebb and flow of breath, the thud-thudding of her feet hitting the ground one after another and the lifting, dropping, lifting, dropping motion of her legs, sending vibrations up through her that she received as though from far away and in slow motion. Even her voice sounded distant and not really hers. She listened to herself answer the things the others asked her, but she didn't know what it was she was saying and she didn't really care; only the onwardness of walking mattered, only that slow thud-thudding that was her feet and her heart and the wounding pulse of her poisoning pain.

She was alone. She was quite alone. She walked a frozen shore in the middle of nothing, with only the solitude to stalk her either side, and she began to wonder whether she really was a Solipsist, the traitor among them.

A brain in a body, a collection of cells in a collection of cells, making its way in a menagerie of other cell-collections, animal and vegetable, wandering the same rough globe with their own share of its dumb cargo of minerals and chemicals and fluids carried strapped and trapped in and by that cage of cells—temporarily—always part of it but always utterly alone.

Like Golter; like poor, poor Golter.

It had found itself alone, and it had spread itself as far as it could and produced so much, but it was still next to nothing.

They had grown up—had they only known it—in one room of an empty house. When they began to understand it was a house, they had thought there must be others nearby; they had thought perhaps they were in the suburbs, or even a well-hidden part of the city, but though they had colonized those other rooms, they had looked out from their farthest windows and tallest skylights and found—to their horror, and a horror only their own increased understanding made them fully able to appreciate—that they were truly alone.

They could see the nebulae, beautiful and distant and beckoning, and could tell that those far-away galaxies were composed of suns, other stars like Thrial, and even guess that some of those suns, too, might have planets around them ... but they looked in vain for stars anywhere near their own.

The sky was full of darkness. There were planets and moons and the tiny feathery whorls of the dim nebulae, and they had themselves filled it with junk and traffic and emblems of a thousand different languages, but they could not create the skies of a planet within a galaxy, and they could not ever hope, within any frame of likelihood they could envisage existing, to travel to anywhere beyond their own system, or the everywhere-meaningless gulf of space surrounding their isolated and freakish star.

For a distance that was never less than a million light years in any direction around it, Thrial—for all its flamboyant dispersion of vivifying power and its richly fertile crop of children planets—was an orphan.

There was this wall. She was coming slowly up to this flat wall. The wall was white and gray and studded with little round stones; to one side there was a larger boulder shaped like a giant door handle. She wondered if the wall was really a door. Somehow, she was sure that Cenuij was on the other side. She could see ice and frost on it. The wall was coming closer all the time and seemed to be very tall; she didn't think she'd be able to see the top. It kept advancing toward her even though she was sure she had stopped walking. Walking had been everything for longer than she could remember; it had been her universe, her existence, her whole reason for being, but then she had stopped, and yet here was this wall coming toward her. Very close now; she could see frozen trickles of water between the small stones, and what might have been small, frosted plants. She looked for Cenuij's eye, peeking through at her from the other side. Somebody else must have noticed the wall, because she thought she heard a shout from somewhere far away.

The wall slammed into her. There seemed to be a safety rail. Her head hit the wall anyway, and everything went dark.

The android saw her falling and rushed forward as Miz shouted out. It couldn't hope to save her properly, but it was just close enough to stretch out a leg and get a foot under her upper chest, slowing her descent just a little before her falling weight took her down and she fell to the stony beach and lay there, facedown and still.

Feril hopped once, unbalanced, then knelt with the others as they gathered quickly around her.

"Is she hurt?" Miz said, as Zefla and Dloan gently rolled her over. There was a small graze on her cheek and another on her forehead. Her face looked old and puffed. Her mouth opened slackly. Miz took her right glove off and rubbed her hand. Feril touched her left glove.

"She's lying in this water," Zefla said. "Let's get her to the trees."

They took her into the forest and laid her down. Feril ran its fingers over the taut left glove again. "There appears to be something wrong with her hand," it said.

The others looked at the glove. "She did cut her hand a couple of days ago," Zefla said. Dloan tried to undo the glove.

They had to cut it eventually. Her hand was bloated and discolored; the original wound oozed from beneath a small, sopping plaster. Miz made a face.

Zefla drew her breath in. "Oh, oh," she said. "Oh, you silly thing . . ." She touched the swollen skin. Sharrow moaned.

Dloan drew his laser, opened the grip, and adjusted the controls.

"What's that for?" Miz asked, staring at the weapon.

Dloan closed the grip again, turned, and fired the gun into the needle litter at his feet; a tiny, continuous red ember burned. Dloan seemed satisfied and clicked the beam off.

"Poison," Dloan said, gently taking Sharrow's wounded hand and laying it as flat as possible on the ground. "Antiseptic? Dressing?" he said.

Zefla was rummaging in Sharrow's satchel. "Here," she said.

"Might wake her up," Dloan said, kneeling so that he could hold Sharrow's hand securely. "Want to hold her down?"

"Shit," Miz said, and took her feet. Feril held her other hand and pinned her shoulders; Zefla smoothed her hand over Sharrow's forehead.

Dloan pointed the laser pistol at Sharrow's wounded hand and pressed the trigger. The flesh spotted, blackened, and split, parting like the skin of a rotten fruit. Sharrow moaned and stirred as the liquid inside spilled out, sputtering and steaming under the laser's power. Miz looked away.

Zefla rocked back and forth, stroking Sharrow's forehead and cheeks; Dloan grimaced and screwed his eyes up as the fumes bubbling from the wound reached him, but kept the laser pointed at her hand, lengthening the incision.

The android looked on, fascinated, while the moaning woman moved weakly beneath him.

They built a fire. Zefla had a last lump of foodslab left she'd been saving; they warmed it with the laser and tried to get Sharrow to eat it. They used a laser to heat some water in the hollow of a stone, soaked a bandanna in it and got her to suck at it. Her face seemed to grow less puffy, and her breathing became slower and deeper. She passed from unconsciousness to something more like sleep. The smell of antiseptic spread around the hollow.

They had traveled only ten kilometers from their last camp; they still had thirty left to travel to the tower at the head of the fjord. Feril thought that given the state of the ground on the far side of the fjord, the Solipsists might be significantly delayed; but it would be a close-run thing, and while it could carry Sharrow until the next camp, it would have to leave soon after darkness if it was to get back to the mouth of the fjord in time to attempt to make contact with the submarine.

"We don't really have much choice, I guess," Miz said. He still felt ill after watching what they'd done to Sharrow's infected hand. His feet ached and his stomach felt as if it were eating itself; he was light-headed and shivery with hunger. He couldn't stop thinking about food. But at least the pain of walking helped take his mind off his empty belly.

"You're sure you can carry her safely?" Zefla asked Feril.

"Yes."

"I could spell you," Dloan said.

The android paused. "Thank you," it said.

"Okay," Zefla said. She lifted the satchel. "Let's go."

The small group of people walked along the cold gray shore under a dark, lowering sky. The tall leading figure walked lightly, even gracefully, but the one following looked too slight to carry the burden in its arms as easily as it appeared to, and the last two in the group were limping.

Above them, a sky the color of gun metal shook free the first few tiny flakes of snow.

Elson Roa watched from the top of a bluff through a pair of high-power binoculars. He saw the leading figure of the group on the far side of the fjord take an object from a satchel and stop briefly while they examined it. Then they replaced the object in the bag.

Roa switched the field-glasses' stabilizers off and listened to their slowly dying whine as the air above the waters of the fjord began to fill with snow, wiping the view out in a swirling gray turmoil of silence. The sniper at his side checked the range read-out on her rifle again and shook her head, tutting.

Roa looked behind him to where his comrades stood, healthy and alert and waiting. A little snow drifted out of the dull expanse of cloud hanging between the mountains and settled gently on their dirtied but still gaudy uniforms.

They moved through a limited world; the falling snow obliterated everything save for a circle perhaps ten meters in diameter consisting of forest edge, rocky shore, and flat water. The patch of the fjord's black surface they could see specked continually with white flakes that vanished the instant they touched that darkness. No waves beat. Where the snowflakes touched the ground, they sat among the rocks and pebbles for a brief moment, then melted. The sky was gone, brought down to an indeterminate low ceiling where the mass of gray-white flakes became a single cloud of chaotic, cluttering movement.

Feril followed Zefla Franck, putting its feet where hers had gone. Sharrow was a slight burden in its arms; her extra weight meant that it had to lean back a little as it walked to keep its center of balance vertical, but it could continue like this indefinitely if it had to. It kept looking around even though there was little enough to see. It maintained its audio sweep, listening for anything unusual.

They had pulled the hood of Sharrow's jacket up over her face when they'd set off; when Feril looked down at one point, it saw that the hood had fallen back, and flakes of snow were falling onto her sleeping face. The soft white scraps touched her cheeks and became tiny patches of moistness. Where they fell on her eyelashes, they lasted long enough for the android to be able to see the shape of the individual crystals, before each unique shape was dissolved by the heat of her body and flowed into the skin around her eyes like tears.

Feril watched for a moment and then pulled the hood back up, sheltering her.

Zefla Franck was leaving footprints now; the snow swarming from the closed and heavy sky was beginning to lie, collecting flake by tiny flake on the rocks and pebbles and the rough-surfaced trunks of the trees at the forest's hem and building small bridges of softness over crevices and rivulets, which had begun to freeze.

The shore became too steep and the snow too heavy; they returned to the forest, walking among the trees in a scarcened filter of flakes, enlivened every now and again as a clump of snow fell suddenly from the canopy above through the branches to the forest floor.

Zefla, with her laser, cut through the tangles and fallen branches they encountered, leaving the charred smell of burned wood curling behind on a cloud of smoke and steam.

Sharrow made occasional small whimpering noises and moved in Feril's arms.

They walked on until it became too dark to see, then stopped to rest. Sharrow slept on, Zefla sat still, Miz complained about his feet, and Dloan offered to take Sharrow. Feril said there was no need. Then they walked on, all but Dloan equipped with night sights. He followed just behind Miz. The falling snow thinned, then thickened again.

Feril could see Zefla Franck's previously well-balanced gait becoming ragged and clumsy, and hear Miz Gattse Kuma's wheezing, labored breathing behind. Dloan slipped and fell twice. They were only about nine kilometers from the head of the fjord, but the ground ahead was rough and much of it was uphill. It suggested they stopped and made camp.

They sat, exhausted, on a fallen trunk. Sharrow lay across their laps, her head cradled in Zefla's arms. Feril found wood and used a laser to light the fire. It erected the tent for them, too. They put Sharrow inside; Zefla wrapped her in the blanket. Miz and Dloan sat at the fire.

"I could go on the last nine thousand meters with Lady Sharrow," it told them, once they had gathered around the fire. "Even if she does not wake up, her palm, applied to one of the tower's stone square's posts, might well open the tower up."

None of them seemed to have the strength to reply; they just stared at the flames of the fire. Snowflakes fell toward it, then were caught in the updraft and whirled away. The snow seemed to be thinning again.

"Alternatively," Feril told them, "I could return to the coast and signal the submarine. Though I'd have to leave now."

"Or you could stay here on guard," Zefla said from the tent, putting Sharrow's satchel under her head as a pillow.

"Or he could head for the tower again," Dloan said. "With a gun, he might be able to hold off the Solipsists for a while.

"I still think we should get word to the outside," Miz said. "Get the sub to call up some air support. Hell, the Security Franchise people didn't bother about Roa's fucking great flying boat, and one lousy fighter-bomber would be all we'd need."

"Nobody sane would take it on," Zefla said, after satisfying herself that Sharrow was comfortable. She hunkered down on the other side of the fire, her voice sounding far away, distorted, by the column of heated air rising between them. "So, we need to get word to the outside, we need a guard tonight, and we need to guard the tower, too, to prevent Roa getting to it first."

"All these things are possible," Feril said. "What would you like me to do?"

They all looked at each other; and they each glanced at Sharrow, a bundled shape in the tent.

"Vote," Zefla said. "I say . . . oh, guard the tower."

Dloan nodded. "Me, too."

Miz made a tutting noise and looked away.

"Feril?" Zefla said.

"Yes?" It looked at her.

"What about you?"

"What—? Oh, I abstain."

Zefla glanced back at the tent. "Guard the tower it is."

They gave the android a laser pistol; the snow had stopped and the sky was clearing.

The fjord was pure black. A clear-blue light came down from Maidservant, gibbous in the sky above; it coated the mountains and the dozens of small, snow-covered islands with a ghostly silver. Junklight sparkled in the northern skies, toward the equator. There were no fires on the far side of the water.

The android flitted away into the trees, silent and quick.

22

The Silent Tower

Z efla awoke in the middle of the night, her bladder full.
She had tried to stave off the hunger pangs by drinking
quantities of water made from snow they'd melted. Miz had
talked about doing some night-fishing through a hole in a
frozen stream, but then had fallen asleep.

Snuggled down between the warmth of Dloan and
Sharrow, she didn't want to get out of the tent but knew
she'd have to. She checked on Sharrow, who seemed to be
breathing peacefully, then got up as carefully as she could,
extricating herself from the others and wriggling her way
out through the tent door. Somebody—probably Miz, lying
cradling the machine gun—murmured behind her, and she
whispered, "Sorry!"

The fire was still glowing. It was light enough for her to
see without a night-sight. She walked downhill through the
quiet carpet of snow and squatted among the trees near the
shore. The night was still and cold and clear. She heard a
couple of muffled crumping noises in the distance, and
guessed it was snow falling off trees.

She got up, fastening her fatigues. Steam filmed up
from beneath her, just visible in the moonlight. Maidservant
stood big and silver above the mountains on the other side
of the fjord; it would be disappearing soon. She looked at it
all for a few moments, thinking how beautiful this place was,

and wishing the ache in her muscles and the hunger and the steady gnawing fear in her guts would vanish and let her enjoy it.

She turned and made her way back toward the camp.

The two figures were about twenty meters from the tent. They wore matt-black suits that covered their faces, and they each held small handguns. They were creeping slowly closer to the tent, coming from the direction of the fjord head down a small ridge.

Her mind raced. Her gun was in the tent. The two figures hadn't fired yet, though they were well within range and must have realized there was no guard posted. They didn't seem to have seen her. If she simply shouted, rousing Miz and Dloan, the two figures might shoot straight into the tent.

She shrank back and ducked, then ran downhill and curved around to get behind them. She tried to go as quietly as she could, slipping twice on buried roots but not making any appreciable noise. She found the rear of the ridge and ran up it, crouching.

The two black figures were right in front of her, still creeping toward the tent. She stayed where she was for a moment, getting her breath back, keeping her mouth wide so that her breathing didn't make a noise.

The two figures were separating; one stayed where he was, crouched on one knee, gun pointed at the tent, while the other started to circle.

Zefla drew both her gloves off, placed them on the snow, and crept down toward the kneeling figure, her hands out in front of her. There was a tickling feeling in her throat, probably because she'd been breathing hard. *Fate*, girl, she told herself, *this is no time to cough, or sneeze, or get the hiccups.* . . . She got within five meters of the crouching figure, then something in the fire collapsed with a snap and a cloud of orange sparks swirled into the air.

She froze. So did the person circling around to the front of the tent. If they turned to look at the kneeling figure in front of her, they'd be bound to see her. She wasn't close enough to make a dive for the kneeling figure. She watched the one near the tent, her heart thudding.

The circling figure kept its gaze on the tent, then moved slowly closer. Zefla relaxed fractionally and crept on toward the kneeling figure, her breath silent. The tickle in

her throat wasn't so bad now. Four meters; she would get to
the kneeling figure with the gun before the other one got to
the tent; three meters.

The snow fell from a tree immediately behind her without any warning.

She heard it, started to straighten as she thought there
might have been another attacker behind her, then—
realizing, but knowing it was too late—pounced, shouting, at
the man in front of her as he whirled around, bringing the
gun up and firing as he rolled.

Miz had woken from a dream. He had been aware of somebody getting out of the tent. He felt stiff and sore and incredibly hungry. He still had the machine gun in his arms.
He started to ease his arms and shoulders into a different
position, then heard a whooshing, thumping noise, followed
immediately by a scream and two shots. He tore the tent entrance open to see a black-suited figure right in front of him
looking to one side, then turning to point a gun at him.

He had gone to sleep dreaming about this; his thumb
flicked the safety an instant before his finger pressed the
trigger. The gun shuddered and roared in his arms, trying to
burrow back down past him and blowing the figure outside
backward, gun firing up into the trees.

Miz threw himself out of the tent. He felt Dloan follow.

There was a body lying in the snow, and an impression
of movement downslope. Miz ran after the fleeing figure.
The black-suited figure dropped the handgun it had been
carrying, dived into the water, swam for a few seconds, then
dived, disappearing in a black swirl of moonlit water.

Miz raised the machine gun and sighted at where the
black suit had disappeared, then raised the gun a fraction.
After a few moments there was a hint of turbulence to one
side of where he was aiming; he corrected and fired, moving
the gun around as though stirring the distant, fountaining
water. The magazine ran out and the gun fell silent.

He remembered the night-sight and clipped it on. The
body in the water floated darkly, oozing warmth.

Miz let the machine gun drop to the ground, then
picked it up and started walking back up to the tent, shaking. He had just realized: the body on the snow had been
wearing fatigues, and Zefla hadn't been in the tent.

A sickness worse than any hunger grew in his belly as he walked, then ran, back up the slope to the tent.

Sharrow had woken with the noise, still groggy; then she saw Zefla's pale, slackly unconscious face, and the blood oozing from the wounds in her chest and head.

Now their earlier roles were reversed, and Sharrow knelt in the tent, tending to the shallow-breathing, trembling Zefla. Dloan looked on, his body shaking more than his sister's. He held her hand, staring at her face, his eyes wide and terrified.

"Call for help," Sharrow told Miz.

"What?" he said.

"Of course," Dloan said, his eyes shining. "The Franchisers. We can call the Franchisers."

"But—" Miz began, then looked from Sharrow's face down to Zefla's. He shook his head. "Oh, Fate," he said with a moan. He took his phone from a pocket and opened it. He tried pressing a few buttons, frowning. Dloan saw the expression and looked, wide-eyed, for his phone. Sharrow dug hers out from her satchel and found Zefla's.

None of them worked; it was as though they had been turned off from outside.

There was little they could do for Zefla. The bullet in her chest had gone right through, puncturing a lung; the front wound bubbled with each shallow breath. The bullet that had struck her head had left a long gouged mark along her temple a centimeter deep; tiny shards of bone marked its edges. They couldn't tell if the round had pierced her skull or grazed off. They sprayed antiseptic on her wounds and bandaged them.

Feril arrived back twenty minutes later; it had heard the noise from its position near the tower. It tried broadcasting a distress message using its own comm unit, but didn't hold out much hope of its being picked up unless somebody was deliberately looking with a targeted satellite.

It put its hands gently to Zefla's head, feeling carefully around, and told them there was a bullet lodged inside her skull near the back.

The android suggested it go on guard now. Miz gave it a machine gun. It closed the tent and left them to tend the wounded woman as best they could.

It knew now that it should have spoken its mind earlier,

when they were trying to decide what to do; it ought to have suggested that it stay here, on guard, but it had not felt it was its place to say anything. They were experienced at this sort of thing, their lives were more totally at risk than its was, and it had not wanted to be thought presumptuous or patronizing.

Fool, fool, it told itself, taking the safety off the machine gun. *Fool, Feril—fool.*

It sat down in a pile of freshly fallen snow near the top of the small ridge above the camp and nursed the gun until the bitter dawn arose.

They set off just after dawn, leaving Dloan behind in the tent with Zefla. She was still breathing shallowly. The bandage around her chest was soaked red, and they had to keep her turned on her side to let her cough up blood without choking. Dloan just sat there with wide, frightened childlike eyes, stroking her hands and whispering to her.

"She'll be all right," Sharrow told him, not believing it but feeling it was the only way to dam his despair. The big, powerful man looked about five years old.

Dloan said nothing but looked at Sharrow with a faint, tremulous smile and kept on stroking Zefla's hand. Sharrow ran her hand over Zefla's pale, hot face and stroked her cheek.

"You'll pull through, eh, girl?" she said, trying to keep the choke out of her voice, then pulled away and stood shakily outside the tent where Miz and Feril were waiting.

She hesitated, then went to the body lying frozen just up the slope from the tent; it had been torn almost in half by the machine-gun fire. Sharrow pulled the black mask off the figure's head, remembering Keteo. It was a woman's face.

Again, she thought at first she didn't recognize it, then recalled the woman at Roa's side in Vembyr, during the auction and then afterward at the docks. It was she. She let the mask snap back and rejoined Miz and Feril.

"Let's go," she said.

They set off into the snow-quiet forest under skies like milk.

Feril knew the fastest route; they moved as quickly as they could, uphill through broken boulders and deformed, wind-blasted trees. Sharrow walked until the android saw her stumble and gulp for breath, then offered to carry her.

She said nothing for a moment. She stood breathing heavily, her bandaged hand hanging at one side. For a moment Feril thought it might have mistimed its offer, but then she nodded.

Feril picked her up easily and strode off through the trees. Miz struggled to keep up; the air was like freezing water in his throat, his legs weak and shaky with hunger and fatigue.

They were fifteen hundred meters away when they heard the firing up ahead.

They stopped for a moment, and Sharrow got down from the android's arms. Machine-gun fire crackled and laser fire snapped; there were sharp explosions that might have been grenade or mortar rounds, and a booming ripple of fire that could have been a cluster munition. Trees around them reacted to the shuddering air, loosing powdery falls of snow. . . .

"What," Miz wheezed, "was all *that*?" His breath smoked in front of his face. "The Solipsists . . . couldn't have had . . . ordnance *that* heavy . . . could they?"

"I believe I heard jet motors," Feril said.

The gunfire and explosions died away, the echoes fading slowly to silence among the mountains.

They listened a while longer, then Sharrow shrugged. "Let's go and see." She looked back the way they had come, as if trying to see the tent. She let herself be lifted when Feril offered her the cradle of its arms again.

A few minutes later they saw the smoke rising above the trees ahead, piling silently up to the calm skies, spreading and fanning in the shining space above the peaks.

They came to the tower half an hour later.

The trees ended four hundred meters from the tower; the slope descended to a delta of tall rushes. The stone square containing the shallow-walled circle with the stubby tower at its center was just as the android had described it, near the straight edge of the fjord's end with the braided river delta beyond.

They looked out onto devastation. The whole small estuary around the stone square and the tower was dotted with smoldering fires, bodies, and wrecked vehicles. The decaying superstructures of a couple of long-foundered boats rested above their still images in the quiet waters of the calm fjord.

It was hard, at first, to distinguish ancient wreckage from fresh carnage; then the android pointed to the trail of bodies that led from a break in the trees on the far side of the river delta and stretched toward the tower. Smoke still rose from most of the corpses.

"Those the Solipsists?" Miz asked it. Most of the bodies were too blackened for any colors to be visible.

The android took a moment to reply.

"Yes," it said eventually.

They could see the two parachutists the Solipsists had dropped; they must have been hit again, because both their bodies were burning, too. Sharrow caught the smell of the individual pyres on the breeze and felt sick. There was just one other gaudily uniformed figure visible, sprawled at the corner of the stone square nearest them.

"Who *did* all this?" Sharrow said. "Was this all the tower defenses?"

The android lifted a hand, pointing toward the forested valley behind the small estuary, then seemed to droop.

"I believe . . . ," it began, its voice small; then it fell over slackly, thumping into the ground and rolling a little way downhill, limbs flopping.

"What—?" Miz said, stumbling after the android with Sharrow.

They lifted Feril's head.

"Fate," Sharrow said. "How do you bring one of these things around?"

"Can't see any switches," Miz said. "Think this was natural? You know—just a fault in the android, maybe? No?"

She looked around the silent mountains, the valley, and the river delta. "No," she said. "No, I don't think so."

They gazed at each other. Miz's face looked strained and gray. Sharrow had never seen him look so old and careworn. She wanted to take his head in her hands and kiss his poor face better.

"I don't like this, kid," he said. "This isn't good." He glanced at the tower, pulling his hunting jacket closer around him. "This isn't a good place."

She unhitched the machine gun from the android's shoulder, pulled it free, and handed it to Miz.

"I know what you mean," she said. "But there's nowhere else to go, is there?" She looked across at the tower. "Not if we're going to get Zef out of here."

Miz took the machine gun and checked it. He shook his head. "I hate it when you're right."

She readied the HandCannon, holding it awkwardly in her right hand; then they left Feril where it had fallen and walked down toward the stone square and the tower—a rough stone stump capped with black.

They passed ancient burned-out tanks and rusting All Terrains and motorbikes, wrecked helicopters and the hulks of small ACVs. The bodies were mostly long-decayed, reduced to bleached bones and faded rags that had been clothes and uniforms, all gone to tatters.

They crossed the field of chin-high rushes, their boots crunching through shallow, ice-dried pools. Miz hauled himself up onto the plinth of the stone square near one corner; he reached down and hauled Sharrow up after him.

They walked through the flat expanse of snow to one of the small stone posts set in a corner of the square. It was like a tiny model of the central stone tower, a stump rising from a black hemisphere.

A garishly colored, motley-uniformed body lay in front of it, facedown, limbs spread; the snow here was pitted with neat holes that ended in shallow blackened craters in the flagstone. Miz turned the body over with one foot, keeping the gun trained on it.

Elson Roa's dead face stared up at the sky. His chest had been opened and burned by a laser. He looked surprised.

Miz looked at Sharrow, but she just shook her head.

He pushed Roa's body off the edge of the stone square, down into the rushes beneath.

The pitted metal cover on top of the post swung back easily. It was on a spring; Sharrow held it back with her bandaged hand. The double-sided handprint was there, just as Feril had said.

Sharrow gave the HandCannon to Miz, took the glove off her right hand using her teeth, then—after a look at the handprint there, and the cryptic legend—put her hand down firmly on the slick chill of the plastic template.

Nothing happened for a few moments. Then the plastic

under her hand lit up and glowed softly; a four-by-five grid of little bright dots appeared on a panel above Sharrow's middle finger and started to disappear at one per second.

Miz and Sharrow looked at each other, then around the estuary, feeling exposed and vulnerable. A wind came out of the valley and ruffled the tops of the trees, scattering snow.

The last of the dots disappeared.

There was a grinding noise behind them; they turned quickly to see two shining metal shell-doors sliding up out of the tower, gradually covering the black hemisphere at the summit of the squat structure and meeting with a hollow clunk.

Another grinding noise came, from the side of the tower facing away from the fjord. Sharrow took her glove out of her mouth and threw it over the low stone wall into the circle. The glove landed unharmed in the snow. She shrugged, stepped over the knee-high wall, and started walking to the tower.

Miz followed her.

On the valley-facing side of the tower, a door had dropped vertically into the floor, revealing what appeared to be another door of black grass. There was a hint of a small space behind the black glass door that the daylight did little to illuminate. A smell of plastic wafted from the tower's entrance. As they looked in, lights came on inside; the Lazy Gun sat on a pedestal in the center of the room, gleaming.

"Yes," Miz breathed.

Sharrow moved forward; another handprint appeared at face level on the surface of the black glass door. She put her palm to it, and with hardly a pause it, too, sank into the floor.

She looked at Miz. He nodded at her. "You go on; I'm staying out here."

She nodded and walked forward, entering the tower. She stepped quickly over the doors that had sunk into the floor and went to the Lazy Gun. It looked real. She lifted it from its plinth and swung it around. It was light but massy; a strange, disturbing sensation, like something from a dream.

So it was real. This was the eighth and last Lazy Gun. Her head swam; she felt dizzy. She put the Gun down on its pedestal again and walked to a hole in the floor where a broad ramp led down beneath the tower.

She went halfway down to the floor below; a softly lit space perhaps half the area of the stone square outside stretched away around her. She saw equipment of a hundred different types, and boxes and cases that might have concealed a hundred more—a billion more, on some scales. There was a strange, carlike device near the foot of the steps, resting on one canted wheel, its single-seat cockpit open. What looked like a fabulously hi-tech suit of armor stood nearby. A rack of bewilderingly complex guns stood to one side of what might have been a cluster of black-body satellites gathered together to resemble a carousel. Something that resembled an old radar unit sat on the back of what was probably a small ACV.

She was still looking for something that looked remotely like a comm set when she heard the firing.

Miz watched Sharrow enter the tower. He felt nervous; there were too many dead people around here. Even the android had keeled over once he'd come back within half a klick of the place.

The wind gusted, lifting snow from the trees in the valley behind the tower and from the stone square itself, blowing it across the square and into Miz's eyes. He blinked.

He heard something like clattering feet coming from behind him. He turned and looked through the cloud of drifting snow.

A huge black four-limbed animal was charging toward him, its head down. Something on its head glittered. Miz stared. The animal was thirty meters away. A sial; a racer; one of the things they raced in Tile, one of the beasts somebody had been naming after his defeats and setbacks for the past half year or more.

He blinked; this couldn't be happening. The animal charged on; its warm breath powered out of its black nostrils and curled in the air. Miz raised the machine gun and fired.

The animal vanished utterly. The noise of its hooves faded a second later, then came back, again from behind him.

He turned: another night-black sial with something glittering on its head. He sighted the gun. When the beast was ten or so meters from him, and he could have sworn he could feel each shuddering hoofbeat through the flagstones under his boots and make out the great silvery spike attached to its forehead and a glinting harness, he fired; that animal, too, disappeared, just like a hologram.

The noise faded, swung around behind him. He turned again: two animals, racing toward him, heads lowered. He glimpsed movement in the doorway of the tower and saw Sharrow. She sagged against the doorway, then fell forward into the snow.

"Fucking *set-up!*" he roared.

He glanced at the two animals tearing toward him through the snow, hooves flinging curves of powdery white behind them. He fired, saw the image flick out of existence, and turned to see two more beasts coming from the other direction. He fired at them, too, until the gun's magazine ran out; then he ran for the doorway.

He realized then that he had seen only one of the first pair of sial disappear. He glimpsed something bearing down on him on his right. He turned to use the machine gun as a club and put his hand to his pocket for his laser.

The firing came again before Sharrow could stumble from the ramp to the doorway; when she got there, she saw Miz firing through a hazy cloud of wind-blown snow. She opened her mouth to shout, and then the pain struck her, incandescing. An instant later the pain shut off abruptly and was replaced by a terrible numbness, exactly as though somebody were using a nerve weapon on her. Her arm holding the HandCannon wouldn't move. Her legs folded under her, and she collapsed against the side of the door, before falling forward into the snow.

She could move her eyes and blink and swallow—nothing else. Her bladder had emptied, and if she had had anything to eat for the last few days, her bowels would have voided. Her heart spasmed, beating quickly and irregularly. Her breathing was shallow, uncontrollable. She had a view forward across the snow-covered stone square to the low circular wall and the dark on-white chevrons of a forested mountain beyond.

She felt the stones beneath the snow ring to hoofbeats like a drum roll and glimpsed movement from the corner of her eye.

There was a scream and a terrible tearing noise, then great hooves pounded past; a pair of camouflage-clothed legs kicked and struggled in the air in front of the flashing hooves, and then the scream gurgled to nothing.

She closed her eyes.

There was a single loud shot and then a ragged thump a few meters away. She opened her eyes to see the black back and haunches of the great beast fall heavily to the snow. A single jacketed arm flopped into the snow beyond the head of the animal.

A sial. One of the things they raced in Tile, with criminals' brains emplaced. She stared at the arm lying loose on the snow and saw movement. She watched the fingers clench, then slowly unfold and go limp.

The sial's hide steamed gently in the cool air. She could see blood on the snow, where the animal had passed in front of her.

She waited. The paralysis went on. Then she heard the squeaking, cramping sounds of somebody walking toward her. Two sets of footsteps.

Two identical pairs of boots came into view; one pair went over to the fallen sial. She could see the person wearing them up to about midthigh level; he was standing near Miz's motionless arm. The butt of a large hunting rifle was lowered to rest on the snow. She could hear other footsteps, but only those two pairs of boots were visible. The pair in front of her tilted as the person wearing them squatted. She saw knees, then a pair of clasped hands, held in front of a smart uniform jacket the color of dried blood and decorated with insignia she didn't recognize; then a face.

The young man pushed the cap back from his blond-browed, gleaming face, revealing a bald scalp. He favored her with an enormously wide smile.

"Why, Lady Sharrow!" he exclaimed. "Fancy meeting you here!" He glanced over to where his twin was also squatting down, still holding the hunting rifle and studying the dead animal.

The one with the rifle saw her looking at him and waved cheerily. He lifted the limp arm lying on the snow in front of him and made that wave, too.

Miz's hand was made to flop up and down. Tears came to Sharrow's eyes.

The young man said, "Yes, and you brought some of your little friends with you. How chummy. What a pity Mr. Kuma seems to have taken all our criticism to heart!"

He laughed, and then she felt herself lifted up by the armpits until she was half resting on her knees. The young man stood behind her, holding her.

"Oh, look," he said. "Isn't that a shame." He tickled her under the armpits. "But Molgarin *will* be pleased."

Molgarin, she thought groggily. *Molgarin . . . that means something. That was what I was trying to remember. Molgarin . . .*

She looked over the bulging, still-steaming corpse of the dead sial to where Miz lay sprawled on the snow, joined to it.

The sial had had some sort of great metal spike secured to its head by a collar fitted around its neck and head. The spike was a meter and a half long and perhaps ten centimeters thick at its base. The artificial horn had pierced Miz through the chest; it protruded from the back of his hunting jacket for nearly a meter. The snow around him was bright with blood. His face looked like Roa's had: slightly surprised.

The tears welled in her eyes. Then the young man let her down and laid her carefully on her back. She had time to see camouflage-suited men with guns slung over their shoulders coming out of the tower's door carrying boxes, and glimpsed two dark, fatly sleek shapes approaching through the air above the valley; as she saw them, they slowed and dropped, and she heard the sound of their jets.

As soon as her back pressed into the snow, her tongue started to slip down her throat, but then the young man turned her over on her side and she could breathe again.

"Don't go away, now," she heard him say. His footsteps sounded in the snow, fading behind her.

He had laid her down where she could see Miz's face. She wanted to look at it for just a little longer.

Then the one squatting by Miz took out a long viblade knife and put it to his neck. She closed her eyes.

When the humming noise stopped and a few more seconds had passed, she opened her eyes again to see the second young man walk past her, carrying a bag.

The noise of the jets was suddenly very close. Their engines shrieked and a great bustling, tumbling cloud of dusty white rolled across the stone square.

Miz's beheaded body leaked blood onto the snow.

Her tears trickled onto the snow, too. The paralysis meant that she couldn't sob.

They put her on a stretcher and carried her toward the bomb-hold of one of the two heavy VTOL bombers, along with their loot from the tower and the equally paralyzed body of Feril.

She was still lying on her side when they carried her across the square, so she was the first to see Dloan sitting at the edge of the trees not far from where she, Miz, and the android had emerged a quarter of an hour earlier.

Dloan sat observing the scene, out in the open where he was easily visible and apparently unarmed. Even from that distance she thought she saw in the way he sat there, in his posture and bearing, something hopeless and terrified and alone.

She watched him watching them all, with no tears left to cry.

Somebody saw Dloan; she heard shouts. Guns were turned toward him. Dloan stood slowly, as though weary. He took something from his pocket and aimed deliberately at the men on the stone square.

He didn't have to fire; Sharrow heard projectile rifles and lasers crack and snap all around her, and she saw Dloan jerk and shake and fall in a small storm of kicked-up flurrying snow.

The firing stopped quickly, and he lay still.

They carried her into the belly of the great dark aircraft.

23

All Castles
Made of
Sand

"**O**f course, I personally—the two of us—bore Mr. Kuma no personal ill will. But you know how it is—orders are orders, eh? Shame about the old Solipsists, too, but such is life; they got involved beyond their depth. We hired them only to attack the Land Car, but then they went and got ideas about beating you to the Gun. They should have backed out when they were told to. But, hey, there I go; I don't want to anticipate whatever Molgarin may choose to tell you. That's where we're heading now, my lady, to Molgarin's Keep in the cold-desert beyond the Embargoed Areas, in *Lantskaar*!" he said, pronouncing the word with a kind of hammy relish. "Exciting, isn't it?"

There were sixteen people secured within the brightly lit bomb-hold of the leading bomber, strapped tightly against its walls in bucket seats: Sharrow, Feril, the two identical young emissaries in their smart red-brown uniforms, and twelve efficiently anonymous men in blanked camouflage suits, mostly armed with lasers and micro rifles. One carried a stun rifle; presumably that was what they had turned on her. She could see properly only because she was so tightly strapped in, her head held back against the bulkhead behind her by a harness. This was not a special security measure for her; the rest of the hold's passengers were similarly tied down. Only she and Feril did not have a quick-release handle clenched in their hands.

The booty from the tower sat webbed and tensioned in front of them in the center of the hold. The boxes and various indecipherable pieces of apparatus bounced and jiggled against their restraints as the airframe around them bucked and swerved and sank and rose, all accompanied by an enormous tearing, screaming noise.

The young emissary had to shout above the racket. "Don't worry about being intercepted by the Rebel States forces or the Security Franchisers; we have an understanding with the former, and the latter can't track us." He rolled his eyes to indicate the aircraft. "We're currently doing over three times the speed of sound at little more than tree-top height. They tell me traveling at this speed so close to the ground is such a terrifying experience for pilots—and the chances of them being able to correct a mistake by the terrain-following automatics so remote—that it's considered kinder to black out the cockpit screens altogether!"

He was silent for a moment, then chuckled as a particularly violent maneuver rammed him and Sharrow hard back against the metal wall. The equipment from the tower seemed to hang above her and the young emissary; she could see the webbing holding it in place going taut and starting to stretch. "Gosh," the young man said, his voice sounding strained as he fought to speak against the pressing g-force. A roaring noise louder than the bomber's engines was drowning him out, anyway. ". . . Hope that stuff's properly secured. Eh, Lady Sharrow? Or we're both meat paste!"

She was still trying to work out if this meant he wasn't an android after all, or if it was just an attempt to deceive her, when she blacked out.

She awoke to open air and the jangling sensation of feelings returning; her flesh sparkled with pain, like a million tiny pinpricks. Even her teeth hurt. She was being carried by two soldiers; one held her under the knees, the other under the armpits. One of the young emissaries was at her side, taking deep breaths and slapping himself on the chest, then rubbing his hands together.

She was carried out from beneath the shadow of the bomber. It had landed on a gritty, dusty desert; the air felt powder dry and bitterly cold. There were low, ash-gray mountains a few kilometers off, forming a bowl around the clinker-dark plain, which was empty save for the two sleek black aircraft and a few trucks and other vehicles. She saw other, smaller shapes curving through the heavy gray skies above the encircling mountains.

The emissary saw her trying to move her head and beamed a broad smile at her as the two soldiers heaved her into a small open car.

"Back with us again, Lady Sharrow?" He held his arms out wide and spun around, boot heels grinding on the grit. "Welcome to Lantskaar!" he said. He leaned on the side of the little open car. "And to Molgarin's Keep."

He watched her trying to look around the featureless desert and the barren hills around it. He laughed. "It's all underground," he said, climbing in beside her. She saw Feril being carried out of the bomber's hold by a quartet of soldiers. "Though there are," the young emissary said, waggling his eyebrows at her, "some incredibly ancient force-field projector-walls that can spring up to trap the unwary in the event of an attack." The car jerked and rolled forward, heading for a long rectangular hole in the plain. "Believe me," the young man said, "you don't want to be standing astride one of *those* when they power up, let me tell you."

He chuckled again as the car angled down a ramp into a dully lit tunnel. The tunnel curved, spiraling down into the ground; a series of huge, meter-thick doors swung or irised open for them. The car's motor whined; behind, she could hear the deeper notes of what she guessed were the trucks. After a while her ears popped. The young emissary started to whistle.

There was a huge, echoing underground vehicle park, full of cars, trucks, light armored transports and tanks. She was carried to an elevator that descended to what looked like the foyer of an hotel. Her skin still tingled and her muscles felt like jelly as they put her in a wheelchair, secured her, and pushed her along a gently lit corridor to what smelled like a clinic.

A male nurse rose from a desk and nodded to the emissary, who patted her on the head and said, "She's all yours, matey."

She was pushed into a surgery. Her heart thudded as

she saw an operating table through a glass screen. A female doctor and two female orderlies appeared, pulling on gloves.

The doctor put something cold to the back of her neck, muttered something, then came around and squatted on her haunches in front of her. "I think you can hear me," she said, talking quite loudly. "We're just going to get you washed and cleaned, do a proper check-up and then let you sleep for a while. All right?"

She stared at the woman: middle-aged, a little plump, hair bunned, brown eyes. She had no idea whether what she'd just been told was the truth or a lie.

The two orderlies stripped her, removed the bandage on her hand, cleaned the wound, and put a temporary dressing on it before they washed her in a warm pool. They dried her with towels: efficiently, neither gently nor roughly. They helped her to stand, then slipped a plain white shift over her head. They supported her from either side and made her take a few unsteady steps, then took her through to a couch. The doctor she'd seen earlier ran nerve-response tests, which tingled but did not hurt. She redressed the hand wound and took a small sample of blood in a vial, which she slotted into an analyzer. The doctor asked Sharrow to speak. She tried but only drooled. The doctor patted her arm.

"Never mind; you should be all right in the morning." She prepared a gas syringe and put it to Sharrow's neck.

The last thing she remembered was the gentle jolting of the wheelchair being trundled along an unseen corridor that seemed to go on forever.

She awoke in a snug bed. She saw a time display in the darkness that indicated it was early evening. A glowing patch alongside proved to be a light switch.

She was in a small room furnished like a cabin. She was lying on her side, curled up in an alcoved bed with a shallow wooden panel down half the open side. She was wearing the shift they had dressed her in earlier. She tried moving her arms and legs, then sat up and after a pause swung her legs out of the bed, holding on to the wall as she stood.

The carpet beneath her feet was deep and rich. The air was warm. The room held a recessed bookcase full of repro books, a desk and chair, a screen that didn't work, and a wardrobe full of clothes, all of which were her size. Attached was a bathroom with various toiletries, though nothing that could cut.

There were no windows; air came silently from porous tiles in the ceiling. It was so quiet, she could hear her heart beat. A lump of black glass the size of an eyeball was wedged in a top corner of the room, from where it would have a view of everything except the bathroom.

She tried the door; it was locked. She felt weak and sat down on the bed, then lay down and fell asleep again.

The Lazy Gun came to her in her dreams. It looked like a man, but she knew it was the Lazy Gun. They were sitting in the small cabin in Molgarin's Keep where she was sleeping.

Hello.

... Hello.

So, what would you like to know? said the Gun.

What do you mean?

What would you like to know? the Gun repeated patiently.

She looked around. Where is Cenuij? she asked it.

Dead, of course, it said. What else?

What about the others?

They're dead, too.

I know, but where are they?

The dead aren't anywhere. Unless you count the past.

Won't I see them again?

Only in your dreams. Or recordings.

She started to cry.

You are the last one, the Gun told her.

What?

You are the last one. You are the last of the eight. You are just like me; I am the last of the eight as well. You are me and I am you. We are one.

No I'm not, I'm me.

Yes, you are you, the Gun agreed. But you are me, too. And I am you.

She kept crying, not knowing what to say. She wanted to wake up but didn't know how to.

Listen, said the Gun. Is there anything I can do?

What?

Is there anything I can do? Just tell me.

What *can* you do?

Destroy things. All I can do is destroy things. It's the only thing I'm any good at. Would you like me to destroy something?

I want you to destroy everything! she screamed. Every fucking thing! All the evil men and compliant women, all the armies and companies and cults and faiths and orders and every stupid fucker in them! All of them! *Everything!*

I can't destroy all of everything, but I could destroy a lot of it.

You're being stupid.

I'm not; I could destroy lots of things and people, but not all of them.

You're mad, she said, wanting very much to wake up now.

Neither of us is mad, Lady Sharrow, the Gun said.

The man got up to leave the cabin.

Anyway, we'll see what we can do.

What do you mean? she said.

About destroying everything. We'll see what we can do.

She clenched her injured hand, trying to wake herself with the pain, but it wasn't sore enough.

What *are* you? she asked it.

The man was at the door. I'm you, the Gun said. I'm the last of the eight.

It winked at her.

We'll see what we can do.

Now go to sleep.

She awoke to a smell of food and saw a laden tray sitting on the desk. She just missed seeing whoever had left it; the room's door clicked shut with a solid, massive sound and sucked itself tightly closed.

She lay there, thinking about the dream she had had, and shivered. Then the smell wafting from the tray dragged her back to the immediate.

The tray contained a breakfast sufficient for two hungry people; she ate all of it. It was midmorning. The screen was working, so she watched the news.

The Huhsz were in trouble because they'd irradiated senior officials on Golter, Miykenns and Nachtel's Ghost; the World Court was under severe pressure to allow the terminally afflicted bureaucrats access to wartime-restricted medical technology. The Court in turn was leaning heavily on the Huhsz for apologies, scapegoats, financial recompense, and guarantees of future behavior, all of which the Order seemed comprehensively unwilling to give. The World Shrine was virtually under siege, and there was talk of force being used; Huhsz cantonment defenses and Lay Reserve Martial throughout the system had been mobilized.

There was a news blackout around the Embargoed Areas and the Security Franchise, with rumors of an air clash between the Franchise forces and the Rebel States. Travel in the far south of Caltasp was restricted.

People were apparently still talking about and commenting on the attempted assassination—seen live on screen on Nachtel's Ghost and still being repeated and re-repeated throughout the system—of some new philosopher-guru from the Ghost called Girmeyn.

She sat closer to the screen, dialed up a news archive, and found the filed item from a couple of days earlier: a studio, a live debate; politicians and religious representatives arguing against Girmeyn, and he winning charmingly but decisively.

Girmeyn looked as she remembered him: black hair and dark eyes, and that strange sense of empowered calmness. Then a figure lunging from the audience, stretching over a table, swinging something. Confusion and shouts and a sequence of brief, wild camera angles, most with people getting in the way; a shot of a vicious-looking sacrificial knife lying bloody on a desk with security officers waving guns behind; Girmeyn bleeding from a head wound, holding one hand up to it, motioning aides and others out of the way with the other hand and talking to the man being held down.

Then came a silent shot from behind glass of Girmeyn, head discreetly bandaged, in a room with the same man; just the pair of them sitting in two small seats facing each other, talking, and the man breaking down, putting his head in his hands, and Girmeyn hesitating, then putting his own hand out, touching the man on the shoulder.

She watched it again, then a third time. The last word on Girmeyn had him in retreat on some asteroid habitat.

She returned to the current news. The usual small wars and civil conflicts, minor and major disasters and the occasional heart-warming filler item.

She sat back in the seat, watching the main news items again. She felt dizzy, the way she had when she'd seen the Lazy Gun and looked into that storehouse of ancient treasure under the stone tower.

After a while she shook her head and switched the screen off.

She showered and afterward caught sight of herself in the bathroom's full-length mirror as she toweled behind her back. She stopped and looked at herself. An artificially bald woman in early middle-age. A dressing on one hand. The skin under her eyes dark. A face that had aged recently.

Alone, she thought. *Alone.*

She wondered what was behind the mirror, looking back at her.

She dressed in a dark suit of trousers and jacket and a pair of heavy, sensible shoes. In the course of dressing she effectively searched the room, but found nothing that would serve as a weapon.

She sat down eventually and watched some screen; an old fast-paced slapstick comedy that kept her from thinking too much. The smartly uniformed young emissaries came calling at her door half an hour later and invited her to an audience with Molgarin.

The two young men walked on either side of her. Two guards followed a few paces behind. An elevator took them even farther down, pausing occasionally while muffled whirring and thudding noises announced what were probably blast shutters opening and closing.

Finally a short corridor walled with roll-doors brought them to a shallow ramp leading up to darkness. The guards stayed at the foot of the incline. She walked up between the two young emissaries; they took one of her arms each, gently but firmly. A rumbling noise behind them closed off the light.

The space they arrived in was a giant circular bunker, black-dark save for a series of twenty or so slitlike projections spaced regularly around the walls, apparently looking out across the cold gray desert to the distant ring of ash-colored mountains she had seen the day before. She wondered if the projections were recorded images, but guessed they were real-time. The sky above the mountains looked clear and thin and blue.

Distance was hard to estimate, but as they marched her toward the center of the bunker, she guessed it wasn't less than forty meters in diameter. The darkness made the encircling desert views shine, hurting her eyes.

The two emissaries halted; she stopped, too, and they let go of her arms.

Ceiling spotlights blazed in front of her, shining down onto a black circular dais; steps were just visible, gradations of shade against shade. The dais was crowned by a tall, plain throne made from a gleaming black material that might have been glass, jet, or even highly polished wood.

The man sitting in the throne was dressed in a sumptuous robe of many colors, though purple and gold predominated. The thick robe hid his frame; he could have been anything between of an average build and obese. His face looked plump but healthy; he was clean-shaven, and his head, covered in short black curls, was bare. There was at least one ring on each of his fingers, and he wore two sets of earrings and a pair of jeweled nostril studs. A brow-brooch glittered over his right eye.

His fingers sparkled magnificently as he clasped his hands lightly together. He smiled.

"Lady Sharrow," he said. "My name is Molgarin. We met once long ago, but I don't expect you remember; you were very young."

His voice was even and quiet; it sounded older than he looked.

"No, I don't remember," she said. She thought her voice sounded flat. "Why did you kill Miz like that?"

Molgarin waved one hand dismissively. "He cheated me out of something that was rightfully mine, many years ago. One of the skills one develops during the course of a long life is that of relishing one's revenge, and both planning and executing acts worthy of that skill." Molgarin smiled. "Finally, though, the truth is that I had him killed to distress you." The smile faded. "Please sit down."

The two young emissaries took her arms again and urged her forward; the three of them sat on the bottom step of the dais, their bodies twisted slightly so that they could still see Molgarin. He put his arms out to his sides slowly.

"I felt that you insulted my young emissaries here," Molgarin said. (The two young men both smiled smugly at her.) "And through them," Molgarin said, "me." He shrugged. "And so I punished you. I always make a point of punishing those who insult me."

"Yeah," the emissary in front of her said. "You should see what we have planned for that *cousin* of yours."

Molgarin cleared his throat, and the young man glanced up at him, then back at Sharrow with a conspiratorial leer. The spotlights reflected on his bald head.

"Whatever," Molgarin said, "the wretch is dead. But please don't imagine that all that has happened has been done to upset you, or as revenge on Kuma. My purpose has rather more substance than that."

Molgarin settled back in his throne, clasping his hands again. "You have—as you have doubtless realized by now—been used, Lady Sharrow. But used for something infinitely more worthwhile than personal gain or individual glory. The interests I am pleased to represent and I myself have little enough concern with the trappings of power. Our concern is with the health of Golter and its system, with the good of our species."

"You're not just another dick-head power-junkie?" she said matter-of-factly. "Oh, that's all right, then."

Molgarin shook his head. "Oh, dear," he said. "Something worse than cynicism must be abroad if even our aristocracy cannot accept that the rich and powerful may be motivated by purposes beyond acquiring yet more money and increased influence." He put his head to one side, as though genuinely puzzled. "Can't you see, Lady Sharrow? Once once has a certain amount of both, one turns to hobbies, or good works or philosophy. Some people become patrons of the arts or charities. Others may—charitably—be said to raise their own lives to the state of art, living as the common herd imagine *they* would live if they had the chance. And some of us attempt not merely to understand our history, but to influence meaningfully the course of the future.

"I grant that, in my case, because I am beyond the jurisdiction of the chancre we call the World Court, I have a greater personal interest in the future than most, because I expect to live to see it, but . . ." Molgarin hesitated, anticipating a reaction where she had given none. He went on. "Yes, I am what we choose to call immortal. I have been so for four centuries and expect to be so for considerably longer than that. . . . But I can see you are not impressed. Probably you don't believe me." He waved one hand. "Never mind."

"He *is*, you know," the emissary behind her whispered.

"Romantic children like your cousin," Molgarin continued, "would try to return us to a golden age that never existed, when people respected the aristocracy and power rested safely in the hands of a few individuals. My colleagues and I believe a more enterprising, more corporate style is required: one that releases the natural resourcefulness and entrepreneurial spirit of humanity, freeing them from the dead hand of the World Court and its miserable, gelding restrictions.

"For this, we—like your cousin—thought it prudent to gather as many of the treasures and achievements bequeathed to us by earlier and more progressive eras as we could, especially given the decidedly feverish atmosphere beginning to be generated by the approach of the decamillennium. Though in our case this sudden burst of acquisitiveness was as much to prevent the artifacts concerned from falling into hands as rash as your cousin's as to assist directly in our own plans, which do not need to rely on such vulnerably physical specifics."

Molgarin shrugged. "It's a shame, really; we thought at one point that your cousin might be of a mind with us. We even invited him to join us, but he proved to have these silly, vainglorious ideas of his own. He has, frankly, been a considerable annoyance to us." Molgarin shrugged. "No matter. Now that we possess all that you have so kindly provided us with, he can be dealt with at our leisure. These . . . gadgets will act as bait, if nothing else." Molgarin smiled thinly. "Your friend Elson Roa learned what happens when somebody at first cooperates and then opposes us; your cousin will find the lesson equally hard, though I intend to draw the process out a little where he is concerned. Conversely, those who help us—like Seigneur Jalistre, whom I believe you know from the Sea House—find the rewards considerable. I think I might give him something from this selection as a present."

Molgarin looked to one side. More ceiling lights came on, revealing Feril standing ten meters away, a bulky collar around his neck. The Lazy Gun was nearby, resting on a thick column of clear glass beside the odd vehicle with the single slanting wheel she had seen underneath the tower, and a dozen or so other bits and pieces of what appeared to be suitably ancient and exotic technology, none of which she recognized.

"Call me a sentimentalist," Molgarin said. "But I thought it only right to rescue everything the tower and its undercroft contained, even though all the rest is baublery next to the Lazy Gun. See—we even brought your little android friend. Molgarin raised his voice fractionally. "You may wave, machine."

Feril raised one hand stiffly and waved.

"It is worried about the restrainer collar," Molgarin explained to her, smiling. "Really, it is safe as long as it takes no more than a step or so from where it is now."

Molgarin got up from his throne and went over to the Lazy Gun. He was a little less plump and rather taller than Sharrow had guessed. He patted the Gun's gleaming brushed silver casing. She noticed that there was some sort of device fitted to it, too: a thick looped metal bar twisted around the right-hand grip, secured with a lock, prevented access to the trigger mechanism.

"This will," Molgarin said, "when the time is right, make life considerably easier for us." He turned to smile at her. "Really, your family has done so much for our cause, despite opposing us at practically every turn, that I feel almost mean that I have had to do what has been done." He moved away from the Gun, though not toward his dais. "Not to mention what has to be done."

Another spotlight came on and revealed a figure standing beside Molgarin. It was she.

Sharrow looked at herself. Her image was blinking in the strong overhead light, looking with an expression somewhere between fear and bewilderment at Molgarin.

This new Sharrow still had all her long black curled hair; she was dressed in a long, conservatively dark suit identical to that Sharrow had chosen earlier and now wore.

Molgarin reached out a hand to the other Sharrow; the woman offered him her left hand. Molgarin curled it up in his.

Sharrow felt the fingers in her own left hand start to ache. She tried to rise, but the young man behind gripped her around her neck while the one in front grabbed her feet.

Her image, hand crushed inside Molgarin's, cried out just before she did.

The pain disappeared, cutting off. She saw her image crying and touching her injured hand with the other.

Molgarin shook his head and smiled broadly at the real Sharrow. "If you only knew the self-restraint I have had to exercise with this toy," he said. He turned and stroked the woman's cheek. She seemed not to notice. "Though of course I have enjoyed her," Molgarin said. He looked back at Sharrow.

"Quite empty," he said, nodding at her image. "Her mind is quite empty." His smile grew wider. "Just as it should be, really."

He drew something from his robe. It was a HandCannon. "Allow me to introduce your clone, Lady Sharrow," he said. He pointed the gun at the woman's face. "Sharrow's clone," he said softly. "This is Sharrow's HandCannon."

The woman looked into the muzzle of the weapon, puzzled.

Sharrow struggled. "You *fuck*!" she screamed.

The clone glanced at her when she yelled, then looked away again. She gave no impression that she had recognized herself in Sharrow.

"Oh, I'm afraid we never really bothered to teach her any languages, Lady Sharrow," Molgarin said. "Never showed her a mirror, either," he added absently. He moved the gun right up to the woman's eye. She drew her head back just a little.

"She's sweet, isn't she, my little day-fly?," Molgarin said, moving the gun from one of the woman's eyes to the other. Her eyes crossed following the weapon's movements.

"I've had her for a couple of years now," Molgarin said conversationally. "I'm only sorry we didn't collect the necessary cells when you were in that mining hospital on Nachtel's Ghost, when I had you implanted with the crystal-virus. Still."

Molgarin continued to move the gun from side to side, then said, "Yes, I've enjoyed her company over the past two years or so. But I have the real thing now."

He fired into the woman's right eye.

Sharrow flinched, biting off a scream and feeling her eyes close on the image of the back of the woman's head disappearing in a red cloud and the body being blown backward into the darkness. She kept her eyes shut, feeling herself tremble uncontrollably; she tried to stop it but could not.

The young man behind her shook her. "Oops!" he whispered.

She opened her eyes, still trembling, her chest heaving. She choked the sobs back and listened to her own breathing, gazing through tears at Molgarin coming toward her.

"Oh, save your grief, Lady Sharrow," he said, putting the gun back into his robe, a small frown joining the faint smile on his face. "She was a blank," Molgarin said, spreading his hands. "A nothing; scarcely human." He laughed lightly. "For whatever that's worth."

He stood looking down at her for a moment, then swiveled and returned to his throne. He sat back with one leg crossed over the other.

"What, Lady Sharrow?" he said after a pause. "No insults, no threats, no curses; no bravado?" He shook his head. "I warn you I shan't be satisfied until you've called me something vile—doubtless involving that disagreeable word 'fuck'—*and* come up with some unlikely and painful-sounding fate you may merely wish on me but which I have the means—and for all you know the intention—of inflicting upon you." He contrived to look terribly amused with himself.

She was still breathing hard, fighting back her terror, trying to find strength from somewhere, from anywhere. She stared at him, now knowing how to express anything she felt.

Molgarin gazed at her with a look of tolerantly amused patience.

Then his expression changed. He frowned and looked up at the slit-views of the desert displayed in a wide circle around the chamber.

"*What?*" he said. He looked distracted. He peered at the screens, turning to look at those behind him. "*What?*" he said again, and raised a hand to one of his earrings. "*How?*"

She looked up. The slit-views of the desert were no longer static sections of a peaceful panorama. Dots danced in the skies above the mountains on three sides. What looked like a cavalry charge was taking place on two of the screens; Keep guards were running from the mounted troops, throwing their guns away.

"Well, do it!" Molgarin said, still with his hand at his

ear and looking away from her. "Now!" he shouted. "Anything!"

She saw the emissary in front of her looking worriedly at the one holding her arms. The one at her feet let go and drew a small laser pistol out of his uniform jacket.

There was sudden movement on several of the screens. A series of great gray explosions lifted slowly from the surface of the desert. They continued to expand and lift. They looked so immense, she expected to hear them, no matter how deep they were, but then they started to fall back in silence.

Molgarin turned back. He glanced at the two emissaries, then smiled shakily at her. "We seem to be—" he began.

The floor trembled and a full third of the slit-views suddenly went dark. Feril was staring intently at the confused scenes portrayed in the ones that were left. Molgarin glanced at the dark screens. The emissary holding the laser pistol stared at them.

"We seem to be under attack, Lady Sharrow," Molgarin told her. "Possibly from that irritating cousin of yours." He seemed to have difficulty swallowing. "I promise you this will be his last piece of romantic melodrama, lady. He'll suffer for this, and you'll watch him suffer." Molgarin looked at the two emissaries. "Mind her," he told them, then put his head back against the throne and gripped its arms tightly.

The topmost step of the dais rushed upward, taking the throne with it on a great gust of air and a thunderous rumble from beneath the chamber; the throne vanished into the ceiling ten meters overhead, leaving a single solid black column in the center of the circular room.

Before the two emissaries could react, the whole chamber shuddered, the remaining slit-views went black, and every light in the place blinked out, leaving utter darkness.

She hauled, twisted, and ducked, bringing the yelping emissary holding her arms tumbling over her back. "No!" he screamed.

There was a sudden snapping noise and a brief stuttering blink of light; then, as she threw herself to one side and the emissary rolled away from her, a scream that became a sizzling, gurgling noise. She lay, silent, on the steps. A smell of roasted flesh wafted over her.

"Twin?" said a tremulous, hesitant voice. It was answered by a bubbling noise. She started to move. "Twin?" the voice said again, an edge of panic in it now. Another bubbling, gurgling noise. She moved closer, correcting, anticipating. A tremor shook the bunker; there was a tremendous crack, and a crashing, tinkling noise off to one side. "Twin!" the voice screamed.

That last anguished shriek was enough. She stood silently, closing her eyes and lashing out with her foot.

"Tw—oof!" The voice cut off.

She stepped to one side; a blink of white laser light fired at where she had just been was enough to show her both of them, captured as though by a flash of lightning: the one who had held her, lying spread out on the floor at the foot of the steps leading to the black column, and the other one, crouched sideways on the floor in front of her, looking toward the steps, holding the laser in one hand and his lower chest with the other.

She swung her left foot at his head. The heavy, sensible shoe connected with a crack that jarred her whole leg. She fell to the floor.

The burbling sound came again from a few meters away, then a noise like a snore from nearby. The bunker shook once more, and she heard what sounded like debris falling somewhere.

"Lady Sharrow?" said a distant voice. Feril.

She said nothing. "Lady Sharrow," Feril said calmly. "I can see you. The laser pistol that the man you just kicked was holding flew from his hand and is lying approximately seven meters to your right." Feril paused. "I do not believe either of the young men will trouble you for the moment," it said.

She stood and walked quickly to her right, still silent.

"Just two steps farther," Feril said. "Stop. The pistol is now a meter to your left."

"Got it," she said, lifting the weapon.

"I believe one of the young men you disabled has the chip key to the explosive restrainer collar I am wearing," Feril said as another tremor shook the floor beneath them. "If you intend to remove it from me, that is," it said. It sounded apologetic.

She swiveled and started walking through the utter darkness. "Am I going the right way?"

"Stop," Feril said. "Yes—you are a step away from the young man you kicked."

She felt down. "So they weren't androids," she said.

"No, I believe they are clones, but otherwise perfectly normal human beings," Feril said. There was a pause. "Well . . ."

The man was breathing shallowly; she kept the gun pointed at where the breathing was coming from, then felt in his uniform jacket. "This feels like a chip key."

The android directed her to it. "The slot is at the back," it told her.

They key snicked in, the collar buzzed alarmingly, then a small white light flashed and the collar clicked open. She removed it and put it on the floor, which trembled again as she set the collar down. More smashing, tinkling noises sounded in the distance.

"Which direction to the Lazy Gun?" she asked.

"Your hand?" Feril said. She shivered, gritting her teeth as she put her hand out into the darkness. Feril held her bandaged hand gently; they walked forward. "Here it is," the android said.

She felt for the device and lifted it. "Great," she said. "Now all we have to do is try to find a way out of this place."

"If I may make a suggestion," Feril said, its voice calm. "While I was standing near it earlier, I had the opportunity of scanning the monowheeled vehicle taken from the tower. It appears to be in working order."

"Hmm," she said. "Or we could just wait here for my cousin to appear."

"Ah," Feril said carefully, "I am not sure about that."

"You're not?"

"I was able to observe the action taking place on the desert surface and in the nearby hills by way of the high-definition screens built into the walls of this place. Those in the first wave of comparatively lightly armed attackers were not identifiable. However those in the second wave, who seemed to be fighting both the Keep's defending forces as well as the first wave of attackers, were almost certainly Huhsz."

"*Huhsz?*" she said into the darkness.

"I believe so. There were certain insignia on the wings of the aircraft forming—"

"Are you sure?" she asked.

"I am sure of what I saw on the screens," Feril said cautiously.

"Fate," she said. Then, "But if Geis is mad enough to start crossing the Areas, they certainly are." She hoisted the Gun to her hip, holding it like a child. "Where's the monowheel?"

"This way."

The floor bucked beneath them, almost throwing her off her feet. Another devastating crash sounded from a distant part of the bunker.

The android helped her into the monowheeled vehicle's open cockpit. She shoved the Lazy Gun into the long footwell past what felt like a pair of hanging pedals, then she sat. There was a small compartment just to the rear of the cockpit; Feril climbed up and stuck its legs into it, sitting on the rear of the vehicle just in front of the tilted monowheel. The vehicle moved fractionally, with the hint of a whine.

"Now what?" Sharrow said, raising her voice above a roaring noise coming from somewhere ahead in the darkness. A gust of hot air blew around them, flinging dust into her face. She closed her eyes.

"Try this," it said. "Excuse me." She felt it lean over her, bending her forward; she heard a click, then lights glowed. The android leaned back again. She looked around at it; its face gleamed softly in the green light spilling from the vehicle's screen and instruments.

"Perhaps you should drive," she said.

"The position here is a little exposed," it told her. "Allow me to navigate."

"All right." She turned back and studied the controls: a twin-stalk hand grip with various buttons arranged on the columns, two pedals for her feet; various dials, screens, and touch-holos, and a head-up display seemingly hovering in midair in front of her.

She pressed a pedal; the monowheel's nose dipped. The other pedal brought it level again. She took the hand controls and squeezed both; her left hand was stiff and hurt a little, but it was bearable. There was a beeping noise from the instruments. Nothing else happened until she let go of the left grip. The monowheel leapt forward, banging her head against the seat's headrest.

"Stop!" Feril yelled.

She released the grip and they stopped quickly. She sensed the android turning behind her.

"Oh well," it said, turning back. "I don't believe you were too keen on that young man, anyway."

"Dead?" she asked.

"Thoroughly," Feril said.

She found the lights and another holo display, switchable between radar, ultrasound, and passive EM. "Hell," she said, "I had a unit like this on a bike once." She adjusted the display to optimum on EM.

She was sitting on the safety harness; she lifted, pulled the straps out, and fastened them around her. The holo display showed the whole bunker ahead of her in gray; the roof had collapsed in at least two places. The ramp she had been brought up was lying off to her left.

There was a muffled rumble from above, followed by another hot gust of air.

"I think we should leave this place fairly soon," Feril said.

"So do I," she said. "Ready?"

"Ready. I suggest you head for the ramp."

"On my way." She pressed the right grip lightly, sending the monowheel humming forward over the floor, then tipped the wheel; the vehicle turned. She looked at the squashed body of the young emissary she'd kicked and then run over. The monowheel was obviously quite heavy.

The other emissary lay still at the foot of the dais. His chest, neck, and face were still cooling. She thought she heard him moan.

She took the laser from her jacket, reached out over the side of the cockpit, and shot him twice in the head.

She paused just once more, at the other cooling body on the floor, then left her image lying there and powered the monowheel down the ramp.

There was a door.

"Just a minute," Feril said. "This seems to require a fairly simple radio code."

The door trundled aside, revealing a short corridor walled with roller doors.

"Well done," she said, moving the monowheel forward.

"My pleasure." The second roller door on the left rippled as a rumble of noise sounded all about them. "The door opposite that, I think," Feril said. "It will require the vehicle's cannon."

"Cannon?" she said, looking around at the android.

It nodded. "I believe this was a robo-tank hunter; a sporting vehicle used by the Vrosal Moguls following the—"

Another blast shook the roller door.

"Aiming and firing controls?" she said quickly.

"You aim the whole vehicle," Feril said. "The pedals control nose angle, the red cursor on the head-up is aimpoint, and the red button on top of the left hand grip fires."

She fired at the door; there was a burst of light from beneath the monowheel vehicle, an ear-ringing bang—and a single small hole appeared in the roller door. An instant later the door bulged and burst open as the shell exploded behind it.

Wreckage tumbled past them; she ducked, glanced back at Feril, who seemed to be unharmed, then eased the monowheel over the remains of the door. The vehicle rolled with uncanny smoothness into a circular-section tunnel fitted with twin toothed metal rails. There were flat rail-cars sitting on the rails; beyond them the tunnel spiraled upward.

"This is how I was brought in," Feril said. "I believe it leads to just below the surface."

"Maybe so, but how do we get over these flat cars?"

"I believe this vehicle is quite sophisticated for our day; I suggest just driving at them."

"All right," she said. She sent the monowheel forward slowly; it climbed over the flat cars as though they weren't there. She looked back and shrugged, then powered on up the spiral tunnel.

There were blast doors, but they had all been opened.

The monowheel hummed up the spiral tunnel for several minutes without incident, eventually emerging into an underground marshaling yard. She heard heavy-caliber gunfire echoing in the distance and saw flashes reflect off the ribbed gray concrete of the ceiling.

"That way, I think," Feril said, pointing past some supporting columns, away from the firing but toward an area of the yard where the view was hazed with smoke.

The monowheel raced over a tracery of tracks, keeping perfectly stable. The vehicle crossed a bridge over another level of the underground yard where smoke billowed up;

past the smoke they found the bodies of a Keep guard and one of the original attackers. The Keep guard still clutched his rifle. He had been beheaded, presumably by the bloody sword hanging by its lanyard from the hand of the other dead man, who lay against the railings of the underground bridge, his tunic nearly blown off by the grenade explosion that had killed him.

She stared at the man's naked right arm as they passed, slowing down for a better look.

She shook her head and accelerated again. The black mouth of another tunnel expanded to swallow the speeding monowheel.

The Advance Tactical Command Team entered the Deep Citadel through an aperture in the roof. They were covered in dust and stank of smoke. A couple of them had been lightly wounded, though really they had been almost unopposed. The Keep's own defenders seemed to have been effectively disarmed by their original attackers, who themselves had not been equipped with heavy ordnance.

One of the Keep's defenders had been captured and made to cooperate; he had guided them here, to the throne room.

The throne itself had gone, vanished into the roof; tech teams were still trying to break into the secure tunnels on the two levels immediately above. They suspected the master of this underground maze had flown and taken their quarry with him. There were many tunnels and escape routes into the desert and the mountains around, and they had not been able to find all of them in the short time they'd had available, between being granted permission to make this incursion and the launch of the attack itself, precipitated by that of the quaintly mounted and lightly armed forces who had preceded them.

They explored the remains of the circular chamber, using night-sights.

Ghosts, thought the Priest Colonel. *We are like ghosts.*

They were almost a kilometer underground, and they feared that once the man who had ruled over this sunken fortress had made good his escape, it would all be destroyed.

"Sir!" a yearfellow shouted from the other side of the black column that filled the middle of the dark chamber.

The Priest Colonel and his aides approached the yearfellow, standing pointing his quivering gun at the body on the floor.

They all looked at it for a while.

A couple of his men wept; several offered up muttered prayers of thanks.

"It's she," a voice said.

"Analysis," the Priest Colonel said. One aide crouched down to the body, unstrapping a bulky piece of equipment from his back pack. "Send the results direct to the Shrine," the Priest Colonel said. Another aide knelt, unhitching a powerful comm unit.

The Priest Colonel knelt, too, and removed one of his armored gloves. He reached out and touched the dead woman's pale, cold hand.

"I want physical tissue samples sent immediately to the Shrine," he said. The first aide took a small vial from his tunic and tore off a strip of flesh left near what had been the woman's right eye. He sealed the bloody scrap in the vial and handed it to another of the faithful, the young yearfellow who had first discovered the corpse.

"Take my own craft," the Priest Colonel told him, removing a ring from his finger and handing it to the yearfellow. "Fly straight to the Shrine. God go with you."

The yearfellow saluted and ran off.

The Priest Colonel stared at the body lying on the floor, as the gene-sampling machine hummed and clicked.

The battle had extended far and wide. The bandamyion-mounted troops had been de-planed from their transports, drawn up ready to attack, and had just begun their advance after the electronic disablement of the Keep's defenses when they had themselves been overwhelmed by the Huhsz forces, their light harness cannon, laser carbines, pistols, and ceremonial swords no match for the Huhsz high-velocity projectile weapons, smart missiles, pulse-shaped tunneling demolition charges and airborne X-ray lasers.

The monowheel sped through the shattered iris of a door low in the foothills above the desert, then turned smartly and accelerated up the hillside, every traversed ridge and boulder a soft ripple of movement as its wheel flowed or its body leapt over the obstructions, leaving only a faint trace of dust behind, while its camouflage-skinned body flowed with constantly changing patterns and shades of ochre and gray. Air roared; the transparent cockpit screen rose liquidly around her of its own accord, reducing the wind-blast.

She pressed the accelerator grip a little harder; the monowheel screamed still faster uphill, forcing her head back against the seat. She let the grip go; they coasted toward the summit of the ridge.

She braked the monowheel with the left-hand grip. The vehicle purred to a halt, then stood perfectly still and silent on its one slanted wheel.

The woman and the android looked down into the bowl of the desert. The battle was a great broad, slow column of smoke and dust over the center of the depression. A dozen or so craters had been punched into the surface of the desert, each a hundred meters or more across and half that deep; smoke piled out of three of them.

As they watched, a gray shape rose quickly out of one of the other craters, twisted once in the air and powered away, climbing rapidly as it angled northeast and took on the color of the sky. Its sonic boom sounded almost soft among the crackling detonations of munitions in the desert below.

She watched the aircraft go, its half-seen outline disappearing over the pink-lit mountain peaks, then she turned and squinted downward. She dragged the Lazy Gun out of the footwell and pointed it over the edge of the monowheel's cockpit, bringing its sights down to her eyes.

Perhaps six score bandamyions lay strewn across the desert, in small groups. A few of their riders were still firing, some of them using the bodies of their dead mounts as barely effectual cover from the armored Huhsz troops.

She looked up to see Huhsz weapon platforms cruising above the killing ground, firing monofilament bi-missiles and cluster rounds almost casually into the fray, their every discharge turning a few more of the fallen bandamyions into chopped meat and killing a rider or two.

A couple of arrowhead shapes circled high above, black on blue. To the south, beyond a distant filigree of contrails, the sky sparkled sporadically. The Lazy Gun showed no more detail.

She moved the monowheel fifty meters along the ridge to where a dead bandamyion rider lay, crushed underneath his fallen mount.

She looked, frowning, at his outthrown arm.

"*They* seem better armed," Feril said.

She turned and caught sight of a last group of riders; just a few black dots against the cinder-gray of the hills four or five kilometers away. A Huhsz gun platform exploded in the air near the group of riders and fell smoking to the ground.

She looked through the Lazy Gun again, turning up the magnification.

The view wavered. The bandamyion riders were like ghosts against the trembling image of the barren earth of the mountains. The group of ten riders ascended quickly to a pass in the mountains, then stopped. One of them stood up in his saddle. Another raised something to his shoulder and a pink spark flamed, washing out the view in the Gun's sights for a moment; she looked away and up and saw first one, then both of the arrowhead shapes high above blossom with silent fire against the blue, and start to fall.

She looked back through the Gun's sights.

The rider standing in the saddle—outlined against the start of the sunset, body made thin and sticklike by the wash of pastel light behind—seemed to look down into the desert. She thought she saw him shake his head, but the quivering image made it hard to be certain.

"That is, perhaps, your cousin," Feril said quietly. "I might be able to contact him, if you like."

She looked up at the android, then over to the rider crushed under his dead mount.

"No," she said, putting the Gun down. "Don't do that." The group of riders at the pass in the distant mountains were barely visible dots, a tiny dark flaw against the pale sunset light. "Just a moment," she said.

The monowheel dipped millimetrically and made the tiniest of whining noises as she got down from it and walked to where the dead man's arm stuck out across the dust from beneath the tawny pelt of the dead bandamyion. The rider's gun lay nearby.

She lifted the rider's cold gray hand up; the sleeve of his tunic fell farther back. She inspected the mark on his wrist.

"What do you see, Feril?" she asked.

"I see a patch of slightly abraded, callused skin, which I would guess extends to a two-centimeter wide ring around the dead man's wrist," Feril said. "There are two immediately adjacent outer rings, which look as though they formed the limits of a wider band of callusing in the past."

"Yes," she said. "That's what I see, too."

She let the dead man's hand fall back to the dust and picked up the light laser carbine that had fallen from his hand.

She walked around the bandamyion, looking for anything else, and saw the Keep-uniformed body of a guard lying half-in and half-out of a shallow trench downhill. She turned him over; he'd been shot with a small-beam laser.

She tried to fire the guard's gun, but it only clicked.

She looked into the distance. "Mind Bomb," she whispered.

She returned to the other side of the dead animal and looked up at the darkening blue vault above, then at the android sitting patiently to the rear of the perfectly still vehicle's cockpit, the tilted monowheel itself curving out behind Feril's slender body like a rounded fin.

"Do you know roughly where we are?" she asked.

"Only to within about one or two hundred kilometers," Feril said apologetically.

"That'll do," she said. "Think this glorified monocycle could take me to Udeste?" She dusted off her hands as she walked back to the vehicle.

"*Udeste?*" Feril's head moved back a fraction.

"Yes," she said. "I was thinking of heading into the sunset and turning right when I saw the ocean, but maybe you can find a more direct route, if this thing has the range."

"Well," Feril said. "I suppose I could, and I suppose *this* could, technically. But aren't there forces between here and there who might attempt to stop us?"

"There are indeed," she said, swinging back up into the cockpit. She patted the Lazy Gun. "Though if we can get the lock off this, they won't be *able* to stop us."

"I am not sure that will be easy," Feril said. "What if we cannot release the weapon?"

She looked into the machine's sunglass-eyes, seeing herself reflected twice. She watched her tiny, distorted images shrug.

"If they get us, they get the Gun, too, and everybody gets to go with a bang." She pushed the Lazy Gun forward into the footwell and sat in the seat, hauling on the harness.

"To tell the truth, Feril," she said, "I really don't care anymore." She glanced up at the android. "You don't have to come, though; just point me in the right direction. I'll let you off wherever. You can say you were abducted; you'll get home."

Feril was silent for a second, then said, "No, I'll accompany you, if you don't mind. Given that you are prepared to risk your life, it would be lacking in grace of me not to gamble the loss of a week's memories."

She shrugged again, then looked toward the sunset, to the pass in the mountains.

The riders had gone. Before she looked away, a single large aircraft powered into the skies beyond and headed northwest, angling across the sunset and dispatching another distantly diving arrowhead shape above as though it was an afterthought.

The monowheel vehicle turned and rolled away down the far side of the ridge, picking up speed as it descended toward a dry valley, then accelerated smoothly away in a trail of chill, falling dust.

24

Fall into the
Sea

The evening light deepened as the monowheel spun quickly down a succession of shallow clinker valleys devoid of snow, vegetation, or significant obstructions toward a range of mountains, then came out into a broad gulf between jagged peaks whose summits still held a snow-pink trace of sunset. They found a wide shelf of sand and gravel that traced a barren contour on that great valley and drove along it; after a few kilometers its surface bore a dusting of snow that thickened gradually as they drove. The tree line was fifty meters lower down.

"Is this a road?" she said, puzzled, as they headed into and out of a long, narrow side valley she'd have thought it easier to bridge at the mouth.

"I believe it is a raised beach," Feril said. "Caused by the waters of a temporary lake, probably formed when a glacier block—"

Feril went silent, then said, "Electromagnetic pulse."

"What?"

The mountaintops on the other side of the broad valley were suddenly blazing white.

She stopped the monowheel.

They turned and looked behind them, but the snow-caped shoulders of the mountain at their back cut out much of the sky.

"I believe the Keep has been destroyed by a thermonuclear device," Feril said.

She watched for a moment as high, feathery clouds above the mountains slowly faded yellow-white, then started the monowheel again and powered on along the sand-and-gravel road.

The ground-shock arrived a little later. The monowheel absorbed the pulse without a murmur, but they saw the snow-smothered ground nearby shake and ripple.

Sharrow and Feril looked up the white mountain slopes on their right, to see them covered with hazy white clouds, gradually spreading and enlarging.

"Oh, shit."

"I believe those are avalanches."

"So do I. Hang on."

They raced along the white shelf of the ancient beach to the shelter of an outcrop of rock. The avalanches were a smoothly building roar of noise that terminated in a blast of icy air and a sudden dimming of the late-evening light; the sky above the summit of the outcrop disappeared. A tearing dim grayness flowed all around the sheltering rock-face, and a whistling noise came through the throaty bellow of the avalanche. They were suddenly surrounded by their own heavy, swirling snowfall.

A noise like thunder sounded down-slope as the tsunami of snow and ice hit the forest.

When the roaring stopped and the last few flakes had fallen around them, they brushed themselves down and went slowly on through a dim white haze across the ice-rubbled mounds of settling snow. She found the cockpit heater control and turned it up.

Feril leaned over the side of the vehicle and peered underneath as they traversed one of the house-high pillows of snow.

"Impressive," she heard the android say. She glanced around. "The wheel beneath has ballooned to this width," Feril said, spreading its hands over half a meter apart, "and appears to grow spikes where it contacts the surface." The section of angled wheel protruding behind Feril was thin as a knife.

"Yes," she said, turning to the front again. "Well, don't lean back."

The parallel road had all but disappeared under the icy

debris and scattered falls of rock. Downhill, through a haze of settling snow, much of the forest had disappeared under the white flows, the shattered trunks of the trees sticking jumbled from the snow like broken bones.

She kept the monowheel on what felt like the right level until they saw a huge flute of ice and snow like a scree slope leading down through the wrecked forest to the flat valley floor. She swung the vehicle onto it and down while the last of the day's light leached from the sky.

They followed the frozen river for an hour through the moonlit darkness, then stopped.

She parked the machine off the white highway of river in the shelter of a C-shaped bay of rocks topped by snow-dusted trees. Feril studied the lock on the Lazy Gun while she stretched her legs and inspected as much of the monowheel as she could by moonlight.

The single wheel was angled at about thirty degrees off the vertical; it looked solid but couldn't be. She remembered the bike back in the warehouse in Vembyr, but even flex-metal couldn't do what this material seemed to be able to. She got Feril to move the vehicle forward a little. The single wheel seemed to flow rather than merely revolve. It was the color of dulled mercury; its chevron-corrugated tread reminded her of the milled edge of a silver coin.

The cannon muzzle was scooped into the chin of the vehicle on the center-line. The shining tubes sticking from the rear, which she had mistaken for engine exhausts, were the recoilless weapon's gas-ports. Feril checked the weapon-state screen and reported that they had another thirty-one shells left of various types.

"I'm afraid the cannon will remain our most powerful weapon," Feril said sorrowfully, putting the Lazy Gun down and tapping the trigger-lock. "This is a cryptogenetic code-lock. It is impossible to open without the correct base-sequence key."

"Well, never mind," she said. "It was always a long shot."

"I am sorry," Feril said. "However, I believe I have worked out the link between your interest in the mark on the wrist of the man you looked at earlier and the reason you wish to go to the province of Udeste."

She hauled herself back into the vehicle. "Took you a while," she said, yawning.

"Yes," Feril said contemplatively. "I am a little disappointed myself."

"Well," she said, "you can redeem yourself by taking the night shift. I'm tired."

"I shall drive with all due care and attention."

"Yes," she said, sliding down into the footwell, yawning. "Lantskaar welcomes careful drivers."

They put the Lazy Gun in the compartment behind the cockpit; Feril sat on the Gun with its legs either side of the driving seat. After a little experimentation, she found a comfortable way of snuggling down into the footwell while the android leaned over to the controls in a position that would have been torturously uncomfortable for a human, but with which it assured her it was perfectly happy.

She slept while Feril drove through the night.

So far, so good.

Eh? What?

I said, So far, so good.

The man who was really the Lazy Gun was sitting in the monowheel cockpit alongside her. There wasn't room for him, but he was there.

What do you want now? she asked the Gun. I want to sleep.

I beg your pardon. I just wanted to say, well done. Sorry I can't do any destroying yet, but like I said, we'll see what we can do. . . .

Yes, yes, she said. Now go away, I'm tired.

All right. Good night, Lady Sharrow.

Good—Fate, I don't believe this; I'm saying good night to my own subconscious.

Of course you are, the Gun said.

Now sleep.

The air was warm around her as she spun through it, safe in the midst of the surrounding cold. The android was at the controls. The antique machine hummed beneath her, transporting her among reflections.

In her dream she hugged the broad neck of the trafe bird.

The sky was an insane blue; an endless curve of land died before the wheel, forever reeling away toward an expanding horizon. The mountains became snow-dusted hills, which became tundra. They rolled across the plains of frozen lakes among the mountains, found old tracks through the hills and skirted the marshy tundra until they found an old turnpike, its metalling cracked like the surface of an ancient painting and dotted with the erupted blisters of ice hummocks.

They avoided settlements and once swung off a better-maintained length of the tundra road to let a military supply road-train pass, but otherwise saw no sign of people. Feril's internal knowledge of Golter's geography didn't cover northern Lantskaar and the Embargoed Areas in great detail, and the monowheel seemed to have no strategic navigational systems whatsoever, but the android was what it described as cautiously certain they were now around the center of the Areas, near the Farvel coast, a thousand kilometers due west of the fjord where they had found the Gun. They had traveled approximately seven hundred kilometers from the Keep.

They saw many aircraft contrails, and on one occasion heard but did not see low-flying jets while speeding through a low forest by the side of a long lake.

The monowheel absorbed the shock of potholes and boulders, leapt larger depressions, and turned its wheel to a tall ellipse to ford rivers. Once, when she was driving quickly up a shallow slope on a hillside toward a long bridge that had fallen into a ravine, the vehicle slammed to a stop as she was still squinting at the revealed rim of broken concrete and thinking about braking.

She turned around to Feril.

"Did you do that?"

"No," the android said. "The vehicle would appear to be what is sometimes called 'smart.'" Feril sounded slightly condescending. "Though not sentient, of course."

"Of course."

"I myself was just about to suggest braking."

"Right," she said. She looked for a way down into the ravine, then whirled the monowheel around toward a hairpinning side road descending into the forest.

She walked, windmilling her stiff arms, by the side of a waterfall in low hills they thought must be near the northwestern limits of the Areas. The android stood in the pool at the foot of the waterfall, the water lapping around its thighs. She was determined not to ask it why it was doing this.

"Hey," she said, peering under the rear of the vehicle. "There's a mark, a gouge or something here." She looked at the android. "What happened to the due care and attention?"

"Oh," Feril said quietly, staring into the water. "That will be a bullet mark."

"A *bullet* mark?" she said.

Feril nodded slowly, still staring at the water. "We picked that up last night at the Lantskaarian border." It looked at her briefly, head turning smoothly to and fro. "It all happened very quickly," it said reassuringly. "By the time I had an opportunity to waken you, we were out of danger. I thought it best to let you sleep." Its voice was soft.

She was not sure what to say.

Feril stooped, dipping suddenly, one hand flicking into the water, then it straightened and walked toward her, a half-meter long fish flapping powerfully in its hand.

She looked at it.

"You said you were hungry," Feril explained. "I suggest we grill the fish with the laser."

She nodded, wondering why they had not thought to ask the android's help when they had all been starving at the fjord.

"Thank you, Feril," she said. She no longer felt hungry, but she supposed she had better eat. "I'll get the Gun."

They reached the Security Franchise strip that afternoon, traversing several military roads in the forested hills while Feril monitored leakages of comm and sensory wavelengths. It guided them away from the roads and the areas where the electromagnetic clutter was thickest; they took to tracks, then paths, then the forest floor, thick with rotting leaf-scales and moss-covered boulders.

They crossed what they guessed was the border into Caltasp by wading the monowheel through a rushing stream beneath a ramshackle electrified fence; the vehicle reduced the portion of the wheel under its body almost to nothing at one point, and at another was actually afloat, in a dark pool under the everleafed trees. Even then, it remained perfectly stable and level in the water, gyros whining distantly. A light flashed on the instruments, and Feril suggested pressing the glowing area; when she did, the monowheel surged forward through the water, leaving a foamy wake.

The machine purred out of the water, rose smoothly up the muddy bank, and entered the forest again.

"Great toy," she said.

"Quite."

They returned through the concentric layers of surface-traveling civilization to forest paths, then tracks, then winding metaled roads in the foothills, then a narrow turnpike, heading arrow-straight through the plantations of low crop-forests. Vapor trails wove a net through the clear blue sky, and twice again they heard low-flying jets.

A third group of jets went right over them; this time there was no warning build-up of noise, just an impression of their shadows—a single flicker across the road—followed by a stunning, titanic slap of sound and the scream of their engines fading in both directions at once while the trees on either side of the road whipped back and forth in the sudden storm, losing scales, twigs, and whole branches. The monowheel reacted to the gust by squatting slightly, but otherwise remained level.

They rolled on.

She had never seen a turnpike in Caltasp so deserted.

"Where *is* everybody?"

"It's a little worrying," Feril said above the slipstream noise. "I've been monitoring the public-broadcast channels, and several of them appear to consist only of a sound track of what I believe is called martial music. Other channels have been showing nothing but old entertainments. There have been a couple of weak EMPs in the last hour, too."

She looked around at it. "You mean nukes?" she asked.

"Perhaps not; they may have been caused by charged-particle weapons."

She turned back, watching the trees stream past on either side. "Either way," she said.

They side-stepped two military convoys by taking once to the forest and once to the hummocked tundra. The turnpike avoided towns and other settlements as a matter of course.

The tundra became huge prairies of grain.

They plowed a course through one vast field to avoid a roadblock, then on an ordinary but straight road accelerated to outpace a helicopter that seemed to be trying to follow them.

She switched roads several times immediately after that, always heading north or west through the dying light of the cold afternoon.

Finally the military traffic became too thick, and they left the metaled ways altogether. They took to tracks and forest fire-breaks, old drove-ways and canal tow-paths. They passed hill-villages and dark-looking towns, old orchards and walled compounds; the monowheel rose and fell and banked and paced through the gloaming.

She thought she smelled something in the air as they rolled down the bed of a half-dried river, over water-meadows and sand banks and through clear shallows between hills bright and clear in the winter dusk. The river splayed out, deepening to become a tree-studded estuary; they took to the bank, then summited a sand dune.

They were facing the sea.

Feril drove through the depths of the night, once she had gone to sleep. They had made good time along the cold beaches of the coast and watched the skies to the south and east flicker and pulse with different-colored lights. Feril picked up officially sanctioned broadcast reports of limited engagements taking place between Security Franchise units—backed by World Court licensed forces—and the armed services of Lantskaar, following acts of aggression and an invasion by the latter; the situation was being contained and there was no need to worry. The broadcast ended abruptly in another strong, electromagnetic pulse.

Stretched forward over the cockpit, Feril only glanced at the monowheel's night-sight display now and again to check on its sensitivity. Sea, surf, beach, and dunes were bright in the moonlight. The strand was flat and smooth in places, strewn with braided streams and shallow pools in others; the monowheel thrummed across it all as though over glass.

She was on a station platform, in the middle of a snowy plain. An old steam train huffed behind the crowd of people. The Gun was there again, but it wasn't saying anything this time; it stayed in the background while she said good-bye to Miz and Dloan and Zefla and Cenuij. They were whole and fit and well, as she'd have liked to remember them. She tried not to cry as she hugged them and said good-bye. She kept thinking there was somebody else there, too; somebody she could see only from the corner of her eye, a faceless figure in a wheelchair, but whenever she turned to look at the figure, she disappeared.

Then she saw Froterin and Cara and Vleit standing behind the others, and they looked great and hadn't aged at all, and she laughed and cried and hugged them, too, and they were all talking at once and everybody was hugging everybody else, all so glad to see one another after all this time, but soon it was time for them all to go, and her eyes filled with so many tears, she couldn't see properly as they all boarded the train, waving and smiling sadly as the old engine went huff, huff, and gradually pulled the dark carriages away from the little station in the snow.

She and the Gun watched the train disappear into the white distance. Then she looked at the Gun and It smiled.

The sleeping woman stirred beneath the android, sighing and turning over in her sleep. Feril pushed the speed up as they flashed past a town, burning in the darkness. More lights flared in the sky to the south, and the broad band of junklight sparkled intermittently.

The monowheel forded two rivers and swam three.

Lady Sharrow woke with the dawn.

The sky was a shroud of low cloud; light drizzle fell. They zipped along the tide-wet shore, leaving their single cryptic track behind on the winter beach. The sky ahead looked dark, solid, and certain after the hollow blueness and the overcast's gray indeterminacy.

The beach went on into the distance, and she let the speed climb until the monowheel would go no faster. The cockpit closed right over and the noise was still colossal. The streaked sand and water flashed at them and beneath them to be pressed and flung, arcing and falling into the whirling vortex that the vehicle left behind as it screamed along the shore, its whole body humming, vibrating like a tensed, quivering animal, their speed so great that its suspension was finally registering bumps and small shocks. She smiled. The dunes to her right were a blur. The velocity readout indicated that they were traveling at about seventy percent of the speed of sound.

Feril was hunched over the rear of the liquid glass. She risked a glance. The android's expressionless face gave no hint of its emotions.

The beach became uncomfortably bumpy and changed to a mixture of sand and gravel; drizzle sounded on the screen like blasted shot. She relaxed and slowed the car until the cockpit glass opened a hole above her head. The roaring noise was still terrific.

"You okay?" she shouted.

"Extremely!" Feril said loudly, and sounded as though it meant it. "What an exhilarating experience!"

She drove on; three hundred kilometers an hour suddenly seemed terribly slow. Surf boomed to their left as the drizzle became rain and the cloud overhead thickened. She took the monowheel into the dunes in the cloud-dark noon.

On the far side of a stinking marsh guarded by ancient, crumbling concrete monoliths and a series of weed-scummed lagoons, they came to the fence. It looked dilapidated but still strong. There was a guard tower nearby, but it was unoccupied and strung with blow-weed.

The cold wind moaned through the hexagons in the fence and the metal support legs of the tower.

They got out of the vehicle. Feril could detect no surveillance devices. She considered using the cannon just for speed, but it would be noisy; she cut the fence's steel mesh strand by strand with the laser instead. The monowheel curtsied through the hole, and they rolled on through the chill levels of marshland beyond.

She brought the vehicle splashing out of a greasy, polluted stream and charged it up the wet-dark sand to the bottom of a dip between two tall dunes.

The Sea House lay in the rain-dulled distance, its dark bulk shrouded in squalls and cloud. Its top hundred meters were hidden, the spires and towers vanishing into the murk like the giant trunks of a petrified forest.

The cold wind gusted; a stench of rotting seaweed flowed around the stationary vehicle like a slimy, stroking hand.

"Ah-ha," said Feril.

"Yes," she said, tilting the wheel toward the slope of

gravel beach beneath and squeezing the throttle. "Ah-fucking-ha."

The monowheel skimmed easily across the weed and pools in the bay, climbed the greasy stones of the causeway's steep sides without a pause and came to rest near the middle of the isthmus, facing the Sea House and standing absurdly on its single disc like a resting bird. She climbed out; Feril remained in the vehicle.

She walked, limping, to the great iron door overhanging the incline at the end of the causeway. Her hands were empty; they shook. Her belly grumbled and she felt faint. The blood pumped and coursed within her, and with each beat of her heart the whole vast edifice seemed to quake and pulse and shiver, as though for all its mountainous solidity, the Sea House was merely a projection, something held in the power of her blood-quickened eyes.

There was no sign that anybody had noticed her approach. Clouds bundled around the House's crenellated slopes, snagged there, and were dragged away again. The rain was cold on her face. She reached the tilted gatehouse and found a heavy stone. She slammed the rock against the great iron door repeatedly. Chips of stone and rust fell together to the damp cobbles. Her muscles ached; the bones in her arms seemed to resonate with each quivering concussion.

"All right! All right!" a voice said. She dropped the rock and stooped to the opened grille.

"What do you want?" the voice said from the darkness.

"In," she said.

"What?"

"Let me in," she said.

"Who are you? What's your name? Have you made an appointment?"

"No. Let me in. Please let me in. It's very important."

"What? No appointment? This is disgraceful. Certainly not, go away. And if that's your car, you can't park there."

"Stand away from the door," she said, stepping slowly backward.

"*What?*" said the small, scratchy voice.

"Stand well away from the door if you want to live," she called, still walking backward. "Stand back!"

She turned and ran, waved to the android in the

monowheel, then dived to the causeway's flagstones, her arms over her head.

The monowheel's cannon boomed eight times in quick succession; immediately following the first blast there began an answering sequence of eight thunderous explosions. After the last, she got up and ran to the monowheel, which was already moving toward her. Feril put out a hand and hauled her easily into the cockpit.

She took the controls as Feril leaned back, sending the monowheel curving down the causeway while debris was still falling from the wrecked gatehouse. As the monowheel splashed into the shallow pools among the weed at the bottom of the causeway, the Sea House's great iron door fell forward in one vast, dusty, smoking piece and slammed into the slope, cracking the causeway and throwing flagstones and cobbles into the air. The rest of the gatehouse's facade crumbled and slid, collapsing into a smoking pile around the fallen door and leaving a huge broil of dust above a ramp of rubble and a dark, gaping breach.

The monowheel sped away, charging around the curve of the bay in front of the Sea House's curtain wall and into the slack retreating waters of the old tide, wading to a point in the towering walls a third of the way around the structure from the wrecked gatehouse.

"There," Feril said.

She turned the vehicle toward the scooped trench of a weed-draped tunnel in the towering granite walls.

The monowheel crept up the stinking sewage outfall to a portcullis of corroded iron bars. A torrent of dirty water fell from a level halfway up the two-meter-diameter grille. She picked up the laser.

"It looks very rusty," Feril said. "Try nudging it."

She sent the monowheel forward; the iron frame creaked, then shifted. She reversed the monowheel quickly. The portcullis fell forward, splashing into the tunnel and releasing the damned-up pond of sewage behind. She heard it flowing past them and almost passed out with the smell.

They traveled another twenty meters up the sewer before reaching a junction beyond which the pipes became too narrow for the monowheel. They looked up; gray light filtered down through a grating. Feril stood on the top of the vehicle and pushed the grating up and back.

The android climbed out; she passed it the Lazy Gun,

then Feril pulled her up to join it. She strapped the Gun to herself while Feril replaced the grating. She handed Feril the laser rifle and kept the pistol for herself.

They were in a broad, damp gallery; tall windows on one side contained not a single intact pane. Rain gusted in. Moss grew on dulled mosaics underfoot as the woman and the android jogged along to the darkness of a doorway. They turned a corner and ran right into a small monk walking toward them, one iron-manacled hand chained to the wall at his side, his gaze fixed on the steaming bowl he was carrying.

Sharrow bumped into the monk, splashing the gruel over his habit and the wall at his side. He looked angry for a moment, then his mouth fell open as he saw the android. His brows furrowed as he looked at their chainless hands. He had time to look frightened, briefly, before Sharrow cracked his head off the stones above his chain-track; he slid unconscious down the wall.

Feril looked back at the prone figure as they ran on.

They climbed what seemed a never-ending spiral of steps rising out of a vast gallery, exiting at the top of a massive stone tower and crossing to the main House over a thin stone bridge, high over an ancient deserted dock where rusting cranes stood pierced with rust and coated with moss. Thigh-thick lengths of rope lay coiled on the rotting docksides like enormous worm-casts.

They followed the chain system through drafty corridors and dark halls, turning each time the number of rails decreased. They had to hide twice as monks passed them in gloomy corridors. The second group carried rifles and were running in the direction of the distant gatehouse.

The chain system's inset hierarchy took them constantly upward and inward, ascending broad shadowy flights of steps, ramps that spiraled and zigged and zagged higher and higher into the middle, then upper, levels of the House. Halls and balconies, tunnels and corridors, filled the stonespace; their feet sounded off paving-slabs, wooden planks, ceramic tiles, and pierced metal. The tracks on the walls were reduced to two, then one as they penetrated the vast building.

Finally they found a corridor whose walls were quite smooth, with no rails whatsoever. They walked cautiously into a small walled courtyard ceilinged with chill gray mist where bedraggled plants lay beaded and heavy with moisture. What appeared to be a well in the center of the courtyard looked down into a vast hall, where they saw tiny figures moving to and fro. A rancid draft of air rose from the well, bringing the noise of small, alarmed voices.

They looked around at the windows facing onto the hidden garden. Feril nodded at a door in one corner.

It wasn't locked. They walked into a short corridor lined with pornographic holos. Feril stopped outside a door. She could hear voices now, too.

They burst in. The girl in the bed gave a shriek and ducked under the bedclothes. The fat, naked man sitting at the screen whirled around, his eyes wide. A senior brother's habit lay folded on a chair. She lasered the screen; it had been on sound only. The naked man put his arms up, sheltering himself from the debris of the exploded screen.

"You have five minutes," she told him, "to take us straight to any 'Honored Guests' who've arrived here in the last three days." She looked at Feril. "Start counting."

The fat man sat up, trying to muster his dignity. He took a breath.

"And you had better fucking know who I mean," she told him, before he could speak, "or you're cooked meat."

"Daughter," the man said, standing, his voice confident and controlled. He pointed to the habit on the chair. "At least allow—"

"Oh, at least *nothing*," she said, suddenly angry. She fired the gun at the floor between his feet. Splinters burst from the varnished wood. There was a yelp from beneath the bedclothes, and the fat man hopped on one foot, holding the other. His eyes had gone wide again. "Move!" Sharrow yelled.

They walked through the apartments; the fat brother limped, leaving a trail of blood. She limped after him, frowning at the red spots they were leaving in a trail behind them. She kept looking back. They climbed steps, crossed a terrace underneath a roof of stained glass, and then the fat man pointed a shaking hand at a door.

She stationed him two meters back from the door, a finger to her lips. "Keep him there," she told Feril quietly. The android stood behind the naked man, gripping his quivering shoulders. She went to the wall at the side of the door and tested the handle. It turned and she pushed; the door swung open.

"No!" the fat man screamed, an instant before his torso exploded open through a giant red crater in his midriff. Blood gushed from his mouth as his eyes rolled back and his entrails flooded out. She ducked and rolled across the bottom of the door, firing.

Feril let go of the man and stepped to the side.

Sharrow jumped up and stuck her head around the side of the door; Molgarin lay on the floor inside, screaming.

"*You?*" she said, frowning.

Molgarin was propped up on his elbows, howling. He was dressed in a dull habit; the HandCannon lay where he had dropped it. The laser had burned deep into one shin and shattered the other; blood pumped onto a dark carpet.

He saw her. "Don't kill me!" he screamed. "Don't kill me! I'm not immortal! I'm an actor, not some warlord! My name's Lefin Chrolleser! I worked in a rep company in Tront! I swear! For pity's sake, *please*! He *made* me do it! He *made* me! I'll take you to him! Please don't kill me!" He put his head back, sobbing and spluttering. "God, my legs! My legs!" He looked back at her, eyes streaming, and wailed, "Oh, please don't kill me, please. . . . I promise I'll take you to him. . . ."

Sharrow looked at Feril. "Could you carry him?" she asked.

The android nodded. "I think so."

She burned the man's leg wound with the laser to stop the blood. His screams echoed through the stained-glass rooms.

They walked unhindered through the midst of the chained. Nobody followed them. Feril carried the moaning man. She limped in front, following his whispered directions.

They took a creakingly ancient lift, descending into the bowels of the House down a circular shaft.

He watched the scene at the gatehouse on the monitor. Armed monks swarmed over the wreckage and ran along the walls. Ancient weapons were hauled out from under tarpaulins inside long-neglected towers; geriatric tanks were trundled out of storage and hauled into positions where their rusty cannons could cover the breach.

He shook his head. He ought to have attended to this. He had been foolish to rely so much—as they had—on the reputation of the place keeping people away.

He checked the bank of broadcast and subscription-beamed monitors again. Most stations local to southern Caltasp were blanked out. The rest of Golter was reporting on the small war that had broken out with the Rebel States. The Court was keeping a surprisingly firm grip on the relevant facts. His own information was that the war had already gone tactically nuclear, and larger weapons couldn't be ruled out. It wasn't the end of the world, but it was depressing and elating at the same time; another pointless war, another increase in Golter's lamentably high background-radiation level and yet more destruction. . . . But this might be the beginning of the end for the World Court. The time might be coming.

He looked at the House monitor screens. They really ought to have proper security surveillance. There wasn't even any surviving record of exactly what had happened at the gate; the recording apparatus had been sighted in the gatehouse itself.

The chamber's rear-interior door chimed. He checked the monitor.

It was that fool Chrolleser. . . . He started to look away. . . . and Sharrow.

He looked back, stunned.

Chrolleser looked feverish and sweaty; he held the HandCannon he'd asked to keep after the fiasco in the Keep. It was pointed at Sharrow's head.

"Sir!" he gulped. "Sir—look! I have her! And she has brought the Gun!"

He closed his mouth; it must have fallen open. He pulled the monitor view back. The two were alone in the long corridor that led back to the old elevator shaft. The Gun was strapped to Sharrow's side. Her eyes looked old and defeated, her face gray and wan. So *that* was who had wrecked the door! He should have guessed.

"Come in!" he yelled, punching the door button. He buzzed the Restricted Library, switched the desk camera on, and directed the transmission to the library, then jumped up from his seat and ran across the chamber, up the flight of stone steps and along the balcony to the opening door.

He skidded to a stop in front of it as Sharrow clicked a

magazine back into place in the stock of the HandCannon, cocked the gun, and pointed it at a spot between his eyes.

Behind her Chrolleser seemed to have fainted, head lolling to one side, even though he was still standing up. Then something moved underneath his bulky habit, and he bent forward. The actor collapsed to the floor, moaning; the android that the team had taken with them from Vembyr slid out from under the back of Chrolleser's habit, holding a laser rifle.

He was aware that his mouth had opened again. He stared from Sharrow to Chrolleser to the android, then back to Sharrow again.

She smiled. "Hello, Geis," she said. The HandCannon in her bandaged hand barely wavered as she punched him in the jaw with her other fist.

"No! No, Sharrow! You've got the whole thing wrong! I captured Molgarin. He's my prisoner. Look, I'm just glad you're safe!" He laughed. "That's quite a right jab you have there, but come on, this is ridiculous. Sharrow. Untie me."

The chamber was big, irregularly shaped on several levels and tall-ceilinged. It was so packed with treasures that it looked like nothing more than a giant junk shop. Geis sat tied to one seat, Molgarin or Chrolleser or whatever his name was to another. The android stood in front of them, the laser rifle in its hand. Geis had bled a little from one side of his mouth. He worked his chin now and again as he talked to her. The other man was mumbling, barely conscious.

Sharrow walked around the big stone table that dominated the chamber's central area and on which she had deposited the Lazy Gun. The enormous table was loaded to overflowing with a whole trove of treasures; the less valuable items were not quite priceless.

She looked up from the casing of the *Universal Principles* to a rack of weapons she recognized from the undercroft of the tower in the fjord. A system of pulleys kept a load of jewel-encrusted harnesses suspended over the table. The harnesses looked about the right size of bandamyions. On the wall behind were a couple of giant diamond-leaf ikons from the time of the Lizard Court. They were each the size of a house, and she had read about them in school; they had been missing for three thousand years. There was a small door underneath the two ikons with wall-tracks leading from it; the chain system extended even to here.

She drew her hand over the ceramic cover of a book probably old enough to have predated the first millennium, and looked around the chamber again, rubbing her fingers together. She thought she recognized some of the more classical treasures from the old gold-mine store, deep under the Blue Hills in Piphram.

"You've always liked a clutter, haven't you, Geis?"

"Sharrow, please," Geis said. "You're making a terrible mistake here."

She turned and frowned at him. "Good grief," she said. "Do people actually say that? Well, well."

She opened the case of the *Universal Principles*. The Crownstar Addendum lay inside, draped over what looked like a piece of cut glass the size and approximate shape of a crown.

"What's this?" she said, hauling the heavy, thickly glittering ring out. There was some sort of writing engraved around the rim; she didn't recognize the alphabet.

"That," Geis said, "is the Crownstar."

"This lump of glass?" She didn't try to disguise the disappointment in her voice. The so-called Crownstar's prongs were cut off-set, like a series of sharp, canted escarpments.

"It's not glass," Geis said, sighing. "It's diamond. A single, pure flawless diamond. Be careful with it."

"Uh-huh," she said skeptically. "Feril?"

The android looked at the torus in her hands.

"It is a diamond," it said.

"See?" Geis said to her, smiling. "The Crownstar."

"Well," Feril said with a hint of apology in its voice, "it might be that, too, but originally it was part of a triple-filament deep-crust drill-bit."

"What?" Geis said, looking at the android as though it were mad.

"Fourth millennium," Feril said. "They lost one drill at ninety kilometers under the Blaist mountains, and the replacement was never used. That must be part of the back-up head."

"What about the inscription?" Geis protested. "The runes?"

"Serial numbers," Feril said.

"Rubbish!" Geis said. He looked furious, but didn't take

the argument any further. Molgarin/Chrolleser groaned in the seat alongside. Geis glared at him. "Oh, shut up!"

Sharrow put the Crownstar back in the casing with the Addendum and closed the cover.

She paced on around the table. She drew an ornamented, jewel-studded sword from an equally impractical-looking scabbard. The sword's edges were thick and flat. She shook her head and slid the sword back into its sheath.

"What exactly is this place, Geis?" she asked as she continued to look around. "Some sort of den?"

"Breyguhn found it," Geis said with a tired air, "when she came in here looking for the *Universal Principles*. After the Sad Brothers refused to ransom her, I meant to use this place to provide apartments for her, even though they insisted she still had to be chained. Later they went back even on that concession, but by that time I was looking for somewhere secure, and I came to an arrangement with the Sad Brothers."

"And where is Brey?" Sharrow asked.

Geis glanced over at the screens on the wall. "Now? Probably having to listen to Tidesong; then they let her eat with the other prisoners."

Sharrow looked around at the tall, shadowy spaces of the chamber. "And you were going to give all this to Brey, were you?"

"Yes," Geis said. "Because she's family, Sharrow. The way you're family."

"Right. And of course, you'd never dream of doing anything horrid to me, would you?"

"Sharrow," Geis said. "I've been trying to help you from the beginning; I *have* been helping you from the beginning. I tried to rescue you from this ... monster, at his Keep." Geis nodded at the man tied to the other seat. "It wasn't my fault the Huhsz attacked at the same time. I'd no idea they were there." Geis sounded bitter. "Some of my forces did get in and found this material here; they managed to retrieve it and bring it to me. Brave men died to rescue this collection, Sharrow. You shouldn't make fun of it."

"Geis," she said, not looking at him, "you've had *minutes* to think up a better excuse than that. I'm disappointed."

Geis closed his eyes for a moment. "You, whatever your name is," he said wearily to Feril. "You must be capable of reason. Please try to talk some sense into my cousin."

"I am afraid that as far as I understand them, I believe Lady Sharrow's suspicions may well be justified, Count Geis," Feril said regretfully.

"You fucking piece of *junk*," Geis roared, shaking the chair he was tied to. "*Untie me!*"

Geis was breathing hard and looked flushed. He had been wearing trous and a slim-fitting tunic top over a white shirt; Sharrow had torn the shirt into strips to tie him and Molgarin/Chrolleser up. She hadn't bothered to put his tunic-top back on and he looked pathetic and vulnerable, stripped to the waist. She frowned at his midriff.

"Geis," she said. "Is that the start of a paunch?"

"Sharrow!" Geis shouted, sucking his belly in. "Stop this nonsense! Let me go!"

"Maybe," she said. "Once you've given me the key to the Lazy Gun."

"I don't have the key," he said. "I *do* have clinics . . . which could perhaps help rid you of that awful thing in your skull which—"

"You don't have the key," Sharrow said, "but you do have clinics where they might be able to crack the lock's genetic code and manufacture a key, yes, Geis?" she said, smiling. "Except you're not supposed to know what sort of key is on the lock. Though, actually you might; old Molgarin here might have told you it was a gene-lock. There was no need to cover up there, but you did." She shook her head. "You're slipping badly, Geis." She looked disapproving. "I have to say I think you're letting the whole family down here."

"Sharrow—" Geis said evenly.

"Oh, Geis, just admit it. You've been following in old Gorko's footsteps, collecting all the things he tried to collect, trying to complete his work, and somehow—I don't know what your absurd scheme actually is—at least to weaken the World Court, even if you can't actually destroy it." She looked at the bank of screens that filled one alcoved wall of the chamber. "Oh—how *is* our latest war going?" she asked. "Does it fit in with your plans, or not?"

"Sharrow," Geis said again, struggling to control his voice. "I know you've been through a tough time recently—"

(She grimaced and shook her head and made a well-not-really motion with one hand.)

"—but you really are being quite thoroughly *paranoid!*"

"What a wonderful idea it must have seemed," she said, ignoring him and crossing her arms as she sat up on the big stone table. "Doing that old Mind Bomb trick again. You know—the one old Ethce Lebmellin did for you, where one signal turns everybody's guns off. But this time doing it with an entire fortress, and it meant your boys—well, not *your* boys, because you couldn't risk your own people being caught, but the people you could use who nobody knew were yours: the Sad Brothers—they could come in like knights of old—with bandamyions! And swords! And flowing capes!"

She clapped her hands. "You'd get it all, wouldn't you, Geis? Miz dead—taunted and played with for months using all that nonsense about the sial races in Tile so everybody thought he was being paranoid, and then finally killing him off with the paranoia made real! My, you must have been creaming your pants when you thought that one up. And you'd have all the things we looked for, all the things you wanted but couldn't be seen to go for yourself, and you set up this dummy"—she nodded at Molgarin/Chrolleser—"to be fall-guy, so you could blame it all on him. No doubt you told him he'd get away, but would he? Would he always be out there so you had something to keep me safe from, or were you going to run him through with your mighty broad-sword, just for me?"

Geis stared at her, appalled.

"And I was supposed to feel so fucking grateful, wasn't I, Geis?" she said, shaking her head. "I was meant to fall into your arms. Or am I flattering myself?" She looked puzzled. "Was that part of the deal or not?"

"I loved you, Sharrow," Geis said, sounding more sad than anything else. "I *still* love you. Just let me out of this and I'll prove it all. I do love you, and I do love this family and our race— Oh, smile your cynical smile if you want, Sharrow, but I mean it. Everything I've had to do has been done for love."

Feril turned to her then and said, "I think somebody is coming." It nodded at the low door set underneath the two giant diamond-leaf ikons.

Sharrow turned to face the door and pointed the gun at it. She heard the chink-chink noise of a chain and guessed who it might be.

The door opened and Breyguhn entered. She was dressed as Sharrow remembered, in a plain gray shift, though the gown was dirtier than it had been. Her eyes looked wild; when she gazed at Sharrow, then at the android, then at Geis, it was with a strange blankness. She carried a pile of books awkwardly in her arms. Her right hand was still joined to the track in the wall via a manacle and chain, but it was steel now rather than iron.

Sharrow let her gun down. "Hello again," she said. "Feril, this is my half sister, Breyguhn."

Feril turned and bowed slightly.

Breyguhn dropped the books at the same moment, revealing a pistol. She fired it at Sharrow's head as Geis half stood and whirled around, whacking the back legs of the chair he was tied to into the legs of the android.

Sharrow felt something smack into the side of her head and spin her around. She slumped against the table, trying to bring the laser up to bear on Breyguhn, then fell to the flagstones, the gun bouncing out of her limp fingers.

She lay there. Her head was sore. As though through a fine mist she saw Feril staggering from the blow Geis had dealt it with the chair. Breyguhn fired at the android; Feril's right leg blew off at the thigh. The android hopped around on one leg, trying to stay upright. Another shot cracked across its chest, raising sparks. It kept on hopping. It still held the laser rifle, but it didn't seem to want to use it. She tried to shout at it to shoot all the dirty bastards, but her mouth wouldn't work. It kept on hopping and hopping, banging into the stone table and stumbling, the rifle still clutched in its hand.

Then Geis shouted something and fell over on the floor still tied to the chair. Breyguhn came over and kept the gun on the hopping android while she pulled at the strips of shirt restraining Geis.

As soon as he was released, Geis stood up, pulled the blunt-bladed sword from its scabbard on the table, flicked one of its jewels so that its blade edges flickered with pink fire, and swung it at the hopping android.

It wasn't a powerful stroke, but it separated Feril's head from its trunk as though its neck had been made of paper. Feril had raised one arm over its head while trying to balance, and that was sliced off in the same blow. The head fell to the floor and rolled under the table; the arm fell onto it.

The android's headless body tottered on its single leg for a second. Geis raised the sword over his head and brought it scything down. Feril's body parted down the middle and fell apart in halves, like something from a cartoon.

Sharrow made a last attempt to raise her hand, then gave up. She closed her eyes.

Are you all right? . . . Hello? I said, Are you all right?
. . . You . . . You again . . . Now what?
This isn't really going as we hoped, is it?
. . . No.
Well?
Fate . . . Who cares?
Nobody, if you don't. It's your life.
. . . Exactly. Oh, I'm tired. Fuck it, just let me die.
No, I don't really feel we've destroyed enough yet. One of us has to. We are each other, after all. We are the last of the eight.
Oh, fuck, yes, sure . . . We'll see what we can do. . . .
That's right. Now wake up.
I don't want to wake up.
I said, Wake up.
No, won't.
Wake *up*!
No, wo—
Now!
No.
N—

People were arguing. Her head hurt and people were arguing. She hated it when people argued. She screamed at them, told them to shut up; it was bad enough the Gun wouldn't give her any peace. Screaming just made her head hurt worse. They didn't seem to hear, anyway.

"You have to *kill* her."

"No! There's no need; I almost had her convinced before you came in."

"Oh, it's my fault now, is it? I save your skin and—"

"I didn't *say* that! That's not what I meant."

"Kill her. Kill her now. If you can't, I will."

"How can you say that! You're her sister!"

Half sister, Sharrow thought.

"Because I know what she's *like*, that's why!"

Shut up, shut up! she screamed at them.

"She's coming around. I heard her say something."

". . . No she isn't. Look at her; lucky you didn't blow her brains out."

"I was trying to."

"Well, I'm not going to let you."

She was tied. Tied sitting to a seat, much like Geis had been. Hands and feet tied—no, taped. Tape over mouth, too. Head hanging forward. Sore. She wanted to tell them to shut up again, but didn't. She raised her head and looked at them.

They stood in front of the table, arguing. Breyguhn was still joined by her chain to the wall. Sharrow didn't understand the chain; Brey must have some sort of special place she could change over from the main system to some private line. At least they had given her a chain of steel rather than iron. Probably a really generous concession for the Sea House. . . .

She had to let her head drop again. They didn't seem to have noticed, anyway. Everything went gray again. Still had sound, though.

"Kill her, Geis. Please keep your personal feelings out of this. This is for—"

"Keep *my* personal feelings out of it? Well, that's rich, coming from you!"

"I *stayed* here for you! My Fate—I came *in* here for you! Who was it found you *this* place? And I could have left; but I stayed for you, for you and the family. I won't let *her* ruin everything. You know she will, Geis. You know what she's like. She won't forgive; she *can't* forgive! Geis, please, kill her. For me. Please. Please . . ."

"I didn't ask you to stay. You wanted to."

"I know, but please, for me . . . Oh, Geis . . ."

"Get *off* me! You stayed because you wanted to, not because of me or the family. You're more attached to that chain than me!"

She thought she heard a sharp intake of breath. She wanted to laugh, but she couldn't put her head back. *Oh, Geis,* she thought, *you were always too literal.*

"How *dare* you! You're frightened! All right, *I'll* show you how it's done!"

"Brey! No! Put that—"

The sounds of a struggle. A shot was fired; she heard a

ricochet nearby. The crack of a slap. Silence, then a cry, then lots of weeping, and some sobbed words she couldn't make out.

"Brey . . ."

"Have her, then!" Breyguhn cried. "It was always her you wanted, anyway. Well, do what you *want!*"

Then the sound of her chain rattling, followed by a door slamming. A door in the place where there were not supposed to be any. But she had seen lots of doors here today. Lots and lots of doors . . . It all drifted away from her again.

Suddenly there was something under her nose and she was sniffing a sharp, noxious vapor, and her head seemed to clear and there was an odd ringing noise somewhere.

Geis squatted in front of her.

"Sharrow?" he said.

She lifted her head. "Uh-huh?"

"Sharrow," Geis said, "I just want you to know that I always loved you, always wanted you to be happy and to be a proper part of the family. You belong with me, not with that criminal Kuma, not with any of the others. They don't matter; none of them mattered. I forgive you for all of them. I understand. But *you've* got to understand, too. The things that were done, they weren't all done by me; there were people who thought they were doing what I wanted them to do, but they didn't know. Sometimes *I* didn't know what was happening. People can be too loyal, you know, Sharrow? That's the way it was, I swear."

Geis glanced at the man still tied to the seat next to hers, the man whose name she'd forgotten but who wasn't Molgarin. He looked dead.

"These people did that," Geis said. "They overstepped the mark, I'm not denying that. But they meant well. Like the crystal virus; that was put in on Nachtel's Ghost, but I didn't know how it would later be used. I didn't know Molgarin would start trying to build his own power base and use you to do it. I didn't know you'd been tortured." Geis looked agonized. He'd put his tunic top back on, she noticed. "At least I knew it was safe, though," he said with an attempt at a brave smile. "I have one of those implanted in my own head; did you know that?"

She shook her head. Of course she didn't know that.

"Yes," Geis said, nodding. "A fail-safe; a way of taking everything with me until I choose to disable the system."

Geis tapped the side of his head. "If I die, the crystal-virus lattice senses my death and sends a coded signal; everything I own destructs. All of it, it's all wired to go: asteroids, ships, mines, buildings, vehicles, even pens in certain politicians' and Corp. execs' pockets; they blow up. You see? Even if they get me, even if the Court gets me, they might start a war. The insurance claims and the commercial disruption alone could wreck everything. You see how important one person can become? Do you understand now?"

She made a little whimpering noise behind the tape. He reached up and gently unstuck the tape from her mouth. It still hurt.

"I understand," she said, her voice sounding mushy. He looked pleased. "I understand," she said, "that you're as fucking mad as Breyguhn, cuz."

She sighed and looked away, expecting to be slapped or punched. Her gaze fell on the table. The Lazy Gun lay there. The lock had been taken off. Geis had had the key. Of course he had.

Something moved on the table a meter from the gun. She started to frown, then her chin was held in one hand while with his other Geis stuck the tape back over her mouth.

"No, Sharrow," Geis said. "No, not mad. Just long-sighted. I've been preparing all this for a long time now, prepared your eventual role in this from way, way back." Geis paused. He was looking very serious now. She got the impression he was considering whether to tell her something important. She shook her head slowly, as though trying to clear it.

There *was* something moving on the stone table behind Geis.

He gripped her knees. "We are the past, Sharrow," Geis said. "I know that. All this . . ." He looked around, and she thought he might see the movement on the table, but whatever was moving there stopped just as Geis turned his head. "All this might help what I've prepared, might serve as rallying points, battle standards, bribes, distractions . . . whatever. But only a new order can save poor Golter, only some new message can win people's hearts and minds. All you see here, however precious it might be to us, might have to be sacrificed. Perhaps we *need* a new beginning, a clean slate. Perhaps that is our only hope." He was talking quietly now.

The ringing in her ears was fading, and she was feeling a little stronger and less groggy. She was able to focus on what was moving on the stone table.

Fucking Fate, it was the android's hand!

Its forearm, the one that had been chopped off by the same stroke that had beheaded it. The arm had fallen to the table, and that was where it was now, crawling over the surface very slowly and quietly, using its fingers.

She felt her eyes go wide and turned the motion into what she hoped looked like another attempt to clear her head.

Geis looked concerned, then said, gently. "Sharrow, this is all a lot for you to take in just now, but you must believe me that I've made sure your name will live forever." He smiled mysteriously. "Not as you might have imagined, but—"

Gods, the arm was heading for the Lazy Gun. She stared at Geis and smiled inanely.

"—well, but in a way you might be rather proud of, even if it was never a way you could have imagined."

She looked for Feril's head. It wasn't under the table where it had fallen. Its body wasn't lying in separate pieces on the floor, either. Then she saw it: both halves of the body were propped against what looked like a giant electrical junction box in one corner, near the door Breyguhn had come through. The head . . .

The head, Feril's head, had been set on an end-post of the weapons rack from the fjord tower, in the middle of the great stone table. From where it was perched—and assuming the android's head could still see—it had a perfectly good view of the Lazy Gun and the hand that was now less than half a meter from the Gun's open trigger mechanism.

Geis was still talking.

"—hate me for what I've done, initially at first, but I know, I really do know that eventually, once all that's going to happen has happened, you'll know I did the right thing."

What was this idiot talking about? She tried to concentrate on her cousin's face and ignore the android hand scraping its way across the surface of the stone table toward the matt silver body of the Gun.

What could the hand do when it got there? The trigger wasn't supposed to be especially stiff, but what about aiming? Would the half-meter length of arm and hand have the strength to turn the Gun, even if Feril could aim it with its head three meters away? What had the sights been set at? How wide a field? Feril would need to point the Gun at Geis; at the moment it was pointing at ... at the casing of the *Universal Principles*.

She stared at Geis, not listening.

Holy shit, she thought. Even if Geis considered the casing of the *Universal Principles* disposable, he wouldn't think the same about the Addendum and his ludicrous Crownstar.

Fate, she might get out of this yet. She felt herself start to cry and was furious with herself. Hope could be more painful than despair.

"Oh, Sharrow," Geis said tenderly, "don't cry." He looked sympathetic. She thought he might be about to burst into tears himself. Revolting. At least this performance was keeping his attention on her and away from the table. "—this could end well yet," he told her. "We're together, don't you see? That's a start...."

The arm and hand crawling along the table had almost made it to the trigger of the Gun. She was trying to watch it from the corner of her eye, staring wide-eyed at Geis and absurdly frightened that just by the intensity of her stare he might guess she wasn't really listening to a word he said.

"—and I'm glad you came here, glad you saw this place—no, really, I am. Because this is my most private place, my sanctum, the one place where I am the real me, not surrounded by flunkeys and yes-men and—"

She found herself wondering where Feril's brain was; if it was inside its head or some other part of its body. She assumed it was watching with the eyes in the head and telling its arm what to do by a comm link, but where from? Stop it, stop it, stop it, she told herself. It doesn't matter.

"—we'll be happy again," Geis said. "We'll all be happy. We have it in our own hands to make it so, and you and I are going to make it happen. Even that criminal you thought so much of, even he'll have something more than he deserved to commemorate him. Because we all have a criminal past, don't we, Sharrow? That's what poor old Golter's had on its conscience all these ten thousand years, isn't it? That first war, and the billions who died.

"Year zero, after twenty thousand years of civilization. That's what we've never really been able to forget, isn't it? But our sentence is almost up, Sharrow. The decamillennium. It'll be just another day like any other, we all know that. But these symbols matter, don't they? That's what all this has been about, from the beginning: symbols. Hasn't it?" He looked upset. He put his hand out to her tape gag, then hesitated. "Oh, Sharrow," he said. "Just say you understand, just say you don't hate me utterly. Please? Will you?" He looked as though he weren't sure whether to trust her or not.

She nudged her head forward in a series of little nods and made little whimpering noises.

Geis's eyes narrowed, then he reached up and took the tape off her mouth again.

"Now," she said, "take all the rest of the tape off me, or the android wastes the Addendum, the Crownstar, and the *U.P.* casing."

Geis looked at her, uncomprehending. He laughed.

"Pardon?" he said.

"You heard," she said. "Turn around very slowly and take a look; the android's hand is on the trigger of the Lazy Gun." She smiled. "I'm serious, Geis."

He turned around slowly.

One of the fingers on the android hand gripping the Lazy Gun's trigger-guard peeled away for a moment and made a little waving motion. Geis went very still.

"Count Geis," a tiny voice whispered in the quietness of the chamber. It was Feril's voice. "I am terribly sorry about this, but I am quite prepared to do as Lady Sharrow says." The eerie, just audible voice from the head perched on the weapons rack sounded regretful.

Geis was still squatting. He swiveled slowly on his haunches to look at Sharrow again. He swallowed.

"Don't talk, Geis," she told him. "Just do it."

He reached slowly around behind her and started to strip the tape away from her arms. Sharrow looked at Feril's head, high above the table on the weapons rack.

"I had no idea you had quite such a degree of survivability built into you, Feril," she said as one of her hands came free.

"It was never relevant before," Feril whispered, its voice almost drowned by the rip of tape being pulled away from Sharrow's feet.

Geis stopped. Sharrow had one hand and one leg free.

She nudged him in the shoulder with her knee. "Keep going," she said.

Geis stood up, shaking his head. "No," he said. "No." He went around the back of the chair.

"What?" she said, glancing at Feril's head. "Geis—"

He stood behind her, a viblade knife in his hand; he grabbed the rear of the small chair with his other hand. "No, I don't believe it'll do it, but if it does . . ." He put his hand on her collar, the knife to her throat.

"Geis—" she said.

"Breyguhn!" he roared. He started dragging Sharrow on her seat backward across the flagstone toward the door. She put her free hand to his arm holding the knife, but didn't have the strength to tear it away. She could only hold on. "Breyguhn!" Geis shouted again.

"Geis—" Sharrow said. She thought she could hear Feril saying something as well, but there was too much noise to hear what it was.

"Breyguhn! I know you're out there! Stop sulking! Get in here! Brey!" Geis got to the door. Sharrow looked back at the table; Feril's head couldn't see them anymore, but the hand and forearm holding the gun was jerking, dragging itself around in one direction, then whiplashing itself back in the other like a skewered snake, gradually scraping the Lazy Gun around to point toward her and Geis. "Brey!" Geis roared.

There was a clinking sound from the other side of the door. At the same time one half of Feril's body, propped up in the corner near the door, spasmed suddenly rigid, bringing the remains tumbling past the electrical junction box and clattering down at Geis's feet. He yelled with fright as Breyguhn came back through the door looking sulky. She still had the gun in her hand.

Geis spun away, letting Sharrow's seat drop sideways to the floor, he hacked at the twitching bits of android body with the viblade, then threw it away and lunged across the stone table, grabbing the sword he had used earlier. He swung it at the body parts moving on the floor.

The hand holding the Lazy Gun clenched. The junction box behind Geis flashed and boomed. The lights in the chamber blazed, then went out. Emergency lighting globes glowed feebly. Geis hacked at the half of the android body writhing on the floor with the great sword, chopping through the metal and plastic and gouging trenches into the flagstones beneath. Breyguhn was screaming. Sharrow used her free left arm and leg to push herself under the stone table, then tried to roll, tearing at the tape still securing her to the chair and looking for the viblade Geis had thrown away.

She heard shots and more screams, then light blazed and there was a noise like a thunderclap and a sound like a million windows shattering.

Breyguhn screamed, loud and shrill. "Stop it! Stop it!"

"I'm trying to!" Geis bellowed.

A great thump made the floor under Sharrow quiver as she finally got free of the last of the tape and scuttled out from under the table.

Her feet splashed. She looked down, then up. Water was pouring into the dimly lit chamber from a half-meter-wide hole in one wall. Geis was still hacking at the android's body; Breyguhn was holding her gun with both hands and aiming at the android's head; the hand clutching the Lazy Gun was jerking and clenching apparently at random, turning and firing the Gun every second or so. One of the diamond-leaf ikons had shattered; it lay in a scree of glittering shards between the door and the sparking remains of the junction box. Molgarin/Chrolleser was dead, arched back in his seat with his eyes staring at the ceiling, a set of great naked bone jaws clamped around his neck like a man-trap, blood leaking from where the curved teeth had punctured. Even as Sharrow stared, the jaws disappeared again.

The water gushing from the breach in the wall was up to Sharrow's ankles. She grabbed the first weapon she saw lying on the stone table: the HandCannon.

Breyguhn fired her pistol again; the shot spun Feril's head around on the post. The Lazy Gun spun around, too, as the arm holding it jammed against the casing of the *Universal Principles*. The Gun pointed straight at Sharrow; she ducked under the table, into the water. A titanic pulse of sound shook the air, followed by a vast crashing, tumbling noise. A cloud of dust rolled forward from the wall, followed by a wave of dirty water that pushed Sharrow toward the other side of the table. She was floating; her head bumped against the underside of the stonework. She pushed forward as the rumbling noise behind her eased. She looked beyond the lower edge of the table, trying to see Breyguhn's legs on the far side of the flooding room, but the dark air was full of dust.

There was a flash from the side and a painting covering one wall began to burn. The dust-filled chamber had shrunk. Half of it, including the door she and Feril had first come through and the balcony where they'd encountered Geis, was now a vast pile of rubble, fallen from layers and levels above, where the ceiling now stretched up into darkness; sparks and water fell out of the heights. The burning painting lit the dusty chamber with a yellow, flickering light. She still couldn't see Breyguhn or Geis. The Lazy Gun was hidden by the piled treasure in the center of the table. The weapons rack Feril's head had been on had disappeared.

Something tumbled out of the darkness above; she dived to one side into the waist-deep water as a massive piece of stonework whistled down and smashed into the stone table, splitting it and hurling everything on it into the air. A wall of water came surging toward her; she was washed toward the small door under the remaining diamond-leaf ikon.

A terrible, thrumming vibration traveled through her legs as the waves slapped and hissed against the electrical junction box where Feril's body had lain.

She waded through the water, slipping on the bank of diamond debris under her feet, then hauled the door open against the sucking weight of water and stumbled splashing up a dark, inclined corridor beyond. She checked the HandCannon as she went, thinking it felt wrong, and cursing when she discovered there was no magazine in it. She stuffed it into a pocket.

Another quaking burst of sound came from behind her, and a great dark fist of smoke pushed out from the chamber, pulsing along the surface of the ceiling above her.

The corridor rose; the water around her legs became shallower. Cables hanging from the ceiling swung back and forth, making her fight her way through, crashing off walls and cable-runs and buzzing metal boxes. Smoke preceded her along the shadowy corridor as she finally waded up some steps and out of the water.

She ducked under drooping, humming cables, through a haze of acrid smoke, a stink of burning insulation, and a scrape of sparks as the broken end of a cable swung back and forth across the damp flagstones.

She straightened on the far side to see Breyguhn standing five meters in front of her, right wrist chained to the wall, her right hand gripping a pistol. She was bleeding from a head wound. The thin yellow light made her look deathly pale.

Breyguhn pointed the gun at Sharrow. "He's gone, Sharrow," she said sadly. "Taken his silly sword and gone." She shrugged. "Frightened the Gun was going to do something irresponsible ..." Breyguhn smiled bleakly.

She took a step toward Sharrow, who retreated a step and then flinched as she backed into the hanging cables. The cable at her feet sparked and crackled.

"Taken his silly sword and gone ...," Breyguhn said in a girlish, singsong voice. She aimed the gun at Sharrow's face. The chain squeaked.

Sharrow ducked as the gun fired; she grabbed the live cable and jammed the exposed end into the chain-track on the wall.

Breyguhn screamed. Her gun loosed off its remaining rounds into the wall as she shook, her wrist smoking.

When the gun stopped firing, Sharrow hauled the cable out of the chain-track.

Breyguhn collapsed like a heap of rags, only her still-smoldering wrist held upright against the wall by the chain.

Sharrow gagged on the smell of burned flesh as she stumbled forward. She turned Breyguhn's face to the light and felt for a pulse. Her half sister's eyes stared up the tunnel, motionless. Sharrow shook her head and dropped the other woman's arm.

Another explosion from the chamber behind blew her off her feet and along the tunnel.

She started running.

There was another door where the chain-track disappeared; she ignored it and ran limping, head pounding, breath ragged, down the tunnel. It ended in a tall space lit from above—and from a downward slope in front—by gray daylight. It smelled rank and fetid and the stone floor was covered with straw. She saw large stalls on either side; harnesses and bridles and tall saddles hung on the walls. There were no animals in any of the stalls. The gray light from the slope in front of her came from another short, high-ceilinged tunnel.

She limped down it, under the barbed teeth of two enormous portcullises, out into the cold drizzle of the day.

She was standing on a weed-smothered slope that led from the foot of the Sea House's towering walls down to the sand and gravel floor of the bay. The sea was a line in the distance, light gray against dark. A broad stone ramp sloped away to the sand pools and gravel banks that the retreated tide had revealed. The gray water piled and hummocked in the distance, out to sea. There was no land visible.

A large animal carrying a single rider was picking its way through the humped shoals of gravel beyond a stretch of sand dotted with shallow pools where the animal had left its hoofprints. As the rider glanced back, the wind lifted his riding cape and blew it out to one side.

She ran down the slope, skidding on the weed, and splashed into the first sandy pool. A sliver of sand-duned land was just visible in the distance around the side of the House's dark walls.

She ran on a way, then stopped.

What was she doing? The bandamyion reared up and turned around, stepping delicately forward across the gravel shoal until it found the relative firmness of the sand again.

You idiot, she told herself. *You've got an empty gun in your pocket. What the hell are you going to do with that? Throw it at him? You should have run the other way, around the walls to the outfall; you could have got the monowheel and chased the asshole on his stupid animal in that.*

Geis brought the bandamyion trotting forward. He was about thirty meters away. He reined the beast in. It stood shaking its wide tawny head. He leaned over the saddle, staring at her.

"Satisfied, Sharrow?" he said. His voice sounded thin and reedy in the cold, salty wind. "Do you know what you've done?"

She just stood there. She wondered what else there was to do. Cold water seeped into her shoes.

"*Do* you?" Geis shouted.

She looked back at the Sea House. It was its usual massive self. If the Lazy Gun was still causing havoc somewhere inside it, at least it hadn't yet decided to destroy the whole thing.

She looked back at Geis and shrugged.

"And I once thought I loved you," Geis said, shaking his head. He said it so softly, she hardly heard him.

Geis drew the jewel-encrusted sword from its saddle-sheath and switched it on; its edges were suddenly lined with pink fire. "I'm going to make you the mother of God, Sharrow," Geis said, urging the bandamyion forward a pace or two.

She wasn't sure she'd heard him right.

"Girmeyn," Geis said. "Girmeyn, on Nachtel's Ghost. He will be the Messiah; a new voice for the new age, a line written under all we've done in the last ten thousand years and a new hope for the next ten thousand.

"He's mine. I had him raised; I held his life, all he was, contained in my hand," Geis said, holding up the hand gripping the bandamyion's reins. "I had him brought up, trained, educated. All that you destroyed in there today," Geis said nodding at the House behind her, "all that was to be his birthright, my final gift to him. But you took it away from him. He's on a Foundation asteroid now; one of mine. That's where Girmeyn is, Sharrow, and he's your son."

Son? she thought.

The bandamyion trotted forward.

"Your son," he shouted. "Yours and your thief friend! Taken out after you crashed on the Ghost; stored while my clinicians found a way to save it, then grown like a clone, only actually born ten years ago, but aged in the tank and fed the wisdom of ten millennia and a set of perfect, optimized stimuli by an AI devoted to the purpose; and all to my design. So he's mine, perhaps more than he's anybody's. But biologically he's yours, Sharrow. Have no doubt."

Son? she thought. *Girmeyn?*

Geis was edging the bandamyion slowly closer, its heavy hooves splashing in the pools of water.

"But you'd ruin that, too, wouldn't you, Sharrow?" Geis said, still advancing. "You'd wreck that plan like you've wrecked everything else, wouldn't you?"

Who, me? she thought.

She could see the facets in the bandamyion's dark eyes now, dull glisters in the gray light. She took a step back, then another. She really ought to have gone for the monowheel.

"I would make you the mother of the Messiah, the mother of God, and you'd spit on it, wouldn't you, Sharrow?" Geis kicked the bandamyion's sides. The spur terminals buzzed and the animal trotted, rolling its great head. She stepped back.

The sword hanging in Geis's hand made a humming noise; drizzle spat and hissed when it hit the pink projected edges, producing little wisps of steam. More vapor smoked from the nostrils of the bandamyion as it vented its warmth to the cold air.

"We're on the brink, Sharrow," Geis said, raising his voice a little. "Can't you tell?" He made a show of sniffing the breeze. "Can't you smell it? We're right on the cusp of something better, something new and *fresh*, and everything I've done has been to prepare for it and make its birth easier. But you'd spoil that, too, wouldn't you, Sharrow? You'd let your vanity, your pride, your own small-minded need for revenge get in the way of a new future for everybody, wouldn't you?"

Yes, she thought, *yes. I've been selfish; that's all I've ever been. And what if the fool is right, and there is a new world waiting? Fate knows it's an old refrain; we always think there's something better just around the corner, and we're always disappointed, but we have to be right eventually, don't we?*

"That can't happen," Geis said quietly, now that he was so close. He nodded slowly. "You're not armed," he said. "I suppose I should be thankful. I'm not sure even knowing he was your son and that he'd die with all the rest would stop you, would it?"

She looked from the huge, heavy face of the bandamyion up to his eyes. Oh, yes, the crystal-virus he claimed he'd had implanted in himself for that pre-prepared act of final petulance. She didn't know if Geis was telling the truth about that or not, but it sounded psychotic enough to be part of his repertoire.

And Girmeyn. Girmeyn now in one of Geis's space habitats. Even if he wasn't her son, how could she kill him?

Easily, she thought, standing there with her feet sinking into the watery sand and the stinking breeze blowing about her. *All of them, all of it—easily.*

How many tyrants had begun by being charming, beguiling, attractive? Still, they all ended up the same.

We are a race prone to monsters, she thought, *and when we produce one, we worship it. What kind of world, what translation of good could come from all that's happened here?*

She saw them all die again: Miz crumpled in the snow, speared through; Zefla, pale and dying in the pathetic little tent; Dloan falling on the cold hillside; Cenuij tumbling past her into the night (and Feril, hacked, blasted, destroyed, even if a week-younger copy would be revived in the future . . . and Breyguhn, too, sacrificed to Geis's plans, and all of them; Keteo and Lebmellin, Tard and Roa, Chrolleser and Bencil Dornay, Fate alone knew how many other Solipsists, Huhsz monks, and nameless spear carriers; everybody who'd suffered and died since she'd stood on the glass shore of Issier with Geis).

And her mother, she thought, as something within her gave way under the pressure of so much remembered death, and she was five years old again, standing in the wrecked cable car surrounded by smoke and blood and broken glass, crying and screaming, bewildered and terrified while her mother raised herself up, body broken and butchered and put her hand out—to touch, to comfort, to caress, she'd thought, she'd been sure—and pushed her out the door into that cold gulf of gray.

She remembered the faceless woman in the wheelchair, from her dream, and the little station in the snow and the waiting train that had gone huff, huff, each vertical jettisoning of smoke and steam like breath, like an explosion.

Gunfire. It was the first thing she really remembered: that scarifying, punishing noise as the cable car rocked and blew apart and the bodyguard's head burst open. It felt like her life began then; it always had. There had been something vague about a mother and warmth and safety from before, but that all happened to somebody else; the person she was had been born watching people die, watching her mother ripped open by a high-velocity bullet and then reach out to push her away and out, a second before the grenade exploded.

All I've ever been was made by weaponry and death.

Not armed, she thought. *Not armed. I am the Lazy Gun, the last of the eight, and I'm not fucking armed, just got this one stupid, empty gun. . . .*

She put her hand in her pocket. Her fingers closed around the HandCannon, feeling the gun's odd lightness and the wide empty slot in the grip where the magazine should be.

Of course, there might be a round in the breech.

A round in the breech, she thought.

She couldn't remember if she'd cocked the gun earlier or not. She'd taken the magazine out of the HandCannon when she'd made Molgarin/Chrolleser take the gun, and she'd put it back in when Geis had come along the balcony toward them, but had she cocked the gun then? Had she sent a round into the breach?

She had no idea. Even if she had, she still didn't know whether whoever had taken the clip back out again had removed a round from the chamber as well.

What if I can kill him? Suppose there is a round in the gun? How many more people die if he's telling the truth?

"I'm sorry, Sharrow," Geis said, and shook his head. The spur terminals crackled again; the bandamyion trotted forward.

Sorry? Of course he was sorry. People were always sorry. Sorry they had done what they had done, sorry they were doing what they were doing, sorry they were going to do what they were going to do; but they still did whatever it was. The sorrow never stopped them; it just made them feel better. And so the sorrow never stopped. Fate, I'm sick of it all.

Geis kicked once more at the bandamyion's flanks, and the animal cantered toward her. Geis raised the sword, swinging it out and back.

Sorry be damned, and all your plans. Fuck the faithful, fuck the committed, the dedicated, the true believers; fuck all the sure and certain people prepared to maim and kill whoever gets in their way; fuck every cause that ends in murder and a child screaming.

She turned and ran.

In her pocket, her hand fitted around the grip of the gun.

The round might be there. How could she not take the chance?

When she heard the bandamyion's hoofbeats right behind her, she dodged to the side and went down on one knee.

She pulled out the HandCannon, aimed, and pulled the trigger.

The bandamyion was turning toward her. In the imperative physicality of that instant she had no idea what she had aimed at, only that she'd knelt and pulled the trigger. The gun fired, spasming once in her hands, and then she was diving to the side, throwing the gun away in the same moment, falling and turning, eyes closing as she dropped and curled up.

There was a quick, keen slicing noise.

Something whacked into her side. The pain burst entirely through her body, making her cry out. She splashed into a shallow pool.

The water was cold. One side of her face and body had gone numb. She raised her head and tried to sit up.

The pain flicked on, making her gasp. She crouched, swiveling in the sandy pool so that she was hunched over; the pain faded.

She had at least one burst rib; she recognized the pain from injuries in childhood and adolescence.

She sat up carefully, shivering, and looked toward the Sea House. The bandamyion was hunkered down near the entrance to the underground stables, licking at some blood on one shank. Its saddle hung half-off, askew over its haunches.

She looked around and saw Geis, lying a few meters away in the direction the beast had been charging. She got up, shouting as the pain came back. She held her arm across her chest, waited for her head to clear, then limped toward the man.

The sword lay nearby on the sand. It was dull, the pink fire that had edged its blades extinguished. From the marks on the sand, it looked as if the bandamyion had taken a tumble. She inspected her jacket over the place where her side hurt. There was no cut; the sword stroke must have missed and she'd been hit by a bandamyion hoof. Her side ached; it felt like more than one broken rib. She supposed she had been lucky, even so.

She limped on, over spots of blood.

Geis lay facedown in a shallow pool, his cloak stuck wetly to him over his shoulders and head. She pulled the cloak back; the water in the pool was filling with red. The GP round had taken most of Geis's neck away.

His face was under water. She pulled at him, turning

him over. Blood poured from the fist-sized hole in his neck. His head hung slackly; his eyes were half-closed and pink water dribbled from his mouth. She pulled him out of the water onto the sand and laid him on his back by the side of the red-stained pool.

There was a muffled explosion from the Sea House. She turned; the bandamyion was jumping and bucking near the entrance to the stables, something at its rear end burning. One final kick sent the animal's saddle smoking into the rocks. The bandamyion turned its head and licked at a patch of scorched hide.

Another explosion sounded from the House, then another and another. She saw debris rise and fall among some distant towers after one blast, and smoke started to rise from the vast building in a dozen different places.

She looked back at Geis's slack, dead face.

A tremor shook the sand under her feet. The bandamyion, just starting to hunker down again, jerked upright and looked from side to side, grunting in distress.

She closed her eyes and waited for the Lazy Gun's own thermonuclear farewell.

There was an almost inaudible rumbling for a few seconds, something close to infrasound felt in the bones and the water and the ventricles of the heart and brain.

Then nothing.

She opened her eyes. The Sea House was still there. A few dark wisps of smoke rose from it. A gray-brown cloud flowed out of the stables entrance and drifted on the breeze. The bandamyion had hunkered down again and looked annoyed at having to get up and move away from the smoke. It trotted along the weeded slope under the high granite walls, shaking its head and snorting.

She sat there for a while, beside the dead man on the cold sands in the foul wind and the soaking drizzle.

Eventually she rose slowly, favoring her injured side.

She looked around. The bandamyion was a still-moving tawny dot halfway around the side of the Sea House. A few small twists of smoke rose among the building's undisturbed topography of towers. In the distance, the waves of the new tide creased gray across the horizon.

Nothing else moved that she could see.

She hobbled to the sword lying on the sand. She tried

switching it on, but its flat edges remained dull. She let it fall back to the sand.

She lifted her face to the drizzle and the evening grayness, staring into the flat expanse of dull sky, as though listening for something.

She lowered her head and stood for some moments. She gazed from the sand at her feet, across the pools to the gravel banks, and on up to the seaweed and the spray-froth beyond, and over that to the gray streaks of gravel and the weed-choked sands that rose into the tall dunes.

She shook her head and limped across the sands to where the HandCannon lay. She picked the gun up, turned it over in her good hand, blew sand off it, and stuffed it into her jacket pocket.

Then she started back, retracing her steps toward the impassive granite walls of the Sea House.

She shook a handkerchief free from her breast pocket as she walked and started tying it around her nose and mouth, using only one hand; her muttered curses accompanying this undertaking were snatched and flung away by the stiffening breeze.

A little later the monowheel vehicle spun backward out of the sewer outfall, pirouetted vertically like a saluting mount, swung down across the greasy slope of stones at the base of the House's walls, dodged uncoordinated gunfire from a nearby tower, and accelerated quickly away across the tide-flooding sands.

About the Author

IAIN BANKS was born in Scotland in 1954. His first novel, *The Wasp Factory*, was published in 1984. His novels include *Consider Phlebas*, *The Player of Games*, *Use of Weapons*, *Against a Dark Background*, and *Ferrsum Endjinn*.

A SPECIAL PREVIEW

*From the pens of three of science fiction's brightest stars
come three long-awaited sequels. Any one alone would
be an event of note. All three together
is nothing short of a Grand Event.*

BRIGHTNESS REEF
BY DAVID BRIN

DAVID BRIN'S Uplift novels form one of the most thrilling science fiction sagas ever written, set in a world brimming with imagination. The *New York Times* bestselling series has received two Hugo Awards and a Nebula Award. Now, after an eight-year absence, David Brin finally returns to his most popular universe with the first book in an all-new Uplift trilogy. *Coming in September 1995.*

BLADE RUNNER™ 2: THE EDGE OF HUMAN
BY K. W. JETER

FANS EVERYWHERE are familiar with director Ridley Scott's dark, stylish, futuristic masterpiece. Now, K. W. Jeter—popularly known as the heir to Philip K. Dick—returns to the steamy streets of twenty-first-century Los Angeles with the continuing adventure of Rick Deckard, a Blade Runner charged with the execution of renegade replicants. *Coming in October 1995.*

ENDYMION
BY DAN SIMMONS

DAN SIMMONS'S brilliant novels *Hyperion* and *The Fall of Hyperion* are among the most thunderously applauded science fiction publications of the last decade, and new readers constantly delight in discovering the awe and wonder of Simmons's gloriously realized far-future universe. Now he returns to continue the immortal tale of mankind's destiny among the stars. *Coming in December 1995.*

*Help us celebrate our Tenth Anniversary with
these blockbuster Spectra hardcovers!*